"You lost childre[...] voice, someone in a [...] answered it, counting them on his fingers.

"My first two sons died of fever; the lord refused us herb-right in the wood. My wife lost two babes young, one from hunger and one from fever. My eldest daughter they raped; killed her husband. The babe died unborn. My youngest son they struck down; he lives. Another daughter they struck down, breaking her arm; I know not if she lives or dies. And my brother's children, that I'd taken in: two of them dead, by the lords' greed. And that's children. I lost friends, my parents, my brother.

"You ask yourselves: if they can take one child, will they stop there? Will all your submission, all your obedience, get you peace and enough food? Has it *ever* worked? You can sit here and let them take you one by one, or you can decide to fight back."

THE LEGACY OF GIRD

edged weapons, even if they had had them to practice with. No one did, the strictest of the laws forbade any

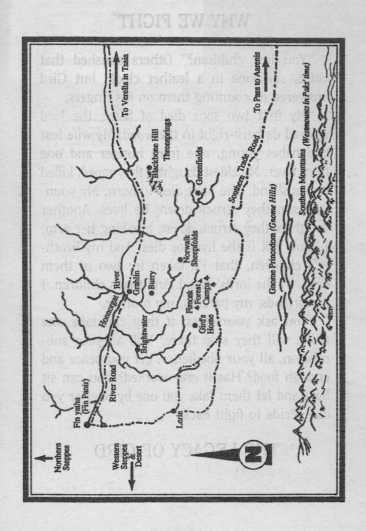

SURRENDER NONE
THE LEGACY OF GIRD

ELIZABETH MOON

SURRENDER NONE: THE LEGACY OF GIRD

This is a work of fiction. All the characters and events portrayed in this book are fictional, and any resemblance to real people or incidents is purely coincidental.

A Baen Books Original

Baen Publishing Enterprises
P.O. Box 1403
Riverdale, NY 10471

ISBN: 0-671-69878-8

Cover art by Larry Elmore

First Printing, June 1990
Second Printing, August 1991

Printed in the United States of America

Distributed by Simon & Schuster
1230 Avenue of the Americas
New York, NY 10020

In memory of Travis Bohannon
a country boy from Florence, Texas
who gave his life to save his family from fire.

Not all heroes are in books.

Acknowledgements

Too many people helped with technical advice and special knowledge to mention all, and leaving any of them out is unfair. But special thanks to Ellen McLean, of McLean Beefmasters, whose stock has taught me more than a college class in Dairying ever did, to Joel Graves for showing me how to scythe without cutting my ankles off, and to Mark Unger for instruction and demonstration of mixed-weapon fighting possibilities. Errors are mine; they did their best to straighten me out.

PART I

PART I

Prologue

The Rule of Aare is rule one:
Surrender none.

"Esea's light on him," muttered the priest, as the midwife mouthed, "Alyanya's sweet peace," and laid the wet pink newborn on his mother's belly. The priest, sent down hurriedly in the midst of dinner from the lord's hall, dabbed his finger in the blood and touched it to a kerchief, then cut with silver scissors a lock of the newborn's wet dark hair, which he folded in the same kerchief. With that as proof, no fond foolish peasant girl could hide the child away from his true father. The stupid slut might try that; some of them did, being so afraid of the lord's magic, although anyone with wit enough to dip stew from a kettle ought to realize that the lords meant no harm to these outbred children. Quite the contrary. With a final sniff, the priest sketched a gesture that left a streak of light in the room long after he'd left, and departed, to report the successful birth. Not a monster, a manchild whole of limb and healthy. Perhaps this one would inherit the birthright magic . . . perhaps.

Behind, in the birthing room, the midwife glowered at the glowing patch of air, and sketched her own gesture, tossing a handful of herbs at it. It hung there still, hardly fading. The new mother grunted, and the midwife returned to her work, ignoring the light she was determined not to need. She had the healing hands, a legacy of a great-grandmother's indiscretion in the days when such indiscretions meant a quick marriage to some handy serf. She hardly believed the change, and having a priest of Esea in the birthing room convinced her only that the high lords had no decency.

In the lord's hall, the infant's future was quickly determined. His mother could be his nurse, but his rearing would be that of a young lord, until his ability or lack of it appeared.

The boy showed a quick intelligence, a lively curiosity; he learned easily and could form the elegant script of Old Aare by the time he had seen six midwinter festivals. He had no peasant accent; he had no lack of manners or bodily grace. He also had no magic, and when the lord lost hope that he might show a useful trace of it, he found the boy a foster family in one of his villages, and sent him away.

It could have been worse. His lord provided: the family prospered, and the youth, as he grew to be, had no trouble finding a wife. He would inherit a farmstead, he was told, and in due time he had his own farm. With his father's gifts, he started well above the average, and as well he had the position of a market judge in the nearest town. It was not enough to live on, but it supplemented his farm's production. He knew he was well off, and shrugged away the hopes he'd once had of being adopted into the lord's family. Yet he could not forget his parentage, or the promise of magic.

In the year of his birth, and far away, the boy already lived who would make his parentage worthless.

Chapter One

"You're big enough now," said the boy's mother. "You don't need to be hanging on my skirts any more. You're bold enough when it's something you want to do." As she spoke, she raked at the boy's thick unruly hair with her fingers, and wiped a smudge of soot from his cheek. "You take that basket to the lord's steward, now, and be quick about it. Are you a big boy, or only a baby, then?"

"I'm big," he said, frowning. "I'm not scared." His mother flicked her apron over his shirt again, and landed a hand on his backside.

"Then get on with you. You're to be home right away, Gird, mind that. No playing about with the other lads and lasses. There's work to be done, boy."

"I know." With a grunt, he lifted the basket, almost hip-high, and leaned sideways to balance the weight; it was piled high with plums, the best from their tree. He could almost taste one, the sweet juice running down his throat . . .

"And don't you be eating any of those, Gird. Not even one. Your Da would skin you for it."

"I won't." He started up the lane, walking cantways from the weight, but determined not to put the basket down for a rest until he was out of sight of the house. He wanted to go alone. He'd begged for the chance, last year, when he was clearly too small. And this year, when she'd first told him, he'd—he frowned harder, until he could feel the knot of his brows. He'd been afraid, after all. "I'm not afraid," he muttered to himself. "I'm not. I'm big, bigger than the others."

All along the lanes he saw others walking, carrying

5

baskets slung over an arm or on a back. A handbasket for each square of brambleberries; an armbasket for each tree in its first three years of bearing; a ruckbasket for each smallfruit tree over three years, and a backbasket for apples in prime. Last year he'd carried a handbasket in each hand: two handbaskets make an armbasket, last year's fee. This year was the plum's fourth bearing year, and now they owed the lord a ruckbasket.

And that leaves us, he thought bitterly, with only an armbasket for ourselves. It had been a dry year; most of the fruit fell before it ripened. He had heard his parents discussing it. They could have asked the lord's steward to change their fee, but that might bring other trouble.

"It's not the name I want, a man who argues every measure of his fee," said his father, leaning heavily on the table. "No. It's better to pay high one year, and have the lord's opinion. 'Tis not as if we were hungry."

Gird had listened silently. They had been hungry, two years before; he still remembered the pain in his belly, and his brother's gifts of food. Anything was better than that. Now, as he walked the lane, his belly grumbled; the smell of the plums seemed to go straight from his nose to his gut. He squinted against the bright light, trying not to think of it. Underfoot the dust was hot on the surface, but his feet sank into a coolness— was it damp? Why did wet and cold feel the same? He saw a puddle left from the rain a week ago, and headed for it before remembering his mother's detailed warnings. No puddles, she'd said; you don't come into the lord's court with dirty feet.

The lane past his father's house curved around a clump of pickoak and into the village proper. Gird shifted his basket to the other side, and stumped on. Up ahead, just beyond the great stone barn where the whole village stored hay and grain was the corner of the lord's wall. The lane was choked with people waiting to go in the gate, children younger than Gird with handbaskets, those his own age with armbaskets, older ones with ruckbaskets like his. He joined the line, edging forward as those who had paid their fee came out and left room within.

Once inside the gate, he could just see over taller heads one corner of the awning over the steward's table. As he tried to peek between those ahead of him, and see more, someone tapped his head with a hard knuckle. He looked around.

"Good looking plums," said Rauf, Oreg the pigherd's son. "Better than ours." Rauf was a hand taller than Gird, and mean besides. Gird nodded, but said nothing. That was safer with Rauf. "They'd look better in my basket, I think. Eh, Sig?" Rauf nudged his friend Sikan in the ribs, and they both grinned at Gird. "You've more than you need, little boy; that basket's too heavy anyway." Rauf took a handful of plums off the top of the basket, and Sikan did the same.

"You stop!" Gird forgot that loud voices were not allowed in the lord's court. "Those are my plums!"

"They may have been once, but I found them." Rauf shoved Gird hard; he stumbled, and more plums rolled out of the basket. "Found them all over the ground, I did; what's down is anyone's, right?"

Gird tried to snatch for the rolling plums. Sikan kicked him lightly in the arm, while Rauf tipped his basket all the way over. Gird heard some of the other boys laughing, a woman nearby crying shame to them all. The back of his neck felt hot, and he heard a wind in his ears. Before he thought, he grabbed the basket and slammed it into Rauf's face. Sikan jumped at him; Gird rolled away, kicking wildly. In moments that corner of the courtyard was a wild tangle of fighting boys and squashed fruit. The steward bellowed; the lord's guards waded into the fight, using their hands, their short staves, the flats of their swords. And Gird found himself held immobile by two guards, with Rauf lying limp on the stones, and the other boys huddled in a frightened mass behind a line of armed men.

"Disgraceful," said someone over his head. Gird looked up. The lord's steward, narrow-faced, blue-eyed. "Who started it?"

No one answered. Gird felt the hands tighten on his

arms, and give a shake. "Boy," said a deeper voice, one of the men holding him. "What do you know about this. Who started it?"

"He stole my plums." Before he spoke, he didn't realize he was going to. In the heavy silence, with Rauf lying still before him, and the courtyard a mess of trampled fruit, his voice sounded thin. The steward looked at him, met his eyes.

"Your name, boy? Your father?"

"Gird, sir. Dorthan's son."

"Dorthan, eh? Your father's not a brawling man; I'd have thought better of his sons."

"Sir, he stole my plums!"

"Your tribute . . . yes. What was it, this year?"

"A ruckbasket, sir. And they were fine plums, big dark ones, and he—"

"Who?"

Gird nodded at Rauf. "Rauf, sir. Him and Sikan, his friend."

"Anyone else see that?" The steward's gaze drifted over the crowd of boys. Most stared at their feet, but Teris, a year older than Gird and son of his nearest neighbor, nodded.

"If you please, sir, it was Rauf started it. He said they were good plums, and would look better in his basket. Then he took some, and Gird said no, and he knocked Gird aside—"

"Rauf struck the first blow?"

"Aye, sir."

"Anyone else?" Reluctant nods followed this. Gird saw a space open around Sikan, who had edged to the rear of the group. Sikan flushed and moved forward when the steward stared hard at him.

"It wasn't so bad, sir," he said, trying to smile around a bruised lip. "We was just teasing the lad, like, that was all."

"Teasing, in your lord's court?"

"Well—"

"And did you hit this boy?" The steward pointed at Gird.

"Well, sir, I may have—sort of—sort of pushed at

him, like, but nothing hard, not to say brawling. But he's one of them, you know, likes to make quarrels—"

The steward frowned. "It's not the first time, Sikan, that you and Rauf have been found in bad order." He nodded at the men behind Gird, and they released his arms. Gird rubbed his left elbow. "As for you, Gird son of Dorthan, brawling in the lord's court is always wrong—always. Do you understand?"

"Yes, sir." There was nothing else to say.

"And you're at fault in saying that *your* plums were stolen. They were your lord's plums, owed to him. If Rauf had given them in, the lord would still have them. Instead—" The steward waved his hand at the mess. Very few whole fruit had survived the brawl. "But your family has a good name, young Gird, and I think you did not mean to cause trouble. So there will be no fine in fruit for your family . . . only you, along with these others, will stay and clean the court until those stones are clean enough to satisfy Sergeant Mager here."

"Yes, sir." And he would be late home, and get another whipping from his father.

"Now as for you, Sikan, and Rauf—" For Rauf had begun to move about, and his eyes opened, though aimlessly as yet. "Since you started trouble, and moreover chose a smaller boy to bully, you'll spend a night in the stocks, when this work is done." And the steward turned away, back to his canopy over the account table where the scribes made marks on long rolls of parchment.

Gird found the rest of that day instructive. He had scrubbed their stone floor often enough at home, and scraped dung from the cowshed. But his mother was no more particular about the bowls they ate from than Sergeant Mager about the courtyard stones. He and the other boys picked up pieces of the squashed fruit and put them in baskets—without getting even a taste of it. Then they carried buckets of water—buckets so large that Gird couldn't carry one by himself—and brushed the stones with water and long-handled brushes. Then they rinsed, and then they scrubbed again. Just when Gird was sure that the stones could be no cleaner had they just been quarried, the Sergeant would find a scrap of fruit rind, and they had it all to do over again. But he did his best, working as hard as he could. By the time the Sergeant let them go, it was well past midday, and Gird's fingers were raw with scrubbing. He called Gird back from the gate for an extra word.

"Your dad's got a good name," he said, laying a heavy hand on Gird's shoulder. "And you're a good lad, if quick-tempered. You've got courage, too—you were willing to take on those bigger lads. Ever think of being a soldier?"

Gird felt his heart leap. "You mean . . . like you?"

The sergeant laughed. "Not at first, of course. You'd start like the others, as a recruit. But you're big for your age, and strong. You work hard. Think of it . . . a sword, a spear maybe . . . you could make sergeant someday."

"Do you ever get to ride a horse?" That was his dream, to ride a fast horse as the lords did, running before the wind.

"Sometimes." The sergeant smiled. "The steward might recommend you for training. A lad like you needs the discipline, needs a place to work off his extra energy. Besides, it's a mouth less to feed at home." He gave Gird's shoulder a final shake, and pushed him out the gate. "We'll have a word with your dad, this next day or so. Don't start trouble again, eh?"

"Holy Lady of Flowers!" His mother had been halfway down the lane; she must have been watching from the house. "Gird, what did you mean—"

"I'm sorry." He stared at the dust between his toes, aware of every rip in his clothes. They had been his best, the shirt actually new, and now they looked like his ragged old ones. "I didn't start it, Mother, truly I didn't. Rauf stole some plums, and I thought we might have a fine—"

"Effa says Rauf hit you first."

"Yes'm." He heard her sigh, and looked up. "I really didn't—"

"Gird—" She put a hand on his head. "At least you're back, and no fine. Effa says the steward didn't seem angry, not like she thought he would be."

"I don't think he is." Suddenly his news burst out of him. "Guess what the sergeant said—maybe I can train to be a soldier! I could have a sword—" Excited as he was, he didn't notice her withdrawal, the shock on her face. "Sometimes they even ride horses, he said. He said I was big enough, and strong, and—" Her stiff silence held him at last; he stared at her. "Mother?"

"No!" She caught his arm, and half-dragged him down the lane to the house.

The argument went on all evening. His father's first reaction to the story of the plums was to reach for his belt. "I don't brawl," he said. "And I didn't raise my sons to be brawlers."

Arin, as usual, stood up for him. "Da, that Rauf's a bad lot, you know that. So's the steward: they've got him in stocks this night, and Sikan too."

"And I'll have their fathers down on me, did you think of that? Oreg's no man to blame his own son, even if Rauf tells the tale aright. If Gird hadn't fought back, Oreg would've known he owed me sommat, a bit of bacon even. And Sikan's father—I want no quarrel with him; his wife has the only parrion for dyecraft in this village. As for this way—it's no good. We can't be fighting each other; the world's hard enough without that. They'll have to know I punished Gird, and I'll have to go to them and apologize."

So it was a whipping on top of his bruises, and no supper as well as no lunch. Gird had expected as much; he saw from Arin's wink that he would have a scrap to eat later, whatever Arin could sneak to him without being caught. But his father was as unhappy as his mother to hear of the sergeant's offer of training.

"It's never good to come into notice like that. Besides, we follow the Lady: would you take sword against your own folk, Gird? Break the village peace in blood and iron?" But before he could decide whether it was safe to answer—the answer he'd thought of, while waiting for his father to come from the fields—his father shrugged. "But if the steward comes, what can I say? They have the right to take you, no matter what I think about it. The best I can hope for is that the steward forgets it."

The steward did not forget. Gird spent the next day wrestling with the family's smallest scythe—still too long for him—mowing his father's section of the meadow. He knew he'd been sent there to get him out of sight, away from the other village boys. He knew his mother had baked two sweet cakes for Rauf's family and Sikan's, and his father had taken them over in the early morning. It was hot, the steamy heat of full summer, and the cold porridge of his breakfast had not filled the hollows from yesterday's fast. But above him, in the great field, his father was working, able to see if he shirked.

He kept at it doggedly, hacking uneven chunks where his brother could lay a clean swathe. There had to be a way. He paused to rub the great curved blade with the bit of stone his father had given him, and listened to the change in sound it made on different parts of the blade. When he looked sideways up the slope to the arable, he saw his father talking to another of the village men. Gird leaned on the scythe handle, the blade angled high above him, and picked a bur from between his toes.

When he looked again, his father had started back up the arable. Gird dared not move out of the sun to rest, but he tipped his head back to get the breeze. Something rustled in the tall grass ahead of him. Rat? Bird? He scratched the back of one leg with the other foot, glanced upslope again, and sighed. Someday he would be a man, and if he wasn't a soldier, he'd be a farmer, and able to swing a bigger scythe than this one. Like his father, whose sweeping strokes led the reapers each year. Like his brother Arin, who had just grown out of this scythe. He grunted at himself, and let the long blade down. Surely he could find a way to make this work better.

By nightfall, with all his blisters, he had begun to mow a level swathe. He'd changed the handles slightly, learned to get his hip into the swing, learned to take steps just the right length to compensate for the blade's arc. The next day, he spent on the same patch of meadow. Now that he had the knack of it, he was half-hoping the steward would not come. He would grow up a farmer like his father, leading the reapers in the field, guiding his own oxen, growing even better fruit . . .

It was the next day that the steward came at dusk, when his father had come in from the fields, and Gird had begun to feel himself out of disgrace as far as the family went. The children were sent to the barton out back, while the steward talked, and his father (he was sure) listened. He wanted to creep into the cowbyre and hear for himself, but Arin barred the way. He had to wait until his father called him in.

There in the candlelight, his father's face looked older, tireder. His mother sat stiffly, lips pressed together, behind her loom. The steward smiled at him. "Gird, the sergeant suggested that you were a likely lad to train for soldier: strong and brave, and in need of discipline. Your father will let you choose for yourself. If you agree, you will spend one day of ten with the soldiers this year, and from Midwinter to Midwinter next, two days of ten. It's not soldiering at first, I'll be honest with you: you'll work in the barracks just as you'd work here. But your father'd be paid the worth of your work, a copper crab more than for fieldwork. And the following year, you'd be a recruit, learning warcraft, and your father will get both coppers and a dole off his fee. 'Twould help your family, in hard times, but your father says you must do as you wish."

It was frightening to see his parents so still, so clearly frightened themselves. He had never really understood them before, he felt. Behind him, in the doorway, Arin and the others crowded; he could hear their noisy breathing. Could soldiering be so bad as they thought? All his life he'd seen the guardsmen strolling the village lane, admired the glitter of their buckles, the jingle of their harness. He'd been too young to fear the ordersticks, the clubs . . . he'd had strong hands rumpling his hair, when he crowded near with the other boys, he'd had a smile from the sergeant himself. And the soldiers fought off brigands, and hunted wolves and folokai; he remembered only last winter, cheering in the snow with the others as they carried back the dead folokai tied to poles. One of them had been hurt, his blood staining the orange tunic he wore, but the world was hard, and there were many ways to be hurt.

He wanted to stand on one leg and think about it, but there stood the steward, peering at him in the dimness with eyes that seemed to see clear into his heart. He'd never spoken to a lord before, exactly. Was the steward a lord? Close enough.

"It would not be a binding oath," the steward said, a little impatiently. Gird knew that tone; his father had it when he asked who had left the barton wicket open. It meant a quick answer, or trouble. "If you did not like it, you could quit before you started the real training . . ."

Gird ducked his head, and then looked up at the steward. From one corner of his vision he could see his father's rigid face, but he ignored it.

"Sir . . . steward . . . I would be glad to. If my father allows."

"He has said it." The steward smiled, then. "Dorthan, your son Gird is accepted into service of the Count Kelaive, and here is the *pirik*—" The bargain-sum, Gird remembered: not a price paid, as if he were a sheep, but a sum to mark the conclusion of any bargain. The price was somewhat else.

The very next morning, Gird left at dawn to walk through the village to the count's guards' barracks. None of his friends were out to watch him, but he knew they would be impressed. The guard at the gate admitted him, sent him straight across the forecourt to the barracks. The guards were just getting up, and the sergeant was crosser than Gird remembered.

"Get in the kitchen first, and serve the food; then you can clean for the cooks until after morning drill. I'll see you then. Hop, now."

The porridge was much like their own, if cooked in larger pots and served in bigger bowls. Gird carried the dirty bowls back, and scrubbed them, under the cook's critical eye, then scrubbed the big cookpots. Then it was chop the onions, while his eyes burned and watered, and chop the redroots until his hands were cramped, and then fetch buckets of clean water. All the while the cook scolded, worse than his oldest sister, while mixing and kneading the dough that would be dumplings in the midday stew. The sergeant came in while Gird was still washing down the long tables.

"Right, lad. Now let's see what we've got, here. Come along." He led Gird out the side door of the kitchen, into a back court, a little walled enclosure like a barton with no byres. In one corner was the kitchen well, with the row of buckets Gird had scrubbed neatly ranged along the wall.

The sergeant was just as impressive as ever, to Gird's eye: taller and broader than his own father, hard-muscled, with a brisk authority that expected absolute obedience. Gird looked at him, imagining himself grown into that size and strength, wearing those clean, whole, unmended clothes, having a place in the village and in his lord's service more secure than any farmer.

"You're a hard worker, and strong," the sergeant began, "but you'll have to be stronger yet, and you'll have to learn discipline. Begin with this: you don't talk unless you're told to, and you answer with 'sir' any time I speak to you. Clear?"

Gird nodded. "Yes . . . sir?"

"Right. You're here to learn, not to chatter. Dawn to dusk, one day of ten . . . can you count?"

"Not really, sir."

"Not really is no. Can't count sheep, or cows?"

Gird frowned. "If they're there . . . but not days, sir, they don't stay in front of me."

"You'll learn. Now, Gird: when you come here, you must be clean and ready to work. If you can't wash at home, come early and wash here. I'll have no ragtags in my barracks. Is that your only shirt?"

"No, sir, but th'other's worse."

"Then you'll get one, but only for this work. Do you have shoes? Boots?"

Gird shook his head, then remembered to say "No, sir." Shoes? For a mere lad? He had never had shoes, and wouldn't until he wed, unless his father had a string of good years.

"You'll need them later; you can wear them here, but

not at home. Did you have breakfast at home this morning?" Of course he had not, beyond a bit of crust; the porridge had just gone on when he walked up to the barracks. The sergeant hmmphed at that. "Can't grow soldiers on thin rations. I'll tell the cook, and you'll eat here all day on your workdays. Now—about the other boys. I want no brawling, young Gird, none at all. If they tease you about going for soldier, you learn to let it pass. No threats from you, no catcalling at Rauf or Satik or whatever his name was. You'll be where they can't bother you, if you keep your nose clean. Hothead soldiers cause more trouble than they're worth; you have your chance, for you and your family: earn it."

An answer seemed required; Gird said "Yes, sir."

The rest of that day was more chores and little that Gird could see as soldiering, although he did see the inside of the barracks, with the lines of wooden bunks and thin straw mattresses, the weapons hung neatly on the walls, the jacks (*inside!* He wondered, but did not ask, how they were cleaned. Surely they were cleaned; they smelled less than his own family's pit.) He swept a floor that seemed clean enough already, carried more buckets of water to the cook, ate a bowl of stew larger than his father ever saw for his lunch, washed dishes until his hands wrinkled afterwards, fetched yet more water (he felt his feet had worn a groove from the well to the kitchen door) and sliced yet more redroots, had a huge slab of bread and a piece of meat for supper, and was allowed to stand silent in a corner and watch the ordered marching that preceded the changing of watch before dusk.

He ran home along the dark lane his bare feet knew so well, bursting with excitement. Meat! He didn't know if he would tell them, because they would see no meat until harvest . . . but it had tasted so good, and the stew and bread had filled all the hollows in his belly. He burped, tasting meat on his breath, and laughed.

They were waiting, and had saved a bowl of gruel and hunk of bread for him; he felt both shamed and proud when he could give it to the others.

"So—they'll feed you well?" His mother wasn't quite looking at him, spooning his share carefully into other bowls.

"Yes. Breakfast too, but I must get there early."

"And do you like soldiering?" she asked, a sharpness in her voice.

"It's not soldiering yet," he said, watching the others eat. "I helped the cook today, chopping onions and carrying water . . . I carried enough water for two days."

"You can carry my water tomorrow," his mother said. His father had yet said nothing, watching Gird across the firelight as he ate.

The time from summer to Midwinter passed quickly. One day in ten he rose before dawn, at first cockcrow, and ran up the lane to the gate where the guards now knew him by name and greeted him. Into that steamy kitchen, larger than his own cottage, where the cook—never so difficult as that first day—gave him a great bowl of porridge before he served the others. As the days drew in with autumn, that kitchen became a haven, rich with the smells of baking bread and roasting meat, savory stews, fruit pies. It was a feastday, however plain the soldiers found the food (and he was amazed to hear them grumble); he had his belly full from daylight to dark. With a full belly, the work went easily. Hauling water, sweeping, washing, chopping vegetables, chopping wood for the great hearths. He learned the names of all the guards, and knew where everything was kept. Two of them were recruits, one from his village and one from over the fields sunrising, tall boys he would have thought men if he hadn't seen them next to the soldiers. He began to learn the drill commands as he watched.

The other nine days passed as his days always had, in work with his family. He was growing into the scythe, or managing it better, and he was allowed in the big field for the first time. Arin took him up to the high end of the wood, where the village pigs spent the summer rooting and wallowing, to help gather them into the

lower pens. They ate their meager lunch in a rocky cleft
up higher than others ever came, a place Arin had
shown him the first year he went to help gather pigs.
He spent a few days nutting in the woods, with his
friends, laughing and playing tricks like the others.
They all wanted to know what he was learning. When
he explained that so far it was just work, like any work,
they wondered why he agreed.

"It *will* be soldiering," Gird said, leaning back against
a bank and squinting up at one of their favorite nut
trees. "And in the meantime, it's food and coppers for
my family—what better?"

"Good food?" asked Amis. He was lean and ribby, as
they all were that year.

Gird nodded. "Lots of it, too. And that leaves
more—"

"Can you take any home?"

"No." That had been a disappointment, and his first
disgrace. Sharing food was part of his life: everyone
shared, fast or feast. But when he tried to take home a
half-loaf being tossed out anyway, it had brought swift
punishment. "The sergeant says that's stealing. They're
getting enough for me, he says, more than I'm worth.
That may be so, though I try. But not one crust will
they let me take out, or a single dried plum." The
stripes had not hurt as much as knowing he could not
share; he had not told his father why he'd been punished.

Teris made the closed-fist gesture against evil. "Gripe-
hearts, is what they are. You watch, Gird, they'll turn
you against us."

"Never." Gird said it loudly, though he could already
sense a rift between him and his friends. "I can share
from my own, when I earn my own: then you'll see.
Open heart, open hands: the Lady's blessing."

"Lady's blessing," they all said. Gird made sure to
put a handful more than his share into the common
sack, that would go up to the count's steward as their
fee for nutting in those woods.

At Midwinter Feast, he stood once more before the
steward, this time in the Hall, and agreed to his next
year's service. His father had stayed home, shrugging

away Gird's concern for his cough. Two days in ten, he thought, they will not have to feed me, and there's the coppers besides. He was proud of the thought that his pay might help with the fieldfee.

Two days in ten made one in five. In the short days of winter, the sergeant set him to learning counting and letters. Gird hated it. Sitting with cold feet and numbed hands over a board scrawled with mysterious shapes was far harder than fetching water from the well, even when that meant breaking the ice on it first. At home he could read tallies well enough, the notched sticks all the farmers used to keep count of stock and coin. But here were no helpful hints . . . you could not tell, from the words, who wrote them. Without the clue that this tally was Oder's . . . when everyone knew that Oder had only a double-hand of sheep . . . you had to know *all* the words and numbers to find out what it said.

Some of the men laughed unkindly at his struggles. "Thickhead," said one, a balding redhead whom Gird had rather liked before. "Perhaps the knowledge could get in, if we cracked it open for you?"

"More like his little wit would fall out," said another. "He thinks with his hands and feet, that one, like most peasants."

Gird tried to concentrate on markings that seemed to jump and jiggle about in the flickering candlelight. Was the sign for three supposed to stick out *this* way, or that? He wiggled his fingers, trying to remember. The sergeant's sword was on the same side as that hand . . . he shook his head, confused once more.

"Here," said the redhead, handing him two pebbles. "Put this in your hand—no, *that* hand—and hold it there. Now call that your left hand, eh? Stonehand. Some signs are stonehand, some are empty hand—you can remember that much, can't you?"

He might have, but he was angry. He clenched his teeth against the temptation. The sergeant intervened. "Let him alone, Slagin. The stone's a good idea, but leave the rest of it. Some boys take longer, that's all. All right, Gird, the cook needs more water."

By spring, the two days in ten of plentiful food had

begun to show. He had always been heavier built than most of his sibs. "More like my brother," his father had said, of an uncle dead before he was born. Now his broader frame began to carry thicker muscle. He had grown another two fingers up, and was straining the seams of his shirt. And that summer he carried a ruckbasket of plums without difficulty.

All that year, Gird worked his two days in ten, and his family settled into the knowledge that he would almost certainly become a soldier. His father continued to teach him the crafts and skills of farming, but with less urgency. His mother let out his old shirt, and made a new one, without pleading with him to stay home. His brothers admitted, privately, that life was a bit easier when he got part of his food elsewhere, and the coppers came in on quarterdays. Rauf tried once to tease him into a fight, calling him coward when he backed off; a few months later he noticed that Rauf crossed the lane to avoid him. And his friends seemed glad to see him, when any of them had time off for foolery, which wasn't often.

So at Midwinter, he gave his oath to the steward, and entered training as a recruit, to sleep in the barracks with the others and learn the arts of war.

Chapter Two

"Your oath to the steward's one thing," said Sergeant Mager. "It's me you've got to satisfy."

Gird, along with three other recruits, all from other villages, stood uneasily in his new orange uniform while the sergeant stalked back and forth in front of them. The other soldiers were inside, enjoying the Midwinter Feast. They were in the little back courtyard he knew so well, with an icy wind stiffening their skins.

"If you make it through training," the sergeant went on, "you'll give your oath to our lord or his guardian. You'll go where he sends you, and fight his battles, the rest of your time as soldier. Some of you—" He did not look at Gird, "—some of you started your training as boys. But you needn't think you know much yet. You all start level."

Level meant the bottom. The senior recruits, that Gird had seen cuffed and bullied by the older men, now cuffed and bullied the new ones. Gird was no longer the cook's helper, but he still hauled buckets of water, scrubbed floors, and now had his uniform to keep clean and mended, besides. The boots that went with it kept his feet from the snow, but chafed badly until he learned how to pack them with oily wool. He had never had to do anything to a bed but fall into it and fight his brothers for the cover: now he had to produce as neat a mattress, as tightly rolled a blanket, as the others. And, lacking a boy to do the work, all four new recruits washed dishes.

Yet none of them complained. Like Gird, they had all been peasants' sons, only one of them the son of a free tenant. It was worth all the abuse to have a full belly all winter long, somewhere warm to sleep. Gradually they got used to having enough to eat, a bunk each, with a warm blanket, whole clothes that fit, boots.

Gird had been hoping to move quickly into training with weapons, but the sergeant had other priorities. They would all, he said firmly, with a hard look at Gird, learn their letters well enough to follow simple orders. They would learn to keep count, so they could help the steward or his agents during tax-time. Ifor, who had been sent from the nearest trading town, could already read a little, and use the pebble-board for figuring. He didn't mind the daily session with letters that was still torture to Gird.

"You'll never make sergeant, Gird, if you don't learn this," the sergeant warned. Gird was beginning to think he didn't care, if making sergeant meant making sense of reading and writing and numbers. He could see, as clear as his hand on the table, how many legs two sheep had, but trying to think of it and write it down made the sweat run down his face. He was the slowest in this, as he was strongest in body. The sergeant insisted that it didn't have to work that way, that many strong men were quick-minded in learning to read. Gird eyed the others wistfully, wondering what the difference was inside their heads. He struggled on. He knew all the marks, now, that stood for numbers and sounds; he could read the simplest words, and write his own name in awkward, shaky letters. But it got no easier, for all his labors.

Besides that, they had to learn about their lord's domain: the correct address for the lord himself, for the steward, for the various officers who came through on inspections. The names of all the villages, and the headmen of each, and the sergeants in all the places the guard was stationed. Once in the lord's guard, they might be sent anywhere within his domain. Most men served away from their homes, at least until they were well along in service. Gird had never really considered the possibility that he might leave and never come back. Going off to war was one thing, but leaving this village—the only place he'd ever known—to make a life somewhere else—that was new and disturbing. He frowned, but said nothing. At least this was better than reading and writing. The lists went on and on. They had to know the right name for each piece of equipment in the barracks, from the tools used on the hearth to the weapons hung on the walls. Each weapon had not only a name, but a name for each part—for each movement with which it could be used—for the command given to make each movement.

When they did begin what Gird recognized as soldier's training, it was hardly different from the games boys played. Wrestling—he had wrestled with the other lads all his life. He was good at it. When the sergeant asked him if he thought he knew how, he answered briskly that he did, and stepped out. Someone chuckled, but he ignored it. They laughed at everything the new recruits did, good or bad. He eyed the balding redhead he'd been told to work with, and cocked his arm, edging in as the boys always did. Something like a tree trunk suddenly grabbed him and he felt himself flying through the air, to land hard on the cold stone floor.

"It's not a game, any more," said his partner mildly. "Try again." Some five falls later, when Gird was breathless, bruised, and much less cocky—and the other man had hardly broken into a sweat—the sergeant called a halt.

"Now you know what you don't know. Convinced?"

"Yes, sir."

"Remember: if we have to crack your head to let in wisdom, we will." The sergeant was serious, but Gird grinned at that. It made sense. His father said much the same, and he'd known all his life that his own head was considered harder than most.

Besides wrestling, there was drill. Gird found he liked that, although he had trouble with some of the sequences, and more than once turned in the wrong place and got trodden on. And pounded, when the sergeant caught up with him. But when it worked, when all the separate individuals merged into one body, and the boots crashed on the stones together, it sent shivers down his backbone. This was really soldiering, something the village folk could watch and recognize, something to show off. If the sergeant ever let them past the gates, which he had not for tens and tens of days.

One late winter day, shepherds came to ask the guard's help in hunting a pack of wolves. The steward agreed, and the sergeant, now mounted on a stout brown horse, led them all out into a miserably cold, bleak day with neither sun nor snow to commend it. Gird marched for the first time in uniform down the lane past his cottage, where his younger sister peeked through the leafless hedge and dared a shy wave. He could not wave back, not with the sergeant's eye on him, as it surely was, for all he rode ahead. But he knew she watched, and admired her older brother, and someday all the others would too. He could imagine himself receiving admiring glances from all the villagers, when he saved their stock from wolves or folokai, or protected them from brigands.

Gird enjoyed the wolf hunt, though it meant that he and the other inexperienced ones spent three whole days trudging through cold damp woods and across even colder wet pastures, looking for wolf signs. It was not until much later that he realized the sergeant never expected them to find any—that's what the gnarled old tracker with his hounds was for—but it kept them out of trouble and far away from the actual hunt. They returned in the glow of a successful hunt, behind the lucky ones who had actually killed two wolves and so got to carry them through the village (Gird and the other recruits had carried them most of the way back, while the hunters themselves told and retold exactly how each spear had gone into its prey.)

With the coming of spring, they spent more of their time outside, and more of it in things Gird recognized as soldierly. Marching drill, and long marches across the fields and pastures. Archery, not with the simple and fairly weak bows his own people used for hunting small fowl in the woods, but with the recurved bows that took all his strength to draw. They learned the use of stick and club, facing off in pairs and later with the older recruits in sections. Gird collected his fair share of bruises and scrapes without comment, and dealt as many.

Days lengthened with the turning year. Soldiers as well as farmers had to put in their due of roadwork, and Gird's weapon on that occasion was a shovel. He hesitated before jamming it into the clogged ditch: was this like a plow? Did he need to perform the spring ritual of propitiation before putting iron in Alyanya's soil? He muttered a quick apology as he saw the sergeant glare his way. It would have to do. He meant no disrespect, and he had brought (on his own time) the sunturning flowers to the barracks well. Although the sergeant had brushed them away without comment, surely the Lady would understand.

He might have known his mutter would not go unnoticed. Even as he tossed the second shovelful of wet clay and matted leaves to one side, the sergeant was beside him.

"What's that you said, Gird?"

"Just asked the Lady's peace, sir, before putting iron to 'er."

The sergeant sighed, gustily, and looked both ways to be sure the others were hard at work before he spoke. "Gird, when you were a farmer's brat, you paid attention to the Lady, and no doubt to every well-sprite, spring spirit, and endstone watcher. I've no doubt who it was tied that bunch of weeds to the wellpost."

Gird opened his mouth to say it wasn't weeds at all, but the proper flowers, picked fresh that morning, but thought better of it.

"But now you're a soldier, or like to be. You need a soldier's patron now, Gird, not a farmer's harvest matron. Gods know I'm as glad of the Lady's bounty as anyone, and I grant her all praise in harvest time. It's right for farmers to follow all the rituals. But not you. Will you stop to ask the Lady's blessing every time you draw steel, in the midst of battle? You'll have a short life that way."

"But sir—"

"You cannot be both, Gird, farmer and soldier. Not in your heart. Did your folk teach you nothing of soldiers' gods?" Gird shook his head, still shoveling, and the sergeant sighed again. "Well, 'tis time you learned. Tir will take your oath in iron, same as mine, and asks nothing but your courage in battle and your care for your comrades. The lords say he's below Esea, their god—" He peered at Gird's face, to see if he understood. Gird nodded, silently; his father had had a lot to say about Esea—a foreign god, he'd said, not like their own Lady, and not like the Windsteed. "But to us it doesn't matter," said the sergeant. "He's god enough for me, my lad, and that should be enough for you. Think about it. And no more flowers around my well, is that clear?"

"Yes, sir." He had not thought soldiers *that* different. Everyone knew the capriciousness of the *merin*, the well-sprites . . . how the water rose and fell, regardless of local rains, how even its flavor changed. Had that well in the barracks yard gone years without proper care? He was sure the water had tasted sweeter after his offering. But he could not argue with his sergeant.

After the roadwork, after the bridge repairs that followed the spring rains, the recruits had their first chance to mingle with the villagers. Gird spent most of that time helping his father and brothers with their work, but found an hour now and then to meet with his old friends. At first they were properly impressed with his growing strength and martial skills, but that didn't last long.

"It's not fair," said Teris, when Gird had thrown him easily for the third time one evening. "You're using soldier's tricks against friends, and that's not fair." He turned away. So did the others.

"But I—" Gird stared at their backs. He knew what that meant. If they shut him out, he would have no one in the village but his family. And his family, just lately, had been irritating him with complaints about his attitude. If the sergeant forbade him to remember all the Lady's rituals, his family insisted that he perform them all perfectly. He could not lose his friends: not now. "I—I will teach you," he offered. "Then it would be fair."

"Would you, truly?" Teris turned around again.

"Of course." Gird took a deep breath. The sergeant might think he knew nothing—or that's what he kept saying—but here he knew more than any of them. "We can say we have a guard unit—we can have a sergeant, a captain—"

"I suppose you'll want to be captain," said Kev.

"If he's teaching us," said Teris, shrugging, "he can be captain. For awhile."

"We need a level field," said Gird. He would teach them marching, he thought to himself. Maybe if he taught them, he wouldn't forget the commands himself. Somewhere in the back of his mind he remembered an oath not to teach "peasants and churls" the arts of war. But marching in step wasn't an art of war. They'd all tried it when they were little boys; they just hadn't known how to do it *right*. And wrestling wasn't an art of war; no one fought battles by wrestling. And archery . . . all boys played with archery. Nonetheless, he took care that the level field they decided on was well out of sight of the guard stations.

In a few weeks, Gird's troop of boys was moving around the back horse pasture with assurance. Bit by bit, as he learned from the sergeant, he transferred knowledge to the boys.

"The little groups are called squads," he said one day. "We have enough to have three of them; it's like pretend armies. Every squad has a leader, and marches together, and you can do real things with it." They built a sod fort in the field, and practiced assaults. Teris, in particular, had a gift for it; he remembered everything Gird told him, the first time.

Now, rehearsing his new knowledge with his friends, Gird felt that his life as a soldier was well begun. That first summer as a recruit, he spent all his free time with them; he saw no reason why their old friendship should ever end. He wished he could show them off to the sergeant. If he could train them, he had to be learning himself, didn't he?

But as time passed, Gird's friends were working too hard in the fields to have time for boyish play. First one, then another, failed to turn up for drill, and then the others refused to do it. They wanted to lie in the long grass and talk about things Gird didn't know: whose brother was courting whose sister, which family might have trouble raising the field-fee this year, all that timeless village gossip. When he tried to argue them into drill or wrestling, they simply looked at him, a look the sergeant had taught him to think mulish and stupid. He gave in, since arguing would not serve, and wished he could live in two places at once.

After harvest, he had less time off himself, and rarely came into the village all that winter. The recruits had begun to learn swordwork, and even Gird knew that he could make no excuse for teaching his friends to use edged weapons, even if they had had them to practice with. No one did; the strictest of the laws forbade any but soldiers to have weapons, and even the free smiths feared the punishment for breaking that law. Besides, the sergeant still insisted that he keep trying to learn to read and write. None of his friends could, or cared to. His father admitted that reading was a useful skill, but wasn't at all sure that it was right for a farmer to know. Gird opened his mouth to say "But I'm not a farmer!" and shut it again. That was the whole point, and they all knew it.

There were other barriers growing, too, between them. He could not tell them what the sergeant said about Alyanya, or what he felt himself. Even the rituals of harvest had seemed a little silly: the twisted wisps of straw, the knotted yarn around the last sheaf, all that was peasant lore, far removed from his future as a soldier. He felt guilty when he listened to the other soldiers' jests; those were his people, his family and extended kin. Yet he wished that the villagers would somehow impress the soldiers—would somehow be more soldierly, so that he could feel pride in them.

And there was the matter of soldier's discipline. For himself, Gird could stand a few buffets when he made a mistake, a few lashes for coming back drunk from the harvest festival trying to sing "Nutting in the Woods." Being clouted by the others was no worse than being mauled by Rauf and the older boys when he'd been younger. For that matter, many families were almost as rough; his father had taken a belt to him more than once, and his oldest brother had pummeled him regularly before he married and moved away.

What he did not like was having to do the same to others. When Keri, a lad from one of the distant villages, mishandled a sword, and the sergeant had them all join in the punishment, Gird told himself that someone who couldn't stand a few buffets wouldn't stay strong in battle, but he didn't like to think which bruise on that battered face had come from his fist. He got a reputation for being strong enough but unaggressive, a little too gentle. The sergeant shook his head at him after seeing him flinch from Keri's punishment. "And I thought you'd be the quarrelsome sort, glad enough to clout others. Well, better this way, as long as you don't mind killing an enemy. But mind, lad, soldiering's not for the faint heart or weak stomach." He was sure he would not mind a battle; it was having to hit someone helpless that made him feel sick to his stomach. This was another thing he could not share with boyhood friends; he knew they would not understand.

Past Midwinter Feast, in the slack of late winter, he found another troubling presence in the barracks. Three of the soldiers, all from Finyatha and rotated here from the count's household, favored Liart. Gird had never heard of Liart before that second winter, when he came back from the jacks one night to find the three crouched before the hearth with something that whimpered between them. When they heard him, one of them whirled.

"Get away!" he'd said. "Or by Liart's chain, you'll rue it!" He had gone to the sergeant, unsure, and seen the sergeant's face tighten.

"Liart, is it? Liart's chain? I'll give them Liart's chain!" And he had stormed out, bellowing. But in the end he had gone to the steward, and come back shaken. "A god of war is a god of war," he'd said then, in the bleak light of a winter morning. "Our lord approves, if someone chooses Liart for patron."

Gird tried to ask, and was sworn at for his pains. Then, later, one of the other men, Kadir, explained. "Liart's followers buy his aid with blood; 'tis said he likes it best if it comes hardly . . . d'you see?" Gird didn't, but knew he didn't want to know. "Liart's chain . . . that's the barbed chain, like the barbed whip they use on murderers, up in Finyatha. Some lords use it, more than used to. Mostly it was thieves and outlaws, in the old days, so I heard. But the thing is, Gird, don't you be asking trouble of Liart's followers; they'll torment you as glad as anyone, if you bring notice to them. I'd be careful, was I you."

A few days later he found a short length of barbed chain on his bunk, as they came in for inspection. The sergeant's eyes met his; he took his punishment without complaint; they both knew he had not put it there. He himself had declared for Tir, as his sergeant had suggested the previous summer, although he had not yet given his oath of iron. That would require a Blademaster, and the sergeant said they would have the chance after they'd given their final oath to the lord when training was over. The sergeant had told him what was lawful for him to know, though, and it was very little like anything the villagers taught.

So when the days lengthened again into spring, there were many things he could not share with old friends. They would have questions he could not answer—that was the best face he could put on it. Likely it would be worse. And he himself, as tall now as any of the guards, would be promoted from recruit come Summereve, when the lord was home from Finyatha.

Later he would remember that spring as one of the happiest times of his life, drenched in honey. He was young and strong and handsome; when he walked along the lanes to visit his family, with the brass badge of his lord's service shined and winking in the sun, the little children smiled and waved at him, tagging along behind. "Gird," they called. "Strong Gird . . . carry me, please?" Girls near his age glanced at him sideways; he felt each glance like a caress. Boys too old to tag him like the younger children watched nonetheless, and when he stopped to speak to someone they'd come close. "Is it hard to be a soldier, Gird?" they'd ask. And sometimes he told them tales of the barracks, and watched their eyes widen.

Once, twice, he had leave to go to the gatherings in the sheepfolds around, where the young men and girls met and danced. He was too young yet—he merely watched—but he enjoyed the music, and the respectful, if wary, glances. His old friends still joked with him, cautiously, but none ventured to wrestle or match arms. He didn't mind that; he didn't want to hurt them, and he knew now that he could.

Even at home, it was a good spring. His father's eyes still showed concern, but his older brothers were clearly proud to have a brother in the guards. Other lads his own age were still "lads" only—too young to marry, too young to inherit a farm, and most were younger sons.

"Sim's boys" or "Artin's boys," they were called, in lumps like cattle. But he, Gird son of Dorthan, he had a name for himself in the village, and a nickname to match, for even the veterans called him "Strong Gird." And on his rare days off, when he helped his father and brothers on the farm, he knew he deserved that nickname: he could outlift any of them, could haul more wood and dig a longer line of ditch. Now he could handle the longest scythe they had, and mow as level a swathe as his father.

"I can't say they've spoiled you for work," his father said one of those nights, when Gird was enjoying a last few minutes by the fire before walking back to the barracks. "You're a good worker; you always were, from a little lad. You're strong, and you've no foolish ideas about it. But I still wish—" He left the wish unfinished. Gird knew what he would have said, but he had never understood it. He would never forget his family, the people of his heart. And, strong as he was, he wouldn't die in battle far away—he would come home to them. Couldn't they understand that?

"I'll be all right, Da," he said, patting his father's shoulder. "I'll be good, and someday—" But he could not name his private dream, not then. It trembled on the edge of his mind, half-visible in a cloud of wishes too vague to express. He would do something wonderful, something that made the village and the sergeant both proud of him. Something very brave, that yet hurt no one but bad men, or monsters.

"Go in peace, Gird, as long as you may," his father said. "I pray the Lady forgives your service of iron."

His father always said that, and it always annoyed him now. Alyanya, the Lady of Flowers, the Lady of Peace, the Lady whose permission they must have each spring to touch the land with plow or spade—Gird thought of her in his mind as a more beautiful form of the village maids. Rahel, maybe, with shining hair down her back, or Estil whose perfect breasts swung dizzyingly with every stroke of the scythe during haying. Those girls, those flower-scented soft-skinned girls with their springtime bodies swaying along the lanes, those girls didn't mind his "service of iron." No, he had seen them glance, seen them smile sideways at him, while farm lads his age received no flicker of eyelash at all.

And surely the Lady herself, whatever else she was, understood the need for soldiers—surely she also admired broad shoulders, strength, the courage of a man with bright weapons in his hand. The sergeant had told him an old tale about Alyanya and Tir, in which the Lady had her Warrior guardian, and was glad of his service. He had never heard such a tale at home, but it made sense, the way the sergeant told it. That the iron of plow and spade was but another form of the iron of sword and spear, and the Lady's consent to one was as gracious as her consent to the other. "Bright harvest," the sergeant's tale had sung, "born of this wedding, child of this marriage—" Girl and Lady, he thought to himself, both know and want the strong arm, the bright steel. But he did not argue with his father, as he had once the year before. His father was a farmer, born and bred, and would die as a farmer—may it not be soon! he thought piously—and he could not expect a farmer to understand soldiers' things.

He walked back through the late-spring night, with starlight glittering in the puddles alongside the lane, as happy as he could imagine being. He was Gird, the local farmer's son who had made good, had made a place for himself in the lord's household, by the strength of his arm and the courage of his heart.

Then the lord count arrived from the king's court. All the guards stood rigid in the courtyard for that: Gird in the back row, with the other recruits. Tall as he was, he had a good view of the cavalcade. A halfsquad of guards, looking somehow older and rougher than those he had met, on chunky nomad-bred horses, followed by two boys that looked younger than Gird on tall, light-built mounts. Behind them, a prancing warhorse with elaborate harness embroidered and stamped on multicolored leathers. And on the warhorse, their lord—Gird's liege lord, Count Seriast Vanier Dobrest Kelaive—a sour-faced young man in orange velvet, black gloves, tall black boots, and a black velvet cap with an orange plume. He looked, Gird thought, like a gourd going bad in storage—a big orange gourd spotted with fungus.

Immediately he suppressed the thought. This was his lord, his sworn liege, and for the rest of his life he would be this man's loyal vassal. His eyes dropped to the horse, the saddle, the tall polished boots. There were his spurs, the visible symbol of his knighthood, long polished shafts and delicate jewelled rowels. The steward came forward; the squires dismounted, handing their horses to grooms. One of them held the lord's bridle; the other steadied the off stirrup while he dismounted. Gird watched every detail. So far he had not had a chance to ride more than the mule that turned the millsweep. But in watching the horse, he heard everything, heard the steward's graceful speech of welcome, the curt response.

He knew, as did they all, that the young lord had been educated at the king's court in Finyatha; this year, at Summereve, he would take over his own domain, and the steward's rule would end. Everyone had liked that idea—or almost everyone—and had told one another tales of the steward's harshness. A young lord, they'd said, their own lord, living finally on his own domain, would surely be more generous. The steward would have to do his bidding, not make up orders of his own.

But now, seeing the young lord in person, Gird had a moment of doubt. For all the complaints he'd heard of the steward's harshness, most years no one went hungry. The sergeant had told him of other lands where brigands or war brought famine. Here, despite the fees, a hardworking family could prosper, as his had, with one brother tenanting his own cottage, and Arin soon to marry. Would things be better under the young count?

Still, Summereve, only a few days away, would bring a great day for both of them. The lord's investiture, in the moments after midnight. He could not imagine what solemn rituals gave one of the lords dominion; the sergeant made it clear that it was none of their business. Perhaps the sergeant himself had never seen.

Village rumor, he remembered, had it that the lords gained their great powers when they took office. But he had never seen any lord, or anyone with powers beyond the steward's ability to ferret out the truth when someone lied. He could not begin to imagine what kind of powers their young lord might have, or use. He pulled his mind back from this speculation to his own prospects. His promotion from recruit to guard private, the next afternoon, would be part of the lord's formal court, the first occasion on which the count would show his wisdom and ability to rule well. Gird had his new uniform ready, had every bit of leather oiled and shining, every scrap of metal polished.

He let his eyes wander to the rest of the entourage. Behind the lord's horse came others equally gaudily caparisoned: young nobles in velvets and furs, sweating in the early summer heat. Young noblewomen, attended each by maids and chaperons, riding graceful horses with hooves painted gold and silver. They began to dismount, in a flurry of ribbons and wide-sweeping sleeves, a gabble of voices as loud and bright as a flight of birds in the cornfield. As the young lord passed his steward's deferential bow, and led the party into the house, Gird felt a surge of excitement. The real world, the great world of king's court, the outside world he had never seen, had come to him, to his own village, and he would be part of it.

Chapter Three

Behind the main mass of the lord's hall lay the walled gardens. To the east, the fruit orchard, with its neatly trimmed plums and pears, its rare peach trained against a southern wall. To the west, the long rows of the vegetable garden, mounds of cabbage like a row of balls, the spiky blue-green stalks of onions and ramps, the sprawling vine-bushes of redroot. Ten-foot stone walls surrounded each garden, proof against the casual thief and straying herdbeast. But not, of course, against the daring of an occasional boy who would brag the rest of his life about a theft of plum or pear from the lord's own garden.

Meris, son of Aric, now the tanner's apprentice, had taken a plum the year before, but it was partly green. This year, he determined to take a sackful, and share them out, and they would be ripe ones, too. The lord's best plum tree, as Meris knew well (for his uncle was a skilled pruner of trees, and worked on them), was the old one in the middle of the garden, the only survivor of a row of plums grafted from scions of the king's garden in Finyatha. Its fruit ripened early, just before Summereve, medium-sized reddish egg-shaped plums with a silver bloom and yellow flesh.

It seemed to him that the young lord's arrival would be an excellent time to make his raid. The lord and his retinue would be busy, and nearly everyone else would be watching the excitement in the forecourt. So as soon as the first horns blew across the field, signalling the approaching cavalcade, Meris left off scraping the hair from the wet hide he was working on, and begged his master to let him go.

"Oh, aye, and if I don't you'll be so excited you'll likely scrape a hole in it. Very well . . . put it back to soak, and begone with you. But you'll finish that hide before supper, Meris, if it takes until midnight."

With the prospect of a belly full of his lord's best plums, a delayed supper was the last thing Meris needed to worry about. He grinned his thanks and darted from the tannery. He had hidden what he needed behind a clump of bushes on the east side of the lord's wall . . . a braided rawhide rope with a sliding loop. Other boys used borrowed ladders, and he'd heard of the smith's boy using some sort of hook tied to rope, but he had found that the looped rope could nearly always find a limb to fasten on. With a little support from the rope, and the skill of his bare feet on the rough-cut stone walls, he had always managed to get over. And the rawhide rope, without a hook or other contrivance, never attracted the suspicious attention of the guard. Once they'd found it, and he watched from the bushes as they shrugged and left it in place. A herdsman's noose, they'd said, dropped by some careless apprentice. Let the lad take his master's punishment, and braid another.

He waited, now, in the same clump of bushes, watching people stream by from the eastern fields. Soon no one passed. He heard a commotion around the wall's corner, from the village itself. Let it peak, he thought. Let the lord arrive. He waited a little longer, then glanced around. No one in sight, not even a distant flock. He swung the noose wide, as he'd practiced, and tossed it over the fence. He heard the thrashing of leaves as he pulled, and it tightened. He tugged. Firm enough.

Standing back a bit from the base of the wall, he threw himself upward, finding a toehold, and another. Whenever he found nothing, he used the rope, but most of it was skill and scrambling. At the wall's top, he flattened himself along it and gave a careful look at the hall's rear windows. Once he'd been seen by a servant, and nearly caught. But, as he'd expected, nothing moved in those windows. Everyone must be watching the forecourt, and the young lord's arrival. He pulled up his rope, and coiled it on the top of the wall. He could gain the wall from the inside by climbing one of the pears trained along it; he needed the rope only for getting in. This time, though, he planned to use it to lower the sack of stolen fruit on his way out. He checked his sack, took another cautious look around, and climbed quickly down a pear tree to the soft grass under the trees.

He heard a blast of trumpets from the forecourt, and grinned. Just as he'd planned: complete silence in the gardens, and everyone out front gaping at the lord. Silly. He was going to be there long enough for all to see, so why bother? Meris glanced around, still careful. No sign of anyone. One of the gates between the fruit orchard and the vegetable garden was open; he could see the glistening cabbage heads, the spikes of onion.

He moved forward. None of the pear trees had ripe fruit, but all were heavy with green pears. One of the golden plums was ripe; a single fruit lay on the grass beneath. Meris snatched it up and bit into it. Sun-warm and sweet, the juice slid down his throat. He spat the pit into the grass and plucked several of the golden plums for his sack. He took a few red plums from another tree, and then found himself at the old one, the "king tree" as his uncle called it.

It was loaded with ripe and overripe plums; clearly the steward had decided to leave it for the young lord's pleasure. Ordinarily, Meris knew, the trees were picked over every day to prevent loss to bird and wasp. But here the limbs drooped, heavy with plums, and the grass beneath was littered with fallen fruit. Wasps buzzed around these; the air was heavy with the scent of plum. Meris stepped forward, careful of the wasps beneath, and started picking.

He had nearly filled his sack, when he heard a door slam at the far end of the garden. He looked over his shoulder. Surely the welcoming ceremonies would have taken longer than this! He could see nothing between the trees, but he heard voices coming nearer. To go back, he would have to cross the central walk, in clear view of whatever busybody gardener had come back to work. But on this side, only a few steps away, was the open door to the vegetable gardens. He could outrun any gardener, he was sure, but he might be recognized. If he could hide for a little . . .

Quietly, he eased through the garden door, still without seeing whose were the oncoming voices, and found himself in unknown territory. To his left, rows of cabbage and onion stretched to the rear of the stable walls. Ahead were the beanrows, tall pole frames with bean vines tangling in them, only waist-high at this season. In a few weeks the beanrows would have been tall enough, but right now he'd have to crawl in between the poles. Scant cover, and once he was among them, a long way to any of the walls. On his right, the low matted redroots, with gourds beyond them, and some feathery-leaved plants he'd never seen before. The wall he'd come through was covered with some sort of vine; it had orange flowers and was trimmed off a foot or so below the wall-height. He saw no one, in the whole huge garden, but he saw no place to hide quickly if someone came in.

He flattened himself against the wall by the open door, and listened. Guards, they sounded like, rough voices. Perhaps the lord had sent them to check on everything—though Meris thought he should have trusted his local sergeant. The voices had passed beyond, and then he heard them coming back, heard the steady stride, the faint chink of metal on metal. Guards, sure enough. He dared a look, saw a broad back in the orange and black striped tunic, no one he recognized. Guards who had come with the young lord, then. They were through; they passed by, and kept going. He listened to their heavy step all the way down the main walk.

He grinned to himself. His luck was holding. In a mad impulse, he darted forward and yanked two onions out of the ground and stuffed them in his sack. And a ramp. Ramps, the onion cousin that none of the peasants was allowed to grow, brought from the old south, so they'd always heard, and sold sometimes on market days for high prices—he would have a ramp of his own, the whole thing. He might even plant it, under the forest edge, and grow more. Then he stood up.

"Hey—you there!" In the time it had taken him to pull a ramp, one of the gardeners had entered by the stable doors. Meris did not wait to see what would happen; he bolted straight for the door into the orchard. Behind him, the gardener's yell had started others yelling. He slammed the door behind him and threw the latch; it might slow them an instant. Then he was off, running between the trees as hard as he could pelt, the sack of stolen fruit banging his thigh.

He hardly saw the group of people strolling along the main walk before he had run into them, knocking one man flat. He heard high-pitched cries, and deeper yells of rage, and kept going, knocking aside someone's grab at his arm. It seemed the orchard had grown twice as wide; tree limbs thrashed his face. Behind him now

were the heavy feet of guardsmen as well. When he
came to the wall, he swarmed up the pear tree as fast as
a cat fleeing a wolf, and gained its top. Here he paused
a moment. The guards were too heavy for the pears;
they'd never be able to climb so high, he thought. Of
course, they'd bring ladders . . . He caught a flash of
bright orange between the trees below, and someone
yelled. Hardly thinking, he snatched an onion from his
bag and fired it at the shape. Another bellow; he turned
to leap into the thicket below. He'd have to risk mash-
ing his fruit. He had no time to lower it carefully; in
fact, he'd have to run off without it if he didn't want to
be caught.

The sergeant kept them on parade in the forecourt
even though the young lord had gone on into his hall.
He might come back out; besides, the peasants were
still milling about in the lane near the gates. When
the noise began, a verberant yell from somewhere deep
in the hall, the sergeant sent squads in at once, one
through the hall itself. Almost as soon as they disappeared into the hall, they came boiling back out again,
running for the gates. Gird, with the other recruits,
knew that something had happened, but not what; the
sergeant silenced them with curses when they asked,
and finally sent them off to the barracks. There they
shifted from foot to foot, nervous as young colts in a
pen. They dared not sit on the bunks made ready for
inspection; they dared not do anything, lest it be the
wrong thing.

Not long after, they were called back. The sergeant
looked as grim as Gird had ever seen him; no one dared
speak. He hurried them into formation, marched them
once more to the forecourt. This time they were told to
form a line dividing the forecourt in half. On one side,
the lord and his steward, and the guardsmen. On the
other, the villagers, crowding in behind Gird and the
other recruits. And between them, his shirt torn half off
his back, Meris son of Aric.

Gird stared at the scene before him, bewildered. He
had known Meris all his life; the younger boy had a

name for mischief, but Gird had thought him safely apprenticed to the tanner. What could Meris have done, to cause such an uproar?

The boy, held tightly by two guardsmen, stood as if lame, leaning a bit to one side. Gird could see a bruise rising over his eye. On the far side of the court, the lord started forward, slapping one black glove against the other. The steward laid a hand on his arm, was shaken off with a glare, and stepped back.

"What's his name?" asked the lord. No one answered for a moment; Gird thought no one was sure who should, or how the young lord should be addressed. Then the steward spoke up.

"Meris, son of Aric," he said. "A tanner's apprentice."

The young lord flung a glance back at the steward, and nodded. "Meris, son of Aric . . . and is Aric here?"

"No, my lord. Aric is a herdsman; your cattle are in the pastures beyond the wood right now; he is with them."

"And the tanner, his master: where is he?"

A movement among the villagers, and the tanner stepped forward. "Here, sir."

"Sir *count*, churl." The lord looked him up and down. "A fine master you are—did you teach your 'prentice to thieve, is that it?"

"Sir?" The tanner's face could not have been more surprised if he'd found himself dyed blue, Gird thought. The young lord barked a contemptuous laugh at him.

"You mean to claim you did not know where he was? You did not know he was stealing fruit from my orchard? From the way he ran straight for that pear tree, I daresay had done it often before. You know the law: a master stands for his apprentice's misdeeds—"

"Stealing fruit?" Gird did not know the tanner well; the man had moved into the village only three years before, when old Simmis had died and left the tannery vacant. But he seemed honest enough now, if perhaps none too bright. "But he begged the time off to see your honor's coming—"

"While you, I presume, were too busy to see your liege lord's arrival, or to supervise your apprentice properly?"

The tanner looked from lord to steward and back again, seeing no help anywhere. "But—but sir—I didn't know. I thought he—"

"You should have known; he was your apprentice. Be glad I don't have you stripped naked and in the stocks for this; the steward will collect your fine later." The lord smiled, and turned to the boy. "And as for this young thief, this miscreant who was not content to steal my fruit, but boldly assaulted my person—you'll climb no more walls, and steal no more fruit, and I daresay you'll remember the respect you owe your lord to the end of your life." The steward moved, as if he would speak, but the young count stared him down. "It is your laxness, Cullen, that's given these cattle the idea they can act so. You should have schooled them better."

The courtyard was utterly silent for a long moment. Then a soft murmur began, like the first movement of leaves in a breeze, rustling just within hearing. Gird felt a wave of nausea, as he realized with the others that the young lord intended far worse than the steward ever had. Even now he could not believe that Meris had assaulted the lord: Meris had never assaulted anyone. His mischiefs were always solitary.

It was then, as his eyes slid from one to another, not quite meeting anyone's as their eyes avoided his, that he noticed the pin clasping the young count's cloak. A circle, like the symbol of Esea's Eye, the Sunlord, but sprouting horns . . . like a circle of barbed chain, the barbed chain the followers of Liart had left on his bunk. And those three, of all the soldiers, were untroubled by the count's malice . . . were eager, he realized, for whatever the count wanted.

What the count wanted, as events proved, was threefold: to terrorize his peasantry, to impress his friends from the king's court, and to leave Meris just enough life to suffer long before dying. Long before the end of it, Gird and many others had heaved their guts out onto the paved court, had fallen shaking and sobbing to their knees, trying not to see and hear what they could not help seeing and hearing. Not even his sergeant's fist on his collar, the urgent "Get *up*, boy, before it's you—"

could steady him. He staggered up, shook free of the sergeant's hold, and bolted across the empty space into the crowd, fighting his way to the gate like a terrified ox from a pen.

He had moved so suddenly, with so little forethought, that no one caught him; behind him the villagers reacted to his panic with their own, screaming and thrashing away from the scene of torture. That kept the rest of the soldiers busy, though Gird didn't realize it. He ran as if he could outrun his memories, down the long lane past his father's cottage, out beyond the great field, the haymeadows, fighting his way blindly through the thickets beside the creek, and through the rolling cobbles to the far side. Then he was running in the wood, staggering through briar and vine, falling over the gnarled roots of the old trees to measure his length again and again. He never noticed when his uniform tore, when thorns raked his arms and face, tore at his legs. Higher in the wood, and higher . . . past the pens where they fed the half-wild hogs, past the low hut where the pigherder stayed in season. He startled one sounder of swine, so they snorted and crashed through the undergrowth with him for a space. Then he was falling into another branch of the creek, and turning to clamber upstream, instinct taking over where his mind couldn't, his legs finally losing their stride to let him topple into the rocky cleft his brother Arin had shown him all those years ago.

For some time he knew nothing, felt nothing, and the hours passed over him. He woke, with a countryman's instinct, at dusk, when the evening breeze brought the hayfield scent up over the wood, and tickled his nose with it. He ached in every limb; his scratches burned and itched, and his mouth tasted foul. Until he was up on his knees, he did not remember where he was, or why—but then a spasm of fear and shame doubled him up, and sourness filled his mouth. He gulped and heaved again. Meris, a boy he had known—a lad who had tagged behind him, more than once—would never walk straight again, or hold tools, and he had worn the uniform of the one who had done it.

He could hear his mother's voice ringing in his head. This was what she'd meant, about taking service of iron, and leaving the Lady of Peace. This was what his father had feared, that he would use his strength to hurt his own people. Scalding tears ran down his face. He had been so happy, so proud, only a few days before . . . he had been so sure that his family's fears were the silly fears of old-fashioned peasants, "mere farmers," as the sergeant so often called them.

Arin came to the cleft before dawn, sliding silently between the trees. "Gird?" he called softly. "Girdi—you here?"

Gird coiled himself into an even tighter and more miserable ball as far back as he could burrow, but Arin came all the way in, and squatted down beside him.

"You stink," he said companionably, one brother to another. "The dogs will have no trouble."

"Dogs?" Gird had not thought of dogs, but now remembered the long-tailed hounds that had gone out with the tracker after wolves.

"I brought you a shirt," said Arin. "And a bit of bread. Go wash." The very matter-of-factness of Arin's voice, the big brother he had always listened to, made it possible for him to unclench himself and stagger to his feet. He took the shirt from Arin without looking at it, and moved out of the cleft before stripping off his clothes. In the clean chill of dawn, he could smell himself, the fear-sweat and vomit and blood so different from the honest sweat of toil. Arin smelled of onions and earth. He wished he could be an onion, safe underground. But the cold water, and a bunch of creekside herbs crushed to scrub with, cleansed the stench from his body. His mind was different: he could still hear Meris scream, still feel, as in his own body, the crack of breaking bones.

"Hurry up," said Arin, behind him. "I've got to talk to you."

Gird rinsed his mouth in the cold water, and drank a handful, then another. He pulled on the shirt Arin had brought; it was barely big enough across the shoulders, and his wrists stood out of the sleeves, but it covered him. Arin handed him the bread. Gird had not thought he was hungry, but he wolfed the bread down in three bites. He could have eaten a whole loaf.

By this time it was light enough to see his brother's drawn face, and read his expression. Arin shook his head at him. "Girdi, you're like that bullcalf that got loose and stuck in the mire three years ago—do you remember? Thought he was grown, he was so big, but once out of his pen and in trouble, he bawled for help like any new-weaned calf." Gird said nothing; he could feel tears rising in his eyes again, and his throat closed. "Girdi, you have to go back." That opened his eyes, and his throat.

"I can't!" he said, panting. "Arin, I can't—you didn't see—"

"I saw." Arin's voice had hardened. "We all saw; the count made sure of it. But it's that or outlaw, Girdi, and you won't live to be an outlaw—the count will hunt you down, and the fines will fall on our family."

It was another load of black guilt on top of the other. "So—so I must die?"

"No." Arin had picked up a stick, and poked it into the moss-covered ground near the creek. "At least—I hope not. What your sergeant said was that if someone knew where you were, and if you'd turn yourself in, he thought he could save your life. And we'd not lose our holding. The steward . . . the steward's not with the count in this. You saw that. But you have to come in, Gird, on your own. If they chase and capture you—"

"I can't be a soldier," said Gird. "I can't do that—what they did—"

"So I should hope. They don't want you now, anyway." Even in his misery, that hurt. He knew he'd been a promising recruit, barring his slowness in learning to read; he knew the sergeant had had hopes for him. And now he'd lost all that, forever. His stomach rumbled, reminding him that he'd also lost plentiful free food. "We can use you," Arin went on. "We always could."

His mind was a stormy whirlwind of fear and grief

and shame. He could imagine what the sergeant would say, the sneers of the other men, the ridicule. And surely he would be punished, for disgracing them so, and breaking his oath of service. Would he be left like Meris, a cripple? Better to die . . . and yet he did not want to die. The thought of it, hanging or the sword in his neck—and those were the easy ways—terrified him. Arin's look was gentle.

"Poor lad. You're still just a boy, after all, aren't you? For all the long arms and legs, for all the bluster you've put on this past spring."

"I'm—sorry." He could not have said all he was sorry for, but a great sore lump of misery filled his head and heart.

"I know." Arin sighed. "But I'm not sorry to think of you working beside me, Gird, when this is over. Come now: wash your face again, and let's be going back."

He felt light-headed on the way, but the stiffness worked out of his legs quickly. His soiled uniform rolled under his arm, he followed Arin down paths he hardly remembered.

"We need to hurry," said Arin over his shoulder. "They were going to start searching again this morning, and I'd like to get you down to the village before they set the dogs loose."

"What—what happened, after—"

"After you bolted? Near a riot, that was, with everyone screaming and thrashing about. It took awhile to settle, and the count had more to think of than you. Then your sergeant came to our place, and talked to father. Said you'd deserted, and they'd have to hunt you unless you came back on your own, and even if you did it might go hard with you. He didn't like the count's sentence on Meris any more than the rest of us, but . . . he had to go along. He took out a few of the men late in the evening, calling for you. I was sure you'd come up here."

"I didn't think," said Gird. "I just couldn't stand it—"

"Mmm. Then the steward came, after dark." Arin stepped carefully over a tangle of roots and went on. "Said we'd lose the holding, the way the count felt.

He'd come down to show off his inheritance to his friends from court, all those fine lords and ladies, and then Meris hit him with an onion—"

"He what!"

"That's right. You probably don't know what really happened. Meris was stealing fruit, thinking everyone would be busy out front, but the count wanted to show the ladies the garden, and hurried through. So when Meris was spotted, he ran straight into the count and knocked him flat, in front of his friends, and then fired an onion at him from the top of the wall. Probably thought it was a guard. Poor lad."

Gird was silent, thinking what sort of man would cripple a boy for such a ridiculous mistake.

"He was wrong, of course, and now we're all in trouble, from the steward on down, but—" Arin flashed a grin back over his shoulder. "At least you didn't take part in it— and if they want to call it cowardice, well, I say brave men have better to do than batter rash boys into ruin."

"I don't want to die," said Gird suddenly, into the green silence of the wood.

"No one does," said Arin, "but sick old men and women. Did you think a soldier would never see death?"

"No, but—but I didn't think it would be like this. If it is, I mean." He didn't expect an answer to that, and got none. Early sun probed through the leaves, shafts of golden light between the trees. The wood smelled of damp earth, herbs, ripening brambleberries, a whiff here and there of pig or fox or rabbit. He was afraid, but he could not shut out the richness of the world around him, the springy feel of the leafmold under his feet. Air went in and out his nose despite his misery.

They came to the straggling end of the lane without being seen. Gird hesitated to follow Arin into the open, but his brother strode on without looking back, trusting him. He could see no one, but a distant shepherd far across the fields. Up the lane toward the village. Now he could see the first cottages, his father's well, the lane beyond, the great fields to his right. A few women at the well, someone (he could not tell who) behind the hedge in front of their cottage.

Arin spoke again. "It's better if you go alone, Gird. Can you do that?"

Cold sweat sprang out all over him. Alone? But he knew Arin was right. The sergeant and steward would know that his brother had gone to bring him in—the whole village knew already—but if he went the rest of the way alone it could go unspoken. Less chance that more punishment would fall on Arin.

The soldiers were just starting out from the gates when he came in sight of them; the sergeant must have delayed as long as he could. They paused, and the sergeant gestured. Gird walked on. His legs felt shaky again, and it was hard to breathe. When he was close enough, he didn't know what to say. He couldn't salute, not with his filthy uniform under his arm, and a peasant shirt on his back. The sergeant's face was closed, impassive.

"Well, Gird," he said.

"Sir," said Gird miserably, looking down at his scuffed and dirty boots. He forced himself to meet the sergeant's eyes. "I—I was wrong, sir." One of the men guffawed; the sergeant cut it short with a chop of his hand.

"You broke your oath," the sergeant said. He sounded weary and angry together, someone who had come near the end of his strength as well as his patience. "Right in front of the count himself—" He stopped. "You're carrying your uniform? Right. Give it here." Gird handed it over, and the sergeant took it, his nostrils pinched. "Take off your boots, boy." Gird stared a moment, then hurried to obey. Of course the boots were part of the uniform; he should have thought of that. His feet, pale and thin-skinned from more than a year of wearing boots daily, found the dusty lane cool and gritty. The sergeant jerked his head at Keri, one of the other recruits, who came to take the boots, and the uniform both. "We'll burn them," said the sergeant. "We want nothing tainted with cowards' sweat." Gird felt himself flushing; the sergeant nodded at him. "Yes, you. You were wrong, and so was I, to think you'd ever make a soldier. I should have known, when you flinched from it before . . ." His voice trailed away, as the steward came out the gates with the village headman.

The steward gave Gird the same sort of searching look. "So. He came back, did he? Or did you track him down?"

"He came back, sir. Brought his uniform; he'd got a shirt from somewhere."

The steward looked Gird up and down. "It's a bad business, boy, to break an oath. Hard to live down. Reflects on the family. The count would make an example of you, but for the sergeant's report: you're strong, and docile, and will do more good at fieldwork than you will feeding crows from the gibbet. See that you work, boy, and cause no trouble. One more complaint of you, and your family's holding is forfeit." He turned to the headman, ignoring Gird.

The sergeant said, "You heard him. What are you waiting for? Get along to work, boy, and thank your Lady of Peace that you still have the limbs to work with. I wouldn't mind laying a few stripes on your back myself."

Chapter Four

In time Gird thought the stripes would have hurt less. He walked back to his father's cottage, that bright morning, with his feet relearning the balance of walking bare, and his skin prickling with the knowledge that everyone knew he had been disgraced. Had disgraced *himself*, he reminded himself firmly. That first time along the lane, no one said anything, though he was aware of all the sidelong glances. He made it home without incident, to find Arin waiting for him.

"You're to clean out the cowbyre," said Arin, handing him the old wooden shovel. "He thinks it better if you keep out of sight."

Gird glanced at his mother, busy at her loom. Her expression said "I told you no good would come of it," as clearly as if she'd spoken aloud. His youngest sister Hara had obviously been told to keep quiet. He wondered if she'd been the one peeking through the hedge earlier. Probably. He took the shovel and went to work.

Across the barton, Arin was mending harness. Beyond the barton wicket, Gird could see a cluster of men in the greatfield. Midmorning now; they'd stopped work for a chat and a drink. He shoveled steadily, piling the dirty straw and manure in the basket, to drag across the barton and toss on the pile just beyond the gate. He wasn't sure why Arin was staying close—did they think he would run again? And Arin hadn't asked what happened up at the manor gates. Gird felt as touchy as after his first sunburn each spring. Every glance Arin gave him seemed to be made of flame.

At noon, Hara passed through the cowbyre with their father's lunch wrapped in a cloth; she gave Gird a cool nod that cut him to the bone. Arin stopped punching holes and lacing straps together, and stretched. He smiled; by then Gird was not sure what that smile meant.

"Come on, then, long-face. It's not what you're used to, but it is food." Arin hardly needed to wash, but Gird was muck to the knees and elbows. He remembered to flick a spatter of clean water out for grace, and washed carefully enough to please the sergeant before going in to get his bowl of mush. It hardly seemed to touch his hunger, but then the look on his mother's face tightened his throat so that he could not have swallowed another bite.

By late afternoon, he had cleared the cowbyre, and when the cowherd brought the animals back to the village, and Arin led their own three into the barton, he had the stalls spread with fresh straw. He washed up quickly, and started milking. He had always liked the cows, even the crook-horned red cow who slapped his face with her dirty great tail and did her best to tread in the bucket. His father appeared as he was milking the second, but said nothing before going on inside. Gird leaned his head into a warm, hairy flank, and let his hands remember the rhythmic squeeze and pull that brought the milk down quickly and easily. The milk smelled good, no taint of onion or wild garlic. He leaned closer, and gave himself a warm, luscious mouthful.

"I saw that," said Arin, from around the rump of the third cow. "You know better." It was the old bantering tone of their boyhood, but it didn't seem the same.

"Sorry," said Gird, wishing he weren't so conscious of the taste of that milk, the richness of it. Their milk was traded to the village cheesemaker; grown men did not drink milk. He felt he could drink the whole bucket. He finished the last quarter, and carried the bucket into the kitchen. From there he could hear the voices in the front room: his father and the steward. What now? he wondered. But his mother, square athwart the kitchen hearth, sent him back to the barton with a wave of her spoon.

He ranged around it, doing every chore he could think of, until his father called him in. It was much like the night the steward had visited to offer him the chance to train: his mother and father sitting stiffly on one side, and the steward at their single table. Arin followed him in. Hara, banished to the kitchen, was as close to the door as she could be, and not be seen by the elders.

"You should know," said the steward without preamble, "what your rashness will cost your father. He must appear at court, the afternoon of the count's investiture. I have spoken with the count, and pled what I can: your youth, your father's record of work, your brothers. But the fact is, the count is angry, and with reason. And your father, head of your family, will be fined. I came to tell him, that he might have it ready to pay, and save himself a night in the stocks."

Gird met his father's eyes. His father in the stocks? For his running away?

"You will attend as well, boy, and it may be the count will have something to say to you. He is your lord; he may do as he pleases. Remember your rank, and try—" the emphasis was scornful, "to cause no more trouble."

When the steward had gone, Gird's father patted his shoulder. "It's all right, Gird. You're here, and alive, and—it's all right." Gird knew it was not. For the first time in his life, he realized that he could do harm he could not mend. He felt at once helpless and young, and far removed from the boyish confidence of a few days before.

"What—how much is the fine?" he asked.

His father cleared his throat. "Well. They want repaid all they spent on your training. It's all in the steward's accounts, he says. Food, clothing, the coppers he sent me, even barracks room. And then a fine for oath-breaking—" Gird had never really mastered figures, but he knew he'd worn clothes worth far more than his family could have bought him. And eaten more, of better food. His father turned to Arin. "I'll have to ask you—"

Arin nodded. "Of course. Will it be enough?"

His father scrubbed at his face with both hands. "We'll see. Gird, you were too young before: come here, now, and see where our coins lie hid."

He had known it was under some stone in the fireplace; everyone hid valuables that way. But not which— and before his father levered out the stone, he would not have suspected that one. Within was a leather pouch, and in that his father's small store of coppers and silvers. His father counted it out twice.

"I saved most of your wages, for Arin's marriage-price, and Hara's dower. There's a hand of coppers, and another hand of coppers. But a fine of double the fieldfee—that's a silver and a hand of coppers, and doubled—" He laid it out as he spoke, handling the coins as gingerly as if they were nettles to sting him. Gird held his breath, thinking of the hours of labor, baskets of fruit and grain, that each represented. "And the uniforms—" The last of the coppers went into a row, and his father frowned, shaking his head. " 'Tis not enough, even so. They might have let you keep the boots, at least, if we must pay for them."

"How much?" asked his mother.

"Eight copper crabs, and that's if the count holds to the steward's say. I doubt he will. It'll be a sheep, then, or a furl of cloth."

"I have a furl, set by," his mother said. "It was for—"

"No matter what it was for," said his father harshly. "It is for Gird's life, now."

"I know that," said his mother. Gird watched as she opened the press that stored her weaving, and pulled out a rolled furl of cloth. His father touched it lightly, and nodded.

"We'll hope that will do," he said.

The lord held court in the yard, with the count seated beneath an awning striped orange and yellow. None of his noble friends was with him; having sat through his investiture at midnight, they had all slept late.

Despite Gird's father's oath to the steward that they would appear, one of the soldiers came that morning to march them up to the manor gates. He had studiously ignored Gird; others had not, small children who had stared and called and been yanked back within cottages by their mothers. Gird's feet were sore, not yet toughened to going bare, and his shirt had already split. His mother had patched it the night before. He was acutely aware of the patch, of his bare feet, of the difference between Gird, Dorthan's son, peasant boy, and Gird the recruit.

That contrast was sharpened when he watched the other recruits accepted into service as they gave their oaths to the count, and pinned on the badges of guard private. None of them met his eyes, not even Keri. One by one they came forward, knelt, swore, and returned to the formation. Gird's heart contracted. For one moment he wanted to throw himself before the count and beg to be reinstated. Then his roving eye saw the stocks, with the stains of Meris's blood still dark on the wood.

Another case preceded theirs. The steward had intended it, Gird knew, as the ritual single case the new lord must judge; he had saved it back from the spring courts. Now he rushed the witnesses through their stories of missing boundary stone and suspected encroachment on someone's strip of arable. Clearly not even the plaintiff and defendant thought it was as important as before, compared with Gird and his father. The count concurred with the steward's assessment, and the loser didn't bother to scowl as he paid his two copper crabs to the winner, and another to the count.

Then it was their turn. The steward called his father forward; Gird followed two paces behind, as he'd been bidden. To his surprise, the sergeant came too.

The count's face was drawn down in a scowl of displeasure that didn't quite conceal an underlying glee. The steward began, explaining how Gird had been recruited.

"A big, strong lad, already known as a hard worker. He seemed brave enough then, as boys go—" He turned to the sergeant.

"Willing to work, yes. Obedient, strong . . . not too quick in his mind, my lord, but there's good soldiers enough that can't do more than he did. Never gave trouble in the barracks."

"And he gave you no hint of his . . . weakness?" The count's voice this day was almost silken smooth, no hint of the wild rage he'd shown before.

The sergeant frowned. "Well, my lord, he did in a way. He didn't like hurting things, he said once, and he never did give up his peasant superstitions. Flowers to the well-sprite, and that sort of thing."

"Complained of hard treatment, did he?"

"No, my lord. Not that. Like I said, a willing enough lad, when it came to hard work, not one to complain at all. But too soft. I put it down to his being young, and never from home, but that was wrong."

"Indeed." The count stared at Gird until he felt himself go hot all over. "Big lout. Not well-favored, no *quality* in him. Some are born cattle, you know, and others are born wolves. You can make sheepdogs of wolves, but nothing of cattle save oxen in yokes. He looks stupid enough. I can't imagine why you ever considered him; if you want to stay in my service, you'd best not make such mistakes again."

"No, my lord," said the sergeant and steward, almost in the same breath.

"Well," said the count, "to settle young oxen, put stones on the load. You had a recommendation, steward?" The steward murmured; Gird heard again the terms his father had told him. The count nodded. "Well enough, so far as it goes, but not quite far enough. Let one of my Finyathans give the boy a whipping, and if his father wants him whole, let him pay the death-gift for his life. Else geld the young ox, and breed no more cowards of him." His eyes met Gird's, and he smiled. "Do you like my judgment, boy?"

Beside him, his father was rigid with shock and fear; Gird bowed as well as he could. The death-gift for a son was a cow and its calf that year. A third of their livestock gone, or his future sons and daughters. He knew his father would pay, but the cost!

The steward muttered again; the count shook his head. "Let the father pay now. What is it to be, fellow?" Gird's father stepped forward, and laid the pouch of coins, and the furl of cloth, on the table. The steward took the pouch and counted the coins quickly.

"The cow?" he said without looking up. Gird's father nodded, and the steward noted it down. "Go fetch the cow," he said brusquely.

"Sir, she's with the cowherd—"

"Will you fetch the cow or not?" The steward's face was white. "It's all one to me whether you have grandsons from this boy."

Gird's father bowed. "I'll go now, sir, may I?" he said, his voice trembling, and backed away. The count laughed.

"'Tis no wonder the boy's a coward, with such a father. At least he's docile." The count waved a hand, and one of the Finyathan guards went off, to return in a few moments with a long rod bound in leather. "And you, sergeant, as you erred in choosing him, I don't doubt you'd like a chance to leave your mark on him?"

Whether he wanted to or not, Gird could not tell, but the sergeant had no choice. That much was clear. Nor did he. He went to the stocks without resistance, hoping he could keep from crying out. He felt the scorn more than the blows, but the Finyathan guard, when the sergeant gave up the rod to him after four or five stripes, had evident delight in his work. The count watched, leaning on one elbow and chatting to the steward without taking his eyes off Gird's face. By the time his father came back with the cow, Gird had bruises and lumps from more than the rod. He had closed his eyes before they swelled shut, not wanting to see his former friends in the guards as they joined in.

He woke face-down in a puddle of water that had been thrown over him, with the count's waspish voice saying "Take the oaf away, and pray I forget all this." His father's arm helped him up; outside the gates Arin too waited, to help him home.

His head rang. He could not have made it without help. His mother and Hara cleaned the blood off, and muttered over the damage done to the shirt. The rest of that day and night he lay wrapped in a blanket, sipping the bitter brew his mother spooned down him at intervals. For himself, he'd have been glad to have wound-fever and die of it, to be at peace, for his old dreams tormented him like haunts, making mock of his pride. He twisted and groaned, until Arin woke and held him.

"It's all right, Girdi. It's over now." But it was not over, and wouldn't be. He was sour with his own sweat, disgusted with himself, and shaking with fears he could not express. If things had gone so wrong so fast, what was safe? Arin's reassurance meant nothing. He remembered the look on the count's face, the delight in cruelty. He might have been killed—really killed—his life had hung on the count's whim.

The next morning he forced his stiff, aching body out of bed. He was not sure he could work, but he knew he must. His mother had yet to remake his shirt from the ragged scraps left after his punishment, so she insisted he stay indoors. His father and Arin agreed. Indoors, then, he worked—back to childhood, he thought, scrubbing the stone hearth, washing dishes and pots, carrying buckets of water from the well. It was hot indoors, breathless as Midsummer usually was. Sweat stung in the welts and scrapes; he ignored it, shrugged away his mother's attempt to put a poultice on the deepest ones. She glared at him.

"You may want a fever, to get out of work, but we've no time for that, lad. Stand you there and no more shifting, while I clean this out again." He felt himself flush, but stood. What else could he do? He had forfeited his chance to adult status. Her fingers were gentler than her voice. The sharp fragrance of herbs worked its way past his misery for a few moments as she stroked the heavy ointment on his back. " 'Tis a bad world, lad, where such things happen. But you see what comes of taking iron to mend them. Remember this: no matter how bad it seems, soldiering makes it worse. It always comes hardest on those with the least. Mind your father, keep out of the lords' eye: that's best. Notice brings trouble, no matter if it seems good at first. Remember what tree the forester chooses."

He'd heard that often and often before. It was not in the Lady's ritual, but it was the village's favorite truth: notice brings trouble. As bad to be always first in reaping as always last; as bad to be richest as poorest. The tall tree catches the forester's eye, and the fattest ox suggests a feast. He had never liked it, since he could not have hidden among others even if he wanted to. What, he had wondered, was the tall tree supposed to *do*? But his trouble would prove the truth as far as the village was concerned, and he expected to hear it many times again.

He was young and strong and healthy; his body healed quickly and he was soon hard at work with his father. But he could not escape the knowledge that he had brought trouble to his family. They had been prosperous, for peasants: three cows, eight ewes, extra cloth laid away, the copper and silver coins that took so long to earn. His father had had a good reputation with the steward, and had no enemies in the village itself.

Now Arin could not marry until they earned the

marriage-fee, but before that came the field-fee and house-fee, and the harvest taxes were coming soon. He could help with the work, but he had to eat, and he brought no more land with him, on which more crops could grow, or beasts graze.

His father said nothing of this. He had no need to say it; Gird knew precisely what it meant, what it would cost them all in labor and hunger to regain even a scrap of safety. His feet toughened quicker than his mind. Daylong in the fields he caught the tail end of comments that seemed intended for his ear. The other men said nothing near his father, but left him in no doubt what they thought. Young lout, they said, set himself up for a soldier and then shamed us all with his weakness. He knew some of them had been as sickened as he, but if they remembered it at all, they didn't say so around him. It was convenient to blame it all on him. He knew, on one side of his mind, that this had always happened so, that once he had done the same, but it still hurt. His former friends stayed away from him, whether because of their fathers' orders or their own scorn he didn't know, and soon didn't care. He was in a deep wallow of misery, just like the bullcalf in the bog Arin had mentioned.

In that first month of trouble, between the event and the harvest, only one mercy intervened. The young count and his entourage left to visit another of his holdings, and the steward conveniently forgot to put Gird on the workroll. In the required workdays, he could work his family's garden and fieldstrip, while his father and Arin worked the greatfield for the count. And he could do day-labor for anyone hiring work done, taking his pay in a meal away from home more often than hard coin. Most of this was unskilled labor, fetching and carrying. Gird carried water for the masons brought in to raise the count's orchard walls, and lugged baskets full of clay and broken rock. It was hard work, even for someone of his strength, and he soon felt the difference the change in food made. He came home so tired he could hardly eat, and fell onto the bed as soon as he'd cleaned his bowl.

At harvest, Gird could not avoid the other men and boys. Harvest time gathered in more than crops; the village people worked together and celebrated together, and the year's stories began to form into chants and tales that would be retold over and over during long winter nights. It was no fault of Gird's that his disgrace so neatly fit the measures of an old song, "The Thief's Revenge" and needed but little skill to change a few words. He never knew who sang it first, but its jangling rhymes followed him down the lanes. "He gave a cry and ran away, as fast as he could run—" jibed the little boys. "Eh, Gird, can you outrun a fox? A pig?"

Now his former friends had their own say. A shrug, a wink between them, a shoulder turned to him. Teris even said "If you were going to make such a fuss, you could at least have saved Meris," which was completely unfair. He could not have saved Meris; no one could. They hadn't. But they blamed him for Meris, and for trying and failing. Some—Amis among them—said nothing, just watched him. Were they waiting for him to defend himself, to argue? But he had nothing to say. He was too tired to argue, too hungry and too miserable.

The girls never looked his way at all, and he was sure they laughed about him in their little groups. He was careful not to watch them openly and court more ridicule, although he had come to the age where the mere sight of a girl leaning to pull a bucket from a well could send his blood pounding. It was slightly easier to ignore the girls if he wasn't with the boys. He quit trying to talk to anyone, soon, and kept to his own family.

With all they had lost, that winter was hard. They could not afford to butcher an animal for winter meat; they would need every calf and lamb next spring to pay the fieldfee. Gird's scanty earnings had gone for the fall taxes, along with two of their sheep. That meant less wool next spring, for his mother to spin and weave, and less cloth to trade or sell. At least they had fodder in plenty, for that had been gathered before they lost the extra animals. And Gird roamed the wood bringing back loads of firewood and sacks of nuts. He avoided the nutting parties of the other boys and young men, avoided the last autumn gatherings of dancers at the sheepfold.

Later, he remembered that winter as the coldest, hungriest, and most miserable of his life, although he knew that wasn't true. There was no real famine; they had beans and grain enough, some cheese. Except for the ritual cold hearth at Midwinter, they had a good fire yearlong. His mother had managed a whole shirt for him, pieced out of scraps, and he had rags enough to wrap his feet. It was the sudden difference, from more than enough to barely enough, that made it seem so bleak.

Meris died in the long cold days after Midwinter. Gird had tried to visit him once, but his family, suffering under a heavy fine as well as Meris's injuries, wanted no contact with another unlucky boy. Meris had had few friends, but those boys loosed their frustrated rage on Gird when they caught him alone, and battered him into the snow. He might have fought back, to ease his own frustration and grief, but one of them got a bucket over his head. The guards heard the noise, and broke it up; when Gird wrestled the bucket off his head, the sergeant was standing there sucking his teeth speculatively. He said nothing, just watched, as Gird made it to one knee, than another, and staggered off down the lane.

That was the last direct assault, but by then Gird was convinced that everyone was against him. The next time he got a bit of work, and a copper crab, he took it to the smelly leanto behind Kirif's cottage, where a couple of other men hunched protectively over mugs of sour ale. He knew it was wrong. He didn't care. For a crab he got more ale than his head would hold, mug after mug, and his father found him snoring against the wall.

That loosed his father's tongue, where the other had not. "A sot as well as a coward! I didn't work so hard to save a drunken oaf, lad; this had best be the last time you spend our needs on your own pleasure." It didn't feel like pleasure then; his head was pounding and his stomach felt as if it never wanted food again. His father was not finished, however. He heard the full tale of his misdeeds, from the time he'd run off to follow Arin on the pighunt as a child, to the stupidity of going for a soldier, right down to his selfishness and sullenness in the past months. He had not told his father about Meris's friends attacking him, or what Teris had said; he realized that it wouldn't do any good now.

He felt almost as guilty as his father seemed to want. It *was* his fault, no getting around it, and if some of the consequences weren't fair, nothing ever had been. Only one of the gods cared about fair, that he knew of, and the High Lord was far away, nothing much to do with the village folk or the soldiers, either one. He went back to work doggedly, determined to pay back enough of the debt he owed so that Arin could marry within a year. He didn't visit the aleshop until after Midsummer, and then with a basket of mushrooms to trade, not good coin his family could use. And he stopped with a single mug, that put a pleasant haze between him and the other villagers.

Arin's wedding briefly lightened his miseries, for his favorite brother would include Gird in the celebration despite anything he'd done. "Besides," Arin said, "you've worked hard to get my fee together. You might have done much less; it wasn't all your fault, after all. I know I can depend on you."

For a wedding, all quarrels ceased. Oreg even donated a pig to the feast. Gird was old enough to wait in the barton with the men, to watch his brother's dance, and join the drinking afterwards, when the newlyweds were safe abed and women were cleaning up the last of the feast. This was not like Kirif's leanto; here was a cask of the strong brown brew from a neighboring vill, and hearty voices singing all the rollicking old songs he'd grown up with, from "Nutting in the Woods" to "Red Sim's Second Wife." He had enough ale to soften the edges of any remarks about him, and joined his loud voice to the others without noticing anyone's complaint.

But this did not last. Arin and his wife took over the

bed he had shared with Gird, as was only right; Gird slept on the floor near the hearth that winter. Arin's wife, soon with child, began to have the childsickness, waking early every morning to heave and heave, filling the cottage with the stink of her illness. Gird, now on the work rolls, had his own duties to fulfill when the required days came around; he could no longer replace his brother and free one worker for the family. When Arin's first child was born, another mouth to feed, they had not yet put by enough for the fieldfee. That year was leaner than the one before.

Soon Gird felt that he would never get anywhere at all. Arin's wife lost a child, but was soon pregnant again. As hard as they all could work was barely enough to feed them; they had no chance to save towards replacing the sheep or cow Gird had cost them. Year flowed into year, a constant struggle to survive. Gird could not miss the gray in his father's hair, the cough that every winter came sooner and lasted longer.

Chapter Five

"I don't see why you care." Gird hunched protectively over his mug. The mood Amis was in, if he turned around to argue, Amis would grab it away. He didn't have anything to trade for another, and this one would barely fuzz the edges of his misery.

"You're turning into a drunk," said Amis, far too briskly. "It's been what—three years?—and all you do is work and drink—"

"And eat," said Gird. "Don't forget that—they tell me all the time at home."

"And eat. You never come out with us—"

Gird shrugged, and took a swallow. Worse than usual,

it tasted, but the bite in his throat promised ease later. "You may want me; the others don't."

"It's past, Gird. So you're not a soldier, so what? We didn't like it that much when you were—"

"That's true. You don't much like anything I do: fight or not fight, run or not run, drink or not drink. If I gave up ale, Amis, would that make me friends? Not likely."

"You know what I mean. Drink for celebration, yes— with all of us, a lot of singing and dancing and rolling the girls—but not this way. Come with us tonight, anyway."

Gird swallowed the rest of the mug he allowed himself, and tried to think past the rapidly spreading murk in his head. Walk across the fields to some sheepfold, listen to a wandering harper play, dance with—it would have to be girls from the other village, none from here would have him. And then back by daybreak, to work— his feet ached, his back ached, all he wanted was his bed. But at home his father's eyes would question silently: what did you take, to trade for that drink? What will you take next? It was my own, he answered that unspoken question. I found the mushrooms, I picked them when you were resting, it's my right—

"All right," he said gruffly. Amis grinned at him, steadied him as he stood. He did not look to see the reactions of the other men drinking in Kirif's hut; he thought he knew exactly what he'd see if he did.

Somewhere on the walk, two others joined them: Koris and Jens, he'd known them all his life. His skin prickled; he was sure they were none too happy to find him coming along. But nothing they said led that way. It was all the common talk of their village, Jens courting Torin and her father's dislike of it, a wager between Koris and his older brother on the sex of an unborn calf, Teris's problems with his wife's mother, how the last spring storm had damaged the young fruit on the trees. The thought passed through his mind that, but for subjects, it was much like the talk of his mother and aunt and sisters, that nearly drove him mad when he had to be indoors listening to it. For all that Jens and Koris talked of the girls, while Effa and Hara talked of the boys, it was the same talk. Who liked, who spurned, who loved secretly—who would be honest, and who lied in all encounters—whose work could be trusted, and who put rotten plums in the bottom of the basket.

He said nothing, having nothing to say, as the cool night air gradually blew the fumes of ale away. They were walking over the higher pastures sunrising of the village—east, as the lords called it. Under his feet the turf made an uneven carpet; overhead the spring stars blossomed as the night darkened. It had been a long time since he'd been out in the dark looking up, his gaze unmisted by drink. Some night-blooming plant—he knew he should know the name, but he'd forgotten—spread rare perfume on the air, and every lungful he took in seemed important, as if it carried a secret message.

They could see the sheepfold from the ridge, dark against the leaping flames of the fire built in the outer enclosure. As they came down the slope, the harpsong came to greet them, first the more carrying notes, then all of them, a quick rhythm that made them hurry. It ended, and voices rose in noisy swirls of greeting, flirtation, argument. Gird lagged as the others moved forward. He saw Jens edge toward a darker corner. There was Torin, who must have come earlier with her friends. Koris glanced back at him, and Gird stepped into the brighter firelight, not quite sure what he was going to do. He hadn't been to one of these since he was old enough to be serious about it. Boys the age he'd been lounged against the low stone wall, or crouched atop, knocking elbows and joking about the older ones.

At least three times a growing season, from early spring to fall, the young unmarried men and women of five villages met at this communal sheepfold. Gird had no idea how the dates were set, only that the word would spread through the young men—tomorrow night, tonight—and those who wished would go. One cold autumn evening, the first year he'd gone, there'd been only three young men and two women, and the music had come from a ragged lad playing a reed pipe. Usually there were more, and always someone from outside, a stranger, to play the music they danced to. But he had not come since he left the guard's training.

He heard someone say his name, across the fire, and his head jerked up. He couldn't see who, even when he squinted against the flames. So. They'd heard the story too, no doubt, and it would all be told over again. He glared at the coals beneath the burning wood, that half-magical heap of colored lights and mysterious shapes that seemed to be struggling to say something. A long hiss ended in a violent *pop*, and he jumped.

"I wonder what it said that time." The girl's voice held humor, as well as warmth. Gird didn't look at her.

"What all fires say," he said.

"Here's home and safety," she said. And then, surprisingly, "Here's danger; here's death."

Gird turned. She had a broad face, boldly boned for strength, not beauty, and all he could tell of her coloring in that uncertain light was that she was darker than he. Big capable hands held the ends of her shawl; she looked like any other young woman. Except for those eyes, he thought, watching the perfect reflection of the fire in them. Except for the mind that said those words.

"You're Gird," she said. "The one who left the guards."

"Yes." He wished he hadn't looked at her.

"Are they hard on you?"

He looked again, once more surprised. "Now?" She said nothing, and he wondered whether he dared be honest. Silence lengthened. No one else came near them; he could feel no other attention, no other pressure than her quiet interest. "At first," he began, "it was worst on my family—my father, my brothers—" He told her about that, the fines they'd had to pay, the extra labor on the roads. She said nothing, only nodding when he broke off. Tentatively, warily, he told her more. The guards themselves had bothered him least— even now that surprised him, that the sergeant, after that one explosion, had been fair, if distant, and the other soldiers neutral. "I'm just another farmer's son to them. They don't bother me, if they see me; they treat me no differently than the others. They never teased—"

His head went down, remembering those who did, whose taunts he could not answer.

"It's like rape," she said. He stared at her, shocked and ready to argue, but she was still talking. "They blame the blameless, the victim: they always do. When the young count's houseparty went hunting our way, and one of them took my cousin, took her there in the street just for the excitement of it, everyone blamed her. My aunt said 'Oh, if you hadn't loitered there,' and the lad who loved her—or said he did—had nothing to say but blame. All her fault, it was, but how could she help it? They blame you, for not preventing what they never moved to prevent."

"But I wasn't—"

"Not your *body*," she said, in a tone that meant he should have understood. Then, "Never mind. If you're not killed, you're still alive; so my cousin said, and married elsewhere a year later, after the babe died. She survived; you will; that's how we all live."

"It's not right," Gird said, in a voice that he remembered in himself from years past.

Her brows went up. "Are we gods, to know right and wrong beyond the law? I hate the way it is, but no one made me a lord."

He would have answered, or tried to, but the music began again. At close range, the harp drowned out soft words, and the others had begun a song. Gird didn't know it, but the girl did.

"Fair are the flowers that bloom in the meadows
Fair are the flowers that bloom on the hill
Each spring brings more to brighten the season
Each winter snowstorm the bright flowers kills—"

She had a husky singing voice, melodic but not strong, that clung to the melody like a peach to a twig, half-enfolding it. Gird could feel her singing along his body, a warm, slightly furry touch. He wanted to sing with her, at least hum the melody, but his throat was too tight. Another song followed that one, this time an even sadder lament that they all knew. He sang, feeling his voice unkink and lengthen into the line of the song; her voice rolled along beside, rich and mellow. At the end of the many verses, he realized that others had fallen silent to listen, and at once his voice broke harshly, ruining the ending. Someone laughed, across the fire-light; Gird flinched as if he'd been slapped, but the girl's hand was on his arm.

"Never mind," she said, under cover of the harper's quick fingering—it would be a jig, this time, and some-one had found sticks to patter. Without really looking at the girl, Gird eased back to the angle between wall and fold, not at all surprised to find she had come with him. She stood closer than he found really comfortable; he could have put his arm around her and found her no closer.

"You know my name," he said, gruffly, unwilling to ask what she might refuse to answer.

"I'm Mali, from the village near the crossing—some call it Fireoak." He remembered that name, from his guards' training; with the name he called up the loca-tion, the number of families, all the details he'd been taught. It surprised him; he didn't know he could re-member all that. He looked down at her.

"You knew of me—"

She shrugged, and the shawl slipped back from dark hair. Something marked the side of her face: a scar, a birthmark. Hard to see in that light, but he could just make out a paler path across her cheek. "Most do; that kind of tale spreads. But Amis told me of you, and your past before the Guards. So I wanted to see you, see what they'd made of you."

"A failure," Gird said, then jumped as she slugged his arm. Hard: he would have a bruise there.

"Only you can make yourself a failure—and you a great strong lad with a head of solid stone—"

He was wide awake, now, as if he'd been dipped in a well. "What *are* you, some foretelling witch—?"

Firelight and shadow moved on her face; he could not read her expression. "I? I'm a farmer's daughter, as you're a farmer's son. I'm headstrong too, so they say of me, and a dangerous lass to cross. If you married me you'd have a strong mother of your children, and a loyal friend—"

"Marry—I can't marry—I'm—"

"A whole man," she said. Gird could feel his ears go
hot; he wanted to grab her and shake her, or disappear
into thin air. He knew he was whole; his body was as
alive to her as his ears, and far more active. Was *this*
how girls his age bantered? Surely she was bolder than
the others.

"I'm sorry," she said then, in a quiet voice. He could
feel her withdrawing without actually moving; she slid
the shawl back over her hair. The withdrawal pierced
him like a blade. He could not stand if it she left.

"Wait!" he said hoarsely. "I—you—I never heard
anyone—"

"It's no matter." She wrapped the shawl tightly around
herself, hugged her arms. "I'm overbold and wild; I've
been told often enough. But I'd heard of you, and how
you had changed, refusing your friends. I thought perhaps I could help, being a stranger—"

"You did." Gird rubbed his own arms, feeling the
texture of his clothes and skin for the first time in—
when?—years? He felt alive, awake, inside and out,
and not only in that way which proved men whole. His
skin tingled. "I'm—I'm awake," he said, wondering if
she'd understand. Hot tears pricked his eyes; his throat
tightened again.

She was looking at him, dark eyes hard to see in that
flickering firelight—but he could feel the intensity of
her gaze. "Awake?"

"It—oh, I can't talk here! Come on!" Without thinking, he grabbed her arm and led her around the wall to
the entrance. She had stiffened for an instant, but then
came willingly, hardly needing his guidance. He barely
noticed someone by the gate turning to look, and then
they were out beyond the walls, on the open fields,
with the firelight twinkling behind them and stars brilliant overhead.

He stopped only when he stumbled over a stone and
fell, dragging her down too. He had been crying, he
realized, the roaring of blood in his ears louder than
any night sound, the smell and taste of his own tears
covering up the fragrance on the wind. She had pulled

free when he fell, and now crouched, a dimly visible shape, an armspan away. When he got his breath at last, he sat up; she did not move, either towards him or away.

"I'm sorry," he said. "I don't—I've never done that before—"

"I should hope not." The tone carried tart amusement, but not hostility.

"I had to get away—I couldn't talk about it there, with those—"

"Only a few of them would still mock you, Gird."

"It's not that. It's—oh, gods, I'm awake again! I didn't know I wasn't. I didn't know I'd gone so numb, and now—"

"Does it hurt, like a leg you've sat on too long?"

He drew a long breath, trying to steady his breathing. "Not—hurt, exactly, though it does prickle. It's more as if I'd been sick, shut indoors a long time, so long I forgot about the colors outside, and then someone carried me out into spring." He turned to her, wishing he could see her expression. "Did you mean that about marrying?"

To his surprise, she burst out laughing, a joyous rollicking laugh that he could not resist. He didn't know why it was funny, but he laughed too. Finally, after a last snort, she quieted down, and apologized.

"I shouldn't *laugh* at you, I know that, but for someone just waking after long illness, you do move fast. Was this how you courted the girls, back when you were in the guards?"

"I didn't, back then—I was too young." Even in starlight, he could see that she'd let the shawl slip back again, revealing her face. His body insisted that he was not too young *now*; he tried to stay calm. "Mmm—would you sit with me?"

She moved closer, spread her skirts, and sat down almost hip-to-hip. "I thought I was, with you the closest person to me on this whole dark night."

She had a scent he had not noticed before; now it moved straight from his nose to his heart. Did all women smell like this? He cursed himself for a crazy fool, to have wasted the years in which he might have learned *how* to court such a girl. He clenched his fists to keep from reaching for her.

"But surely—" His voice broke, and he started again. "But surely you have someone—someone in your village—?"

Her low chuckle warmed his heart. "Alas no, Gird. For I'm the forward, quick-tongued lass you heard tonight; I will not guard my tongue for any man's content, though I swear by Alyanya there's no malice in it. And though I'm big and strong enough, and a good cook, I'm not much for threadcraft. My spinning's full of lumps, and my weaving's as bad as a child's. My family's parrion has always been in threadcraft, though my great-aunt taught me her parrion of cooking—she said I'd been born with a gift that way."

"My mother and sisters have threadcraft enough," Gird said. "But a parrion of cooking they'd welcome, even more in herblore than bakecraft." He could hardly believe they had come so fast to discussion of parrions. Wasn't that the last part before formal betrothal? He could not remember; he could not think of anything but the girl herself—Mali, he reminded himself firmly— and the smell and feel of her.

"Mine is that," she said, the weight of her coming now against his arm; he shifted it around her shoulders, and she leaned into him. Where she touched him, her body seemed to burn right through their clothes; he felt afire with longing for her. It was a struggle to speak calmly. He took another long breath of the cold, clean night air.

"Your father?" Gird thought it likely her father wouldn't agree, given his own reputation. But she shook her head, in the angle of his arm, where he could feel it.

"Grandmother's our elder, and village elder too—the magelords don't like it, but they agreed. She'll be glad enough if anyone wants me, and you're a farmer's son, in the same hearthing. But what of your mother?"

"She'll be happy." He leaned closer, to smell her hair. Was he really talking of marriage with someone met just this night, and by firelight? Could she be a witch—or, worst of all, a magelady pretending to be peasant, disguised by her magic?

"I have to tell you about this," said Mali, struggling upright for a moment. He looked at her; she had one hand to the mark on her face. "I'm no beauty, besides my loud tongue. Many call me ugly, for this scar if nothing else."

"What happened?" It was a chance to breathe, to remind himself of the customs of his people.

Mali made a curious noise that Gird could not interpret, somewhere between a sniff and a snort. "I wish I could claim it came from defending my cousin against the magelords—it happened the same day—but in fact it was my own clumsiness. I was carrying a scythe to my brother in the fields, and tripped. When I came running back, looking for sympathy, there was my cousin in the lane. No one had time for me then, and no wonder. I thought to save my grandmother trouble by treating it myself, but failed to put herin in the poultice, so it scarred. My own fault." She laid her warm hand on his. "But I will understand if you change—I mean, it's not fair. I've landed on you this night like a fowler's net on a bird. You must have a free choice, a chance to make up your own mind. See me in daylight, and then if you still wish—"

Contending thoughts almost silenced him. Gird eyed her. "Is it that you think you can get nothing better than the coward of the count's own village? Was I just a last chance for you, is that what you're saying?"

She sat bolt upright. For an instant he thought she was going to hit him again; the place she'd slugged him before still ached. "You *fool!* If you don't want me, just say so. Don't make it my fault."

"I didn't—"

"You did." She was breathing fast, angry, and he waited. Finally she went on. "I was curious. I'd heard—what I told you. For myself, barring I like a roll as well as anyone, I'd live alone rather than marry anyone's last chance. Then meeting you—Amis said you were gentle, but he didn't say how you sang." Her voice trailed away. "And you're no coward, whatever *you* think."

"You don't think a man knows himself best?"

Laughter burst out of her again. "Who could? Can water know it's wet, or stone know it's hard? What could it measure itself against? I know my feelings, but my grandmother knew I was meant for herblore, not needlecraft or weaving. So with you—did your father or mother think you would make a soldier?"

Surprise again. "I—don't know. Not really, I suppose, although they feared I could be—"

"Cruel?" He could see her head shake in the starlight. "No, not like that. You can do what you must, but you take no pleasure in giving pain." He was eased by that, and his suspicions fled. A strange girl, like no girl he'd known (but what girls had he known?) but not a cunning one. If she said she liked him, then she did. Gird cleared his throat.

"I would like to—" Lady's grace; he didn't even know how to ask. But Mali had moved nearer to him again, her shoulder against his, her fragrant hair once more against his face.

"You should wait until sunrise," she said. "You might change your mind."

Gird laughed. "Sunrise," he said, "is too far away. Or do you want to go back and find witnesses to make it formal?"

"I want no witnesses," she said, in a low voice that was almost a growl. "Not for this." She folded her shawl, and lay back upon it, arms wide. "I swear by the Lady, that for this night I am content."

And content were they both by sunrise. Gird had thought he knew how it went between men and women; it was no secret after all, and any child saw it often enough growing up. But Mali's body, sweet-scented and warm on the cool hillside grass, was nothing like his imaginings—or far more. He could not get enough of touching her smooth skin, her many complex curves all ending in another place to enjoy with tongue and nose and fingers. And she, by all evidence, enjoyed it all as much as he did. They had fallen asleep at last, to be wakened by the loud uneven singing of Gird's friends on their way home. Mali chuckled.

"They want to let you know it's time to go, but without interrupting. You know, Gird, they are your friends. You must forgive them someday."

Right then he would have forgiven anyone anything, or so he felt. A pale streak marked distant sunrise. With a groan, he pulled his clothes together. "I don't want to leave."

Mali was already standing, shaking out her shawl. "If you wish, you know where."

"You know I want to marry you."

"I do *not* know. I know you enjoyed my body, and I enjoyed yours, but there's more to marriage than that. But I like you, Gird. I say that now, after hearing you sing, laugh, and cry—more than many girls do, before they wed. Look on my face in daylight, and decide." She turned away to start home. Gird caught her arm.

"Why not now?"

"What of your work today? What of your family? Go home, lo—Gird. Go home and think whether you want a big, clumsy, loud-voiced wife with a scarred face. If you do, come see me in daylight. Ask me then—"

"I'm asking now!"

"No. I'll not answer now. Daylight for both of us, then." And she pulled away and was gone. Gird stared after her, then followed the distant voices of his friends toward home.

He caught up with them within sight of home. By then it was light enough to see their expressions; he could feel himself going red. Amis elbowed Jens.

"You see I was right. He just needed to get a little fresh air—"

"He got more than fresh air, I'll warrant. Look at his face. If I'd gone out like that with Torin—"

"You wouldn't. You'll be learning how in your marriage bed, Jens."

"I know how." Jens shoved Koris, who shoved back. "It's just that with her father—"

"Come on, Gird," said Amis, throwing an arm around his shoulders. "Tell us—you drag the girl out in the middle of the dancing, did you just throw her on the ground, or what?"

He could hear the undertones in their voices—they weren't sure if he was going to be angry, or sulk, or what. He felt like singing, and instead burst out laughing.

"That's new," said Amis. "I like that—Gird laughing again."

"Be still," he said, ducking away from Amis's arm and the finger that was prodding his ribs. "You were right: I admit it. I needed to go dancing—"

"You didn't dance," said Jens.

Gird shrugged. He could feel more laughter bubbling up, like a spring long dry coming in. "I did well enough," he said.

"Watch him go to sleep behind the hedges today." Koris grinned, but it had no bite to it. "You may be tired by nightfall, eh?"

Gird grinned back. He felt that the bad years had never happened; he felt he could work for two days together. He drew a long breath—sweet, fresh air of dawn—and said nothing more. He had never expected to be happy again, and now he was.

He came in through the barton, aware of the stale, sour smell of the cottage after the freshness outside. All very well to fall for a girl, to marry her—but where would they sleep? He'd have to build a bed. He'd have to earn the marriage fee for the count, and the fee to her family for her parrion. He'd have to—

"You're looking blithe this morning," said Arin, from the flank of the red cow. Milk hissed into the bucket. Arin's voice had sharpened, in the difficult years, but he sounded more worried than angry.

"Sheepfold last night," said Gird. He took down the other milking stool, and a bucket.

"You? I thought you'd gone to Kirif's."

Gird washed the cow's udder with water from the stable bucket and folded himself up on the milking stool. The brindle cow flapped her ears back and forth as he reached for her teats, and he leaned into her flank and crooned to her. "Easy, sweetling—I was at Kirif's first, and then Amis came along and we went over to the fold—"

"Good for you," said Arin. "Meet anyone?"

He might as well admit it; it would be all over the village by the time they came to the field. "You always meet someone at the fold," he began, but he couldn't hold the tone. "Someone," he said again. "Arin, there's a girl from Fireoak—"

"Where?"

"Fireoak. Sunrising of here. You know, Teris's wife's sister married into Fireoak. And her parrion is cooking and herblore—"

"Teris's wife's sister?" said Arin, with maddening coolness.

"No. Mali's parrion. The girl I met."

Arin's eyebrows went up. "You were talking parrions? In one night?"

"We did more than talk," said Gird, stripping the first two teats and going on to the next.

"You can't mean—you're not betrothed? Gird, you know you have to ask—"

Gird grinned into the cow's flank and squirted a stream of milk at Arin, who had come to stand by her hip. "Not betrothed, but more than talk. Lady's grace, Arin, you know what I mean. And I will ask for her, just you wait."

"But are you sure? The first time you've been out with the lasses since before—" he stopped short, and reddened. Gird laughed.

"Since before I left the guards, you mean, and you're right. So you think it's like a blind man's first vision, and I should wait and see? So she said, but I tell you, Arin, this is my wife. You'll like her."

"I hope so," said Arin soberly. "Best tell Da."

"After milking." He finished the brindle cow, and took both buckets into the kitchen.

His mother gave him one look and said "Who?"

Gird looked at her. "Is it so obvious?"

"To a woman and a wife? Did you think I was blind, lad? No, you're a lad no more. Man, then. You've found a woman, and bedded her, and now you want to marry."

"True, then. What d'you think?"

She looked at him, a long measuring look. "About time, I think. *If* you're ready. You've spent long enough sulking—"

"I know," he said, to forestall what was coming. She shook her head at him, but didn't continue the familiar lecture.

"Well, then—I don't know where the fee's coming from, but you can earn that. What's her parrion?"

"Herbcraft and cooking." He held his breath; his mother had always talked of finding a wife with a parrion to complement hers: another weaver or spinner, perhaps a dyer.

"Well enough. No lad—man—takes advice of his mother, but you think now, Gird—is she quarrelsome? The house will be no larger for cross words." That was said low; Arin's wife was still in the other room, and she had brought, his mother had said once, a parrion of complaining.

"Not—quarrelsome." She had said she was freespoken, but nothing in her voice had sent the rasp along his skin.

"Best tell your father." She gave him a quick smile. "If she's brought you laughter again, Gird, I'll give her no trouble. It's been a long drought."

His father, still hunched over his breakfast, brightened when Gird told him. Arin's wife said nothing, briskly leading her oldest out the front door. His father leaned close.

"Comely, is she?"

"She's—" Gird could not think of words. She had been starlight and scent, warmth and strength and joy, all wrapped in one. "She's strong," he offered. His father laughed.

"You sound like the lad you were. Strong didn't give that gleam to your eye, I'll warrant. There's more to the lass than muscle. When will you go to her father?"

"Soon. I—I'm not sure."

His father whistled the chorus of "Nutting in the Woods" and laughed again. "Young men. By the gods, boy, I remember your mother—" Gird was shocked. His mother had been his mother—that capable, hard-handed woman in long apron, spooning out porridge or carding wool or weaving—all his life. His father had gone on. "Hair in a cloud of light around her face, and she smelled like—like—I suppose all girls do, in their spring. Never a young lad can resist that, Gird; we all go that way, rams to the ewes and bulls to the cows, and spend the rest of our days yoked in harness—but it's times like this make it worthwhile."

"Eh?" He had not followed all that; his father's words brought back Mali's scent, as if she stood next to him, as if she lay—and he pulled his mind back with an effort.

His father thumped the table. "To see sons ready to wed themselves, strong sons: that's what's worth the work, Gird. To see you with your eyes clear and your mind on something but the past."

Gird shrugged. The self of yesterday, the self that had had nothing to hope for, was gone as if it had never lived.

"'Tis the Lady's power," said his father. "She can bring spring to any field." This no longer embarrassed Gird; he had returned whole-hearted to his family's beliefs.

His visit to Fireoak began auspiciously. Mali's own mother had seen his mother's weaving at the tradefair years before.

"She has the parrion for the firtree pattern," the woman said. She was as tall as Mali, but spare, her dark hair streaked with gray. "If she has not the parrion for the barley pattern, I would be glad to trade." Gird knew that his mother had wanted the barley pattern for years, and had never been able to work it out herself. She had bestowed the firtree pattern on Arin's wife's aunt; surely she would trade with his wife's mother. He nodded: no commitment, but possibility.

Mali herself was kneading bread, her arms flour-smudged to the elbows. The scar she'd told him of was obvious enough, along the right cheek, more broad than deep. He didn't care; he had known he would not care. It was hard to be that close to her, in the same air, and not holding her. Her eyes twinkled at him: agreement. Then she looked back at the bread dough and pummeled it again. He could feel once more her fist on his arm, the strength of her. She was strong inside and out; his knees weakened as he remembered the feel of her body all along his on the starlit grass.

"Mali's not the quietest girl," said Mali's father. He was not so dark as Mali and her mother, a brown square man with a graying beard, almost bald. "She's got a quick tongue."

"Gird knows that," said Mali, flipping the dough up and slamming it down again.

"Like that," said her father. Gird smiled at him.

"Better a quick tongue than one full of malice," he said, misquoting the old proverb on purpose.

"Oh, aye, if it's not quick into the pot. Good cook; her parrion's valuable." That began the bargaining phase. A daughter's parrion was a family's most valuable possession, the secrets and inherited talent of generations of women passed to a chosen carrier. A valuable parrion enriched the household gaining it, and impoverished those left behind. The lords' fee for marriage was the same for all of the same rank, but he would owe Mali's family for her parrion.

At least it meant that her family found his acceptable, and she must have agreed as well. Despite all the lords had done, the people had never come over to thinking that girls had to go where their families bestowed them. Marriage was, in the old rituals, the mingling of fires on a hearth—and if either failed to kindle, the marriage could not be.

Arin had come along for the bargaining phase, since Gird was neither holder nor heir. Gird and Mali escaped to the smallgarden, there to stand awkwardly staring at each other, in full view of her village. An amazing number of people seemed to need to go back and forth in the lane. Gird knew none of them, but noticed the same small boys driving the same goats up and down, a girl in a red skirt carrying a basket—full, then empty, then full again—past the gate. Mali finally began to laugh.

"It's true—they're just seeing how long we can stand here, and expecting one of us to turn tail and run."

"The scar doesn't matter." The words were out before he thought; she flushed and it showed whiter. "I'm sorry," he said.

"No—I'm used to it. I *thought* you'd come anyway, and I thought you'd still—but I'm blushing because it's my fault."

"Fault?"

She looked away past his shoulder. "I had heard of you; I went there to meet you, and no one else. And meeting you, I wanted you—and then—"

"And then I wanted you. So?"

"So—I still want you, but—don't bring it back to me, years from now."

"No." He moved closer to her, ignoring the women now carrying buckets past on their way to the well. "No, it was meant. The Lady meant it, maybe, or some other god." He put his arm around her waist, and she leaned on him. He could have carried her off to the barton, then and there, but Arin came out looking pleased.

"So—we have work to do, Gird, to earn your fees."

He knew he had turned red; he could feel the heat on his face. "Ah—yes. Mali—"

"Don't tarry," she said. Then she leaned against him again, and kissed him, and whispered in his ear. "We may have a Lady's blessing already."

Chapter Six

The only awkwardness came when he had to bring Mali before the count's steward, to have her transferred on the Rolls. Luckily the count himself was not in residence, but the steward might have decided to invoke the rule himself.

"So—you're marrying, young Gird?"

"Yes, lord steward." Gird kept his eyes down.

"About time—you've loafed long enough." The voice was chilly; Gird watched the fingers holding the pen tap on the edge of the parchment. "Look up at me, boy."

The steward's face was older, grayer, but otherwise unchanged. Gird met those ice-blue eyes with difficulty.

"You brought the marriage fee?" Gird handed it over, the heavy copper coins slipping out of his hands much faster than they'd come in. "And this is the girl—" The steward looked her up and down, and then glanced at Gird. "You chose strength, eh? A good worker, I'll be bound—none too pretty—" Gird felt his ears burning; Mali's face had gone mottled red. Her scar stood out, stark white, from brow to jawline. "Wide hips—good bearer. Any mageblood in your line, girl?"

"No, lord steward." Her voice was husky, almost a growl.

"No, I daresay not. Nor would breed mages, is my guess. Waste of his lordship's time, your sort, bar the fun of it." The steward looked back down at the parchment. "Mali of Fireoak, daughter of Kekrin, son of Amis, wed to Gird of this village, son of Dorthan, son of Keris. Fee paid, permission granted to farm with Dorthan. That's all then."

They ducked their heads and went out quickly, both of them flushed and angry, but too wise to speak of it. First to Gird's father's house, for Mali to lay her first fire on the greathearth; every old grannie in the village was there to cry the portents of that flame. Gird held his breath. She put the splinters down in the Star pattern, and above them the tripod of fireoak, brought from her own family's hearth, and then struck the flints. Once—would have been too soon. Twice—a fair omen, but not the best. On the third strike, a spark leapt from her tools to the tip of the fireoak splinters, and kindled living flame. Now she moved quickly, laying the rest of the fire in ritual patterns: this twig over that, this herb, a twist of wool from her father's sheep, an apple-seed from their tree. The grannies muttered and flashed handsigns at each other; Gird was worried, but his mother smiled happily. It must be all right, then.

He and the other men left then, trudging through the back kitchen, then the cowbyre, into the narrow, cramped barton where the women had laid out the wedding feast on planks. This would be the refusing, he knew: Mali's parents would come, and try to persuade her to go home. She would first refuse them, with the door open, then—when they argued longer—close and bar the door to them. After a ritual greeting to her mother-in-law, and a prick of the finger to get two drops of blood, one for the fire and one for the hearthstone, her parents would knock again. And now, as a member of this household, she would greet them as honored guests.

All this time, Gird endured the jokes of his friends and his brothers and father. He had heard such jokes all his life, finding them funny once he was old enough, but now, waiting for Mali to become his wife, and not her parents' daughter, he was not amused. What did these grotesque fantasies have to do with Mali? He swiped irritably at his brother, when Arin tried to tie the traditional apron on him.

"You have to, Gird. You're her husband now; don't you want children?"

Gird looked at the apron, its ancient leather darkened by generations of celebrants. It was ridiculous. Bulls didn't need such a thing; why did the gods demand it of humans? He could remember sniggering in the corner when Arin danced in the apron, and wondering how his brother could approach his wife in his own skin afterwards. His friends had come nearer, warily, ready to help Arin force him into it if necessary. He sighed, and let his arms fall.

"All right. But I still think—" He said no more; their hands were busy with thongs and lacings. "I wonder how old this custom is—"

Mali, when she came out, bit her lip to keep from laughing. At least, he hoped that was suppressed laughter on her face. He felt a fool enough, strutting around like a young bull first meeting heifers, and nearly as big. She wore the maiden's vest of soft doeskin embroidered with flowers, laced tightly behind, where she could not reach it, a tradition as old as his apron. The men began to stamp the beat, their deep voices echoing off the barton walls as they chanted. Gird stamped as hard, feeling his face redden, hating it—but the old rhythm began to move him.

The steps were only partly traditional: part was each new-married man's invention. The jiggling thing on the apron was ridiculous, yes—but it was not *merely* ridiculous. Gird strutted the length of the barton, whirled, skipped a step, backed—and closed on Mali. Her eyes were bright, twinkling with laughter; she glanced down, pretended shock, looked skyward and reeled backwards, to catch herself with a clutch at Gird's shoulder. The watchers howled. She snatched her hand back, a maiden caught in indiscretion, and turned away. Gird circled her, faced her again, put his hands behind his back and waggled his hips. For an instant she grinned delightedly, then covered her face with her hands, brushed past him close enough for her skirts to catch on the apron, and then leaped like a startled deer.

Clearly, the dance was not embarrassing Mali—she played into the jokes as heartily as most men. Gird took heart, then. They could make their families laugh—their private joke, if their red faces came from exertion, and not from the shouts and laughter of others. They spun it out, circling and dodging between others and the tables, playing parts they only half understood. When they were both dripping sweat, Gird gave her a little nod, and his next rush carried them both into the cowbyre, where a stall had been laid with fresh straw for this occasion.

Here she had to unlace his apron, and he to unlace the maiden's vest she wore, to replace it with the matron's looser vest, his wedding present to her. Her fingers on his legs, his waist, brushed tantalizingly; the apron would be hardly more obvious than his response if she didn't hurry. He fumbled with the vest lacings.

"Did they have to lace it so tightly?"

"That was my sister," said Mali, breathless. "She

wanted to see me faint, I think. Don't break the laces, remember." If he broke the laces, they'd have to give her family a sheep. He grunted and worked carefully. Finally the last knot came loose, and Mali drew a deep breath. "Ahh. Better." She worked her arms out of the vest carefully, and turned to him.

Gird handed her the matron's vest his mother and sisters had made. "You'd best get this on, if you don't want to spend the rest of the feast in here."

Mali chuckled as she looked him up and down. "Eager, are you?" She twitched her shoulders, putting the vest on, and Gird felt his pulse quicken. "But we'd better hang these out, or they'll come in to help."

"I'll do it," said Gird. The apron and vest had to be returned to each family, and the first step was to hang them on the appropriate pegs outside the cowbyre. A roar greeted him as he came out and put them up. Two of his friends were ready to grab him and keep him out, but he was quicker and managed to dart back into the stall with Mali.

Someone outside began another song, in which the women joined as well. Mali hummed the melody, and sat swaying a little back and forth. Gird stared at her. He wanted her—wanted her even more than on a hillside in the dark—but on the other side of the wall the whole village was waiting for this. It was one thing to be roused by someone else's marriage rites, he was discovering, and quite another to fulfill all the rituals with everyone watching him. Or not exactly watching, but not indifferent, either.

Then Mali turned away, and burrowed into the straw. Gird watched, bemused. There was nothing in this stall; he'd cleaned it himself, that morning, and laid the clean straw carefully. Mali grunted, and came up with a stoppered jug and something wrapped in a cloth.

"You are a witch." Gird pulled the stopper out when Mali passed him the jug. He sniffed. "What's this?"

"My aunt's favorite. And I'm not a witch, but you don't know all the rituals. Groom prepares the stall, but the bride bribes her new mother-in-law to supply it."

Gird sipped cautiously; a fiery liquid ran down his

throat and made him blink. "Lady's blessing—that would bring—"

"Trouble if the lords knew of it." Mali took a swig, and opened her eyes. "My. No wonder she wouldn't let me taste it before." She unwrapped the cloth, and Gird saw a half-loaf of bread and some cheese. They ate quietly for the rest of that song, and the beginning of the next. Then either Mali's aunt's potion or Mali herself—warm and spicesmelling beside him—drove out his lingering embarrassment. He rolled toward her on the clean straw, and she embraced him. It was as satisfying as the first time, even when he roused to the ring of faces peering down at them.

"You went to sleep," Amis said, grinning. "We could hear you snore all through the singing."

Gird looked past them at the opening; it was nearly dark. Mali, her skirts back down around her knees, started rebraiding her hair. When he looked at her, she winked, and wrinkled her nose. "Well," he said, "did you eat all the food, or can we have some?"

They had to lead more dancing, that night, in the final Weaving that took them in and out of every cottage in the village, and around all three wells. Then at last it was over: all the food eaten, all the songs sung, all the dances danced, and a few hours to sleep (this time only sleep) until dawn brought work and their first day as a married pair.

Despite his mother's approval, Gird had worried about Mali's quick tongue in the house, when she had to share that cramped kitchen with two other women and the children. His mother's health had begun to fail; she was querulous sometimes, and Arin's wife could never weave to suit her. But Mali left the loom alone, and took over all the kitchen work. The other two had no more scouring and scrubbing to do, no more washing of pots or kneading of dough. Gird had never known how much difference a parrion for cooking could make. All women cooked, and many men; food was food. Now he realized that food differed as much as weaving. Mali's bread was lighter, her stews more savory, her porridge smooth, neither lumpy nor thin. She gathered herbs in the wood, and hung them to dry; they gave the cottage a different, sharper smell. She even knew how to make cheese.

With no kitchen work to do, Gird's mother could concentrate on weaving, and let Arin's wife do all the carding and spinning. They traded Mali's cheese for extra wool; his mother sent three furls to the trading fair in the next village, which brought them precious coppers, almost as much as the marriage fee even that first year. Gird's mother had always liked weaving better than anything else. Now she produced furl after furl, trading to the dyer for skeins of colored yarn, rich golds and reds and dark green. With those, she could weave patterned cloth that brought a higher price, combining the barley pattern Mali's mother had taught her with color.

The other cheesemaker in the village was getting old, and people began to bring Mali milk. She traded herbs to the older cheesemaker for one of her tubs, and made more cheese. For every five, a hand, she could keep one. Her cheese was not as good as some, she admitted— she would not try to sell it at a tradefair—but in the village it brought them what they needed to feed the extra mouths.

Gird's first child was born just after Midwinter. Mali had gathered the herbs she said she needed back in the summer, and as usual the village grannies came to help with the birthing. Gird had not realized how much his status would improve, first as a married man, and then as a father. Now all the grown men spoke to him by his own name. In the rest breaks they would wait for him before starting a conversation. Teris, who had been married more than a year, now treated him as an equal, an old friend. For a few days he resisted this, remembering Teris's accusations. One bleak day when they were both in the cowbyre, Mali wormed the old quarrel out of him, and counseled forgiveness.

"You can't change the past, love. If he's a good friend now, why not?"

Gird found that his old grudge looked very different

when he got it out and tried to explain it to Mali. "You make every thing so simple," he complained.

"It's not simple, but it's over. He erred, back then—did you never err?"

"You know I did, but—"

"Well, then, let be. He blamed you unfairly; if you refuse his friendship now, you'll be blaming unfairly."

"Are you ever angry?" He looked down at her; she had the baby at her breast, and he could smell her milk and the baby's scent overlaying her own.

Mali knotted her brows, thinking. "Angry . . . yes. When things happen, not later. If I'd been here, and seen someone hurting you, then I'd have been angry. Otherwise—'tis like a bit of old milk in the pan that sours the new. All life would sour if we held anger. So I yell, and throw things, and scour it all away, right then, so the next day won't sour."

"But when things aren't *right*—"

Mali shifted the baby to the other breast; he noticed how the baby's sucking had changed the shape of her nipple before she pulled her vest across to cover it. "Is this about Teris, or something else?"

Gird chuckled; he wasn't sure why. "Something you said that first night. And talking with the men in the village council. Things have changed since my father was a young man, and more since his father's day. And not for the better."

"Taxes?" Taxes were up again, the field-fee higher for the third year in a row.

"Not only that." Gird rolled on his back and tried to think. "The law itself has changed. Old Keris was telling us yesterday about the way it was back then. No guards here, for one thing, and fewer everywhere. No lockups. No stocks, no whippings."

"Old men always think their youth was golden," said Mali, stroking the baby's back.

"He saw the lords' magic himself, he said." Gird looked for a reaction to that and got it; Mali stared at him, shocked that he would speak of it openly. "He said they used to show it all the time, use it for aid in drought and storm."

"What was it like?" Her voice was barely above a whisper.

"He saw them call rain, he said. Bring clouds out of a clear sky, gather them up as a shearer gathers the tags of fleece, and then call rain down." Gird cleared his throat and looked around. No one else was in hearing. "He said, too, that the old lords would warm the heart to see, not like our count. That everyone wanted to please them."

"Old men's tales," said Mali, but without conviction.

That year the spring rains came timely, and a rich harvest rewarded their labors. Arin's wife had another baby in the fall; by Midwinter, Mali told him she was pregnant again. The cottage seemed to bulge at the seams already . . .

The dun cow lowed, her hoarse voice as loud as if she'd been in the cottage. No, she seemed to cry. No, no, no . . . o . . . o. Gird palmed his burning eyes and wanted to groan a refrain to it. No. He was not ready to get up and help that cow; he wanted to lie where he was and sleep. But the cow was not giving up; with the stubborn insistence of a deprived bovine, she let out another long plaint. Most cows tried to edge furtively into the woods when about to calve, but this one wanted someone there . . . yet refused to do it where it was convenient. Gird rolled on his back, grunting at the ache in his shoulders from plowing, and slowly sat up. He heard his father's harsh breathing, the catch in every inhalation. One of the children snored: probably Rahel. The cow called again, this time answered by the two in the cowbyre. Gird stifled an oath, and sat up, feeling around on the floor for his boots.

Outside, the predawn light in the sky only made the barton itself darker. Gird carried a splinter of oak from the fire, its tip bright orange, almost flaming in the breeze of his movement. Tucked in his tunic was the scrap of candle he'd light if he needed it when the time came: no use to waste candle if daylight came before the crisis. The dun cow had stayed out of the byre last night, as she did every time she calved. She would be

in the thicket near the creek, if he was lucky. Outside
the barton, the lower meadow looked silver-gray under
a sky sheened with dawn. Heavy spring dew wet his
boots through before he came to the thicket, guided
more by the cow's voice than his sight, though it grew
lighter moment by moment.

In among the gnarled and twisted scrub, though, he
could barely see, and staggered more than once over
root or stone. Stupid cow, he thought, as he had thought
for three years now. Staying out in the cold and dark,
hiding yourself in the thicket, when you know you'll
want my help. There she was, a large hump of shadow
among lighter, flickering shadows. Down already, grunting and panting, her tail thrown back out of her way.
He pulled out the candle, found a smooth stone to set it
on, and with a wisp of dry grass and breath, blew the
splinter into a flame. The cow's big eyes reflected it,
making three flames where there had been one. For a
moment his mind wandered: did the cow see a reflection of flame in his eyes? Was that why she looked
afraid? He lit the candle, picked it up, and walked
closer, crooning to the nervous cow. *Have a heifer*, he
begged silently. *Have a heifer this time.* A contraction
moved across her girth; a bulge extruded below her
tail. A pearly blot inside . . . a hoof. That was good,
unless the other leg was back. He couldn't quite see.
Another contraction, and he could: two hoofs and a
nose. A normal delivery, so far, with the shiny black
nose already free of the sack. Now it was light enough
to see the shapes he needed to see. He tipped the
candle, quenching it against the damp grass with a hiss,
and tucked it back into his tunic. His feet were cold.
The cow groaned again, a softer sound but eloquent of
struggle. Gird stroked her flank, and began the calving
chant.

"So, cow, gentle cow, quiet cow, so . . . Birth calf,
milk calf, little calf grow . . . so cow, kind cow, good
cow, so . . . Life come, growth come . . ."

Another contraction, and another, this one longer,
pushing the shoulders out. The shoulders came, all in a
rush, as always, and the wet calf lay still a moment,

hind end still in the cow. Then the rest of the body followed. The cow made a noise Gird never heard save in those moments after calving, almost a murmur. The calf's ear flicked. With a lumbering rush, the cow heaved herself up, and the cord broke. She shook her head at Gird, who went on chanting until the wildness left her eyes. The cow nosed around the calf, licking it clean of the birth sack, licking it dry, murmuring, encouraging. The dun cow was a good mother cow. The calf shook its head, waggling both ears, and tapped its tiny front hooves on the ground as it tried to figure out how to stand. The cow licked on, still murmuring. The calf pushed one front leg out, then another, and heaved itself to a sitting position, then fell over. But it tried again, and again, its ridiculous little ears flicking back and forth with each effort. And it was a heifer, the year's good luck, for he could keep it.

Gird was never sure what made him look away from the calf, to glance between the knotted limbs of creek plum and hazel, but there across the meadow walked a creature of grace and light. Tall, lithe, so inexpressibly lovely that his throat closed. What was it?

The creature turned, as if feeling his glance, and looked toward him. A voice came, bell-like but slightly discordant.

"And what are you thinking, human, alone before dawn on this unlucky day?"

Gird could find nothing to say, only then remembering that it was the spring Evener, the day and night of equal length, when the creatures of night ruled until truedawn, and the creatures of day could not wander the dusks unscathed.

"The cow called," he said finally. The black-cloaked figure came nearer, hardly seeming to touch the ground.

"The cow called. Cattle to cattle: as your masters would say of you. Less than cattle, we think you, worse."

He could see the face now, inhuman but beautiful with a beauty that called human hearts and eyes. Pale against the black cloak, wide eyes starry bright. Was this a treelord? He had heard tales of them but no one he knew had ever seen one.

"No, I am not one of those dreamsoaked lost singers," the figure said. Gird shivered. He had said nothing; it had picked the thought out of his mind. "I am what they were, and should have stayed, had they any pride or wit at all. Your kind, when they know us at all, call us kuaknom."

He had never heard that word. Kuak, that was the old word for tree—and the nomi were the windspirits that hated order and served chaos. Kuaknom: that would be—

"Old lords," said the being, now just outside the thicket. "Very old, human slave. Firstborn of the elder races, lords of power and darkness—"

"The fallen treelords," Gird said, having finally put it all together. The treelords who had quarreled with Adyan the Maker, so the tales went, and turned against their kin, and riven the forests that used to cover the land in a great battle.

"Not fallen, little man," said the kuaknom, with a smile that sent ice to Gird's heart. "Not fallen—but changed. And on this night, until truedawn, those witless enough to wander abroad are our lawful prey. You, little man—"

Gird flinched as the kuaknom reached for him. The cow grumbled, in the way of new mother cows, and rattled her horns against the hazels. And a shaft of red sunlight, sharp as an arrow, stung his eyes; he flung up his hand, and the kuaknom backed away, muttering in its own language. Then again, to him:

"You are safe, human, by that one gleam of sun, but I curse you for it. May your loins wither, and your beasts fall sick, and the strength of your arm fail when you need it most." Even as Gird squinted against the sunlight, it was gone, a shadow across the field.

He sat a long time, bemused, until he heard Raheli's shrill voice calling for him. Was such a curse dangerous? Would he die, lose his manhood, his cattle, his strength? The cow continued to groom and nurse the calf, who showed all the sturdy life of a healthy young bovine.

*   *   *

Nothing befell to make him think the curse had force until the following winter. He had consoled himself that it was, after all, delivered in sunlight, which ought to make the words of the dark powerless. He had given more than his usual share to the rituals of Alyanya and even contributed freely to the lords' offering to Esea. Esea was, after all, a god of light, who might be expected to offer protection against the powers of darkness. When the rest of the year went well (the other two cows also calving heifers), he counted himself lucky.

But that was the winter of the wolves, the worst that had been seen since Gird's childhood. It began even before Midwinter. They had heard the wolves howling night after night, but none of the stock had yet been touched. The headman had gone to the steward, asking the guards' help to hunt the pack, but the steward had refused. Some of the men had gone out to the more distant folds, to help the shepherds watch. Arin went, over his mother's objections, twirling his long staff and grinning at Gird as he walked away.

Gird was hauling dung to the pile when he heard the shouts. He hauled himself to the top of the barton wall. There they came, across the snow, a cluster of men moving awkwardly. Carrying something—no, someone —he slid down, and went through the cottage without stopping to speak. His father was already out in the lane. Together they moved toward the group—and then he could see it was Arin they carried, Arin whose blood stained his clothes and dripped scarlet on the snow.

They got him into the house and stretched on the table. Gird felt his own heart pounding, slow but shaking his whole body, as he saw Arin's wounds. Then his mother pushed him aside.

"Go fetch water," she said. And to Arin's wife, "Get those children out of here—into the kitchen—"

Gird went out to the well; the men stood around silently, shoulders hunched against the cold. He lowered the bucket into icy black water and drew it up. As he turned to carry it in, Amis turned to him. "Is he—?"

Gird shook his head. "I don't know."

"Kef's gone for the steward," Amis said. Gird nodded

and went back inside with the bucket. Coming in from the clean air, he could smell the blood as if it were a slaughterday. He gave the bucket to Mali, who reached for it, and went to stand behind his father.

Arin had long bleeding gashes on his legs and arms; one hand was badly mangled. "He was trying to choke one of them with it," offered Cob, one of the men who had carried him in. Gird's mother said nothing; she and Mali were cleaning the wounds with one of Mali's brews, and wrapping them with the cloths the women kept. Arin looked as white as the snow outside against the dark wood of the table; he did not move or speak. "He bled all the way back," said Cob, into the silence.

Gird's mother gave him a fierce look. "You might have tied these up then," she said.

Cob spread his hands. "We had nothing but our dirty clothes; I would not give him woundfever."

Gird's mother opened her mouth and shut it with a snap. Gird could imagine what she would have said to him. But Cob had done the best he knew, and Cob was not her son.

The door opened, and someone coughed. Gird turned. The steward was there. No one said anything; the steward came nearer. In the dim light his face was stern as usual, but Gird thought his eyes softened when he saw Arin's wounds.

"Wolves, or folokai?" he asked.

"Wolves, sir," said Cob. "At the sheepfold, they were, and Arin come to drive them off—"

"Alone?" asked the steward.

"No, sir. But he went first, and it seemed the wolf drew away—just the one, that we could see. He went to chase it a bit, and that's when the pack ran at him, and then the rest of us ran out with torches, and drove them off him."

The steward moved closer yet. Gird's mother put out a hand, as if to stop him, and drew it back. The steward laid his hands on Arin's shoulders.

"Heal him, sir?" asked Gird's mother in a choked whisper.

The steward looked startled, then shook his head.

"No, I can't do that—I have not the power." He looked closely at Arin's wounds. "I doubt he'll live—he looks to have lost too much blood—"

"No!" Gird's mother grabbed at his sleeve. Gird felt his heart contract with pity for her and Arin both. "It's not fair—he alone against the wolves—"

The steward pulled free. "I'm sorry. It's a shame—I'll take his name off the work rolls—if he lives, he'll be unfit to work until well into summer. If he dies, I'll remit half the death fee; he deserves that much."

"And more," someone muttered behind Gird. The steward's head came around, but the mutter had been too low to identify. Even Gird had no idea who it was.

"And I'm sending down a sheep," said the steward. "He will need meat broth to mend, if he can."

"Thank you, sir," said Gird's father. His mother nodded. The steward glanced around the room, as if looking for an excuse to say something else. His gaze lit on Gird.

"At least you have another son, a strong one. And this one—Arin, is it?—has sired already, hasn't he?"

A wave of hot fury rolled over Gird. He knew the lords considered them cattle, but the steward rarely made it so clear. Arin had bred; Arin's children lived; Arin himself—the laughing, steadfast, honest brother who had saved his own life more than once—that Arin did not matter to the steward, and even less to the lord who ruled the steward. He himself was just another bullcalf; if he died, the steward would shrug as easily. By the time he'd mastered his anger, the steward had left, and the other men not of the family. Gird's oldest living brother, a cottager in his own holding, had come; he and Gird stood beside the table.

Arin opened his eyes and stared vacantly at the ceiling for a moment. Then his eyes roved until he met his mother's. "Lady bless you," he said. "This is home?"

"Home," she said. "We'll soon have you well . . ."

"Not so soon." His voice was so weak Gird could hardly hear it. "If I die—"

"You will not die!" Arin's wife had come back in, and clasped his hand.

"If—you will take care of the children?" He looked at Gird, not his older brother or father, and Gird answered, feeling in an instant the weight on his shoulders.

"I will, as my own."

"Good. The wolf—I was—frightened." His eyes sagged shut, and his head rolled sideways.

It was late that night before he spoke again. By then the sheep had come, a carcass already cleaned, and Mali had a broth cooking, rich with herbs as well as meat. By then, too, they knew the old tracker and the guards had already gone after the wolves. Too late, Gird thought bitterly. But he held his tongue. Arin roused briefly, asked for water. He could not lift his head to drink; Gird put an arm under his shoulders and lifted him. He could feel the heat through his shirt. Was it a good sign, that Arin was warm again, or a bad sign of woundfever? He didn't know. He felt the trembling of Arin's muscles as he drank; when his mother had wiped Arin's mouth, Gird let him down as gently as he could, and pulled the blanket straight. Arin's eyes were bright, but not quite focussed.

"Issa?" His wife moved up and took his good hand. "I will try, but—I am afraid the wolves have done for me."

"No—" she breathed.

"Yes. You will have a place here. Gird will take care of you."

"Arin—" began his father. Arin interrupted him, talking in broken phrases, without heeding any of them.

"I saw—a place—the Lady's garden. Flowers in the snow. Gird. Little brother—remember what I said."

"Yes, Arin," said Gird. He had no idea which of the things Arin had said over the years had come to him now, but he would forget none of them.

"You are more a soldier than you know. But don't give up the Lady's bounty, Gird."

"I won't." His vision blurred, and he realized he was crying. It felt strange to be looking *down* at Arin. Arin's eyes roved, and found his father's.

"You—told me not to go—" he murmured. His father shrugged. Gird looked at him sharply. Could he say nothing? But the firelight glittered on the tears that ran down his face. Although tears were nothing unusual among the village men, Gird was still surprised. His father cried rarely; now his shoulders shook with silent sobs. "Don't cry," said Arin, quite clearly. "I chose, or the Lady chose my time—" He said nothing more; his eyes closed. Gird watched the blankets for the rise and fall of breath.

In the hours of watching that night, in the flickering firelight, as their words to each other gradually failed and all was silence but for the snoring of Arin's oldest and the thin wail of Gird's youngest when he woke hungry in the turn of night, Gird felt the weight of manhood settle on his shoulders. He looked from face to face, seeing in the exhaustion of his father's the truth that he was now—must be now—the head of their family, in fact if not in law. Here, in this room: all that his father had made was now his to protect, support, defend.

When Mali had fed the baby, she came to sit beside him, her hand on his. He looked into her eyes, and saw her absolute confidence that he could do what he must, that they were safe with him. It was not true. He felt simultaneously the cold menace without, all that winter stood for, of famine, wolves, cold, even the lords' ravaging taxes, and the cozy seeming security within. How could he stand between, one mortal man? Cold sweat came out on his face; he felt himself shiver as if someone had poured a bucket of icy water over him. Mali squeezed his hand. Her warmth, her strength leaned against him. He was not alone, then—there was another pair of arms, another strong back. Enough? It had to be enough. He could feel through his skin her awareness of his feelings, and her impossible joy that fought all his despair with laughter. His fear did not frighten her, nor his weakness weaken her.

Arin was still alive at dawn, when Gird and his father began the day's work. Gird eyed his father, noticing what he had not before—how weak his father had become in the past few years. That great frame had bent; the broad hands that had frightened him were stiff, knobby with swollen joints. His bush of yellow hair had gone gray. Had this begun while Gird was sulking, before his marriage, Gird wondered? Not that it mattered; somehow his father had become an old man.

All that day, he thought about it while doing his work. Sim would not come back—some old quarrel that had been far over his head when he was a boy had sent Sim out to make his own way. Now that he had a cothold, he would be a fool to give it up. And if Arin died—he hoped fiercely that Arin would not die, but knew that hope alone could not save him. If Arin died—when Arin died, since even if he lived through this he might die before Gird another way—Gird would have it all to care for. Arin's wife Issa—the children—Mali—his own children now and to come—his parents. In the bleak light of that late-winter day he admitted to himself that his parents might not live long.

Arin lived another two days. He said nothing more that they could follow, although once the fever rose he muttered constantly, tossing and turning restlessly. He could not drink the broth Mali had made; Gird was almost ashamed to take a bowl of it, but they could not waste food. The sheep was already dead. They all drank quietly, avoiding each others' eyes and trying not to hear Arin's moans.

Not long after Arin died, just after the first thaw, Gird's father dropped suddenly one day, and lay twitching. By morning he, too, was dead. The steward came again, to value the cottage and the lord's property therein. Gird had the death-fee to pay, part in coin and part in livestock—his precious heifers, two of them—and then the steward confirmed him in his father's place, as "half-free tenant of this manor," whose clothes and few personal tools might be handed down to his heir. The rest—the land, the cottage, the livestock, the major tools such as ox-yoke, plow, and scythe—were the lord's, and he was "allowed" to use them.

Chapter Seven

He loved the feel of the scythe, the oiled wood smooth under his hands, the long elegant curve ending in its shining blade. Facing the uncut grain, with the sun over his left shoulder throwing his shadow ahead of him, he paused for the first of the harvest prayers.

"Alyanya, gracious Lady, harvest-bringer . . ." That was the oldest reaper, away on the other end of the field, to his right.

"Lady of seed and shoot, Lady of flower and corn . . ." That was the oldest granny in the vill, holding a wreath of harvest-daisies high.

"As the seed sprouts, and the green leaf grows, as the flowers come, and the seed swells . . ." And that was the Corn-maiden, who would wear the wreath while they reaped.

"So we with our blood offer, and you with your bounty reply . . ." All the reapers, their response ragged with distance, but sincere—and Gird with the others had nicked the heel of his palm with the scythe-blade, and squeezed a drop of blood to flick on the ground. Then he smeared the rest on the blade itself, to return his strength to the cut grain. Garig, the headman, blew a mellow note on the cow's horn, and the harvest began.

Gird swung back his scythe and swept it forward and around. The wheat fell away from his stroke, as if swept by a gust of wind. Step forward, swing, sweep . . . and another swathe turned aside for him. That old rhythm reclaimed him, required—so early in the day—hardly any effort. Step, swing, sweep, return. Step, swing, sweep, return. On one side the standing grain, and

96

before him the diminishing row he worked, and on his left side the bright stalks lying with their heads on the short green grass. The ripe wheat gave up a smell almost as rich as bread baking. Beneath the stalks lay a secret world, tiny runs that showed as he worked his way along.

He looked up, to see his way, and realized he was nearly halfway. Pakel, the oldest reaper, was only a third along his row—but no one expected him to be fast, not at his age. Still, he moved as smoothly as ever, and Gird knew he would be working just that well at day's end. Gird went on. Step, swing, sweep, return. Something flickered in the stalks ahead of him, and he smiled. So the little ones, the harvest mice, had realized their day was come? He took another stroke, and another. Another mousetail, just escaping his blade to leap deeper into the wheat.

Gird reached the end of his row long before Pakel was through. He stopped to whet his blade from the stone looped to his belt. Behind him, three men worked on the half-field he'd begun, in staggered rows, as three others followed Pakel. It was the custom to harvest in halves, all reapers in each half working the rows one way, to "fold the field" as it was said. Gird walked back up, outside the fallen grain, and took a pull from the water jug one of the women held. He didn't need it yet, but it was wise to drink on every row. Then he began another row behind the last man on his half.

The little cut on his hand itched, as it always did. The sun was higher, and the smell of the ripe grain richer. A little breeze ruffled the wheatears and brought up the green smell of the haymeadows nearer the river. Step, swing, sweep, return. This was the best time of the harvest-day, when he had one swathe down, and his body had warmed and loosened to the work. The scythe swung and sliced almost on its own; his body was merely the pivot for its swing, leaving his mind free to wander. He enjoyed the evenness of his cuts, the smooth stubble he left behind, the proof of his skill. He saw every tiny blossom of the weeds within the grain: the starry blue illin, the delicate red siris, like drops of blood. Overhead arched a cloudless sky, a harvester's boon, and out of it came the song of a kiriel, sweet and piercing. He felt the prickle of stubble on his feet, the sleeves of his shirt on his arms as they swung.

This—not the other—was the right use of his strength. He felt as if he could swing the scythe forever without tiring. Row after row, selion after selion, flowed away behind him. The sun's heat, which a few years ago had worn him down by midday, now seemed to give him its energy. He remembered, as clearly as if it had been that morning, the first time he'd taken a scythe to swing. Arin's scythe, that had been, and his first cuts down in the haymeadow had been ragged as if he'd ripped at the grass with his hands. Now Arin was three years dead, and he was the leading reaper, the strongest man in the village, able to provide for his own and his brothers' children as well. He did not let himself think of the children who had died, his two eldest sons, one of Arin's, in a fever. It might have been that kuaknom's curse, or chance, but it was over.

He stopped to drink at the end of the row, and rubbed his hands together. He could just feel the pressure at the base of his thumbs from the grips; the right had shifted. He spat on the handle and worked the grip back and forth slightly. There. He tapped a splinter under the bindings to tighten it, and swung the scythe lightly to check . . . yes.

Across the field he could see Arin's oldest lugging water up to the fieldmasters. Another selion or two, and it would be time for the noon break. He was not tired, but he was hungry, his belly reminding him how long it had been since that crust of bread before dawn. He could smell cooking food even over the rich smell of ripe grain around him. They were supposed to lunch on the lord's bounty when harvesting the great field, but that bounty had been less each year. Back before Arin's death, it had meant meat as well as bread, and barrels of ale. In his childhood he remembered harvest meals of roast meat, bread, cheese, and sweet cakes, heavy with honey and spices. Last year, bread and meat broth only; the men had grumbled, but what good did that do? The steward would not kill one of the lord's sheep or cows for grumbling alone. He had not grumbled; he could not afford to, with two families to support. It did no good to become known as a grumbler. He'd eaten his bread and broth, taking an extra helping while others complained.

He looked ahead critically. They might finish the great field in two days, at this pace, and then begin the harvest of the individual strips. Would the weather hold? It had been a dry spring, and they'd all prayed for rain, but rain now would add nothing to the harvest.

At the noon meal, the steward handed out round dark loaves and bowls of thin soup. This year no one grumbled. Gird ate silently, steadily. The more he could take of the lord's bounty, the better for his family. Arin's boy, as a water carrier, could eat with the harvesters this year. He came to sit by Gird, a boy as quiet and shy as Arin had been cheerful and open. Gird wondered if seeing his father die had changed him—but he'd been a quiet baby, for all that.

"Mali's coming out to bind," said the boy—Fori, his name was, though they seldom called him by name. He was "Arin's boy" to the whole village. Gird frowned.

"She should not: she's too near her time."

"Ma has the sickness," said Fori, ducking his head. Gird sighed. Issa loathed fieldwork, and although she was not as good a weaver as his mother had been, she would spend all her time at the loom. Leaving all the other work for Mali, Gird thought—but she also had the sickness, no one could deny it. No one with the sickness could come into the harvest field; throwing up on the first day of harvest was the worst of bad luck. And it was no fault of Fori's, what Issa did or did not do. But he worried about Mali. Big and strong as she was, every child seemed to take more out of her; she had not looked well this time.

"Make sure she has enough water," said Gird. Fori nodded. He had not finished his bowl of soup, but sat dangling his hands.

"Eat! You take all you can get, lad." The boy slurped up the rest of his soup.

"It's not as good as Mali's," he said through a mouthful of bread.

"No, but Mali didn't have to cook it. It's not from our stores. When you're doing the lord's work, you feed from his bounty: that's custom."

Gird followed his own advice, and went back for more. At least the steward wasn't stinting them on amounts—no one frowned when he picked up another half-loaf of bread and refilled his bowl.

When he was full, he lay back in the shadow of the old fireoak at the field's corner until the horn blew. The afternoon's work was always harder: the field seemed to swell with heat, lengthening every selion. Gird was soon back in the rhythm of the work. His mind seemed to hang on every close detail now, unwilling to soar abroad as it had in the morning. His shadow, at first a squat dark figure close beneath him, lengthened with the hours. He was still far ahead of the others, overtaking one after another on their selions, and swinging away beyond them. Yet no one minded: he was, he sensed, their pride as well as his own. Gird Strongarm, they said, grinning as he came past.

On the outer edges of the field, the women and older girls were binding the cut grain into shocks. None of his or Arin's girls were old enough yet: only a woman who had bled could gather in harvest. But he could see Mali's peaked hat busy among the others. Some years she worked first among the women, almost as much faster than others as he was. This year, she lagged, slowed by the coming child that made bending difficult.

By dusk, when he could feel the damp coming out, more than half the great field was down. Now the men joined the women in binding the last grain. Again tonight, they would eat the lords' bread and meat—if there was any meat, Gird thought. Surely there would be. He found Mali, and led her up to the serving line. She moved heavily, and beneath the day's sunburn, her skin was pale.

There was meat, although the steward's men doled it out one slice to a loaf of bread. A pottage of beans, cheese, and a wooden cup of ale completed the meal.

"No sweet cake?" Gird heard someone ask. The steward's men said nothing, handing a serving to the next in line.

"I heard the steward tell the cooks they need not kill another sheep—that the great field would be done early enough that there'd be no evening meal tomorrow." Mali kept her voice low.

"What?" Gird stared at her. "That's—we can't be done by noon, and if we work the afternoon, he has to feed us."

Mali, her mouth full of meat, merely shrugged. Gird tore off a hunk of bread and chewed it, thinking hard. The custom had always been to feed them for any part of a day spent on the lords' work. When they finished harvest a bit early, they had time for a rest before the meal, even a bit of singing. He worked his way through the bean porridge, which lacked the flavor of Mali's, and wondered what could be done.

As it happened, Mali was not the only one to have heard the steward's words. The men gathered cautiously after dark, in the lane near Gird's cottage.

"Not fair," said Teris. "We work faster, and they punish us—"

"So we can work slow, if Gird can hold back," said Amis's uncle.

Gird felt himself flushing. "It's not my fault," he said.

"No one said it was. But if being fast loses us a feast, maybe being slow will get it back."

"Course, he's already told the cooks," said Amis. "Might be even if he has to feed us, it won't be much. No meat, anyway. And he'd be angry with us. Is it worth that?"

"Where's Garig?" asked Pakul. "What does he think?"

"Garig's in the steward's back pocket," said someone too softly to make out.

"We can't do aught without him," said Gird. "It's not fair, I'll stand to that, and do what I can, but we need Garig. It's only he can speak for us to the steward, anyway."

* * *

"I'll say what I can." Garig sighed, though, and Gird was sure he'd come back with nothing. "The steward— the steward's told me some of it."

"Of what?"

"What's gone wrong. There's a place—somewhere far off, I don't know—where the lords come from, back when they come. It's where they traded, over the mountains. It's gone."

"Gone? How can a place be gone?"

"Raided, I suppose, like a town the nomads have burned. Anyway, the lords got gold and jewels that way, and now they don't."

"So what's that got to do with us?" asked Teris. "We need to eat, same as always, and it's always been if we do the work on the lord's field, he feeds us."

"The count's squeezing *him*," said Garig. "So he's squeezing us—that's the truth of it. He has to send more—"

"We can't." Mutters of agreement with that, a low-voiced growl. "Might's well join the Stone Circle—"

"None o' that!" Garig's voice rang out. "We'll have none o' that talk here. D'you want the guards down on us? They're outlaws, no better than brigands, that bunch."

Gird agreed, but silently. He had heard more than one mention of the Stone Circle in the past two years. All he knew about them came from such brief encounters. The steward had warned Garig that anyone found helping a member of the Stone Circle would be turned out, if not killed outright. According to him, they were lawless, lazy farm lads who tried to get higher wages by threatening the farms—burning grain and hayfields, attacking herds in pasture, and so on. The other stories Gird had heard were of young men who saw no chance of marrying or having a place to farm—whose families could not spare the food, no matter how hard they worked. He tried not to think about it, about the disappearance of four or five younger sons from his own village in the past three years. Somewhere, the stories went, was a great circle of stones bigger than any mortal man could move, and into that circle fell miraculous showers of grain and fruit, more than enough for all who came. And the stones protected anyone who found the way inside, that was in the tales too. From that mysterious place, the movement took its name, promising peace and plenty in the days when "all men are stones of the circle, and none must run and hide."

"I'll speak to the steward," Garig said, sounding more angry than understanding. "I'll try—but no promises. And if there's slacking tomorrow, we could all be in trouble."

The men stood awhile in the lane, grumbling softly, when Garig had gone into his cottage and slammed the door. Gird was glad enough to stand there, in the warm darkness. Inside his own cottage, Issa's sickness fouled the air, and the children bickered over their meager supper. He tried to tell himself that they were doing all right, better than some others, but it was poor comfort.

The next day, Gird worked as slowly as he could. Garig had said that the steward had consented to another evening feast, if the work took them past midafternoon. Mali could not come, but Issa was doing her best raking up the fallen heads of grain into baskets. He was worried about Mali. She had not looked really well since losing the one of the twins. This baby should be her last—would be, if he had to force the herbs into her himself. He grinned at that thought. Mali might be weaker, but she was as headstrong as ever.

They finished the greatfield before dark, but not long before. Gird noticed that everyone came to the feast quietly, with none of the usual songs and laughter. There was meat, sure enough—not abundance, but some, and plenty of bread and cheese. He made sure that Fori and Issa ate heartily, and stuffed himself. Tomorrow he could begin cutting their own strip, grain that would feed them and help pay the fieldfee.

It was dark, the thick dark of a cloudy night, with enough wind to keep the leaves rustling uneasily.

"What?" Gird asked softly.

"We want to talk to you." That was Teris, he could tell. Gird sighed.

"Do you have nothing better to do than—"

"Shhh. Not here. Come along with us."

"Who's us?"

"I told you he'd make trouble." Tam's voice, this time.

"I'm not making trouble. I just want to know what—"

"Come *on*." Teris had his arm, and shook it. "We'll talk, but someplace safe."

Gird let Teris lead him along the lane, between two cottages that he was sure were Garig's and Tam's, and down between a barton wall and the gurgling stream. The night air smelled wet and green; he could pick out scents he never noticed by day.

"There's someone here needs to talk to you," Teris said. Gird felt his heart begin to pound. Someone in the dark, someone he didn't know? He remembered all at once that Teris's mother was reputed to be a dire-witch, laying curses on those who crossed her. "Go on," Teris said into the darkness. "Ask him."

Someone he could not see cleared his throat and said "Teris says you know about soldiering."

"No."

"Yes," hissed Teris. "You do."

"We need—we want someone to teach us."

"Who?" asked Gird. He thought he knew already. Instead of a spoken answer, he heard the click of stone on stone, and then felt a stone pressed into his palm.

"You know," said the voice. "The farmer's only hope . . . the only thing what won't burn in the fire that's coming . . ."

"But you're not soldiers," he said. "You don't—"

"We need to know how. We're getting enough, almost, now—if we only knew how to fight, and had weapons—"

"It won't work." Even here, where he was sure no one listened, he kept his voice low. "Running at 'em in a mob, like—they'll just ride over you and ride over you—"

"We have to *try*." His eyes were more used to the dimness; he could just make out Tam's face and the gleam of his eyes. Tam's weaker eye wandered off-focus, then came back. "We can't be soldiers; we don't have the training—"

"You!" Gird snorted. Tam couldn't throw a rock straight, let along make a soldier. "You'll just be killed, and they'll take it out of your families and the rest of us. Use sense, man! You'd have to know how to march, how to use your weapons together—"

"You could teach us," said the stranger, now a hunched black shape against the faint gleam of the water. "You were teaching them to march, Teris said. It was forbidden, but that didn't stop you. And then—"

No one had brought up his cowardice to him for years. They'd accepted him, he thought, once he grew up and married, once he was bent to the same lash as the rest of them. What had they told this stranger, that his voice changed when he said "And then—?"

"I—can't," he said hoarsely. "I—I don't remember enough of it."

"You remember enough to know that an untrained mob is hopeless. You can't have forgotten it all. I didn't." Teris again, hectoring as usual.

"I—"

"You're scared still, aren't you? After all these years—"

"He was my *friend!*" It came out louder than he meant, and he muted the rest of it. "I could not be part of what did that to him. *That's* why I ran, and if you want to call that cowardice, fine." He had never explained it to his friends before. Now the words poured out of him. "If you think I feared blood or pain, why d'you think I stayed in 'til then? If you remember so well, Teris, you must remember the beatings I got. You saw my bruises."

"Well—yes. But they said—"

"*They* called it cowardice, and my father bade me accept that. 'Twas hard enough on us, without causing more trouble. And that's what's really wrong with them— that they'd think cowardice is not wanting to cause pain."

"But you haven't joined—" and the stones clicked again.

"No. I had the family to think of, not just my own but

my brother's. Once already I'd caused them all trouble; my mother died of the young lord's enmity, when he refused us the herb-right in the common wood. And the Stone Circle when it started was young lads, unmarried and mostly orphans: they had no family to suffer if they were caught."

"So—?"

Gird sighed. That bleak vision of his nightmares edged nearer, tried to merge with reality. "So—who will feed my wife, my children, if I go off to teach the Stone Circle how to march in step? Who will plow the field, or tend the beasts? If it could happen, and an army of peasants took the field, who would feed *them*? Some must plow and plant, some must spin and weave, or that army would die hungry and ragged, too weak to fight the spears."

"Is that what you plant for? That army, or your family alone?"

Gird spat rudely at the stranger's feet. "I plant for the lord, like all the rest, and we live on the spillage from the tax-cart—dammit, you ask questions like the steward laying blame for a cracked pot! You know my name, but hide yours; why should I listen to you?"

The stranger's head moved, as if listening for something, than gave Gird a long, neutral stare. "You know it's getting worse. You know we have no chance to resist without the knowledge you have. And you sit there, smug as a toad, giving good reasons to a bad argument—why *shouldn't* I put a thorn in your backside? You think I have no family, or these others? Those lads who joined Stone Circle years back are fathers now, just as you are. Those that didn't rot on the spikes. You think your children will thank you, for leaving them helpless before enemies?"

"They would not thank me for throwing them in prison to starve, either."

"Take 'em with you."

"No."

"At least tell us something, something we can use."

"I—" Gird looked around; there were four or five crouched nearby. He was sure of Teris and Tam, but not the others. Was Amis there? He could not tell. "I don't think it will work, even if I taught you—even if real soldiers taught you. The best way for us is to work and keep our peace; what you do only makes the lords angrier, raises the taxes higher—"

The stranger growled, and stood. Gird stood too, and they faced one another a long moment. Then the stranger laughed softly. "It's coming, Gird, whether you like it or not—you will see, and I hope you see before you suffer more deeply than a man can stand. I lost my family; I would not wish that on anyone. My name is Diamod, when you want to find me again."

Gird turned away, wondering if they would let him go. No one touched him. He felt his way along the wall of Tam's barton, and then let his feet remember the way along the lane to his own cottage. Teris. Tam. Three or four others, who had not spoken so that he could not know who they were. Did they think he would tell Garig or the steward? His heart ached at that. His hands ached to strike something, anything. He would help them, if he had no family to think of. He could imagine himself teaching them as he had taught Teris and Amis and the others. But he could not risk Mali and Issa and the children.

He got back to bed without waking anyone up, and fell into heavy sleep. Dreams troubled him. In his mind's eye, he could see them, ragged, workworn, scarred, hungry, running in uneven clumps and strings to strike at the horsemen with their poles and scythes, their sickles and clubs. Behind the horsemen, the lords' army waited, trained soldiers in good armor, with their sharp swords and pikes. But they had nothing to do, for the horsemen could deal with the peasants. At the end— He woke with a jerk and a chopped-off cry. Beside him, Mali turned over and groaned softly, then snored.

In the thick darkness of the cottage, he seemed to see the past years as a painted streamer like the ones the lords sometimes carried on horseback. Hard work and hunger now, yes—but he had known hard work and hunger as a child. Yet his children were thinner than he had been, hard as he worked. He had never accumulated the store of coppers and silvers that his father had had beneath the hearthstone when it was needed. If something did happen with his own children, or Arin's, he would not be able to do what his father had done.

The next morning, he was still thinking about it as he shoveled manure. What could he do? He could not imagine sneaking away from the village some nights, to train Stone Circle members, coming back at dawn to work, but he could not imagine taking his whole family into an uncertain future, either. He was mulling this over when he heard shouts from the lane, and the heavy roll of hoofbeats.

He went through the kitchen to find Mali and Issa and the children starting out the front door.

"Get back!" he shouted. They made way for him. He could see, now, people in the lane nearer the center of the village. Amis was headed out his front gate, and Gird moved slowly toward his own. He could hear the loud complaints, the bellowed orders of the guard sergeant, the cries of children. It must be the Stone Circle man, Diamod, he thought, but he didn't see him. Had someone seen him? Reported him? He realized suddenly that his friends might think he had, if that was indeed who the guards were after.

It looked as if the guards were trying to search each cottage and barton. The noisy crowd surrounded them, not actually resisting but somewhat obstructive. The guards, some mounted and some afoot, moved toward Gird's end of the village. Now he could see faces he recognized, guards and villagers alike. An old woman, Teris's mother, was arguing with one of the soldiers, clinging to his arm, shaking it. He wrenched free of her and she staggered away, to be caught by her daughter. A child darted out into the lane ahead of the horses, and Amis went after him. The soldier riding the lead horse yelled something at him; Amis, intent on the child, shook his head and lunged forward.

Although he was behind the others, hardly out of his own dooryard, Gird saw exactly what happened. The

soldier's arm moved, and Amis turned, his shoulder
already hunching against the expected blow. The soldier's mace caught Amis full in the face, that familiar
flesh disappearing instantly in a mush of blood and
broken bone. One tooth flew free, a chip of white
spinning in the hot sunlight before it fell out of sight
behind the other bystanders. Gird felt something prick
his hand, and looked down to see the handle of his
shovel broken like a dry stick; he opened his hand and
let the pieces fall.

As if in a dream, all motion slowed. One by one those
at the back of the crowd turned to run, their eyes
white-rimmed, their mouths open. Even before Amis
fell to the ground, they had opened a path for the
soldiers, those in front scrambling back, afraid to turn,
afraid . . . and the soldiers' horses, their high necks
streaked with sweat, ridged with lather where the reins
rubbed, setting their ironshod hooves down one by
one, so slowly that it seemed they could hardly catch
the terrified fugitives. Amis lay huddled, blood pooling
in the lane, soaking into the dust, both hands covering
his ruined face. One of the horses, bumped hard by
another, placed a front hoof in the center of his back so
slowly, with such precision, that Gird had to believe it
was a deliberate choice. He could hear a terrible crunch
over the other sounds, the thunder of hooves, the
screams—

And motion returned to normal, the crowd flowing
back along the lane in a panic, the leaders running flat
out, arms wide. Behind, the horses surged, the soldiers
yelled, their weapons slicing from side to side. Gird
stepped back, between the plum trees; it was all he had
time for before they were past, horses bumping and
trampling over the slow and clumsy, in pursuit of the
fleetest. From the corner of his eye, he saw Diamod,
cause of the whole incident, slipping quietly from the
back of Amis's cowbyre to make his way over the fields.

Gird swallowed the same bolus of rage and fear that
he had chewed and swallowed so often before. Now it
was Amis on the ground, dead or dying he was sure,

and then it had been Arin torn by wolves, and before that Meris.

Amis breathed in difficult, jerky snorts. Gird laid his hand against his neck; the pulse was thin, irregular. Was Amis conscious at all? He should say something. What could he say?

"Amis? Can you hear me?" Stupid enough, but something. Amis's hand twitched; Gird laid his own over it.

"You've got to *do* something!" That high voice was Eso, always ready for someone else to do something. "Get him to safety—wash his face—"

"Be still," growled a deeper voice. Amis's father. He knelt beside Gird, his face as gray as his beard. His hands shook as he reached out to his son. "Is he—?"

"He's dying—I saw the mace hit his face, and horse trampled him—" Gird gestured at the pulped mess of Amis's back.

"And if they come back, they'll but hurt him more." Amis's father held his son's slack hand. "Gird—get a plank or bench."

Gird nodded, and backed away on his knees. He shivered, nauseated, and barely made it to the trampled verge before throwing up, the morning's food and a life's bile together. Then he went into the front room, where Mali stood with her fist against her mouth, white as milk, and ripped the legs off one of the benches without a word. The long plank banged against the doorpost as he went out, and he almost lost control again. Amis. Kindly, cheerful, steady Amis, who had taken him to the sheepfold gathering to meet Mali— who had farmed alongside his strip for ten years, who had never done one thing wrong but be where a mace could destroy him—

Amis's father and Gird wrestled Amis onto the plank; that long, lanky body felt *wrong*, as if it were a boneless sack of seedcorn. He was still breathing, a hoarse rattle, in and out, that bubbled the blood on his face. What had been a face. Gird thought of the cheerful brown eyes, the nose lopsided from a cow's kick, the wide mouth.

Amis's wife had fainted; Mali sat beside that crumpled heap, comforting the younger children, as Gird and Amis's father carried him through, all the way into the barton. There they sponged the blood off his back, rolled him over. Gird turned his head aside and retched again. They could do nothing. Amis's breathing filled the barton with pain. One of his brothers came, and stood beside them, watching. Amis's wife, finally, biting her kerchief, holding their youngest baby close. Mali came to stand behind Gird, and put a hand on his shoulder.

Amis never woke, and when he finally quit breathing Gird could not at first turn away. Only the noise of the returning Guard, angry voices and the clash of weapons in the lane, loosened the paralysis that had locked his joints in place. He stayed calm in the turmoil that followed, giving his evidence to the steward in a slow, deep voice that came to him for that occasion. Amis had never been known as a troublemaker; his lunge at the guard's horse was a grab for the child who had run unknowing into danger. The steward nodded, shrugged, remitted part of the death-fee, and evicted Amis's wife to live with Amis's father. Another family, strangers relocated from another vill, moved into it.

And Gird put a sack of grain at the far edge of the wood, with two stones on top of it. It was gone the next day.

PART II

PART II

Chapter Eight

The first scream brought him out of his musings; he looked across the ploughed strips to see nothing at first. Perhaps someone had spilled a kettle of hot water. He scratched the back of one leg with his other foot, and clucked to the oxen. They leaned into the yoke. Then another shriek, one he would have known anywhere. Raheli! He dropped the plowhandles, and started across the field at a run. Then the horses came, from between the cottages, and crashing through the back gate of his barton. Lords' horses, with the bright orange and green and yellow he had seen going in the manor gates the day before. Another scream, and another, shriller—one of the little girls? He had yelled himself before he realized it, a deep roar of rage and pain. Up the field, another plowman answered.

"Stop, you!" yelled one of riders, waving something at him. Gird paid no mind, charging toward his own gate. Now he could hear a man's voice, yelling, and more screams down the lane. The same rider yelled "Guards! Ho!" The horsemen closed toward him, the horses plunging with excitement. Behind them now he could see footsoldiers in Kelaive's bright orange. The sun glittered on their helmets, on riders' buckles and saddlefittings, on the stubble of last year's grain. Gird took a breath, slowing to see how he might get by. Now one of the riders was above him, the tall dark horse snorting and prancing.

"Get back, fellow!" the rider said. Gird peered up at a narrow pale face. "It's nothing to do with you. Get back to work!" The voice had fear in it, as well as

arrogance. Was he armed? Gird tried to circle the
horse, but the horse spun, and blocked him. "Get
back!" the man said, louder. Gird looked aside; the
guards were almost on him, their cudgels ready. Another scream, this one a man's death-cry, ending in a
gurgle. Gird flinched, and shivered—it had to be Parin,
he was the only one inside. His belly churned; his
vision blurred. Then pain stung him awake; the rider
had slashed his back with a whip. He spun, fury once
more driving out fear, but the guards had him, four of
them. For all he could do, it was nothing—they had
him face-down in the fresh-plowed furrows, choking on
dirt, two of them on his back, as the screams went
on—and then died away. When they let him up, the
other plowmen were back at work, and the riders were
gone, and the grim-faced guard sergeant gave him his
warning.

He knew before he came inside what he would find.
The shattered barton gate, the ewe he had brought in
for nursing lying dead in the barton, her guts strewn
wide, their one pig gone, the cottage doors smashed,
the great loom broken: that was bad enough. But there
lay Parin, his face one curdled mess of blood and shattered bone, and there lay Raheli, naked, the slight
bulge of her belly that had promised so much to her
and Parin. He knelt beside her, so full of grief he could
not breathe. When he felt that first warm breath on his
hand, he could hardly believe it. Alive? After the blow
that had split her face all down one side, and drenched
her in blood? After that blade or another had bared her
ribs on one side, and sliced deep into her hip? After the
beating, and the rape? He looked at the body he had
not seen since she became a woman. Even at that
moment, he noticed—and hated himself for noticing—
the white beauty of her skin, the full young breasts, the
long curve of back and thigh now streaked with blood.
Her breath touched his hand again, and he drew a long
shaky breath of his own. Alive. He had to do something—

He looked around the room again, seeing destruction
everywhere, and out the front door, now splintered—

something stirred, there. He could not leave Raheli, but he must; he had to get water, rags, something. He stood too quickly and his head spun. Staggering, he made it to the door and then crouched, heaving all he had eaten into the trampled torn dirt of the yard.

Then he looked up and saw the rest of it.

She must have been at the well, for the blood trail started there, and the water jug lay broken beside it. Girnis lay sprawled between the well and door, her slight body twisted as if she'd been thrown against the wall. And Pidi, where was Pidi? Gird found him on the far side of the well, fists jammed into his mouth, trying not to cry; a hard blue knot on the side of his head and a welt on his back.

He was shaking with rage and grief; he could hardly lower the bucket to the water. The weight of it full dragged on him, steadied him; he got it up, and scooped a handful for Pidi, who said nothing but drank it.

"Stay here," he said to the boy; Pidi nodded. Gird went to Girnis; she was alive, but unconscious. Her left arm was crooked, and swelling: broken. He glanced around for something to splint it with, and caught sight of someone, a kerchiefed head, over the sidewall. It disappeared; he did not call. He found a piece of the splintered door, and tore a strip from his tunic. Girnis did not stir when he handled her broken arm. Should he carry her inside? No. Girnis would do well enough out here until she woke, he thought, and knew that he wasn't thinking as well as he should. But Raheli needed him. He took the bucket inside, breathing hard through his mouth. The cottage stank of blood and brains and slaughter. He had killed animals more cleanly—but he could not stop to think of that.

Raheli's face, if she lived, would have a scar from hairline to jaw. He was not sure she would live. The blade that had cut her had gone through into her mouth, come near her eye—might have broken her jaw or her cheekbone as well, he couldn't tell. Raheli had had the parrion of herbal wisdom from Mali; it was not his knowledge. Blood pooled under her head; her scant breaths gurgled. Blood in her mouth, what if she choked? He looked wildly around, and this time found the scattered bedding, the cooking cloths for straining, the cloths for women in their time. As quickly as he could, trying not to think beyond the immediate wound, he pressed the cleanest rags into her wounds. The long shallow gash along her ribs had nearly quit bleeding anyway; the deeper wound where the blade had met her hip oozed steadily, reddening the cloth. Her face— her face was hopeless, he thought at first, as blood soaked one cloth after another.

"Gird?" He jumped, swore, and turned to glare at the light that poured in the broken door. Then he saw it was a woman, though he could not make out her face against the light. "Is—is Raheli alive?"

"Just." His voice grated and broke; he wanted to burst into tears. Hard enough to be alone with this, but harder with someone else.

"Let me see." She came up to him, and now he could see it was Tam's aunt, old Virdi. Her breath hissed out. "Aahhh—Lady's Peace, she's bad—"

"I know that." He had never liked Virdi, but she had the healing in her hands, so his mother had said. And no scorn to her for not saving Mali—healing in the hands was nothing in a plague of fever.

"The lord, he did this?" He thought he heard derision in her voice, and bristled. Next she would ask why he'd let it happen. But when he glared at her, her eyes were soft, not accusing at all.

"He did. I was—plowing. They—" He could not go on.

She nodded. "I saw across the fields—the guards knocked you down, there were too many. Lady's Curse on Mikrai Pidal Kevre Kelaive: may he never know peace."

He had never heard a woman lay a curse before, but there was no doubt Virdi had done just that. So simple? He shivered, suddenly cold. Her hand touched his head, dry and chill as a snake.

"Near broke your head, they did, too—" He had not

realized that he'd been hit, but where she touched him was a heavy pain—and then it was gone, and she was rubbing her hands briskly on the hearthstone. She gave him a quick smile. "Rock to rock; the hearthstone's strong enough." She pointed, and he saw a little crack he didn't remember seeing.

Her hands on Raheli's head hardly seemed to have weight; they hovered, touched as light as a moth on a nightflower, retreated. She sighed, then lifted the cloths he'd laid on that torn face, and hissed again. "Get me more water—and—" a quick look at the hearth, now fireless, "—go to Tam's, and bring a live coal."

"But will she die while I'm—?" Gird didn't finish the question, for she interrupted.

"Not if you're quick about it." She had poured the remaining water in the bucket into the one unbroken pot, and he took the bucket and went out. Pidi still crouched by the well, but now he was crying, shoulders heaving. Gird drew another bucket of water, and found the dipper somehow unbroken, caught in the hedge. He squatted beside Pidi.

"Come on, lad—let me see—" Pidi looked up, eyes streaming.

"I—I couldn't—" He winced as Gird touched the lump on his head.

"You couldn't stop them. Neither could I."

"But—but they—they hurt Raheli—and Parin tried to fight—"

"Pidi, listen. I have to get fire. Can you stay here?"

"Raheli? And—and Girnis! They—hurt her too!" The boy grabbed Gird's arm with both hands, threatening to overturn the bucket. Gird set the bucket carefully aside, and gathered up his youngest child, letting him sob. He wanted to do that himself, would have given anything for a strong shoulder to cry on, but all the ones he'd known were gone. He patted the boy's back, carefully avoiding the welt on it, and carefully not thinking. Enough to comfort one who could be comforted. "I'm so sorry," the boy was saying between sobs. "I'm so sorry—"

"It's not your fault." Gird tried to keep his voice

steady, soothing, as if Pidi were a sheep caught in a briar, a cow with her head through a gap. Finally the sobs quieted to gulps. Gird unhooked the boy's hands and moved him away far enough to see his face. "Here—let me wipe that for you—" Pidi nodded, mouth set tight, and Gird cleaned his face. "Now—I still have to go get a firestart, from Tam's house. Will you stay here quietly?" Pidi nodded, solemnly, tears threatening again. "I'll be back," said Gird. Pidi said nothing.

He saw no one on the way to Tam's cottage, though he was aware of a stir in the village, of people watching him and ducking from his sight. All the doors were shut. He knocked on Tam's door, and Tam's wife, white-faced, opened at once. She paled even more when she saw the blood on his clothes.

"Virdi sent me for a firecoal," he said, as calmly as he could. Tam's children were huddled around the hearth, silent and staring. "Our fire's out." Tam's wife nodded. Without saying a word, she went to her hearth, and took a burning brand, far bigger than the custom was. She offered it with a stiff little bow, and he took it gingerly.

In the sunlight, the flame was pale, hardly visible; he could feel the heat of it as it blew back toward his face. He knew by that he was walking fast, too fast. Pidi waited in the yard, sitting now by Girnis. He nodded to the boy, and stopped to pick up some splinters of the door.

Inside, Virdi had Raheli's face clean of blood, but for the wound itself. She had her hand over Raheli's cheek, her expression withdrawn. Gird stepped carefully around her and laid the only fire pattern he knew, the shape the men used in the open. The brand from Tam's house lit it instantly, and warmth returned to his hearth. He went back out for the bucket, and picked up more wood. For an instant, he wondered if it was bad luck to burn doorwood, but then shrugged. How much worse could his luck be? He put the bucket down beside Raheli, and laid the wood carefully on the fire.

"Is there a boiler left?" asked Virdi suddenly. Gird

looked around the chaos in the room, and then went to check in the back room. There he found a single metal pot, the one Mali had used for steeping her herbs, dented but still whole. He took it to Virdi, who nodded. "Good. Start heating water in it—put it near the fire, but not in it. And then clean your hands. I'll need your help."

They had Raheli's wounds bound, and her body covered with the cleanest cloth, when the steward came. All that time anger had grown in Gird's heart, anger he had controlled so long that he had half-forgotten some of it. Now it grew as swiftly as a summer storm-cloud, filling him with black rage. He had tried so hard: he had suffered so much already. In spite of all he had brought up three of his own children, and two of Arin's—he would have had his first grandchild the next year—and the lords could not let even one hardworking farmer alone, in peace.

Yet when the steward came—an old man, now, slightly bent but still capable of rule—Gird said nothing of it. He heard what he expected to hear: he, as head of his household, would bear the penalty for his son-in-law's attack on the count's son and his friends, and for his own attempt to get to his cottage to defend them. The loss of the cottage he expected, immediate eviction, fines, loss of all "so-called personal" property, damages assessed for the breakage of the lords' property in the cottage.

"The count remembers you," the steward said slowly, his eyes drifting from the broken loom to the smashed door. "He will be content, he says, if you sign yourself and all your children into serfdom, become his property in name as in fact." He paused, and his voice lowered so that Gird could hardly hear it. "Were I you, Gird, I would flee: he'll name you outlaw, but you would escape for a time. Otherwise—you well understand what kind of man he is; he would take delight in all you fear, in far worse than you have seen, in this manor. I have done all I can."

"You serve him." That was all Gird dared say, and he clamped his mouth on the rest of it.

"I serve him—I gave my oath, long ago, to the count's father; had he not died young—but that's no matter. I break my oath by this much—to warn you, to say that for this night I can promise you no pursuit. Say you will clean and mend what you can by midday tomorrow, when you must be evicted: I will tell him that."

It was all the kindness left; years later Gird realized what the steward risked, and what he would suffer if anyone found out what he had done.

Chapter Nine

All the times he had thought about leaving, it had never been like this. He had imagined sending the children away somewhere (but where?), going himself to join the little band of rebels he had first met—but not this terrifying journey. He was sure they were leaving a trail a child could follow through the narrow wood. Anyone would expect him to go that way—but what other way was there? He could not have strolled past the manor itself with Raheli on his back.

It still worried him that he'd left the cottage such a wreck. It wasn't his fault, he knew that, but a lifetime's work and care nagged at him. He should have—

Ahead, two rocks clacked sharply together. Gird halted, breathing hard. Behind him, he could hear Fori's breathing as well, on the other end of the litter. Raheli was heavier than he'd guessed. Pidi, beside him, glanced up and Gird nodded. Pidi clicked two pebbles in his hand, mimicking the stones' sound. Another clack, this a triple. Pidi replied with the triple of triples Gird had taught him. Trouble, that was. Danger, trouble, need help—any of those.

Raheli moved on the litter, and moaned softly. Gird

looked over his shoulder. Blood had seeped through the pack of moss on her face, staining it dark. He heard a twig crack, and looked ahead. There were three, coming down the slope. One was Diamod. He could have wished it was someone else.

"Gird—what is it?"

"You haven't heard?"

"Only the rock signals of trouble, that someone was needed. Yours?" Diamod looked past him at the children.

"Aye. My daughter's hurt bad; they killed her husband. Outlawed me, for what he did, and for trying to get to her—"

"I'm sorry." Diamod actually sounded sorry; Gird had been half-certain that he would dare amusement or scorn. "So—you're fugitives now?"

"Yes. I don't know if Rahi will live—"

"Later. Now we must get you away." Diamod waved the other two men forward, and they took the handles from Gird and Fori.

"These are smooth!" said one, clearly surprised.

Gird hawked and spat. "Scythe and shovel handles," he said. "I'm outlawed anyway; might's well bring something useful."

Diamod grinned at him, then sobered as he looked at the others. "Are all these coming?"

"Fori's my brother's son. His wife died last year, in childbirth. The other two are mine, and have no place in that village."

They set off again, faster for the unwearied strength of the two men carrying Raheli. Gird strained his ears backwards, expecting to hear any moment the cry of hounds, horses' hooves crashing in the leaves behind them. But he heard nothing, only their own hard breathing, their own footsteps.

They followed the water up out of the wood, past the cleft Arin had shown Gird all those years ago, where the Stone Circle visitors had waited for so many nights. Up a narrow, rocky defile, and carefully around the west slope of the hill, keeping as much as possible to the low scrub. Gird looked up once or twice, seeing folds of land ahead he did not know, but looked back oftener. When would the pursuit come, and how bad would it be?

By noon, when the sun baked pungent scent from the scrub, they had found another watercourse, this one winding away to the south. Along its banks low trees formed dense cover. Diamod lagged far behind, watching for pursuit, as the others paused for a brief rest. Gird dipped water from the creek, and bathed Raheli's face.

She was awake again, lips pressed tightly together, eyes dull. He did not want to speak to her—what could he say?—but she questioned him. "Where—are we?"

"South of the village, beyond the hill. We had to leave, Rahi."

"Parin—they killed him—"

"Yes."

Her hand strayed to her belly, as if feeling for the child within. "I—don't want to lose the baby—"

"Virdis said you would not, unless you got fevered. She gave me herbs for you." He dug into the roll of clothing and bandages for the little packet of herbs. Rahi shook her head.

"I'm fevered now—I can tell. If I lose it—" Her voice trailed away, and her eyes fixed on some distance Gird could not fathom. Then she looked at him directly. "The little ones?"

"Pidi has a lump on his head, but he's all right. It would take more than a lump to damage him. Giri has a broken arm. Here—you need to drink—" Gird lifted her as gently as he could, but Rahi flinched and moaned. He could feel her fever burning through the wrappings Virdis had put around her. She sipped a little water, then shook her head. He laid her back down. She alone, of all his children, reminded him of Mali—she had that same hair, the same quick wit. He could not lose her. But her fever mocked him. Of course he could lose her, as he had lost his parents, his brother, his brother's wife, the babies that had died. He could lose her quickly or slowly, as the fever raged or died, or as pursuit caught them.

He looked around at the others. Giri, her arm bound

tightly to her side, looked pale and sick; she had never been as strong as Rahi. Pidi, whose lump had matured into a spectacular black eye, sat watching Gird alertly. Fori, much like Arin but with Issa's slender build, sat hunched with his head down, breathing heavily.

"Fori?" Gird put a hand on his shoulder, and Fori jumped. When he looked up, his face was streaked with tears.

"I should have stopped them," Fori said, through sobs. "I—I should have been there."

"I, too—but we weren't. And if we had been, we'd have been dead as Parin is now."

"But she's—"

"Your cousin, and my daughter."

Diamod came back before he could say more, breathing hard as if he'd been running a long way. "I saw guards on the near side of that first hill, moving slowly. Not the way we'd come, exactly—I don't think they have a trail. But we can't stay here. We must move under cover, and keep moving."

This time Gird and Fori took the litter again, and the other two men took their bundles. One of them led the way southward, summering as Gird thought of it, keeping them along the creek bank as the water deepened and broadened, then leading them eastward, sunrising, up a tributary. Diamod lagged behind, overtaking them again near dark, when they'd stopped under a clump of pickoak where a spring came bubbling up from the rocks.

"They didn't follow," he said, before anyone asked. "They've put someone up on the hill—I saw a glitter up there—but no sign of real pursuit. We must stay out of sight of that hilltop, and no fire, but we can think now where to take the—your daughter."

Gird hoped his face did not show all he felt. "She's fevered now," he said, ducking his head. Raheli had said nothing, all the afternoon, but she seemed to be in a sick daze. He had gotten her to drink a little twice, but nothing more.

"She needs shelter, and a healer. Have you any family in another village?"

Gird shook his head. "Only my wife's—my dead wife's—family, over in Fireoak. But I don't know where that is from here, and even so they might not take her."

One of the other men turned to him. "Fireoak? My sister married into that village. They don't have much trade, those folk, but they're kindly."

"We can find Fireoak easily enough, but it will be days of careful travel. We're a day or more from the sheepfold where the dances are."

Gird nodded. "I know that."

"For healthy men it would be a day's journey, but carrying her, and with the others, it will be two, I think. Then from there to Fireoak is—"

"A day, like this. But it's the only shelter between, that fold."

Mali's parents, like his own, had been dead some years, but her brother was alive. He squatted beside the litter and laid a hand on Raheli's head.

"Mali's child?"

"Aye." Gird felt restless, in here where he could not see.

"We heard there'd been trouble your way. Your name was mentioned." Gird was sure it had been, if the guards had been by. "They said a man died—?"

"Rahi's husband, Parin. He was inside; he tried to fight them off."

"Mmm. And you?"

He felt the rush of shame again. "I was out plowing—when I heard her scream, I tried—but the guards got to me—"

Mali's brother shook his head. "None o' us can stand against them. It's no blame to you. Well. I reckon we can take her in, see if she heals—and the younger girl?"

"Has a broken arm."

"She's welcome here too. The lords come here rarely, and one woman—one girl—but the thing is—"

"You can't let us stay. I know that." Gird sighed, heavily. "I—I'm an outlaw now, we both know that. Trouble for you. But if you'll care for them—"

"We will."

"Then I'll leave now, before I bring trouble."

"Will you tell us where?"

"No. What you don't know, you won't be withholding. If Rahi lives, I may come through again sometime."

Mali's brother nodded. "I can give you a bit of food—"

"Save it for Rahi—I'm giving you two more mouths to feed, maybe three if she doesn't lose the child—"

"Never mind. We're glad to help Mali's daughters. May the Lady's grace go with you."

Gird almost answered with a curse—what grace had he had from the Lady this several years?—but choked it back. The man meant no harm, and maybe the Lady meant no harm either. He and Fori eased out of the barton, keeping close to the walls and low, until they came between the hedges that edged the fields of Fireoak. Back up the grassy lane—the plough-team's lane, he was sure—to the heavy clump of wood that reminded him of the way the wood had been when he was a child. Here no lord had thinned it, and the oak and nut trees made a vast shade.

Diamod was waiting, with Pidi; the others had disappeared. Gird and Fori scooped up the sticky paste of soaked grain, and ate it from dirty fingers. For the first time, Gird felt like a real outlaw. No fire, no shelter, no table or spoons—only the knife at his belt, and the farm tools he had carried away.

"And now?" Diamod asked. "What will you do now?"

Gird looked sideways at him. "What is there to do, but try to live and fight?"

"You had said you were thinking of teaching us what you knew of soldiering."

Gird wiped sticky fingers in the leafmold, and scowled at the result. "I had some ideas, yes. But your people— were they all farmers before?"

"Most of them. I was a woodworker, myself. There's a one-armed man who was a smith, but crippled for forging long blades."

"But most have used farming tools, sickles and scythes and shovels and the like?"

"Yes—but why?"

Gird had crouched by the trickle of water to scrub his

hands clean; now he flipped the water from them, and leaned back against a tree. Something poked him in the back, and he squirmed away from it.

"You can't fight soldiers as an unarmed mob; we know that already. It takes too many—and too many die. Drill would help; having a plan and following it, not rushing around in a lump. But weapons—that's the thing. We'll never get swords enough, not with the watch they keep on smiths. I'd thought of making weapons from the blades of scythes or sickles, but that too would take a smith willing to work the metal, and then training to use them. I had just begun sword training myself; I'm not any good with a sword." He paused to clear his throat. Diamod was scowling, and now he shrugged.

"So? Are you still saying there's no way peasants can defend themselves?"

"No. What I'm saying is we have to use what we have. The tools the men are used to—the tools we can make, or that we have already—and then learn to use those tools for fighting."

Diamod looked unconvinced. "Are you saying that ex-farmers with shovels can stand up to soldiers with pikes and swords?"

"If we can't, then we're doomed. I don't know if they—we—can. But we have to try."

"And you'll teach us."

"I hope so. There's something else—"

"What?"

"Just an idea. Let me tell the others about it later."

Diamod led Gird, Fori, and Pidi through the woods that lay between Fireoak and the next holding to the east. Gird tried to keep in mind how they had come, but soon found all the trees, trails, and creeks blurring in his mind. That night they spent in the wood, eating another cold meal of soaked grain. The next day, they followed a creek most of the day, coming at last to a clearing where the creek roared down a rocky bluff. At the foot of the waterfall, a rude camp held a score of men.

In the center of the camp was a circle of stones

around the firepit, symbolic of their name, but actually used for seating. The lean blackhaired man who appeared to be the leader did not rise from his stone when Diamod led Gird forward.

"So this is Gird of Kelaive's village, eh?" The man looked worn and hungry, as they all did. Diamod started to speak, and the man waved him to silence. "I'll hear Gird himself."

Gird stared at him, uncertain. So many strangers— not one familiar face beyond Fori and Pidi—upset him. He could not read their expressions; he did not know where they were from, or how they would act.

"Have you ever been out of your vill before?" asked the man, less brusquely.

"Only to trade fair, one time, and to Fireoak when I was courting," Gird said. The man's voice even sounded strange; some of his words had an odd twang to them.

"Then you feel like a lost sheep, in among wild ones. I know that feeling. Fireoak's in your hearthing, anyway—hardly leaving home and kin, like this. Diamod has told us about you—that you sent grain, the past few years, after your friend was killed—"

"Amis," said Gird. It seemed important to name him.

"And now you've run away to join us. Why?"

Gird got the tale out in short, choked phrases; no one interrupted. When he finished, he was breathing hard and fast, and the others were looking mostly at their feet. Only the blackhaired man met his eyes.

"Outlaw—this is what you chose. After telling Diamod you would not consider it—"

"While I could farm," Gird said. "Now—"

"You can't farm here," the man gestured at the surrounding forest. "So what skills do you bring us?"

Gird was sweating, wishing he could plunge away into the trees and lose himself. What did these men want? Were they going to grant him shelter or not? "I thought I would do what Diamod asked before: teach you what I know of soldiering."

Someone snickered, behind him. The blackhaired man smiled. "And what do you know of soldiering, after a lifetime spent farming? Did you bring swords, and will you teach us to use them? Or perhaps that scythe slung on your back will turn to a pike at your spellword? Diamod told me he had found someone, a renegade guardsman, he said, to teach us soldiers' drill, but what good is drill without weapons?"

The tone of the questions roused his anger, and banished fear. "Without drill you couldn't use weapons if you had them. With it—with it, you can use whatever comes to hand, and make a weapon of it."

"S'pose you'll lead us into battle wi' sticks, eh?" asked one man. Others chuckled. "Fat lot of good that will do, a stick against a sword."

"It can," said Gird, "if you've the sense to use it like a stick, and not try to fence with it." This time the chuckles were fewer; he could see curiosity as well as scorn in their faces.

"'Course," said the black-haired man, "we've only got your word for it, that you can fight at all."

"That's true." Gird relaxed; he knew what would come of this. They wanted to see what Diamod had dragged in, but it would be a fair fight. "You want to see me fight?"

"I think so." The blackhaired man looked around at the others. "Aye—that's what we want. Show us something."

"Let'm eat first, Ivis," said one of the other men. "They been travelin' all day."

"No guest-right," the blackhaired man scowled. "Until this Gird proves what he is or isn't, I'm not granting guest-right."

"No guest-right," said Gird. He was surprised to find outlaws following that much of the social code. Food was more of the soaked grain, and a cold mush of boiled beans. Looking around, Gird saw only the one firepit, and no oven. The blackhaired man unbent enough to explain.

"Sometimes the lords hunt this wood, and their foresters use this clearing. So a fire here is safer than one elsewhere in the wood; folks is used to seeing smoke from about here. We tried to build an oven once, but they broke it up when they found it."

"Where do you go when the foresters come?" asked Gird.

"That you'll find out after you fight. *If* you convince us to let you stay."

When Gird had eaten a little, he stood and stretched. The others went on eating, all but a strongly built man a little shorter than he was. Gird glanced at the black-haired man, who grinned.

"You'll fight Cob; he's our best wrestler. Used to win spicebread at the trade fair that way, as a lad. Show us how a soldier fights, but no killing: if you're good, we can't afford to lose you or Cob."

"All right." Gird had seen Cob's sort of wrestler before; he would be strong and quick. But the sergeant had taught his recruits many ways to fight hand-to-hand, and which ones were best against which kind of opponent. Gird watched Cob crouch and come forward in a balanced glide, and grinned to himself.

Although he knew what to do, it had been a long time since he'd done it. He got the right grip on Cob's arm, and put out his own leg, but his timing was just off, and Cob twisted away before he was thrown. Gird avoided Cob's attempt at a hold, but the effort threw him off balance and he staggered. Cob launched himself at Gird, knocking him sideways, and threw a leg across him quickly. Gird remembered that—it took a roll, here, and a quick heave *there*, and suddenly he was on top of Cob. Under him, the man's muscles were bunched and hard. He was not quitting. Gird did not wait for Cob's explosion, but rolled backwards suddenly, releasing his grip. Cob bounced up and charged. This time Gird was ready; he took the wrist of the arm Cob punched at him, pivotted, and flung Cob hard over his shoulder onto the ground.

Cob lay blinking, half-stunned. Gird heard something behind him, and whirled in time to catch another charge, even as the blackhaired man said "Triga—no!" Triga's mad rush required no great skill; Gird used the man's own momentum to send him flying as well. He landed hard and skidded an armlength when he landed.

Cob whistled, from his place on the ground. "You

could've made money with that throw, Gird. Teach me?"

Gird looked at the blackhaired man. "Well?"

"Well. You can fight—not many overthrow Cob. I'm sorry about Triga, but glad to see you have no trouble with him. We can use those skills."

"And the rest?"

The blackhaired man frowned slightly. "I am not the only leader; the Stone Circle is made of many circles, and each has its own. You must convince us all that this is something we need, and can use. I still do not see how sticks and shovels will let us stand against soldiers with sharp steel."

Gird started to say that he wasn't sure, but realized that these men didn't want to hear that. Those eyes fastened on his face wanted certainty, confidence, the right answer. The only answer he was sure of was drill. "You have to start with drill," he said. He knew they could hear the certainty in his voice about that. "You have to learn to work together, move together. Let me show you."

"Now?" someone asked, as if it were absurd to start something new so late in the day.

"You can't start sooner," said Gird, quoting the old proverb. Several of the men chuckled, but it was a friendly chuckle this time.

"Start with me," said the blackhaired man. "My name's Ivis." He stood and the rest stood also. Cob, cheerful despite his fall, had climbed to his feet, and reached a hand down to Triga.

Gird took a deep breath and tried to remember the expression on his sergeant's face. "The first thing is, you line up here." He scratched a line in the dirt with his toe. "You, too, Fori—come on. Pidi, just stay out of the way. Two hands of you here, and two behind, an armslength." That would make two ranks of ten.

When the front ten had their toes more or less arranged on the line he'd scratched, he looked at them again. They slouched in an uneven line, shoulders hunched or tipped sideways, heads poked forward, knees askew. Triga was rubbing his elbow. Those behind were

even more uneven; they had taken his armslength liter-
ally, and the short ones stood closer to those in front
than the tall ones. This was going to be harder than
he'd thought. His boyhood friends had been eager to
play soldier.

"Stand up straight," he said. "Like the soldiers you've
seen. Heads up—" That sent one of them staggering, as
he jerked his head up too far. Someone else chuckled.
Ivis growled at them, and they settled again. Gird did
not like their expressions: they weren't taking this seriously at all. Only Fori and Cob and Ivis looked as if
they were even trying. "You three—" he said, pointing
to them. "You get together here in the middle. And
you others—look at them, how they're standing. Like
that is what you need. Feet together, toes out a little.
Hands at your sides. You in the back row, make a
straight row—" Gradually they shifted and wiggled into
something more like military posture. Gird wondered if
he had looked like that at first. Maybe this was the best
they could do, for now.

"Now you have to learn to march." He glared, daring
anyone to laugh. No one did, but he saw smirks. His
old sergeant would have had something to say about
that, but he had never dealt with outlaws, either. "You
all have to start with the same foot—"

"Like dancing?" asked Cob. Gird stopped, surprised.
He'd never thought of it as like dancing, but all the
dances required the men to step out with the same
foot, or they'd have been tripping each other. He thought
his way into the harvest dance he had led so many
times. Wrong foot.

"Like dancing," he said finally, "but not the same
foot. The other foot, from the harvest dance." Surely
they all danced it the same way. "Think of the dance,
and then pick up the other foot." Slowly, wavering, one
foot after another came up, until they were all teetering
on one foot. All but two had the correct foot. Those
looked down, saw they were wrong, and changed feet.
"Now one step forward." The double line lurched
towards him, out of step and no two steps the same
length. Gird felt a twinge of sympathy for his old ser-

geant. Had it been this difficult? "Straighten out the lines," he said.

He kept them at it until his voice was tired. By then they could break apart and reassemble in two fairly straight lines, and they could all pick up the same foot at the same time. But when they walked forward, their uneven strides quickly destroyed the lines. He was sure they could have danced it, arms over each others' shoulders, but they couldn't fight in that position. He'd told them that, and a few other things, and remembered some of the words his sergeant had used.

They were ready to lounge around, eating their meager supper, but Gird remembered more than his sergeant's curses.

"We must learn to keep things clean," he said.

"Clean!" Triga had scowled often; now he sneered. "We're not lords in a palace. How can we be clean—and why should we?"

"Soldiers keep themselves clean, and their weapons bright. I spent my first days in the guard scrubbing the floor, washing dishes, and scouring buckets. First, it keeps men healthy—you all know that—and protects against fevers. And second, it means that you know your equipment will work. A weapon's no good if the blade is dull. And third, I stink bad enough to tell any forester there's a poor man here: so do you all, after the drill. D'you want hounds seeking us? It's warm enough: we should all bathe."

Sighing, Ivis and Cob heaved themselves up, and the others followed. Gird led them to the waterfall. Once well wet, the men cheered up and began joking, splashing each other. Pidi had found a clump of soaproot, and sliced off sections with his knife. Soon the creek was splattered with heavy lather.

When Gird felt that the grime and sweat of the past days was finally gone, he washed his clothes as best he could, and saw the bloodstains from Parin and Rahi fade to brownish yellow. The other men watched him, curious, but some of them fetched their own ragged garments and tumbled them in the water. Gird smiled when he saw them laying out the wet clothes on bushes, as he was doing. Diamod brought him a clump of leaves.

"Here—rub this on, and the flies will stay away. Otherwise you'll be eaten up by the time your things are dry."

"I should've washed clothes first—now it's near nightfall. But I have a spare shirt."

"Most of them don't."

But even in dirty clothes, the men stank less, and carried themselves less furtively. Gird, with a clean shirt tickling his bare knees, suggested another change in their customs.

"Why not bake a hearthcake on one of these stones? 'Twouldn't be bread, exactly, but it would be hot, and cooked—"

"If we had honey we could have honeycakes, an' we had grain," said Triga. Gird began to take a real dislike to Triga.

"There's always bees in a wood," he said crisply. "And stings to a bee, for all that."

"There's none knows how to make the batter, Gird," said Ivis. "We've no mill or flour. All we know is crush the grain and soak it—if you know better, teach us that."

Gird thought of the millstones left behind—but he could not have carried them and Rahi. He looked at the stones used as seats, and found one with a slightly hollowed surface. Then he went to the creekside, and looked for cobbles. He could feel the other men watching him, as if he were a strange animal, a marvel. But millstones, the cottage millstones, were no different. A hollowed stone, like a bowl, and the grinder. Some people had flatter ones, with a broader grinder. It had to be fine-grained stone, and hard. He picked up several cobbles he liked, and hefted them, felt along their smooth curves with a careful finger. Yes.

Ivis had the grainsack out for him when he returned. Gird wondered if it was grain he'd grown, or someone else's contribution. It didn't matter. He dipped a small handful, and poured it onto the stone, then rubbed with the cobble. It wasn't the right shape—neither the bottom stone nor the grinder—and the half-ground grain wanted to spit out from under and fall off. He worked steadily, ignoring the others, pushing the meal back under the grinder with his finger. He was careful not to lick it, as he would have at home: thin as they all were, they must be keeping famine law, when all the food was shared equally.

When the first handful was ground to a medium meal, he brushed it into a wooden bowl that Ivis had brought. It was not enough to make any sort of bread for all of them, but he could test his memory. Cob brought him a small lump of tallow, and he took a pinch of salt from the saltbag he'd brought himself. Meal, water, fat, salt—not all he liked in his hearthcakes, but better than meal and water alone. He stirred it in the wooden bowl, while the fire crackled and Pidi brushed off the flattest of the stones facing the firepit. The tallow stayed in its lump, stubborn, and Gird remembered that he needed to heat it. He skewered it on a green stick, and held it over the fire, catching the drips in the bowl. Finally it melted off, and he stirred it in quickly. He felt the stone, and remembered that he should have greased it. The stick he'd used for the tallow was greasy now; he rubbed his fingers down it, and then smeared the stone. The stone was hot, but was it hot enough? He poured the batter out. It stiffened almost at once, the edges puckering. Hot enough. With his arm, he waved heat toward it, to cook the upper surface. Mali had had the skill to scoop up the hearthcakes and flip them, but the only times he'd tried it, they'd fallen in the fire.

The smell made his mouth water and his belly clench. He looked up, and saw hungry looks on all the faces. Now the upper side was stiff and dull—dry, and browning. He hoped he'd put enough tallow on the rock. He slid a thin twig under it, and it lifted. He got his fingers on it—hot!—and flipped it to Ivis. Ivis broke it in pieces—each man had a small bite—and then it was gone. But if his fighting had gotten their respect, this had gotten their interest.

"I thought you were a farmer, not a cook," said Ivis.

"My wife was sick a lot, that last few years." Gird gestured at the bowl. "May I give my son that?"

Ivis nodded. "Of course. It's fair; he had none of the hearthcake itself." Pidi grinned and began cleaning the batter from the bowl with busy fingers and agile tongue. "But tell us—what do we need?"

Gird thought about it. "Millstones—we can use this, but we can't carry it along, not if the foresters come here. But we can put millstones in another place, if you have a particular place."

"Where I came from, we all had to use the lord's mill," said Ivis.

Gird shrugged. "That was the rule for us, too, but most of us had handmills at home. Always had. The lord's mill was a day's journey away—we had no time for that. And then if you did go, you'd have to wait while he ground someone else's, and might not get your own back. Anyway, we can have millstones for hand milling—it'll take time, is the main thing. We can't have bread every day. Tallow, we need, and a bit of honey if it's available. Salt—I brought some with me, but we'll need more—"

"There's a salt lick downstream a bit," said Cob. "I can show you."

"And if we want lightbread, we'll need a starter. Do you ever get milk?"

"D'you think we live in a great town market, where we can buy whatever we like?" asked Triga.

From the tone of the response, others were as tired of Triga's complaints as Gird was. Gird waited until the others had spoken, then said "No, but I think you're not so stupid as you act." Cob grinned. Triga, predictably, scowled. Gird turned back to Ivis. "How long have you lived out here?"

"Me? A hand of years—five long winters. Artha's been here longer, but most don't stay that long. They move on, or they die."

"You've done well, on beans and grain."

"There's more in the summer. We find herbs, do a little hunting, rob a hive once a year—no one wants to do it more, with all the stings we get. We do get milk sometimes, when we venture in close to a farmstead. Not all of us, o' course. Milk, cheese, trade honey or herbs for a bit of cloth . . ."

Cloth, in fact, was one of the hardest things to come by. Gird, remembering his mother's hours at the loom, and the value of each furl, did not wonder at this. To share food was one thing; to share the product of personal skill was another. The outlaws had learned to tan the hides of beasts they hunted—"Stick 'em in an oak stump that's rotted and got water in it"—but good leather took more than that; many of the hides rotted, or came out too brittle to use for clothing.

As he listened to Ivis and Cob, and thought about all that this group needed, he thought back to his sergeant's comments about the importance of supply. Soldiers did not grow their own food, or raise their own flocks, or build their own shelters—this, so they could have the time to practice soldiering. But these men would have to do it themselves. Could they do that, and learn to be soldiers as well?

Chapter Ten

The next morning, Gird realized that the others were all looking to him for leadership, and not only in military training.

"Do we work on drill before breakfast, or after?" asked Ivis.

"After," said Gird, to give himself time. His clothes were still damp; he turned them over and hoped the morning sun would dry them. Then he eyed the trees, and realized it would be a long time before the sun came into the clearing. Breakfast was another cold mess of soaked grain. Gird was already tired of it. He was spoiled, he supposed, by having had a wife and daugh-

ter with a parrion for herbs and cooking. Pidi leaned
against him as he ate, and Gird put an arm around him.
He wished he could have left the boy with Mali's
brother—he was really too young for this. Fori sat on
Gird's other side, carefully not leaning, but clearly nervous among so many strangers.

"Do you have a plan beyond training us?" asked Cob.
Gird glanced at Ivis, who seemed interested but not
antagonistic.

"When Diamod first came to our village," Gird said,
"he wanted to learn soldiering. Wanted me to teach all
of you. I thought he meant *you* had a plan—whoever
your leader was."

"We've tried things," Ivis said. "And the other
groups—I know they have. Captured a guards' storehouse, one did, and burned it out, but that brought
more guards, and they took prisoners—finally killed
them. Robbed a few traders, but that's—we don't like
to be brigands; that's not what we're here for."

"And that is?"

Diamod leaped into the discussion. "We've got to be
the peasant's friend—free the peasants, somehow, from
the lords—"

"That won't happen!" Triga stamped his foot in emphasis. "There's always been lords and peasants. But if
we can make them understand they have to be fair—"

"Now *that* is what will never happen." Cob stamped
both feet. "Lords be fair indeed! They wouldn't know
how, and why should they? Nay, 'slong as we've got the
lords over us, they'll do their best to keep us down, and
take every bit they can. Does the farmer leave the
sheep half a fleece, or feed a cow and not milk her?"

"A *good* farmer leaves the beasts alive and healthy,"
muttered another man. Gird could tell this was an old
argument, comfortable in their mouths as their tongues
were. He knew its byways as well, having heard them
all in his own village. He cleared his throat, and to his
surprise they all quieted and looked at him.

"You have no plan," he said, as if musing. "One
wants to teach the lords how to rule, and another wants

to end their rule, and I suppose some of you would like to go and live peacefully far away, if you could."

"Aye—" More than one voice answered him.

"I used to think," Gird went on, "that it was best to work hard and live within the lords' laws. That if a man worked hard enough, honestly enough, everything would be right in the end. That's what my father taught me, and times I did other than he said, we all suffered for it. I determined to follow his advice, and trust he was right. But I was wrong." He paused, and looked around. Pidi was trembling a little in the arc of his arm; Fori's face was set. The others watched him closely, and did not move. "I told you a little—about my daughter and her husband—but not all that led me here. It began long before, and over the years I built a wall of the stones I swallowed—stones of anger and stones of sorrow. A wall to keep myself at peace, and safety within— and it did not work." He ran a hand through his thinning hair, and scrubbed his beard. "I don't know if any law is fair, but the law the lords put on us is not fair, and no man can live safe under it. I don't know if all the lords are alike, but some of 'em—Kelaive, for one—are not only greedy, but cruel. They like to hurt people; they like to see people suffer. Such men cannot rule wisely, or fairly. And when such men rule, no one can live an honest life." He drew a long breath, gave Pidi a squeeze, and then pushed him gently away. He could not say what he was going to say, with his arm around his youngest child.

"I have taken that wall down," Gird said. "Those stones—those stones I will throw at our enemies. Those stones, which I bring to this circle—because the Lady herself cannot give us peace unless we drive off the alien lords who rule us."

"But we can't," said Triga. "We are too few—"

"Now, in this place, yes: we are too few. But there are more farmers than lords, more servants than lords. Few have joined you, as I did not join you, because they too think we are too few. They do not wish more trouble than they have. But if we can show success, they will come. I'm sure of it."

"Yes!" Cob stamped his feet again. "Yes, you're right. Gird's right," he said to the others. Most were nodding, smiling, clearly pleased with what Gird had said. And Gird, putting his arm around Pidi again, wondered if he could possibly perform what they were sure he had promised.

Serious planning began after a short review of yesterday's drill. He had realized that the clearing was really too small and too cluttered for serious drill; he could not march his two lines of ten five steps without someone having to step over or around a log or stone. And in the noise they made while drilling, a squad of mounted guards could have ridden up on them without anyone noticing.

"Do you have anyone out looking for foresters?" he asked Ivis.

"Usually someone goes downstream, and someone goes upstream," Ivis scratched his jaw and looked thoughtful. "We use stone clicks for signals. But today everyone wanted to hear what you said." In other words, Gird thought, just when it was most dangerous, they had no guard set. That would have to change.

"What about at night?"

"No, no one goes out at night. The foresters don't travel at night."

"But—" He wondered how far to go. Would Ivis be angry? It had to be said. "At night, you could see the glow of their fire—smell smoke or cooking food—and be warned."

"I suppose." Ivis didn't look eager to wander the forest at night; Gird could understand that. But Diamod had seemed to like sneaking about the village—maybe he could. He glanced at Diamod, who smiled brightly. He still did not understand Diamod, and he wondered if he ever would. The other men seemed to feel the way he felt—would have felt, if he'd left home under any other circumstances, he reminded himself. They were here because they had to be. But Diamod seemed to be enjoying himself.

"Someone should go out now, and be sure no foresters are coming," he said to Ivis. Ivis nodded, but did nothing. "Who will you send?" Gird asked.

"Me? But you're—"

"Do you *want* me to take over as leader? Is that what you're saying?"

Ivis sat silent a long moment, his face somber. Then he looked Gird in the face. "I haven't done much," he said. "Just—just tried to keep them together—talk to farmers about food—but I don't *feel* like a leader. I never did. They started listening to me after Rual died, but I never wanted it. They're used to me, but you'll do better."

"It's not something you and I should decide," Gird said, almost before he thought it. "If this is about fairness, and ruling fairly, then they should have a say."

"Triga will quarrel," said Ivis. Gird shrugged.

"Let him quarrel. He won't do more; he didn't like landing on the ground." He looked around at the others, now lounging around the clearing in the attitudes of men trying to hear a private conversation without seeming to listen. "Ivis and I were talking," he began, not raising his voice. They edged closer. "He asked me if I wanted to be leader."

"You! We don't even know you," Triga said. Predictable, Gird thought. He's so predictable.

"Quiet now—you can argue later." He put a bite into his voice, and Triga subsided. The others were attentive; he could not tell if they approved or not. "Ivis—do you want to tell them what you said to me?"

Ivis swallowed, gulped, and finally repeated most of what he'd said. "I think he'd be a good leader," he finished. "He's strong, and he has a plan. And he knows more than just soldiering. I'd rather follow him."

"And I," said Cob quickly, giving Gird a wide grin. "I want to learn how to fight like that."

"Yes," said some of the others, and "Gird—let's have Gird." Triga was obstinately silent until everyone else had spoken. They all looked at him, and he turned red.

"Come on, Trig," said Cob. "You know you want to—it's just your stubbornness."

"What if he's a spy?" Triga said. "How do we know he isn't a guard in disguise?"

"I'm not that stupid!" Diamod glared at him. "I was

in his village; I met his friends. They told me a lot—"
He gave Gird a long look, steady and measuring. "A lot
about his past. They couldn't all have been lying. He's a
farmer and a farmer's son, and if you think he's not, you
can argue it with me. Knife to knife."

"Enough," Gird said. "We can't be spilling each other's blood over little quarrels, if we want to fight a war.
Triga, d'you think Diamod's lying?"

"No." It was a sulky no.

"Do you think *I* am? I'll have no one in my army that
thinks I'm a liar." He felt ridiculous, speaking of an
army when what he had was twenty ragged, hungry,
untrained men and one boy, but he saw the others
straighten a little. If coward was a word to make men
flinch and bend, maybe army was a word to straighten
their backs and make them proud. He saw Triga's face
change, as he realized that he might actually be thrown
out of the group. Fear and anger contended; fear won.

"No—I don't think you're lying." Slightly less sulky,
and somewhat worried.

"These others agreed to have me as their leader—do
you?" He kept his eyes locked on Triga's; he could feel
the struggle in the man.

"I suppose. For awhile. We can see." Cob and Diamod
looked angry, but Gird shook his head.

"That's fair. You don't completely trust me, but you're
willing to give me a chance." Triga's jaw dropped in
surprise; he had been braced for an argument. Gird
looked around at the others. "I told Ivis I would not
take the leadership on his word alone. You have all
chosen, as you have a right to do—and I thank Triga for
trusting as far as he can. None of us can do more than
that."

The others sat back, their expressions ranging from
puzzled to satisfied. Triga said nothing, but looked as if
he were chewing on a new idea.

"Now. We need to send out watchers, to let us know
if anyone comes. Ivis says you usually had two; I'd like
to send four—two of you, and my son Pidi and my
nephew Fori. They need to learn the forest."

"It's my turn," said Ivis. "And Kelin—" Kelin was

a slight brownhaired man with one shoulder higher than the other. He did not quite limp when he walked, but his stride was uneven. Gird nodded.

"Pidi knows many useful herbs," he said. "My daughter taught him."

Kelin grinned. "Then let him come with me: all I know is flybane and firetouch. And sometimes I miss firetouch until I'm already itching."

"Three pairs of clicks," said Ivis, as they left. "That's the danger signal. "You pass it on, whichever way it comes, and move away from it. Cob knows the trails."

When they had gone, Gird surveyed the clearing itself. If they had to leave it untouched, so that foresters who used it would not know they'd been there, he could not move the logs and stones used for seating to give more room for drill. They really needed a campsite the foresters did *not* use. This one could become a trap, particularly if his people became effective against the lords. So what did he need in a campsite? He thought about that as he roamed the clearing, pacing off distances, and trying to listen for clicks.

Water. Good drainage, and room for the jacks trenches he would have them dig; the disgusting stench just behind a trio of cedars was entirely too obvious. Level ground, uncumbered, for drill, but enough trees for cover. A cave would be nice, shelter from weather and a place to store food and equipment. While he was asking, why not a forge with a skilled smith? He remembered that Diamod had said one of the men had been a smith, a one-armed man—there he was. His name was odd, a smithish name: Ketik.

"Ketik—"

"Aye." He had a rough voice, and stood canted a little sideways, as if missing the weight of his arm. The stump was ugly, a twisted purple lump of scar. He wore no shirt, only a sleeveless leather jerkin.

"If we found another campsite, what would we need for a forge?"

Ketik stared at him out of light-blue eyes. "A forge? Don't you see this arm? I'm no smith now."

"If we had what is needed, couldn't you take an apprentice? Teach someone?"

Ketik snorted, a sound half-laughter, half-anger. "Could you teach someone to swing a scythe by telling them? Wouldn't you have to show them? Do you think smithery is so simple?"

"Not simple at all," said Gird quietly. "It is a great mystery, and our village had no smith at all. We shared one with Hardshallows. But we will need a smith—"

"And not all are weapons smiths," Ketik said.

"I know. What I'm thinking of wouldn't take a swordsmith. But we would have to have our own forge."

"A good fireplace," Ketik said rapidly. "Fuel—fireoak is best. Someone to make charcoal, because you'd need to be able to refine ores sometimes. Leather for the bellows, and not the rotting, stiff mess these idiots make in old tree stumps. Real leather, properly tanned. Tools, which means iron: ore or lump iron from some smelter. Both are illegal. An anvil. Someplace with water, too, and a way to disguise the smoke. Satisfied?"

"We will need to move anyway," Gird said. "We might as well look for what we need."

"What we need is the gods' blessing and a fistful of miracles," said Ketik. He sounded slightly less irritated now, as if challenging Gird had eased his mind.

"You're right," Gird said. "But though we need Alyanya's blessing for a good harvest, we still have to plow and plant and weed and reap."

Ketik laughed aloud. "Well—you may be the leader we need after all. I never heard of a one-armed smith teaching smithery, but then I never heard of a farmer teaching soldiering, either."

Triga had come close while they were talking; now he said, "I said last autumn we should find a new campsite."

Gird nodded, ignoring the rancorous tone. "Did you find someplace you thought would be good?"

"Me?" Triga looked surprised. "They wouldn't listen to me."

"If you already know a place—"

"I know another place than this, but it might not be what you want."

"How far is it?"

"A half-day, maybe, or a little longer." He pointed across the stream. "Sunrising. It's swampy; the foresters never go there."

Gird opened his mouth to say that the last thing they needed was a swamp, and closed it again. If Triga was trying to be helpful, why stop him. "I think we'll need more than one place, but that sounds useful. If we're pursued—"

"It's like a moat, I thought," said Triga.

"As long as we have a bridge over it—one they can't see."

"Gird—about the grain—do you want us to grind more today?" That was Herf, who had been tending the fire when Gird awoke. Triga looked sulky and opened his mouth; Gird shook his head. "Triga, tomorrow or the next day I'd like to see your swamp. Right now, though, the grain comes first."

Triga said "I could go look for a path through the swamp."

"Good idea." Gird had never seen a swamp, and had no idea what one would look like. Were they flat? Sloped? Did they have high places that were dry? "If you find a dry place inside it," he said slowly, "like the castle inside the moat—?"

"I'll look." Triga actually seemed cheerful—for him—as he waded across the stream and turned to wave back at them. Gird shook his head and turned to Herf.

"Now. How much grain do we have?"

When Herf showed him their meager food stores, and the way they were kept, Gird could hardly believe the band had not starved long ago. Sacks of grain and dry beans were sitting on damp stone under a rainroof made of small cedars with their tops tied together. Gird prodded the bottom of the sacks and felt the telltale firmness of grain rotted into a solid mass. Beans had begun to sprout through the coarse sacking. Herf had tried to store onions and redroots in a trench, but most of them were sprouting.

"I know," he said in answer to Gird's look. "Once they sprout, the redroots are poisonous. But I couldn't dig them in any deeper here, without proper tools. The ground's stony."

"Well." Gird squatted beside the trench, and brushed the leafmold off a healthy redroot sprout. "My da used to tell about his granda's da—or somewhat back there— about the time before the lords came, when our folk grew things in the woods."

"In the *woods*?"

"In fields, too, the grain—of course. But redroots and onions and such—some we don't grow now—along the streams, and in the woods. We can't eat these—maybe we should plant them now, and harvest in the fall."

"We can still eat the onions—"

"Some of them, yes. But why not plant the others? Spread 'em around in the wood—no one'd recognize them as plantings, and they'd be where we knew—"

Herf frowned, thinking hard. "Then—we could grow the greenleaves, too, couldn't we? Cabbages, sorli—"

"Maybe even sugarroot." Gird poked at the leafmold. "This here's good growing soil for some crops. Herbs, greenleaves—grow 'em along the creekbank, we could. You know how hard it is to haul water to the greenstuff in summer—we could plant it where it needs no help."

"Aye, but breadgrain and beans—we can't live on greenstuff and redroots alone."

"Right enough. For now—you get your grain from farmers, right?"

"Or steal it from traders—but that's rare."

"When we take it from farmers, they go hungry—so we can't afford to let any rot—"

"It's the best I could do!" Herf puffed up almost like a frog calling.

"I'm not saying it wasn't. But if we find a new camp-site, maybe we can do better. Besides—did you ever see the big jars the lords use?"

"Jars?"

"Aye. Brown, shiny on inside and outside. Like our honeypots but bigger. They're almighty heavy and hard to move, but grain and even meal stay dry inside them."

"And where would we get such? We don't have a potter."

Another miracle to wish for, thought Gird. They needed some pots—at least small ones. In his mind's eye, his future campsite had sprouted another fireplace, although it wavered as he looked at it. He'd never seen a potter's workshop. He knew they had a special name for the hearth in which they cooked their pots, but not what it looked like. But he could see as clearly as if he stood there the kitchen of the guard barracks at Kelaive's manor, with the great jars of meal and beans, the huge cooking kettles, the shiny buckets, the longhandled forks and spoons, the rack of knives. If he was going to have an army, he would have to have a kitchen capable of feeding it—and storerooms—his head ached, and he shook it. What he had was a sack and a half of grain, some of it rotted, less than a sack of beans, a few sprouting onions, and redroots that might be edible in half a year. An open firepit, two or three wooden bowls, the men's belt knives. He sighed, heavily, and heaved himself up.

"All right. We'll grind some of that grain, and make hearthcakes tonight. But we're going to need more grain, and I know the villages are short right now. Some of the men hunt, don't they? How often do they bring anything back?"

"Not that often. There are only two bows, not very good ones, and the arrows—"

"Are as bad. I can guess that. Anyone who can use a sling, or set snares?"

Herf shook his head. Gird added those skills to the list in his head, and told himself not to sigh again. It would do no good. He wished he hadn't sent Fori off; the lad had a talent for setting snares, and had once taken a squirrel with his sling. Come to think of it, slings could be weapons too.

"All right." He raised his voice. "Come here a bit, all of you. There are some things need doing." The men came closer, curious. "If we're going to be an army," he said, "we have to organize like soldiers. Food, tools, clothing—all that. We're starting with what we have. The first thing is to get all the rotten grain and beans apart from what's good, and protect the good from the wet. Then we're going to plant the sprouted redroots, scattered along our trails, so that we'll have them next fall. They'll get bigger, you know, and double or triple for us. Who here has used a handmill?" That was usually women's work, although many men helped grind the grain. Two hands raised. Gird nodded at them. "Herf will give you the grain—you saw how I did it yesterday. We're making enough hearthcakes for everyone tonight. Unless the foresters show up, of course."

By midday, all the clothes washed the previous evening were dry. Gird pulled on his trousers happily; he did not feel himself with his bare legs hanging out. The two volunteer millers had produced almost a bowlful of meal, and Herf had used Gird's clean shirt to hold the little good grain in one sack while he scraped out the spoiled and turned the sack inside out. The bottom end was beginning to rot. Without Gird having to suggest it, Herf decided to rip out the stitching there and sew the top end shut, so the weakest material would be at the opening. Since he seemed to know how to use a long thorn and a bit of twine to do it, Gird left him alone. Two other men had gone out in both directions along the creek, with the sprouted redroots, and were planting them. Gird reminded them that there was no good reason to plant them close to that campsite, since they would be moving somewhere else.

Fori appeared unexpectedly in midafternoon with a pair of squirrels he'd knocked down, showing off to Ivis with his sling. He had skinned and gutted them already, and had the skins stretched on circles of green wood. Gird grinned at him, delighted. But two squirrels would hardly feed twenty hungry men—they had no soup kettle.

Herf had the answer to that, showing Gird how hot rocks dropped in a wooden bowl could make the water hot enough to cook without burning holes in the bowl. By this time, he had all the good grain in one sack, and the dry beans separated from the damp, sprouting ones. Gird had wondered if they could also grow beans in the wood, but beans liked a lot of sun. Reluctantly, he had buried the smelly remnants of spoiled grain and beans.

Now Gird sliced up onions, his eyes watering and burning, to go in with the squirrels and one dry, wrinkled, unsprouted redroot. Herf added the beans he'd put on to soak that morning.

The guards came back in the dusk to the smell of roasting hearthcakes and squirrel and bean stew. Gird had already found another, besides Diamod, who would be willing to stand night guard; these two had eaten, and when Ivis and Kelin returned with Pidi, the night guards went out. Gird had also drilled the others, in the afternoon, and insisted on their cleaning up. He was pleased to notice that Ivis and Kelin stopped to wash hands and face in the creek before approaching the fire.

They had only three bowls to eat from; these passed from one to another, along with the two spoons. But compared to the night before, it was a festive meal. Even Triga made no complaint. Ivis came to sit by Gird, and said, "I made the right choice."

"It won't always be like this," Gird said, thinking of all the things he had to do. "We were lucky that Fori got those squirrels."

"But it feels different." Ivis wiped his mouth with his tattered sleeve and grinned, teeth bright in the firelight. "You know what to do."

Across the fire, Fori was basking in the praise of older men; Pidi was showing Herf the herbs he had brought back in his shirt. They were feeling at home here; Gird wondered if the young adjusted more easily. He was not sure what he felt. The blinding pain when he thought of Rahi was still there; when it hit, he found himself turning in the direction of Fireoak, *willing* himself across the woods and fields between to be with her. She might be dead by now, or still struggling in fever. He could not know.

He was beginning to know the men around him, and already knew that several of them would have been friends if they'd grown up in the same village. Cob reminded him of Amis, with his matter-of-fact friendliness. Ivis was more like Teris—responsibility made him truculent, but once freed of it, he was amiable and mild-tempered. Gird told himself that these were mostly farmers—men like those he'd known all his life—and in time would be as familiar as the men of his village, but for the moment he could not quite relax into kinship with them.

That night before he dropped off to sleep, he made an effort to speak individually with each of them, to fix their faces and names in his mind. Then he burrowed into a drift of leaves, with Pidi snuggled close to his side. It was still hard to sleep, in the open, knowing he had no cottage to return to, but he was tired, and the strain of the past few days overcame him.

The next morning brought complications. Instead of cool spring sunshine, the sky was cloudy, and a fine misty drizzle began to penetrate their clothes. The foul stench of their ill-dug jacks oozed across the clearing. Gird was sure they could smell it in the next village, wherever that was. He wrapped his leather raincloak around the sacks of grain and beans. The night guards arrived back at camp hungry, while Herf was struggling with the fire. Smoke lay close to the ground, making them all cough. After the previous night's feast, plain soaked grain seemed even more dismal than usual. Gird's joints ached; he wished fervently for a mug of hot sib. He heard low grumbles and mutters, and Triga's voice raised in a self-pitying whine.

This would never do. Gird strode back into the center of the clearing as if the sun were shining and he knew exactly what to do. The men looked up at him, sour-faced.

"Triga, what did you find yesterday?" Triga, interrupted in mid-complaint, looked almost comical. Then he stood up.

"I found that swamp I told you about—" Someone groaned, and Triga whipped around to glare in that direction.

"Never mind," said Gird. "Go on—and you others listen."

"I walked all around it—that's why I came back so late. There's three little creeks goes into it, and two comes out. I don't know what the middle's like yet—there wasn't time—"

"Good. That's where we'll go today."

"All of us?" Herf asked. "It's raining."

"It's raining here, too," Gird pointed out. "You'll get just as wet sitting here complaining about the rain, as walking along learning something useful. Maybe we'll find a cave, and can sleep dry."

They didn't look as if they believed him, but one by one his fledgling army stood up. He grinned at them.

"But first," he said. "We're going to do something about *that*." And he pointed toward the jacks. "It stinks enough to let anyone know a lot of men have been here, and it's making us sick as well."

"We don't have no tools," someone said. Kef, that was the name. Gird grinned again.

"I brought a shovel, remember? I'll start the digging, but we'll all be doing some—because there's more to it than just shoveling."

He had spotted a better site the day before. Now he took his shovel and tried it. Here a long-gone flood had spread across the clearing below the waterfall, and left a drift of lighter soil, almost sand. He started the trench he wanted, and gave the shovel to Kef. "That deep, and straight along there," he said. They really needed a bucket, too, but they didn't have one. He'd have to use the wooden bowls for the ashes. The men watched as he scooped ashes and bits of charred wood from the side of the firepit into one of their bowls. "You, too," Gird said, pointing at the other bowls. "We're going to need a lot of ashes."

"But I though ashes only worked in a pit," said Ivis.

"Best in a pit. But a trench is like a little pit. Ashes on top, then dirt, after you use it."

"Every time?"

"Every time—or it won't work. The guards kept a pot of ashes in the jacks; I started doing that at our cottage later, and ours smelled less than most." He looked at them, noticing the squeamish faces. "The worst part," he said carefully, "is going to be burying what's already there." He was pleased to note that no one asked if they had to.

It took longer than he'd hoped, with only the one shovel and small bowls to carry ashes, but at last they had the worst of the noisome mess buried, strewn with ashes, and a new bit of clean trench for that morning's use. Gird covered it up himself when they were all done, and marked the end with a roughly cut stake poked in the ground.

"Now we clean up," Gird said, "and then we go look for Triga's swamp. He's right—if we can find a safe way into it, that the foresters and guards don't know, it could be a very handy place."

Chapter Eleven

Triga led the way, with Gird behind him, and then the others. Gird had asked Ivis to be the rear guard, staying just in sight of the others. Within the first half-league, he was wondering how this group had survived undetected so long. They talked freely, tapped their sticks against trees and rocks as they passed, made no effort to walk quietly. Finally Gird halted them.

"We're making more noise than a tavern full of drunks. If there's a forester in the wood anywhere, he's bound to hear us."

Ivis turned a dull red. "Well—Gird—we don't like to come on 'em in surprise, like—"

"The foresters? You mean they know—"

"It's sort of—well—they'd have to know, wouldn't they? Being as they have to know the whole wood. But what they don't actually *see* they don't have to take notice of. My brother's one of them, you see, and—"

"And on the strength of one brother, you trust them all? What about the guard?"

"Oh, the duke's guard is a very different matter—very different indeed. But they don't venture into the wood except when the duke's hunting. And then they're guarding him, not poking about on their own."

"And—duke? Your lord isn't Kelaive?"

"Gods, no! I've heard about him, even before you came. Our duke's Kelaive's overlord, just as the king is his."

"So the foresters of this wood know that a band of outlaws lives here, and expects you to make enough noise coming so they can avoid you. What if they change their minds? Surely your duke's offered a reward."

"My brother wouldn't take a reward for me," Ivis said earnestly. "And if he captures the others, I'd be, right in the middle."

"What if he's transferred, or killed, or one of the other foresters gets greedy?" Ivis said nothing in answer; from his expression, he had thought of this before and tried to forget it. Gird looked at all the others. "Listen to me: an army does not go about expecting its enemies to get out of the way. We can't fight like that. Cannot. Perhaps Ivis's brother has enough influence on the foresters of this wood, but we will not always be in this wood. We have to leave it someday, and you must know how to move *quietly*. And we must be alert—we must find the foresters before they find us, and never let them know we were near. Understand?" Heads nodded, some slowly. "Now—the first thing—no talking while we march. No banging on stones or tree limbs. Walk one behind the other, far enough that if one man stumbles, the others don't fall too. Triga, you should be far enough ahead that I can just see, and you shouldn't be able to hear us—you listen for anyone *else*. If you go too fast, I'll click pebbles twice; if I click three times, stop. You give two double clicks if you hear foresters. Ivis, if you hear anything behind us, give two double clicks. The rest of you—if you hear two double clicks, stop where you are and do not make a noise. Clear?"

Again, heads nodded. Gird hoped that there were no foresters out that day, so they could get in at least one practice before it was needed. He waved Triga ahead, waited until he was almost out of sight on the narrow trail, and started off himself. Behind him, the noise of the others was much less, although he could hear an occasional footfall. Triga led them fairly quickly, and

Gird had a time keeping him in sight and avoiding obvious noisemakers. But his followers grew even quieter, as if they were listening for themselves, and learning from their own noise how to lessen it.

The double-click he had been half-waiting for startled him when it came. The others had frozen in place; Gird took a final step and a stick broke under his foot. He grimaced, and looked back along the line. Cob, behind him, grinned, wagged his head, and made the shame sign with his fingers. Gird shrugged and spread his hands. When he looked ahead, Triga had stopped just in sight. Gird could hear nothing now but the blood rushing in his own ears, and the faint trickle of water somewhere nearby.

The click had come from behind him, and now he saw a stirring in the line, silent movement as one man leaned to another and mouthed something. Gingerly, Gird took a step back toward Cob, placing his feet carefully on soggy leaves and moss. Cob leaned back to get the message, then forward to Gird.

"Ivis. Said we were a lot quieter, but should practice stopping. He may do it again."

Gird wished he'd thought of suggesting it, but at the same time wanted to clobber Ivis. His heart was still racing at the thought of being caught by foresters. He nodded, instead, and murmured "Tell him not too many—we have a long way to go." Cob nodded, and passed the message back. Gird waited what he thought was long enough for it to reach Ivis, then waved Triga on, and started again himself. He almost trod on the same stick, but managed to stretch his stride and avoid it.

Triga's swamp, when they came to it, appeared first as softer mud in the trail, and then a skim of sib-colored water gleaming between the leaves of some low-growing plant with tiny pink flowers. Ahead was an opening in the forest, with tussocks of grass growing out of the water.

"We have to turn here, if we're going around it," said Triga softly to Gird. The others had come up, but were squatting silently in the dripping undergrowth on the dryest patches they could find.

"Have you ever been out in it?"

"When I was a lad, once. There's someplace out there with plum trees; I could smell the flowers."

Gird sniffed. It was just past blooming time for the plums in his village, but wild plums came both earlier and later. He didn't smell any.

"Did you find the trees?"

"Finally—after I got wet to the thighs, and then when I got home my da beat me proper for running off from the goats—but there's a dry hummock somewhere, with plums."

"Right out in the middle, I'll bet," said Cob. "O' course, we're already wet."

"There used to be a path partway in," said Triga. "Follow me and step just where I do." And with that he was off again. The others fell into line.

Triga's way led alongside the bog, and finally came close enough so that Gird could see how big it was. Despite the drizzle and fog, he could just make out the forest on the other side, a dark massive shadow. In the bog itself were islands crowned with low trees tangled into thick mats. After a short time, Triga came out from under the trees, and stepped onto one of the tussocks. It trembled, but held him up as he took two steps and hopped to another. Gird looked at it distrustfully. How deep *was* that dark water? And what was under it?

"One at a time," he said, and reached a leg across to the black footprint Triga had left. He didn't like the way his foot sank in, and stepped quickly to the gap between tussocks. The mud sucked at his feet, and let go with a little plop. Across the gap, and onto another tussock. Now he was out in the open, where anyone could see him—anyone sitting snug under the forest edge, for instance. His neck prickled. One of Triga's footprints had a finger of murky water in it; when Gird stepped there, his foot sank to the ankle.

"I don't like this," said someone behind him, and someone else said "Shhh!" Their feet squelched on the wet ground, and Gird cursed silently as icy water oozed through his boot.

Only six of them had started into the bog, when the

first foothold gave way and Herf found himself hip deep in cold, gluey muck. He yelped; three gray birds Gird had not noticed fled into the air with noisy flapping of wings and wild screeches. Triga stopped and looked back, grinning. Gird said "Wait!" as softly as he thought Triga would hear.

They could not explain what happened without talking; Gird sweated, but endured the noise as best he could, while they established that yes, Herf had stepped carefully in the now-sinking footprint, and yes, all the footprints had been getting wetter, and no, it was clear that nobody else could make it. Herf, sprawled across the tussock with one leg stuck in the mud, was grimly silent.

"All right," Gird said finally. "First we get Herf out, and back on solid ground. Then all of you in the forest start circling the bog, and looking for other ways in. Don't get stuck."

"Don't walk on moss," Triga added. "It looks solid, but it won't hold you up."

"We can't come back the way we came in," Gird went on. "So Triga will have to find us a way across. And now we know that a group trying to follow us would bog down—"

"Although the tracks are easy to see," said Cob.

"Right. If we use this, we need a way in that we can all take, and that they can't see."

Getting Herf loose was no easy matter, and involved five men getting themselves wetter and muckier than they had intended. Two more got stuck, although not as badly.

In the meantime, Gird and the others perched on tussocks noticed that water was creeping up around their feet. "We have to keep moving," Triga said, unnecessarily, and went on, aiming for one of the brush-covered islands. By the time all of them had made it there, to crouch under the thick tangle of limbs and new leaves, they were mud to the knees and breathless.

"I didn't know it would be worse with more than one," said Triga. Gird accepted that as an apology, and nodded. At least some of the little trees were plums, tiny fruits just swelling on the ends of their stems. Water dripped on him, sending an icy trickle down the back of his neck and along his spine. He hoped his raincape was keeping the grain and beans dry. If he had to be wet and cold, it should be for a good purpose.

"We'd better go on," he said. "And if there's a way for each of us to pick his way safely—that might be better than stepping in your tracks."

"It's that kind of grass." Triga showed them again. "Not that other, with the thinner blades; it grows on half-sunk moss, and you can go right through. This stuff is usually half-solid, but you have to keep moving. Try to pick your way several tussocks ahead, so you don't have to stop except at places where trees grow. All those are safe. I think."

"Look at this," Cob said. He pointed to a delicate purple flower on a thin stalk. "I never saw anything like that."

"They grow in bogs," Triga said. "A little later, the whole bog will be pink with a different flower—the same kind, but larger. The purple ones grow only on the islands."

Gird looked at him. This sounded less and less like the knowledge gained on one clandestine visit as a child. Triga reddened.

"No one could find me here," he said. "I used to come here a lot, before I left home."

"And not after?"

"The others didn't want to see a swamp, they said."

"Well, we're seeing it now. What else do you know about it?"

Triga began to lead them across the little island to the bog on the far side. "There aren't many fish, for all this water. Lots of frogs, though, and little slick things like lizards, but wet. Birds—different kinds you don't see anywhere else. Some of them swim in the bits of open water, and dive. Most of them wade, and eat frogs and flies. Flowers. One island has a wild apple grove, and one has the best brambleberries I've ever eaten. Wild animals: something like a levet that swims, long and sleek, and levets, of course. Rabbits sometimes—

I've surprised them grazing the grass on the islands. Deer come to the edge to drink and once I saw one where the apples grow. They jump very fast and carefully."

They began to cross to the next island, this time picking individual ways, with much lurching and staggering. But no one fell in the mud, and they all arrived safely and somewhat drier, but for the rain. This island had fewer trees, and starry blue flowers as well as the tall purple ones.

"In midwinter," Triga said, as if someone had asked, "the bog may freeze on top, but you still can't trust the moss. If the ice is thick enough to walk on, then it's safe, but not otherwise. Most years it freezes that hard after Midwinter. But the thaw comes early—I don't know why—and I've put a leg through the ice more than once."

This time they did not pause, but went on across the island and back onto the bog. Gird lurched and barely kept himself from falling into the muck.

"I'm thinking this might make a better farm than a castle," he said.

"Farm?" Triga glanced back at him, teetered, and regained his balance.

"Plums, apples, brambleberries, all guarded by this muck. I'd wager that in full summer the flies are fierce."

"So they are. The worst of them aren't out yet, the big deerflies."

"Onions would grow on the edges; redroots on the islands."

"Some of these grasses have edible seeds," Triga said. "My mother's father, he showed me some of 'em. As much grain as wheat, almost. That's what the birds come for, the swimmers."

Gird was about to ask how the swimmers could find space to swim, when they came to a stretch of open water. Under the dark sky, with the drizzle falling, it was impossible to tell how deep it was. "Now what?"

"We've gone too far down. Turn up this way, upstream."

Gird could not see any movement in the water; it lay blank and still, dimpled like hammered pewter by the falling rain. Grunting, he followed Triga to the right, trying to pick his way. Eventually that space of water narrowed, and narrowed again, until he could leap across to a tussock that lurched under him. He grabbed the tallest stalks, and managed not to fall. Something hit the water with a loud plop behind him; he broke into a sweat again.

"Frog," said Triga. "Big one—he'd be a good dinner."

"You eat *frogs*?"

"What's wrong with that? They're good."

Gird shuddered, and tried to hide it. That was the explanation for Triga's attitude, he was sure. Anyone who would eat frogs would naturally be quarrelsome and difficult. "They're . . . cold. Slimy." He remembered very well the little well-frog he'd caught as a boy: the slickness, the smell, the great gold eyes that looked so impossible. His father had shown him frogspawn down in the creek, and he'd prodded it with a curious finger. It had felt disgusting.

Triga shrugged, looking sulky again. "It's better than going hungry. Food's food." He gave Gird a challenging look. "I ate snakes, too." Gird's belly turned. What could you say to someone who ate snakes and frogs?

"You eat fish, don't you?" asked Triga, pursuing this subject with vigor.

"I had a fish once." Gird remembered the bite or two of fish that he had eaten on his one trip to the trade fair as a youth. They had bought a fish, all of them together, and tried to cook it over their open fire. He could barely remember how it had tasted, though the smell was clear enough. It hadn't been as filling as mutton. He met Triga's expression with a grin. "The fish in our creek were about a finger long—the little boys caught them, but no one ate them."

From the looks on the others' faces, Triga's revelations about fish, frogs, and snakes were explaining his behavior to them as well. As if he'd realized that, he led them on faster, landing with juicy splashes on his chosen tussocks. Gird followed at his own pace, carefully. Snakes, too. There might be snakes out here, worse snakes than the striped snakes that wove through the stems of the grain, or the speckled snakes by the creek. He wanted to ask Triga how big the snakes in the bog could be, but he didn't want to admit he didn't know. Did they swim?

A sweet perfume broke through his concern about snakes, and he realized they were almost to an island whose scrubby gnarled trees were covered with pale-pink blossoms. Apples. Gird drank in the delicious scent, so different from the rank sourness of the bog itself, or the faintly bitter scent of the purple flowers. He climbed onto the rounded hump of solid ground with relief. Triga had thrown himself flat on dripping grass, and seemed back in a good humor; he smiled as Gird and the others crawled under low, snagging limbs to join him.

"This was always my favorite," he said. "Wild apples here, and crabs at the far end, two of them."

Gird crouched beside him. "What I don't understand is what made the islands. Why isn't the bog all bog?"

Triga shrugged. "I don't know. The way each island has its own trees and flowers, it's almost like a garden—as if someone planted them that way. But who or why I have no idea."

"Are any of the islands large enough for a camp?"

"No—probably not. I thought so, but now I see just six of us on one of them, I realize they're too small. The biggest has nut trees—not as tall as most nut trees—that would give good cover around the edge. But I think even twenty of us would crowd it. Certainly if you're going to be finicky about the jacks. Out here I always perched over open water."

The drizzle had stopped, but the apple limbs still dripped cold water on them. Gird looked out between the twisted trunks and caught a gleam of brighter light glinting from water and wet grass. It reminded him of something. He sat quiet, letting the memory come . . . he'd been crouched under another thicket, another time . . . dawn, it was . . . and the shadow had come, the thing that claimed kinship with the elder singers, but claimed also to be different. Kuaknom, it had been. Gird looked across the wet and dripping bog, now slicked with silver as the sun broke through for a moment. There across the uneven wet mat of moss and grass was an island, its trees like miniatures of the forest, bright flowers shining along its shore.

"I know who planted this," he said. It had come to him, with the beauty of the moment, the glittering, brilliant colors outlined in silver light.

"Who?" asked Triga.

"The singers. The old ones." He shivered as he said it. Was it bad luck to name them? Would it bring the illwishers here?

"You know *them*?" asked Triga, sitting bolt upright.

"No . . . no, but I know the tales. And I met one of their—the ones that went wrong, the kuaknomi."

"Gods take the bane!" Triga flicked his fingers twice, throwing the name away. "Don't speak of them!"

"But the others. I know they did. A garden, you said, each island like its own bed of flowers or fruit. I don't really like it, Triga, but it's very beautiful."

"Even the frogs?"

"Even the frogs."

The sun vanished again behind low clouds, and by the time they reached the far side of the bog, a light rain was falling. Cob scraped the muck from his worn boots with a handful of moss.

"I never thought I'd be so glad to find a muddy trail in a forest," he said. "And now we have to walk all the way back around to get home."

Gird gave him a warning look, and he was quiet. They all were, listening to the many sounds of the rain, the almost musical tinkling of the drops of water in the bog, the soft rush of it in the leaves overhead, the plips and plops of larger drops falling to the forest floor. Where, Gird wondered, was the rest of his troop?

Rock clicked on rock somewhere in the wet distance. One click. What was that? Gird peered around, seeing nothing but wet leaves and treetrunks. His heart began to pound heavily. He blinked rain off his eyelashes, and wished fervently that he'd let the damned grain rot, and taken his leather cape along. Then at least he wouldn't have rain crawling through his hair, trickling down his neck. He didn't mind arms and legs; he was used to being wet—but not his *head*. From the expressions the others had, none of them liked it. Hats, he thought to himself. We have to make hats, somehow. Every summer the women had plaited grass hats that lasted the season; they threw them away after harvest.

"Were we quiet enough?"

Gird leaped up and barely stopped the bellow that tried to fight its way from his throat. Ivis was grinning at him, along with the rest of the men who had gone around the bog. Rage clouded his vision for a moment as his heart raced. He felt he would explode. They were all watching, with the wary but smug look of villagers who have just outwitted a stranger. Another cluster of raindrops landed on his head, cold as ever, and it was suddenly funny. They *had* outwitted him, as fair as any trick he'd ever seen.

"You—" he began, growling over the laughter that was coming despite his rage. "Yes, damn you, you were quiet enough." A chuckle broke loose, then another. "Now let's see how quietly you can march home, eh?"

They were not as quiet, for the rainy spring evening began to close in fast, and they had to hurry. When they came to the clearing, Gird was glad he'd told Pidi to stay and mind the fire; they all needed to crowd near the glowing coals. Pidi had cooked beans, flavored slightly with the herbs he'd gathered.

Next morning was damp and foggy, but not actively raining. Gird woke stiff and aching, with a raw throat. Around him, the others were still sleeping, Pidi with the boneless grace of all small children. Gird pushed himself up, cursing silently, and crouched by the firepit. He held out a hand to the banked fire—still warmth within. But dry fuel? He peered around in the dimness. Someone—Pidi, he supposed—had made a crude shelter of stone, and laid sticks in it. They might be drier than the rest. He poked the fire cautiously with one of them, uncovering raw red coals. After a moment, the end of the stick flared. Dry enough. He yawned until his jaw cracked, then coughed as the raw air hit his sore throat. Sleeping wet in wet clothes—he hadn't done that for years. He'd never enjoyed it.

Alone in the early morning gloom, he let himself sag into sour resentment. Forget the hot sib. What he needed was a good stout mug of ale. Two mugs. Maybe they could build barrels and brew? No, first they had to have a dry place to sleep. A drop of cold water hit his bald spot. No, first they had to have hats. He added more sticks to the fire. Some of them steamed, hissing, but enough were dry to waken crackling flames. Someone across the clearing groaned, then coughed.

"Lady's grace, I hurt all over," he heard someone say. He felt better. If he wasn't the only one, it didn't mean he was too old for this. Another groan, more coughs. "I'd give anything for a mug of ale," said another man. "Sib," said someone else. "Anything but beans or soaked wheat," said yet another. Gird felt much better. The soldiers had grumbled in the barracks, when he was a recruit. They'd grumbled when it rained and they had to work in it; they'd grumbled when it was hot and sweat rolled out from under their helmets. Grumbling was normal. He was normal. And he knew exactly what the sergeant had done about grumbling.

"Time to get up," he said briskly.

A startled silence. A low mutter: "Gods above, *he's* up. He's got the fire going." He heard more stirrings, and turned to see men sitting up, clambering to their feet, rolling over to come up on one elbow. He grinned at them.

"Can't fight a war in bed," he said. Utter disbelief in some faces, amused resignation in others. Pidi, who had not walked to the bog and back, came over to the fire, all bright eyes and eagerness.

"I found most of the roots and barks for sib." He showed Gird a small pile which Gird would not have recognized. "There's no kira in sight of camp, and you told me not to leave—"

"Good for you," said Gird. "Do you know how much of each?" *He* certainly didn't. Pidi nodded.

"But it takes a long time. Do you want me to start it?"

"Go ahead. We need it."

While Pidi started the sib, Gird went off to the new jacks trench, along with several others. Already the camp smelled better, he thought. Certainly the men looked better, even grumpy and stiff as they were. That hike in the rain had accomplished something.

"We need to set up work groups," Gird said without preamble, as they gathered near the fire. "A hand to each group—" They began shuffling themselves into clusters of five. Gird had thought of assigning them to groups, but decided to let them pick their partners—for now, at least. With his knife, he shaped chunks of bark peeling from a fallen limb into the familiar tallies of the farmer. "One notch for food, two for tools, three for camp chores. Two groups get a food tally, and one hand each for the others. We'll drill after breakfast, then the groups go to their assignments—"

"What's food for?" asked Triga. "We're the ones get to eat?" No one laughed. Gird shook his head.

"Those with a food tally go looking for food: hunt, gather herbs, tend the things we plant, later. Ivis, how did food donated by farmers come to you? Did someone tell you it was there, or did you go ask?"

"Every so often someone would come to the wood, and leave a feathered stick in a certain tree—that's for Whitetree, the nearest. Fireoak usually brought the food itself, put it just inside the wood. Diamod traveled about so much, he'd know, or he'd see it and bring it in, or come get us to carry it. And sometimes, when things were very bad, one of us'd sneak into the village and beg."

"Which is dangerous for them and for us both. And I suppose too much hunting would bring the foresters, wouldn't it?"

"Aye. They don't mind rabbits and hares and such, but the duke likes his deer hunts."

"Well, we'll have to do something. Fori's good with his sling, and he can set snares: that's something you can all learn. We need a better way to let the villagers know when we need something, and what it is. With a few more tools, we might be able to gather more food and lean on them less." Gird handed the first food tally to the group Ivis was with. "You know the local village; you've got kin there. Find out what they can send, and when. What is the most trouble to them. When they've had trouble, and what gave them away. If they can't send food, find out if they can send sacks, boxes, a bucket—anything we can use to store or prepare the food we have. Even little things: a small sack is better than none."

"The other food tally." Gird handed it to the group Fori was with. "Go some distance away from this camp, and then look for anything edible you can find. Birds' eggs, birds in the nest, rabbits, squirrels—most creatures are having young about now; look for their hiding places."

"Frogs?" Triga was not in that group, but he spoke up anyway.

"When you're carrying the food tally, you can catch us frogs, Triga," Gird said.

"And you'll eat them?"

Gird swallowed hard. "I'll do my best. Now—you *are* with the tool tally. You all know we need a lot of things we don't have. Another shovel, axes, chisels. A shepherd's crook would be handy for pulling down vines with edible berries; a drover's stick for beating nuts from the nut trees next fall. We need pots to cook in, bowls to eat from, baskets or sacks to carry what our gatherers find, spoons, buckets, rope: every one of these will help us make more of what we need. Whoever holds the tool tally will work for that day on one of the things we need."

"I can make baskets," Triga said. Everyone stared at him; usually women made baskets. He reddened. "I used to plait the grasses in the bog," he said. "First just for something to do, and then to see what I could make."

"Could you make a basket from anything around here?" asked Gird. He did not want to make another trek to the bog so soon.

Triga stared around, uncertain. "Maybe . . . I can try . . . but it may not work right the first time."

"That's all right. If you find a way, it's time well spent. Any of the rest of you like to whittle?" One man raised his hand. "Good—why don't you start whittling some spoons, and bowls if you find the right chunks of wood. You others try it—anything's better than nothing."

"What about the guard we send out to listen for foresters?" asked Ivis.

"From the last group, those with camp chores tally. Two go out, and three will have plenty to do here. Gathering wood for the fire, tending the fire, and some other things I've thought up. But first—we didn't do any drill yesterday, so let's line up."

This time they lined up quickly and almost evenly. They all started on the same foot, and they marched almost in step from the firepit to the stream, still in lines. Wavery lines, but lines. Gird showed them how to turn in place to the right and left, and then had them march around the camp as a column of twos. They had to weave in and out of trees, and they were soon out of step, but the pairs did manage to stay side by side. By this time Gird was warm and had worked the stiffness out, so he sent the two groups with food tallies off, and picked two guards from the camp chores group. One of the remaining three he sent in search of the driest wood he could find, one sat by the fire, and Gird beckoned to the last.

He had had the idea that they could weave lengths of wattle, as he'd used for the barton gate, and the fence between his smallgarden and his neighbor's. Wattle laid at an angle against a log might give some protection from wet. He explained what he had in mind to Artha, a very tall, loose-jointed man nearly bald on top. Artha had vague, hazy blue eyes, and the least initiative Gird had seen.

"But I don't—that wattle, now, we allus made it wi' the sticks i' the ground, like. Put the sticks down in the wet mud, my granda he said, and then put the vines through, back and forth, back and forth—"

"But the sticks don't *have* to be in the ground," Gird said. The times he'd mended his gate, without ever taking it down, he knew that. Artha stood slack-handed, his jaw hanging. Gird realized that this was going to take firmness, as if Artha had been a child. "Artha, bring me some sticks, about so long—" He spread his arms to show the length.

"All right, but I dunno how you'll do it lessen you put them sticks in the mud first—"

"Never mind, just bring me the sticks." Artha ambled off, and Gird searched up and down the streambank until he found a willow sprouting multiply from the muck. He cut the pliant sprouts and stacked them.

By midday, Gird looked around the busy campsite and smiled to himself. The voices he heard all sounded content; one man was even whistling "Nutting in the Woods." His sergeant and his father had both been right: idleness was a fool's delight, and work brought its own happiness. Triga had created one lopsided basket from the same willow sprouts Gird was using, and then torn it down to make it "right" as he said. Now he was halfway through again. It didn't look quite like any basket Gird had seen, but it was going to be a useful size, he could tell. The man who liked to whittle— Kerin, that was—had turned out three recognizable spoons. He'd pointed out that he needed something to rub them with, to finish them, and one of the others had experimented with Gird's collection of cobbles. Gird and Artha had made one length of wattle, not quite an armspan wide by twice that in length. Gird held it up to the light: it would no more keep water out than a basket, he thought. But it would support something *else*. Leaves? A deerhide?

Late afternoon brought the food gatherers back. First came the hunting and gathering group, with a miscellany of edibles. Birds' eggs from different kinds of nests: small, round and beige, pointy and blue with speckles, streaked with brown on beige. They'd found a rabbit's burrow, and while the blind, squirming kits had been very small, there were eight of them. Fori had knocked another squirrel out of a tree, and they'd found a squirrel nest—but that led to near disaster, when Fori, precariously wrapped around the slender bole, had met a furious mother squirrel face to face. Fori had come down faster than he went up, losing skin off his arms. "But I have a nose, still," he said. They had also, on the advice of one of the others, dug up the roots of the thick-leaved grasslike plants that grew along the stream lower down. One man had the bight of his shirt full of last fall's nuts: some were rotting or sprouting, but some were still whole and sweet.

Ivis's group had come back with little food, but other important treasures. "Gars says he never used his granda's old stone tools—even his granda didn't—but look—" and he emptied a well-worn, greasy leather sack. Gird looked at the odd-shaped bits of stone curiously. He could remember seeing clutter like that in someone's cottage . . . and old Hokka had used a sickle set with tiny stone blades. But he'd never used stone tools himself. "They're sharp," Ivis said, as if he'd asked. "Gars thinks some of them had handles—wooden handles—but I don't know how they'd fasten. But you can cut with them." Some were obviously blades, thin shards of stone like broken pottery. Others were rough lumps with a sharp edge, like handax heads, or chisels. Kerin poked at them.

"I could use these . . . it would be easier to make a bowl with this than a knife . . ." Gird nodded; that got him off the hook.

"Fine—try them, and if you can teach someone else—" He turned to thank Ivis, but Ivis was still grinning.

"That's not all. Look here—" Wrapped in a wet cloth, he had brought seedlings of the common greenleaves: cabbage, lettuce. . . . The villagers had liked the idea of the outlaws growing some of their own food, and he'd been given as much as he could carry without crushing it. One of the men carried a small round cheese, and another had a large lump of tallow. He had also thought to ask for things Gird hadn't mentioned: beeswax, soap, thread. "Best of all—" Ivis nodded at the last member of his team, who pulled a bundle from under his shirt. It was cloth, something rolled into a lump—but the deepest, most intense blue Gird had ever seen.

"What is *that*?" he asked.

Ivis grinned. "You know the lords won't let us have blue clothes—"

"Yes. I never saw any."

"This is old, from my grandda's time. He used to say that the blue was expensive—it came from some kind of blue stone, from far away north—but before the lords came it was a favorite color. Good luck color. Anyway, my brother says if you're serious about overturning the lords, best we'd have some blue shirts."

Gird unfolded the bundle carefully. Two blue shirts, each decorated with intricate embroidery around the neck, flowers and grain in brilliant colors. The old woolen cloth was as sound as ever. "Where had they kept this? Not even a moth hole . . ."

"I don't know. My brother's the eldest; he knew about it and I didn't. But I do remember my grandda's stories. What do you think?"

"I think it's good luck," said Gird, refolding the shirts carefully.

Chapter Twelve

On a bright, blustery day in early summer, Gird led his troop eastward through the wood. There were twenty-four of them now, and every one of them carried his own spoon and bowl as well as his own belt knife. Each had a hat, plaited of grass and oiled against rain, and a staff about his own height. Each had three flat hard loaves of bread tucked into his shirt. And they marched quietly through the wood, with Diamod scouting ahead, and Triga bringing up the rear.

They were on their way to meet another of the Stone Circle groups two days away; Diamod (as usual) made contact. Behind them, the forester's campsite was clean and bare; they had moved all their gear some days back to another site Gird had found. Gird found himself about to whistle, and didn't. They were all doing well, including the new ones. He'd been surprised when three more came from his old village: a friend of Fori's, Teris's son Orta, and Siga, a single man about ten years Gird's junior.

They had told him all the latest news: how the steward had come to Gird's cottage only to find it stripped to the bare walls. He had taken that for Gird's impudence, but the villagers had done it, hiding every pot, tool, and bit of cloth. Gird had felt tears burning his eyes when the boys showed what they brought—his people, his neighbors, had cared that much, to risk themselves to save his things, and then to send their sons with it. Irreplaceable treasure indeed: two hammers, three chisels, his awl and his axe, a shovel blade, a spokeshave, a plane, a kettle, a longhandled metal spoon, firetongs, the cowhides that had been stretched across the bedframes, a furl of cloth that still showed rusty bloodstains . . . "We couldn't carry it all," Orta had explained. "But if you go back, or send someone, there's more."

His eyes still burned, thinking of it. He blinked the tears away, and told himself to keep his mind on the journey.

Part of that involved watching out for forage along the way. They had all learned, since he came, to make use of whatever food came along. Gird had even eaten one of Triga's frogs; he was sure it wriggled in his throat, but he had to admit it tasted like food. More or less. Some of the others refused, but most followed his lead. He still didn't like frogs for dinner, but better that than hunger. Now he scanned the undergrowth on either side for edible berries and fruits, herbs and mushrooms. Fori, still the best slinger in the troop, would be watching the trees for squirrels or levets.

Gird wished it had been possible to leave Pidi with someone. The boy was too young for this, he told himself again—but then again, the boy was not as young as he might be. The black eye had faded, leaving only a faint dark stain beneath, but the little child he had been, thoughtless and carefree, had not come back. Pidi seemed happy enough—he laughed sometimes, and scampered through the woods like a young goat—but he would never be carefree. It would have happened in time, Gird knew, but—he shook that thought away. There was no safe place for Pidi. Home had not been safe. That led him to Rahi, and the black sorrow pierced him again. She had lost the child, in fever, and when he'd last heard, a few days ago, she was still too weak to get up.

A gust of wind roared by overhead, whipping the forest canopy and letting a flash of sunlight through. *The Windsteed in spring seeks the far-ranging Mare . . .* he thought, clicking his tongue in the rhythm of the chant. This was late for the Windsteed's forays, but what else could it be? He accepted the omen, and let the wind blow away his dark thoughts. It never paid to argue with the gods, any of them.

That night he insisted that their temporary campsite be set up as neatly as the old one. No one argued. Fori lopped a sapling to make a handle for the shovel blade, tied it snugly, and began digging the jacks trench. They would have no fire, but they ate their beans (cooked the night before) from bowls, with spoons. Even plain beans tasted better that way, not scooped up with fingers. Almost before he said anything, the correct tally group had gathered up bowls and spoons to wash them in the creek by the camp; when they were done, everyone stripped down and bathed.

The full measure of what he had accomplished became obvious when they met the other Stone Circle group the next afternoon. They had come out of the wood, and angled between some brush-covered hills, and down a crooked stream bed. The other group had a guard out to meet them—that much Gird could approve—but they could smell the camp long before it came in sight. He noticed that his men wrinkled their noses as well. He had not intended to bring them in as a formal drill, but they began to fall in step, rearranging themselves into a column.

They came into a space set off by a rocky bluff on one side, and house-high thickets of pickoak on the others, to find unkempt men lounging around a smoking fire.

Someone had stretched a line between two trees, from which flapped something intended as laundry, but Gird could not recognize one whole garment. His own troop fairly strutted into the clearing, and came to a smart halt without the command he forgot to give. The others stared at them, wide-eyed as cattle staring over a gate. The one who seemed to be the leader, a redhaired man whose sunburnt nose was peeling, stared as hard as any. Then he got up from his log.

"I don't believe it. Diamod, you said these were farmers?"

Diamod smirked. "I said these were farmers who had learned soldiering. Was I right?"

"You—and *you* must be Gird." The man came forward, looking Gird over with interest.

"I'm Gird, yes."

"And you were a soldier?"

"Years ago I was a recruit. Then a farmer. Now—what you see."

The man looked along the column, and swallowed. "What I see is hard to believe. How long have you been training them?"

Gird squinted, thinking. "Since late-plowing time. I was finishing plowing the day it happened."

"I didn't tell him *everything*," Diamod interrupted.

"And you did that much that fast. Can you teach us?"

"I might, aye. But there's more than just marching in step."

"Swordfighting, of course. Or do you use spears?"

Gird laughed. "We don't use swords or spears—where would we get them?"

The man's face fell. "But—what do you fight with? Not just sticks, surely."

He had not intended this kind of entrance, or a display of the other things he'd been teaching his men, but this was a chance he could not overlook.

"Aruk!" he said. Behind him, twenty-four sticks came up, to be held stiffly in front of each man. Gird took a step forward, clearing the necessary space, and said, "Form—troop." This was tricky; they'd only been doing it right a few days, and it looked anything but soldierly if someone forgot. Properly, it took them from a column to the parade formation in smart steps and turns, each pair coming forward and spreading to the sides. It might have been wiser to simply face the column right or left and pretend that was the same maneuver—but if this worked, it was far more impressive. He did not look around; he wanted to see how these others reacted. From the even tramp behind him, and the heavy breathing, they were doing it right. From the faces in front of him, it looked professional.

Now he turned, as neatly as he could, and looked at his troop. They had all made it into place, still with sticks held vertically before them. Now came the interesting part. He gave the commands crisply, and the sticks rotated: left, right, horizontal, vertical, all moving together in an intricate dance of wood. No one was off-count today; he was proud of them.

"But—" the redhaired man said. Gird spun around to him.

"You fight with a sword?"

"Not very well yet, but—"

"These sticks are longer than swords. You can't fence against a sword, no, but you can poke with it—just as you'd poke cattle through a gap. D'you think soldiers are harder to move than cattle, if you hit them right?"

"Well—no. But I thought—"

"If you want to learn from me—what's your name, anyway?"

"Felis."

"Felis, if you want to learn from me, the first thing is to clean up this stinking camp!" He had not quite meant to be that rude, but a gust of wind brought the foulness thick into his lungs.

"But what's that got to do with—"

"Yes or no."

"Well, yes, but—"

Gird glared around at the men in the camp, most of whom were sitting up more alertly now, sensing a fight coming. Two were not; they lay against the rock face, with another crouched beside them.

"What's wrong with them?" Gird asked, pointing.

Felis glanced that way, then shrugged. "Sim has some kind of fever, and Pirin has the flux—"

"And you ask why the stink matters! Didn't you have jacks where you came from? Didn't the grannies teach you about any of that?"

Felis flushed dark red. "We don't have any tools, hardly, and it's not so easy out here away from the towns—"

Gird snorted. He felt good, the righteous anger running in his veins like stout ale at harvest. "You thought soldiering was easy? You thought fighting a war was going to be easy?" His sergeant had said something like that more than once—he had the rhythm right, anyway. Felis glared at him, but said nothing. Gird went on. "You ask any of these men—Ivis, or Diamod—if *we* had more than this when I started. You ask them if someone can smell our camp from as far away."

Some of the men were standing now, coming forward slowly. Gird could not tell if they came in support of their leader, or from curiosity. Felis looked around, seeking support.

"There's no way—we don't have good ground here, for digging jacks and such. It's hard enough to find enough to eat, and—"

A taller man intervened. "So what would you do, stranger, if you had command here? Or is it all talk?"

Gird raised his brows ostentatiously. "Do you want us to show you? Or had you rather live like this?"

"Show us!" Felis spat. "Go ahead—let's see what you can do."

"Your people must help," Gird said. Felis shrugged. "I won't make them. You can try."

"You're giving me command?" There was a moment's absolute silence, on everyone's indrawn breath. Felis paled; his jaw clenched. Then he spread his hands.

"For one day, for what you can do. I'll be interested. Of course, we've nothing to share for supper." Gird was sure that was a lie, but he smiled.

"We brought our own, and enough for return," he said. Then he turned his back on Felis, taking that chance, and dismissed his own men "—to your tally groups."

Raising his voice to reach all the men in the camp, he said, "You have two bad problems. The first is your jacks, which is making you sick with its filth. No need to ask where it isn't—but you need a good deep trench far away from the creek."

"The ground's all rocky hereabout," said the tall man. "We can't dig it with our fingernails."

"Fori." Gird put out his hand, and Fori handed him the shovel blade. "Here's a shovel, if you can put a handle to it. Anyone here can cut a pole, or—"

"I'll cut a pole," said the tall man. He turned on his heel and stalked off. Gird watched him for a moment, then went on.

"What do you have to carry things in?" he asked the group at large. After a moment's silence, someone pointed to the kettle on the fire, and a large wooden bowl. Gird smiled at them. "That's more than we had," he said. "We had no kettle. But we don't dirty a kettle with filth. Triga, I'll want some baskets. Any of you men know how to make a basket?"

"A *man* make baskets?" asked one with a low whistle. Gird put out his hand to stop Triga (and Triga's arm was there—predictable as always) and said "Don't laugh; Triga's a good enough soldier to know that supplies help win wars. Learn from him; we need baskets to haul that stinking waste into the hole you—" He nodded at the tall man who had cut his pole and was bringing it back, "—are going to dig for it."

"I'm not moving any of that filth!" snarled someone across the firepit. Gird heard mutters of agreement, and the amused chuckles of his own men.

"Move the filth, or move yourselves," Gird said. "It's killing you—and you know it."

"That's not all," came Ivis's voice from behind him, "he'll have you bathing, and if you get a cut, he makes you scrub it out with soaproot. Besides, nobody wants to eat in this stench. Just get rid of it."

Gird grinned at his people, and walked over to the firepit. The kettle on it gave off a thin steam, but he could not tell what was in it. The overall stink was too strong. "What is it?" he asked the man tending the fire.

"Grain mush. It's been grain mush for months, 'cept when someone snares a rabbit, or finds a berry patch."

"No bread?"

The man squinted up at him. "You a housewife? I never learned to make bread. Besides, it takes things we don't have."

"You'll get them." Gird patted the man's shoulder, and left him peering backwards, stirring ashes instead of the fire.

Now for the sick men. He knew he'd been lucky that none of his own troop had sickened yet. Although he'd tried to nurse his mother and Mali, he knew very little of the healing arts. Cleanliness, of course—everyone knew that the fever spirits thrived on foul smells and dirt. They grew fat and multiplied on what made healthy men ill. It was nearly impossible to be clean enough to keep them all away (his mother had insisted that even a speck of old milk left in the bucket could feed enough spirits to ruin the next batch) but the cleaner the better.

The stench worsened as he neared the sick men. One of them had red fever patches on his cheeks; his breath was labored, almost wheezing. His eyes were shut, and he didn't pay any attention to Gird. The other, pale and sweating, had vomited; the man with him was wiping his face clean. Gird felt a tug at his sleeve, and turned. Pidi, almost as pale, had come up beside him.

"I picked some breakbone weed on the way—it might help for the fever. But I didn't bring any flannelweed."

"Boiling water," said Gird. "See if they have another pot, and be sure you get the water well upstream." Pidi went off, and Gird forced himself to squat down beside the sick men. The caretaker glared at him.

"Ya canna' do aught for 'em. This'n'll die by morning; feel his head." Gird reached out to the fevered man, whose forehead felt like a hot stone—dry. "And this'n, bar he stops heaving, he'll go in a day or two. He's lost all he can, below, and I can't get 'im to the jacks we got, let alone the jacks you say you'll dig."

"You know flannelweed?" Gird asked. The man shrugged.

"I'm no granny, with a parrion of herbs. What be you, man or woman?"

Gird took hold of his wrist, and squeezed until the bones grated; the man paled. "Man enough, if strength makes men. But I'd be glad of a woman's parrion of healing, if 'twould save lives. Have you sought a healer?"

"Aye. Felis brought one from the vill, a hand or more of days ago, when it was just Jamis here. But she was like you, all twinchy about the smell. Said we'd have to clean it up afore she could do aught. So's Felis told her what he told you, and she huffed off, about holding her nose."

Gird let go of the man's wrist, and picked up the rag sodden with vomit. "This'll do him no good here, but to make him heave again." He tossed it away, and turned back to the sick man, who was staring at him with the frantic look of a trapped animal. "If we can find flannelweed, and get you to a clean place—I'll try, at least." He made himself touch the man's hands, filthy as they were, and managed not to flinch when the man clutched at him.

"Please, sir—please—"

"I'll try." Gird looked at the sulky caretaker. "You can go clean up; I'll get my people to carry them."

"You're welcome to it." The man stalked away, clearly furious, rubbing the wrist Gird had bruised.

Gird looked around. Herf, in the tally group for camp chores, had picked up the stinking rag on a stick, and was carrying it toward the stream. He could hear the solid chunks of the shovel at work somewhere among the pickoaks. Ivis came up.

"Are you going to want to move them? I can have someone cut poles—"

"Yes, and I'll need a bucket of clean water, if you can find one. Does anyone but Pidi know flannelweed?"

"I'll ask. Those rags on the line aren't really clean, but they're cleaner than that—" Ivis pointed to the sodden rags under the two men.

"We'll need them, but not here. No sense in dirtying them now." Gird unhooked the sick man's fingers from his hand, one by one, and stood up. Pidi was coming back down the slope with a bucket of water—had he had to go all the way up to find clean? Triga, Gird saw, had a cluster of men around him—presumably he was making a basket and showing them how. Artha—who, Gird wondered, had told him?—was carefully scooping ash from the cool side of the firepit into a sack of some kind. The cook looked furious, but wasn't interfering.

Gird went to look at the stream, and shuddered. It looked as if hogs had wallowed in it, and it smelled worse. All along the banks, except at a crossing, were the uncovered remnants of a long encampment. Flies swarmed over them, rising in a cloud when he came near. Some of the filth had fallen into the stream and was far too wet to shift easily. It had been foul so long that rocks in the stream were slimed with luxuriant green weed, its brilliant color clear evidence of the steady supply of filth. It would be best to move the camp entirely, but he could not do that by himself.

"Gahhh." Diamod had come up behind him. "This is worse than I recall. But perhaps you've changed my nose for me."

"It's a damned shame," said Gird. He was angry again, but this time with a slow, steady anger that would burn for days. "It's hard enough to think of fighting the lords, with their soldiers and their weapons. We can't be fighting ourselves, too. There's no village this bad; these men came from better. They should know."

"So did we, but we didn't do it until you made us. Be fair, Gird, when you were a boy, did you do more than your father demanded? Or your sergeant?"

"I grew to a man," Gird said, growling, and forcing away the memory of his boyhood sulks. Had his mother really had to threaten beatings to get him to clean the milk pails? Had his father clouted him more than once for leaving muck on the tools? He sighed gustily. "True, I was the same way. But now—they're men, they should know better."

"Teach them, like you taught us."

"I wish I could move the camp. Now. This moment."

Diamod grinned. "Tomorrow, maybe: the way you're going, you could do that."

Gird stared moodily at the mess near his feet. "We can't move all this tonight. Ashes, I suppose for the rest." He turned and called Artha. "There may not be enough—but try to spread ashes on all of this. Upstream and down. Don't step in it."

"No, Gird."

On his way to see how the trench was coming, Gird passed Triga, who held up one of his "fast" baskets, a flat, scoop-shaped affair. "Gird, it might go faster if we had something like a hoe, to scrape the stuff right into the basket." A solution creating another problem, Gird thought, but one of the local men looked surprised and said "We have a hoe—course, it's just wood—"

"Fine," said Gird. "Triga, I don't think we can move it all tonight, but see what you can do with that." Triga nodded, not sulky at the moment. It had to be eating frogs, Gird thought, that made a man so touchy on some things so reasonable when given a problem to solve.

The steady thunk of the shovel led him to the trench diggers. The tall man who had cut the pole for the shovel handle was jabbing the dirt with another, pointed pole to loosen it for the man with the shovel. Four others—two of Gird's, and two locals, were picking out rocks ahead of the shovel. The trench was deep enough, and reasonably straight, but it would never hold the accumulation on the banks of the stream. This would do for current and future use.

"Fori—" Fori was on the shovel at that moment; he looked up. "We're going to need another hole for the old stuff. Not a trench; just a pit. Let's put it farther back in the wood, away from this." Fori nodded, and shouldered the shovel. The other men looked from Gird to Fori, and back to Gird. "Artha's got the ashes; I told him to go ahead and use them where they are, but he can get more."

"Does Triga have carriers yet?" asked Fori.

"Yes, and a hoe for scraping up." Gird glanced up at the sky; it wasn't long until sundown. "We can't finish tonight, but we can get a start on it."

The tall man leaned on his pole and looked at Gird. "You remind me of my da. He was always one for starting a job now."

Gird smiled. "I was just thinking of my own da." He turned away, sure that Fori could handle that little group by himself. By now, Pidi should have hot water—and he'd forgotten that he'd sent Ivis to find someone to find flannelweed. And where were the food tally groups?

Back in the clearing, he noticed a controlled activity. Pidi crouched over a bucket of steaming water, chatting with the local cook, who looked much less sulky. Felis, of all people, was gathering the dry rags off the line. Ivis, Cob, and Herf were crouched near the sick men; a stack of sticks had appeared by the firepit; and much of the clutter of the campsite was gone, replaced by clumps of gear that he suspected were not really organized. But it looked better, and he could walk across the open space without tripping over bits of wood and someone's rotted boot. His own men and the locals were moving about as if they had something to do and were doing it. The cook waved to him, and Gird veered toward the firepit.

"This boy says he's yours—right?"

"Right." Gird tousled Pidi's hair. "My youngest."

"You got nerve, dragging your boy along to a war."

Gird gave him a hard look. "I had no choice. They threw me out of my holding, because my daughter's husband tried to defend her—and I hit one of them—so did Pidi, for that matter, boy that he is."

"Oh. Your daughter—she died?"

Gird could feel his head beginning to pound; Pidi laid a hand on his arm, and he realized he'd made a fist. "No. She's alive, last I heard, but she lost the baby. And she may die. I don't know."

The man gulped, and looked away. "I'm sorry." After a pause, in which Gird tried to get his temper locked down again, he said, "The lad brought me herbs, for flavoring. Wild onions, too. Most lads don't know that."

"His mother and sister both had a parrion of herbcraft. Pidi learned quickly."

"This's not ready, Da, but it might help." Pidi pointed to the steaming bucket, in which Gird could now see leaves steeping. He sniffed the sharp-smelling steam.

"At least it smells good." He dipped some in his own

bowl, and took it over to the sick men. Now he'd have to remember not to eat from his bowl until he could wash it. But Ivis had found a wooden cup the fevered man had used. Gird poured the hot liquid into it carefully. Ivis and Cob had stripped off his clothes, and washed him with the clean water they'd brought. Gird had no idea what the fever was; the man had the sour smell of sickness, but nothing he could recognize.

"Will he rouse at all?"

Ivis shrugged. "He opened his eyes when we first touched him with the wet cloth, but said nothing."

Gird held the steaming cup under the man's nostrils; they twitched. "Let's lift him, and see if he'll drink."

Cob looked worried. "The healer in our village said if they're not awake, don't make them drink."

"Just a sip." Gird was sure the man was really dying, but felt he had to try. Ivis lifted him, and Gird held the cup to his lips. When he tried to pour a little in, it dribbled back out. Gird sighed. "Well. If he wakes, we can try again."

"Do you think he'll wake?"

"No. But I'm no healer; I could be wrong."

They turned to the other man. Gird helped Herf bathe him with clean water, and wrap him in the cleanest clothes they could find. Gird hated touching the man's clammy skin; it reminded him of tending Issa, who had been sick so often. They gave him a drink of clean water; he did not heave it up at once, so Gird felt more hopeful. He looked across the campsite, and saw Triga and someone else dragging loaded baskets away toward the pickoaks. Artha was back at the firepit, gathering more ashes.

"Do you think they would share our food?" asked Cob. That was what Gird had been thinking; he simply did not know.

"If they would, we'd have them in our troop before midnight," said Ivis, grinning. "I still think it was that first hearthcake, Gird, that settled your place in our camp."

Gird grinned back. "You were tougher than that. I thought it was Fori's squirrels. But you know the customs: if they eat our food, and we don't eat theirs, that's their obligation and our protection. And they've already said they won't share."

"Felis said it. Felis may be wishing he hadn't been so clever."

"We can offer." Gird stood up and headed for the firepit again. At this auspicious moment, one of his food tally groups returned, gleefully carrying the carcass of a young pig.

"If they won't share now," breathed Herf, "they're so crazy we don't want them."

"How did they get that?" muttered Gird. "They haven't been down robbing some farmer's pigsty, have they?" When the commotion died down, he learned that they'd come across a sounder of wild swine, feasting on mushrooms and old acorns under the pickoaks. One fell to a lucky shot by one of the slingers Fori had been trying to teach.

"I guess there were enough of us, so the most of them ran, and that one—it just knocked him flat, and then we landed on him, and slit his throat."

"And the others didn't come back. We were lucky." Gird looked at his smug foragers, spattered with blood and dirt, and then around at the locals, who looked as hungry as wolves.

"We caught him, but he lived in your wood," Gird said loud enough for all to hear. "We would share the feast."

The local men in the clearing looked at Felis, who spread his hands. "All right. But all we have is grain mush."

Gird breathed a sigh of relief. They *should* share food both ways; that made the obligations equal. "We would be glad to share freely, all we have with all you have." He would like to have insisted that all of them, locals and his men alike, clean up before eating, but with the stream so foul that was impossible. He called his troop together, while the cook and Diamod fashioned a spit for roasting the pig, and supervised the washing of hands in clean water. No one argued; they seemed almost proud to demonstrate their superior habits to the locals. That led to a flurry of handwashing by the locals as well, and Gird was content.

Soon the smell of roasting pig overcame the worst of the camp's stench. The cook caught the dripping juices off the pig, and stirred them into the mush, along with salt from Gird's pouch. By the time the pig was done, Gird's appetite had returned full force. With roast pig, mush, and the bread they'd brought, everyone had plenty to eat, and the conversations around the firepit were friendly. Then one of the locals got up and sauntered toward the creek.

"Use the new trench," said Gird. The man stopped.

"But it's dark. I couldn't find it."

"Cob, help him."

The man opened his mouth to complain and shut it again. Cob was up, with a brand from the fire. "This way," he said.

"But we always—" the man said, looking at Felis.

"Do it," Felis said. "They fed us our own pig; they can tell us where to put our own jacks."

Gird was up before dawn; the rank smell had gotten into his dreams, and he'd been pursued through dark tunnels by something with poison fangs and bad breath. His own men were curled up neatly enough under the edge of the pickoaks, where the smell was least. The locals were sprawled anyhow around the firepit. Gird went to the jacks, then picked his way to the firepit and poked up the fire. It was going to be a clear day, but dew had soaked the stones; he dared not sit down until they dried. He went to look at the sick men, and found that the fevered one had died in the night. The other was asleep, breathing easily. He put more wood on the fire, until it crackled, and then took a bucket and started upstream. On his way back, he met Fori with the other bucket.

"I thought this must be where you were," said Fori. "And I knew you'd want more good water."

"Another fifty paces up, there's a clean creek coming in from one side. I went up that to a pool—I think there's a spring under it."

"That's what Pidi said, when I asked him. Felis is asking for you."

"Is he?" Gird went back down, stepping carefully as the water tried to slosh out of the bucket. Felis would have waked with one of two plans, and Gird hoped the man had sense. He doubted it; anyone who couldn't stay out of his own mess could hardly be called sensible. Besides, it was never easy for a man to give up leadership.

Felis, however, had taken a third route Gird hadn't thought of. "I talked to everyone," he said, as soon as Gird came into the clearing. "They want to follow you. They think you know how to run an army." Gird set the bucket down by the firepit, and blinked. He hadn't expected Felis to ask the others himself, privately.

"What about you?" he asked.

Felis darkened with the easy blush of the redhead. "I wish I had done what you did," he said. "I wish I'd thought of all that. All I thought of was fighting itself—I kept trying to learn swordfighting—"

Gird met his gaze. "Do you want to learn my way, or go your own?"

"I'll stay, if you'll let me."

"You fooled me," Gird said. "I thought you'd be angry, and go away."

"I *am* angry," said Felis. "But you did it fairly, and not to make me angry. Did you?"

"No. At least—" remembering his own anger of the day before, "—at least, I didn't start that way. It seemed such a waste."

Felis's followers had been watching their conversation from a distance, furtively; when Gird and Felis smiled at each other and clapped hands, everyone relaxed.

That day was spent cleaning up the camp as best they could, while the new members learned how Gird's system worked. Supper was less a feast, for no lucky catch rewarded that day's hunters. But the camp stank less, and Pidi had given two draughts of flannelweed to the man with flux. He had not died, at least, and had not heaved all day.

"What now?" asked Felis, as they sat around the dying fire. "Are you going to drill us for a few hands of days, and then go take over another group?"

Gird yawned and stretched. He was very tired. "No," he said. "No, I have another plan. The Stone Circle must learn drill, and all the soldiering possible, but we'll never have enough outlaws to fight a war. We've got to have a way to train *everyone*. At home. While they farm, or make pots, or whatever it is they do."

"How?" asked Cob, beside him.

"Tomorrow," said Gird. "I'll explain it all tomorrow."

Chapter Thirteen

The newcomers, Gird discovered, had already grasped the idea of traveling quietly, with scouts ahead and behind. He led them back up the stream they had camped beside. The sick man looked as if he would definitely recover; they carried him in a pole-slung litter. All of them carried some piece of equipment, for Gird did not intend to return to that camp until it had had time to clean itself.

"I suppose you want us to dig a jacks trench every time we stop?" asked Felis.

"Yes." Gird was ready to glare, but Felis merely shook his head, and grinned. They were halted for a noon rest on the shady side of a hill, where the scrub grew barely more than head-high. Summer heat shimmered on the slopes around them, and baked pungent scents from the scrub.

"So will you tell us your plan now?"

Gird looked around at the others. They were all listening; he wondered how they would react. Was there a better time? He thought not. But instead of answering Felis directly, he asked, "How many men did you have when you started?"

Felis frowned thoughtfully. "I didn't start it—but

there were three hands when I came. Then Irin died, and then two more came, and then six, but one of them died soon; he'd been hurt. Three hands, four—it went up and down."

"And how many other groups are there, and how large do you think they are?"

Felis began tapping the ground, as if a map, to remind himself. "I heard of one away westward—beyond your village—Diamod went there once and said they had less than two hands of men. North and west, another, but I heard that one was captured and killed, all of them. Two hands, maybe three. South and east, someone told me of a large group: five or six hands of men, maybe more. But I heard they have fields, and can feed themselves."

Gird nodded. "That's what I thought. There may be more groups, but nowhere more than the farmers can support. We can't feed ourselves. So a day or two of travel between groups—each one drawing food from two or three villages—and the villages are so poor. Four hands is a large group; five is too large for most. And without proper care for the food they *do* get, some of it is wasted. Diamod told me several years ago there were enough in the Stone Circle to fight a war, but ten soldiers here and fifteen there and twenty over here don't make an army. They have to be together. Organized. Training together."

"But I don't see—"

"We need the Stone Circle: we need a place for men to go when they've been outlawed or have lost their holdings. But we need an army more. And we need an army that can feed itself during training, house itself during training, clothe itself—"

"It's impossible!"

"No, I don't think so." Gird let his eyes wander from face to face. "We were all farmers, craftsmen—we fed ourselves, housed ourselves—and in the evenings, off-season, we sat around our bartons or our homes and talked."

"Yes, and you yourself would have nothing to do with fighting when you still had your holding," said Diamod boldly.

"That's true, because you wanted me to sneak away and teach you drill—go away from my home, and my work, and risk discovery both ways, to teach strangers. I say now I was wrong. But what I told you then still has force. Suppose you had said, 'Let *us* teach *you* how to fight and defend yourselves—here in your own village, you and the men you know best fighting shoulder to shoulder to protect your own against the lords.' Do you think I might have answered differently?"

A long silence. Diamod opened his mouth and shut it. Felis pulled a grass stem, chewed it, and spat it out. The others said nothing, but all the faces conveyed shifting thoughts and emotions. Finally Triga said, "You mean for us to go into villages and teach farmers what you've taught us—by ourselves?"

"It won't work," said Herf suddenly. "It can't—the lords would see it, their guards would. Right under their noses, peasants drilling? They'd be hung on the spikes by nightfall."

"There aren't guards stationed in every village," said Ivis. "If they would have their own scouts out, to see anyone coming—"

"Better than that," said Gird. "Think how our villages are built. Every cottage, nearly, has its own—"

"Barton!" said Fori, eyes suddenly alight. "Walled in—no one can see, but over the back gate—"

"That's right," said Gird. "Bartons. Big enough to teach a few men to march together, use sticks. No one notices when the men go into a barton of an evening, or the noise that comes out of it—men telling jokes, drinking ale—" He could suddenly feel it, the mellow flow of liquid down his throat that would ease his joints and make the old stories new again.

Felis pursed his lips. "Not everyone in the village will do it—what about those who don't? What if they report it?"

"Start small. One or two, let the locals decide who else to ask. Nobody in my village would've reported it to the steward, though some wouldn't come. Let 'em stay home. And if the guards do come, what's to see? A group of men talking and singing, same as any evening."

On face after face, Gird could see the idea take root and grow. He watched its progress through the group. It would work; he knew it would work. It had come to him in a flash of insight so intense that it waked him out of a sound sleep. He had been planning to try it, but the attack on Rahi had come first.

"So: you train us, and we train them. Just those of us here could reach five, six hands of villages, and if every village trained four hands of men—"

"But would we try to move in with them? Someone would surely notice that—"

Gird nodded. "I know. I'm not sure what the best way is, but I'm sure that training the farmers at home is part of it." He stretched, relieved that they seemed to understand his point and agree. "But right now, each one of you must know everything *I* know—and be able to teach it. And if you know something I don't, you must teach me."

"You don't know everything?" asked Felis slyly.

"No. I didn't know how to plait baskets or cook frogs; Triga taught me that." Triga grinned and raised a fist. "We all share some knowledge—the farmers among us, at least. But many of us have special skills, something extra, which we can share with others."

By Midsummer Eve, Gird had both groups drilling with sticks. They camped apart, for he still could not feed both at once. One campsite lay just within the east side of the wood, and the other was near (but carefully not in) Triga's bog. But the flow of information, skills, and supplies went back and forth almost daily. They drilled apart three days, and came together on the fourth, to practice larger group movement outside the forest, on a grassy hillside.

Both camps had the clean, tidy look of a good master's workshop—and it was a workshop, as Gird explained often. If they had an army someday, of farmers who had trained in their bartons, they would have to have camps in the field, and those camps would have to have jacks, kitchens, shelters for wounded, space to store supplies. Here, in small groups, they could learn what worked, and later they could show others.

As summer days lengthened, the food-gathering groups were able to bring back more and more supplies. Gird insisted that some of these be stored for emergencies. They dried fruit on lattices of plaited grass, cut the wild grain and threshed it, dug edible tubers, honed their skill at slinging and throwing. Archery was harder. Of the four bows between the two groups, one had broken early, and it seemed no one could make good arrows. Still the best of them occasionally hit a bird or rabbit. Each camp had its own handmill, and when there was grain to grind, they had bread. Gird toyed with the idea of trying to brew some ale, but they really couldn't afford the grain. Maybe after harvesttime, he thought—next winter would be cold and dismal enough, without giving up ale entirely.

Gird rotated all the men through all the tally groups, but noticed which had special abilities. The whittlers, sure of an appreciative audience, worked even when not on actual tool duty, fashioning spoons and bowls, dippers and pothooks. Some of the men took to the old stone tools, and one liked to spend his spare time chipping new blades from flint cobbles. No one sneered, now, at those who could make useful baskets, or sew neat patches.

On Midsummer Eve, lacking ale, they drank the fresh juice of wild grapes and sat out under the stars, singing the old traditional songs. Like Midwinter, Midsummer was a fireless night, but this one was not dark and cold. In the freshness before Midsummer dawn, when every sweet scent of the earth redoubled its strength, Gird lay in the long grass and wished they could have women with them. The other men, too, were restless, remembering the traditional end to all those traditional songs, when the brief hours of darkness were spent first hunting the elusive flowers said to bloom only that night, and then celebrating them. Gird thought of his first night with Mali, of all the Midsummers he'd spent with her. A breath of air moved, wafting still more scent past him, and he rolled up on one elbow. She had been dead, and he had not gone back out, but now he was out, and he could not stop thinking about it.

Of course it would not do. He made himself get up and walk around the others, who pretended to be asleep. The two or three who were really asleep risked dangerous dreams, on Midsummer night. They snored, or muttered, and tossed uneasily. He did not wake them, walking farther away into the stillness. Dew lay heavy on the grass, gray-silver in the starlight, in the slow light of dawn that rose from the east in faintly colored waves.

Two days later, he had just come from the eastern camp, and was nearing the other, when Diamod met him on the trail.

"I have to tell you something," he said. Gird stopped. He had made a rule that they not talk on the trail, even when chance-met like this. But Diamod's expression declared this an emergency.

"What, then?"

"Your daughter Raheli—"

Gird's heart contracted; his vision hazed. "She's dead." Despite the two reports he had had, he had continued to worry, sure that she might yet die of her injuries or her sorrow. He had worked harder, to keep himself from thinking about it, but her face haunted him.

"No—she's come."

Relief and shock contended; he felt that the ground beneath him swayed. "Come? You mean—come *here*? They wouldn't keep her?"

"They would have been glad to keep her; she would not stay. She has come here, and she insists she is joining us."

"*No!*" That was loud enough to send birds squawking away in the forest canopy overhead, and loud enough for any forester to hear. Gird bit back another bellow and lowered his voice. "It's impossible. She can't—"

"You come tell her that. She followed me here from Fireoak—I didn't even know she was following until I reached the wood, and then I couldn't—I didn't think I should—send her back. Or that she'd go."

Rahi alive, and well enough to walk so far—that was as much as he'd hoped. More. He wanted to see her, hold her, know she was whole and strong again. He remembered the blood on her face, on her body. When he looked at Diamod, the man seemed to have understood his very thought, because he nodded slowly.

"Yes, she has a terrible scar, and no, she seems not to mind. She wore no headscarf. Something else, she's dressed like a man."

Gird shook his head, shrugged, could not think of anything to say. Most headstrong of his children—how was he going to convince her to leave? If she had come this far, it would not be easy, and if she refused to obey him, it would cause him trouble with the men.

"What has she said to the men?" he asked Diamod.

"She said she was your daughter, and must see you. She had told me she meant to stay, but when I left she had said nothing else to the others."

"Thank Alyanya's grace for that," said Gird. He shivered, flicked his fingers to avert the trouble, whatever it had been (and he could guess well enough) and started on toward the camp.

The other men were all busy, carefully busy and carefully avoiding the tall, strongly built person in trousers and man's shirt who sat motionless on a log, back toward him. Gird paused to look at her. From that distance, in that garb, she looked like a boy, her short dark hair (she had cut her hair!) rumpled, her big hands busy with a knife on a stick of wood. What was she whittling? When had she learned to whittle—or had she known, and he not known it?

He came toward her; the other men's glances at him alerted her, and she turned, then stood. She stood very straight, as she had when expecting punishment in childhood—she had been the one of his children most likely to defy him. Now he could see the ruin that blow had made of her beauty, a scar worse than her mother's, puckering the corner of her mouth. Her jaw had been broken, by the unevenness of it now. Her eyes held nothing he had seen before, in her years as child and maid and young wife. They might have been stones, for all the softness in them.

He could not bear it. He could not bear it that his daughter, his (he could admit it to himself) favorite, could look at him so. "Rahi—" he began. Then he found himself reaching for her, sweeping her into his hug despite her tension when she felt his hands. She stiffened, pushed him back, then stood passively. That was worse. He held her off, searching her face for some part of the girl who had been. "I'm sorry," he said. "I didn't think—"

"I came to stay," she said, as if it were a ritual she had memorized. "I came to fight. I am strong. I have no—no family ties."

"Rahi—!" He was appalled. But she went on.

"No child, no husband, nothing—but the strength of my body, the skill of my hands. I can be useful, and I can fight."

The other men had vanished, into the trees. Gird did not blame them; he was grateful for their tact. He was also sure they were listening avidly from behind every clump of leaves.

"I can't marry again," Rahi went on. "I'm—too noticeable. Imagine going before a steward or bailiff. And the healers say that fever may have made me barren, as well as killing my—the—child. And I don't want to marry again. I want to do something—" She snapped the stick she'd been whittling, and flung the pieces away. "Something to end this, so no other young wife will see her husband die as I did, and then have it be his wrongdoing—" She looked up at Gird, eyes suddenly full of tears. "I have to do this, Gird, here or somewhere else."

She had not called him Da, or the more formal father: she had called him Gird, like any of his men. That was another pain, even closer to the deep center of his heart where father and child were bound in ancient ties. He blinked back his own tears, and brushed away those that had run down his cheeks. His beard was wetter than he expected.

He tried to stay calm. "Rahi, love, we can't have

women here, in the camps. Not to fight—and it's not fair otherwise. It's not safe."

"Was I safe tending my own hearth at home?" she asked bitterly. "Is any woman safe? Are we safer when the strongest men are off in the woods playing soldier?" Gird grasped at the weak end of that.

"That's going to change; I thought of a way for men to learn soldiering in the villages." He explained quickly, before she could argue, and when he finished she was nodding. "So you see—" he said, easing into it.

"I see," she interrupted. "I see that the men will get some training, and then you'll take them away to a battle, leaving the women unprotected."

"That's not what I meant!"

"That's what it will be. You know that. Remember, years ago, when you told me I was as good as another son? After Calis died? I know many girls aren't that strong—but not all men are as strong as you, yet you've got Pidi here—little Pidi that I can sling over my shoulder—and you think I can't—"

"It's not just strength. You know that." Gird was sweating; he could feel it trickling down his ribs, and his hands were slick with it. "What about—you know— all those women things—"

Rahi stared at him a moment, and then snorted. A chuckle fought its way up, and she was suddenly convulsed with laughter. "Oh, Da—oh, Lady's grace, it still hurts when I laugh, but— You mean you never *knew*?"

"Knew what?" He could not imagine what she thought was funny about the problems having women in camp could bring.

Her hand waved, vaguely, as she tried to stop laughing, and hiccuped instead. "Mother never told you? All those years and you thought—" she shook her head, laughing again. Finally, eyes streaming tears, she regained control. Now, flushed from laughter, she looked like his daughter again, like her mother—all the warmth and laughter that Mali had brought into his life regained. Gird stared at her, halfway between anger and delight. She took a long breath, with her hand to her side, and explained. "Da, women have ways—herbs, brews—we're not like cows, you know. We're people; we understand our bodies. If it's a bad time—and I agree, fighting a war would be a bad time—we take care of it and don't make a mess. I can't tell you; it's *our* knowledge."

"But Issa—"

"Oh, Issa!" Rahi shook her cropped hair. "It doesn't work for some women, or they won't bother—that kind wouldn't want to learn soldiering anyway." She chuckled softly, a gentler sound. "I thought I would never laugh again, and here the first time I see you, I disgrace myself—"

"It's no disgrace to laugh," Gird said. He wanted to reach for her again, hug her, stroke her hair as he had when she was a small child. But she was a woman, and a woman who had suffered too much to be treated as a child. "Even after sorrow—it comes, sometimes, when no one expects it."

Rahi nodded. "Mother used to say it was the Lady's way of making it bearable. Tears in joy, laughter in sorrow, she said, were a sign of the Lady's presence." She reached out to him, her hand almost as large as his own, and patted his shoulder. "There—now I've grieved, and laughed, and called you Da again, which I said I would not do, were I your soldier. But I'm staying."

And from that decision he could not budge her, not then nor that night nor the next day. Their argument was conducted in the spurious privacy of the camp, with everyone not listening. Between bouts, Rahi demonstrated her usual competence, fitting her contributions of work and skill in effortlessly. Gird began to notice covert grins, sidelong sly looks at her, at him. The skin on the back of his neck itched constantly from being looked at. His ears felt sunburnt. Rahi did not take part in the drill sessions, but she was clearly watching and learning the commands.

After the afternoon's stick drill, Ivis lingered when the others dispersed to their assigned groups. "Your daughter—" he said, his eyes down.

"Yes." Gird bit it off. He was going to have to talk

about it, without having solved it, and it could do nothing but harm.

"You told us."

"Yes." He'd forgotten that, by this time. He looked at Ivis, who was staring past his shoulder. Gird resisted the temptation to look around—was Ivis looking at Rahi?

"She's a lot like you," Ivis said.

"She's—what?"

"Like you. Gets things done. Strong—more than one way."

Gird grunted. He could see where this was leading, and he didn't like it. Had Rahi been talking to them behind his back?

"She hasn't said anything, but we couldn't help hearing a little . . ."

Gird squinted up at the bright sky showing between the leaves, and asked himself why Mali hadn't had all boys. Life would have been a lot simpler. "She wants to stay; you all know that. She can't. She's stubborn, like her mother." *And me*, his mind insisted silently. "Stubborn on both sides," he admitted aloud. "But it's impossible."

Ivis dug a toe into the dirt and made a line. "She's not like most women."

Gird snorted. "She's like all women. Wants her way, and expects to get it. But with Rahi, it's even more so. Her next older brothers died, in a plague. That may have been it, though Mali—my wife—she was a strongminded woman too." As if she were alive again, he heard her voice in his ear, as she had warned him that first night at the gathering. *I will not guard my tongue for any man*, she'd said, and she'd kept that vow. Along with all the others. And had taught Rahi the same, if teaching had anything to do with what was born in the blood. He could feel his own blood contending. If only Rahi had been his son—but then it might have been Rahi dead, and his (her?) wife left. Gird shook his head. That was too complicated; what he had was complicated enough. How could the men respect a leader who couldn't make his daughter obey?

"We think she's earned it—if she can, if she's strong enough—"

"Strong enough! Of course she's strong enough; that's not the point."

Ivis cleared his throat noisily. "Gird—it *is* the point. To us, anyway. You've worried about some of the men here having the strength to lead, or the courage when it comes to a real fight. She's—she's your daughter, and we know what happened. She should be here."

Gird stared at him. "You think that? But if I let her—what about others?"

Ivis cleared his throat again. "The—the one thing I did hear her say, to Pidi, was that women could train at home too. In the bartons."

In the bartons I don't have yet, Gird thought furiously. In the bartons that are safe—if they are safe—only because the men always gather in the bartons. Again a memory of Mali forced itself into his consciousness, the day of their wedding when she had faced the ridiculous ceremonies with no embarrassment whatever. Were women really just humoring men with all that squealing and shyness? Could they—he had no doubts about Rahi, who could probably ride wild horses if the chance occurred—could *other women* really learn to fight, use weapons, *kill*—alongside men?

Ivis was watching his face with a wary expression. "She said I shouldn't say anything to you," he said.

Gird glared at him. "I thought you said you hadn't talked to her!"

"I haven't. I would have, but she wouldn't. Said it was up to you and her to work out, and I should stay out of it."

"Giving you orders, eh?" For some reason that amused him; he could feel Rahi's resentment of someone's interference, her fierce determination to convince Gird by herself.

Ivis grinned, catching the change in Gird's mood. "You notice I didn't obey."

"So how many of them agree with you?"

Ivis relaxed still more. "I didn't talk to all, but all I asked agreed that they would let her stay."

Gird muttered one of the old guards' curses he hadn't used in years; Ivis clearly had never heard it and didn't understand. "Go away, then. I want to talk to her." Ivis vanished, as if whisked away by magic. Gird looked around for Rahi. There she was, grinding grain as placidly as any housewife by her hearth. He had a sudden sinking feeling, as if a hole had opened in his chest, and let his heart fall out on the ground. Could he possibly be about to do what he was going to do? He swallowed against the feeling, and called her. She looked up, smiled, and came to him. He noticed that she had, even in that moment, scooped the ground meal into a bowl, and laid another atop it to keep out dirt.

This time he looked her over as if she were a real recruit. Within a finger of his height, broad shouldered, as Mali had been. Thin, from the fever, but with strength in her arms. The scar down her face made her too distinctive to send into a village or town—but she could still see out of both eyes, and had two good arms and legs. He had men with less. She stood there calmly, not arguing. Not intending to change her mind, either; he could feel the force of that determination as if it were heat from a fire.

"I don't think you understand," he said without preamble, "how hard it is for me. I've already seen you lying at my feet in a pool of blood. I don't think I can stand seeing that again."

Her face paled. "You don't understand how hard it is for me," she said. "I *lost* that blood, lost my husband, lost my child, and could not strike even one good blow to stop it. I *know* I cannot stand that—I will not be that helpless again. Not ever. Either you teach me, or—I don't know, but I'll learn somehow."

"And die somewhere I never know." Gird sighed, near tears again. "And that will be my fault, as it was my fault for not protecting you before. You give me a hard choice, Rahi." She opened her mouth, but he shook his head. "You would say, as your mother said often enough, that it is a world of hard choices. All right. I give in, on this one thing. But if this kills you, Rahi, make sure it is not because you failed to learn what I could teach."

If she felt triumph, she did not show it. Only in the

corner of her eye, the little wrinkle twitched, whether
from surprise or delight, he could not tell, and would
not ask.

"And you were right," he went on, "to call me 'Gird'
when you first came. If you would be a soldier, then it
is for that you are here, and not as my daughter."

She nodded, gravely. "Yes, Gird."

"And if you—if you need—" Now her eyes crinkled
in what could only be laughter. Gird glared at her.
"Dammit—!"

"Gird, if I cannot stay as a soldier, for some reason, I
will tell you at once, and go. But it is not likely, even
without what I know of herbs: the healer said so."

His arms ached to hold her, comfort her, restore to
her the promises of her childhood—the promises all
children should have. But it was too late for that. She
looked content with what life had left her; he had no
choice now himself. Her future was no more doubtful
than his—and, he thought sourly, the only doubt was
when they'd be strung on the spikes, not if.

But when she returned to grinding, and he saw by
the glances passed around the campsite that everyone
understood, and accepted his decision (he could not
believe many of them actually approved) he was able to
return to planning with a lighter heart. If he could
establish training in the villages, bartons full of trained
men—his mind put other women in that picture, and
he hastily blanked them out—in time they would outnumber the lords and their guards. Would any of the
guards come over? They had come from peasant ranks.
If they saw their friends and family actually fighting,
would that make a difference? He let himself imagine a
series of battles in which the peasants stood their ground,
in drill array, using their sticks and shovels, pushing
back the guard and then the lords themselves. Of course,
he still didn't know whether the sticks would work as
he saw them in his head.

He sighed. Time to start the next level of training.
He had in mind straw-stuffed dummies tied onto logs,
to simulate horsemen. It would help if he'd ever actually ridden a horse, and knew in his own body how

firmly a horseman could sit. He'd seen men bucked off—he remembered trying to ride calves—but that was not like a soldier on horseback firmly in the saddle. Still, it ought to work. If they could unseat horsemen, they could ambush mounted patrols. Even more important, if they could unseat horsemen—even one horseman —even a straw dummy tied to a log—it might convince the farmers in their villages that it was worthwhile spending all those hours learning to drill and use a stick.

Making the straw dummy was quick work, in the hot days of tall grass and long afternoons. Cob suggested weighting the body with rocks; Triga had the even better suggestion of seating a real person on the log, and pulling him off slowly—to see how a person felt— and then making the dummy feel the same. That turned into several days of experiment, with one after another trying to keep his seat on the log with friends pushing and pulling from one or both sides. Gird took a turn, wondering if it felt anything like riding a real horse, or if it could be a way to learn. It was easy to wrap his long legs around the log and hang on, but hard to keep his balance when someone yanked his arm. After his second fall, he watched Ivis on the log.

"We don't need the straw dummy," he said, "As long as we pad the ends of our sticks, and remember that this one is a friend. Whoever's up can tell us which moves are hardest to counter."

The rider—Ivis, then others—was equipped with a reed "sword" and laid about vigorously to simulate resistance. Slowly at first, then with increasing confidence and speed, they all learned where to strike a rider to throw him off balance. The game became so popular that Gird had to remind them that there were other ways—and enemies—to fight, or they would have spent all their time knocking one another off logs.

Rahi, in the meantime, had merged almost invisibly into the troop. Gird was acutely aware of her presence for the first few days; then he went off to the other camp, and when he returned it was as if she had always been there—but as a soldier, not his daughter. She did not avoid him, exactly, but she did not spend her free time with Pidi, or with Gird, and even seemed to steer clear of Fori. She had her place in drill, and made no more than the usual beginner's mistakes. As he would have expected, she learned fast. Gird waited for something to go wrong, but nothing did.

It was now nearing harvest. After harvest the fieldfee collectors would be out; Gird wanted to introduce his barton idea to at least a few villages before then. For that he needed seasoned older men, men the farmers might trust as similar to themselves. They had to be proficient in the drill (although he didn't expect them to teach the farmers much in the short time until harvest—but they had to impress them.) And—perhaps most important—they had to be reliably close-mouthed. He himself would go, of course. Ivis had developed into a trusted lieutenant, as had Cob. Diamod was known in five or six villages as a Stone Circle organizer. Felis, who might have been another possibility, had broken his wrist on his last "ride" as a target, and would not be fit until after harvest.

After long discussions, Gird chose four villages to test his idea: Fireoak, Harrow (where Felis's group had supporters), Whitetree, where Ivis's brother lived, and Hardshallows. Cob and a man from Felis's group went to Harrow, Ivis to his brother, Gird to Fireoak, and Diamod to Hardshallows. They were to spend no more than two nights in the village, and talk to no more than five men.

Chapter Fourteen

Coming into Fireoak on a late summer day, as an active rebel organizer, was very different from leaving it as a fugitive who had only the ghost of an idea for rebellion. The two of them joined a stream of workers coming in from the fields: harvest markers, who went into the fields before harvest to make sure the boundary stones didn't roll an armspan one way or the other—herders prodding slow-moving cows toward home and milking time. Gird flared his nostrils, enjoying the scent of cow. He had never understood those who thought cows stank. Pigs stank; dogs stank; even people—but cows had a rich, joyful scent, as befitted animals who lived on fresh grass and herbs. Their droppings had never disgusted him. Someone—he could not right then remember who—had told him once that a man should keep only those animals whose smells were pleasant to him.

The Fireoak farmers and herdsmen knew perfectly well the two were outlanders, but they knew Diamod and had heard of Gird. They sauntered down the lane, dusty and brown as the farmers with them, and no one spoke to them. Slow, traditional talk rolled by: harvest chances, taxes, a remedy for stiff ankles followed by a joke about the cause, comments on cows and weather and the uncommon number of rabbits that summer—a joke directed at Gird, which he well understood and knew better than to answer.

"Pop up and down everywhere, they do," someone said a second time, to see if he would rise to the bait. "Got so common, we might think they's people."

Then the village, with its familiar cottages, the wattle

fences between smallgardens, the walls of bartons rising behind. It was at once strange and the same: so like his own village, and yet not his village—and his village was not his village. Gird sniffed: bread, cheese, the vegetables they had not yet planted for the camps, ale somewhere—his mouth watered. Children wandered about, too thin but not yet starving, noticing the strangers but warned away from saying anything by quick gestures from their elders.

He would have passed Mali's brother's cottage, if Diamod had not jabbed him in the ribs. It looked different by daylight, from the front. He remembered Rahi's harsh feverish breathing in the barton out back, the gray light of dawn when he'd eased out the gate into the field beyond. Now he saw a low fence enclosing a ragged smallgarden, the beaten path to the front door. And in the door, a thin girl, yellowhaired, who held one crooked arm as if it pained her. Her face whitened, and she ducked inside. Gird turned to see Diamod wink before he walked on.

Gird came to the door, stepped out of his boots, and said "Girnis?"

Mali's brother's wife, a face he barely remembered from that one night, said "You're Gird? Gods above, what do you mean—come in, don't stand there!" Gird picked up his boots and ducked beneath the low lintel. It was dark inside, and would have been cool if not for the fire on the hearth. By that flickering light, Gird could see Girnis standing flat against the wall between a loom and a wheel.

"Is—is Rahi—?"

"She's alive, and well, and stubborn as ever." Gird looked at the wife, whose lips were folded together. What had he walked into? He had not asked Rahi all that had happened here, but perhaps he should have.

"I thought—" the woman began, then closed her mouth, and twisted her hands, and finally said again "I thought you were leaving Girnis with us. To be ours."

"I did," said Gird, surprised. "I said so; I was grateful."

She looked at him hard, then her mouth relaxed a little. "You didn't come to take her?"

"Of course not! Why would you think—"

"Raheli left. When she didn't come back, we thought she was with you, or dead—we didn't hear of anyone being killed. And then we thought, if you wanted her, you might want Girnis, but she's—"

"She's not Rahi." She was the child of Mali's illness, the twin that lived, but never as vigorous as a singleton. "I wouldn't take her. Girnis, let me see you."

Girnis came to him, shyly but now unalarmed. Her arm had healed a little crooked—not so bad, when she held it out. But she stood with it up, as if it were still in its bindings, and it was thinner than the other.

"Does it still hurt you?" he asked. She nodded.

"Mother Fera—" she glanced toward the woman, "—says I should move it more, but the joint hurts, Da, when I try."

"Let me feel." Gird took her arm, conscious of its thinness, and the faint tremor—nervousness? pain?—that met his touch. He bent and straightened it slowly, stopping when he met resistance and heard her indrawn breath. He could feel nothing wrong but stiffness, but he was not a healer. "I'm sure your aunt has tried heat," he said, "and herb poultices. I think myself it would be good to move it more. Sometimes things hurt when they're healing. A few times a day, anyway—I think you could do that." She nodded, solemnly. She was quiet; she had always been quiet, the quietest of his children, but not slow. Just quiet, in a house full of noisy ones.

The woman had moved nearer; she looked less alarmed. "We've had an offer for her," she said. "She has a mixed parrion, she says?"

Gird nodded. "Yes. She has Mali's parrion of herbcraft, and Issa's—my brother's wife's—parrion of embroidery. Issa was a weaver, as well, but died before Girnis learned enough."

"I am a weaver," the woman said. "I can teach her, if her arm strengthens. But—will you let us arrange the marriage?"

"Of course. I told you—if you in your kindness will have her, she is your daughter, and yours is the right to speak for or against."

He heard boots in the barton, and stiffened, but the woman called through the house: "Gird's here. It's all right."

After that awkwardness, he was surprised to find that Mali's brother was enthusiastic about the possibility of training within the village.

"Of course, the bartons," he said. "You're right, Gird, and I don't know why we hadn't thought of it before. Had no one to teach us, I suppose. I know—let me think—I know two hands of men who would join here, at once. What about weapons?"

"Drill first, then weapons," said Gird. He and Barin were sitting on the cool stones of the barton, drinking ale to celebrate. He could feel a delicate haze leaching the tiredness from his bones.

"What about women?" asked Barin.

"Mmm?"

"You've got Rahi now. I'm Mali's brother, after all; I remember what she was like and how relieved the family was when you offered for her. Will you take women like that in?"

Gird shrugged. "*I* would myself, but I can't force another group to do it. What about you?"

"I don't like the thought of seeing my wife—but after all, she could be cut down for no reason, as Rahi was. Most of them won't want to anyway, but for a few—why not?"

The following night, five other men visited Barin's, presumably to finish an open barrel of ale before the beginning of harvest, when it was bad luck to have one. They talked village gossip until the stars were thick and white, then Gird spoke his piece. Less open than Barin, they still agreed it was a good idea. The longer they talked it over, the more they liked it—except that only two of them thought women should be allowed to join.

"They talk too much," said one of the men. "Let them find out, and it'd be all over the village by dawn."

Barin laughed. "And who was it let out the secret of Kinvit's lover, last winter?"

The others burst into laughs; the man who had complained of women talking too much said "But it wasn't my fault!" Gird chuckled. It was always the same; the loosest mouths complained that others gossiped. *Their* tales were always true, and if the wrong story got out, it was never their fault. Finally the man came around, laughing at himself. "All right," he said. "I got drunk; I opened my mouth, and out fell Kinvit and Lia, doing what Kinvit and Lia had been doing since harvest. No nosy old granny could have done worse." But he was still opposed to having women training in the village. Gird did not push him, letting Barin do most of the talking. They would all know, by now, about Raheli; they would all assume that Gird had a special reason for allowing women to fight. And that was perfectly true.

In the end, the men voted to organize a barton meeting, and gradually recruit new members. Gird promised to send someone—"It may not be me," he pointed out—to train them. "Consider him a sergeant," he said at first, but even in starlight he could see the dislike they had for that name, associated as it was with the lords' tyranny. "What would you call him, then?"

They talked back and forth, suggesting and arguing, until one of them said "We're like a bunch of cattle milling in a pen, waiting for the herdsmarshal to set us on our way."

"Marshal!" said Barin, smacking his leg with his fist. "That's good—and it's not a word we would fear to have overheard. Marshal. And the rest of us are—"

"Yeomen," said Gird. "That covers all of us, farmers and craftsmen alike. Any but lords. And no one will ever know, from talk of it, what it is."

"I do like that," Barin said. "The yeomen and the marshal meet in the barton tonight. As long as we need only those two ranks—"

"But we've got another!" It had come to Gird in another of those flashes of insight. "Marshal—that's one of us traveling, coming to train you. But even in the village, you'll need a leader—that's the yeoman-marshal. And then yeoman for everyone else."

"And someday—" Barin said. He didn't have to finish. They all drained the last of their ale, and stamped their feet in agreement. Gird could see it—the flow of men out to the Stone Circle, to learn. The flow back in, to train those in the bartons . . . and back out, to the fight they all knew must come, and then back, to take up their peaceful lives. As natural as breathing, or the cycle of seasons. He knew from experience that ale could make things seem simpler than they were in morning's light, but this was going to work.

Work began in earnest when he returned to the camp and conferred with the others who had gone out. All the villages had shown an interest—not surprising, since they had talked to men already known to be Stone Circle sympathizers. Two of the others had noticed that the villagers shied from the usual military rank terms of sergeant and captain, but they had not come up with alternatives. They nodded when Gird told them about marshal, yeoman-marshal, and yeoman.

"That'll do," said Ivis. "They won't mind that—it's nothing like the guards. Best of all, we can talk about it in front of anyone—even a guard sergeant—and he won't know what it is." Gird nodded.

"They thought of that, too."

"Will we all be marshals?" asked Cob. "I mean, when we're drilling here, that's going be to confusing."

"None of us are marshals yet," Gird said. "And some of us may be better than others at teaching. Besides, we still don't know enough." In his mind, the wheel of the year turned, grinding the moments away. How long before the first snowfall? Before full winter? Four bartons to train, this winter—maybe more. "After harvest," he said, "we need to bring one man from each village here, to drill with us, and see how the larger units work. When the taxes are paid, no one takes much notice if someone travels to visit relatives. In the meantime, our own harvest: I hear the fieldfees are up again, and we cannot starve our allies."

For the next few hands of days, they drilled only briefly, spending most of their time gathering food and preparing it for storage. No casual nutting and berrying, this time, but a planned harvest of the woods and fields, that must be done before the lords came to hunt, in the days after the fieldfees were paid. Gird had planned food storage sites both in and away from the camps, so that if one were found and destroyed, others would be safe. They could not hunt, and risk foresters preparing for the lords' visits seeing their smoke or smelling the blood, but they could gather fruit, tubers, berries, and stow them away. Into storage pits lined with rock went redroots and onions: their own harvest had been abundant. Other roots and tubers, bulbs and nuts, were stored with them, along with apples and plums and dried berries, bundles of herbs, strips of necessary barks. Their own baskets stored grain as well, harvested from the edges of common pastures, along streambanks, and in Triga's bog. Gird moved from place to place, checking the growing stores, and trying to foresee what hazards they must survive.

After harvest, the lords would come to hunt the large wood; Gird moved everyone to the tangle of hills where Felis's group had lived, and the only game worth hunting was wild boar. If they stayed out of the pickoak scrub, living uncomfortably in the lower brush, they should avoid the occasional hunting party with a taste for pig. The men grumbled, but only slightly. Gird found work for them even in the chest-high thickets of brush.

"We might need to come this way and hide, and it would be good to have paths they can't see from the opposite hill." So his troop crawled and twisted through the thick growth, hacking out paths wider than the rabbit-trails they found. Rahi sniffed the hacked ends of the scrub, and said she thought some of these were medicinal, stunted by soil or dryness. She began making a collection of twigs, bark, roots, and brewed a variety of pungent bitter concoctions which she insisted he taste. They all made his tongue rough up in furrows; they tasted as if they ought to do something good. One made him sweat profusely.

At last Ivis's forester friends sent word that their duke and his friends had returned to the city; the forest was theirs for the winter. By this time the autumn rains were beginning, turning their trails to cold gray mud.

Gird wished he had a stone cottage, with a great roaring hearth; his knees ached constantly. Instead, he had the three main campsites he'd found for winter, two backed into the south face of a hill, and one deep in a grove of cedars and pines. His favorite had a clean-running creek, small but adequate to their needs, and the surrounding trees had all dropped their leaves, letting in the low winter sunlight. The other south-facing camp had a larger stream, but he was somewhat worried about floods, come spring. Even in the slower autumn rains, they had to cross the stream on fallen logs. The men called that one Big Creek, and the other Sunbright; the most secluded campsite they called Cedars.

No one grumbled when he insisted they go right on working, rather than huddle in the first shelter they could contrive. He did not know if they were learning to think ahead, or if they simply accepted his orders. But wet and cold as it was now, winter could only be worse. The shelters he had planned went up quickly: wattle frames for side and roof, thatched with whatever they could find, mostly wild grass. Gird realized, as they wrestled with the grass between rains, that he should have had them out scything it earlier. Next year, he thought. And by then he would need another scythe or two. And some sickles. They smeared mud on the insides of the walls. Triga suggested another plan: poles braced against a tree, lashed together, and then wattle woven to make a circular peaked shelter. After building a couple like this, he admitted that it took more work, and gave less interior room, but the two they had made a welcome change, like extra rooms, during that winter.

The newly designated yeomen marshals arrived for their training while this was still going on; Gird had to stop for a couple of days to give them intensive training. But they were almost as impressed with the troop's camp organization as with the drill. This, in turn, helped convince the last doubters among his soldiers that such organization was important. If it could impress strangers, then it was not just a matter of comfort.

The yeomen marshals stayed a hand of days; on the

last day, Gird discussed with them the way they'd
organize and train during the winter.

"By spring," he said, "I'd like to have your yeomen
ready to drill with another barton. Someday we'll have
to have bartons able to come together quickly."

"What about recruiting new bartons?" asked the
yeoman-marshal from Hardshallows. "I know you wouldn't
want to risk it in your old village—the steward, I hear,
is still furious about you, and the men who left after
you—but we're less than a day's walk from Hawkridge
to the west, and not much more from Millburh, down
our own stream."

Gird had hoped no one would suggest that yet; he
had wanted to be sure the barton idea would work
before starting more. But he could not actually stop
them—these were not *his* men yet—all he could do was
make them sneaky, if they'd already decided. In the
pause, while he tried to think how to answer, Barin
from Fireoak spoke up.

"I think we should wait until we have at least two—
maybe three—hands of yeomen, all drilling well. How
else could we show them what we mean? And if—I
don't mean to be illwishing, but if this doesn't work—if
we find that our neighbors *do* tell the lords' men, then
better only a few bartons die, than many."

Gird nodded, glad he hadn't had to say it himself.
"Barin's right, I think. If your barton grows and pros-
pers, and you're sure it's safe, then I will not tell you
not to tell the next village. But we're like a man starting
a journey with a heavy load: it's better to take a few
slow steps, and be sure it's balanced and will hold, than
to set off at a run and have the whole thing fall apart."
His hands mimed the falling load, and they all laughed.
"One village at a time. I think myself it would be better
if only one in each barton knew the name of the yeoman marshal in other bartons."

"But if he dies?"

"Each of you tell one of your yeomen—not someone
you usually work in the field with—how to contact *us*,
here. And let us know the name of that person. Later,

everyone will know everyone, but for now, as Barin said, *if* someone tells, it's better that only a few die."

When the yeoman marshals had left, Gird and his troop used the hand of days between the last of the autumn rains and the first of the snows to transport and stow the food and supplies the villages had given them, cut and haul wood for their fires, and add such refinements to their shelters as time and ingenuity allowed. When that first bank of blue cloud rolled across, cutting off the slanting autumn sun, and dropping the temperature, Gird felt that they were as well prepared for winter as possible.

This did not mean he had thought of everything. His own well, in the foreyard of his cottage, froze only in the bitterest winters, and only after midwinter. The clear-running creek that was one of the reasons for choosing Sunbright froze solid before Midwinter, and they must either melt snow and ice for water, or carry it (a cold, heavy load that sometimes froze before they got it home) from a spring some distance away. He had thought to dig the jacks trenches ahead, before the ground froze, but had not realized that the "loose" dirt from them would freeze, and have to be chopped into chunks to fill the trench.

Problems had the advantage of helping Gird keep everyone busy. In the villages, winter boredom led to quarrels and occasional fights. Here, such dissension could be fatal. So his four tally groups had assigned chores, and whenever the weather allowed, Gird chivvied everyone out for a march or drill practice. He divided the groups slightly differently. One brought food from storage, and another cooked it, while the camp chores group had to maintain the fire, the jacks, and the supply of water. The tool groups were set to repairing tools broken or chipped, and to making useful items for the camps. One of the things the villages had sent (at Gird's request) was yarn; Rahi taught several of the men to knit, using smooth-polished twigs as needles. Knitting was an unusual parrion; she had had it from Mali's brother's wife, in the time she lived there, and liked it much better than weaving.

Midwinter was a different kind of problem. Gird had always known when Midwinter was coming because the village headman said so. Here, he realized, everyone thought of him as headman, and he should know when to celebrate Midwinter. He looked up, at a heavy gray sky. The days were still getting shorter, so it wasn't Midwinter yet. He felt that it would come in a hand or two of days, but he did not know when it would be, or how to find out. But missing the Midwinter celebration was unthinkable.

He asked the others. Most thought it would be "soon" but no one had an exact date. Would it matter? At that thought, a colder chill ran down his neck. Of course it mattered; Midwinter and Midsummer were the ends of the axle on which the year turned. He had to know. He had to find out. Now that the men knew he did not know, they were looking at him nervously.

"How did you find out last year?" he finally thought of asking Ivis.

Ivis flushed. "Last year—well—we all went into one village or another, near Midwinter, and celebrated there." And before Gird could decide to do the same, he said, "I don't think we can, this year—we're too many."

"True, but we can ask." Ivis' village was too far away, across the wood, but one of them could make it to Fireoak and back. To Gird's surprise, Fori asked to go.

"I can stay with Barin, and ask about Girnis. And the barton."

Gird nodded. "Good—but be sure you're back *before* Midwinter."

Fori set off the next morning with a sack of food and everyone's prayers. Gird watched all the faces staring after him, and said, "Since you're all so glad to be outside, get your sticks." A general groan, but not so dismal as he'd expected.

Stick drill had progressed a little farther. Felis, once his arm healed, was able to demonstrate what he had learned of swordsmanship. Gird suspected it wasn't much, but he himself had never gotten that far. One thing he did know was the length of swords Kelaive's guards had used. He asked the others; the duke, Ivis said, carried a longer sword, but no longer than from waist to ground. He had seen him standing with its tip resting on the ground. So, Gird thought, a sword could have a blade that long, or shorter. He asked his one-armed smith, who mentioned curved blades and broad-bladed swords, but agreed on length. That meant that a longer stick could fend off a sword—not fence with it, to lose chips as the sword chopped—but if the stick could hold the swordsman back, the sword could not harm the person with the stick.

It seemed reasonable, but they had to test it. Slowly, Gird insisted. Carefully. No more broken bones, if possible. Felis took those of his original group who had learned the most about swords, and these faced Gird, Cob, and a few others Gird thought he could trust to stay calm.

The sticks were nowhere near spear length, but about the length a man would choose as a walking staff, or for guiding cattle. So far they were not all the same length, although a broad hand would cover the difference. Gird had watched them in use over the past season, noticing carefully what went wrong most often, when the sticks clashed in ranks, which grips did not hold. Now, with Felis well again, they would see. He felt a little silly, standing there with a real stick facing an imaginary sword, but what else could they do?

Felis waggled his wooden "sword" and swiped at Gird. Gird lowered his stick, and pointed it at Felis, who sliced at it. Before the "sword" struck, Gird jabbed the stick at Felis's face. Felis jerked back, and his sword stroke went wild.

"Wait," said Felis. "Try that again, slower." It would not be slow in battle, but they were only learning. Gird nodded, let Felis begin his sideways swipe with the sword, and then jabbed again. Again Felis jerked his head back, and this time, while he was still off balance, Gird jabbed again, and got him in the chest, gently. Felis grunted, then straightened. "I can't—I think I'm just not good enough—but if you keep poking that at my eyes—I have to back up."

"Let Cob and Arvan try it," said Gird, stepping back. Arvan advanced with his "sword" and very little enthusiasm, to meet Cob. Here Cob was the shorter by a head, yet with the length of his stick he could force Arvan off balance.

"It's too easy," said Felis, scratching his thick red beard. "These sticks we're using for swords don't have the weight of a real weapon. If someone got a blow in, it would jar your stick aside—"

"But could they?" Arvan was frowning. "Cob, just hold it still—let me try." He swung hard at the stick, and managed to bat it aside, but it swung back on rebound, and Cob needed little force to control it.

"But suppose there were more than one swordsman," Felis said. "If you have more than one coming in, you can't just poke one. The other one will poke you."

"That's what the formation is for," Gird said. "If it works." This time he and Cob lined up facing Felis and Arvan. When they lowered their sticks, and jabbed, the two "swordsmen" found themselves giving ground, flailing uselessly with their shorter weapons.

"Just remember," Felis said, "that even an accidental blow with a sword is going to take chips off that stick. It won't last forever. Can you do real damage with it?"

"I don't know." Gird tapped him in the chest again. "If I did that much harder, you might fall down; I might even break your breastbone, or a rib."

"You'll have to swing it to knock someone flat, most times." Triga, watching, entered the discussion. "And if you swing it, that gives time for a fast swordsman to slip in and kill you."

"*And* if you swing it," Felis pointed out, "it can foul on someone else's stick who's fighting another opponent."

"Mmmph. I thought we could try this—hold still, now, I won't really hit you hard." Gird jabbed at Felis's face, then tapped his chest, and then slid his hands down to swing the stick like a flail. But Arvan chose that moment to dart in and put his "sword" to Gird's neck.

"Like that," Felis said, grinning at Arvan and Gird both. Gird glowered at Cob.

"And where were you, partner?"

Cob looked rueful. "Standing watching you, when I should have been watching Arvan. We have more to learn, yeomen."

"We could whittle a point on these sticks, and fire-harden it," said Triga.

"It's still not going to go through any kind of armor. Even if it did, it would catch there, and I'd be standing there with a dead soldier on the end of my weapon, looking foolish." Gird scratched his beard vigorously, as if that could clear his head. "I thought if we hit them in the chest hard enough—or in the belly—that would knock them down, maybe even out."

"Hit them in the face—that makes 'em back up, and they'll worry about losing an eye—"

"True, but—" Gird thought about that. "We need a way to kill them, or we'd be standing all day poking poles at them. I did think of some farm tools—the shovel, the mattock, the scythe—but they all have to be swung. And you're saying, aren't you, that anything we swing will be clumsier than a sword?"

Felis half-closed his eyes, and began swiping the air. Gird stared, then realized he was imagining himself swinging various farm implements. Gird tried to guess which, from Felis's movements, but except for the sickle (a short swing, with a snap to the wrist) he could not be sure which was which. Felis opened his eyes, made a few passes with his "sword," and grinned. "I think there's a chance with a mattock—and even a scythe, though the grips would have to be moved around. But it wouldn't be easy."

Gird heaved a dramatic sigh. "None of this is easy. If it was easy, someone would've done it long ago."

Rahi spoke, for the first time in a drill session. "What if two or three worked together? One with the stick, to force the swordsman's attention, and one or two with weapons more likely to kill, but slower."

"That's fine, if we outnumber the enemy," said Felis. "But in battle—"

"Wait," said Gird. "That might work—and we had better outnumber them, Felis, facing steel with wood. Let's try it."

Felis shrugged, but stepped forward again. This time Rahi stood beside Gird with one of the sickles. She was on his left, but then looked at her sickle and quickly changed sides as Gird lunged at Felis. Felis backed, his attention necessarily on the stick in his face. When Rahi came forward, he tried to swing at her; but the pole caught him in the angle of neck and shoulder. Arvan swung at Rahi, but missed as Cob's pole got him in the chest, and then poked again at his face. Rahi could easily dodge Felis's wild strokes, and she swung, stopping just as the sickle tip hooked into his side. Then, slow for the exercise, but smoothly, she swung back, pivoting, to come forward again and take Arvan in the belly. They all stopped and stood up.

"It works in slow motion," said Felis doubtfully. "And I don't know how we'll practice it fast, not without killing each other."

"We still need someone with a stick for every swordsman." Gird scratched again, and stared at the stick. "And some behind with the other weapons, the killing weapons. Not that the sticks can't kill. But there's something I'm not seeing. Anyone else?"

"Well—you ever see that old-style stickfighting, on fair days?" asked Cob.

"No—the only fair-day I ever went to had one wrestler not as good as you, and a man who could throw knives."

"They started it like a dance," Cob said. "One man tapping a drum, and them tapping the sticks together. It was pretty, like watching horses in a field, tappity-tap. Then they started going faster, and faster, and about then I realized it was a kind of fighting. I'd have learned more, only I was there to make a few crabs wrestling, and my friends had bet on me. I asked one of them later, and he said it was old, something our great-great-grand-das would have known about."

"Do you remember any of it?"

"Only the first bits, the slow part. But it'd be good

practice, anyway. Get us used to the feel of something hitting the sticks."

It took longer than Gird would have expected before he could match Cob's pattern; his knuckles felt as if he'd hit them with hammers. And that was with both of them being careful. Triga, who'd been to the same fair, and thought he remembered the stickfighting very well, tried to start fast and ended up sucking his split knuckles ruefully. At least he wasn't angry—but there had been no frogs to eat for days. Arvan picked up the movements quickly, as did Felis, but Padug, who had been Felis's other star pupil at swordsmanship, was slower than Gird. By the time Fori came back, to announce that Midwinter Feast should be celebrated in eight days, most of them were still fumbling their way through this new drill.

Midwinter itself was the coldest and darkest Gird had ever known. No one was sick—Alyanya's grace—but that meant no excuse for any fire whatever. And the rituals of Midwinter had always involved the whole family: each member had his or her assigned role. He had asked the men, and located an eldest son, youngest son, the oldest and youngest overall. Rahi had to take all the women's roles; Gird hoped the gods would understand and accept their intent, and not demand the precision only a whole family could provide.

At dusk on the first night, all their fires were quenched, and the hearths brushed clean. Water, fire, ritual earth (though they had no garden or ploughland), each handled with due reverence—the icy air breathed with respect and affection both. Rahi, not surprisingly, remembered all the women's verses: she had been, once, the youngest daughter, then the eldest, and with Mali's death and her marriage, Alyanya's representative in Gird's home. Together, finally, hands cupped around symbolic light, they sang the Darksong. That was in the middle of the night, when Torre's Necklace stood high overhead. From then until dawn, they huddled together, telling old tales of their childhoods, their fathers' tales, as far back as any could remember. Their breath steamed silver in the starlight, each speaker like a tiny chimney. Then—best of omens—a clear dawn to Midwinter Day, and Rahi set the circle pattern of twigs for the new fire. In a great circle, hand to hand, they watched her light it, on the lucky third spark.

They had their feast, as well, for Gird had hidden a comb of honey, and dripped it liberally over hearthcakes and grain mush. Besides that, they had deer, hunted safely long after the lords had gone back to their city. They feasted in comfort, around the roaring fires, and spent the second long night singing more songs than Gird had ever heard. All it lacked was ale; he missed the warmth in his throat and belly, though not the aching head when he woke.

The rest of that winter was hard, but not as hard as he'd feared. When the snowmelt began, with the myriad tinkling music of dripping icicles, they were all still healthy. No one had lost fingers or toes to the cold; no one had had lung fever.

Twice he'd been able to send men to the four original bartons, to check on their training. All had a full three hands or more in training; Hardshallows had five. And they were still recruiting, though cautiously. Fireoak had discovered a man who thought Kelaive would pay him for rebel names. He had changed his mind, Barin reported, when they explained it to him personally. Fori's report of that explanation was fuller than Barin's; the barton had expressed their opinion of him with force—the man would limp for awhile. Gird winced, but accepted it. Better one man beaten than many killed—or even one. He felt slightly better when he found, still later, that the one who had hit the man in the head with a pot was his wife, now an accepted barton member.

Hardshallows reported that it had indeed started a daughter barton, down in Millburh. Growing slowly, but Millburh had a resident guard post, almost a fort. They had to be careful. As the weather lifted, the barton in Ashy, Felis's old village, sent word that it, too, had contacted another village: Three Springs, which had passed the word to two other vills in the same hearthing. As soon as the spring plowing was over, those bartons would be sending elected yeomen marshals to train with the main force.

It was all moving faster than Gird had expected. He still could not quite believe that he'd been away from his own home almost a year—and was alive, leading a growing number of disaffected peasants in what was clearly going to be an army. And yet they'd had no clashes with the lords, no trouble with any of the guard forces. It would be easy to be careless, moving through the green and fragrant woods of spring, with flowers starring the pastures beyond, with the birds carolling overhead.

We don't have an army *yet*, he reminded himself firmly.

Chapter Fifteen

All that spring and summer, the movement spread, like ripples from a dropped stone. The Stone Circle began to become what it had always claimed to be, the center of a wider movement of rebellion. The first bartons ventured out of their villages to drill with Gird in the fields. Their yeomen marshals contacted Stone Circle supporters in other villages. Distant Stone Circle outlaws, living wild in the woods and hills, sent messengers to find out what was happening. Gird would not let any more stay with him; he knew they could not support more where they were. But he sent those he thought would make good teachers and leaders, both to new bartons and to outlaw groups. Gradually—sometimes painfully—he discovered which of his people could do that work, and which of the outlaw groups were honest rebels, and which were brigands.

He insisted that the groups he led provide as much of their own food as they could. That summer was even busier than the one before, as strangers came and went, learning and taking back what they'd learned, while the work of supporting his own troops still had to be done. He saw no end to it, the things he had to do, remember, foresee. But he noticed that some of his people were learning to think ahead for themselves, learning to think how something used one way for a lifetime could be useful for doing something else.

He heard, late that summer, that a distant barton had ambushed a lord's taxman, and shook his head. "That'll start us trouble," he muttered.

Triga cocked an eyebrow at him. "You were hoping to have a war without trouble?"

"I was hoping to have a war when we were ready for it. Not in bits and pieces, here and there, where they have the advantage."

"What I heard was the barton got the money, all of it, and killed the taxman and his two guards. Sounds to me like the barton had the advantage."

"As long as they didn't take anything that can be traced. Where can they spend those coins? And on what? I hope they've sense enough not to go to a smith. They start trying to buy weapons, and we'll see trouble we haven't thought of yet." Gird doubled his own outposts and guards, expecting the worst. Sure enough, mounted patrols swept through the country, both in the wood and beyond in the hills. Gird's men were very glad of their low paths through the scrub. They came back to find that one of their winter camps, Sunbright— deserted now for several hands of days—had been found. The patrol had destroyed the little they'd left behind, and they would certainly know where it was the next winter.

But the patrols, after that double raid, stayed away. From their contacts in the villages, they heard of more trouble—searches of cottages and barns for illegal weapons, men taken on suspicion of rebel activity and beaten or—in two cases—killed outright. Only one of these was actually a Stone Circle supporter, and he had not been a member of the local barton (being, as the yeoman marshal put it, too hotheaded to wear a hat without its catching fire.) These searches and arrests actually increased support for the rebels: after all, if you could be arrested for nothing, why not join?

Gird split his group into threes, and sent each one to a different area for the rest of the summer. They drilled together only a few times, and cautiously, with watchers on all the nearby heights. During harvest, and the lords' favorite hunting time after it, more patrols came. But they'd been expected, and they found nothing but the same deserted camp they had found before. Once the winter storms began, Gird knew no more patrols would come. That winter was like the previous one, except that he began to try to keep accounts of his troop. He had begun with simple tallies, marked with wheatear, sickle, and flower, but he needed lists of all his people, and their villages, and the bartons and their yeoman marshals. Rahi brewed a brownish ink, but he had nothing like the smooth parchment the sergeant had had to write on. He struggled for awhile with the pale inner bark of a poplar, but finally gave up in disgust. He hated writing anyway.

That spring, the spirit of unrest made the whole countryside uneasy. Gird was not quite sure now how many bartons there were. The long winter months were ideal for conspiracy; each barton wanted to claim a daughter barton or two. That meant more than doubling, over the winter. Requests came in for Gird himself, or one of his senior instructors, to come inspect and drill not just one barton, but several. Gird and the others agreed on basic rules for drilling bartons together —how far the drillground must be from any village, what kinds of lookouts to set, what the signals would be, and what common commands all bartons should know. But he knew it was futile; in time, they would be discovered.

On those days of drill, Gird noticed first one blue shirt, then another. They had three at the camp now. Those who wore the blue held themselves proudly, aware of defiance. Gird insisted they have another shirt or cloak to throw over it, should an enemy show up. It would be hard enough to switch from drill to some innocuous activity, without having to explain away a forbidden blue shirt.

They could not, in these short sessions, teach all the new people all they themselves had learned. Gird felt the push and pull of time, the sense of things moving fast and slow at once: the lords could not long remain unaware of all that went on around them, but his people were not ready yet. They needed more time, more drill, and he needed to know more himself. When he thought of gathering all the bartons, in a full army, and meeting the lords with theirs, he was terrified.

Time ran out before he was satisfied with himself or the bartons, after Midsummer and well before harvest. He had gone to the gathering place for the sheep of five villages, so much like the pens where he had met Mali, but far to the north and east. Norwalk Sheepfold, they called it locally, the usual stone-walled shelter, back to the winter winds, with a fenced yard before it. It lay in the hollow of grassy hills, a half-morning's walk from the nearest village, where no troops were stationed anyway.

As usual, Gird came to the meeting site before anyone else, met the shepherds who would be their lookouts, and gave his instructions. Then he squatted in the lee of the sheepfold, eating a chunk of hard cheese, to wait for the first barton to arrive.

When it came straggling along, hardly any two yeomen in step, and weapons every which way, Gird winced. He knew it had formed recently, but that did not excuse the shambling, uncertain line, the complete lack of organization. He began, as always with a new barton, with an attempt at an inspection. As always, he found more than one thing wrong.

"You got to take care of yer own scythe, Tam!" Gird yanked the blade loose and just stopped himself from throwing it on the ground. They couldn't afford to lose a single scrap of edged steel. But every single time he had to check the bindings himself—it was enough to infuriate the Lady of Peace herself. Tam's jaw set stubbornly; the others stared, half-afraid and half-fascinated. Gird took a long breath and let it out. "This time get it tight," he said, handing Tam the blade. He could feel the tension drain away as he went down the line, looking at the other scythes. Most were in reasonable shape, though he wondered if they really would hold against horses or armor.

Fifteen men and three women. Eleven scythes, one pruning hook, two sickles, three shepherds' crooks, two simple staves. Everyone had a knife, and all but one of them were sharp. Before they began the actual drill, he looked around the skyline. Nothing but a flock of sheep to the north, whose shepherd waved from the rise. Safe.

"All right. Line up." They had done this before, taught by Per who had learned from Aris, who had learned from Gird the year before in Burry. They moved too slowly, but they did end up in straight lines, three rows of six. Tam was still trying to jam the end of his blade into the notch of the pole, tamping it against the ground. Maybe he'd learn, before he died.

"Carry." They stared at him, then half the group remembered that that was a command, and wobbled their weapons, clearly unsure where the "carry" position was. *Don't rush it*, Gird reminded himself, remembering the defections after his last temper tantrum. *They have to learn from where they are, not from where they should be.* "Carry," he reminded them. "On your left shoulder—this one—because you have to be able to carry your weapon a long way, and without hitting anyone behind or beside you, or catching on theirs." He reached out and took a scythe from someone— Battin, the name was—in the front rank, and showed them. "Like this."

By the time they were all able to follow the basic commands at a halt, the sun was nearly overhead. Gird looked around again. The northern flock was out of sight over the rise, but another moved now across the slope to the west, and its shepherd waved elaborately. Good. Two more bartons coming to drill. Even so, even with the shepherd's signals, he would take the usual precautions.

"Weapons into the sheepfold," he said. "Another barton's coming in." Much more quickly than before, they obeyed, laying the scythes out of sight behind the low walls of the pens. Two of the women began to cut thistles with their sickles, gathering them into their aprons. The men with shepherds' crooks leaned on the low-roofed lambing hut and began talking sheepbreeding. The others hid in the lambing hut itself. Gird sat on one of the walls, and caught his breath.

"Sir? Gird?" That was Per, the nominal yeoman marshal of this barton.

"Just Gird, Per. You've got a good group here." It would be a good group after a year of enough to eat and heavy training, but it would do no good to say that.

"I'm sorry about Tam's scythe. I—there's so much I don't know—"

"Don't worry. You can't do it all; that's why I tell them they have to maintain their own weapons. You've done a lot: eighteen, and fifteen scythes."

"Three women," muttered Per. Gird shot him a glance. "You believe the lords' sayings about women, Per?"

"Well, no, but—"

"Our women have suffered with us all these years. We never kept them safe; they've borne the lords' children, and lost them if they had one touch of magic: you know that. Now they ask to learn fighting with us: if our pain has earned that right for us, theirs has earned it for them."

"But they're not as strong—"

Gird bit back another sharp remark, and said instead, "Per, we don't ask anyone to be strongest, or stronger. Just strong enough."

"Whatever you say."

"No. Whatever you finally see is right—dammit, Per, that's what this is about. Not just my way—not just Gird instead of your lord or the king, but a fair way for everyone. You, me, our women, our children. Fair for everyone."

"Fair for the lords?"

Gird snorted, caught off guard. "Well—maybe not for them. They had their chance." He pushed himself off the wall. The incoming bartons had joined somewhere along the way, and were marching some thirty strong, all in step and clearly proud of themselves. He could not tell, at this distance, exactly what weapons they carried, but at least some of them were scythes. Per's foot began to tap the beat as the formation came nearer. Gird let himself think what they could do with some decent armor, some real weapons. They were marching like soldiers, at least, and impressing the less-experienced group he'd been working with. He called those in the lambing shed out to watch as the yeoman marshal of Hightop brought the formation to a halt.

They had a short rest, then all three bartons began drilling together. Almost fifty, Gird reckoned them up, a half-cohort as the lords would call it, most with staves. For the first time, Gird could *see* them facing real troops, the lords' militia, with a chance to win. He marched them westward, away from the sheepfolds, got them reversed, reversed again, and then tried to convince them that when the column turned, it turned in only one place. Those behind were not to cut the corner, but march to the corner, and turn. Again, and another tangle. He sorted it out, and got them moving again.

It was then that a shepherd's piercing whistle broke through the noise of their marching. Gird looked around, already knowing what it had to be. There, to the east, a mounted patrol out of Lord Kerrisan's holding; already they'd been spotted. He saw the flash of sunlight on a raised blade. His mind froze, refusing to work for a moment. Someone else saw them, and moaned. He turned to see his proud half-cohort collapsing, some already turning to run, others with weapons loose in their hands. The sun seemed brighter; he could see every detail, from the sweat on their faces to the dust on their eyelashes.

"We have to get away," said Per in a shaky voice. He heard the murmur of agreement, a grumble of dissent.

"We'll never make it," breathed someone else, and a heavy voice demanded "Who *told* them we were out here?"

"It's a random patrol," Gird answered, without really thinking about it. "A tensquad, no spears—if they'd known we were here they'd have sent more, and more weapons. Archers, lancers." He glanced at the horsemen, now forming a line abreast. One of them had a horn, and blew a signal. Two of the horsemen peeled off, rode at an easy canter to either side. "They're circling, to pen us—"

"But what can we do?" asked someone at the back of the clump that had once been a fighting formation.

I ask for a sign, and I get this, Gird sent silently to the blazing sun. *Lord of justice, where are you now?* A gust of wind sent a swirl of dust up his nose, and he sneezed. "I'll tell you what we can do," he said, turning on his ragged troops the ferocity that had no other outlet. "We can quit standing here like firewood waiting the axe, and *line up! now!*" A few had never shifted; a few moved back, others forward. Two at the back bolted. *"No!"* To his surprise, his voice halted them; they looked back. "Run and you're dead. We're all dead. By the gods, this is what we've been training *for.* Now get in your places, and pick up your weapons, and *listen* to me."

The others moved, after nervous glances at the slowly moving horsemen, back into their places. Gird grinned at them. "And get those weapons *ready!*" Far too slowly, the scythes and sickles and crooks and sticks came forward. At once Gird could see what was wrong, besides not having anything but a knife and short cudgel of his own. They could face only one way, and he knew, knew without even trying it, that they'd never reverse in formation, with weapons ready. There had to be a way—what could work? In his mind, he saw his mother's pincushion, pins sticking out all ways—but then how could they move? There was no time; the horsemen were closing, still at a walk, but he knew they would break to a trot or canter any moment. They must be a little puzzled by a mass of peasants who weren't trying to run, weren't screaming in fear.

"We have to kill them all," Gird said, as calmly as if he knew they could do it. "When they're close enough to fight, they can recognize you. The only way you can be safe back on your farms, is if you kill them all. That's

what all this drill is for, and now you're going to use it."
All those eyes stared right at his, blue and gray and
brown. He felt as if someone were draining all the
strength from his body; they were pulling it out of him,
demanding it. "You can do it," he said, not pleading
but firmly, reminding them. Never mind that this wasn't
the best place for a small group of half-trained peasants
to fight a mounted troop. Make do, make it work anyway. Miss this chance and you'll not have another. *I'll
be safely dead*, he thought wryly.

Almost automatically, the formation had chosen the
side facing the horsemen as the front. Gird walked
quickly along it, nodding, and then, talking as he worked,
shifted those on the flank and rear to face out. "If they
come from two directions, we have to be ready. You
turn like this—yes—facing out, and you behind him—
yes, you—you put your crook here. You, with the stick—
poke at their eyes."

"But do we hit the horse or the man?" asked someone behind him. This group had never drilled against
even imaginary horses.

"The horse," said Gird. "If you hurt the horse, either
it'll run or the man will fall off. Now think—you want to
open a big hole—"

He heard the hoofbeats louder now, and faster. Sure
enough, they were trotting towards him, eight horsemen
with their swords out and shining in the sun. The
horses looked huge, and their hooves pounded the dry
ground. The two sent around the peasant formation had
stopped: clearly they were intended to prevent run-
aways. The horsemen yelled, a shrill wavering cry, and
Gird yelled back, instinctively. His motley troop yelled,
too, a sound half-bellow and half-scream of fear. Two of
the horses shied, to be yanked back into line by their
riders. The peasants yelled again, louder; the riders
spurred to a full charge. Belatedly, the other two riders
charged the back side of the formation.

He was still thinking *I hope this works* when the
riders crashed into the block of peasants. The horses'
weight and speed drove them into the formation, but
five of them died before they cleared the other side.

Gird himself slammed his cudgel into one horse's head, leaping aside to let it stagger past into the sickle of the woman behind him. The rider missed his swing at Gird, but got the woman's arm; someone buried a scythe in his back before he could swing again. Two riders were dragged from their mounts and stabbed; another took a scythe in the belly before sliding sideways off his horse, screaming. Gird saw one of the women with a simple pole poke one rider off-balance; someone else caught his sword-arm and stabbed him as he fell.

It was over in minutes. Ten horsemen lay dead or dying on the ground; seven horses were dead, two crippled, and one, spooked, galloped away to the west. Gird looked around, amazed. The woman who had lost an arm sat propped against a dead horse, holding the stump and trying not to cry. Eight were dead; two others badly hurt. But—but peasants on foot, with no weapons but the tools of their work, had defeated armed men on horseback. Not an equal fight, but a real one.

He knew he should say something to them, but he couldn't think of anything fitting. He looked around the horizon, and saw only the sentinel shepherd, waving that no danger neared. Per came up to him, bleeding from a gash on his scalp, bruised, amazed to be alive. They all were. Per nodded at the woman who'd lost an arm, and said "Gird—I see now."

"Do you?" He felt a thousand years older as his fury drained away. It had to be better to die this way, fighting in the open, than rotting in dungeons or worked to hunger and sickness, but those silent bodies had been people a few minutes before. That woman had had two hands. He nodded at Per, and walked over to crouch beside her. Someone else had already torn a strip of cloth from her skirt to tie around the stump. "You—?"

She had gone pale, now, the gray-green pallor before fainting or death, but she managed a shaky smile, and moved her other hand, still gripping the sickle. "I—killed the horse."

"You did."

"I—fought—they—died—"

"Yes."

"All?"

"All."

"Good." With that she crumpled, and before they had finished sorting out the dead and wounded, she had died.

"Nooooo!" That scream came from one of the other women, who fell sobbing on the dead one's body. Then she whirled to face Gird, her face distorted. "You let her die! You—you killed her—and this is what happens—" She waved her arms to encompass the whole bloody scene. "You said fight to live, but she's dead, and Jori and Tam and Pilan—" Her voice broke into wild sobbing. Gird could think of nothing to say: she was right, after all. The woman had died, and seven others, and the two worst wounded would probably die, even if their lord didn't notice their wounds and kill them for that. The ten horsemen had probably had lovers or wives, maybe children—the weight of that guilt lay on his shoulders. But another voice, thick with pain, spoke out.

"Nay, Mirag! Rahi's dead, but she died happy, knowing she'd fought well. Not in a cage in the castle, like young Siela, when she tried to refuse that visiting duke, and not hanging from a hook on the wall, screaming for hours, like Varin. Gird promised us a chance, not safety."

"You say that, with that hole in you, with your heart's blood hot on your side? What will Eris say, tonight, when she has no one beside her; what will your children say?"

The man coughed, and wiped blood from his mouth. "Eris knows I'm here, and she knows why. If she weren't heavy for bearing, she'd be here herself, and the little ones too. This is best, Mirag. Rahi's satisfied, and I'm satisfied, and if you keep whining along like that, I'll say out what I think should happen to you!"

The woman paled, and her mouth shut with a snap. The man looked at Gird.

"She's not bad, Marig—Rahi's her sister."

"I'm sorry." It was all he could say. Marig shrugged,

an abrupt jerk of her shoulder; the man beckoned with a finger and Gird went to him.

"D'you know much of healer's arts?" Gird shook his head. "Might should learn, then. If I'd been able, I'd've put a tighter band on Rahi's arm. You'll need that craft, Gird."

"You'll get well, and be our healer," said Gird, but the man shook his head.

"Nay—this is a killing wound, but slower than some. Blood'll choke me, inside. But you'd best get all away, before more trouble comes."

A flick of memory, of his old sergeant's words long ago, came to Gird. "We won't leave wounded here, to be taken and questioned."

The man grinned tightly. "I hoped you'd think so. Make it quick, then."

"Is there anyone you'd—?"

"You'll do. You made it work." Gird grimaced; he had to have someone else agree, or it would feel like simple murder. He called Per over, and Aris, the yeoman marshal of Hightop. The wounded man was still conscious enough to give his assent again, and Aris, slightly more experienced than Per, saw at once why it must be done.

But neither would do it. So Gird took his well-worn dagger, and knelt by the man's side, and wondered how he'd feel if he were lying there, bleeding inside and choking, and how he could be quickest. Worst would be weakness, another pain that did not kill. So he put the whole strength of his arm into it, slicing almost through the man's neck.

The other badly injured man was unconscious, having been hit in the head, and then trampled under a horse. He quit breathing, with a last gasping snort, just as Gird reached him. Then it was only the hard, bloody work of dragging the corpses together onto a pile of brushwood and thistles, stacking what weapons they could use to one side. The group from Per's barton left first, to enter their village as best they might without attracting attention. They dared not carry any of the spare weapons, and Gird cautioned them not to take personal belongings from their friends' bodies.

"They'll know someone was here," he said, "to start the fire. But if you're carrying a tool or trinket someone recognizes, they'll know you, too, were part of it. This way it can seem that everyone from this village died, and it might spare you trouble." Not really, he knew: there was going to be trouble for everyone—but there had always been.

They seemed calm enough, even Marig. She had quit sobbing, at least, and she laid the locket she'd taken from her sister's neck back on her without being told twice. "Can't we even take Tam's scythe?" one man asked. "We don't have that many." His own crook had shattered. Gird shook his head again.

"With so few scythes, everyone will know that Tam's is with you. It'll be taken, but not to your village." He nodded to Per, who started them off, in trickles of two or three, moving indirectly.

Aris had the other two bartons ready to move out; each one carried his or her own weapon, and some of them carried a second, taken from the fallen. Gird dithered over the swords. For one of them to be found carrying a soldier's sword meant instant death—but to lose all those blades— In the end he let them decide, and ten volunteers belted swords they could not use around their peasant jerkins.

"Are you sure you need to burn the bodies?" Aris asked. Gird said nothing; he'd never imagined doing anything else. It was in all the tales. "We'll need a good start of them," Aris went on, when Gird didn't answer. "They'll have horses near enough—we don't know but what the smoke could be seen a long way, and the horses might come anyhow, and find us on the way. I don't know—I don't know if I could lead another fight today."

"You could if you had to," said Gird, plunged once more into how different it was in stories and reality. But Aris made sense, and he looked at the stacked bodies. The smoke would draw attention; someone would come, and that someone would likely be mounted, and ready for trouble. No smoke, and another patrol would go looking for the first—might not find them right away—but to let the dead lie out unprotected? He squinted up, and saw the first dark wings sailing far up. That alone would draw attention.

"All right," he said, finally. "No fire." *Lady, bless these dead—these brave and helpless—* Aris nodded, clearly relieved, and set off with his bartons. Gird angled away from them, his own new sword heavy at his side. *Did I do the right thing?* he asked himself. *Am I doing the right thing now?*

He looked back from a farther ridge, some hours later, and saw a column of dark wings. The woman's face came to him, that face so composed, even as she died, and the thought of dark beaks tearing her face, gouging out her eyes—he stopped abruptly, and threw up on the short grass, retching again and again, and scrubbing the dried blood on his hands. Nor could that be the end of it: he had started something, back there, that no crow could pick clean, and no fox bury the bones of—he had started something, like a boy rolling a rock down a hillside, and the end would be terrible.

Word of the Norwalk battle spread as fast among the lords as among the bartons. Gird, sifting reports from his runners and spies, spared a moment for amazement at the varying interpretations. By the end of the first day, that column of carrion crows had attracted another patrol. By the end of the second, the little village of Berryhedge had been put to the torch, and the villagers—those who had not fled the first night—were dead or penned in the nearest fort's yard, to be dealt with at the next court. The other two bartons had made it home safely, and so far their stolen blades had not been discovered. Bruises and cuts alone were not suspicious; too many of the farmfolk suffered injuries in their work year-round for that to be a sign of collaboration. But all the lords' guards were alert, watching for smoke from illicit fires, searching for weapons, stopping travelers on the roads. It was, some said, a huge army—an invasion from the neighboring kingdom of Tsaia—the private war of one lord on another—the peasant uprising that had been feared so long. On the strength of one escaped horse, and its tracks, someone even decided that it had been an attack by cavalry, using peasants as infantry. No, argued another: it was an alliance of horse nomads and peasants.

To Gird's surprise, some bartons now wanted to march out looking for patrols to fight. He reminded them of the dead and wounded, the village destroyed. But this was the first time that his people had fought, in military formation, against their old enemies, and they were elated.

"I can't see why you aren't happier about it," Felis said. "It worked, just as you said it would. Losses, yes: you had warned us, no war without deaths, without wounded. We understand that. But it worked. If we keep drilling, keep working, we can stand against them. And there are more of us; the numbers are on our side."

"I am happy." Even to himself, Gird did not sound happy, and he knew it. "I am—I just see the other side. Felis, we have only one real chance: we have to do it *all*, and do it right, because if we don't, then everyone who dies has died for nothing."

"It's not for nothing; it's for freedom." Felis scratched his sunburnt nose, and stalked around a moment before coming back to plant himself in front of Gird. "Look— you found a way for us to stand against their weapons and their training. It worked. Not even with the best of us, who've been training years now, but with one barton so new they hardly knew their left feet from their right. If you can do it with that, you can do it with anyone. Lady's grace, Gird, the day you walked into our camp I wouldn't believe you could get my men to pick up their own filth. But you did. What's wrong now?"

Gird could not answer. He knew, as he knew the ache in his bones, that it was not that easy. It could not be that easy. But they needed him to say it was, to cheer them on, to give the simple answer he knew was not enough. He felt himself resisting, as he had once or twice when the steward put pressure on him, as if he were a tree, rooting himself deep in the ground. The one thing he knew, the one thing he had to give, was his own certainty when he was right—and if he did not know he was right, he could not say it.

Felis, he could see, did not like his expression or that refusal to rejoice in their victory. Nor did others, who visibly damped their own glee when he was around. He should do it—but when he opened his mouth, stretched it in a smile, nothing came out. *We won*, he told himself, and the depths of his mind, cautious as any farmer to the last, said *We won that time*.

He was not even sure what it would take to win, in the way he meant win, in the way that would bring lasting peace. He threw himself into more planning, trying to calculate how many yeomen they had by now, and where, and trying to picture the larger country in which his war would now take place. A few soldiers had defected, men ordered to burn their own villages, or seize their own relatives, men who faced in adulthood what Gird had faced as a boy. They knew more of tactics than he did, and insisted that he had to have support in the towns, as well as the farms.

Meanwhile, the conflicts continued. Another ambush, and another. A guard encampment attacked at night; another village burned, and its fields torched. Like it or not, ready or not, it was on him; he must fly on that wind, or be left behind. Gird drove himself and those he knew best, traveling far to meet the yeoman-marshals of other bartons, to speak to those who were not sure, who were afraid. By autumn, he was moving far beyond the villages and fields he knew best, trusting those he had trained to keep his own group working, to find a safe wintering. This next year would see whole villages rise—even before planting time—and he had to be ready to lead his army in the field.

Chapter Sixteen

Something rasped, in the dry winter bushes, a sound too small for a cry, too great for a wild thing slipping away. Gird crouched, stock still, wondering whether to run now or investigate. It could be—it was probably—a trap. Someone had talked, and the town guard were out here to catch him. The sound came again, and with it another, like a sob choked down. Trickery, it would be. They were trying to lure him that way. But even as he thought this, he was moving, carefully as he might, threading his way through the prickly stiff brush.

In the gloom, he nearly stepped on the naked, bruised body that lay curled on its side. He stooped, after a hard look around that showed nothing but more brush. A man, an old man with thin gray hair and beard. One eye had been gouged out; the other showed only blood-shot white behind an enormous bruise. The man's pale skin bore many bruises, scratches where the bushes had torn at him, whip marks on his back, burns on his hands and feet. Yet he was alive, his breathing unsteady and loud, but strong enough, and he had a steady pulse at his neck.

Gird squatted on his heels, considering. It was already cold, and would be colder with full night. An old man, beaten and burned, missing an eye—he'd likely die by morning, left here with no covering and no care. But inside the town, the barton waited. Even now they'd be gathering, waiting for him, waiting for the hope that only he could bring. And the old man might die anyway. Gird touched the old man's shoulder, then wished he hadn't, for the bloodshot eye opened.

"No . . ." breathed a tremulous voice.

"You're safe," said Gird, knowing he lied, but not what else to say.

"Cold . . ." came a murmur.

"It's all right." His mind went back to his own home, the times he'd teased one of the women for that soothing "It's all right," when it wasn't. He could understand that now. It didn't make things all right. With a gusty sigh—too loud a sigh, he thought instantly: it would carry in the quiet twilight—Gird stripped to the waist and laid his shirt, sweaty as it was, on the old man's body. He had to have his dark jerkin for later . . . but he could spare the shirt.

"I'll help you," he said, and put his arm under the old man's shoulder. Groaning, and obviously trying to smother it, the old man managed to get his arms into Gird's shirt.

"You—should not—"

"I can't leave you here to die," said Gird. He couldn't help it that the words came out harsh, not comforting. He was late, and he was going to be later yet, and if he had to climb in over the wall, he was very likely to be seen.

"Who?" Now wrapped in the shirt, the old man had recovered scraps of his dignity; he asked with little volume but much authority. Gird chose to misunderstand the question.

"Who beat you? I don't know; I just found you. You don't remember?"

The old man held up his hands—longfingered, graceful hands, for all the ugly burns—and said softly, "Esea's light be with you, the High Lord's justice come to you, the Lady of Peace lay her hand on your brow—" He paused, as Gird scrambled back, careless of noise. "What's wrong?"

"Don't curse me!" It was hardly louder than the old man's murmur, but the anger in it carried.

"Curse you?" The old man chuckled, a breathy sound much like the whuffling of a horse. "Lad, it's a *blessing* —I'm giving you my blessing. Don't you know that much?"

Gird shifted uneasily. "What I know is, the longer we

stay here, the likelier we'll be seen. Whoever beat you—"

"The senior priest at Esea's hall," said the old man. He was sitting up on his own, now, looking with apparently idle curiosity at the burns on his feet. "He called me a heretic, and held what he would call a trial by fire. I call that torture, but the law permits it. And as I lived still when he was done, they stripped and beat me and threw me off the wall."

"You should be dead!" said Gird, and then reddened, realizing how it sounded.

The old man chuckled again. "That's what the high priest said, in other words—that I should be dead, for the harm I'd done and might do, and he did his best. The gods, however, sent you—" He reached around, in the gathering darkness, as if groping for a staff, then stretched his hand to Gird. "Here, then. Help me up."

"But you can't—"

"I can't lie here in the cold in your shirt. Come now—give me your hand. It's not so bad as you think." Gird reached out, and felt the man's hand slide into his. It was bony, as old hands are, with loose skin over the knuckles, but stronger than he expected. And he could not feel, against his own horny palm, the crusted burns he expected. The old man staggered once, then stood, peering about. "Ah—" he said finally. "There they are." Gird looked, and saw nothing but the chest-high bushes disappearing into evening gloom. "If you will wait," the old man said, more command than request, and he plunged into the tangle without making a sound. Gird waited, although he was definitely going to have to climb the wall. The barton would be wondering if he'd been caught.

When the old man came back, he had a very dirty ragged garment slung around his shoulders, over Gird's shirt, and some kind of covering on his feet. It looked, in that light, much like the rags peasants wore wrapped around their feet in winter, when they had nothing better.

"Now, lad," he said, far more briskly than Gird would

have thought possible. "Now we can go into town without fear."

Gird opened his mouth to argue, but instead found himself retracing his path through the bushes, the old man's hand clenched firmly on his elbow. The old man's other hand held Gird's staff. Without fear? Did the old man plan to ask the gate guards to let them in, when he'd been beaten and left for dead? What was he?

When they came to the gates, the postern was still open, and the last few townspeople were hurrying in. A row of torches burned brightly, lighting their faces for the guards to see. Gird tried to shy aside, into the shadows, but the old man's hand forced him to walk right up the middle of the trade road, into that golden light. He thought frantically how he could get out of this without alerting the guards, and glanced sideways at the old man.

In torchlight, the old man looked altogether different. Smaller, crook-backed, with a dry seamed scar where his eye had been, not the red dripping socket Gird had seen. Almost bald on top, and a wisp of pure white at his chin, a patched leather cape over a rough wool shirt (and it doesn't even look like my shirt, thought Gird), patched leather breeches on bowed legs, feet indeed wrapped in dirty rags. He leaned on Gird's arm, and the staff, as if his legs could hardly bear his weight.

"Ho, there!" One of the guards stepped forward, lifting a torch to peer at their faces. "And who be you, coming in so late—don't know your face!"

Gird opened his mouth, and found a name in it. "Amis of Barle's village, m'lord, and m'father's father Geris, come to pilgrimage at th'shrine."

"Should've come earlier; the gate's closed to outsiders."

At this the old man mewled, an infantile wail of misery and disappointment. The guard grinned, insolent but not unkind. "Never seen anyone needed a miracle more, and that's a fact. Got any honey to sweeten the sib, Amis of Barle's?"

"Honey, m'lord?" Gird let his jaw hang down stupidly, and patted his "grandfather's" hand. "We's no bees, m'lord, that's for them's got orchard trees. But we's barley-cake—" He fished in his jerkin for the stale end of barley cake he'd saved from breakfast, and offered it. Whatever was going on, he was supposed to pretend stupidity and meekness. The guardsman looked at him, long and steady, then pushed it back. "If that's all you've had, coming in from so far, keep it. Now, gransire, we've had an upset today, and I'll have to see your hands before you enter."

"Hands?" asked Gird before he thought. The one on his arm squeezed hard, hard as a strong young man, and released him. The guard nodded.

"In case a thief tries to sneak back in," he said. "He's hand-branded, that one, and we're to look at all strangers, especially those with one eye gone. I'm sure your gransire isn't the thief, but I must look." And he took each of the old man's knotted hands, and looked at the palm. So did Gird—and saw nothing but old pink skin, marked by heavy work. The guard jerked his chin up. "Get on in, fellow, you and your gransire, and be sure you're not up to any mischief this night. Beggars' steps on the winter side of Hall, and no laying up in someone's doorway."

"Thanks, m'lord." Gird found himself pulling his forelock before he thought of it, and edged by the guard with care for his companion.

Once through the town's wall, the old man used his grip of Gird's elbow to guide him toward the main square. The streets were busy yet, full of people who knew exactly where to go. Gird had his own directions, from the gate, but he went where the old man wanted him to—he had no choice.

In the square, a few stalls still had shutters open. A bakery, its main doors closed, sold the remnants of the day's baking out a broad window. From one stall came the sour smell of bad ale, from another the stomach-churning scent of hot oil and frying meat. Gird swallowed his hunger, and found that his tongue now responded to his own will.

"I've somewhere to go," he said gruffly. "Can you find a safe place?"

"Better than you," said the old man. "Could you have come through the gates alone?"

Gird grunted. Of course he couldn't, not that late, but if it hadn't been for the old man, he wouldn't have been that late. "I don't understand you," he said. "You were hurt, you could hardly move—"

"We can't stand here in the open talking," said the old man. "I want my supper." This last became a weak whine, suitable to the aged cripple he seemed to be, and Gird was not surprised to see a couple of guards walk by, scanning the faces as they went.

"I don't have anything but that barley cake," said Gird, and added unwillingly, as the guards paused, "Granther, you know that. It took all coppers we's got to make this trip for your eye. Here—" He fished out the barley cake, and broke it, as the guards watched. The old man took his share in a shaky hand, almost whimpering in his eagerness. A drop of spittle ran down his chin into his beard, glittering in the guards' torchlight.

"Beggars' steps over there," said one of the guards gruffly, gesturing across the square. Gird bobbed his head, hoping he looked stupid and harmless. The guards moved on, stopping to joke with the baker's lass, as she reached to close the shutters at the window. The old man touched Gird's arm, pushing him gently towards the beggars' steps.

When they sank down on the lowest of the five steps, Gird stuffed his piece of barley cake back into his jerkin, and said again "I have somewhere I must go. Can you stay here? Will they find you?"

In the dimness, the old man's face was suddenly more visible, as if a candle had been lit inside it. "Lad, I can stay here, or go, or stay with you, and they will not find me—have you seen nothing this evening?"

"Riddles," said Gird. "You give me tricks and riddles—"

"I give you light in darkness." The old man's face shone brighter, then dimmed. "But the blind cannot see light, and think darkness is reality."

Gird stirred on the cold step, not sure what he could say. The old man was mad, and no wonder, with what he'd been through. He must have been one of *them*— perhaps one of their elder mages—and he'd angered someone. They'd taken their revenge, and wrecked his mind as well as his body. Probably as bad as the rest of them, when he was whole, but now— "I need to go now," he said, as gently as he could. "I'll come back to you."

"Yes," said the old man. "You will." He bit off a chunk of the barley cake, and started chewing it. Gird watched a moment, feeling a strange confusion in his mind, then shook his head and got up.

The meeting place, when he finally found it, was a merchant's storeroom crowded with nervous men, at least a dozen of them, and lit by two candles. He'd expected only the elders of the barton, but apparently others had insisted on coming. Was this a trap? He tried to see the corners of the storeroom as he gave the password again, but darkness lurked behind bales and boxes as if it were alive and twitching. His neck itched; he wanted to whirl and look behind himself, but he controlled that urge.

Calis, the only man he'd met before, limped forward to shake his arm and then grinned broadly at the rest. "I told you he'd come. Whatever happens, he'd come."

"He's late." That was a square-built, black-bearded man, with a look of authority and the weathered face of someone out in the open most of his life.

"He's here. That's what counts." Calis shook his arm again. "Lady bless you, Gird, for coming. You'll lead us, eh? Make us free?"

Calis had not sounded that simple back in Harrow, when he visited that barton's drill. Then he had seemed a possible leader, someone who could organize a barton, start its training. Gird looked around as calmly as he might, trying to figure out what had gone wrong here. Fifteen men, no women—that was still common enough, despite his urging. None very young: quite right, at such a secret meeting; young men talked too much. None very old. Four held themselves with a kind of furious rigidity: men used to command, perhaps, pretending a passivity they could not feel? Gird smiled at the black-bearded man. "Hurry makes the fleet fall, and the aim wide: I came as I might, to come safely."

"You would preach safety in war?" That was another of the four he'd noted, a tall brown bear of a man leaning against the stacked boxes across from him.

"I preach nothing, being no priest. As Calis will have told you, I expect—" He glanced at Calis, whose gaze slid past him. So. Trouble indeed. "I teach what seems obvious to me, that wild rebellion against the king but causes death and torment."

"And this is what we came for?" The brown man pushed away from the boxes to confront him. "We came to hear the same song the priests sing: obey, submit, seek peace from the Lady in your hour of death?"

"Gird, *tell* them. Tell them what you told us at Harrow."

The worst trouble: treachery. Their first rule was never to mention one barton in another, to say only "there" or "that other place" or "his barton." Gird shook Calis's hand from his arm, but without violence, and tried to decide where the worst danger lay. He could not fight fifteen, were they all of the same mind, but it was just as likely that Calis had tried to entrap honest rebels as well as one rebel leader. If he could but find them out, and lead them. A dense silence packed the room thicker than the men. Someone behind the black-bearded man coughed. Was it a signal?

Gird glanced around the group, meeting all eyes but Calis's. In the candlelight, all glittered; he could not tell false from true. He lifted his hand for silence, though all were quiet, and began.

"You know the times are bad. You know they're getting worse. Bad enough when peasants are murdered at their work, when wives and mothers are raped and beaten, left for dead with their babies crawling in their blood. Worse, when the craftsman's skill is bought with pain and threats, when a smith must make shackles and chains for prisoners, not plows and harrows for farming. Bad enough when merchants' goods are stolen for the rich, and they must cheat the poor to survive." He looked from face to face. There was one closed, tight with anger—for old wrongs, or for his words?

Another sat slack-jawed, as if he could drink Gird's words in, taste them on his tongue. There in the dim shadows at the back, two heads leaned together, mouth to ear.

"You know there's been fighting—everyone knows that. Men and women have died, for trying to save their own lives. You know that all the times farmers and craftsmen and merchants have tried to fight against trained soldiers, they've been killed, and their families with them. What I'm telling you is about another way."

"A way for peasants to fight soldiers?" asked the black-bearded man.

"A way for peasants to *be* soldiers." Gird paused. That was the nub of it, and enough to have him hanged. He sensed a stirring back in the shadows. Well, he need not mince words now, having already convicted himself, and maybe boldness would gather a few to his side. "The difference between soldiers and hopeless fools willing to die is training. Not fine swords, nor magic, but training—the training soldiers have."

"And you can give us that training?" *That* voice came from wealth and privilege, with its arrogant sonorities. Gird smiled straight at it.

"I? I'm a farmer: I *give* nothing. But I know how you can *earn* that training, and that's my reason here." Out of the gloom sea-green eyes stared into his. He could just make out a foxy brush of hair, a slender figure no longer lounging in the shadows but upright, alert. Odds it was some noble's son, come to spit rebels with his guards around him to keep him safe.

"Gods know, farmers give nothing." That voice again, this time clearly belonging to green eyes and an arrogant set of head and shoulders. "That sounds like kapristi talking, if a farmer knows what kapristi are." He didn't, but he caught the muttered "Gnomes!" of another.

"Farmers earn their bread," Gird said, working his toes in his boots to ready himself. It had to come soon. "As craftsmen do, and merchants too, most times. What's earned feeds; what's given rots the belly. What's taken—" He stopped as light dazzled his eyes, light that polished the blades drawn against him. He saw no source, but it centered on the brown man.

"What's taken belongs to the taker," said he, amusement ruffling the edge of his voice. "Traitors taken, in this town, belong to me." He stood easily, weaponless, but from behind the stacked boxes had come two guards, with pikes, and four of the other men had drawn swords. To Gird's surprise, the green-eyed man wasn't one of them: his face drew back, shocked into loss of its earlier dignity. Calis stood dithering, clearly wondering whether to seize Gird or retreat to the safety of shadows.

"What's taken," Gird said, meeting the brown man's eyes, "chokes the taker." His fingers clenched and loosened, and he realized then that he'd left his stout staff with the old man on the beggars' steps. *Idiot* he told himself. *You're asking the gods for a miracle*. The brown man gave a smile that might have been genuine admiration.

"You're brave, at least—no whining craven like most of your type. Too bad you didn't choose honest soldiery, fellow—"

"I tried," said Gird, keeping his voice level with an effort. He was not sure why he bothered to answer, save that he had no plan, and saw little help in the faces of the others. "As a lad, I joined my count's guard right willingly. But then—"

"What?" asked the brown man, lifting a hand to halt the guards who had moved a step nearer. Gird looked at him, seeing nothing like the vindictive arrogance of his own count. Those eyes might have been honest; that mouth had laughed honestly, at things worth amusement, not at others' pain. Well, it would serve nothing, but he would tell this man the truth, and if one of them lived after this night, that one would know it had been told.

"The lord of our village came from the king's court with his friends, to celebrate his coming of age. One of the village lads chose that confusion to steal plums from the lord's orchard—" Gird paused, and the man nodded for him to go on. Despite himself, his voice trembled over the next phrases, and he forced more breath into it, almost growling at the end. "So our lord had him taken, which was just enough, and had him tormented and finally maimed, which was not just, not for a few plums. And he enjoyed the sight, gloating over the boy's pain, and I—" He stopped again, drew in a great breath. "I was hardly older; I'd known Meris all my life." His accent thickened, he could tell the brown man had trouble following it now. "I knew—I knew someday they'd tell me the same, to hurt or kill some poor lad as only wanted a handful of plums or a truss of grapes. Kill m'own folk, maybe, if in a bad year th'cows wandered. I couldna do that—could not—and so I ran, and it fell hard on my own folk even when I came back."

"You're from Kelaive's domain," the brown man said, softly. "That insolent pup, worst of a bad litter. I'd heard that tale differently."

"Certain so, if *he* told it," said Gird, caught up as always in that old pain, but also, suddenly curious to know how Kelaive told it.

"Not from him: his sergeant told one of my guards, and it passed to me on one long march—a good soldier ruined, he said, by a bad lord's whim, and the blame fell on him, too, for not knowing how to keep you." The man shook his head. "Well. You know the law, that's clear, and your place in it. You had a bad master; that's no excuse—"

"And what would be?" asked Gird, his voice tight with unshed tears and old anger still caged. "Would my mother's death, when that count refused the simples of the wood to us? Would our hunger, in a bad winter when Kelaive danced in the king's hall and laid double taxes on, to buy himself more gowns? Would my daughter's pain, her own babe by her lover dead, and her raped to bear a stranger's child? Cows stolen to make his feasts, sheep taken to give him wool—by all the gods, we farmers may not give, but we take better care of our least creatures than you lords do of us. Prod an ox and it kicks, and even a beaten cur will turn and bite your heel—"

"Peace, fellow!" The brown man stared at him. "Esea's

dawn, but you've a long tongue in your head, and wit in that thick skull. A hard use dulls most tools, but those of high temper—" He stopped, gestured, and the four drawn swords rasped back into their sheaths, though the guards stayed as they were, poised just behind him. "See here: would you take service with me, you and your family safe from Kelaive, and quit this nonsense? You'll be killed, elsewise, and your family take the brunt of Kelaive's bad will: by law I must report those rebels I seize."

He might have done it, had not Calis seized his hand and rushed into speech. "Yes, Gird, yes! He's a good lord, he is, and fair and just—he'll keep his word to you—" But under the rush of words was fear, and in the other eyes he saw the same fear trembling. He shook off Calis's hand, and met the brown man's eyes.

"You will protect me, you say." The brown man nodded, gravely. "But what of these others? You may be trying to be a good lord, sir—" The sir came out slowly, but inexorably, "—but here are those who thought you bad enough to join a plot against you." He waved his hand around at those who clearly wished they could be invisible. "You may be better than Kelaive—I daresay you are, and it should be easy enough. But you can't protect all those that need it, and it looks like you haven't protected all your own, even."

The brown man looked around; Gird watched the men flinch as he looked at each one slowly. "Cobbler. Wheelwright. Cloth merchant. Baker's helper. You think to make a government out of such as these, farmer? Who'll make your laws? Who'll judge in your courts?"

"Honest men, sir." He didn't want to say "sir," to someone who would either kill him, or be killed, this night, but he found himself doing it anyway. And he could not hate this man, who was so much more reasonable than Kelaive.

"Honest *merchants*?" Scorn edged the brown man's voice. Gird noticed one of the men stiffen: that had gone home. "You think to find honest judges from a tangle of merchants who pour water in the milk, or chalk in flour they sell you. Or among farmers who put the bruised fruit in the basket first, or craftsmen who put as much base metal in gold or silver as they can?"

"As near there as among nobles, sir," Gird said, and braced himself for the blow that would surely come. The brown man glared at him, showing anger for the first time. "At least among common men, of different trades, there's a chance they'd stick to a measure, not make different weights and measures for each case."

"Damn!" The brown man clenched his fist then opened it. "You *are* a man, after all. I hate—it's too bad you cannot bring yourself to take service here." He glanced aside, at the black-bearded man who had been one of the swordsmen. "Remember what I said, Caer? Squeeze the mud, and it turns to stone; beat the ore and get gold: from the pressure we put on them, such comes out. I would be proud if son of mine had courage to speak so before a deadly peril, had wit to think in bondage." He turned back to Gird. "Death it must be, but a man like you does not fear death. I swear no torment; come quietly and I'll ensure the headsman's single blow. If you must fight, then I cannot interfere, and not all wounds kill cleanly."

For some reason he could not define, Gird felt a change in the room's atmosphere, as if a shutter had opened, letting in fresher air and truer light. He smiled at the brown man. "Sir, it's not my way to give in so easily. But I will admit that had my lord been like you, I might not be here."

"Were my subjects like you, Gird, I might not be here either." He looked around again. "Out of these weaklings, these trimmers, you'd make an army? Were you to have the chance to try, I'd wish you luck of it, but worry none."

Some bright image stung Gird's mind, and he said "Well—if you have no worry, you could let me train them, as a wager, and see if they can withstand trained arms."

The man laughed openly. "Well, indeed, fellow! Wit and tenacity combined! Let you train a score or so of malcontents to harrass my guards, and for a wager— that passes wit, Gird of Kelaive's domain, and near approaches madness. And I should be mad to take such wager."

"But why are you here, if you fear nothing from them?"

The brown man scowled, and a quick flicking glance to the green-eyed youth in the shadows conveyed some urgent menace. "You ask much, fellow. But if you think only subjects have troubled families, and because you will soon be dead, I'll tell you. That—" He flicked a hand at the green-eyed youth, "That's my son, one of them. A true-son, of my lady's breeding. I came because he came, and knew he came because that bold tailor, there, came to me and warned me. My son's of an age to seek adventures, to throw off fatherly wisdom, and stir up excitement—to seek, in a word, such midnight meetings, secret societies, all that."

"I tried to tell you—" began the youth, but his father's gesture stopped him.

"He would say that he's done this for me: the lad lies, and all my beatings never stopped him. He feels deprived, that his brothers' share of my wealth is larger. They've increased it; he's squandered his. So he joins conspiracies against me, but with no real conviction. He'd most likely have confessed this one in another season."

"Your son. You love him?"

"Love! He's my son; he's my blood and bone—but he's as craven as any of these fools about to spend their last breath in prison."

"You'll put him there too?"

"Him? No; he's my son. I may send him off to serve with the king's army against the nomads, though. Let him freeze his rump in an icy saddle for a winter, and see if he learns wisdom."

"And so a rich young man, who's had all the chances to do better, gets off with a half-year's exile from home, while the poor wretches with him must die—"

"It's necessary," said the brown man roughly.

"Oh, it's necessary," said Gird slowly, drawling it out in caricature of his own peasant accent. "And it's that makes it necessary for us to fight. When it comes down to it, your justice is to save your own blood, and kill what stands in the way."

"So does anyone!" snapped the man, his patience clearly fraying.

"No, sir. I've seen it myself, villagers sharing their few bits of food so the fewest died. We was all hungry, sir, each one of us, but we didn't grab for self alone. You don't have to believe it, but I've seen, and I know, and so does most of these others."

Suddenly, as if he were suspended in the air at the very top of the room, Gird saw himself from outside, his own heavy-boned weatherbeaten face, his shaggy thinning hair, his heavy arms gleamed with sweat, his old leather jerkin a little loose where the past months of travel had thinned his belly. Baggy-kneed breeches, patched and stained, worn boots badly in need of resoling, no weapons but fists like knotted lumps of hardwood.

And he saw the brown man, and even into the brown man's mind—saw the slight awe the brown man felt, and the fainter tinge of disgust that such a lout should speak sense, when his own son had none. He saw the candlelight quiver on a guard's helmet as the man shifted slightly; he saw the sides and backs of the other heads watching him. And he saw the green-eyed man, that had looked older but was only a youth, sliding a throwing knife from his sleeve, as he looked at his father.

He was back in himself, yelling "*No!*" in a bellow that raised dust from the boxes, and throwing himself at the brown man so fast that the guards could not react. He hit the brown man square, and knocked him sprawling, just as the blade came spinning out of the dark, catching light and flickering. It missed them both, and stuck in the floor, quivering. The guard on that side had seen the blade whirl past; he turned to face the thrower. The other guard moved forward to swing at Gird, but met instead the black-bearded man, who had yanked his sword out to take Gird from behind. Their weapons rang together, and Gird managed to roll off the brown man and get out from under them.

Then a second blade flashed through the light and

caught Calis in the throat, even as he pointed a finger to the green-eyed man.

"Traitor," he said. "Call my father in, will you? Try to warn him?" And as Calis choked in his blood and died, the green-eyed man had his own sword out, and came into the fight on his own. He caught the black-bearded man under the ribs from behind, then parried the guard's pike stroke and danced away. "Brother in law, are thy ribs sore enough?" The black-bearded man had fallen, hardly an arm's length from Gird, and blood rolled out from beneath his hand. The brown man scrambled back, grabbing the fallen swordsman's weapon.

Gird saw this in a strange inside-out way which left him dazed for the moment. He had wedged himself between two boxes, and tore at one with his hands, hoping to loosen a slat he could use to fight with. Now the other three swordsmen had their weapons out—but not all on one side. Two struck at the brown man, one defended; one of the pikemen, by this time had fallen to another thrown knife, from whom Gird could not see.

Of all the outcomes to such a meeting, he'd never imagined this, a fight between nobles—and not only nobles, but father and son. Across the room, he saw one of those he thought true rebels slip toward the door. Another caught his eye, lifted spread hands. What could they do? Clearly nothing, but escape—this was no brawl for unarmed men to meddle in. He could not help watching, though, as the father stood ground over the black-bearded man, fencing cautiously against his son's supporter. It was madness to stay—the son must have arranged his invitation, planning to blame the father's death on a stranger, a troublemaker from another land. Yet—as he saw from the edge of his vision another of the onlookers slip out the door—yet he had to know who would win, who would be pursuing him.

The fight went on, the clash of blades surely loud enough to draw notice. None of the combatants bothered with Gird; he might have been a spectator at a wagered match. He wondered if any of those who left were going to alert the city guard. He wondered more at what he saw. The green-eyed son, for all the faults his father claimed, a most skillful swordsman, pressed his father's ally back. The second guard, after a few cautious chopping strokes with the pike, tried to pin his opponent in a corner, but he was taken from the side, by the third man, who opened his belly. The guard groaned and sagged to the floor.

Now the brown man and one friend faced three: his son and his two allies. Gird eyed the fallen pike: he could use *that* if he got hold of it, but how? And to what use should he put it, besides escape—and he could escape now, if he would. Instead, he watched, fascinated, the struggle before him. The brown man, when his guard fell, gave no sign of fear or alarm, but fought the more hardily, his blows coming swift and strong against two, while his remaining friend fought his son. Yet he had to yield ground, backing away from his wounded son-in-law. The green-eyed man opened a gash in his opponent's arm, just as the father managed to slice deeply into one of the two he faced. That one dropped his sword tip to grab at the wound, and the father's sword slid into his neck. But not unscathed—his other opponent stabbed deeply into his thigh, and he staggered. In an instant, he recovered, so that his eager opponent, careless, found himself transfixed on a blade that pierced him to the backbone. His legs failed, and he sagged from the blade, dragging the brown man's arm downward.

Then the son turned, from a deathstroke to his father's friend, and raised his sword. And then Gird moved, scooped up the guard's fallen pike, and swung it like a quarterstaff to knock the son's sword aside. Leaping over the welter of blood and bodies, he tackled the son as he might have tackled a runaway calf, bearing him to the floor with his own great size.

Silence, curiously loud in his ears. Someone groaned; several someones breathed harshly. Under him, the green-eyed man heaved up without success; Gird put a knee in his back and dared look back at the carnage.

He met the level gaze of the brown man, the father, now tightening a belt around his bleeding thigh. When he had it knotted to his satisfaction, the brown man pushed himself to his feet, and moved unsteadily to Gird's side, looking down with an expression Gird could not read.

"Well, Jernoth, you've given me quite a problem this time. What can I do with you now?"

"I never meant this—" The voice was husky and strained, with what besides Gird's weight on his back Gird could not tell.

"Maybe not: but you meant mischief enough. What can I do?"

"Kill him," said Gird, without thinking. The brown man's intense gaze shifted to him.

"Kill my son? Who, if others die, might be my heir?"

Gird felt the tremor beneath him, the shiver of hope. "You'd have killed me, sir, as hasn't done you any harm, but saved your life twice this night. Why not him, that did the harm with intent? Do you think such a one should rule—do you think he'll be better than Kelaive?"

"Quiet, you stinking serf!" said the captive. "It doesn't matter what you want. I'm a noble; he won't kill me."

Gird ignored this, and looked straight at the brown man's drawn face. "Sir, a farmer has to cull as well as foster: it's part of good husbandry. Isn't a ruler like a farmer, seeking to improve the quality of his domain?"

"My son—blood of my blood—"

"Your son tried to kill you, and not even openly, in challenge. He's the cause of all these deaths. He was plotting you say, and not for the first time. Any farmer culls stock; foresters cull trees. You'd cull us peasants. Try the knife's edge on your own cheek, before you shave another. Sir."

The brown man picked up the pike Gird had used, and placed the point against his son's neck.

"Get off him."

"Are you—?"

"Get off him, fellow." Gird slid back, catching the son's elbows as he tried to get his arms under him.

"He's lost less blood than you, sir."

"Indeed. And I'm supposed to think you care which

of us lives? Such as you hate all nobles; you'd be glad to see us all dead."

"No." Gird sat on the son's hips, one hand clamping the other's elbows behind his back, and fished in his jerkin for the roll of thongs he kept handy. He got it out, plucked one from the tangle, and quickly lashed the younger man's elbows together. "No, sir, I don't hate you, personally. I think you don't see clearly, but you may be trying the best you know how. At least you aren't like Kelaive. And I'm not going to let your son up to kill you, with you so weak."

"And you weren't thinking of taking this pike to me if I fell?"

"No. That's not what I'm here for." He pushed himself up, wondering if the brown man would now swing at him with the pike. He was unhurt; he ought to be able to dodge it easily enough.

"No. I suppose you weren't." The brown man regarded him thoughtfully. "You were here to teach my subjects how to fight my army, but you weren't here to play my son's game and kill me." His eyes closed briefly, and he sighed. "Damn. What a tangle this is—and I wonder why the city guard hasn't been beating the door in? We've made noise enough. Perhaps Jernoth bought them off, too."

"There's no one you can trust," said Jernoth savagely. His father let the pike rest heavier on his neck, and he was silent.

"He could be right," the brown man said. "And I'm not sure I could fight my way home, like this." He looked at Gird. "And what about you?"

"I've no wish to die, when your traitor son lives, and no wish to spend time in your dungeons, either."

"No—damn you, fellow, you keep making calm sense when any normal serf would be shivering in a heap. The others all ran away, and I doubt they're sleeping sound now. What are you, anyway? Have the gods laid a call on you?"

"No." Gird shook his head firmly. "My folk followed the Lady of Peace; she teaches submission. And your gods support you."

A clatter of boots on the street outside stopped him; something crashed into the shop beyond the door.

"You should have run when you could," said the brown man.

"You could acknowledge my help," said Gird. Then the guards were in the room, their torches sending wild flickers of bright orange across the calmer candlelight. They skidded to a halt, their pikes at Gird's back.

"M'lord Sier," said the one with a knot of bright yellow at his shoulder. "Someone reported noise—" His voice trailed away as he looked around him.

"Treachery, sergeant," said the brown man.

"This lout?" asked the sergeant.

"No." The brown man smiled at Gird. "That fellow came to my aid; the traitors lie dead, all but one." He looked down at his son, and the sergeant's breath hissed in.

"Lord—Jernoth, m'lord?"

"Lord Jernoth. And two of these others." He pointed, and the sergeant's breath hissed again. Clearly he recognized them all. The brown man's orders brought him to quick attention. "Sergeant, send word—I will need a cart; I've been wounded. This—fellow—" He waved a hand at Gird. "If he had not saved me, you would have a new sier this night; he is a stranger, but welcome in the city for three days, for his service. See he gets a tally from the guardhouse, meals and beer; I brought nothing with me, not so much as a copper crab."

"Yes, m'lord Sier." The sergeant eyed Gird with dubious respect.

"And then Lord Jernoth must be straitly confined until I pass judgment; it is ill done to hurry such a decision." This he said facing Gird directly; but somewhere in the tone of his voice, Gird sensed that he would come to follow Gird's advice.

From there, things went smoothly; the guards bound the young man more securely, then hauled him to his feet and away. Another tended the brown man's wounds, and yet another had already sped away with messages. The sergeant opened his belt-pouch with deliberate slowness, and pulled out a flat wooden tally, one end stamped with the Sier's mark.

"This here's a meal tally, good at any inn but the Goldmark or the White Wing—them's only for nobles." He took his dagger and made three scores across the tally. "That's for a day's food and beer; they'll break off the end each time, to the next line. Understand?"

"Yes, sir." Gird wondered if he was really going to get free this easily.

The sergeant lowered his voice and went on. "What I heard was there was a meeting of conspirators, to hear a stranger, an outsider who came in to start trouble. Have any idea who that was?"

"Me, sir?" Stupidity was always a safe mask for a peasant.

"And then here you are, without a mark on you, but the Sier says you saved his life. Me, I wonder if you meant to do that—but his orders is my life, as they say, and he says let you bide here three days on free meals and beer. All I say is, you'd best be gone by sundown that third day, or the sier might have remembered something he wants to ask you. I would."

"Yes, sir."

"And I don't suppose you'll be having any quiet little meetings with rebels while you're here, either."

"No, sir."

"All right. Go fill your belly, and stay out of my sight."

Gird went out into the dark street, only to be stopped by an arriving troop of guards, who let him go when he showed his tally. He tried to walk like someone with honest business, but the events of the past hour or so were beginning to touch his feelings, as well as his mind. When he got to the main square, he edged his way around it, touching the walls of one building after another, until he found the beggars' steps.

Chapter Seventeen

"You had an interesting evening?" The old man's voice was soft, but clearly audible. Gird jumped, then crouched quickly beside him. "Here's your staff," the old man said, brushing his knuckles with it, as if he could see in the dark. Gird clutched at it, consoling himself with its smooth oiled strength. If only he'd had it with him . . .

"You'd have gotten yourself killed," the old man said, even more softly.

"You—what do *you* know about it?"

"Shh." Gird felt a strong, bony hand on his forearm, and the faint warmth of the old man's body leaning against his. In the brief silence, he was aware of other movement on the beggars' steps, movement that might have been the restlessness of disturbed sleepers.

The old man's body was warmer than he'd thought at first; along his right side he began to feel as if he sat before a fire. He had not thought he could sleep, but now he felt himself sinking into that warmth, as the exhaustion of the day and the night's exertions landed on him. It was so comfortable—and he could not, at the moment, feel threatened.

He woke at dawn, when the great bells of Esea's Hall rang out to declare the sun's daily triumph. The sound crashed through him, shaking him out of peaceful dreams, and for an instant he thought he was being attacked. The old man's hand on his arm quieted him. Gird looked around wildly. The others who had spent the night on the beggars' steps were stirring, sitting up, stretching. The man beside him—was someone else. He jerked his arm back.

"Easy," the old man's voice said, out of a different face. "It's just a face." It wasn't a *very* different face, after all: still old, still with the same basic shape. He looked less feeble, this morning, and was certainly not blind— "A miracle, remember? We came for that."

"But—"

"We should find something to eat." The old man stood, and Gird unfolded himself, less stiff than he'd expected to be. "What is that?" the old man asked.

It was the tally the guard sergeant had given him. "It's—I can get food, at an inn. A tally from the sier."

The old man's wispy white brows raised. "So—the sier himself. I knew it was important, but—"

Gird had had enough of the old man, who was certainly not the helpless, tortured creature who had aroused his pity the evening before. "I will share my breakfast with you, but then—"

"You wish I would go away. I worry you, don't I?" That face was not guileless at all; Gird was more than worried. Whatever this was—and he was no longer sure it was a man and not some kind of demon—it kept forcing him into impossible situations.

"I have business," Gird said, through clenched teeth. "I only wanted to help you, and—"

The thin hand, so very strong, slid under his elbow and gripped his arm as if to steady a fragile, tottering oldster. "And you think I've brought more danger on you, more trouble. And you think *I* was blind, as I know you are. Come along, Gird Strongarm—I know you, and you will know me better before this day is done."

As before, he could not shake that grip, and found himself walking where the old man willed. To the public fountain, to wash his face and hands. To a cheap inn, where he bought hot, meat-stuffed rolls from the serving window, getting double the amount because he refused the ale that the servant offered. To a crooked alley, where they leaned against the bulging wall of a baker's oven, and ate the rolls, while cats wound around their ankles, begging. The food steadied him, and restored the town walls and streets to their normal colors, no longer bright and scintillating as if he had a fever, but ordinary, subdued, under a gray wintry sky.

"You are better now," the old man said, still clutching his elbow. Gird looked down at him.

"In body, yes. But you—what are you?"

"What I told you. A priest of Esea, presently in difficulty with his fellow priests. You have my gratitude for your service—"

"You didn't need me!" Fed, awake, alert, Gird had been remembering that whole sequence of events. "You only seemed hurt—you tricked me."

"No." The man's voice was low. "No—I could have died. I almost did. You do not understand—you could not—all that happened to me, or what my powers are. But I was near death, when you found me: that is true. You saved my life."

"But you healed—" Gird could not quite say it; his fingers wanted to make warding signs.

The man sighed. "Gird, we need to talk, you and I. You have done me a great service; so far I have done you only a small one, which you don't yet realize. You do not trust me—and no, that's not reading your mind; you smell of fear. But we should both leave this town, before we find more trouble than your strength or my powers can handle. Will you trust me for that?"

"I know I have to leave," Gird muttered. "He said so, and—and I don't know towns, that well. But I have tallies for two days more."

"Which no one will be surprised if you use to get food for travel, and then leave. That's what the sier would expect you to do. If you stay in Grahlin, they'll begin to wonder if you have more people to meet."

"Can I use the tallies again so soon?" asked Gird, staring at the ragged break on the end as if he thought it would speak to him. The old man chuckled, but it was a friendly chuckle.

"We don't have to go to the same inn. Besides, the sier gives these tallies to many men—to anyone on his service that day. Didn't you notice that the inn servant scarcely looked at you?" Gird had not noticed; he had been trying to see if anyone were following them. "You can use both tallies at one inn; tell them you want food to travel. They'll be used to that."

So it proved. His request brought no comment, and the servant handed over a cloth sack bulging with bread and cheese, and a jug of ale. On the old man's suggestion, Gird had retained the bit of wood with the sier's mark on it, left when the last of the tally was broken. That got him past the gate guards with hardly a glance. The old man had left ahead of him; Gird was tempted to go out the other gate, but felt it would not be fair.

The old man waited just out of sight of the gate, squatting in the windshadow of a tree beside the road. As Gird came alongside, he stood up and began walking with him, steadying himself with Gird's staff.

"Let me start with what is strangest to you," he said without preamble. "My powers and my knowledge."

Gird grunted. He was trying to think how he was going to explain to the others that his foray into the town had been not only useless, but disastrous. They had lost their one contact; the sier knew his face. Worse, the sier knew he had active enemies. Yet they needed someone in this town; it was sitting right there where the trade road met the river road, and soldiers based here could ruin any plan he might make for the whole area. That might be more than a year away—he knew that—but still the town could not be ignored.

He jumped as the old man's hand bit into his elbow. "Listen," the old man said. "You need to know this."

He did not need to know anything except how to get the old man to leave him alone, he thought sourly. They did not need a renegade priest of their enemy's god who might revert to orthodoxy at any moment and turn them in. But the twinge of pain got his attention, and he listened unwillingly.

"I am a priest of Esea," the old man repeated. Gird managed not to say that he knew *that* much. "You clearly think of Esea as a power of evil—from the way you reacted to my blessing. But Esea, in old Aare, where your lords came from, is the name we give the god of light. The sun is his visible form, but it is not the god."

"*Sunlord, Sealord, Lord of Sands and Chance . . .*" muttered Gird, unwillingly.

"You learned that verse in childhood, no doubt. So far as it goes, it's accurate enough. Our people worshipped Esea, the Sunlord—though only peasants called him Sunlord. Sealord, that's Barrandowea. Ibbirun, the Sandlord—more feared than worshipped. And Simyits, god of chance and luck. We had other gods, many of them, including your Lady, Alyanya the fruitful." The old man looked at Gird calmly, as a man might look at an ox he was thinking of buying. "Tell me, what do you have against Esea?"

"Esea's the lords' god. He brings droughts, dries springs, overlooks wells. The *merin* hate him, and he withers the flowers we bring to please them."

"I see. Because you think of Esea as the Sunlord, and in dry weather you see more sun?"

Gird shrugged. "I'm no priest. But so the grannies said, in our village. If there's a drought, never let a priest of Esea near the wells: they'll call the sun's curse on them, and the water will fail."

The old man snorted. "Do they think priests need no water? That we need no food, so a failing harvest means nothing?" Then he shook his head. "No, I'm sorry. It's natural enough, that you'd blame outlander gods for your troubles, and even more natural, when your rulers are as bad as they are."

"Yes, but you—"

"I'm human. As human as you are: not a demon, not a god. I am of the old blood, of Aare—kin to your lords, if you look at it like that." He walked on a few paces, glanced sideways at Gird, and said, "I see you do look at it like that. And no wonder. But there is much you do not know. The old Aareans had powers, all of them, which none of your people had. Now this cold land has thinned our blood, some say, or the gods of your people have sought vengeance. I think all that is ridiculous."

Gird fastened to the little he had understood. "You are the same blood as the lords—as that sier, or my old count?"

"Not close kin, but of the same origin—from Aare across the sea."

"But—I have seen no powers, in the lords." Even as he said it, he remembered the uncanny light that had come to a dusty, dark storeroom when the sier willed it. "Except—"

"Except last night. First with me, and then with the sier." He caught Gird's hand as he was about to make another warding sign, and said, "Stop doing that. It won't work, because I'm not what you think, but it is annoying. You'll convince anyone on the road I'm an illwisher." There was no one on the road, before or behind. Gird scowled. The old man sighed. "Gird, our people *had* power, and now most of them don't, or they have little. I have, and the sier has, and of course I know about the sier—I have known him for years. We have talked together, dined together—I've been his guest—"

Gird struggled to break the grip on his wrist; the old man was feeble—had to be weaker than he was—but he could not get free. He yanked back again and again, panting, without success. The old man merely smiled at him, a sunny, friendly smile of perfect calm and joy. "Let—me—go!" Gird said finally, when force had not worked.

"When I'm sure you have understood what I'm saying. Not until." The same quiet smile, but Gird felt the threat behind the words.

"Understood, or accepted?" he asked, still angry.

"Understood. Esea's Light, Gird, if I had wanted to charm the wits from you, I could have done it any time."

"Could you?" He glared at the old man, wondering if that had been the answer all along. Had he been charmed into thinking the man hurt, charmed into taking him into the city, charmed into going unarmed into that trap? That peaceful smile seemed to fill his eyes, as if the old man were suddenly larger; warmth and peace seeped into his mind, washing the anger away. But he clung to the core of it, stubborn as a stone in the earth: he might be shifted, but he would not be changed. The old man sighed, at last, and that imposed warmth and peace left him abruptly. He was shivering in a cold wind, aware of sleet beginning to sting the left side of his face.

"Well. Maybe I couldn't, at that. Not now, anyway. The gods must know what they're doing." The old man shivered now, too. But he was still smiling, if ruefully.

Gird looked around. They were on a rise, where the wind could get at them from any angle, and the sleet bit into him. The road ran on eastward, past an outcrop of rock that offered no shelter. Downslope to the right, downwind, scrubby grass thickened to knee-high scrub, and he thought he could see trees in the distance. "I'm cold," he said. "I'm going to find shelter, and if you won't let go of me, you'll have to come too." He was sure he could drag the old man, if he couldn't get rid of him.

"Good idea," the old man said, and nothing more until they had tramped through the scrub into the meager shelter of a leafless wood. Gird hunkered down behind a fallen log, and dug into the dry leaves. Deep enough. He pointed, and the old man crouched there, releasing Gird's wrist. Gird found fallen branches to stack on the windward side, then piled leaves to cut the wind under the log. He kept working, as the sleet came down harder, to cut poles and make a low roof over them. The first flakes of snow floated between the chips of falling sleet as he finished, and crawled under it.

The old man had dug out the leaves to form a nest, and huddled in it. Gird put the sack of food and the jug where he could reach them, and squeezed close to the old man. He was not as cold as Gird had expected—but then he had never been as feeble as Gird expected. Beyond the edge of the shelter roof, more flakes danced. The hiss and rattle of sleet lessened, and that magical silence that heralds falling snow spread around them. Snow clung to the edges of fallen leaves, forming a fantastic tracery until more snow covered the ground in unbroken white.

Gird stared at it. He had slept fireless in winter before, and he had food and ale, but how was he going to get back to his troop? He had expected to spend some days in the town—to leave with enough food to reach the next town—and then to return, with a guide, through three different bartons. He had come to the town from the south; now he was east of it, in a country he had never seen, which was rapidly disappearing under snow. Snow in which his tracks would be all too obvious, in which he could not hope to travel unnoticed. In which he could starve, or die of cold. Beside him, the old man snored, the easy sleep of the old. *He* was warm enough, and unafraid—and what did he have to be afraid of, if he could heal himself of such wounds as Gird had seen? If they had been real.

Gird reached out and pulled the sack of food to him. Don't look too far ahead, his Da had said. There are times to plan for planting and harvest, and times to eat the food at hand, and be grateful. Inside were bread, cheese, a slab of bacon, an onion. He looked at the sleeping man, and sighed, and put the sack aside again. They could share it when the old man woke.

As it happened, the old man woke before he did; Gird had not meant to fall asleep, but the silence and monotony had done it. Outside the shelter was dark, cold, and the silence. Within, the old man had made light, and radiated warmth like a hot stone. He was holding his finger—his *glowing* finger—to a ragged chunk of bacon, which sizzled and dripped onto bread beneath it. It had been the smell of cooking bacon which roused Gird, and it was the sight of it cooking at the old man's touch which sent him out into the dark and cold in one panic-stricken rush.

"Come back!" the old man cried. "I was cooking it for you!"

Gird crouched in the snow, uncertain, shivering . . . half with fear, and half with the cold. Snow caressed his head, his cheeks, his arms and hands, icy kisses like those of the snow maidens that lived in the far north. The old man's head poked out of the shelter.

"It's all right. It won't hurt you. I promise." What good was the promise of someone who could cook bacon with his finger, and make light out of nothing? What good was the promise of someone who could change faces? But the smell of the bacon went right to the pit of his belly; his mouth watered. A lump of snow fell on his head, and he shuddered. Fear and warmth and food, or cold and hunger and—more fear. He was moving before he knew it, back to the shelter, praying fervently to whatever gods might be out this dark night to protect him from one old man.

Once face to face with him again, Gird could find nothing specific to fear. His hands were the gnarled and bony hands of any old man, holding out now a chunk of bread with a chunk of hot bacon on top. Gird looked at the food, but did not take it. "We must share," he said hoarsely.

"I don't like bacon," the old man said, almost wistfully. "A slice of a lamb roast now, or even beef—but I never could eat bacon without trouble. Go on, you take it."

Gird looked him in the eye. Could he not know the customs of Gird's people? Were their people so different? "We must share," he said again. "I cannot take food from you, if you do not take it from me." Or rather, he thought to himself, I *will not* take it and put myself in that kind of relationship.

The man shrugged. "It was yours to start with; I merely cooked it. You don't prefer it raw, do you?"

Gird sighed. Either he was ignorant, or he was being difficult. His head ached, and he didn't want to explain it, but he was going to have to. "It's important," he said. "You cooked it; that means you have the hearthright, the fire-right. I cannot take—no, I *will* not take your food unless you take some from my hand, because that would mean you were my—you had the right to give or withhold food, and I needed your protection."

"Oh." The old man looked surprised, but drew his hand back. "Is *that* why your people first brought food to ours when they came?"

"Did they?" Gird had no idea what had happened when the lords first came. "What did your people do?"

"Made a very large mistake, I think," said the old man, as if to himself. "What should they have done?"

"Were they seeking aid in hunting, or against an enemy? Or were they starving?"

"No—at least not as the chronicles tell it."

"Then if they wanted an alliance of hearthings, they should have offered food of their own, and all shared."

The old man pursed his lips. "And what would it mean to you, if they ate the food offered, but offered none."

"That is the way of accepting the giving hearth as the leader—as the protector."

"Could they offer something else, in exchange? Arms, protection?"

Gird shook his head. "No—what protection could someone without food offer? The strong hearth has food to offer; the weak accepts it, and gives service for protection. If they wish friendship, it is as I said: food shared, both ways. Or more, if more than one are meeting. Famine rule, that can change things, but not always."

"Famine rule?"

"In famine, all share equally, without obligation, even if only one provides. But it must be declared, and accepted."

"This is worse than I thought," said the old man, grimacing. "We were so *stupid!*" He put the bread and bacon down, and said, "Will you take something from the sack and share it with me?"

"I can't cook it," Gird said, frowning. It didn't have to be cooked food, of course: bread was already cooked, and cheese was cured. But he had not actually provided this food—it belonged to the sier, who was an ally of the old man. Some people might argue about that. "Do you accept it as my food?"

"Yes."

"Then I offer this cheese and bread, my hearth to yours." Gird set the bread and cheese between them, then broke a piece from each and held out his hand. The old man took the pieces gravely, and offered Gird the bread and bacon again. This time Gird took it, hoping the bacon was still hot. But he waited until the old man had taken a bite before taking one of his own. The old man had not said the ritual words, but he was sure of the intent, and between only two, that was enough.

The bacon was still warm, and succulent; the grease-soaked bread made a comfortable fullness in his belly. Gird ate quickly, wasting no time, but his mind was full of questions. As soon as he had gulped down the last bite of bread, he turned to the old man.

"What did you mean, your people had made a mistake?"

The old man, eating more slowly, had not finished; he swallowed the cheese in his mouth before answering. "Gird, among my people the customs differ. Offering food is the sign of subservience: servants offer food to masters. I'm afraid when your people came bringing food, my people thought they were acknowledging their lower rank."

Gird sat quietly a moment, thinking this over. The food-bringers, food-givers, ranked *lower*? When everyone knew that those who can afford to give without taking in return are the wealthy and strong? It was backwards, upside down, inside out: no one could live with a people who believed that. They would kill each other. They would believe—that the strong and wealthy are those who can take without giving— He found he was saying this aloud, softly, and the old man was nodding. "But that's *wrong*," he said loudly. His vehemence was swallowed in the snow, lost in that white quiet. "It can't work. They would always be stealing from each other, from everyone, to gain their place in the family."

"Not quite," said the old man. He sighed heavily. "Then again, maybe that's part of the reason why things have gone so badly up here. Back in Aare, there were reasons for that, and safeguards. At least, I think so. It had to do with our magic, our powers."

"Like the light. And cooking with your finger?"

"Among other things, yes. Among our people, rank came with magic—the more magic, the higher rank. One proof of magic was the ability to take, either by direct magic, or by compelling—charming—someone to offer whatever it was as a gift."

Gird thought carefully around that before he let himself answer, but it was the same answer that sprang first to mind. "But how is that different from the bullying of a strong child, who steals a weaker's food, or threatens him into giving it up? It is stealing, to take like that." And it was precisely what the lords had been doing, he thought. What they had always done, if this man was telling the truth.

The old man also waited before answering, and when he spoke his voice was slower, almost hesitant. "Gird, our people see it as the natural way—as calves in a herd push and shove, seeking dominance, as kittens wrestle, claw, and bite. And in a herd of grown cattle, is not the stronger dominant? Yet this doesn't mean constant warfare in a herd, only a mild pushing and shoving: the weaker ones know their place, and walk behind—"

"But men are not cows!" Gird could not contain his anger any longer; he felt as if it were something physical, bright as the light he still did not understand. "We are not kittens, or sheep, or birds squabbling in a nest—"

"I know." The old man's voice, still quiet, cut through his objection as a knife cuts a ripe fruit. "I know, and I know something has gone very wrong. But in our own home, in Aare, that sparring for dominance among our folk had its limits, and those limits were safe enough to let our people grow and prosper for many ages. We were taught—*I* was taught—that with such power comes great responsibility—that we were to care for those we governed as a herdsman cares for his herd—No, don't tell me, I understand. Men are not cattle. But even you might use that analogy—"

And he had, the night before, talking to the sier. Gird shivered, not from cold, when he thought of it. No wonder it had gone home, if the man thought of his common folk as cattle already.

"I still think it's wrong," Gird said.

"It may be. But right or wrong, it's the other way 'round from your people, and that means my people didn't understand them from the beginning. We assumed your people intended to submit, agreed to it without conflict: that's what our chronicles say. So whenever your people resisted, our people thought of that as a broken contract—as if you had gone back on your word."

Gird tried to remember what he had heard of the lords' coming. Very little, though he had heard new things from the men he had been training. Most of the stories began after that, with the settlements growing near the new forts and towns, with the "clearing" of old steadings, the forced resettlement of families, the change in steading custom to conform to the new village laws. Everyone had thought the lords knew they were unfair, knew they were stealing—but had they not known? Had they thought that all they did was right, justified by some agreement that had never been made?

"Not all," the old man said. "Some things were forbidden in old Aare, which our people do here. The worship of the Master of Torments, for example: that they know is evil, and those who do it are doing it knowingly against the old laws. A contest of strength or magery is one thing, but once it is over, the winner has obligations to the loser, as well. But the basic misunderstanding, Gird, I believe I discovered tonight, from you. Your way seems as strange to me, I confess, as mine must seem to you—but strangeness is not evil. What we do with it may be evil."

"When you offered me that food," Gird said, "were you then declaring yourself lower in rank? Or were you trying to fool me into thinking that's what you were doing?"

The old man started to answer, then stopped, then finally said, "I thought—I think I only meant to calm you, to make you think well of me. In one sense, that is claiming a lower rank, because it means I care that you think well of me—in another—I don't know. I didn't think, I just did it."

"I felt," Gird said carefully—carefully, because he did not want to hurt this old man, even now, "I felt like a stubborn animal, being offered a bait of grain if it will only go through the gap."

A grin, across that close space. "You are stubborn; you would not deny that. I did not mean you to feel that, but given what your people think about offering food, wouldn't anyone feel so in such a circumstance? Have you ever—"

"Yes." Had the men he had fed felt that way? Demeaned, degraded? But it was not always so; he had taken food himself, gladly, acknowledging temporary weakness. Sick men had to be fed by healthy men, children by adults, infants by mothers. Was milk from the breast demeaning to a baby? Of course not. Yet—he worried the problem in his mind, coming at it from one side then another. The old man sat quietly and let him alone. "There are times," he said, "when it is right to be the one fed. Times no one minds. If someone's sick or hurt—or children—but grown folk, healthy grown folk—they feed themselves. In a way, living on another's bounty is like being a child again. Maybe that's why it means giving obedience."

"Probably." The old man nodded. "It's interesting that you have the importance of having food to give, but absolute prohibition against taking it by force from each other. The force is used against the land, I suppose, in hunting or farming."

"Not against," Gird corrected. "With. To help the land bear more. Alyanya is our Lady, not our subject."

"So you see even the gods as those who can give, not those who take?"

"Of course. If they have nothing to give, they are not gods, but demons." Gird nodded at the cold dark beyond their shelter. "As the cold demons steal warmth, and the spirits of night steal light from the sun."

The old man smiled. "This day is stealing my strength, Gird, and I cannot hold this light much longer. Not if I'm to have warmth enough until dawn. But before the light goes, I have an apology. I have withheld the courtesy of my name, although I knew yours. I am Arranha, and I am glad to have you as companion in this adventure."

Gird turned the name over in his mind; it was like nothing he had heard. "I thought the lords had many names—four or five."

"So they do, but priests have only one, and mine is Arranha." With a last smile, Arranha let the light fail—

the light Gird had yet to understand, and the cold, snow-clean air gusted for a moment under the shelter. Gird felt Arranha curling up in his leafy nest, and thought of walking away. But he could not blunder through a wood in the dark and snow, not and hope to live until morning. With a silent but very definite curse, he lay down, wriggling his way into the leaves until he was curled around Arranha. His back was cold, but Arranha, protected on the inside, was warm as a hearth. Gird was sure he could not sleep—then began to worry that they might sleep their way into death in the cold— and then slid effortlessly into peace and darkness.

Chapter Eighteen

The next morning was cold and raw but Arranha was awake, and a milder warmth filled their shelter. Gird rubbed his eyes, and looked out to see snow covering all, under a gray sky: the light was silvery. The old man sat hunched, staring at his hands. Gird watched him warily. Was he about to do something? Was he doing something now, something Gird could not see? Then a cramp in his back jabbed him, and he had to stretch. Arranha turned to him, and Gird continued with a yawn that cracked his jaws.

"Sorry," he said afterwards, but even to himself he did not sound sorry. Arranha merely smiled. Silently, he divided the rest of the bread and cheese, and Arranha shared it. The jug, when he shook it, was full. He looked at the old man, who smiled again.

"I filled it with snow, and melted it. It's not ale, but it will do." Gird sipped, found it water with only the faintest taste of the ale that had been in the jug, and drank thirstily. Arranha went on. "It is not snowing now, and I think it will not for some hours. If you wanted to travel, now is a good time."

Gird scratched his jaw beneath his beard. "What about you? I would help you to someplace safe."

Arranha laughed aloud. "Safe? For me? Gird, I am safer with you than anywhere else I can think of, in the world of men."

"But surely you have friends—"

"None so rash as to harbor me now, when Esea's Hall of priests has declared me heretic and traitor. They intended to kill me, Gird—you saw that."

"But—sir—" Gird tried to think how to put it. The man was a priest, and had great powers, but he would hardly be accepted by Gird's troop of peasant rebels. He began as delicately as he could. "I have my work— you seem to know that, and what it is—and the people I work with, my people, they—they won't take to you."

Arranha showed neither anger nor surprise. "You do not want me with you?"

Gird found he was scratching his ear, this time. "Well—it's nothing against you yourself, but—you're one of *them*, sir. One of the lords, and that's who we're trying to fight. Sir."

"Do you know what you're fighting for, Gird, or is it all against?" Gird must have looked as puzzled as he felt, for Arranha explained. "Do you have a vision of something better, a way to live that you want, or are you fighting only against the lords' injustice and cruelty?"

"Of course we have ideas," Gird said. They were bright in his mind, those pictures of what the world should be like. He was sitting at the old scarred table in his own cottage, with Mali and the children around it, all of them with food in their bowls, laughing and talking. In the cowbyre were his three favorite cows, all healthy and sleek; his sheep were heavy-fleeced and strong. He could look around the room and see his mother's loom with a furl of cloth half-woven, tools on their hooks, Mali's herbs in bunches, the sweet smell of a spring evening blowing in the window. Outside would be the fields, with the grain springing green from the furrows, the smallgarden already showing the crisp rosettes of vegetables, the beans reaching for their poles with waving tendrils. From other cottages as well he could hear the happy voices, even someone singing. He felt safe; he knew the others felt safe. That was what he wanted, what they all wanted.

"Can you tell me?" asked Arranha gently.

Gird tried, but the memories were too strong, too mixed: sweet and bitter, joyful and sorrowful, all at once. His voice broke; his eyes filled with tears that were hot on his cheeks, and cold on his jaw. "It's just—just peace," he said.

Arranha sighed. "Coming to peace by starting a war is tricky, Gird. You've never known war; I have."

Gird set his jaw, and blinked back the tears. "It's war enough, when my family and my friends die for nothing."

"No. It's bad, but it's not the same. You're starting something bigger than you can see. Much bigger. You need a better idea of where you're going, what you will need. Do you know anything at all about law?"

Gird sniffed, rubbed his nose on his arm, and thought about it. Law. There were the customs of his village, and the customs all his people shared, from the days when they lived in steadings within a hearthing. Then there were rules the lords made, and that law he had had to memorize when he was a recruit. "A little," he said cautiously. Arranha looked at him, as if wondering what that meant, and sighed again.

"This is going to take longer, and it would go better in a warmer place. Where would *you* go from here?"

The abrupt change of topic jarred; Gird wondered what the old man was up to. Something, surely. But he was tired of arguing, of his own emotions. Let the old man come along, at least for now. "We left the city by the east gate," Gird said. "And then we walked east, and then south but only a little. So back south, and a little west—I don't know this country well, up here."

"The way you're speaking of, there's a village called Burry—is that what you meant?"

"Aye." In Burry, the barton was already five hands strong, and the yeoman marshal had relatives in three other villages.

"Can we reach Burry today?"

"No. But there's a place—" Gird did not want to talk about it, and Arranha did not press him. He ducked out of the shelter, into the distanceless light of a cloudy day over snow. They were going to leave tracks, clear ones, and the place they had slept would be obvious even if he tried to take down the shelter. But he could not see the road from here, or hear any travelers. Perhaps no one would happen by until another snowfall.

He led Arranha further into the wood, away from the road. The silence scared him; it felt unnatural. He reminded himself that he was not used to being away from a village in winter. Even near camp, he could hear the noises of other people. It might be nothing but this unfamiliarity that had his neck hair standing up, a tension in his shoulders. Arranha picked his way through the snow with little apparent effort, though he left tracks. Gird made sure to look, every so often.

When they came to the trail Gird had taken toward the city two days before, he almost walked across it without recognition. Its white surface lay smooth in both directions, trackless. He turned and led Arranha along it, as he looked for the place they could shelter overnight.

It was getting darker, and he was afraid he might recognize it in snow, when he spotted the three tall cedars above a lower clump, and turned off the trail. Arranha had said nothing for hours. Now he said, "Is this a village?"

"No—it's an old steading. Cleared by your folk, to settle a village." He wasn't sure that was why it had been abandoned; it might have been much older than the lords' coming. "It's empty," Gird added. "No one lives here, or nearby." He pushed through the bushy cedar boughs, shivering as they dumped their load of snow on him, and entered the old steading. He bowed, courteously, to the old doorstep, still centered between the upright pillars that had held the door. On either side, broken walls straggled away, outlining the shape of the original buildings in brushstrokes of stone against the white snow.

When he looked back, Arranha had pushed through

the cedars as well, and was bowing as Gird had, though he looked uncertain of his welcome. So he ought, Gird thought. This was old; this had belonged to no one but his own people, and Arranha was a stranger.

"Do you know how many lived here?" Arranha asked.

Gird shook his head. "It was a steading; my Da said a steading was three or so families. Less than a village— four hands, five? A large steading might have more, but I think this one was small." He led the way again, past the empty useless doorway, along what had been the outside of the main building, to an angle of low wall in what had been an animal shed or pen. Here two corners had survived the original assault and subsequent weather, to nearly enclose a space just over an armspan wide, and two armspans long. Gird thrust his hand into the cold snow in the larger space outside, feeling about, and grunted. "Here—help me lift this." *This* was a lattice, woven of green withes and vines, and lightly covered with leaves; it would have been unnoticeable lying flat among the ruins. Now, it fitted across the space between the walls, an instant roof.

"You knew this was here—you had it ready!" Arranha sounded excited for the first time.

Gird let himself grin. "Aye. Thought it up. Looks like nothing but old walls, but it's as good as a house. Almost." He had lifted his end carefully, so that the snow did not slide off; it was heavier that way, but it would look less obvious. He hoped. When they had it braced in place, he looked at it again. Those two side walls had been intended to support a slanted roof, he was sure—he hoped his roof would slant enough to drip on the wall, not inside. The end wall should be lying within the enclosed space; he reached into the snow again, and found the end. He pulled it out, careful to bring its load of snow with it. This piece was light enough for one to move; he shifted it until it almost closed the gap. Now they had a small house, its walls chest-high, topped with slanted roof with its back to the north wind. Its floor was almost snow-free, because that snow had come out with the end wall.

"You thought this up?" asked Arranha.

"Not all of it. I thought of wattle for temporary roofs, in our camps, but others thought of leaving sections where we might need them. And a man in Burry thought of putting the piece down where you might want no snow when the shelter was built." As he talked, Gird braced the foot of the wattle enclosing the end with rocks. His hands began to go numb; he blew on them. Then he reached into his jerkin, and brought out one of his thongs. "We have to tie the roof on, or any little puff will blow it away." Arranha took the hint, and began lacing the roof to the end hurdle.

Inside the shelter, it was quite dark. Gird felt around in the protected corner, and found the dry sticks he'd bundled, and the little sack of meal. He thought of the time it was going to take to start a fire with a firebow, and sighed. It would be sensible to ask Arranha to start the fire with his finger—if that worked, and if it cooked bacon it should—but he hated to ask a favor of a lord.

"If you would let me, I will start the fire," Arranha said quietly. Gird backed out of the shelter and looked at him. No visible haughtiness, just an old man pinched with cold after a long day's walk in the snow.

"In that far corner, then. There's wood; I'll find more." Arranha nodded and ducked inside the shelter. Gird did not stay to watch; he gathered an armload of wood, and came back to a shelter that let chips of light out between the chinks of the wattle.

Inside was warmth and firelight—none of Arranha's magicks. Was Arranha tired, or simply being tactful? Gird did not know, or care; he was glad enough to see a warm fire. The jug was nestled near the fire, and Arranha had found the niche in the wall with the cooking bowl. He had poured the meal into the bowl, but looked as if he did not know what to do next.

"Let me." Gird reached for the bowl, and felt the side of the pot. Warm, but not hot enough. He scrabbled around the floor of the shelter for small pebbles and pushed them into the fire. "For cooking," said Gird, to Arranha's surprised look. "I'll drop them in the jug, to make the water hot quicker. That way it won't crack the pot."

By the time the mush was done, Gird was ready to eat the bowl as well. He swallowed hard, handed the bowl to Arranha first, and forced himself to match spoonful for spoonful the pace Arranha set. They scraped the bowl clean; with a sigh, Gird took it outside to scrub it clean with snow. After a final visit to the outside—Gird insisted on showing Arranha the proper place to use as jacks—they came back to the fire, ready enough for a night's sleep.

Or so Gird expected. Instead, Arranha did whatever he did to brighten the light until Gird could see as clearly as in daylight. From the recesses of his clothes, he pulled a scroll. Gird blinked. The man had been naked; Gird had given him a shirt. Then he had had clothes of some kind—but Gird still didn't have his shirt back—and now he was taking things he had not had out of clothes he had not had. He did not like this. But the alternative was, again, a cold night alone in the woods—and here was warmth and light and someone alive. He gave Arranha the look he would have given one of his men who pulled a stupid trick, but Arranha did not react to it.

Arranha pointed to the scroll. "Can you read that?" Gird peered at it, his long-forgotten struggles with reading sending cold sweat to his brow. The list looked familiar, the lengths of line and numbers made it certain.

"No—but I know what it is. It's the Rule of Aare. I've seen it before; we had to learn it in the Kelaive's Guard."

"And what does it mean?" Gird stared at him, and Arranha nodded encouragingly. "The first one, for instance. What does it *mean*—how does it tell you to live?"

"Surrender none," said Gird. "That's obvious enough. Grab and hold what you've got. Don't quit. Don't give anything up."

"And what is 'anything'?"

"Anything—oh, lands, I suppose. Money. Power. Whatever they've got that they value—"

"Value," said the priest, in that tone that made Gird think he meant more than he said. "Things of value—

think, Gird." He was thinking, and it made him restless. He wanted the ale he had had the night before, to ease the ache in his joints. He wanted to get out of this cold cramped shelter and take a walk across open, sunlit fields. He scowled, hoping that it would pass for thought, and ready to be angry if the priest laughed. The priest did not laugh. "Value," he said again. "Gird, what do you value most?"

"Me?" All the usual answers raced through his mind: money, food, ale, the pleasures of the body, possessions, a better bull for his cows. Then slower, deeper, the people he knew, the way of life he wanted to live. But for that he had no words, no way to say it. "Not just money," he said slowly. "Not things to buy or use, exactly. Friends—a good master, fair dealing in the market and at tax time—family—" Children, he would have said, but it was ill-luck to name them.

"Peace," said the priest, casting that name over ordinary life without turmoil or undue trouble, as Gird himself had said that morning. "Justice." And that stood for all the fair dealing, market or court or steward's assessment, for a lord who would not trample young grain on a hunt, or refuse the use of medicinal herbs in his wood. "Love," the priest said last, and it covered family and friends well enough, all the complicated relationships that made a life more than existence.

"But the law—" began Gird. The priest held up his hand, and Gird stopped short.

"The *old* law," said the priest, "said nothing of peace or justice or love, because everyone agreed on their importance. And the first Rule, 'Surrender none' meant precisely that none of these should be given up: not peace, not justice, not love."

"But—" began Gird again, and again the priest stopped him.

"Surrender none," the priest repeated, this time in a tone of command that would, Gird was sure, have held an army spellbound. "None—none of the Rules themselves, and none of the great goods the Rules were intended to preserve. Our people have forgotten that. Our priests have forgotten that. We have taught them the wrong meanings of those simple commands, and it is these, acted out, which brought them to such actions as trouble you. They think they are meant to grasp more and more, and hold it tightly, sharing it with none, when they were meant to surrender no opportunity of doing right, of spreading Esea's light, the High Lord's justice, Alyanya's peace."

Gird thought of the other Rules, so painfully learned when he was a recruit. If indeed the first meant *that*, then how could the second, the third, be interpreted? "One, for me, and one, for you" had looked, to a peasant boy, like a clear description of the present situation: one rule for the masters, and one for the serfs.

"No," said the priest, with a sigh. "It's easily read that way, and that is in fact the way they read it *now*, paying tribute to Simyits the Two-faced, the Trickster, the lightfingered lord of luck and gambling. But it reminds us to share, as children do, as we did tonight— one spoonful for you, and one for me. Your people do the same."

"But the others?"

"Define the vigilance necessary to protect the code: touch not, nor ask, nor interfere, where it is not necessary, where it is not your business; but if it is, then go far, swift, silently—never let justice lack because of distance or time or idle chatter. Face the door, yes: evil overwhelms the careless. Learn all the arts, to judge fairly, but staying alive is imperative, or the good judge cannot exist to judge."

"It's—it's like a grape-leaf," said Gird, his mind awhirl. "On one side dark green, shiny, and on the other silvery fuzz—can it be the same Rules? And even if it is, what matter to us? We were never *of* them."

"Gird, if a man use a stick to beat a cow, instead of guide it, does that make the stick evil? Would you burn the stick, for being a bad stick, or clout the man?"

"The man, of course, but—"

"The Rules of Aare were a tool of law, a stick, if you will—once men used them well, to guide themselves to better actions, and now they use them badly, to beat other men. You're going to need a stick like that; before you throw this one on the fire, take another look at it."

"It still sounds like trickery," said Gird. He looked closely at the priest, watching for anything he could interpret. Nothing but interest. "If the Rules can be read both ways, then there's something wrong with them. Why not write laws that can't be read wrong?"

"Try it," said the priest. A smile twitched his lips. Gird felt the back of his neck getting hot. Somehow the man had made a trap, and he'd walked in. Even though he didn't feel the teeth yet, it was still a trap.

"I could," he muttered sourly, thinking hard. What was the trap? "It's not that hard to say a man shouldn't steal his neighbor's sheep, or put offal down his neighbor's well."

"And if the sheep got into his garden, or the neighbor had stolen something from him?"

"If we had fair courts, to settle the first problem—"

"Very good. And how will you make fair courts?"

The priest was taking him seriously. The trap must have very fine teeth, because he couldn't feel them yet, and the man was asking what he'd thought about before.

"Fair courts should have someone who knows something about the argument—the kind of argument—"

"Another serf?" asked the priest. This was extraordinary, and Gird paused to look again for any signs of ridicule. None.

"I've wondered about that," he said cautiously. "A farmer to judge disputes between farmers, a tanner to judge between tanners. But then if a farmer and a tanner have an argument, who? If it's someone who started as a peasant, say, then he'd need some training, same as if he wanted to be a soldier."

"Let's suppose you have your judge," said the priest. "A fair man, who knows enough of both sides to understand it, then what?"

"Plain laws that anyone can understand," said Gird. "Fair dealing between master and man, between crafter and crofter. If the law says 'no stealing' that's plain enough—"

"And what is stealing?" asked the priest.

"Taking what's not yours," said Gird. "That's obvious."

"But think, Gird. We all take some things that aren't ours: air, water, sunlight and starlight—"

"The water in my well was mine." Gird clung to that. Air? Sunlight? He'd never thought of himself as "taking" them. There was plenty left for everyone else.

"The water in your well came from somewhere else, and someone else put it there. Have you done one thing to make it grow, as you work to make your cabbages grow?"

"No." He'd never thought of it that way. It was his well, as it had been his father's well, and he had felt lucky to have a well of his own. His well, his water. But he *had* worked, himself, to get each year's crop of barley and oats and cabbages and onions, to take the cows to be bred, to birth the calves. He himself had fed and brushed his animals, pruned and manured his trees, plowed and harrowed and planted and harvested his fields. The water was just *there*, more in a wet year and less in a dry year, but always there, without his thought. Given, like the air and the light. And he had taken.

"Would you call that stealing from the gods?" asked Gird. Or, he wondered to himself, were the gifts of flowers and herbs to the *merin* spirits really a form of payment, and not praise?

"No, I think not. They gave us to this world, and gave to it also those things we need and cannot make for ourselves, by any labor. To take a gift is not stealing. But I wanted you to think about your law. If you want more than riots, if you want more than killing the magelords and then each other, you must have law."

Before he could stop himself, Gird blurted "But I don't know anything about it."

Arranha smiled. "You were just saying you knew what kind of laws you wanted. And once you knew nothing about fighting, but you learned. You can learn this, if you care enough about it."

"From you?"

"From me you can learn some, but not all. You don't trust me, even now—" He looked closely at Gird, as if to see into his mind. Gird hoped the uneasy feeling inside wasn't the priest's inner sight. "So we must find you teachers better suited to your nature and experience. What do you know of the kapristi, the gnomes?"

"The gray rockfolk? Dire fighters, fair dealers, is what I've heard. Not much friends with humans—"

"Not with *our* folk," the priest agreed. "Before we came, your people had no problems with them. Some of ours . . . well, you've heard me admit that our folk have gone widely astray from Esea's path, and not alone in their treatment of you. Some of the wildest thought the kapristi were easy prey, being small and seeming meek. Tried to hunt them, ahorse and afoot. Ignored their boundary markers, tried to move you peasants onto their land to farm or mine."

"And?"

"And were deservedly killed by the kapristi. That's not what my former colleagues would say, of course, but it's true. They never tried to invade human lands, or attacked humans where they had not been attacked. But once roused, those small gray folk are as dangerous fighters as any you could hope to train. As well, they live by a code of law that they boast is the fairest and most settled in all the worlds and peoples."

Gird could not keep back a grin. "There is such a law?"

"They claim so. I have met them myself, Gird, as a student of law. They like my people little, but they were fair and just with me. But it is a strict law, so strict that I doubt you'll find humans agree to follow it. They take no excuses, the kapristi, as they make none; they value fair exchange so highly that they believe free gifts are dangerous, fostering slackness. Would you go so far?"

"No, among our people, gifts are a sacred duty. Alyanya's blessings are gifts—"

"Yet the gnomes would say you return fair exchange, duties of worship, for such apparent gifts, or the gods take vengeance. That's their explanation for what's gone wrong with our people. Impiety, failure to return proper service, and the gods punish by withholding the gifts."

"And what do you say?"

Arranha sighed. "I say that my people have erred, by being ungenerous. We value free gifts, even if we misinterpreted your people's offer of food. Perhaps free gifts are dangerous for gnomes; for humans I think they are necessary. But with the loss of powers came fear, so our people grasp more, and give less, than they did. This hurts you, and you, in turn, will hurt them. That cycle has no end, unless you wish it—unless you declare an end, someday, and forgive the rest of the injury."

Gird felt his forehead knot. "What has that to do with justice?"

Arranha smiled at him, serene once more. "You will find out, Gird, when it is time."

Gird felt unaccountably grumpy at that, as if he were a child being told to ignore adult concerns for now. He was, after all, a grown man—widowed—the father of grown children. Arranha seemed to read this on his face. "I'm sorry," he said. "I didn't mean to confuse you. You are no child; I know that. But I do not know myself exactly why the god sent me to you, or you to me. I was as surprised as you, when you stumbled onto me in that ditch. The god wants something from both of us—"

"Not *your* god!" Gird said.

"Then yours. Believe me or not, as you will, but I have been a priest, a true priest, and I know: your god has shaped your life to some purpose, and I am now part of that purpose. I think—I believe—that some part of that is helping you learn how to shape the future beyond the coming war. Whoever leads your people needs to know more than soldiering."

Gird ducked his head. Of course he had thought about it, wondered if the gods had drawn him toward the leadership that now seemed certain. But it did not do to question them too closely, to bring yourself to their notice. The old man was strange, too strange; he wished he'd never found him. And yet—something about him attracted, as the warmth of a fire in cold attracted. Certainly he knew that they must plan for something beyond war; it was what had bothered him since Norwalk.

"I don't know," he said. "I just don't know."

"But you will," Arranha said softly. "You will know, because you must know, and you will teach others."

Suddenly this solemnity in a tattered shelter in snowy woods, this serious discussion of legalities and philosophies, struck Gird as ridiculous. He snorted. "Aye—I can see now: the great gods who could choose you or anyone else will choose a peasant who can hardly read—a serf and son of a serf, who is better with cows than people—to teach a whole people about law. That's wisdom."

Arranha leaned forward. "Do not mock them, Gird. If they have chosen you—and I think they have, and you suspect it, beneath that banter—they will make you what they need. Better clay that can be shaped to their will, and then fired, than broken shards of earlier firings."

The laughter had gone, fleeing down the hollow corridors of his mind a nameless fear. "I am not mocking," Gird said. "I was wishing for miracles."

"Those, too, you may have. For now, you have me: no miracle, but an Aarean with some small magicks."

"Which once I would have called miracles," said Gird, sighing. "Well, Arranha, you may be right. But at the moment I cannot stay awake." The old man chuckled, released his light, and Gird fell asleep in the glow of the banked coals of their fire.

The next morning was colder, but brighter, as the clouds began to break and a thin sunlight poked through them. Gird and Arranha dismantled the shelter; Gird gathered more wood to replace what they'd used, and tucked it into the corners of the walls. Arranha watched as Gird tried to scatter snow over the wattle sections, now laid flat again. Gird wondered if the face he wore now was truly his own, healed of the injuries, or a face maintained by magic (how?) to fool him. And how was the barton at Burry going to react to this man? He could not lie to them, and pretend Arranha was other than he was.

"Do you ever wonder how our magicks work?" asked Arranha when they had started along the trail.

Gird, who was ahead, swinging his arms to warm up, shook his head. "I never saw any, until I met you. Not save the healer's hands that some have, to take away the pain and lay it aside."

"Your people have *that*?" Arranha's voice had sharpened.

"Some of them. Not many." The cold air speared into his lungs; he had to talk in short gasps, and wished Arranha would ask no more. But he could feel the pressure of Arranha's curiosity at his back, as if it were a stinging fly between his shoulders.

"You've seen it yourself?"

"Felt it m'self. Take the pain of a headache, or a blow. Lay it aside, on something doesn't feel pain, like a rock." He blew out a great cloud of steam, trying for rings. It was good luck to blow rings, the holy circle. "Most of 'em use herbs, for fevers. Singing charms, for demons, if they have the parrion—" He stopped, aware of the intensity of Arranha's interest. Had he said more than he should?

"Singing charms—" murmured Arranha. "Esea's light, what we've missed! What's a parrion, Gird?"

"Parrion's a girl's—" Well, how could he explain? "It's—what a mother gives—or an aunt—family things. My mother, she had a parrion of weaving. Certain patterns were hers, and the loom—but it's not like giving someone a cow. The steading—the family—knows a girl's ability. Her parrion is that, plus what the women give her. I don't know all of it; men don't have parrions, exactly."

"So that's it! Gird, in the old chronicles, my people record that yours used to have a group of elders in each—steading, is it?—and mentioned parrion. But it's not recorded what that was."

Gird nodded, on surer ground now. "Three elders, there were. One was of the hunters, one of the growers, and one of the crafters. The hunter was a man, the crafter a woman, and the grower might be either."

"And the crafters were weavers? Potters?"

"Toolmakers, builders, anything we made. Of course all know something of it—anyone can build a wall."

Even as he said it, Gird wondered. Anyone could build a wall if someone good at building walls gave directions. Some walls were better than others.

"Hmm. Did women make weapons?"

"Of course. Why shouldn't they?"

Arranha crunched along several strides before answering. "Among our people, it's thought bad luck to let women make weapons. Their blood shed during the making could weaken the weapon's hunger for blood, make it weak."

Gird stopped short and turned; Arranha nearly crashed into him. "Blood *weaken?* You mean you don't blood your hearths, or your foundations?" From the shocked expression on Arranha's face, they did not. Gird's mind whirled. These lords were even stranger than he'd thought. To take food without giving meant strength, but blood shed meant weakness: another refusal to give, he thought that was. Yet they had magical power to heal themselves—why should they be afraid to give blood where it was needed? And what would this mean in a war? He was not about to explain the power of giving blood to this alien priest. But Arranha was quick; he had seen it for himself. His eyes widened even more, and his mouth fell open.

"It's—the giving again. Esea! I would *never* have thought of that. The food giver is stronger—the blood giver is stronger—and *that's* why our people found women ruling your steadings. And that's why your people follow Alyanya: the Lady gives harvest—food—and blood. I—am—amazed." He shook his head, like someone recovering from a hard blow. Then, softly, "And I see that you can never accept our laws. If you are to have your own, you will have to forge them from your own beliefs."

Gird, although he heard this, felt a fierce exultation warming his whole body. He had been afraid of the lords so long, afraid of their cruelty, their wealth, their power. It had never occurred to him that they might be *afraid*, that they might be weak where his own people were strong.

But Arranha was still talking. "Gird, remember: if

this is the strength of your people, and you are their proper leader, then it will be demanded from you—you will be their symbol—"

Gird shrugged. "Do you think I'm afraid to give?"

Arranha looked at him a long moment. "No—you've shown that you can. But I think you do not understand how much you may have to give—"

Gird shrugged again, this time irritably. "I may die; I know that. It's likely. We all may. More than that, no man can give." Arranha started to say something, closed his mouth, and shook his head. Gird cocked an eyebrow at him, but the old man merely waved for him to lead the way.

So what had *that* been about, Gird wondered, as he continued toward Burry. He had already lost his wife, most of his children, his home, his beloved cows (he wondered who was milking the dun cow, and if she had settled again). The children he had left might die, and that would hurt—that would worse than hurt; he knew he could hardly live through it, if more happened to Rahi or Pidi or Girnis. He himself could be captured, tortured, killed—but he could not imagine anything else. And by being where he was, he had consented to those losses, if they were demanded of him.

"I still think you should talk to the gnomes," Arranha said suddenly, after a long silence.

"I don't know any gnomes," Gird said. That should settle that. Besides, he had a winter's work to do with the bartons, keeping the training going. He would send someone else to recruit in another town, someone who had been in a town before, maybe.

"I do," Arranha said. "They have much you need to know. For example, leaving law aside, have you ever drilled two or three cohorts together? Do you know how to place them on a battlefield when cavalry threatens? Do you know what to do about archers? Or the kinds of magical weapons my people have?"

"We won at Norwalk against cavalry. We practice pushing men off horses," said Gird, feeling stubborn. Of course it wasn't really pushing men off horses; it was pushing men off logs, and he had to hope it was much the same thing. Arranha had said that the gnomes had fought the Aarean lords—and won. He would like to know how they'd done it. What he could remember of the sergeant's lectures on tactics had most to do with controlling unruly crowds, clearing the village square, hunting wolves. He had a sudden terrible vision of what his ignorance could mean if he led all his bartons out to battle and did something stupid—so stupid that the lords won easily, and his own people were dying, captured. He shook his head, banishing that ill-luck.

"Besides," he said, "you say the gnomes give nothing away. Why should they teach me soldiering for nothing? Or law?"

"You might have something valuable to trade," Arranha said. Gird waited for him to explain, but he didn't. So what did he have? Nothing but his own strength, the allegiance (for now) of some hands of half-trained peasants, his own burning desire for peace and justice. Arranha had said the lords violated the gnomish borders. But would they trade for that, when they could defend themselves as well as Arranha said? Would they trade bad neighbors for good?

"Would you talk to the gnomes if they would talk to you?" asked Arranha, breaking into this line of thought.

Soldiering beyond what his sergeant had taught, ways to make laws fair for everyone. Would it work? He had nearly got himself killed in that town, for knowing so little; he did not want to be the one to get all his men killed. And he did want peace, and justice, on the other side of battle. What would the others think, if he went to the gnomes? He thought about that. He had good marshals, now, who could keep the camps going, keep the bartons going, until he came back. It would be a season or more, he knew. But was he trusting Arranha because of some wicked magic?

"I will think about it," he said, looking back to see Arranha's expression. "I would need to tell my—my friends."

"Of course. If you would take my advice, go to them without me—so you can be sure there is no power of mine involved—and discuss it. If they agree, and you agree, then I will take you."

the same thing. Arrumba had said that the gnomes had fought the Aeran lords—and won. He would like to know how they'd done it. What he could remember of the sergeant's lectures on tactics had most to do with controlling unruly crowds, clearing the village square, hunting wolves. He had a sudden terrible vision of what his ignorance could mean if he led all his barons out to battle, and did something stupid—so stupid that the lords won easily, and his own people were dying, captured. He shook his head, banishing that ill-luck.

"Besides," he said, "you saw the gnomes give nothing away. Why should they teach the soldiering for nothing? Or law?"

"You might have something valuable to trade," Arrumba said. Gird waited for him to explain, but he didn't. So what did he have? Nothing but his own strength, the allegiance (for now) of some bands of half-trained peasants, his own burning desire for peace and justice. Arrumba had said the lords violated the gnomish borders. But would they trade for that, when they could defend themselves as well as Arrumba said. Would they trade had neighbors for good?

"Would you talk to the gnomes if they would talk to some," asked Arrumba, breaking into this line of thought. Soldiering beyond what his sergeant had taught, ways to make laws fair for everyone. Would it work? He had nearly got himself killed in that town, for knowing so little. He did not want to be the one to get all his men killed. And he did want peace, and justice, on the other side of battle. What would the others think, if he went to the gnomes? He thought about that. He had good marshals, now, who could keep the camps going, keep the barons going, until he came back. It would be a season or more, he knew, but was he trusting Arrumba because of some wicked magic?

"I will think about it," he said, looking back to see Arrumba's expression. "I would need to tell my—my friends."

"Of course. If you would take my advice, go to them without me—so you can be sure there is no power of mine involved—and discuss it. If they agree, and you agree, then I will take you."

PART III

PART III

Chapter Nineteen

Winter wind had scoured the sky clean of clouds; autumn rains were past. The next clouds would bring serious snow, but that was likely days away. Gird followed Arranha across the frostbitten grass, his farmer's mind noticing every sheep dropping, every wisp of wool caught on a thornbush.

"I feel uneasy, out in the daylight like this," he said finally, when a fold of ground hid them from the wood in which they'd spent the night.

Arranha gave a brief smile back over his shoulder. For an old man, he was remarkably quick across country. "We are beyond Gadilon's domain, remember?"

"They wander beyond, often enough."

"Not this way. Kapristi taught Gadilon's sires caution, Gird. It was his great-great-grandfather who tried to start a war with them."

"I still can't believe—"

"—that those little folk could defeat the magelords? Nor could my people, at first. But you, you want to defeat them with peasants—is that so different?"

"Well—we're bigger—"

"And not so disciplined. Even with the bit of drill you learnt from your count's sergeant. You need more; your people need more: law and drill both, which to the kapristi are but branches of the same tree. Or, as they would say, two ends of one rod."

"Rod?"

"Measuring rod, or staff of justice. *One measure suits all lengths*: that's one of their sayings. *One law serves justice; many laws serve misrule.*"

"I think I will like that," said Gird slowly. "That's a

problem I know, well enough—right there in the Rule of Aare, it is, though you say it wasn't meant to be like that."

Arranha smiled peacefully at him. "Truth is greater than either of us, Gird. I might mean to speak truly and be mistaken: I'm no god. And you might find it where you didn't expect it."

A little higher on the slope, something marked the rough grass . . . a straight line, he realized, that went on across the slope, and around the edge of the hill, to reappear on the next elbow west. He could not tell if it went beyond that. Neither fence nor wall nor plowed furrow—but a line in the grass, as if it had been closely mown perhaps two handspans wide. He nudged Arranha. "Is that the track of some demon?"

"You saw it! Good. That's the kapristi boundary line. Many humans don't notice—"

"Any farmer would," said Gird. "How do they mow it so evenly? How do they keep the line? I don't see any endstones."

"They don't need endstones: it's their domain, and they set the line where they will. Our people no longer dispute it, and yours never did, being wiser."

"And now?"

"Now we call, and then wait. Remember what I've told you: they're absolutely honest and fair, but they demand the same of others. They give nothing; fair exchange is their rule. They will not take simple courtesies amiss, but they will not return them. Expect no thanks, if a bargain is struck, and don't expect to get any more for asking please." Arranha led the way up to the boundary, and called upslope in words Gird did not know. "Kapristi speech, of course," he answered Gird's question.

"But no one's around," said Gird.

"No humans, no. But a dozen kapristi could be a stone's throw from here, and you'd not know it unless they wanted you to. This is *their* land, Gird; make no assumptions about what you do not know."

I'm not, Gird thought silently. He watched the slope above them, as it roughened into rocky outcrops of some gray stone streaked with black. Rockfolk. Elder folk, like the blackcloak, the kuaknom, he had seen. Like the treesinging elves he had not seen. Even more like the dwarves of legend, who sang gold out of the deep mountain rocks, and made jewels by squeezing rock in their hard fists. Folk created before humankind, who might see humans as he saw the Aarean magelords: intruders, dangerous, enemies.

Rocks moved, coming down the slope. He blinked warily, and they were not rocks, but small gray men. Kapristi, not men, he reminded himself. Gnomes out of fireside stories, all cautionary: what happened to the man who tried to cheat a gnome, the woman who hired a gnome to clean the chimney, the child whose goats strayed over the gnome's boundary. As a child, he'd thought that last story silly, but back then he'd assumed that the gnome lands had a tall wall around them, that the boy must have pretended his goats got in as an excuse to climb the walls and see for himself what treasures the gnomes had.

The gnomes (he felt slightly more comfortable with his peoples' name for them in his mind) moved with steady precision, nothing at all like men slipping and clomping down a slope. Six of them, all looking (to his eye) much alike. They loosed no shower of stones, no bits of turf, to roll before them. They had narrow clean-shaven faces (or did they not grow beards?) under close-cropped dark hair. Although they barely came up to his chest, he could not have confused them with boys—no boy moved with such economy, or had such hardness of face. They all wore gray: belted jerkins over long-sleeved shirts, narrow gray trews tucked neatly into gray boots. Jerkins and trews might have been leather; the shirts were wool.

Meanwhile, Arranha had bowed and spoken again in their angular tongue. Gird heard his own name mentioned, and glanced at Arranha, then looked back at the gnomes. The apparent leader was looking at him, a speculative look that made Gird feel like a carthorse up for sale. He could feel his ears and neck getting hot. Finally, Arranha turned to him again.

"Gird, this is Lawmaster Karik—that's not all of his name, but that's the polite way for a human to speak to him. I have told him about you, and he has agreed to speak with you. He has not, however, agreed to let you enter kapristi lands: he will speak with you here, across the line."

If it had not been for Arranha's gaze, Gird would have turned on his heel and stomped away. They didn't trust him, that's what it was, and he had done nothing to earn their distrust. *Yet*, said a voice in his mind. Arranha had told him of the Aarean nobles' attempt to take gnomish lands; they had reason to distrust humans.

Gird choked back all he wanted to say, and bowed awkwardly at the gnomish leader.

"Lawmaster Karik—"

"Gird? You have no clan-name?"

"Dorthan Selis's son was my father; but our clan name was lost. Our lord was Kelaive, whose subject-name I refuse."

"Ah." A gabble of gnomish between the leader and another of his group. Then the leader turned back to Gird. "It is that you have no master? No clan? No allegiance? You are without law?"

Gird stared. What were they driving at? He looked at Arranha, who said nothing, and wanted to smack that smug smile off the priest's face . . . except that it wouldn't work. He cleared his throat, and then realized that a wad of spit could be misunderstood. He swallowed it. The gnomes waited, motionless but not unattending.

"Lawmaster Karik, our lord destroyed our law." That got attention; he could almost feel the intensity of their interest. "I came seeking law—a way to make things fair."

"*Things* are fair, human farmer: it is living beings who may choose unfairness. Are you a god, to know justice and give judgment?"

Gird shook his head, hoping the gnomes had the same gesture. "No god at all, Lawmaster, but a man seeking knowledge. I know *unfairness* when I see it: short weight, shoddy work, carelessness that causes

injury, stealing and lying—but Arranha has taught me
that knowing wrong is not all I need to do right."

"And he brought you here? Or did you seek us on
your own?"

"I—he would have taught me his rules, Lawmaster.
He showed me that the magelords have broken the
Rules of Aare, changed their meanings . . . but I want
nothing of those old rules. I want new rules, better
rules, that cannot be so misunderstood."

The Lawmaster turned to Arranha. "Here is a strange
being. You told us once that the serfs had no wit for
law."

"I was wrong." Arranha bowed, first at the Lawmaster,
then at Gird. "When Gird and I first met, I thought he
was a common outlaw—a rabble-rouser who wanted
only vengeance for injuries done. And indeed, he had
suffered injuries enough. But he has more—"

"Indeed." The Lawmaster's dark, enigmatic gaze returned to Gird. "And you, Gird son of Dorthan son of
Selis, you must know we give nothing: that is fairness,
good for good and evil for evil. What can you give, for
the knowledge you seek?"

"My pledge. Arranha said you had no law between
your people and ours except by steel. If our side wins, I
pledge a rule of law that protects all boundaries, yours
and ours, and my own strength to enforce it."

"You could be killed in a season, and your debt to us
would not be paid. Or your cause could fail, easily
enough . . . though I hear you are trying to teach
discipline to idle human rabble . . ."

"Not idle, Lawmaster, but by the magelords' illwill."

"Hmph." The Lawmaster looked hard at Gird, then
said, "Will you give the pledge of your hand and heart,
to do all in your power to restore justice to these
disputed lands?"

"Yes."

"Then come over the boundary, and I will teach."

For all that he had thought he was nervous under an
open sky, Gird found that winter season mured in the
gnome's halls almost intolerable. Rock beneath his feet,

rock overhead, rock walls never far away on either hand. Nothing to see but rock, however finely dressed. He saw no beauty in the austere fluting of columns, the majestic proportion of the ceremonial halls. His hosts soon knew this, and his most constant guide once sniffed, "If you want splendor, Gird, if you want stone wrought into the likeness of beasts and birds and trees, studded with shining jewels and clad in gold and silver, if you want harp music and singing, you should have chosen our cousins. Dwarves chose splendor; they are all gold and blood, generous or deadly as the passion takes them. But you wanted law, you said, and that is what we live."

"You do trade jewels," Gird said. He had seen them once, laid in a precise pattern on black cloth for an apprentice to value.

"We do. We are rockfolk, after all; the rock speaks to us as trees speak to the sinyi." The gnome sighed heavily at Gird's blank look. "*Elves*, that is: the first-born singers, those of silver blood. The rock is ours, and the rock returns to us in its treasures what we give of wisdom and loyalty."

"Like cows," Gird murmured; the gnome glared at him.

"It is nothing like cows. You *eat* cows."

Gird did not argue—he could not win arguments with the gnomes—but he thought it was the same. He had loved his cows, cared for them, and out of that love and care had come the bounty of milk and meat and hide.

Most of his time, especially at first, he spent with Lawmaster Karik in a quiet, brightly-lit room lined with shelves full of books—the first he'd ever seen—and scrolls.

Lawmaster Karik insisted that Gird must learn to read and write—to gnomish standards—and calculate with their figures.

"Law is too important to be left to your memory," he said. Gird could tell that this, like most that he said, was not negotiable. "You must write it down, and in courts of law it must be there for reference. Likewise contracts: you understand the importance of honest exchange, but how can that be adjudicated if the terms of the contract are in question? It must all be written down."

"But my people don't usually read and write," Gird said.

"They must learn." Lawmaster Karik tapped the heavy slates on which he had marked the gnomish runes. "If it happens that some cannot learn, then someone who reads and writes must stand for that person before the law. We have few so lacking in wit; we must hope that among your people it is also rare. Is it true you know nothing of written speech?"

Gird felt himself flushing again; in a moment he would start sweating. "They—I tried to learn, when my lord's guard recruited me."

"Well? Can you read, or not?"

He was sweating; he felt huge and clumsy and stupid next to the precise gray figure of the gnome, whose face never showed emotion. "Very little," he said unwillingly.

"You will learn. As it is a necessary precondition to your learning how to devise a workable system of law for your imperfect people, and as we did not ascertain before we contracted with you to teach you law, it is to our loss that this is assigned, and you will not incur any greater obligation because of it." The gnomish clerk who accompanied Lawmaster Karik to the lessons noted this down; Gird suddenly realized that what he had done originally had also been put down as a written contract. "You must learn rapidly, Gird, if you are to be in time to begin your war in the correct season."

To Gird's surprise, the gnomish script came easier than the Aarean had—or perhaps it was the absolute lack of distractions, and his fear that he might have to stay there forever if he did not learn. More quickly than he dared hope, he was able to sound his way through a passage of law that the gnomes had translated for him. They had turned aside his attempts to learn their language: "There is not time," all of them said.

"If it is when a contract made that one party agrees to

hold the other not liable in case of death, then it is lawful for the death of that second party to clear the obligation from his own heirs, but if that second party has partners in work, then it is not lawful, even if it is so when the contract is made." Gird came to the end of that proud of his ability to read, but unsure of the implications for a farmer whose cow dies before it is delivered to the buyer.

Lawmaster Karik said, "A cow cannot be a party to a contract: the death of the cow has nothing to do with it. It is the death of the farmer that might apply, if the buyer agreed that the farmer's death meant the farmer's heirs need not deliver the cow."

"But if he has not paid for the cow, why should he expect it if the farmer has died?"

"Suppose he has paid for it, expecting it to come."

"That's not how we sell cows," Gird said. He knew about that; no farmer in his right mind would pay for a cow that did not stand foursquare and in milk before his eyes. The Lawmaster looked at him, and he felt that he must have said something stupid.

"Let it not be cows," the Lawmaster said. "Even among men, it is common that one buys something for delivery later. One may provide cloth to a tailor, who will make clothes of it. One may send fruit or cheese or grain to a fair, and expect goods or coin to come back." Gird had to admit that some people did things that way; he thought it was unnecessarily risky. "You, yourself," the Lawmaster insisted. "You send men out to bring back supplies, do you not?" He did, but most of those were gifts, not paid for, and he knew very well what the gnomes thought of that. To prevent more argument, he nodded.

"So if someone buys something not present, and the person selling it should die before delivering it . . . then, if it was agreed beforehand, his death cancels the debt?"

"That is what that passage says."

"But does the seller's heir keep the price?"

A flicker of interest on the Lawmaster's face. "An

excellent question! That is in the following passage, which you may now read."

Gird cursed himself silently, and put his thick finger on the first symbols of the next line. Another miserable passage of legalese. The matter turned, he learned as he read, on whether the goods exchanged for the unde-livered goods were perishable, consumable, or durable. If someone traded soft fruits for grain, the grain to be delivered, the soft fruits might have spoiled, or been eaten, before the nondelivery occurred (counting, the gnomish law specified, the days between making the contract and expected delivery, before nondelivery could be charged.) Perishable goods fell under one section of law, and consumable goods under another.

"For example," the Lawmaster said, "if someone trades cloth to a tailor for clothing made . . . if the tailor cuts the cloth, but then dies before the garment is made . . . you see that cloth is consumable, and properly so. That is a different situation from a tailor who sold that cloth to someone else, and then died. In the first case, supposing the original contract to have had a death clause, the tailor's heirs would not have to return the cut cloth. But in the second, they would owe the price they received for it."

The more he studied, the more Gird saw that the gnomish law did make plain sense. Absolute honesty, absolute fairness in exchange: all the laws came down to this, and nothing intruded. They had a rigid rank struc-ture, but rank had nothing to do with law . . . at least, the law of exchange, which made all equal . . . that "one measure for all" that Arranha had mentioned. He could see how it would work among humans—at least, among humans who wanted it to work. It was what he wanted for his people, fair laws; surely they all wanted the same.

Lawmaster Karik began to give him simple cases to examine. Gird found judging harder than he had ex-pected, particularly when Karik insisted that intent and circumstance made no difference to the law.

"If someone means well, but does ill, the ill is still done—and the consequences still exist. Besides, if intent forgives wrong, then any wrongdoer can claim good intent."

"But it's obvious," said Gird. "I could tell if someone meant to do wrong, or just erred."

"Could you? Suppose someone stole a measure of grain, claiming it was to save a family member from starving . . ."

"Find out if the person is starving," said Gird promptly.

Karik shook his head. "Suppose the thief had plenty of grain of his own, but chose to steal someone else's rather than fulfill his own family obligation. Suppose the thief had money, with which to buy grain, but again chose to steal it. Suppose——"

"All right." Gird held up his hand. "I understand. But surely there are times when circumstances make a difference."

Karik nodded slowly. "There are. No code of law can speak to all circumstances, even among gnomes, and among your undisciplined people I foresee great confusion. But for every exception you make to a rule, Gird, more will try to force their circumstances into that exception. As plants growing between set stones force them apart, the roots of the plants seeking every weakness in the stone." Gird suddenly realized that Karik identified with the stone—that all the rockfolk would—where his sympathies had always been with the plants that broke stones apart. Even when it meant mending a wall, he had admired the delicate mosses and ferns that had persevered in their attack on it. He pushed this thought away, and came back to the subject. He had always assumed that the gnomes would feel as he did about Kelaive's treatment of Meris, that the punishment was far more than a boy's prank deserved. Now he asked.

Karik listened to all the details before saying anything. Then he had questions Gird had never thought of, and only after offered his opinion.

"The right relation of punishment to wrongdoing is a subject in itself," he began. "In our law, the obligation is to restore, so far as possible, the right relation between the parties. Thus if you should steal a measure of grain, you would have to replace it—or its value—and also pay a fine to the court, to cover the cost of trying the case. We use punishment only for younglings, but some human systems extend punishment to adult humans, and in our view fail to distinguish properly between punishment and restoration. Some things, of course, admit of no restoration: injury that results in permanent loss of function, death, the breakage or loss of some singular, irreplaceable object. This is difficult to judge, although we have standards.

"In the case you speak of, you are not arguing that the wrongdoer was not guilty, but that the punishment was too great. On that basis alone, I would agree. But if the fine for a theft of so much fruit were a certain amount, the thief's age would make no difference. Circumstance should not change the judgment, assuming the law to be just in the first place. Kelaive seems to have had no law beyond his own pleasure: this does not make the boy's thieving less wrong, but adds another wrong—the lord's wrong—to it."

"I still think there are times—" Gird began. Karik waved him to silence.

"You have never lived under a just code of law; you cannot be expected to understand how it would be. We shall do our best to teach you, and hope you can teach others, and in time your people may approach justice." With that Gird had to be content.

In the course of learning law, Gird answered the gnomes' questions about the way he organized his troops. He had not forgotten what Arranha said about the gnomes' fighting ability. Perhaps he could find something to trade for their knowledge—but nothing occurred to him. The offer came, to his surprise, from the other side, many hands of days after he had made good progress with Karik.

He and Arranha met with a group of gnomes in one of the formal halls; Arranha had explained that he'd been asked to translate. After a few exchanges of formal greetings, one of the gnomes spoke steadily for several minutes. Finally Arranha turned to Gird.

"They would like to contract with you to provide

military knowledge in return for your help in a specific battle. They think you need this knowledge, and may not win your war without it; they have been impressed by your diligence in your study of law, and your lawful nature. But, they point out, you seem to have no knowledge of strategy, and little of tactics. This they can provide. Are you interested?"

Of course he was interested, but for what kind of battle did they need his help, if they could defeat the magelords on their own? He framed that question as tactfully as he might, for Arranha to translate, but the gnomes could follow his speech well enough and began to answer at once. They could give him no details until they knew more of his abilities, but they wanted the Aareans lured into a trap . . . the Aareans were too wary, now, to come after gnomes if nothing else was involved.

Gird stared at the blank grayish faces, all too aware of his own limited experience. He wanted—no, *needed*— the expertise they had; he had been allowed to see a unit of gnomish guards drilling once, and he lusted after that knowledge. But what would it cost? By their own law, they had to deal fairly with him . . . though his notion of fairness went far astray from theirs. Was this a place in which they overlapped?

They did not rush him. He sat a long time, or so it seemed, in silence, and when he finally nodded, and then slowly read the contract and signed his name— shakily, but legibly—they bowed stiffly and left him alone with Arranha.

The next day, Lawmaster Karik introduced him to Warmaster Ketik, who turned him over to Armsmaster Setik. Not for the first time, he wondered if the gnomes chose their names to sound like beetle-clicks. It was not a question he could ask. Armsmaster Setik had the first scar he had seen on a gnomish face, two of them, in fact. Gird had expected a larger, brawnier gnome, but Setik was built like all the rest. He walked around Gird like a child around a trade-fair wrestler, looking him up and down, then snapped a question at the interpreter who had come along.

"Are all humans your size, he asks?"

Gird shook his head. "No—they come from this high—" he gestured, "to this high—a hand taller than I am. Some are built thin, and some heavy, at every height."

"And what are your weapons?"

Gird listed them—the ones they'd used so far, and the ones he'd thought possibilities. The Armsmaster listened in the usual expressionless silence, and then uttered a brief comment which the interpreter did not immediately explain. "What?" asked Gird finally. The interpreter's mouth twitched.

"He said 'Ridiculous!' "

Gird felt the back of his neck getting hot. It was *not* ridiculous; he had won a battle with just those weapons. The Armsmaster watched him out of black, shiny eyes like seeds. Gird struggled with his anger, all too visibly he was sure, and said, "It worked well enough." This time the Armsmaster's question was obvious enough that he began answering before the translator finished, squatting to draw on the floor with his finger the little battle of Norwalk Sheepfolds. The Armsmaster sat on his heels, watching, absorbed in the recital. But ultimately unconvinced; when Gird finished, he began a rapid commentary in gnomish, and Gird knew, before the translator began, that it was critical.

"He says you were lucky. He says you made fundamental errors in placement of scouts, signalling methods, and in choice of ground. He says if you do that very often, you will kill all your people and lose your war."

Gird had long suspected that his apparent success at Norwalk Sheepfolds had been more luck than skill, but he did not like hearing that hasty analysis by someone who hadn't even been there. Someone who was used to drilling with experienced (and disciplined) gnomes, who would not have to stop a panicky rout just before a fight, who had time to pick the right ground, and dependable people to work with. He wanted to say all that, until the gnomes understood, but the Armsmaster's shiny dark eyes offered no sympathy. He wanted to say they'd won anyway, despite his mistakes (if the problem had really been his mistakes) but he met a closed, expressionless face that was not about to change its mind.

"So what should I have done?" he asked, not quite successful at keeping the sarcasm out of his voice.

"He says you will know when he has finished training you."

Gnomish military training was to the training his old guard sergeant had given as Mali's cooking had been to his mother's. He had been proud of his troop's drill—now, for the first time in his life, he saw absolute precision, and realized how sloppy even his old sergeant had been.

"It did not require much to impress peasants who had nothing," the Armsmaster said. The three units of gnomes who had just shown off would have impressed anyone, Gird was sure. They had moved forward, backward, sideways, opening and closing ranks, had marched one unit through another, and had come out the other end of a long string of commands in the same close, crisp formation they'd begun. "You will not get this, from your humans who are not all the same size and shape. But you can come closer than you have."

Gird felt like a clumsy, not-too-bright recruit again, trapped in the middle of a formation of gnomes not quite shoulder high on him. But he learned—learned not only how to move, but why. That notion of a pincushion that he had had, when he ran around turning his people in place at Norwalk: that had a name, and the right commands to achieve it whenever he wanted, from any other formation. He had always assumed that he needed a large uncumbered space for drill; the gnomes taught him to move a unit quickly and precisely in a room cluttered with supplies, to judge the space available and come up with the commands needed.

He discovered that the wrestling ability which had dumped both Cob and Triga was the very first level the gnomish younglings learned. Armsmaster Setik dumped him repeatedly, no matter what approach he took.

"You're too short," he complained once, bruised and winded from several hard falls. "I can't get a grip on you—and besides, you rockfolk are stronger." Setik grabbed his wrist and pulled him up.

"We are not stronger. We know how to use our strength. Can you lift that?" *That* was a barrel of meal. Gird shrugged, and tried. It was heavy, but he had lifted heavier. Setik put his arms around it and heaved, but it did not lift. "You see? You are stronger, in plain strength. It can be very useful. But you do not know how to use that strength. You want to jump at me and do the work yourself. Make *me* do the work."

They drilled with sticks very similar to those Gird's people used. Setik insisted they must all be the same, no matter the size of the fighter. Gird thought that was another expression of the gnomish need for order, but Setik disagreed. "First: they must all be the same so that your fighting formation can have the same intervals without chancing an accidental blow. Second: they must all be the same so that when one breaks, or someone drops one, that fighter will be comfortable with any replacement. Each weapon has its own best blows; some are similar, but in battle a single mistake chances death. Chance is your enemy, Gird—do not depend on luck. Depend on skill, drill, strength, endurance, tactics: what you know, what you can do. If that is not enough, chance will not save you."

"But what about our tools? I thought we could use farm tools—we did use them."

Setik snapped a command at one of the others, who went jogging off to the gnomish armory, and returned festooned with agricultural implements. Setik picked up a scythe. "Show me how your people used this at Norwalk."

Gird hefted it, enjoying as always the very balance and swing of it, then shifted the handgrips for a better overhand stroke, and lifted it. It made an awkward chopping weapon, harder to control than a mattock, but it could reach over others and deliver a solid blow to a head or back. He had seen only two of the successful strokes, both oblique downward swings that ended in a soldier's back. He demonstrated on the straw-filled leather dummy set up in the middle of the chamber.

"I thought at first of swinging it as usual," he explained. "It could take off a leg. But the backswing's too dangerous—there's no way to control it in formation."

"That's what I thought." Setik scratched his head. "We had a weapon more like a mattock, used with a similar stroke but easier to handle because it balances better. That great long blade out there, and the curving handle, make this one very unbalanced. And even you, with your strength, could not swing it sideways at head level."

"Even if I could, the greatest danger is to the person on my left and behind. I've seen someone killed like that in harvest, a scythe-tip buried in his belly."

"Good *individual* defense," Setik muttered. "One man against several armed—that might work. Sharpen the outer edge of the blade as well. But not a good formation weapon. I suppose you use the shovel like the pole?"

"Yes, but it has that edge."

"Hmmm. What we call a broadpike. It would also work with a sharp downward stroke, but that would not fend off the enemy's. These little things you mentioned, sickles and firetongs and such—good for brawls, maybe, or defense when surprised by an enemy while working— but not for your army." Setik went down the list, explaining and demonstrating why each tool was not worth using as a weapon, "unless you have nothing else. But I would not waste my time drilling with them. If you are fighting with trained units against real soldiers, you need a formation weapon. We use polearms, to give us reach, a hauk in close fighting, and archers . . . do your people know archery at all?"

A hauk, when Gird asked, was a short stick, a club, which could be used for training, or for cracking heads—it reminded him of the guards' billets and maces. The gnomes in formation had hauks thrust into their belts behind their backs, ready to grab when needed. Gird learned how to handle all the gnomish polearms correctly; Setik recommended that he settle on one, fairly easily made, for his own army. "A simple spike on the end of your pole will do," Setik said, "and any smith can make that from scrap metal—those scythe blades, for instance. A real pikehead is better, and you could use broadpikes, but that takes more metal, and more skill in smithing. Sharpening the pole itself is better than nothing, but wood alone is not likely to penetrate metal armor—if that's what they're wearing."

Setik knew exactly how footsoldiers with pikes should maneuver against cavalry; Gird's rude guesses, based on practice with men on logs, came close but would, Setik said, cost him too many soldiers. Archers were the worst threat; the gnomes dealt with enemy bowmen by having better bowmen of their own. Gird was not sure his people could learn that fast. He himself had never been better than average with a bow. And the art of making good bows and good arrows— strong enough to be useful in war—had passed from his people to the Aarean lords. Peasants had not been allowed to have bows, or make bows; what they had now could take small birds and animals, but no more. Setik shook his head, and explained to Gird again just how much damage an unopposed group of archers could do. The implication was clear: learn this, somehow, or die for its lack. Gird began to consider who among his people might know a clandestine archery expert— someone far to the north, who might have friends or family among the horse nomads, whose bows the Finaareans respected, perhaps.

Days passed; Gird was no longer sure how many. The gnomes did not celebrate Midwinter, and refused to interrupt his lessons for it. He hoped the gods would forgive him, this once—perhaps, since he was under-ground, among gnomes, they would not know. That didn't seem likely; the gnomes certainly thought that the High Lord, the great Judge, knew everything above ground or below.

He felt stuffed with new knowledge, things that made perfect sense during the lessons but came apart in his mind afterward like windblown puffballs. The Warmaster had been appalled to discover that Gird had no idea how many of the lords there were, or how many soldiers they had. That Gird could not draw an accurate map of Finaarenis and the surrounding lands. That he did not know who the king was, or how the king was related to the various nobles, or how the land was governed. They poured all this into him, day after day, every minute of his waking hours filled and overfilled with new knowledge. He had never known there was that much knowledge in the whole world, and he wished he hadn't found it out. Even with the gnomes' organizing skills, he found himself remembering the name of a town when he wanted the number of stones of grain needed to feed a hundred men on march for two hands of days, or coming up with the right way to place scouts to watch a tradeway when he wanted the command that split a column marching forward into two columns, one of which was veering off to the right. He could imagine himself in the midst of battle calling out the exceptions to liability for delivery of spoiled perishables instead of the right commands, and he sweated all the worse for it.

This struggle was no easier that he did not know how long it would last: how long he had to learn what—he now agreed—he needed to learn. Years would not have been enough; he had started with a bare half-year, if he was going to lead the war in the next season. He would have fretted about that, if he had had time. Instead, the worry seeped into his other thoughts like a drop of dye into water, coloring every moment with fear he had not named. He would have discussed it with Arranha, but the priest was often away when Gird returned to his assigned quarters and fell into bed.

At last, with no warning (at least nothing he had noticed) he and Arranha were summoned to the largest of the ceremonial halls, where a crowd of gnomes had assembled. Silently, Gird noticed; there was none of the whispering or chattering of a human crowd. Lawmaster Karik (one of the four or five he had finally learned to recognize at sight) led Gird to the front of the chamber, and spoke lengthily in gnomish. Then he turned to Gird.

"It is time to send you out, if you would be at your encampment before your people are sure we have killed you. Remember your contracts with us; we have delivered to you that which we promised. You have your obligation."

At least he knew the correct response. "I acknowledge receipt of your knowledge and training; I admit my obligation, and swear to fulfill it to the length of my life."

"Witnessed." That brought a stir, and the chorus from all. "Witnessed."

A chill went down his back. He fully intended to carry out all he had promised, but that "witnessed" meant uncounted gnome pikes at his back if he failed.

Chapter Twenty

He had known he missed the sun—even the thin, cold sunlight of winter—but not until he came out into that remembered beauty, and rested his gaze on a horizon impossibly distant, did he know how much. Tears stung his eyes. It had hurt, in ways he could not define, to have his vision trapped between walls so long. It had hurt to have sounds reverberating in those walls, quiet as the gnomes had been. It had hurt to smell no live wind, with its infinitely varying smells, its constantly changing pressures on his skin. They had led him out into a morning of softly falling rain, a cold spring rain that still held a threat of late snow. Between the showers that fell curtainlike here and there he could see long tawny slopes, dark patches of woodland, the soft lavender and muted burgandy of sap-swollen buds coloring what had been gray. He heard the soft whisper of the rain on sodden grass, the distant gurgle of water running away downhill, a vast silence between the sounds where nothing would echo. Cold and damp as it was, it soothed the inside of his nose, easing with smells of wet earth and rock the dry itch from a season underground with only rockdust and gnomes. His own human smell, that he had been aware of as unlike the others, disappeared into that freshness.

"We will see you at Blackbone Hill," said Armsmaster Setik, who had come out with Gird. Arranha was staying behind awhile, but had told Gird he would follow him later. Gird wondered if Arranha knew about Blackbone Hill; the gnomes mentioned the name only when Arranha was not around.

"Yes," said Gird, drinking in another breath of that air, wondering why the ragged, uneven landscape of duns and grays seemed so much more beautiful than the careful sculpting of the gnomes' halls.

"You have the maps."

"Yes." As he looked at the land, now, the maps he had been taught to use seemed to overlay it. He would go *that* way, and find a tiny watercourse to lead him north and west, then leave that one by a steep-browed hill, and find another beyond the hill, and then the wood he almost thought of as *his* wood . . .

"And—" Setik looked up at him with an expression Gird could not interpret. "I found it most satisfying; for a human, you are—are not unlike a kapristi in some ways."

Gird turned, surprised. The Armsmaster had been even less outgoing than his other instructors, if possible. Gird had assumed he would be glad to rid himself of a clumsy human oaf. Setik's brow was furrowed slightly, his scars pulled awry.

"You are by nature hasty, as all the lateborn are: hasty to laughter, to anger, to hunger—but you forced foresight on yourself, and withheld haste. You have a gift for order, for discipline, for what we mean by responsibility."

"You are a good teacher," Gird said.

The gnome nodded. "I am, that is true. But the best teacher cannot turn a living thing from its nature: I could not make stone grow and bear fruit like a tree. I could not teach a tree to fly. Even among us, who are much alike, some have less talent for war than others. You have it, and you have what is rare with us—what war requires that the rest of our life does not need, and that is a willingness to go beyond what is required, into the realm of gift."

Gird was both puzzled and fascinated. All he had heard, from Lawmaster Karik, showed the gnomes' distrust of gifts, and until now he had not suspected the gnomish soldiers thought differently. Setik smiled suddenly, a change as startling as if rock split in a manic grin.

"War calls for more than fair exchange; we soldiers know what the lawgivers cannot understand. Even among us, I say, are some who freely give—and in war that giving wins battles. You have that; from what you say, it is a human trait." Abruptly, he stopped, and his face changed back to its former dourness. "Go with the High Lord's judgment," he said. Gird glanced back at the entrance to the gnomes' caves, so nearly invisible; there stood several others, watching and listening.

"You will not take thanks," he said to Setik, "but among my people it is rude to withhold them. I will thank the gods, then, for sending me to such a good teacher of war, and ask their grace to keep my mind from scrambling together what you so carefully set apart."

If he had believed the gnomes had any humor whatever, he would have said Setik's black eyes twinkled. "Soldiers of one training are as brothers of one father," the gnome murmured. "Go now, before someone asks awkward questions."

Gird nodded, saying nothing past the lump in his throat, and headed downslope. He stepped carefully across the boundary, and did not look back until he had traveled well out of sight of that unambiguous line.

The gnomes had shown him a small, exquisitely carved model of the lands they called *gnishina*, all drained by the great river Gird had never yet seen, from the western plains to the sea. All his life Gird had lived among low hills and creeks whose windings made no sense to him. He had thought the world was made lumpy, like redroots in a pan, until he saw the gnomes' country, with great mountains rising behind a line of hills.

The model made sense of what had seemed random hummocks. He had not understood the gnomes' explanation, but the great concentric arcs of rock were obvious enough, with the river dividing them like the cleft of a cow's hoof. Rows of hills, variously shaped by the different kinds of rock in them (he understood that much; everyone knew that red rock made rounded slopes, and white rock made stepwise ones) bowed sharply away from the river, to run almost parallel to the southern mountains as they neared them. Between the hills ran the creeks and rivers, all tributaries of the Honnorgat. These stream valleys had formed natural routes of travel. Moving a large force north or south was easiest near the Honnorgat; moving it east or west was easiest away from the great river.

Once more under the open sky, he could interpret the hills before him for what they were: the flanks of a great arch. Going north, he would cross white rock to yellow, and yellow to brown, then travel west to come back to yellow and white. Just so a man might run his finger from the side of a cow's hoof to the cleft, then forward to the point—and find hoof wall again. More importantly, with his understanding of the whole region, and the maps the gnomes had provided, he would know where he was—where his army was—and how to get where he wanted to go. He hoped.

Human lands were scarcely less perilous than the gnome princedoms, though their perils were less uncanny. Gadilon might not trouble his gnomish neighbors, for fear of their retribution, but he had no intention of letting a peasant uprising unseat him. Gird was hardly into that domain when he saw the first patrols, seasoned soldiers whose alertness indicated respect for their new enemy. Whatever had happened while Gird was underground with the gnomes, it had ended all complacency in the outlying holdings. Gird spent an uncomfortable half-day lying flat among dripping bushes as the patrols crossed and recrossed the route he had planned to take. When dark fell, he extricated himself, muttering curses, and edged carefully around the hill and down a noisy watercourse. Here the water noises would cover any he made.

Even with his caution, he was nearly caught. If the sentry had not coughed, and then spat into the water, Gird would never have known that the dark shadow of a boulder was actually a person. He stopped where he was, wondering if he'd been seen. Another cough, a muttered curse. Gird crept away from the stream's edge, feeling the ground under his feet carefully. He could not stay here, and he could not go back—not without knowing where the other soldiers were. He made his way into the tangle of rocks on that side of the stream, and eased his way up onto one of the huge boulders. From that height, he could just see a twinkle of firelight downstream and below. The sentry had probably been told to climb where Gird now was, but up here the night breeze was cold and raw; the man had slid down to get out of the wind. Gird flattened himself on the cold hard stone and thought about it.

With his gnomish training in mind, if he'd been the person responsible for that camp, he'd have had sentries upstream and down, and scattered through the woods. Scattered where? His un-gnomish experience told him that men, like the sentry whose cough had revealed him, cared for their own comfort. No matter how wisely a commander had sent them out, they would each choose a place that combined the maximum of personal safety and comfort with sufficient—to that individual—performance of the assignment. If he could figure out what that was, he could get around the camp in safety. If he made a mistake, they would all be after him.

One simple answer was to backtrack upstream and swing wide around the camp. That would work if he didn't then run into another patrol. He could think of no reason why Gadilon would have another patrol out to the south, but who could read the lords' intent? Or he could try to angle away from the stream, through the brush and woods, and hope to avoid any other sentries without losing so much ground. If the streamside sentry represented the distance from the camp that all of them were posted, that should be possible. He was still debating this with himself when he heard horses' hooves in the distance, a cry of alarm from the camp, and a trumpet call. The sentry below him gasped, and started back for the camp at a run, falling over rocks and bellowing as he went.

Gird stayed where he was, trying to understand what was going on. More lights appeared: flickering torches moving between the trees. Loud cries, shouted commands, responses from distant sentries. He felt a little smug that they were coming from the radius he'd guessed. He wished he could get closer, and had started down from the rock when he heard the unmistakeable clash of steel on steel. More yelling, more screams, more noise of hoofs, weapons, another trumpet blast cut off in mid-cry. He could hear noise coming his way, as several men thrashed through the undergrowth, stumbled over obstructions. They came near enough that he could hear their gasping breath, the jingle of their buckles and mail, the creak of leather. Behind them were more; someone shouted "There they go!"

With a crunch of boots on gravel, they were beneath him. He could just make out two or three dark forms against the starlit water, the gleam of starlight along a weapon's blade. One there was wounded, groaning a little with every gasping breath. Gird lay motionless, hoping no one would notice the large shadow flat on the top of the boulder.

"Don't let 'em get away!" he heard from downstream. "Follow that blood trail." One of the men below him cursed viciously.

"We got to move," he said. "They'll find us, and—"

"Per can't go farther," said another. "We'll have to fight 'em off."

"We can't." A pause, then, "We'll have to leave 'im. He's the blood trail, anyway. They find him, dead, they'll think that's it."

"No! They'll know he couldn't have got this far alone. 'Sides, he's my sister's husband; I'm not leaving him."

"Suit yourself." One of the shadows splashed into the stream, and started across. The other threw a low-voiced curse after him, and backed against the rock on which Gird lay.

Now the pursuers were in sight, the light of their torches swinging wildly through the trees. Gird saw rough, bearded faces, men wearing no livery, or even normal clothes, but the skins of wild animals roughly tanned and crudely fashioned. They carried swords and pikes, stained already with blood. Gird dared not lean out from his perch to see the men at the foot of his rock—but he suspected that they were Gadilon's soldiers, in his livery, and these others were—what? Not any he had trained, he was sure, but who? Gadilon's peasants?

He slid back carefully over the crest of the boulder, hoping that their attention was fixed on the men below. What happened then was clear enough by the sound of it: a low growl of anticipation from the pursuers, a challenge by the one man still able to fight, and bloody butchery thereafter. It did not last long. One of the attackers said, "There was another—look here, he took to the water."

"No matter. We'll find 'im by day, or let 'im carry word to his lord—he'll get no comfort of it. One back from each patrol will do us no harm." Then the speaker raised his voice to carry over the stream's chuckle. "Hey—you coward! You count's man! Go tell yer count what happened, and tell 'im 'twas Gird and his yeomen! Tell 'im to shake in 'is boots, while he has 'em to shake in."

Gird felt the blood rush to his skin at that; he nearly jumped up where he stood to deny it. How *dared* they use his name! His ears roared with the pressure of his anger; as his hearing cleared, he heard one of the men laugh.

"Diss, what're you playing at? D'you really think the count'll believe this night's work was Gird's?"

"What do I care? If he thinks it's peasants, he'll ride

his peasants harder, and spend less time looking for brigands. If he blames every robbery and ambush in his domain on peasants, isn't that good for us? And if he doesn't believe it—if he thinks to himself it's a trick of brigands—he'll wonder why brigands would lay that crime on peasants. If maybe we're allies. And the peasants . . . if they'll skimp to send grain to Gird's yeomen, why not to us—if we convince them we're with them."

Gird dug his fingers into the rock to keep himself from plunging right into that—which was the same, he knew, as plunging a knife in his neck. The brigands all laughed; he heard them stripping the bodies of the count's soldiers, before they left them naked and unprotected in the night, to return to the fire and carouse with the guard-sergeant's ration of ale. Gird heard them ride away, in the hours before dawn. He waited until he could see clearly before slithering down from his perch, stiff and miserable, to see for himself what they'd done.

The dead soldiers looked no different from any other dead; he had not forgotten, in his half-year with the gnomes, how the dead looked and smelled. He squatted beside them and closed their eyes with pebbles. They were enemies, but not now his; he had not killed them, and he felt he owed them that basic courtesy. They had stiffened; he could not straighten their limbs. But he found mint already green beside the creek, and laid a sprig on each of them. Then he plucked a handful of it, and went toward the deserted camp. There he put mint on each of the dead, soldier and brigand alike, unsure why he was doing it except that it felt right. This was not his fight; he disliked both sides with equal intensity.

The brigands had stripped the soldiers of weapons, armor, clothes, and money (or so Gird judged, finding a couple of copper crabs trampled into the ground), but had left behind what food they had not eaten themselves. Gird saw no reason not to take it. He stuffed the flat loaves and half a cheese into his shirt. At the soldiers' picket lines, he found the cut ends of ropes where the brigands had stolen the horses; continuing downstream, he found another dead soldier, the downstream sentry.

He went as warily as he could, aware that he now had two sets of enemies: when Gadilon found out about his patrol, these hills would hum with soldiery, but at the same time the brigands would not be happy to find a real Gird in their midst. By midday, he had put a good distance between himself and the site of the brigand attack, but he felt no safer. The gnomish maps told him that he needed to cross all Gadilon's domain, south to north, then open sheep pastures shared between several lords and peasant villages, before he would be back in territory he knew by sight. The nearest barton —as of the previous fall, he reminded himself—was a group of shepherds who called their settlement Farmeet.

His most direct route took him across a trade road that connected Gadilon's towns with those in Tsaia to the east and Ierin, the most southwesterly town in Finaarenis. The gnomes had pointed out that he must, eventually, control traffic on this road in order to secure either southern quadrant of the realm. Like the River Road, along the southern bank of the Honnorgat in the north, the southern trade road allowed the lords to move soldiers and supplies easily from one fortified town to another. Gird himself found moving across country easier, but the gnomes had insisted that no organized army could travel like a single man or a small group.

Gird made it to the road with only one more close brush with a patrol (he had hidden in a dense cedar as the men rode by underneath, discussing the deaths of their friends in the ambush Gird had seen. He was dismayed to find that they assumed peasants had done it—and that the peasants and brigands were in league.) Now he peered from a thick growth of plums, all white with bloom, at a rutted track that seemed deserted. A horseman had ridden by sometime before; he'd heard the hoofbeats, and he could see fresh tracks overlying older ones. He leaned forward a little, shivering the plums, and the bees in the blossoms lifted with a whine to their buzz. Bees didn't bother him (he wondered where their hive was), but he still could not tell if anyone was on the other side, watching. The soldiers had said something about closing the trade road, keeping the peasants from using it or crossing it. That would take sentries all along the way—surely they weren't doing that—but he would hate to take an arrow in the neck finding out.

Something chuffed, across the track. Gird held very still. A deer burst through the plums there, paused in the track, ears wide and tail high, and chuffed again. Even as Gird heard the snap of a bowstring, an arrow thunked into the deer and it staggered, limped a stride, and fell awkwardly. Three men dressed alike crashed through the undergrowth, lashed the deer's carcass to a pole, and disappeared back into the wood on the far side of the road, without a glance toward Gird. Their silent cooperation convinced Gird that they worked together constantly, but he had no idea whether they were foresters, soldiers, or brigands. Or, for that matter, poaching peasants. He could hear their progress through the wood; taking a chance that anyone else watching would be attracted by that noise, he darted across the road and into the trees, then swung wide of their path.

He wished he dared speak to them. That archer had been powerful and accurate; that's what the gnomes said he needed. If those were peasants, poaching deer, then he might find a useful follower. More likely an arrow, he reminded himself. Too risky.

He made it safely to Farmeet, only to find the shepherds far less outgoing than he remembered from the summer before.

"I heard you was taking on Gadilon's patrols," said one of the shepherds, not quite looking at Gird. "Heard as you come on 'em sleeping, and killed 'em lying there, and took their clothes and all . . ."

"No," said Gird. "That was brigands."

"How'd you know?" They were all very still, sitting hunched as shepherds do, their long crooks angling up over their shoulders.

"I was there, hiding from the soldiers, when the brigands came." They said nothing, but he could feel their disbelief. It was unlikely, he had to admit; to such as these, unlikely was nearly the same as impossible. Only a complete story would do; they would suspect anything less. Keeping his voice low and matter-of-fact, he told it all, from first sighting the sentry to laying mint on the bodies.

"Good you did that," said the oldest shepherd, nodding. "Shows respect to the Lady, that do. Proper to do it for both sides, too."

"They said they was you?" asked another.

Gird nodded. "They did, and they meant it to confuse both Gadilon's men and our people."

"We heard things this past winter." The oldest shepherd poked the fire. "You'd gone down to the underworld, we heard. Talked to that one—has the horned circle, you know what I mean?"

"Liart—" breathed Gird.

"Aye. No good, that one. Them's follows him likes hurting. Our lord's got some like that in his service. Heard you made bargain with 'im, anyhow. That's where you were, eh? Is it?"

"No." Gird wondered where that story had come from, the lords or the brigands or simple imagination. "No, I was with the kapristi—the gnomes, the little rockfolk."

"Ah. They're not *his* followers, what I hear."

"No. They follow the High Lord; I went to them to learn about law—what's wrong with the lords' law, and what might replace it."

A younger shepherd spat. "Anyone can see what's wrong with the lords' law—it don't take muckin' about underground to see that."

"Hush, Dikka. This'll be more, what Gird's talkin' about."

"When this war's over," Gird began, hoping they could think that far ahead, "we'll have to have fair laws, if we're to have peace. Most of our people don't remember how it was before the lords came. What we do now's a mix of our old customs and their laws—it makes no sense, as anyone can see—you're right there. But what to do about it—that's something else."

"And you saw beyond the war, to the peace? Ah, that's good." The oldest shepherd finally turned to look directly at Gird. "You want the peace, do you? And not just the fighting?"

"That's right."

"And you know a fair law for all of us then, when it's over?"

Gird shook his head. "I know a way to devise such a law—but it will mean many of us working on it. You, too, perhaps."

"Not me—but I'll be glad to think on it, that someone is. So you've naught to do with the horned chain?"

"No." He let it stand baldly, like that; they looked at him a long moment, then all nodded.

The oldest shepherd said, "You have an honest look, and nothing that fits one of the horned chain worshippers. So I say—" gathering the others with his eyes. "I say he *is* Gird, and not that fellow as stopped by a hand of days ago, claiming Gird's name and asking our help."

"What!" They had said nothing of this before. The old man grinned, showing the gaps in his teeth.

"Aye—another Gird was here, if we believed him, which we didn't. Big fellow, like you in that. Grinned a lot with plenty of teeth. Said that great powers was with him—and us if we joined him—and the lords would be cast down and trampled in the dust. Our sheep'd grow fat and have golden fleece, the way he told it—you'd think he'd been talking to the Master Shepherd and not the Master of Torments."

"So what did you do?" asked Gird, fascinated. The shepherds all chuckled.

"Do? We's no more'n stupid old shepherds, lad. Us can't think o' none but sheep and wool—can't make an onion from a barleycorn, nor sheep of mice, no more'n make soldiers of th' likes o' us, can you now?" The exaggeration of their accents was so pronounced that Gird found himself grinning; they grinned back, well pleased with his reaction. "He wanted a barton here;

we said we's no barton—we's shepherds, not farmfolk. He says what's Farmeet, then, as he's been told it's a barton—and we says it's a bitty sheepfold, no more'n that, just a lambing shed and pen. He was not happy wi' us when he left."

Gird sniffed elaborately, reference to the old saying about onions and barleycorn, and said, "I smell an onion in this seedsack, so I do—" They laughed uproariously.

"It works both ways," the old shepherd admitted. "No onions from barleycorns, but no hiding an onion from anyone with a nose. But them's certain as they smelled stupid, afore ever they got here; we's no reason to argue with 'em."

"How many?" asked Gird. The old shepherd held up his hands and spread them twice: four hands of men, about the size he'd expected.

The little Farmeet barton had only two hands of yeomen: six men and four women. It would probably spend the entire war herding its sheep, shearing, spinning wool, but it had already served him well.

From Farmeet, he made it safely to Holn, where the rumors the brigands had spread had not yet come. Other rumors had. Already conflict had started, and the lords were raising all their troops, planning to crush the peasants before the summer came. They would move, Gird was told, on Kelaive's domain first, sweeping east across the lands where he had been known to dwell. Gird's own people had runners in all the southern villages, waiting word from him; Holn's runner had already gone to tell Ivis and Felis he was back, and another runner waited any message he wanted to send.

What he wanted, desperately, was a pause in time—a few days when nothing happened, so that he could get back with his own troop and make plans. But it could not be, and he understood it. He listened late to the yeomen of Holn, spreading the maps the gnomes had provided and running his finger along the lines. Then he slept, for a few hours, and had a last conference with the barton, warning them about the brigands who claimed his name. He had no time to stop and teach them the new drills the gnomes had taught him; they would have to learn later, when they rose. For now, he must get to his own troops as quickly as possible.

Although he knew the country near Holn, he was glad to have a local guide, who knew just where the patrols had been going. The first bits of green were showing in hedge and wood; wild plum frothed white, and tiny pink flowers starred the rumpled grass that had green at its roots. Cold wet air gusted past him, carrying occasional snowflakes, spurts of rain, and gleams of unsteady sunlight. He could smell the growth in it, the spring smell that made new lambs throw their tails over their backs and frisk as he and his guide went past. There was a pasture with cows, the herder in his leather cape standing hunched against a flurry of hard raindrops, and here was a ditch brimful of racing water, clear as deep winter ice in a bucket. Gird would have frisked if he could, and he chuckled to himself at the thought of a middle-aged farmer-turned-rebel, throwing his tail over his back to dance in a spring rain.

They saw no patrols that day, but between showers Gird thought he saw a smudge of dark smoke blowing away somewhere to the east. He asked his guide, who shrugged.

"There's been burnings, this winter past. A whole grange, we heard of: every bit of grain and hay lost, and the stones cracked, some of 'em. The lords were making everyone burn the stubble in the fields, last harvest, so's no one could hide in it. Hayricks, too, some places."

From Holn to Sawey, where Felis waited in the barton of a farmer called Ciri. It was dark, quiet but for dripping off the roofs—too quiet for a village on an early spring evening. His guide led him to the back gate, clicked the pebbles in his pocket together. Someone answered the clicks from within, then pushed the gate open for them. Inside was the good smell of food, cows, leather, oiled wood, and the sight of friends' faces. They hugged, smacking each others' shoulders.

The gnomes' impassive dourness faded from Gird's mind—these were men, humans that he knew, faces alive with passion for one thing after another.

"At last," Felis said. Others echoed him. Gird took a deep breath. There was no going back now; there had been no going back from Norwalk, but now he could not hesitate. It was truly "at last" and he must do what he had come to do. They were watching him, relieved to see him but still a little uncertain. Hoping he was over whatever had bothered him after Norwalk Sheepfolds—*needing* him to be over it—but unsure that he was. They reminded him of boys watching a father whose uncertain temper determines the quality of their life. *I am sure,* he told himself. When he smiled at them, their faces relaxed.

"At last which?" he asked Felis, intentionally lightening the moment. "At last I am here to settle an argument, or so that you can tell me you don't want me, or—"

"You know," said Felis, rubbing his nose. How, Gird wondered, had it gotten sunburnt so early in the year?

"I do, but I'm not sure you do. Yes, this is the year, and yes, I have learned things we can use, and yes, we start now. Tonight."

He felt the change in the tiny enclosure: relief, eagerness, and—as always—fear.

"I told you," said one of the local men, in the corner. Gird smiled at him, raising an eyebrow; he flushed. "Some said you'd say wait, like you did last year, but I knew. I knew you had not lost your courage."

Felis jumped into that. "Only a few, Gird, and no one—"

"It's all right." He felt calm and light, certain now where he was going with this group, and for the next few days. After that— "I could not say what I thought was wrong; you know that saying things is not my skill. I'm a plain farmer, same as any of you. I was as glad as any, we'd won at Norwalk, but I knew something was wrong, and now I know what."

"And that is?" asked Felis, a challenge in his tone.

Gird stretched, and let himself hunker down in a corner comfortably.

"You've heard of the gnomes' soldiering, haven't you?" Felis scowled, but nodded. "Well, they've taught me a lot. Norwalk *was* lucky. I had to learn better—and I have—and with what I know now and you can learn quick enough, even the gnomes think we can win."

"What did you trade them?" asked Ciris, whose barton it was.

"Our—*my*—pledge that we would respect their borders, deal fairly with them—" That got nods, and muttered agreement. "—And our help in one battle: they want to trap the magelords in a place called Blackbone Hill."

This caused less comment than he'd expected; if the gnomes wanted their help, they must think Gird's army was good, and that meant good fortune. Gird had his doubts, but wasn't about to share them. Not yet.

"We're not in the same camps," Felis told Gird, when the other men had left and he and Gird were sharing a heap of straw. "The patrols began to come too close. Ivis thought we'd do better spread through several bartons. He said his forester friends told him the duke was planning a raid around Midwinter. So we left, and let out word to one of the brigand gangs that the camps had supplies in them. They moved in; the duke's men caught them—and recognized them, too; the leader's someone the duke's wanted for years. We hope that's convinced the duke that *his* peasant uprising was really a brigand gang in his wood. Ivis's brother agreed to say in the duke's court that the leader had been coming to him, threatening him."

Gird shook his head, half in admiration of their ingenuity, and half in concern. "Not all brigands are that gullible," he said, and told Felis about that other band he'd run into.

"So what will you do?"

"Fight my war, and let them fight theirs. People will recognize the difference soon enough." He told Felis about the shepherds of Farmeet. Felis chuckled.

"Everyone thinks farmers are stupid, and shepherds

are the stupidest: lords and thieves alike. But tell me, what is 'your war'—how will we fight, and when, and where?"

"And have I seen the gods themselves, and is the overworld paved with gold and walled in crystal? You want all the answers at once? In the dark?" Beside him, Felis made a sound between a snort and a sniff; Gird relented. "All right. What I heard is that the lords have raised their army, and plan to start by clearing from Kelaive's domain east. We will take all the bartons from Hardshallows eastward, and move north—away from them, for now—and strike for the River Road."

"Why?"

"Even if we won here, we'd still be caught between the south trade road, the River Road, and the trade road between Finyatha and Ierin. Their supplies would flow freely; ours would not. If we cut the River Road, we've cut Finyatha from Verella, in Tsaia—"

"Tsaia! You're not thinking of fighting there—"

"Tsaia's king is kinbound to this one. The gnomes say things are as bad there. Our bartons on the east reported interest in neighboring vills inside Tsaia."

"But I don't know where Tsaia is, except eastward."

Gird grinned, in the darkness; Felis sounded as much affronted as frightened. That was good. "You will know, when we get there. Now: this is what we must do to win in Finaarenis alone. We must be able to feed ourselves, control the food supply—and that means the trade roads, as well as protection for the farmers, and certain towns—"

"You sound—different—" Felis sounded uncertain again.

"I am, in a way. It's all very different than we thought. It's more than raising three or four bartons at a time to attack a small force. Right now the lords have trained soldiers with good weapons; they have stores of supplies; they have control of towns and roads—and, if we're honest, of much of the countryside. We should have more yeomen overall, but you know how it is—if we seem to be losing, some of those will go home and forget they ever heard of us. Our people have almost no experience, our weapons— Oh. That reminds me. Changes there, too."

Felis rolled over; the straw rustled. "All right. I'm convinced. You've come back ready to lead us to glory, full of as many new ideas as when you came into my camp that first day. But unless the gods put their touch on you, you still need sleep, and so do I."

Chapter Twenty-one

In less than a hand of days, Gird stood facing his first army: the bartons from Hardshallows, his own village, Fireoak, Whitetree, Harrow, Holn, and the original two Stone Circle groups. After his experience with the gnomes, their "straight" lines looked crooked, and their marching seemed as ragged as goats dancing along a path, but he said nothing of that for the moment. They were there, bold, timid, nervous, confident, in every possible mood he might have expected. With them had come the food he had told them to put by for this purpose; each had brought his or her sack of grain and beans, onions and redroots, even strips of dried meat.

What he had not expected so soon was the ragtag clutter of refugees that had come with them. His own village had come all in a lump, convinced that anyone left behind would die. After all, everyone knew where Gird had come from, and Kelaive had never been slow to make reprisals. Most of Hardshallows followed its yeomen, for the same reason, and Fireoak, in the same hearthing, feared the same trouble.

So besides the yeomen, Gird had all the others to worry about: small children, pregnant women, old men and women who could scarcely totter. They knew nothing of camp discipline. He had to double, then triple, the size of the jacks; smoke from the cookfires marked the sky with unmistakeable evidence of their presence. When nothing happened for a few days, the oldest and youngest began to treat it as a holiday—spring, and no work to be done. Grandparents sat and chattered, children screeched, mothers festooned every bush with laundry.

Most of those who were young and strong wanted to join the bartons—better late than never—but Gird took only a third of them. The others he assigned to his traditional tally groups, with Pidi (now beginning to show his growth) to teach them the necessary foodgathering and camp skills. This group he knew could not keep up when the army began to move, but he had no safe place to send them; they would have to do as best they could.

As for the bartons, he had all of them change from varied farm tools to the long stick and the hauk for weapons. The farm tools went to the nonfighters, with a few hours of instruction. Once all his units had the long sticks, drilling them began to look more like drilling a real army. Gird imagined good, hard, steel points on the ends of those sticks, but what they had were sharpened wood: not good enough, but cheap and available. He imagined a lot more drill, but they had no more time than they did steel.

What he did have was willing spies. When the enemy army set out from Finyatha, runners passed the word from barton to barton. Gird knew within a few days, while the army was still days north of Hardshallows.

"Why don't we move *now*?" asked Ivis and Felis. Gird tapped the map the gnomes had made him.

"We can't be sure they aren't getting information the same way we are."

"But no one would tell the lords about us—not farmers—"

"Felis, think. They burned Berryhedge, didn't they? Took the survivors, beat them—do you think there's anything about the Berryhedge barton they don't know? They burned three other villages we know of last winter, taking prisoners each time. Some yeomen got away; some didn't. Some of those they caught will have told all they know—from pain, from fear, from hope of saving a child . . . whatever. Most of our people want to be free, but many of them are scared—and so they should be. Some of those scared ones will help the lords, simply out of fear."

"But I still don't see why—"

"Look again. If they know we're moving north, they'll most likely turn and come after us. They could catch us on the move, before we get to the River Road. I don't know all that country; I need to see it, so that when we come to fight there, I can choose good ground."

"The gnomes taught you that, too?"

"Yes." He looked up, and saw a sulky expression in Felis's eyes. Ivis was merely puzzled. "Felis, I'll be glad to teach you all the gnomes taught me—to teach all of you—but right now I don't have time. Now. When the army has passed the lower ford, there, they'll be unlikely to turn back until Hardshallows. In spring, that stream runs deep and rough. That gives us time to get well north of them before they turn—and if we're lucky they'll go on to my old village, to get word from the steward there."

Cob said "What about the lords' magic—did you learn anything about that? Is it real, and what can they do?"

"It's real." Gird rumpled his hair with both hands. He could have done without that question. The next would be what could he do about the lords' magic, and the answer was, nothing. "Some of them have lost it—that may be why they've changed for the worst. They're afraid they'll lose all their power without their magic to fight for them. But some have enough left— they can make light, call storms, compel men to obedience, change their faces—"

"Are you sure?"

"Yes. Lucky for us that most of them don't have it any more; we'll be fighting soldiers who have no more magic than we do."

"Better weapons," said Cob gloomily.

"Better for fighting unarmed peasants. Remember that most of 'em have been sitting around guarding some noble's home; the ones that have experience got it with horse nomads—not with foot troops who use polearms. They belong to different lords; they'll have a divided command; they aren't used to drilling together. We are."

The lords' army did exactly what Gird had expected. They moved at a leisurely pace down the trade road from Finyatha toward Ierin, waited for a contingent of troops from Ierin, then swung southeastward, following the west bank of the Blue all the way to Hardshallows. His spies told him they burned that deserted village after fording the stream, then stopped to celebrate a victory. Supposedly, the enemy forces now numbered about 300 soldiers, and that many again of servants, guides, packers, and other noncombatants. This was by no means all the force the lords had at their disposal. Ivis's duke was rumored to be on his way with his personal guard—a hundred strong, some of them fresh from the northern frontier.

By this time, Gird and his army were on the move. His original Stone Circle troops now numbered just over fifty; these he considered his best trained and hardiest. The bartons already risen contributed over a hundred, and the newest yeomen—the hardiest of the refugees—added another sixty or so. Then there were the refugees themselves, some of whom might be able to fight, at least a single blow: over two hundred of them.

Moving this motley group turned out to be harder than Gird had expected. Although he and his Stone Circle troops were used to traveling, many of the others had never been out of their villages until now. They did not understand maps, and the farther Gird led them from familiar country, the more unhappy and nervous they became. Some of the older people simply stopped, refusing to go on. For the first few days, it seemed that Gird was constantly being asked to persuade someone's father or mother to keep going. "Not another step!" burned itself into his memory, along with "How many times have I told you—!" addressed to a wailing child.

It was not what he'd planned. It was not anything like what the gnomes had advised. But what could he do? They were his people; he had to take care of them. He led them by the safest ways he could find, avoiding villages where soldiers were quartered. He could not hide the movement of so many from everyone, but most of the peasants would not report them. What worried him were the few who might.

Gird paced back and forth nervously. It was much harder to hide a camp for three hundred than a camp for fifty; the jacks stank almost as far as the road when the wind blew right, and he could not convince his yeoman marshals that any guard sergeant would know what that smell meant. They would not make the trenches deep enough, and insist that the users cover it all. As for the cookfires—he looked back over his shoulder at the wisps of smoke rising into the forest canopy. At least they had trees here, and something to cook. He had to remember that, and the times when they'd had nothing. Farmers around here had been generous, though it was hard to persuade them to stay on their farms and grow food when their barton training gave them confidence. They wanted to fight, now, not plow and plant and reap. He himself would have changed places gladly, in peace, but they wouldn't believe it. For a moment he felt a scythe in his hands, the lovely long swing back and forth, the bite of the blade into ripe wheat. But that was past, and now he had a camp to care for.

"Gird?" Raheli had come up to him, more quiet-footed than he would ever be. In the dimming evening light, the scar on her face stood out whiter than ever.

"What, lass?" His lass she would always be, the child he had held in the moments after birth, the laughing girl who had put flowers on the endstones and danced in the starlight with her lover . . . the girl he had not been able to protect. He could not get away from that.

"There's trouble nearby; a runner came in."

"How much trouble?"

"Farmer's place burning, soldiers all around."

"One of ours?"

"They say not. He came to a meeting awhile back, over to Whitford, and he'd been giving food to the local barton, but not drilling there. 'Tis said he's a lord's bastard, and got his cottage-right that way."

Gird grunted. Peasant jealousy again. "Not his fault, if it's true. Family?"

"Young wife, two children. Quiet man, they said. Hard worker, but kept to himself."

Gird interpreted that his own way. If his village had resented his getting the cottage, they'd have made life hard on him; such a man might keep to his own hearth with good reason. Had the soldiers interpreted his solitude as rebellion? "What of him and the family?"

Raheli shook her head. "Don't know yet. Soldiers took two off along the road, but it looked like a woman and girl." Her voice shook; Gird's would if he spoke, and he knew it.

"They killed him, then," Gird said huskily. "Otherwise, they'd take him along." To watch, to feel his own shame. The same shame and rage he felt still, when he thought of it. He turned away, blinking back the tears. "Well—we'll have to keep a good watch; there's naught more we can do."

It was near dawn when a sentry found someone crawling through the wood on elbows and knees, sobbing. Instead of killing the intruder at once, he dragged him along to the main campsite. Gird, coming from the jacks to the cookfire in hopes of a quiet mug of sib, heard the commotion as the sentry reported to the night marshal.

"What's this?" he asked, strolling over. The sentry's catch was a lean, dark-haired man who stank of smoke and burnt wood. He stood hunched and shivering, his hands cradled to his chest.

"Says he's a farmer, got burnt out," said the sentry. "Says they beat 'im, burned his hands."

"Come to the fire," Gird said. The sentry and the night marshal both helped the man, who staggered as if he was near collapse. They got him seated by one of the firepits, where the flickering light of the morning cookfire showed a strongboned face smudged with ash and soot. A welt stood out along one side of his face; one eye was swollen, and his hands, when he held them out, were blistered on the palms, as if someone had forced them onto a hot kettle. His shirt was scorched up one arm, with the red line of a burn beneath.

"You need to drink," Gird said. The morning cook had shifted to the other side of the firepit; he reached for the dipper in the sib kettle and paused. "Is your mouth burnt? Would cool water be better?"

"Water," the man said faintly. Before Gird could get up, the cook had turned away, and came back quickly with a bucket of cold springwater. Gird held a dipperful to the man's lips. He sucked it in noisily, swallowing so fast he nearly choked.

"Easy. There's plenty." Gird filled another dipper, and glanced at the cook. "Where's Rahi? We're going to need a good poultice for his burns." The cook nodded, gave another stir to the porridge, and went off. When the man had finished the second dipper of water, he shook his head at the offer of another.

"Thanks . . ." he said. Tears made a clean track through the dirt on his face, glittering in the firelight. "I—I thought—"

"You're safe," Gird said. It was not strictly true, but he was safer here than where he had been. "What's your name?"

"Selamis." An unusual name for a peasant, Gird thought, but Rahi had said he might be a lord's bastard. Some of them had unusual names. The man's mouth worked a moment, then he said, "It's—not a village name. I'm not from there."

"It's not a man's name that matters," said Gird. "Selamis is as good as any other. I'm Gird—that's Jenis, and that's Arvi." He craned around to look. "And the cook's Pirik. How did you get away?"

Selamis grimaced. "Tunnel—you—your men said, at Whitford that time, we should all have a way out, tunnel or hole in the wall, something like that. I had one in the woodshed, just under my barton wall. Not big. They threw me in there, after—after they were done—and said they'd take me off to the duke's court come morning. So—I managed to move th' wood, get the trap up—"

"With your hands burned like that? Brave man." Gird flexed his own hands, imagining how it must have hurt to move anything.

Rahi came then, with her bags of herbs and a chunk of tallow. "Get him clean," she said to Gird without preamble. He nodded, and dipped a bowl of water from the bucket the cook had left there. While Rahi worked the tallow and herbs together in a bowl to make a poultice, Gird washed Selamis's hands gently, then his arms and face. The man winced, but did not cry out. Rahi smeared the burns and the welt on his face with her poultice, and bound his hands in clean rags. "It will hurt," she warned. "Anything touching burns hurts, even air. But it will keep them clean, and under the blisters they should heal without much damage."

Once he was bandaged to Raheli's satisfaction, Gird and the night marshal, Arvi, helped Selamis to the jacks and then settled him on a blanket. By then it was dawn, light enough to see the paler line around his mouth from pain and shock. Gird told one of the others to keep an eye on him; he himself had more than a day's work to do. He half expected the soldiers who had burnt the man's farm to come looking for him, but his scouts reported that all the soldiers from that farm had headed back to the nearest town.

It was afternoon before he came back to see Selamis in daylight. The man was drowsing uneasily, twitching and shifting in the blanket. He muttered indistinct words that sounded almost like an argument, then cried out and woke completely. Tears stood in his eyes. Gird squatted beside him, and laid a hand on his arm.

"Pain, or worry?"

"It—hurts a lot."

"Aye. I'm sorry we've nothing better. Are you hungry yet? Can I bring you water?" The man nodded for water, and Gird fetched it, then lifted him to drink. When he was through, Gird let him down gently.

"How many people do you have here?" the man asked, looking around. Gird blinked, thinking.

"Oh—two or three hundred, maybe more. It varies. Does that surprise you?"

"I thought—bartons—a few men each—"

"Some bartons are small, no more'n two or three hands of men. Others are larger. But you weren't in a barton."

"No. I—they didn't like me much." The expression on his face was curious; Gird would almost have said spoiled, but the man was too old, and had worked too hard, to be a spoiled child.

"Rumor says you're a lord's bastard." He watched for a reaction, and got it. Selamis's face closed, hardening; his eyes seemed to chill from warm brown to the color of icy mud. "You won't let me stay?"

"Why wouldn't I? I care more for honesty and courage than blood; that's what all this is about." That had surprised the man; Gird wondered again just what he'd been through.

"My—my sponsor assigned me that cottage," the man said quickly. "I didn't have anything to do with old Kerith being evicted; I'd have taken her in myself, but she wouldn't come—"

"I'm not blaming you," Gird said. Clearly someone had, and Selamis still felt he had to explain himself. He could believe that the local barton might have shunned the man, unfair as it was. But unfairness at the top made everyone unfair. "Here you will have the trust you deserve: if you are honest and brave, you will find loyal friends who care not at all who your father was—or your mother, for that matter. If you've suffered from both lord and peasant, you may find that hard to believe, but it's true."

"You're peasant-born?"

Gird laughed. "All the way back, near's I can find out. Farmer after farmer, born to plow and plant and harvest, to tend my stock."

"But they say you're a great general," Selamis said. Something in the tone rang false; Gird looked at him a moment, but couldn't place what bothered him. He laughed again.

"I'm no great general, lad; I know how to do a few things well, and keep doing them. As long as they work, we'll survive. The gods have been with us, so far."

"You believe they care who wins a war down here?"

"You don't?" Gird looked him up and down. "You don't think the gods gave you a bit of extra strength, to open your trap door with burned hands? You don't think they hid you from the soldiers as you came through the night—that they led you to our camp? I'd say you've had some bounty of the gods already—"

"But my family—"

Gird laid a hand on his shoulder. "I'm sorry. The last thing you need now is a scolding, and you still weak from what happened. I've cursed the gods myself, more than once, in such trouble." He patted the man's shoulder, and levered himself up; his knees seemed stiffer every day. "I'll talk to you again, but for now you rest."

He had gone only a few steps, when Selamis called "Gird—" Gird turned. The man's face had gone white again, and he was shaking.

"What's wrong?" Gird asked, coming back to his side.

"I—I can't—" Selamis shook his head violently.

"Can't what?"

"I can't *lie* to you!" That came out loud enough to attract attention; Gird glared at the faces turned his way until they turned back. He knew they would be listening anyway. He sat heavily beside Selamis, facing him.

"What's this now?" he asked, in the tone that had always gotten the truth from his children. Selamis had started crying, the rough, painful sobs of someone who cried rarely. "Easy, now, and tell me what it is you've lied about."

"They sent me," Selamis said, so softly that Gird could hardly hear him between sobs. "They sent me."

"Who? The soldiers?" Selamis nodded; Gird chewed his lip, fighting back the rage that spurted up in his mind. He looked away; he was afraid of what Selamis would see in his face. "Sent you to spy on the camp? To betray us?"

"Yes." That was as soft as the other; he heard fright as well as misery in Selamis's voice. Gird waited it out, staring at his fingernails, until Selamis went on. "They—they killed my son. Said they'd—they'd keep my wife and daughter—in prison—so if I didn't come back they could—could—"

"I can imagine," Gird said. He could hear the iron in

his own voice. When he closed his eyes it was as if he could see all of them together, all the men and women and children taken hostage in the past years—beaten and raped and tormented and killed—he opened his eyes, and stared hard at the leaves on the ground in front of his knees. "Why you?"

"Because I'm a lord's son," Selamis said bitterly. "He—he put me there, where everyone hated me; he knew I would have no friends, no one to turn to. They said I owed it to my father, that my only hope was with him. I would—if he had asked, as from a son, I would have done anything for him, but they *forced* me—"

"And your hands? Was that to make us believe?" Selamis shook his head. "No. That was the guard captain; he knew me before, as a boy. Just to remind me what he could do, he said. He's one of them—the horned circle—" His head rolled again. "I can't—I can't stand it—what they'll do to her—to my daughter—and I can't lie to you—what can I do?" Gird pulled him up and cradled him in his arms. There was nothing to do but endure, and Selamis surely knew that. Yet the pain the man was feeling would be like the pain he felt when he found Rahi—when Amis was killed—when Meris was tortured. He held Selamis with all the love he felt for all of them, all the ones who suffered in person or through those they loved.

"It's all right," he said, knowing as always that it was not all right, not yet. It was as much promise as reassurance. It would be all right someday; he would make it that way, make a world in which such things did not happen—or if they did, someone who cared would work to change them.

"But my *daughter*, my little girl! I have to go, I can't—"

"You can't go. You're hurt. And you can't betray us now; you don't really want to. You want to save your child, as any father would—as I did, and failed. I won't lie to you, Selamis. Your child may die, and die horribly. I can't promise anything better for her. But you can help me, help me make a better land than this." Selamis was still sobbing, but less wildly. When he was finally silent, Gird laid him down gently. "You are a brave man, Selamis. Brave to come here, brave to tell me—and brave enough for whatever comes of it." He left him then, and told one of the healers to watch Selamis closely. She peered at Gird, as if she could see his churning belly and the rage in his heart, but said nothing. He was grateful for that.

He was not grateful for the wariness of his marshals, who accosted him before he made it to the cookfires for his supper.

"Are you sure he can be trusted?" asked Felis. "I heard he was sent—"

"He told me that himself," said Gird. "If he tells me himself, that stands for something."

"He might have thought we'd heard something from the villagers."

"Have we?"

Felis scowled. "No. But we might. He wasn't liked."

"He wasn't liked because he was some lord's bastard, and the lord arranged a cottage for him. One of theirs was evicted. Not his fault. He wasn't in their barton because they didn't want him, but he gave food. They've got his wife and daughter, threatened him with what you'd expect if he didn't betray us—and *he* told me that. Himself. That's not like a spy."

"Not if he's told you everything," Felis said. Behind him, Ivis and Cob said nothing, but their eyes agreed.

Gird's own doubts vanished in a perverse determination to have Felis be wrong. "We'll watch him, but I say he's honest, and we can trust him. Are we to make the same mistakes they do? It's a man's own heart says what he is, not his father's bloodline. Men aren't cows."

"No, some of them are foxes." Felis stomped off, his own fox-red hair bristling wildly. Ivis and Cob laughed.

"He could be right, all the same," said Ivis, dipping out a measure of beans. "No better way to convince us he's honest than to confess something. I've done it m'self as a boy."

"And what if he *is* honest? How would you have an honest man act?" Ivis shrugged and did not pursue the subject. The next day, when Gird insisted they move on, Selamis was able to walk. Rahi said it would be many days before he could use his hands.

They had been threading their way between the domain of Ivis's duke and that of a count, to his east. North of that, they would come into the domain of the sier Gird had saved. Although the main lines of the hills ran across their way, gaps existed: ways known to herders, hunters, foresters. Gird had his scouts out all around; for several days they found nothing but their own people.

Then about midmorning on the fourth day, the forward scouts reported that soldiers were blocking the next gap to the north. Gird halted the ragged column and thought about it. They could swing west, here, between two lines of hills, and take the next gap . . . but that would mean stringing his whole line out, down on the streamside. Here that meant open land, arable. They would be trampling young grain they might want to eat, come winter . . . and they would be visible from hills on both sides. Downstream, westward, was a largish village with a permanent guard detachment. Could the blocked gap be intended to push him into a trap?

"How many in the gap?" he asked his scouts.

Fingers flashed. "Two hands. Four in sight, and the others in the trees on either side."

"Did they see you?"

"No—I don't think so." The scouts exchanged looks, agreed on that, and went on. "One of 'em said as how it was boring. They'd been told to guard the gaps—all of 'em—but they didn't think anyone'd come this way, not with the good bridge downstream."

Two hands of guards, but well placed in a narrow gap. The noise of battle would bring more—that had to be the intent, that or some similar trap. Overbridge, the village, had a barton but Gird had not called on it yet. His scouts reported that the Overbridge farmers seemed to be at normal work in their fields. Gird looked around. All his people were watching him, waiting for him to make a decision. The longer he waited, the more nervous they would be—and the more likely that some child would get loose and go off noisily, to reveal where they were.

"Six hands," Gird said. He pointed to Felis and Cob. "Three each from yours. Ivis, have four hands ready for support, if we need it. The rest close up and be ready to get everyone across and through the gap *quickly*. If there's a real fight—if they have more hidden that the scouts missed—they'll have reinforcements coming, from both upstream and down. That won't hurt us as long as we know it's coming, and have reached higher ground before they do." He placed pebbles on the ground to show them what he meant. "If they do come after us, let 'em get right up in the gap, and then turn on 'em. Be sure you don't cross the water until all of us are across and out of sight. If they see us, I want them to think we're all the trouble they have."

Six hands of men—three from the original Stone Circle outlaws and three from Fireoak barton—followed Gird and the original forward scouts. They crossed the rushing little river upstream of the gap, at a narrows where the forest almost met across the water, going single-file as quietly as they could. Then they worked their way upslope, hoping to flank the ambush. Gird was not at all sure this would work; he would have expected his own maneuver. But if the guards were still expecting ignorant peasants, they might have no one on the hilltop to watch for it.

His idea almost worked. Gird spotted one of the guards at the moment the guard spotted him, and yelled. More yells, and the noise of movement. Gird held his group still. It was possible that the guard had not seen them all, and in a moment he would know where all the guards were.

"Come out here, you!" the guard said. "Who are you, skulking about in the woods?" He sounded as much nervous as angry.

Gird did his best to look frightened; he could hear the others clearly now, and then they came in sight. Seven . . . eight . . . nine . . . in yellow and green uniforms. They carried short swords; two had bows slung over their shoulders. That was a mistake; he hoped they would not realize it in time to cause him any trouble.

"Answer me, serf!" said the guard, bolder with his friends around him. "You know the rules: no one's allowed on the hills now."

Gird would like to have said something clever, but he couldn't think of anything. The man was three long strides away—farther than that for the men behind him—and Gird would have to be fast or the bowmen might get their bows into action. Someone behind him, trying to move closer, rustled the leaves; the guard's eyes widened. "Are there more . . . ?" His voice rose, as Gird charged straight ahead.

They had swords in hand, but swords could not reach him. Not if the others came in time. Gird thrust the point of his stick at a face that had blurred to a white blob; the man staggered back. Someone's sword hacked at his stick; he felt the jolt, swung the tip away, and jabbed forward again. The guards were yelling, surprise and fear mixed together. Gird paid no attention to them; he could see his own men on either side of him, jabbing again and again at the soldiers who flailed wildly with their swords, stumbling into trees. The two bowmen backed quickly, reaching for their bows.

"Bowmen first!" yelled Gird—the first thing he'd actually said, in words, and lunged at one of them. His stick caught the man hard in the chest; it didn't penetrate, but the man staggered and fell. He gave Gird a look of such utter surprise that it almost made Gird back a step—but instead he thrust again. This time the point caught the man in the neck, slid off to one side, and pinned his shoulder to the ground. Gird leaned on the pole. It was surprisingly hard to force the point in . . . but the man was clawing at his throat, his face purplish. Gird pulled the stick back and clouted him hard on the head. The soldier fell limp; when Gird checked, he was not breathing.

Around him, the fight was ending in a wild flurry of blows, counterblows, and bellows. The sharpened sticks worked, but clumsily: driving a sharp point of wood through clothing and flesh took strength and weight; once spitted, the enemy was even harder to free. Most of Gird's people had done what he did: use the point to fend off attack and throw the swordsmen off balance, then finish them with a blow to the head. It worked because they outnumbered their opponents, but Gird knew that would not always be true.

"Get their weapons," Gird reminded his people, as they finished off the last of the soldiers. "Knives as well: we can use everything. All their food, any tools." The dead soldiers had not worn armor. Gird shook his head over that; they must have assumed that the peasants had no weapons worth wearing armor for.

"Boots?" asked one of his still barefoot yeomen.

Gird nodded. "Clothes, if you want 'em. Felis, take two hands and go downslope; watch for their reinforcements. We made enough noise to rouse a drunk on the morning after. Cob, you take a hand back to hurry our people along." Gird helped drag the bodies into a pile out of the way. He did not bother to look for herbs of remembrance: these were his enemies; he had helped kill them, and it would be an insult to lay the herbs on them. Only one of his people had been hurt, a young yeoman who had a knife wound on the arm to remind him that fallen enemies were not necessarily dead.

Chapter Twenty-two

Soon he could hear the rest of his people coming. They were hardly past, moving much slower than he would have liked, when he heard hoofbeats from the stream valley. No one had said anything about a mounted contingent nearby, but it made no real difference. Felis sent a runner back up: twenty horsemen, five bowmen and the rest with swords. Dust back down the trail, as if more were coming, though he couldn't say if those were horsemen or afoot.

"Good," said Gird, surprising those around him. He hoped it was good; it would be good if they won. "Fori, take eight hands—go *that* way—" Downstream that was, "—through the woods two hundred paces, then go downslope and wait for my call. You'll be coming in on their flank or rear. The rest of you, come with me."

The entrance to the gap trail offered the horsemen a gently rising slope from the narrow fields near the river, a slope gradually steepening as the trees closed in. Gird placed his troops across the point of this triangle, inside the trees, with the center set back a horselength. He watched the horsemen as they rode back and forth near the river, clearly looking for signs of a crossing. One of them went upstream, and came back at a gallop, yelling. The group milled about, then formed into a double column and headed for the gap trail.

Gird was surprised at that. Could they really be so stupid? Sunlight glinted off their breastplates and helmets—these would be harder to kill, but they were trusting too much to their horses and weapons. At the last moment, as the leaders came under the edge of the forest, some caution came to the leader, for he held up his hand and the troop reined in. The bowmen had their bows strung; they reached for arrows. Gird gave the signal anyway. On either side, his men ran out, carefully keeping their formation, poles firm in their hands.

The rearmost horses squealed and tried to back away; their riders spurred ahead. Two bucked, and one unseated its rider, who fell heavily. The first two riders had also fallen, shoved from their saddles by skillfully applied poles. One lay stunned; the other had rolled up quickly, and was doing his best to defend himself with his sword. Behind him, the other riders had tried to charge forward, but their horses shied from the sharp points of the sticks, swerving and rearing. The riders cursed, spurring hard; they could not reach Gird's men with their swords, and any who were separated were quickly surrounded, and pushed out of the saddle. Three of the bowmen, however, had managed to set arrow to string. Two of the arrows flew wide, but one—by luck or skill—went home in the throat of the man about to unseat the bowman. He managed to fit another arrow to his string, and this one narrowly missed Gird. Now his companions realized what he was doing; the remaining horsemen clumped together, protecting the bowmen in their midst, so that they had time to shoot again and again.

Gird smacked the man nearest him with the flat of his hand. "We've got to get them *now!*" he bellowed. His people surrounded the horsemen several men deep, but were showing no more eagerness to face the frightened horses' hooves than the horses were to face their poles. "Stand there and they'll get you all!" he said, flinging himself past those in front to snatch at one horse's bridle. Its rider aimed a vicious slash at him; Gird ducked, and thrust his belt-knife into the underside of the horse's jaw. The horse reared, screaming and flailing; Gird caught a hard blow from one hoof, but lunged again. His men yelled; he saw another dart forward, and another. The bowmen could not hit them now without shooting through their own companions. Horses and men screamed; it smelled like a butchering. Gird grabbed for another bridle, and nearly fell; he had slipped in a gush of horse blood. Too bad, his mind said as if from a distance, that we have to kill the beasts for their riders' sake. And where, his mind went on, are those others that made the dust cloud?

As if in answer to that question, an even louder uproar erupted somewhere behind him. Gird whirled, slipped to one knee in the carnage, and staggered back up. There—downstream a little—it sounded as if Fori's group had engaged the enemy support without waiting for Gird's call. Or had he called? He couldn't remember. He was out of breath, and his leg hurt. When he looked down, he could see a rent in his trousers. The horse's hoof, probably. He took a deep breath, and bellowed. Those who looked around, he waved toward the new noise. "Fori's men," he yelled. "Get in *line*, idiots, before—" his breath and voice failed together. Someone put a shoulder under his arm; he would have shoved help away, but for the moment he could not.

He let himself be helped to the edge of the trampled ground.

Someone handed him a waterskin; he drank, wincing as someone else prodded the gash on his leg. Now he could breathe, and see: all the horsemen down, and half the horses, in a welter of blood. Some of his own dead this time, more wounded. Tending them were women he distinctly remembered from the refugee group . . . what were they doing down here? He had to get back to the fighting, he reminded himself. When he tried to get up (when had he slid to the ground against this tree?) his leg refused to take his weight.

"Your arm—" said someone behind him.

"It's my leg," he growled, but glanced at his arm anyway. A bloody gash had opened it from near his shoulder to his elbow; he stared at it, surprised. He didn't remember that. A broad-faced woman with tangled reddish hair sluiced the blood off with water from a bucket, laid a compress of leaves on the gash, and wrapped it tightly with a strip of cloth. She touched his head; he winced and pulled back.

"Quite a lump," she said cheerfully. "We might's well call you Gird Hardhead as Gird Strongarm."

"But Fori—" he said.

"Quiet. It's all right."

He wanted to say it was not all right, not until the fighting was done and they were safely away. But something with teeth had hold of his leg, and was trying to pull it off. He blinked, grunted, and resolved the monster into two people, one of them holding his leg still while the other cleaned out the ragged wound. It seemed to hurt a lot more than it had; he didn't know if that was good or bad.

"Gird?" That was Fori's voice; Gird fought his way through the haze of pain and exhaustion to focus on Fori's face. Pale, but unmarked; he looked more worried than anything else.

"I'm fine," said Gird. He would be fine; it was not all a lie.

Fori grinned. "It worked," he said. "Just like you wanted: we took their reserves in the flank before they

knew we were there. And then the others from here—
from the first fight—came and got them between us.
We lost a few—"

"How many, each side?" Thinking about the fight
might clear his head.

Fori's hands flicked, counting it up. "Eight hands of
reserves, afoot—our match. Then four hands of horsemen,
and two hands in the gap itself: fourteen hands, seventy
altogether. All dead. Of ours, eight dead, and four
hands wounded, some bad."

Cob's head appeared beside Fori's. "Gird—we're going
to move you now."

"Move me! I can move myself!" He lunged up, but
firm hands pushed him down.

"No. We aren't going to lose you because you walked
all your blood out." Gird would have fought harder, but
his body did not cooperate. He let himself relax onto
the rough litter, and endured a miserable bouncy trip
to whatever ridiculous site Cob or Felis had picked for
a camp.

He woke to firelight, and listened to the voices around
him before opening his eyes. He knew at once he was
indoors, in some large, mostly bare room. It did not
smell like he imagined a prison would smell, and the
voices around him sounded tired, but satisfied, happy,
quietly confident. Then, in a lower tone, someone said,
"What about Gird—do you think—?"

"He'll be fine," said the voice of the red-headed
woman who had tied up his arm. "If he hadn't tried to
fight the whole battle himself—"

"Did you ever see anything like it!" That was no
question; the speaker's voice carried raw emotion.
"Throwing that horse down like a shepherd throws a
lamb—"

Did I? wondered Gird. He could remember nothing
but the first horse rearing over him, and the hoof raking
his leg. Now he came to think of it, that had been the
other leg, not the one with the bad gash.

"—Like something out of a tale," the young voice
was going on. Others chimed in, a confusion of details
almost as chaotic as the battle itself. Gird felt himself

flushing. They made it sound as if he'd waded single-handed into the entire Finaarean army.

"If *he* dies—" began someone else in a hushed voice.

Gird opened his eyes. "I am not going to die," he said firmly, glad that his voice carried his intent.

Several men laughed. "I told you," said Cob. "He's too stubborn to die." Under that confidence Gird could hear relief in his voice. He tried to hitch himself up and his pain lanced through his head.

"Don't move," said the red-headed woman beside him.

"You could have said that before I did." Gird cleared his throat. With the headache, his other pains awoke again, and he wished he'd stayed asleep.

The woman grinned down at him. "Cranky patients get well faster," she said. "Soup?"

"Water." She and another supported his shoulders as he drank, then propped him up. The various pains settled down to a steady but bearable level, and he realized he was hungry after all. And curious: what exactly had happened, and where were they, and who had taken over when he fell on his face? Someone handed the woman a bowl of soup, and she lifted Gird's head so he could drink it.

He saw movement in the group around the fire. Then his most experienced fighters were around him. "You're wondering what happened," said Felis, almost smugly. Gird glared as best he could. Felis had become a good leader, but he could be unbearably smug.

"We were all standing around the riders, having poked and prodded them into a huddle, wondering what to do next, when you jumped out and—"

"I remember that," Gird said. "It's what comes after—"

Cob shrugged. "You grew about four hands taller, sprouted wings and horns, and started throwing horses around like sheep. No: you didn't really get bigger, but you *looked* bigger. Yelling your head off and covered with blood, and you did throw at least one horse right on its side—I saw that, and so did everyone else. The rider that sliced your arm—you threw him, too, across one horse and into another. The riders panicked, even the bowmen. I think we could have stood there watching you finish them all off, but that was boring after awhile, so we tried it for ourselves."

"What hit my head?"

"I didn't see that. We heard the others coming, and Fori's attack yell, and you told us to go help him. I ran off with my group; when I got back, you were sitting against a tree, not saying much of anything, while Elis here cleaned you up. It was hard to tell which blood was yours."

Felis broke in. "The new formations work perfectly, Gird. Even in the trees—I admit I'd wondered if that practice going between trees was good for anything, but now I know it is."

"Of course, we outnumbered them," said Ivis. "Two to one."

"More than that." Gird shifted, testing the limits of his pain. "They were stupid enough to come to us in pieces. We had three to one on the first group, more like five to one against the horsemen."

"But—oh." Gird could see by their faces that they were working this out for themselves.

"Remember what I told you. What counts is how many against how many at the point of contact. If they're not in the fight, they don't count."

Fori spoke up. "But we were even against their reinforcements, at first. And we were moving them—I think we could have won."

"Probably. I hope so. But you'd have had more losses, and a harder fight. We're good, lads, and better than before, but it never hurts to let them make it easy for us. If we can take them at good odds, why not? Now—where are we?"

They chuckled, slightly sheepish chuckles. Cob said, "You aren't going to like this."

"What?" He tried to roar, but it didn't come out as a roar, more as a peevish growl.

"We're in Overbridge. In the soldiers' barracks."

"You *idiots*!" That time it did come out as a roar, and faces turned to him. He struggled to sit all the way up, and nearly made it.

"Listen to me." Cob had a hand on his chest, with weight behind it if he didn't lie back. He lay back, simmering. "There are no more soldiers in Overbridge. The ones we killed were stationed here; the barton is sure none got away. The nearest beyond are past Burry, at a road crossing. We sent word to Burry—and you know the Burry yeomen." He did know the Burry yeomen, as determined as any; if they swore no one would get through from Overbridge, no one would. "This village is delighted with us—those guards camped here all winter drinking up the ale and rolling the local girls, even a few with babies coming. We killed them without trampling the fields, or involving the local yeomen. They *begged* us to come in, offered us food, even the little ale the guards hadn't found—"

"Ale—" said Gird meditatively. *That* should dull his headache. "But we can't stay here," he said, looking around to see if he could spot a likely jug.

"Of course not." Cob reached back, and someone handed him a jug. He dangled it in front of Gird's nose. "But for one night, while certain persons take their well-earned rest—"

"You do have sentries out?"

"Of course. Don't we always do what you tell us?"

Gird heaved himself up on his uninjured elbow; someone behind him helped him up until he was braced against the wall. He got his hands around the jug, and sniffed it. Yes, just what he needed. He took a long swallow that warmed his throat on its way down. He offered the jug to Cob, who shook his head.

"I've had some. Now, about our wounded: three of them won't be able to travel for days, maybe weeks—" Gird took another swallow, and felt the edge come off his aches and pains. Behind the throb in his head, his mind was beginning to work again. Wounded who could walk tomorrow—in two days—not for a long time. Members of the Overbridge barton who wanted to come along rather than stay home and farm. Villagers who wanted to meet the man who had thrown down a horse. Felis wanted to tell him about the weapons they'd taken from the dead soldiers and those found in the armory. Ivis had questions about food supplies for the next march, and Rahi—when had she appeared at his side?—Rahi had one of her herbal brews that puckered his mouth after the ale.

He woke next in the cool colorless light of dawn, his head pillowed on Rahi's lap; he looked up to see her slumped gracelessly against the wall, snoring. His head throbbed; he could not tell if it was the ale or the lump. He tried to reach up to scratch his itching hair, but chose the wrong arm; his wince woke her, and she smiled at him with a look that turned his heart. He could not stand for her to be here, for her to be leaning over him as he had so often leaned over her.

"You put me to sleep," he said quietly, holding her gaze. "You told them to give me ale, and then you had that brew—"

Rahi grinned. "You needed the rest, and you'd have stayed up all night, arguing and keeping everyone awake. Besides, we wanted to clean your wounds again. That hurts."

"Not so badly now," he said, moving arm and leg gingerly.

"You told us, clean makes fast healing. And we have two healers, now. From Overbridge."

"We still need to move, leave here before someone comes." Some large army they could not handle, a commander smarter than the one that had let Gird pit his entire force against three separate smaller ones.

But that day was spent reorganizing after the battles. Gird fretted less as he realized it was not entirely faked for his benefit, and less still when one of the healers had time to draw the pain from his head and lay it on the soldiers' hearth. Where, she insisted cheerfully, it really belonged. He thought to ask about Selamis, who had been traveling with the noncombatants, since he could not hold a weapon.

"He looks bad," said Ivis. "Sad, miserable—I suppose part of it's the pain. But his wife and daughter—he can't help thinking about them." Ivis's losses were far in his past, a young wife dead of fever, children never born alive. Gird thought he knew the anguish Selamis was feeling now (where was Girnis, his other daughter? She had married a lad from Fireoak, but neither of them had come to the wood when Fireoak village broke up. He had not asked Barin about her, not wanting to know.) He looked around but did not see him. Ivis interpreted the look correctly, and said "He's explaining the accounts to Triga."

Gird felt as if someone had poked him with a pin. "Accounts? He can read?"

"So he says." Ivis could not, and was glad of it. "Says he can calculate, too. And write."

"I'll keep him busy," Gird said. "We need someone who can keep track of what we have."

Meanwhile, his army had gathered all the clothing and equipment the soldiers had had—those with no shoes or boots tried on the soldiers' until they found some that fit or were comfortably large and could be stuffed with rags or tags of fleece. The soldiers' clothes, washed in the stream and dried on bushes, became shirts and tunics for those with no clothes, and patch material for those whose clothes needed patching. In the soldiers' kitchen were the huge cookpots he remembered, and longhandled utensils. The heavy storage jars would be impossible to carry along (and now, he thought, I know why their army needs wagons), but the food stored in the pantry would fit into sacks. They had fifty-nine swords now (some had broken during the fights), four bows gathered after the battle and another forty found in the armory. Gird spared a moment's thanks that the soldiers had chosen to go after them with swords instead of carrying those bows along. Best of all, the armory had racks of pikes, eighty of them.

Gird limped over to the racks and touched one gleaming tip. He lifted it from the rack and felt the balance. Not *that* different from the sticks—the gnomes were right about that, too. And if they carried them for a few days, the new weapons would feel normal.

"That should go through a little easier," Felis said behind him. Gird noted that Felis did not specify *what* it would go through easily. He knew that some of them were still shaken by their own violence, by the knowledge that they, too, were men who could kill.

"We have the gods to thank for this," Gird said. He turned and looked at those who had followed him into the armory. They all nodded; eyes down. "We earned the victory this time. But it will not come so easily again." They did not like hearing that, but it was the truth, and he could not lie to them. He had won at Norwalk Sheepfolds in spite of his own mistakes, because the enemy had not expected anything. He had won here, as easily as he had, because of the enemy's mistakes. Some day he would face a commander who made no mistakes, and then—He shook his head. Time enough for that later. Now they must thank the gods who had been with them, who had helped them.

His people had no rituals for celebrating victory in war, because they had not fought a war—at least not in living memory. Gird conferred with the oldest men and women he could find; none of them knew the right ritual. In the end, Gird combined the thanksgiving ceremonies for Alyanya's permission to open the ground —which should hallow their use of the steel they carried—with the harvest prayers for those who had died in the past year. Sweating with both nervousness and pain, he limped from the soldiers' barracks to the bridge over the stream, and threw in a ritual handful of grain, of flowers (gathered that day by village children), of mint leaves. The oldest granny laid a fire in the center of the village square; he led everyone in a slow dance around it. The fire burned bright, upright and clean: did that mean the gods were satisfied? He did not know. He felt both sadness and contentment, grief worn out with time, as the harvest lament always left him. The fire spurted up, suddenly, burning blue as the summer sky; Gird felt a wash of heat across him, as if he'd been dipped in it—but he was not burned, and the fire had fallen back to its wooden roots in an instant. All the hair stood up on his neck. *They said something,* he told himself. *And I'd better figure out what it was. . . .*

*   *   *

It had looked simpler on the model in the gnomes' hall. Gird wiped sweat off his forehead and scowled at the stragglers moving along the trail past him. Go north like this, they'd said, and capture this stronghold, they'd said, and then send part of your force over here to capture this other stronghold which controls . . . it had made perfect sense. There, with gnome soldiers. He could almost understand the gnomish disapproval of undisciplined humans.

He had not planned the capture of the Overbridge guardpost, and it had fallen into his lap, eighty good pikes and all. He had neither planned nor expected the other results of that victory: the bartons that had suddenly decided to leave home and join his army, the lords who decided to punish him by burning farmsteads where no one yet had even thought of joining him, the utter confusion and chaos which had erupted in a few hands of days all over the central part of the kingdom. He *had* planned a march north to the River Road, to isolate (if not capture) Grahlin, the city in which the Sier of Sorgrahl ruled, and he was instead spending days he could not afford in skirmishes with the sier's very capable mounted patrols. Remembering that brown man and his courage, he was not surprised to find that the sier made none of the mistakes other commanders had made.

He would have been glad to avoid Grahlin, but it was important for several reasons. It controlled access to the Honnorgat along one of its major tributaries, the Hoor. It sat athwart the River Road, which here bowed away from the Honnorgat to avoid seasonal flooding at the confluence with the Hoor. And the sier's large garrison would be as much trouble behind him as it was in front or on either flank.

It would have been easier—much easier—without all his unexpected allies, especially the noncombatant followers. They had no place to go; he understood that. But he wished fervently that they would find another no-place besides his army. They could not move quickly, and would not move silently. Even now, when his face should have warned them away, some of the children were calling out to him. The adults shushed them, but only after the fact.

At the moment, he was trying to work his way around to the west of Grahlin. They had tried it before, but this time Gird hoped that the sier would be busy with eight hands of men who had gone east, with forty of his precious pikes. They were supposed to convince the sier that they were leading the whole army that way, but if these stragglers didn't move faster (and more quietly) a stupider man than the sier would realize what was happening. Even as he thought that, the last of the noncombatants trudged by, and his rear guard grinned at him. He knew only about half of them. The rest were new, from the incoming bartons.

Gird fingered the tally sticks tucked into his shirt. Eight hands of pikes was less than a quarter of his army now; he found it hard to keep the rapidly changing numbers in mind. New people came in daily; supplies flowed in and out like water in a basket dipped in and out of a river. The gnomes had insisted that no one could manage a war without knowing his own and the enemy resources, but he could not do that if they kept changing. At least he would soon have someone who could *really* write and cast accounts. Selamis had been able to read everything Gird showed him, including the maps, and he said he could write. When his hands healed, they'd know.

The rear guard had passed; its marshal nodded at Gird, who fell in beside him. This was—Adgar, he remembered. Once of Felis's troop, then his own—the kind of man he liked as marshal, a solid farmer.

"I got the word by runner," Adgar said. "The sier's men took the bait, and are chasing our eight hands eastward."

"Lady's grace be with them," said Gird. His scouts had not reported any nearby enemy troops eastward, but things changed fast. "Our front's crossed the Hoor, and made it over that first ridge."

"Be nice if they could get right up to that guardpost without being spotted." Adgar hawked and spat. "We could use more pikes."

Gird said nothing. The sier's men, he was sure, had their weapons with them, not hanging on an armory wall. They would have to earn any pikes they got from Grahlin. Something stung his sunburnt ear, and he swatted it. In another hand of days they'd either stop to find flybane or be eaten alive.

By midday, the end of the rear guard was across the Hoor; the noncombatants were supposed to be sitting quietly in the woods, while the front waited for the rearguard to close up. Gird moved up to lead the rearguard, and noticed that his ragtag followers were following orders, for once. Heat and exertion had given them the will to stretch out in the shade and wait. Even the children were silent as he led the rearguard past them. He wished he could rest; he had gulped swallow after swallow of cold Hoor water and his belly gurgled. The ridge beyond was steep; he stumped up it, using his stick, until he saw the blue rag tied to a low limb. He halted, and clicked the pebbles in his left hand.

More clicks answered. Cob stepped out of the thick undergrowth, and waved him on. "It's working," he said. "They left the guardpost as soon as they saw our patrol go across the road." It had been a small group—purposely small, to draw out the guard detachment without giving them any reason to call for help.

"Horses?" asked Gird. Cob nodded.

"But they're fast, the fastest we have, and the land's broken down there. Good cover." He did not add, as he might have days earlier, that if all went well those guards would soon have better to do than chase fugitives. He knew from experience now that all did not always go well.

He led Gird up to the front now, where his other forty pikes would lead the rest across the open ground between the hill and the guardpost. If Gird was right, few if any were left inside. If Gird was wrong, they were going to be full of arrows, but he would not think of that. Instead, he took a last look at the sun, hoped the "fugitives" had had enough start to lead the guards a good distance away. Then he nodded at Cob, and set off at a quick walk across the short grass.

It felt very open, out here under the sky, away from hedges and trees. In the shadow of a distant clump, cows stopped chewing to watch them walk by. Gird forced his eyes away from the cows and their calves and back to the guardpost. It was designed like a fort in miniature, but its walls were no higher than barton walls. Most of the time it functioned as a toll station, collecting a fee from travelers using Grahlin's bridge over the Hoor. It did boast a tower, all of three men high, from which a sentry could survey the bridge and the road into Grahlin. Or, as Gird thought, the road *away*.

So far no alarm had come from the guardpost. Gird squinted at its tower; he could see no one up there. But a thin column of smoke climbed into the sky from somewhere in the guardpost. He muttered a curse. At the least they had left a cook behind—a cook who might chance to look out a window idly. He looked along the road as they neared it. Nothing westward—so he should hope, having sent a small group to block the road well out of sight of the guardpost. Eastward, this late in the day, no traffic moved between Grahlin and the bridge, as he'd expected.

Now they were on the road itself. Gird sent units around both sides of the guardpost, which continued to look as innocuous as a cottage, including the smoking chimney. The little tollbooth on the road was empty. The guardpost's main entrance, a heavy wood gate, was closed, but the postern stood open. Gird had planned to break down the gate, which a drunken guard in a tavern had reported to one of Gird's fascinated agents was "only there to impress serfs; it wouldn't keep out a hungry ox, let alone a determined soldier." But given an open postern—it was either a trap or great good fortune.

Great good fortune turned in an instant when the cook—a tall woman with two buckets of garbage in her meaty hands—backed out the door into the men Gird was sending in. She let out a scream that would have shaken slates from a roof, and flailed about with the buckets. In the narrow space of the postern, they couldn't get at her without killing her, and no one wanted to do that. Then her screams roused the hand of guards left at the station, and Gird heard them blundering around inside as they tried to figure out what was going on.

"*Quiet!*" Gird bellowed. To his surprise, the woman was instantly silent, her mouth hanging open. Her eyes bulged out in almost comical panic, and she dropped the buckets with a loud clatter. Gird took her by the shoulders, moved her aside, and said "Be still." She nodded, still with her mouth open. "Follow me," he said to Cob, and plunged through the door.

Already one of the guards had arrived at the narrow passage that led to the postern; Gird lunged with his stick, wishing he'd had sense enough to take a pike instead. His weight and speed forced the man back, but the wooden point would not go through the breastplate. He jabbed again and again; the man retreated, but slowly. Now he was out of the passage. Another guard came up beside him. Cob leaned on Gird, giving him more weight to use. That was fine, but he couldn't use the point on more than one at a time, and the passage was too narrow for two to stand abreast. He would have to push his way out, and take his chances until Cob and the others got through.

He took a deep breath, and bellowed a wordless cry as he lunged. The guard backed two steps; Gird hit his chest hard, and the man staggered and went to one knee. *Faster*, Gird told himself, shortening his grip and running out the end of the passage. Cob and the others were at his heels; he struck at the second man's face. Then Cob was beside him, then another. Cob had a pike, and the man who had fallen died on it. Gird saw a stairway up the outside of the tower, and a man halfway up. He had a horn, and was lifting it to his lips.

Gird threw his long stick, end over end. It spun in the air like a wheel; the man saw it coming, dropped his horn, and screamed. He ducked; the stick hit the stone above him and shattered. Gird had no time to watch this. One of the others had jumped at him as he threw. Gird threw himself to one side, and pulled his hauk from his belt. The sword knocked a chip from it, and the guard grinned triumphantly just as someone else's pike took him in the back. Gird grabbed the sword out of his hand, and looked around. Four guards lay dead or dying; the small courtyard was full of Gird's men, and the guard on the tower stairs was slumped against the wall.

"Sling," said one of Gird's men smugly. Fori was not the only one, now, who could hit something with a slung stone.

"We're not through," Gird reminded them. "Get this place secure, and get four—no, six—hands to the bridge." He went for the tower, and panted his way up the steps. The guard there was unconscious; Gird dumped him off the steps for someone else to kill, and continued to the top of the squatty tower.

From there he could see dust rising from the distant horsemen who were chasing his fast patrol. A score of them, at least, by the dust. Below, he heard the noise settle into the busy murmur of purposeful activity. He looked the other way. There were six hands—most of his remaining pikes—almost to the bridge. Almost a third of them were wearing blue shirts. Gird grinned. His yeomen had begun wearing them when they expected a good fight. Gird himself still had the one Ivis had brought to their first camp, but he was saving that for the day they really needed luck.

Today they needed only the time the fugitives were buying. Gird had all his yeomen in place well before sundown, when the pursuers might be expected to return. A carefully selected group of followers straggled across the fields, although they did not straggle nearly so well when they tried. They kept closing up into neat lines, until Gird yelled at them again. The returning horsemen, trotting briskly in formation toward their own guardhouse, could not help but notice the milling mass of people in the field; they turned aside to investigate. As soon as their backs were to the road and the guardhouse, Gird's signal sprung the trap, and up from roadside ditch and out from the enclosure came the yeomen with their long sticks and their new-won expertise in unhorsing cavalry. One, indeed, wheeled instantly and rode for the bridge to alarm the city beyond, but found himself cut off by the pikemen.

Gird hurried his people into position for the reaction that was sure to come. He wanted both ends of the bridge secure, breastworks on the rocky west bank of the river, a defined perimeter that included the guardpost and the bridge. Late that night, he was sitting over a table in the guardpost with Selamis, interpreting the records that they'd found.

"This is tolls," Selamis said. "Last year by this time they'd had—let me see—almost twice as much road traffic. Numbers and weight are both down. So his income will be down—"

"But he's rich; he'll have treasure in a storehouse—"

"He has to pay his troops, feed his troops, pay his suppliers. Where do you think his money comes from?"

"Fieldfees," said Gird, almost bitterly. Selamis shook his head. "Fieldfee's the least of it. Road tax, bridge toll, market tax, building tax, death fees, marriage fees—not just on farmers, on everyone. Smiths won't make his weapons for nothing. He has to find them the raw metal, pay someone to bring it here." Selamis's hands were still tender, but he could turn the pages himself now. "Look at this. Cloth merchants' stonage last year—"

"Stonage?"

"Stones' weight—didn't your village use that?"

"But cloth is furls."

"Not in bulk. The rough measure of stonage is what team it takes to start the wagon on the level. If you've ever been in a big market town, in the square, you'll have seen the tracks, where they test it. The town's market judge has a hitch—can't use the traders' horses, they could be trained wrong. Double-double-hand-stone, a thousand stones, that is, if a pair starts it. If it takes another pair, it's counted as two, and so on. It's only rough; I was told once that a thousand-stone load will break down to more than that, unloaded, but it takes too long to do that. Most lords just raise the load-fee." Selamis liked to talk, and explained things clearly. Gird was fascinated at the variety of knowledge a lord's bastard had collected. When he aked, Selamis shrugged and seemed to answer frankly. "I was in his household until I was shoulder high to a grown man—they taught me reading, writing, figures, something of law and more of custom. Their custom."

"And then fostered you to farmers? Why?"

"I don't know." That was a door slammed in his face. "I suppose my father decided he had enough bastards around."

Gird thought of asking which lord had been his father, but thought better of it. The man was upset enough already. He yawned, honestly if tactfully, and suggested a few hours sleep before the inevitable attack from Grahlin. As it happened, the attack did not come at dawn, when Gird had expected it, and he got almost a full night's sleep before someone woke him up to ask his advice in an argument between two families whose children had started a fight.

Once he'd dealt with that (giving each child involved an unpleasant camp chore which took him far away from the others: the mothers might have thought of this, and let him sleep), he went out to look at the bridge by morning light.

Chapter Twenty-three

Full daylight, and nothing moved on the road between the city and the bridge. Gird stalked along the lines, glowering into the distance. He could not attack the city; he knew nothing about attacking cities. They had to come out here, where he could fight them. So far the sier had been willing to do that, and Gird had assumed he would come to get his guardpost and his bridge back.

"I don't like this," said Felis, when the sun was a hand higher. Gird didn't like it either. He wondered what the sier was doing instead of sending his troops out. That brown man would not give up his power easily. Even as he thought this, a shout from the bridge brought his head around. He could see nothing but one of his own yeomen waving an arm; he waved his in reply and jogged on.

Under the bridge in the early morning, the Hoor had flowed steadily northward, toward the Honnorgat. Now, even as Gird watched, that flow diminished, the water's color changing from clear green to murky brown. Then it was gone, and the wet rocks and mud gleamed in the sun before they dried. Fish flopped frantically in the puddles, splashing the water out. Sinuous gleams flashed up the bank and into weeds: watersnakes.

"Esea's curse," someone said softly. Gird felt trapped with everyone looking to him for answers he did not have. He had never seen a river disappear like that, and neither had anyone else he'd known.

"Fish," said someone else, and he saw several of his yeomen slithering down the bank to grab for fish in the puddles.

"Get back!" he yelled. Whatever it was had power to spare; where a river disappeared it could return. His people stared at him, and turned to climb back out. He wondered how much water they'd drawn, how many buckets and skins and jugs they had for their need. Expecting the worst, he sent someone to check on the kitchen well at the guardhouse; it was empty, which did not surprise him.

What surprised him was that nothing happened. Around midday, a runner came in from the eastern contingent reporting that they had fought two stiff engagements, come off intact, but had to retreat up the River Road eastward. That meant they could not help if he needed them, but he had expected that. The fish trapped in their puddles died, and stank by mid afternoon. The nearest creeks to the west were barely trickling; beyond them, the flow seemed normal. Gird sent a small party north to the Honnorgat; they reported that the big river seemed completely normal. Although it was not particularly hot for the time of year, everyone felt thirsty—which was partly the knowledge that they had no source of water, Gird knew.

He sent those who could not fight away westward, with a score of yeomen, to make camp by the nearest good water source. He hoped it would stay good. He had a feeling that the sier had decided to move to a new battlefield, one on which Gird had no strengths at all.

Afternoon wore on to evening, cloudless and still. As the sun set, the sky took on a strange bronze-green color; everything seemed to glow from within in that uncanny light. No one had actually suggested that they might abandon their position, but Gird noticed too many sidelong looks, too many whispers. He wished he had even the ghost of an explanation to give them. Instead, he had an itch between his shoulder blades and the feeling that something very bad was going to happen when he least expected it.

Early in the night, he decided to pull back his people on the far side of the bridge, except for the scouts dispersed in the fields. He felt a little better then, but not much. He was bone-tired; he'd walked the lines all day, trying to see something that would explain what was going on. But he could not settle to sleep. Most of the others had, worn out with tension, but Gird stalked back and forth, in and out the gate, grumbling to himself.

He had just been to the jacks when he heard a resonant *pooot* that sounded like a novice hornplayer, followed by a shattering crash that resolved into a splash-edged roar. The ground trembled beneath him. Gird spun to see water erupting from the kitchen well, glittering in the starlight, higher and higher, a trembling column far higher than the tower. Cold mist washed over him, then a splatter of drops, then a flick of solid water falling. The ground bucked and groaned; he fell heavily. He saw the well split, as a cracked waterskin splits if squeezed. Water roared out of a cleft in the ground, waves of it now rolling toward him.

No one could have heard him, but no one needed to. That noise, and the shaking ground, had everyone awake and moving. But the guardpost's enclosed space was already knee-deep in water, water that surged and heaved, seeking a way out. *At least the main gate's open*, Gird thought, struggling to keep his feet in the racing water. He was soaked already, and the water was rising. Other struggling shapes in the darkness clung together; screams rose over the deep-bodied roar.

"The gates!" Gird yelled. "Get out the gates!" He didn't know if anyone could hear him, but it felt better to yell. He fought his way through the water, now thigh-deep, and lost his footing just as he came to the gates. The water threw him, tumbled him, dragged him toward the dry riverbed, but before he reached it was shallow enough for him to get back to his feet. He angled away from the river, shouting for his marshals. In the starlit, windless night, he could see only the vague shapes of guardpost, toll station, and bridge, dark moving blurs that might be his men, and the glittering surface of racing water.

Then the ground heaved again, and the guardpost disintegrated into individual blocks of stone and pieces of wood, as a final gout of water spurted even higher, and fell with an indescribable noise on the mess below. Gird's ears ached with the silence that followed; his yeomen's cries seemed thin, more like buzzing flies than human sounds. He was cold, cold all the way through, wet and shaking. He looked toward the distant city, and saw a faint glow move through the air toward it, to vanish behind its walls.

Anger followed fear so closely that he was still feeling the chill when he found himself bellowing at his people to be *quiet* and pay attention.

"What *was* that?" came a plaintive wail.

"Magic," Gird said firmly. "Now—who's where? Felis? Cob?"

Answers came, shakily at first, and then more firmly. Not everyone. Cob had been inside, sleeping in the guards' barracks; he hadn't answered. Gird shivered, remembering the way the guardpost walls had wavered. Anyone who hadn't made it out before they fell could be crushed—or drowned. Gird splashed through the water, only ankle-deep now, to the near end of the bridge. He looked down, unsurprised to see water in the river, rising water. Too late for the fish, but the frogs croaked happily. If I were the sier, Gird thought,

I would attack while the enemy was still disorganized. How long did the sier expect him to be disorganized?

He got most of his wet, shivering, miserable yeomen back into some kind of order, weapons in hand. One watchfire, on the west side, had survived; he sent a hand of men across the River Road to search for dry fuel. With a makeshift torch in hand, he clambered into the jumbled mess of fallen stones and mud that had been a tidy guardpost. Orange light glistened on wet rock, gleamed on stretches of rippled mud, and turned the slow but steady flow over the lip of the kitchen well to a fiery glaze. Some of the odd shapes were bodies: a naked foot stuck out from under a stone, a dead face, mouth clogged with mud, screamed silently from its pool of water. Gird shuddered. Someone in the darkness coughed, then retched. Someone else groaned.

All through the rest of the night, they searched the wreckage for anyone alive. Most of those in the ruins of the guardhouse were dead or dying, crushed by fallen stones or drowned—or both, it was hard to tell. Daylight made visible to all what those with torches had seen in the night: an uneven pile of rubble, mud, and the smashed remains of whatever had been inside it. One by one they dragged the bodies out. Too many bodies. Gird raged inwardly at the unfairness of it. Felis, red hair thick with mud, crushed when the tower fell: he had been a burr in Gird's boot, from the first day, but he had also done his best. Cob was alive, but lame; a falling stone had smashed his foot. Gird looked at all the bodies, all the injured. Twenty-three dead, eleven injured who could not walk. Worse than any battle he'd fought so far. They would have to dig a grave—and for that matter, new jacks. They would need litters for the injured. Food—all the food stored in the guardhouse was gone. He was not sure whether to trust the water that still came from the shattered well, trickling away through the mess. It came to him suddenly that no one had blessed this well for a long time. Its *merin* might have deserted it, or been angry with the men who took its water and gave no thanks. Perhaps that had made it vulnerable to the magelord's magic.

He sent someone to find herbs for the dead, and flowers for the well. If any good spirit still lived in that water, he wanted it to be happy, to know that the men there now respected it. He laid the proper herbs on each of the dead, muttered prayers for their traveling souls, and scattered the flowers on the water. They swirled in an unseen current. Gird took that as a sign that the *merin* accepted his offering, and dared to taste the water. It was sweet.

"Do you know what it was?" asked Cob, when Gird paused beside him.

"Magic," Gird said. "The sier's magic, I'd guess."

"What can we do against it?"

Gird shrugged. He had no weapons against magic, nothing but Arranha's word, and the gnomes' word, that the magelords were losing these powers, that he could defeat them with ordinary soldiers.

"If that's what they used to be like," Cob said, "I'll quit cursing my grandfather's grandfather for giving in. No one could stand against that."

Gird cracked his knuckles. "I don't know. Most of us are alive, and he's not come out to fight us yet. Maybe it takes something out of 'em."

Cob spat. "He hasn't come out to fight because he doesn't need to. He can do this again and again—"

"If he could do it so easily, he would have before." Gird spoke slowly, feeling his way into the truth. "He sent his soldiers, his patrols, because that was easier, until we blocked the road that he needs. Besides, he hasn't followed it up. If he could, I think he would; he's not a stupid man."

"You know him so well." Cob rarely indulged in sarcasm; Gird thought it was the pain of his foot.

"I met him, last year," Gird said. Cob stared at him. "When I came to visit the barton—what I thought was their barton. It was a trap, but not for me alone."

"And you met the sier?"

Gird nodded. "Met him and—" He did not want to tell Cob all the details of that meeting. "He's—an interesting man," he finished lamely. Cob gave him a long look.

"It should make a good story sometime. If we live to

hear it." He tried to shift his legs, and bit back a groan. "Last thing I needed—damn that rock!"

What bothered Gird most was not knowing what else the sier could do. If he could dry up a river and then send water out a well, breaking the ground around it, what could he do with fire? Could any one of Gird's cookfires turn into a huge inferno? Could the sier move hillsides the way he had moved water? Or call a whirlwind? If he could move water at such a distance, could he influence men directly, even kill? Twenty-three dead now—in minutes—at no risk to the sier or his army. He shook his head as if flies were after him; this would not do. He needed to know more.

Selamis, called back from the nonfighters, stared at the sodden ring of destruction in apparent shock.

"You're a lord's son," Gird began; Selamis's eyes came back to him, wary now. "I met one of their priests, who said they'd had great powers before, but now these were waning. He said one reason the magelords bred with our people was in hopes of getting more mages. Do you know anything about that?"

Selamis didn't answer for a long moment, his eyes roving across the mud and rubble. "I never saw anything like this," he said finally.

Gird grunted. "Did you ever see the lords use any magic?"

"Yes. My fa—they could make light. Some of them did, anyway. I saw one *call* someone once, I suppose you'd say. A quarrel among servants, almost a brawl, and when he came they all quieted, even smiled. Not like they were hiding the anger, like they didn't feel it."

"What did he do?" Gird had not missed the change in Selamis's tone when he spoke of servants.

"He gave his judgment, scolded one—but they didn't mind. They couldn't, with that feeling."

"You felt it too?"

"Partly. It was—" Selamis seemed to struggle for the right words, his hands waving a little. "It felt good," he said finally. "Peaceful, like a hot afternoon. Safe."

"Mmm." Gird thought what that could mean for a

commander. To have his soldiers feel safe, confident—he remembered that the brown man, the sier, had given him a feeling of confidence. He had thought he didn't want to kill the sier because of his own attitudes; had the sier been influencing him? And if he could do that, could he make others feel fear and confusion? He asked Selamis.

"I never saw anything like that," he said. Gird eyed him thoughtfully. Something about the man seemed odd. He was only ten years younger than Gird, but seemed younger than the other men his age; Gird kept wanting to call him "lad." Was that his magelord blood? Arranha had said the lords discarded their halfbreeds who had no magical talent: was that why Selamis had been fostered away?

"Did you ever do any magic?" he asked bluntly. Selamis's eyes widened, then narrowed.

"No." It was a flat no, inviting no more questions. Gird ignored that.

"That priest I met, he said bastards with magic were adopted in, and those without fostered away as small children. You talk as if you stayed with the lords longer— did they think you might have it?"

Selamis reddened, and turned away. "I have no magic. I am only a bastard, and my father sent me away—he never said why. I hadn't done anything wrong—" *But to be a bastard,* Gird thought, *without the talent they hoped to breed in you.* He didn't like the whine under Selamis's words. A few years of luxury too many; perhaps he thought he should have had it forever.

"What about fire? Could they make something burn, something far away?"

"Like this?" Selamis looked around. "I don't know. Light a fire, yes, by touching the wood, but I never saw anyone do it from a distance. Except—" His brow furrowed. "—the priests of Esea, in Esea's Hall, once. They said it was the god lighting the fire on the high altar, but I always thought it was the priests; they had that look, that concentration."

So Selamis had been to Esea's Hall—with his father? Gird did not ask; he had more immediate worries.

"Is there any effort to it? Does it tire them?"

Again a curious expression crossed Selamis's face, caution mixed with something else Gird could not interpret. "I think so. I remember hearing that."

"So if one man, say, did that with the water, then he might be too tired to do more today?"

"He might." Selamis pursed his lips. "They said it was like any other strength—a weak man would be exhausted from lifting what a strong man could carry easily. The man who did this might have been able to do more, or this might have been the work of more than one using all their strength."

Gird scrubbed at his face; he felt he had been awake forever. "And you could not say which, could you?"

"No." Selamis looked around again. "Did you lose the maps, in that?"

Gird had forgotten his maps and the records he had found in the guardpost. "I—must have." They would be crushed under the rocks, soaked and blurred, even if he could find them. He glared at the rubble. "Now what will I do—I can't draw maps!"

"I can," Selamis said. "My hands are almost healed—and I remember the maps well enough. Let me look; I might find something." He stepped carefully onto one of the tumbled stones.

"Go ahead," Gird said. He didn't think Selamis would find anything useful, but there was always a chance. Others had picked through the rubble salvaging what they could; though most of what they found was smashed beyond repair, some weapons survived intact.

Around midmorning, two of his scouts returned to say that at least sixty foot soldiers were on their way, carrying pikes. With them were a score of bowmen. Gird could just see the dustcloud. He had only a few bowmen worth the name, although his yeomen had been practicing with the bows taken at Overbridge. He had plenty of time to withdraw, but he did not want to withdraw. He still had almost twice as many yeomen as the reported force, and thirty of the good pikes. Unless the sier could make the river itself flood, they should be able to hold the bridge, at the least. He sent all his wounded west, to stay with the other noncombatants.

"You're sure about this?" Cob asked. Gird could feel the attention of others; he wished Cob had not asked.

"Sure enough," he said. "He wants it, or he wouldn't have done all that. We thought it was important before; now we know it is."

"But if he has more magicks—"

"We'll pull back. Ordered retreat—" He had never actually done that, but the gnomes had told him how it should work. "They can't take us with sixty, even with good pikes—"

"Alyanya's grace," said Cob, wincing as someone bumped his foot. He had tried to insist that he could stay. Gird insisted that he go. He wished he could do the same with Rahi, who was perfectly healthy, but he knew better than to try. She had taken all his ideas about women, and her individual situation, and recast them into something that he did not yet understand. It was hard to think of her as his daughter, although the memory of her as a child and young woman still lived in his heart. He knew she had killed, now—he had been told, after Overbridge, about Rahi—but he still thought of her with her bag of herbs, her poultices.

He realized that he was standing there thinking about Rahi because he needed someone to replace Cob, and she was the logical choice—would have been, if it weren't that she was his daughter, and a woman. He had *said* it was the same rule for everyone—had he meant it? His mind flicked over the other possibilities. His senior people already had their responsibilities. There was Selamis, but he was new; he had never even drilled with them. He wondered if he could blame it on gnomes. They had been worse than surprised when he told them that women were in the bartons. But Arranha had said that the magelord women were trained to war—or had been.

He looked around. Cob had never said anything, but Gird knew Rahi had been his chosen second. She was busy now, supervising Cob's unit in raising the breastworks on the downstream side of the bridge. They had no shields that would hold against arrows; they would have to crouch behind their scanty walls and hope. Maybe he wouldn't need to say anything at all. But as if she felt his gaze on her, she looked around, and waved.

The enemy force came in sight now, marching along at a good pace. Gird felt his belly tighten. They looked ordinary enough, and if he'd had real pikes for all his yeomen, he'd have been confident. It was going to be hard, bloody work with wood alone against their armor and steel, but it could be done. Had been done. Gird placed his few bowmen on either side of the bridge, where they would have the broadest target.

They came closer. Behind the soldiers with pikes he could just see the bowmen. He heard a shout, and they halted as neatly as even the gnomes could have wished. Their bowmen drew and released; the arrows flew up and burst into flames. Gird stared, as surprised as if a cow had suddenly grown fleece. Someone in his own lines screamed, then chopped it off.

The flaming arrows landed close behind his lines, but no one was hit. By that time, another flight was in the air; belatedly, Gird told his own bowmen to let fly. The second enemy flight fell closer. One missed Gird by a fingersbreadth; he felt the heat of the flames. His own bowmen saw their arrows angle away from the formation, as if they had struck something.

"What is *that*?" someone asked. Gird had no answer. He was beginning to wonder if his two-to-one advantage was an advantage at all. The enemy bowmen released another flight; the yeomen were looking anxiously up to watch the arrows fall. Two of them were struck full in the face. Another four were struck as well, and all six burst into flames, as if they'd been soaked in grease. The other yeomen backed away from them, and at that moment the enemy pikemen charged across the bridge.

Gird's bowmen tried again, and this time hit some of the enemy, but most of them made it to the breastwork. Even as he rallied his yeomen, Gird realized that he had made more than one serious mistake. They had never fought across a breastwork before, for one thing. Raising it for protection from arrows—which hadn't worked anyway—had meant raising it higher than his people usually thrust with their sticks. They were awkward now, handicapped by the breastwork, unable to coordinate their moves as usual. And although they had practiced against each other, they had never faced a trained polearm unit before. The sier's soldiers knew exactly how to handle their pikes over a wall—Gird's yeomen had no advantage of reach, and the disadvantage of poorer weapons and training.

Worse was to come. Rahi's yell brought his head around, and he saw her pointing downstream, to the north. He could just see the cloud of dust, and the dark dots within it that were men on horseback. One of the gnome warmaster's favorite sayings raced through his head: "War rewards the prudent and farseeing, and punishes the unwary. It is what you do not know about your enemy that destroys you." He had not known horses could ford the Hoor downstream from the bridge; he had not known about that kind of fire arrow; he had not known that he did not know. He was not sure he knew what would get them out of this alive.

Already some of the sier's pikes were atop the breastwork, forcing a wedge into his line. If they divided his force, all was lost. Gird raised his voice over the din, calling them back to rally around him. Rahi looked over her shoulder, nodded, and got her unit rearranged into a tight mass, backing away from the breastwork one careful step at a time. Keris, on the upstream side, did the same, not quite as neatly. The sier's pikes overran the breastwork and pressed them hard, but the yeomen managed to come together and sort themselves into rows and columns again.

Gird could just see the approaching cavalry over the heads of the fighters. Would they surround his force, or attack one side? And how would the sier's commander order the pikes? He felt no fear, only disgust with himself for leading his people into this trap—a mistake from start to finish—and the stubborn determination to get them out if possible.

The sier's commander (Gird had finally picked out the dapper little man in a helmet decorated with streamers) had no doubts at all. He disengaged abruptly on what had been the front, shifted his pikes sideways, and left Gird's flank open to his bowmen. Gird's own archers, gifted for once with both initiative and skill, let fly before Gird even realized what had happened, and skewered the front rank of enemy bowmen. But the second rank sent fiery arrows into Gird's closely-packed troop—and anyone hit was instantly engulfed in flame. Gird himself tripped one victim and tried to roll him, but the man was dead—consumed—after the second scream. Gird hardly felt the blisters rising on his arms for the cold chills that raced down his back. It had to be more magicks—no fire burned like that. His formation roiled; he could feel their terror. Frantic, his bowmen tried again, downed four more of the enemy.

And the enemy pikes slammed into what had been their right flank.

Gird struggled with his own fear and confusion, shouted orders he only hoped were right. Their poles were as long as the enemy pikes—just longer—they *could* hold them off if they made no mistakes. He threw himself into that line, giving his yeomen his own energy, his own strength. His line stiffened, straightened . . . and behind him, he heard the cavalry coming, a thundering roar.

War is full of mistakes; it forgives none. The gnomes had said that, too. Sometimes the winner was the commander who made the fewest mistakes, or managed to correct them. Gird spun, with a final slap on the shoulder to one of the line facing pikes, and bellowed encouragement to those facing horses.

This, so apparently dangerous, they had done before. The yeomen braced their sticks and pikes, ready to prod the riders off balance. The horses, as usual when faced with an obstacle too large to jump, slowed, shied, ducked away from the line. Their riders spurred them on, whacked them with the flats of their blades, but the horses refused. Gird would have called his line to attack, but he could not do that with the pikes opposite. He heard a yell from the remaining enemy archers, and several horsemen turned aside, to return with archers riding double.

"Look out!" someone yelled, as if there were anything they could do. The archers grinned—six of them, Gird counted. The riders backed off slightly; those with archers mounted turned their horses' heads away, so that the archers had the best possible angle. Gird sent up a wordless prayer to any god who might be paying attention—though he suspected he had been stupid enough to make them all turn their backs—and received no miracle. The archers made a slow and elaborate dance of taking arrows, nocking them—

"Front two, *now*—second two, reverse!" It was outrageous, hopeless, and impossible, but better than standing like sheep in a pen. The front two ranks on that side of Gird's formation followed him in a ragged charge at the horsemen; the second two—who had been supporting the two on the pike side—spun and faced outward to replace them. Gird did not stop to see if it worked, or how neatly they turned. He was running straight for the mounted archers, screaming as loud as he could; when he saw one archer draw, the arrow aimed at him, he threw his stick, end over end, and dove for the ground.

He felt the heat of the flames, but the arrow missed him. The horse, alarmed at an attack from the rear, crowhopped and whirled, fighting its rider; the archer grabbed too late for the rider's belt and slid off, landing hard on his back. He heard screams: one of his men had been hit by a fire arrow. But more had followed Gird's lead; horses squealed and bucked, spun and reared, and all but one archer fell off.

The other riders tried to cut Gird and his yeomen off from the fallen archers. Gird ducked under one horse's neck, got his arm under the rider's leg and heaved; the man fell off the opposite side, cursing, and cut his own horse trying to strike at Gird. The horse squealed, shied, and collided with another in time to spoil that rider's stroke. Gird had his hauk out, and popped the next rider hard on the knee. He heard it crunch. Then he saw one of the archers, standing, with his strung bow over his shoulder, reaching up for a lift onto horseback. The rider was leaning out and the archer took his wrist. Gird's hauk got the archer in the angle of neck and shoulder just as he left the ground. The man sagged, pulling the rider down and sideways; before the rider realized his danger, Gird had yanked back on the archer, and dragged both off the horse. He put a deliberate heel on the bow as he smashed the archer's head, and then the rider's.

"Gird! Here!" He followed that yell and found a tight cluster of his men, protected by their sticks, holding off a milling crowd of horsemen. Gird dived into that protection just as a sword opened a gash across his shoulders.

"We got the archers," said one of the men proudly.

Without archers, the horsemen could not quite reach and kill the yeomen; Gird was able to maneuver the survivors of his raid back into the main group. These had recovered enough control to withstand the pressure from the sier's pikemen, though Gird realized he no longer outnumbered the enemy by anything like two to one.

Time passed, with sweating, grunting, miserable fly-bitten flurries of effort and equally sweating, miserable, and fly-bitten stretches of exhaustion, when both forces had run out of breath and will. The sun moved on towards evening, and Gird had not been able to move his yeomen anywhere. But no reinforcements had come for the sier's troops, either. They were locked together like two stubborn bulls that have shoved head against head without yet establishing dominance.

What broke the stalemate was Gird's twenty other yeomen, coming back from the distant campsite to find out why they had had no orders. They came marching along, singing "The Thief's Revenge" as loudly and unmelodiously as twenty men could do, while behind them came such of the noncombatants as wanted to flourish a shovel or pick and learn to march in step. In actual numbers, they were too few to matter, but as fresh troops coming onto a field where all are exhausted, they had an effect beyond their numbers. The sier's men withdrew a step, and then another. Gird did not order a charge; he was near falling down himself, and knew his yeomen did not have strength left for a charge. The sier's pikes withdrew an armslength, a pike's length—the horsemen rode between, and the sier's pikes turned to march away. Gird let them. He was glad enough to see them go.

There was no question of holding his position. Too many had died, demonstrating that he did not have what he needed to hold it. Gird watched the low evening sunlight gild the backs of the sier's men as they withdrew to the far side of the bridge, and formed again. His own yeomen gathered the bodies of their dead, ignoring the sier's fallen. It would be foolish to strip the bodies in sight of their companions. Too many, too many: Gird cursed his foolishness, his stupidity, and even the time he wasted cursing them.

"At least you got us out of it," Rahi murmured, as he gathered them again to march away.

"No thanks to me," Gird said. "I got us into it."

"You always said a lesson that leaves bruises is never forgotten."

He looked at her, but her steady eyes did not reproach him. "I said that?"

She grinned, a white flash out of her dusty face. "Often and often. When that witch of a dun cow kicked me. When Gori hacked his ankle with the scythe—" Gori, her older brother, his first son, who had died of a plague. Rahi went on. "One of your favorites, that was, along with 'Think first, and you won't bleed after.' "

Gird snorted. "I didn't remember that one, did I? Gods' above: I thought about what I would do, not what they would do."

But if Rahi did not reproach him, others would. He would reproach himself for this day's stupidity. He would learn from it—he had to, to make the deaths worthwhile—but he would not forget that he could have chosen differently, and those men and women would still be alive.

Chapter Twenty-four

In this chastened mood, Gird spent the next hand of days ensuring that his camp was as safe as it could be. He examined those who wanted to train as yeomen, and assigned them to units to replace those who had died. He visited the wounded, steeling himself to endure criticisms which no one actually voiced. He was sure they said more behind his back.

To his surprise, his recent defeat brought in as many recruits as his earlier victories. Hardly a day passed without one or three or six men or women straggling into camp, asking a chance to train and fight for "the new day." Some had traveled hands of days from distant farmsteads; others came from villages and towns only a few hours away. Some were enthusiastic youths, children—as Gird saw them—hardly off their mothers' breasts. They stared wide-eyed at his veteran yeomen; he could practically see "glory" written on their foreheads. When he tried to explain how hard a soldier's life could be, they hardly listened, their eyes wandering to the alluring strangeness of campfires, women in trousers carrying pikes, men practicing archery. Gird sighed, turned them over to one of the more dour yeoman-marshals, and tried to ignore their eager glances when next he passed them as they scrubbed pots or dug jacks trenches.

Older recruits posed other problems. Some had a grievance against a particular lord, and wanted Gird to ensure vengeance. These could turn sour when they found that everyone had a grievance, and Gird thought no one's private reasons more important than another's. Some were obviously the misfits of their villages, quarrelsome bullies who thought Gird would supply weapons and food and an excuse for their violent behavior. Some were spies, as Selamis had been originally, some were crochety old men who were sure they knew how Gird should run his army, and some were soldiers changing sides, born peasants and now returning to their people—who *also* knew how Gird should run his army. Few of them shared Gird's concern for the time *after* the war, for the kind of land they would have. And they all knew less than they thought they did.

Gird dealt with these as well as he could. What bluff honesty and forthright explanation could do, he did, but when that failed he resorted to his strong right arm and a voice that could, as one of his marshals said, take the bark off a tree at twenty paces. He had the least patience with whiners and those who could find, as the saying went, one grain of sand in a sack of meal.

The army grew, nonetheless, and Gird found that Selamis's ability to read, write, and keep accounts was invaluable. He no longer had to keep in his head the members of each unit, with its marshal and yeoman marshal. Selamis suggested—tactfully—changes in nomenclature, preserving the name "barton" for the original use, and calling tactical units "cohorts" no matter how many bartons went to make them up. Gird agreed, after scowling at Selamis's neat script for a long moment. The gnomes had had names for the units, based on size, from the five-gnome *pigan* to the hundred-gnome *gerist*, but the language of his own people had nothing but "horde" and "skirra." The former meant everyone in the steading or hearthing who could fight, and the latter meant a small raiding party sent to steal livestock. He did not like using one of the magelords' words, but cohort was better than the others.

With Selamis and his most experienced yeomen, Gird worked out a new, more uniform, organization. His cohorts were upwards of 120 hands—though the term "hand" began to fall out of use with the larger unit. Each cohort would have a marshal, and at least four yeoman-marshals. Where bartons had joined to form cohorts, their yeoman-marshals would serve;

otherwise the most experienced yeomen could be chosen. Each cohort would divide into tally-groups for camp work, and each tally-group would be supervised by the yeoman-marshal for that section. When the army divided for some reason, Gird would appoint one of the marshals to command whatever group he himself was not with—which led to the title of "high marshal" for such a situation, and—over Gird's initial protests—"Marshal General" for himself.

"They don't have to call you that," Selamis pointed out.

"Thank the gods! Why should they? A general is one of those fancy officers in gold-washed armor with a plume to his helmet; I'm not—"

"But you are, in one way. Commander of the whole army. It's for the records, Gird, and if you send orders—"

"Flattery." Gird eyed Selamis dubiously. The man had good ideas, but he had too many of them, too fast, and was too tactful by half in presenting them. Gird could not doubt his bravery—he had asked to start training while his hands were still sore—but he could not overcome the feeling that Selamis was just a little too smooth.

Somewhat to Gird's surprise, the sier had caused no more trouble—no patrols had come in pursuit, and the guardpost near the bridge was left a pile of rubble. Gird's eastern troop—half-cohort, he reminded himself—returned after several hands of days, full of their own stories of battle. They had "almost" held the sier's cavalry; they had seen no sign of magicks.

Ivis made no comment on Gird's mishaps, but did get him aside to discuss Selamis. "Are you making a yeoman-marshal out of *him*?"

Gird raised his eyebrows. "I hadn't thought. Why?"

"He wasn't in the barton in his village."

Gird sighed. "We went over that. He was an outsider; he'd been given someone's cottage—"

"I don't entirely trust him." Perversely, Ivis's distrust made Gird feel obligated to defend Selamis.

"He's not like us, I'll admit, but he's good enough."

"He was telling Kef what you thought about the

lords' powers," said Ivis. "As if you'd told him to. Did you?"

"Well—no. But I don't see that it matters, unless he lied about it. What did he say?"

"Just what you've told me, mostly, and you thought the others should tell you if they'd heard anything more."

"That makes sense. If I'd thought of it, I'd have done the same."

"Yes, but—" Ivis shook his head. "I can't explain it, but he's—he's not solid."

"His wife and daughter died. We heard three days ago, from someone who saw it. He knows—that would unsettle anyone." Gird did not say how Selamis had taken the news; he was not sure himself what that white-lipped silence meant, that was followed so soon by apparent calm. He looked off across the camp, where Selamis at that moment was chatting with someone while scrubbing a kettle. Harmless enough; what was it that unsettled Ivis? Gird remembered that Diamod had unsettled him, with the difference between farmer and craftsman, an indefinable shift in attitude.

By this time they had moved the main camp, shifting west away from Grahlin, and south along one of the arcuate band of hills. Only one of the gnomish maps had been recovered; Gird was trusting Selamis's memory for the rest. The maps looked much the same to him, barring the use of a brush instead of a pen.

The larger camps, and richer resources of summer, allowed refinements he had missed before. One of their number claimed to have made his own brews before, and combined the seeds of early-ripening wild grasses with gods only knew what to produce a potent brew. The taste varied widely from batch to batch, but no one was asking for flavor. Gird found it relaxing to sip a mug in the evening after dark, when the weight of the day's worries seemed to bow his shoulders and put an ache in every joint. It had been a long time—many years— since he could end most days in a pleasant if hazy mood. He had, he told himself, earned it.

It was on one such evening, after a day spent settling

the petty disputes which so often infuriated him, that he found himself faced with six newcomers, all women, and all with a grievance. His head had ached since before dawn with the coming storm that drenched the camp in afternoon, and brought a foul stench from the jacks. No one else admitted to smelling it; he'd had to bellow at the marshals before they reassigned their tally groups to digging a new one. Even after the storm, it was hot and sticky, with hardly a breath of breeze and clouds of stinging flies; nothing would dry, and his boots were sodden. For supper they had only cold porridge left from the morning; the storm had caught them by surprise, and all the fires had gone out. So Gird had retired to his favorite stump with a pot of Selis's brew, and let the stuff work the day's irritations out of his consciousness.

He was not happy to be interrupted by the newcomers, and the woman who talked the most had a sharp, whining tone that set his teeth on edge. She had a complaint about the duke's steward in their village, and a complaint about the barton's yeoman-marshal, who did not welcome women. She wanted to tell him in detail about a legal dispute involving one woman's husband's mother and a promised parrion which had then been withheld, as proof of the unreasonable attitude of the steward. His eyes glazed after awhile. He was acutely aware of her disapproval, and that made him even less willing to be sympathetic. The other five women stood shifting from foot to foot as they listened, clumping behind Binis, the speaker, as if she were some sort of hero able to protect them. She didn't look much like a hero, a tall scrawny dark-haired woman with a big nose and very large teeth, hands too large for her wrists . . .

He never did remember when the vague annoyance sharpened into active dislike, and the dislike into anger. Along the edge of his memory was the sight of Binis's face, the expression changing from surprise to dismay to anger and contempt, the faces behind hers mirroring hers as if she were in fact the only real person there—his memory blurred, after that. The next thing he knew, Kef had waked him with the news that Binis

was gone, and with her the five newest yeomen. That
was the next morning, broad daylight, far later than he
usually woke.

"She's gone to tell the sier where we are," warned
Kef. "You really made her furious—"

"I said what I had to." Gird rubbed his face, hoping
the headache would go away, and wondering what, in
fact, he had said. He hadn't drunk that much, and the
stupid woman shouldn't have kept nagging at him.

"I know, but—" Kef peered at him. "You should be
careful, Gird; that stuff Selis makes would take the hair
off a horsehide."

"I'm *fine*." He wasn't, but he would be with a can of
cold water over his head and something to eat. If they
had anything left. He clambered up, stifling a groan as
stiffness caught him in every joint, and looked around.

Something was wrong. He couldn't tell exactly what,
but instead of the busy, determined life of the camp he
sensed uneasiness, an almost furtive bustle in the distance, and ominous stillness around him. None of his
cohort marshals were nearby, and yet he saw no drill in
progress, and heard no tramp of feet out of sight. He
smiled at Kef, and started toward the hearth. It was
bare; the fire burnt out and the stones barely warm.
One cookpot sat to the side, and in it was one cold
sodden lump of porridge.

"That's yours, then," said a woman walking by—Adar,
he remembered after a moment. Widowed, mother of
two surviving.

"You've eaten?" he said to Kef, who was still hover-
ing near him.

"Oh yes. Hours ago. I mean—"

"You mean I overslept because I was drunk," said
Gird, and prodded the porridge to see how firm it was.
He broke off a smaller lump and ate it with difficulty,
watching Kef's eyes. They wavered, not meeting his
gaze.

"Well—you had a lot to do last night—"

"Is that what they all think?" He took another small
lump, and gulped it down without trying to chew it. The
stuff would hold slates on a roof in a gale, he thought.

"Oh no. I'm sure they don't—although some—I mean someone said, but I don't know who—"

Gird finished the porridge, cold and gluey as it was, and thought about it. Rahi'd told him to be careful about drinking too much, but she'd always said that. Tam and Amis, too—but that was years ago. And some people always complained that others drank too much. Far as he was concerned, it was those who had neither head nor heart, trying to deny others what they themselves couldn't enjoy. Yet he remembered old Sekki well enough, who always smelled of sour ale and staggered when he walked, day or night—who died in a stinking puddle of his own vomit, one night. The sergeant had pointed him out to Gird and the other recruits—and he knew the sergeant's warnings against drunkeness didn't come from lack of taste for it.

So—had he been drunk last night, and had he thrown away five good yeomen (he wouldn't count Binis) by losing his temper in a drunken rage? Evidently some of the others thought so. Could they all be wrong? They'd all been wrong before, but so had he.

His head throbbed, and the porridge sat uneasily in his belly. He hadn't been really drunk, but then again he had to consider how the others felt, what they thought. He picked up the cooking pot and started for the creek.

"Where are you going with that?" came a sharp voice from behind him. He turned, and grinned at Adar. She reddened.

"Going to clean it," he said. "Don't we have a rule, that laggards to table clean the pot?"

Her mouth fell open, then shut with a snap. "But you—but you're—"

"I can dip water and scour, Adar," he said mildly. "And one thing about rules, they're for all of us. I'm no different." He turned away before she could offer, and stumped down the bank. The first splash of cold water went on his face, then he dipped the pot, scooped up a handful of sand and small gravel, and swirled it around. When he felt with his fingers, the gluey coating of dried-on porridge was still there. Blast. He'd have to really work at it. He looked around for rushes or reeds. Adar was standing on the bank, watching him.

"Here," she said. "This makes it easier." She handed him a lump of porous gray rock, very light for its size. Scrapestone, or scourstone: he remembered seeing similar lumps for sale in city markets, priced far above a village peasant's ability to pay. Mali had always used rushes. But the scourstone took the porridge off the pot quickly, and his knuckles hardly hurt at all. He gave the stone and the rinsed pot back to her.

"Does it pass your inspection?" he asked.

A smile tugged at her mouth. "Better than my breadshovel did yours. I never would have expected *you* to know how to clean pots."

He thought of saying it was simple enough, like most women's work—which had been his father's comment when his mother was sick—but he thought better of it. Simple work could be hard, and since it had to be done, better those who did it should take pride in it.

"When my mother had fever," he said, "my father bade me do kitchen work—my brother's wife was sick, too."

"Ah. And can you cook?"

He grinned, remembering burnt porridge and bread that baked stone hard outside but soggy within. "No, not well. I've tried, and we didn't starve, but no one would choose my porridge or bread. The Lady gave me wit to plow and raise the grain, not prepare it." He did not mention his hearthcakes, which had helped him win over a campful of hungry men. They were poor fare compared to real food, and he knew it.

"You have a brewer's taste for ale," she said, then colored again. "I'm sorry—I didn't mean—"

"Yes, you did. And I gather you all agree. How much *did* I drink last night?"

"Too much," she said. "A pot or so, that I know of."

He wanted to explain about the pain in his knees and hips and shoulders, the steady ache that sapped his strength some days, the tension and fear, that ale relieved. But he remembered—and knew she remembered —the tonguelashing he'd given young Black Seli for getting drunk in a tavern and blabbing about the nearest barton. Black Seli's excuse had been a fever, and he hadn't put up with it. *Rules are for all of us. I'm no different.* Why had he said that, right out loud. It was true, but still. No one knew how hard it was, dragging a mob of ignorant peasants through one battle after another. He looked at Adar, and realized that she was not going to accept that argument. Neither would he, if someone else gave it.

Gird sighed, heavily, and said, "Well, you may be right. Times before, I drank too much, and I thought I had my reasons."

"Most men have," said Adar. "At least they say so."

"Yes. Well, I can't stop last night now—"

She cocked her head at him. "No—and you can't stop the results of it, either."

He had not thought Adar was so forthcoming. She'd been a quiet one, hardly speaking in drill, always busy at some task but never chattering with the other women. *You said women had brains too*, he reminded himself. *You said men should listen to them.* But it was different, Rahi or Pir and this stranger. He wasn't going to justify himself to her, and he wasn't going to make promises, either. He climbed the bank, regaining the advantage of height, and looked down at her.

"I'll have to try," he said. Then he went on, to hunt for at least one of his cohort marshals.

Kef caught him halfway across the camp, by which time Gird was sure that the problem was much bigger than he'd thought. All the firepits were cold, when someone should have been brewing sib and baking for the noon meal. Those few he could see all looked to be tying up bundles.

"Gird! Red Seli wants to see you." Kef was breathless; he must have run some way. "Back there," he said, waving an arm to answer Gird's unasked question. "In the woods near the spring."

"Where are the other marshals?" asked Gird. Already he knew they might have deserted.

"Ivis took his cohort up the river, to gather fuel; Sim's looking for a better campsite—"

"Better than this?" Gird looked at the clean-running creek, and the heavy woods around that hid them from almost all directions. And they had watchers on the high rocks, the only point that overlooked the camp.

Kef looked down. "They're afraid Binis will tell," he said. "Or those new ones."

"So they all decided to move while I slept."

"They tried to wake you, but—" Kef's voice trailed off. Gird's headache was no worse than the pain in his heart. *He* had told them the importance of a leader's ability to stay alert, to wake quickly and able to deal with emergencies. He had shown them—and would they distrust him now, because only once he drank too much ale? Could he not have *any* relaxation?

He remembered the gnomes suddenly, their stern faces and inflexible rules. Their warmaster would have had something to say about "relaxation," and not what he would like to hear.

"What did I say to Binis?" he asked Kef.

"You don't remember?"

"If I remembered, I wouldn't need to ask you, now would I? Tell me."

Kef looked down, scuffed his toes in the leafmold, and then stared past Gird's shoulder. "You said—you said you didn't care what the steward had done, that the yeoman-marshal had a right to run his barton any way he pleased, and if he didn't want a gaggle of whining women treating war like a village brawl over oven-rights that was fine with you, and if she didn't have a better reason than that for joining up, she'd never last a day of camp discipline—that you had enough half-witted, lovesick wenches hanging around already, bothering your soldiers with nonsensical notions —that for all you cared she could take her ugly face to the duke and see what good it did her—"

"I said *that*?"

Kef nodded. "More than that—and livelier than that, if you take my meaning. You brought up every god I heard of, and a few I haven't, and threatened to unbreech her in front of the whole camp and tan her backside."

"Oh gods." His heart sank. He had never suspected

himself of that kind of thing. He thought Binis was ugly, and just the sort of woman he disliked, but that was no excuse for what he'd said.

"That's when Rahi tried to get you to be quiet—"

"Rahi—!"

"And you told her to shut her damnfool mouth or you'd show her you were still her father—"

"Mmph." Humor pricked his misery. "I daresay she didn't take that well."

"No—she said ale was no one's father, and stormed off—that's when Binis left. And the others."

Gird scrubbed his head with both hands. Worse than he'd thought. Worse then he'd ever imagined—how could he have *done* such a thing? He could see, with the clear vision of the morning after, just how that would affect all the women. He had had no problems with them before; they had done all he asked of any soldier, and now—he shivered. "Where's Rahi?"

Kef was staring at the ground again. "Gone. She went off with Sim. I—I think she'll be back."

At least his son had been far away, off scouting with a small group in the west. Maybe he could get this straightened out before Pidi came back. He had the feeling it was going to take a long time, and a good bit of unpleasantness.

"Well. Thank you for telling me." That surprised Kef; he had expected anger, Gird could see. "I needed to know what had set everyone off. Now I do, and I'm not surprised."

"You're not?"

Gird shook his head. "No—why would I be? I didn't know what I was saying, Kef—you don't have to believe that, but I didn't. That's not an excuse; I've told you all that, and it has to apply to me, too. I was wrong to get drunk, wrong to say all that to Binis—"

Kef scuffed the ground again. "That yeoman-marshal, he did say as how she's hard to live with—always picking quarrels, complaining—that's why he didn't welcome her—"

"That's as may be." Gird took a deep breath, and let it out in a long sigh. His head still hurt, but he could see, between the waves of pain, what he should have done, and would have to do now. "I was still wrong, and I can't afford to be wrong like that. Red Selis first, and then I'll find the other marshals: we need to have a conference."

Red Selis, who had taken over Felis's unit after the guardhouse defeat, was so relieved to find Gird sober, cooperative, and reasonable that he looked almost foolish. Gird did his best to project calm confidence. They discussed the transport of water to an alternate campsite, if one were found, and the possible storage of some equipment near the spring in case they came back to this site later. When all this was settled, Gird looked Red Seli straight in the face.

"I played the fool last night, and you have cause to mistrust me—what about it?"

Red Selis' face turned redder than his hair. "Well, I—I was going to say, sir—since you mentioned it first—it's not that we don't trust you—"

Gird resisted the temptation to shake him. "Of course you don't, right now: what I'm asking is, do you want to quit? Go home?"

"Quit!" Startled, Red Selis stared slack-jawed a moment, then shook his head. "No, 'course not. Just for one bit of temper? It's just that—I dunno, exactly, but—"

"If I'd done that in the midst of battle, it could've killed us all," Gird said harshly. "If someone else had, I'd be ready to break his neck for him—might even try. It's worse for me—I'm supposed to be showing you how. Tell you what, I never knew it to take me like that before—not that I recall. It won't do: you know it, and I know it. That's well and good: no more of it for me. But to mend last night's bad work—I have to know if you'll trust me on this, long enough to see that I mean it."

"Well—yes." Red Selis looked thoughtful. "I never—I mean I thought you'd be angry, like, that we'd seen you—"

"I am angry, but with myself. It's not your fault."

" 'Twas *my* cousin made the brew—" muttered Red Selis. Gird had forgotten that.

"It's not his fault either. You've heard me say it to others: the rule's the same for all. I was flat stupid, that's what it is, and it won't happen again." As he said that, he wondered—how was he going to tell when he'd had too much? Surely it wouldn't mean giving up ale altogether? He could see sidelong looks from those of Red Selis's cohort who were close enough to hear. At least they were there, and not on their way home.

By nightfall, Gird had visited each of his marshals. Sim had not found a really good campsite; the army was dispersed among several temporary sites, and, to Gird's eye, had lost perhaps one in seven. He didn't do a formal count, and no one told him. Gird had not seen Rahi all day; he had not wanted to ask Sim about her. He had asked the marshals to gather everyone briefly, and in the dusky forest light of early evening he faced his army in a clearing not big enough for them all. He could feel hostility, fear, and even more dangerous, detachment—too many of them had decided they didn't care what he did.

"How many of you," he began, "saw what happened last night?" Arms waved, and a general growl of assent. "And how many of you saw it coming? How many noticed I was drunk before that?" Fewer arms, and a subdued mutter. Finally one clear voice from behind a screen of trees.

"I seen it days ago, the way you started goin' to the ale-pot every night. Said to my brother, you just watch, and he'll go the way of our uncle Berro, see if he don't, and you did." That brought a scatter of chuckles, but some nodding heads.

"Well," Gird said, "you were right. I just hope your uncle Berro never made such a fool of himself, and never said so much he wished he hadn't said."

"I always heard as how drunks say what they really mean," said someone else, challenging. A woman's voice. Gird had expected that.

"My Da said, the first time he found me drunk, that a drunk's mind was two years behind him, at least." He paused, looked around, and felt a flicker of interest from them. "If you'd asked me, back when I had a home and a wife and children, if I thought women could make soldiers, I'd have said no. I'd never seen one, and neither had any of the rest of you. When Rahi came, my own daughter, I doubted her at first. But she had nowhere to go, and I knew my own blood was in her."

"And you told her—"

"Aye. Drunk, which I shouldn't have been, I told her a bunch of nonsense. Maybe I do think that, down in the old part of me, in my past. But here and now, I mean what I've said afore about women. You know what that is, and how I've made the rules here. And kept them, until now. I let my own daughter—and you that have daughters know what that costs—choose to put her body in front of pikes and swords. I meant all I said, and my pledge is still that what laws we make afterwards will be fair to women as to men."

"Fine, then, when you're sober—but what if you're pickled in ale when you write the laws?"

"I won't be." He waited a moment, to see how they'd take that, and was surprised at the change in the atmosphere. Most of them were listening, were believing him. The others were uncertain now, no longer detached or hostile.

"I may be pigheaded, but I'm not that stupid: I made a mistake, a big one, and it's cost all of us, not just me. I'm not going to do it again."

"Going to let someone tell you to quit?" asked the same woman's voice. Gird had not thought farther than keeping away from ale altogether.

"Good idea," he said, surprising her. "Who would you trust?" A long pause was followed by several muttered suggestions, mostly marshals. The woman spoke up again.

"Rahi?"

"Tell you what," Gird said. "I'll talk to Rahi, Cob, those others you mentioned—and as far as the ale goes, they can tell me what they think. Is that fair?"

This time almost all of them agreed. "But what about Binis?" asked another woman. Gird nodded, and waved quiet those who tried to hush her.

"She's right. What I do from now on is one thing, but what I did to Binis and those others is another—something I have to deal with. What I thought is I'd go after her, find her. Apologize—"

"No! She'll turn you in."

Gird shrugged. "If she does, it's better than her setting the sier on all of you."

But this provoked more discussion and argument. Gird waited it out. Finally, Red Selis seemed to speak for most when he said, "It's already happened; if she's gone to the sier, then she's gone—we don't want to lose you as well. If she comes back, you can apologize then."

"She won't be back," said someone else. "But the redhead has the right of it. You're no good to us dead or captured."

"I should tell her—" Gird began, when a voice behind him spoke out.

"Tell her what?" It was Rahi; he turned to see her standing there as if she'd never been anywhere else.

"I'll tell *you* I'm sorry," he said. "About last night—I didn't know how drunk I was."

"Very," she said. Her mouth quirked. "More than I ever remember. I hope you learned something from it."

"I did. And I was going to find Binis, and tell her—"

Rahi shook her head before he finished. "Best not. I've got her settled for now, best I could do."

"What?"

"Where did you think I'd gone off to? Someone had to be sure she didn't put the sier's men on us right away. I let her have her say—and she's got a tongue on her almost as bad as yours, when she's roused—and finally convinced her she wouldn't get any profit out of the steward, besides it not being everyone's fault. But she hates you still, and she'd be glad to do you an injury if she could. You can't mend it; best end it."

The meeting broke up into clumps of people talking, a few arguing, some coming to Gird to thank him for speaking, some edging around him. He spoke to all who approached him, feeling Rahi's attention at his back like a warm fire. Finally everyone wandered off into the gloom, and she came up beside him.

"You were stupid," she said quietly. He heard the steel underneath.

"I was. I don't know—"

"Mother said when you were young you drank like that sometimes. Came home ready to fight anyone."

"I don't remember—before I met her, yes, but after—"

"Only a few times, she said, but when she was dying she bade me watch for it. Help you if I could."

"You helped me here. I'm sorry, Rahi." He would have hugged her, but she stood just too far away, his daughter no longer, making sure he knew it. That, too, pierced his heart with a pain as great as all the rest.

She heaved a sigh much like his, and her hands turned, gesturing futility. "I don't think you can understand what your ways have meant to women—beyond what you saw in it." He raised his brows, inviting her to speak, but she shook her head. "You can't understand; you've never been where we were. But don't take it back, whatever you do. Not for me or for any of us. You'll lose—lose more than soldiers from your army, if you do."

"I don't mean to, Rahi. You keep me straight, eh?"

She grinned, a little uneasily. "I'll tell you you're drinking too much, and you'll curse at me."

"To no effect; the gods know what curses to take seriously. I tell you now, when I'm sober—do it, and I'll listen, or you can lay a hauk across my skull and let sense in. Did you hear me tell the others? Well then—it goes for you, too."

Chapter Twenty-five

In the next few days, there was no sign that Binis had carried out her threat to expose the army to her sier. Gradually, by ones and twos, those who had fled returned. Gird, having apologized publicly, would have liked to forget it had ever happened, but knew that it had. In fact, the longer he thought about it, the worse it seemed: first a defeat, and then a drunken temper tantrum. He would have to do something to redeem himself.

His first choice of action was the disruption of a taxday at a market town west of them. Most towns had a garrison of troops, either belonging to the local lord or to the king. This made enforcement of special fees and taxes much easier. As well, the townsfolk felt even more at risk than poor farmers, and were less willing to lend their skills to Gird's supporters. Although most farming villages now supported a barton, few towns did, and those bartons were small and timid.

This time, Gird made sure, through his spies, that none of the lords were actually in Brightwater before he planned his attack. He would face fewer than a hundred soldiers—well trained and equipped, but unsupported by magicks—and he had the support of bartons in all the surrounding farm villages, as well as shaky support from a faction of artisans in Brightwater itself.

Brightwater lay in a valley between two ridges, just where a stream had cut the western ridge to join the one that ran northward toward the Honnorgat. Most of Gird's army had been east of it; he moved two cohorts onto the ridge west of the town, and waited. The town was too small to infiltrate beforehand; even with the summer fair approaching, the local troops were being cautious. He could not count on help from the two hands of yeomen in the barton there, either; they had formed only that winter, and had no regular place to drill. But as he'd expected, the approaching fair, and the incoming traders, distracted the local soldiers; they kept close to the town, scrutinizing traders, and did not bother to scout the woods. Once the fair began, the soldiers gave up even a pretense of patrol. They had enough to do in the town and the meadows around it. Traders who had not made it through to Grahlin on the River Road had turned aside and come here; the fields south of the town were thick with their camps.

On the day before the tax would be collected, a second contingent of soldiers arrived from Finyatha, wearing the king's colors and carrying pikes. Selamis, watching this with Gird, announced that the enemy now had 150 soldiers in the town. Gird scowled, and sent scouts to check back along all the roads to make sure there were no more surprises. Then he called Rahi over.

"We'll want every yeoman who can carry a weapon, and they need to be *there*—" He pointed across the valley to a wood below an outcrop of streaked yellow rock. "When we come down here, the fight'll slide that way, and they'll be placed right to land on 'em—"

"You're sure?"

"Naught's sure but death, but it should be so. They can't go the other way, without getting into the rapids where the streams come together. Handy of the Brightwater folk to build their town on *this* side of the river. If things go well for us, I'll want our reserves right down there by the bridge when they retreat that way."

In the event, it happened as Gird had planned. His two cohorts made it to the edge of the fields just south of the town unobserved; the traders who might have seen him were in the market square, complaining bitterly about the tax being exacted. The soldiers stood around the market square, menacing the traders. The few traders' servants took one look at Gird's ragged but determined army and dove under the wagons, too scared to give an alarm. By the time they reached the town's inadequate wall, with its gates standing wide for the fair, a few soldiers did see the peasants coming, and tried to sound an alarm, but in the confusion of a fair, that alarm went unanswered until Gird and his men were well inside the town.

It was less a battle than a bloody slaughter, as his first cohort took a section of guardsmen in the rear. They had been stationed around the market, to keep the merchants in until the tax had been collected; they could not turn and combine fast enough to defend themselves. Many of the people in the market had their own grievances, and joined in the fight with savage glee. Gird saw one woman lobbing cheeses at a line of soldiers just before they fell; a shepherd yanked back one man's head in time for a yeoman's knife to slice his throat. Gird's battle plan dissolved as everyone entered into the fray on one side or the other. When the tax officer fell, a swarm of peasants and merchants tore at the sacks holding the fees, and dove after the shower of coins that spilled out.

On the other side of the market, the soldiers had a chance to regroup and settle themselves to fight. Their trumpets blared signals; they locked shields and started forward. Gird managed to get his cohorts back together, not without difficulty, and forced a way through the surging crowd, even as the crowd fell away from the soldiers' swords.

The two groups met in the market square; Gird's had the advantage of numbers, and forced the soldiers back into one of the narrow lanes opening onto the square. At this point, the citizenry re-entered the fray by throwing things out of windows—mostly at the soldiers, but some of the missiles landed on Gird's group. When a ripe plum splattered on his head and dripped sweet sticky juice down his face, Gird was instantly reminded of that first row in his own village. He kept his cohorts moving, and the soldiers, increasingly unsure, retreated faster.

The town gates on the east opened onto a narrow strip of land between the walls and the river; as with most towns, the bridge was not in the town proper. Here the soldiers tried to rally, but they had no real hope against Gird's larger number and longer weapons. They backed raggedly south, along the town walls, toward the fields where the traders had camped, and the bridge that would let them across the river to a road leading safely north. But Gird's reserves were just where he had expected, and the soldiers were caught between.

Gird was just ordering the bodies stripped of weapons, when a stream of bellowing men ran out of Brightwater's east gates. His cohorts reformed instantly. The men slowed, and a small group approached cautiously.

"Who's in command?" asked a tall, heavyset man in a trader's gown. He was used to command himself, by his voice. Gird stepped forward.

"I am Gird."

The man's worried expression eased. "Gird—I've heard of you. You have to do something! They're rioting in there; they've killed the council, and they're looting in the market—"

Gird shrugged. "What did you expect? I daresay they're hungry."

"But you—but I heard you were different—that you had studied law or something of that sort, that you had some notion of order."

Gird gave him a long, level look. "Are you asking me to bring order to the city?" He heard a stirring in the ranks behind him, but ignored it.

The man's eyes shifted, and he turned to glance at the other equally worried men behind him. Gird noted that they all looked prosperous; their clothes had no patches and their faces had good flesh.

"Well, I—I can't. I don't know anyone else—they said you could control the peasants."

"Is that what you want?" asked Gird of the others. A few nodded; the rest looked confused. Gird felt a sudden surge of excitement. Was this the start of the new society he had dreamed of? A chance to set one town on the right path? It was a chance, whether or not it was the right one. He nodded, abruptly, and saw on their faces that they were more glad than frightened. He hoped his cohorts would agree. He turned to them, scanning their faces quickly. Some looked as confused as the traders; some looked eager, and a few angry or unwilling. Those he called out, and sent as scouts to patrol the roads.

"We've been asked to help Brightwater regain its order," he said. One of the merchants mumbled something; Gird ignored it. "I want no looting, no idle mischief: you know what I mean. These are our people, same as farmers; we need them and they need us. We'll let them see if they like our rule, if they think it's fair."

He took in only one cohort, replacing wounded with sound yeomen from the others, and marched them in as if for drill practice. The crowd in the market dispersed, to stand flattened against the walls. He could hear some dispute at a distance, angry voices and clangs and clatters; that would have to be dealt with, whatever it was, but for the moment he had to control the center of town.

It looked far worse than the count's courtyard: dead bodies, some that stirred, broken pottery and foodstuffs scattered and trampled, market stalls torn down, broken, their awnings ripped and flapping in the breeze. Once he had his troops in the market square, it occurred to him that he had never explained how to organize a city. He wasn't sure himself.

The traders and merchants who had come after him now sidled up, looking even more alarmed. "You have to say something!" hissed the leader. Gird nodded, but let his silent gaze pass across the square, catching the eyes of those who watched, noting their expressions. Then he nodded, sharply, and raised his hand for silence.

They stared back at him, much like the first men he had met in the wood. Perhaps the same common-sense would work with them.

"You've heard of me," he began, not sure they had. "I'm Gird; we're peasants seeking a better way to live. We fight the lords who tax and tax—" A ragged, half-hearted cheer interrupted him; he held up his hand again and it ended. "You've seen peasants fight before, out of desperation, but we are not desperate. We know a better way, a fairer way, and we want to see that for everyone. These men—" he pointed at the traders, "—came out and asked me to bring order to Brightwater. I would rather bring justice—is that what you want?"

A sulky-looking man slouched against a wall yelled out, "What matters what we want? You got the weapons; you'll do what you want."

Gird shook his head. "No: if Brightwater prefers chaos to order, you may have it. Do you?"

"Me? I want my rights, that's what I want."

"That's what we want for all." Other heads nodded. Gird noticed unfriendly looks aimed at the sulky man. He raised his voice to carry beyond the square and said, "Where is Jens, the harnessmaker's assistant?"

"Here!" Gird had never met Jens, yeoman-marshal of the Brightwater barton, but he liked the compact young man with bright blue eyes under a mop of chestnut hair. Jens had his entire barton together, and they were standing in what could pass for a double row.

Gird turned back to the others. "This is the yeoman-marshal of Brightwater barton. He will help me restore order, and bring justice to your town. He knows you, and you know him; what he says is said in my name." He looked at Jens. "Do you know what fighting is still going on? Are there more lords' men here?"

Jens shook his head. "No, sir. I think that noise is at the council chambers, people taking things, but no more soldiers."

"All right then. We need this square cleaned up—" Gird looked around. "Wounded by the well, so the healers don't have far to go for water. Dead outside the walls—we'll need men to dig graves. Those whose stalls are broken, you can start repairing them." He pointed to the woman he remembered throwing the cheeses. "You—what about your stall?"

She pointed at a jumble of broken wood and ripped cloth. "That was it, sir, and how I'm to get another I don't know—"

Gird pointed to two of his yeomen. "Help her fix what she can. Selamis—" Selamis was at his shoulder, staring bright-eyed around. Gird glared at him. "*You* can take accounts—who had what space, who needs help to repair stalls or houses. Anything else you find out." He looked at Kef, one of the marshals he'd brought along. "You take a half-cohort and settle that riot, or whatever it is. Rahi, you take the rest and make sure everything else is quiet."

Gird stayed in the square with Selamis, trying to get a sense of the town's organization. It was far more complex than his village, or the army. The artisans were not simply "craftsmen" as he had supposed: each craft had its own standing in the town, and rivalry between crafts became apparent as he listened. Within each, too, were hierarchies and rivalries. So a tanner's apprentice might jostle a dyer's apprentice with no more than a curse in response, but a potter's apprentice ranked a tanner's. The finesmith had nothing to do with the blacksmith, and Brightwater boasted both a weapon-smith and a toolsmith. In Gird's village, anyone might peg a bench together or frame a cowbyre; here carpenters and joiners were separated by custom and caste. He wondered what Diamod would say about that, then remembered that Diamod was off scouting. Then there were merchants, some as specialized as the salt seller, and some as general as the importer who handled any and all goods transported across the mountains, from needles to silks to carved buttons in the shape of sea monsters. The houses towered two and three stories tall; those of the wealthiest were clustered in the south-west corner.

An uneasy stillness gripped the town soon after Gird's yeomen occupied the soldiers' guardhouse. Gird did his best to keep everyone busy, insisting that streets must be cleaned of dead bodies ("Yes, the rats too!" he had yelled at someone who asked) and debris. When it was possible, he restored goods to the merchants who had owned them—although he could not clean and mend what the fight had soiled and broken.

He settled such minor disputes as were brought to him the first day with what wit he could muster, al-though some of them seemed frivolous. Why would someone in the aftermath of a battle want a judgment against a neighbor for using the neighbor's balcony as one end of a laundry line? Why pick this moment to complain that someone's son was courting a daughter without the father's permission? He realized that the Brightwater yeoman-marshal, though well-known and considered to be honest, had the low status of a "mere" harness-marker's assistant; whatever he said on an issue was immediately appealed to Gird. Gird might have found this funny (after all, they were preferring the judgment of a discottaged serf), but he had no leisure to savor the joke.

That night, Gird found himself invited to dine with the principal traders, who had, he was sure, their own ideas about his notions of justice. They offered beef and ale, raising their eyebrows when he refused the ale, and insisted that they each take a bite of the bread he brought before he would eat of their meat.

"We had heard you liked ale," one of them said, too smoothly. "If you prefer wine—"

"I prefer water," Gird said, smiling. "In war, I've discovered, the drunkard has half the men of a sober man, and less than half the wit."

They laughed politely, and came to the point rather sooner than he expected. What did he mean by justice, and how would he insure that traders would be respected and treated fairly? Gird answered as the gnomes had taught him: one law, the same for all, of fair weights and measures. A market judicar, backed by a court to which all parties could appoint representatives. He sensed that some of the traders were satisfied by this (he had never believed that all traders were inherently dishonest), but that one or two were appalled. One of these last walked with him back to the guards' barracks, complimenting him on the discipline of his troops. Gird felt as he had when the steward complimented him on the sleekness of a calf.

"And you yourself," the man went on, his voice mellow as the ale Gird had not drunk. "So different from what I'd expected—truly a prince of peasants." Gird controlled his reaction with an effort. Did the fellow think peasants had never heard lying flattery before?

The calf the steward had praised so highly had been taken as a "free gift" to his count's marriage celebration. "I'm sure you will not misunderstand—" The voice had a slight edge in it now; Gird braced himself for the thorn all that rosy sweetness had been intended to conceal. "Some of my colleagues are—alas—less than frank with you. They have their own standards, not perhaps what you would understand, being so honest yourself."

Gird was tempted to say "Get on with it, man! Is it gold you want, or someone's life?" He merely grunted, and walked on a little faster. The man's hand touched his sleeve, slowing him. Gird glanced ahead, to the torchlight where his men were on guard at the corners of the market square.

"There's fair, and there's fair," the man was murmuring, his hand still on Gird's arm. "A man like you, peasant-born—good solid stock, I always say, Alyanya's good earth—" That came out of him as harshly as a cough; Gird would have wagered that the man had never given Alyanya a thought in his life. "I just want you to know I'm your friend; you can trust me. And as a token, I have a little gift—" The little gift came heavily into Gird's hand, round and smooth, with a slightly oily feel. He knew without looking that it was gold, the first gold he had ever touched. With anger and revulsion came curiosity: he wanted to peer at the coins, to see if it was one of the fabled gold seadragons, or the more common (by repute) crowns. He opened his hands and let the coins ring on the cobbles of Brightwater's main street.

"You dropped something, trader!" he said loudly. Heads had turned at the sound of gold hitting stone; he himself would not forget the almost musical chime, or the edges of the five coins against his fingers.

"You stupid fool!" The trader's voice was low and venomous. "You might have been rich, powerful—"

"I might have been your tool, or dead," said Gird softly. Then, louder, "Best pick them up, *sir*; there's been enough coin scattered today."

"If you dare tell anyone—" began the trader, crouching and scrabbling over the cobbles for his coins. "I'll—"

"You're threatening me?" Gird's voice rose, the day's frustrations and his anger getting the better of him. "You snivelling little liar!" The trader's hand slid into his gown, and the torchlight glinted on a thin blade; Gird batted it aside, hardly aware of the shallow gash it gave him. He could heard his men coming to see what was going on. His second swing felled the trader as if the man had been a shovel leaning on a wall. Gird stood over him, sucking his knuckles. He wished the man would stand up, so he could knock him down again.

"What happened?" Jens, the Brightwater yeoman-marshal had come with the others. Gird didn't answer until they had all arrived, perhaps two hands of his own yeomen and those citizens of Brightwater who had been on the street and brave enough to hang around when trouble began. He looked around the circle of faces.

"This one came with me into the city, tried to bribe me, and pulled a knife when I refused his bribe. Tried to tell me the *others* were dishonest."

Jens snorted. "That doesn't surprise me. Short weight, scant measure, stone-dust in the meal, and it's been said for three years that it's his bribes to the council chair that preserved his license to trade here. They're not all bad."

"I didn't think so. But it's this sort of thing I'm going to get rid of." Gird looked around the faces again, seeing varied expressions from glee to worry. "An honest man doing honest work should be able to survive that way—one reason he can't is cheats like this. If you want my help, that's what the cost is to each of you—I won't tolerate bribes, cheats, lies. One rule, the same for all, and fair enough to let a man live if he's willing to work honestly."

"And women?" asked one of the two women there. He nodded.

"And women. Same rule—no more being cheated because only a man can hold a cottage or craftcot. Earn the pay, get the pay."

"I'm for that," she said. Gird wondered who she was; she looked smaller than any of his women, but her face had the same resolute expression.

"What about him?" asked Jens. "Are you going to kill him?"

Gird was startled; it had never occurred to him, but from Jens' voice and the reactions of the townsfolk, no one would think it odd if he sliced the man's throat on the moment. "No," he said. "We've proclaimed no laws—he could claim he didn't know—"

"Not if he was dead," someone muttered. Gird ignored that.

"It's got to be fair," he insisted. "The lords kill for whim; we don't." That *we* included those around; he saw by their faces that they realized it, and were surprised. "No, this'n goes back to his own wagon, out there, *with* his money, all of it, and the other traders must know." As he said it, he realized that he would have to do part of it himself. They were still not accepting Jens or even one of his own marshals. He wished he could have a mug of ale; his belly needed it. He pushed that thought away, and pointed to two of his men. "Simi and Bakri—you carry him. I'll come along and explain. Jens, you come too: I can't stay here forever, and they're going to have to learn to respect you. The rest of you—back to your posts, and call out replacements if you need them."

Fires were still flickering in the traders' field; Gird could see a cluster of dark forms around the one where he had eaten. He hailed them, as his yeomen carried the trader toward the fire. By the time they laid him down, he was beginning to stir and groan.

"This man," Gird said, "told me some of you were dishonest, and then he tried to bribe me. I dropped his gold on the street—he got it back, threatened me, and then drew a knife." He pulled up his sleeve, and showed the fresh gash still dripping blood. "So I knocked him down, and here's his purse. Anyone here know how much he had, so they can verify it?"

The other man who had seemed upset at Gird's original comments on fair trading scuttled forward. "I'm his partner—I know—" and then his voice trailed away. Gird could imagine what he was thinking. Supposing he did know how much his partner had had, should he give that amount, or something higher—and claim Gird had stolen it—or something lower, and let Gird keep the bribe he would be sure Gird had taken. Gird looked past him to the trader he had already picked as the most trustworthy. He had asked Jens about him, on the way out, and Jens said he had a reputation for fair dealing.

Gird carried the purse to the trader. "He gave me five coins, gold I think, but he picked them up when I dropped them. Would you hold his purse?"

Reluctantly, it seemed, the trader reached for it, and then upended it into one of the wooden bowls they'd eaten from. "Five gold crowns," he said. "Three silver crowns, and two copper crabs." He stirred the coins, picked up one of the golds, and bit it, then examined it closely. "And this one is false—poor Rini, he couldn't even bribe honestly." Several of the others chuckled. The trader looked hard at Gird. "I presume you have a reason for bringing him back here rather than slitting his throat for him?"

"I don't do that," Gird said. The gash on his arm was beginning to sting, and he felt suddenly foolish and countrified, standing there with his sleeve torn and blood dripping down his hand. He did not like the feeling, or those who made him feel so. It should have been obvious why he came; it had been obvious to him.

"Well." The trader cleared his throat. "He won't trouble you again, I daresay, and if you intended to be sure none of the rest of us offered you bribes, I may say that some of us would not, anyway."

He sounded almost angry; Gird realized that from the trader's point of view they might resent being lumped with the dishonest one. "I didn't think all of you would," he said. "But it seemed fair to return him here, where he was known, and make sure you knew his purse was with him."

"Oh." The trader's voice had changed. "You were not

accusing us of being his accomplices? Of sharing the bribe?"

That had not even occurred to Gird; it opened new insights into the ways merchants thought—not reassuring. "No," he said firmly. "I thought before that most of you were honest, but one or two—" he carefully did not look at the unconscious man's partner, "—were less happy about what rules I might make. I spoke to you, sir, because you seemed honest before, and Jens said you were."

"Jens? Oh—that—uh—"

"The yeoman-marshal of Brightwater barton," Gird said.

"I thought he was a harness-maker's—"

"I was a farmer," Gird interrupted. "And now I'm the marshal-general." It was the first time he had used the title Selamis had come up with; it felt strange in his mouth, and sounded strange on his ear. He went on before the traders could comment on it. "We consider all yeomen equal, whatever their skill. Yeoman-marshals guide each barton; marshals train yeoman-marshals and command cohorts."

The traders looked a little dazed; the one who had been speaking before said, "Is it like a guild, then? More like that than an army, it seems—"

Gird knew nothing of guilds, and did not want to admit it right then. "It's enough of an army to fight a war with," he said. "But we think beyond war, to the way people should live in peace." Their faces were still blank, carefully hiding what they thought. Gird felt the day's work heavy on his shoulders, and wanted a quiet place to sleep before anything else. "You take charge of him," he said to the traders, waving at the one who had opened his eyes, but still lay flat. Then he turned and headed back for the town.

He would have fallen into bed without even cleaning the knife-gash if one of his men hadn't insisted on washing it out. They had saved him a bed—a real bed—in the barracks. He was asleep as soon as his head went down. He woke in full day, with sunlight spearing through the high, narrow windows and all the other beds empty. Someone had pulled his boots off, and laid a blanket over him. He felt stiff and dirty; somehow it was worse to sleep clothed in a bed, inside.

Outside he could hear what sounded like normal town noises. No screams, no clash of weapons. He stretched, shoved his feet into his boots, folded the blanket, and looked around. Weaponracks on the walls, but no weapons: the soldiers had used them the day before, and his men had them now. He could smell cooked food. He followed the smell and came to a wide-hearthed kitchen. Someone at the hearth looked up and saw him.

"There he is. Bread? Cheese?"

"Both." Gird looked around. "Where's the jacks? And a well?" He followed gestures and found the jacks, then a long stone trough fed by a pipe in the wall of the barracks court. A thin trickle leaked under the wooden plug; when he pulled it out, a stream of cold clean water raced along and out the open drain at the far end of the trough.

"Clean shirts inside," called someone from within. Gird pulled off his filthy one and used it to mop himself with water. Someone had left a chunk of soap—real soap—on the rim of the trough. He scrubbed, feeling more human by the moment. For that matter, he might as well be clean all over; he shucked his boots and trousers, and scrubbed himself all over. Yesterday's gash on his arm reopened, stinging, but it looked clean, a healthy pink. When he was done, he replugged the pipe, and looked for somewhere to lay his wet clothes. Rahi was standing in the kitchen doorway, chuckling and holding out a blue shirt.

"You!" He could not have said why it bothered him then, but somehow being found wet and naked, alone in a walled yard after his bath, was not the same as bathing with others in a creek or pond. He dropped the wet clothes, snatched the shirt, and then held it away. "Blue? But I don't have a blue shirt—"

"You do now. Go on, put it on; they're asking for you, a whole gaggle of them." She had brought trousers as well, somewhat too large but clean and whole. As he dressed, she picked up his wet clothes, sniffed them, shook her head and dumped them back in the trough. "These'll need more than rinsing."

That day Gird found himself having to explain in more detail than he had yet devised just how he thought the law should work. He discovered men of law, who explained at great length why his simple measures would not do, and why the law had nothing to do with justice, and a great deal to do with precedent, custom, and the maintenance of commercial stability. Gird listened until he could not stand it, and then roared at them; they turned pale and disappeared, and he thought no more of them. He let each craft, each kind of merchant, present an appeal: Selamis sat beside him and wrote them all down. Brightwater had plenty of clerks who could read and write, but Gird trusted Selamis more than the strangers. He was not surprised to notice that Selamis talked easily to the merchants, even the richest, or that they seemed to prefer him to Gird.

Then he gave them all his plan, which combined (he thought) absolute common sense with absolute fairness and honesty. When everyone complained, he was sure he'd gotten it right: it pleased no one completely, but everyone slightly. Somewhat to his surprise, the grumbling died off, and the townsfolk and traders went back to their work. He had expected more trouble, not shrugs and winks and return to business as usual.

Many of his yeomen had never been in a town as large as Brightwater. Gird spent the next several days straightening them out, and insisting (until his voice nearly failed) that his rules applied to them, too. It was always possible that a townsman's gift of a pear or meat pasty to the man patrolling the street was not intended —or taken—as a bribe, but Gird could see clearly where it might lead. If someone wanted to give supplies to the army as a whole, as the farm villages had done with their gifts of food and tools, then Gird insisted it had to be done openly. Selamis had to record the gift, and then Gird would distribute it among all the cohorts as needed. Only a few yeomen were obviously looking for bribes, or extorting gifts, whichever way it could be described. Gird shocked his followers and the townsfolk by discharging those few, publicly, and explaining why. After that, the problem seemed to disappear.

He himself had a chance to see inside a rich man's home for the first time, when the surviving master merchants and craftsmen invited him to dine. He had never really thought about what would go into all those rooms, had envisioned even a king's palace as a glorified peasant cottage, but with everything whole and in abundance. The guard barracks had reinforced that notion: it was larger than his cottage, but the furnishings were much the same. Now, when he stepped onto glazed tiles of blue and white, when he saw the tapestries hung from walls, the carved and inlaid chairs and tables, the shelves crowded with things whose purpose he could not even guess, he realized how wrong he had been. The dining hall lay at the back of the house, facing a walled garden—but a garden made more for viewing than using. No cabbages, no redroots, no onions or ramps—but bright ruffles of color he did not even know. Two fruit trees were trained against opposite walls; their fruit gleamed like jewels among the leaves.

The meal itself surprised him as much as the house. He had assumed rich men ate more of the same food that he ate—what else was there? He peered suspiciously at a translucent yellow-green liquid in a glossy blue bowl, and waited until the others had dipped their spoons (their *silver* spoons) into it before trying it. It tasted like nothing he had ever imagined; he could have drunk a kettleful of it. That was followed by a stew of vegetables and fish, then a roast of lamb, rolled around a grain stuffing flavored with herbs. He had not known lamb could taste like that. Then came a dish of fruit with a honeyed sauce, then an array of cheeses, white, yellow and orange.

By this time, he had had more food than his belly would hold with comfort. The merchants nibbled on, watching him covertly. He wondered if they knew he was calculating how many of his yeomen just one such meal would feed. They might—and they might be worrying about it, too. He looked around the room, noticing the soft-footed servants who had brought and removed all those dishes. One of them met his gaze with an angry challenge; Gird gave him a slight nod. He refused the last three courses, explaining that he never ate so heavily in the midst of the day, and when he left he felt as if he should take a bath and wash it all off.

"And that's an honest one, they say," Gird reported to Selamis and several of the marshals that evening. "Not so rich as the one the mob killed, not cruel or unfair to his laborers and servants. I saw just that one part of the house, from the entrance to the dining hall—but if the rest is anything like it—"

"It would be," said Selamis, the corners of his mouth twitching. Gird glared at him.

"You know all about it, I suppose; you may even know what that green stuff was that looked like ditchwater and tasted—oh, gods know how it tasted, but it was good. But men like that, they have a lot to lose. They've done well under the lords; they won't stick with us if they don't do well under us. But if we bend the rules for them, we're betraying our own people."

The marshals nodded seriously, but Selamis lounged in his seat, almost smirking. Gird wanted to clout him. It was hard enough making the marshals accept him when he was invisibly efficient; when he put on airs, it rubbed everyone's hair backwards. Gird glowered at him.

"I suppose you think *you* should have gone to that dinner? You, who would know all the names for that kind of food, and which of those pesky things on the table were for what use? I see the way they talk to you first—maybe they should've asked you." Gird paused for breath, puffed out his cheeks, and made a rude noise. "But they didn't ask you, Selamis: they asked me. They know where they stand with me, even if they don't like sharing table-space with a big stupid peasant who doesn't know what to do with a silver spoon. You're in between: not one nor t'other, not true peasant nor true lord. *We* don't care if you're a bastard or not, but they do. Yet you push it in our face that you're more like them."

Selamis had gone first red, then white, then red again. "It's not my fault," he said, glaring at Gird. "I can't help it that I know figan soup when I hear of it, or what the things are. Or that the better—the merchants and such are comfortable with me."

"No, I suppose not." Gird was half-ashamed that he'd let his temper loose, but the silent support of the marshals, who had never liked Selamis that much anyway, stiffened him. "What is your fault is the way you use it. If you're one of us, *be* one of us; don't be smirking in your ale when you know something we don't."

From the traders he found out where the king's army had been all this time. It seemed that after reaching Gird's village, they had had word from Gadilon about an army harrassing his domain—an army headed by a terrible, cruel commander named Gird. Gird thought back to his near encounter with the brigands in Gadilon's forest, and managed not to laugh. The king's army was busy, the traders said, in the south and east, convinced that that was the main peasant force. And the traders had heard only vague rumors of trouble in the north until they were near Brightwater—and then the rumor had said the trouble was up on the River Road, near Grahlin.

"We were near Grahlin," said Gird, not specifying when, or why they'd left.

"I don't expect the king has heard that yet," the trader said. "Sier Sehgrahlin has much of the old magicks, but not the way of calling mind to mind. Even if he could, the king could not hear, nor any with him. There's no one much left with that, but the king's great-aunt, and she's too old to matter."

"Where is she?" asked Gird.

"In Finyatha, of course, in the palace. Amazing lady; she came to the market there once, when I was a boy, and my grandfather sold her a roll of silk from the south. She looked at me and said 'Yes, you may pet my horse,' and my grandfather clouted me for presuming. I never asked; she saw it in my mind. She told my grandfather so, and he said I shouldn't even have been thinking it, and clouted me again."

"What was the horse like?" asked Gird, suddenly curious.

"A color I'd never seen; I heard later it was favored in Old Aare: blue-gray like a stormy sky, with a white mane and black tail, and what they called the Stormlord's mark on the face, a jagged blaze that forked. But it was the fittings that fascinated me: that white mane was plaited in many strands, each bound with bright ribbons that looped together. The saddlecloth was embroidered silk—I was a silk merchant's child, I could not mistake that. Then when she mounted, she sprang into the saddle like a man—and rode astride, which the horse nomad women do, but no merchant woman I had known. My grandfather told me later all the magelords do, men and women alike, but they think it is presumptuous in lower ranks."

Gird returned to the topic that seemed to him more important. "But if she is the only one—and the sier in Grahlin has no such powers—then his messengers must find the king's army before the king will know and come north?"

"Yes. If he even calls for him: did you not know that Sehgrahlin is the king's least favorite cousin? They have been rivals for years; Sehgrahlin refused to send his troops on this expedition, although he has some up north, guarding against the horsefolk. He will not like to ask the king for help, that one; he will do his best to drive you out of his domain with his own powers."

He had done that, Gird thought, but what more would he do? He asked the merchant, who shrugged. "He might help Duke Pharaon—they've hunted together a lot, and he once loved Pharaon's sister—but he married into the Borkai family. Those he would help, but they lie away north of you, north and west, right on the nomad borders." The trader knew what the gnomes had not—or what they had not bothered to teach Gird—

which lords lived where, and how they were related. Gird had Selamis write it all down, although he suspected Selamis might know some of it already. Then he asked about the one magelord family the gnomes had mentioned, and the trader's expression changed. "Marrakai! Where would you have heard about them? They're not even in Finaarenis; Marrakai's a duke in Tsaia. No magicks, that I know of, but probably the best rulers in both kingdoms: honest, just, and put up with no nonsense. If that brigand you say is using your name wanders into Marrakai lands, he'll find himself strung high before he knows it."

The trouble with towns, Gird realized when he had been there a hand of days, was that they were harder to leave than villages. He would like to have had a town allied to him—but he could not hope to protect Brightwater against a full army. No army had come, but one might. Their barton had grown, swelled with sudden converts, but he didn't trust that. The newly elected council of merchants and craftsmen wanted him to stay (one told him frankly that it was cheaper to feed his army than pay the bribes and taxes of the earlier rulers) but he had not won his war. When the gnomes sent word that it was now time to redeem his pledge to help them at Blackbone Hill, he was glad of the excuse—but he left most of his army near Brightwater, under the command of Cob, whose broken foot was nearly healed.

Chapter Twenty-six

Under a milky sky, the crest of Blackbone Hill loomed dark and inhospitable. Gird had expected the darkness, but not the shape, which made him think uneasily of a vast carcass, half-eaten. Sunburnt grass, like ragged dead fur, seemed stretched between the gaunt ribs.

"There's them says it's a dragon," Wila, his guide, said nervously. Clearly he thought it was something. Gird forced a grin.

"If 'tis, 'tis dead, long since."

Wila shook his head. "There's bones, up there. All black, black inside and out. Seen 'em myself."

"Dragonbones?" Despite himself, Gird shivered. No one had seen a dragon, but the tales of Camwyn Dragonmaster proved that dragons had lived, and might still. Even the lords believed in dragons; one of the outposts up on the western rim was called Dragonwatch.

"Dunno." Wila paused, and hooked one foot behind his knee, leaning on his staff. "All the bones I seen was too little, unless a dragon has almighty more bones than other creatures. If they'd been normal bone, I'd have said fish or bird—something light, slender. But black like that—and no one could think that hill's just a hill, like any other."

Gird glanced upslope again: true. Something about the shape of it, malign and decrepit, made the hairs on his neck crawl. "Why's anyone live here, then?" he asked.

"Well, now." Wila switched feet, and leaned heavily into his staff. Clearly this was a question he'd hoped to answer. "In the old days," he said, "before the lords came out of the south on their tall horses, this was uncanny ground. The Threespring clans claimed the east side for spring sheep grazing—it's not so bad then, with new grass and spring flowers. The Lady tames all, you know," he added, and dipped his head. Gird nodded, and swept his arm wide, acknowledging her bounty. "Then the Darkwater bog folk, they claimed herb right to the western slope, and the land between rock and bog."

"Herb-right to *that*?"

"Aye. In the old days, that is, when the Darkwater bog folk gave half the herbalists in this region, they gathered the Five Fingers from that very rock, the Lady's promise to redeem it, they said." He peered closely at Gird. "You do know the Five Fingers—?"

Gird nodded. "But where I come from, only the wise may say the names—I have heard, but cannot—"

"Ah—yes. I forgot. You're from the overheard, aren't you?"

"Overheard?" Gird hadn't heard *that* term.

"Where the kuaknomi overhear the blessings and overturn them. That's what I was taught, at least. Where the kuaknomi overhear, only the wise may say the name of any sacred thing, lest a prayer be changed to curse."

"They don't come here?"

"Well—there's them as says Blackbone Hill has felt their touch, but aside from that, no. We have the truesingers here, the treelords."

"Elves?"

Wila snorted, then coughed. "That's coarse talk of them, lad. What they call themselves is truesingers. Sinyi, in their tongue."

"You *speak* it?" Gird could almost forget the coming battles for that.

"A bit." Wila put both feet on the ground, and picked the staff up. "Best be going, if we're to be past the Tongue by dark." And despite Gird's questions, he would say no more about elves, but led the way at a brisker pace than Gird expected from someone his age. What he did say, briefly and over his shoulder, had to do with the human settlement now nestled at the hill's steeper end. "Lords forced it," he said. "Broke apart the Threesprings clans, and settled a half of 'em here, and put in two brothers from the bog folk, and set them all to digging in the hill. Came out as you'd think: fever and death, broken bones and quarrels, but the lords want what comes out the mine shaft, and never mind the cost. Send more in, when too many die. It's a hard place, Blackbone, and no hope for better."

"But the barton—"

"Oh, well. The barton's together, and they'll fight— they're good at that. Come the day—"

Come the day, Gird thought, and no one will have to live in a place like this, ever again. The black, disquieting hill loomed higher as they plunged into one of its gullies, angled downslope, then up and across to another. He had been days coming here, after the gnomes' message arrived, passed from one guide to another.

Blackbone was as bleak as its hill, a cramped village of dark stone huts locked in by steep slopes. It stank, not with the healthy smells of a farming village, but with rot that would never become fertility, human waste and garbage piled on barren stone. A thin dark stream writhed behind the row of dwellings, too quiet for its rate of flow. Wisps of sulphurous steam came off it. As a mining village, it had no farmsteads; the barton, Gird found, had adapted to circumstances, and met in the mine itself.

"They dunna come 'ere," said the yeoman-marshal, Felis. "They come to the outside, we got to haul it that far, and load their wagons. Inside they dunna come."

Gird found it hard to endure even the outer tunnel, as daylight faded in the distance. Now he was out of sight of the entrance, sweating with fear, and hoping the barton would think it was the heat. Around the gallery where they drilled, torches burned, smoking. In that dim and shaking light, the men and women looked like nightmare creatures, monsters hardly human. He had already noticed that they were all grimed with the black rock. Now their eyes glittered in the light, the whites unnatural against dark-smeared faces. He glanced up, seeing the dark rock overhead far too close.

One of the women grinned, teeth white against the darkness. "You're no miner, eh? The rockfear gripes you?"

No use to pretend. "It does. I'm a farmer, used to no more than a bit of roof between me and the sky."

She laughed, but not unkindly. "At least you don't lie. Lead us out to fight, then, and you'll be free of this rock." The emphasis on "you" caught his attention.

"And you? Do you want to stay here?"

"Nay—but what do I know of farming? I'd go to other mines, could I." Some of the faces nodded agreement, others were still, with a stillness Gird had never seen.

He had no time to wonder at that, for the detailed plan of battle had to be made that night. Now that he'd

seen for himself the shape of the land, the way the dark
rock loomed over the wagon road into Blackbone, he
could mentally place his few archers where they could
do the most good. The barton members nodded when
he spoke, but he wondered if they understood at all.
None of them were archers. Most of them had never
been out of Blackbone in all their lives. They knew
digging and hauling, enough carpentry to build ladders
and simple boxes, and not much more. They'd been
drilled with picks and shovels. Gird felt the edges filed
onto the shovels and wished he could have such metal
for better weapons.

One of the men nodded. "They 'ad to give us good
steel, see, or it wouldn't be no use against this rock."

"But no smith," said the woman who had asked him
about rockfear. "They brings us the tools, but takes no
chances we'll make swords."

Deep in the ground, away from natural light, Gird
lost track of time and would have gone on all night, but
they had candlemarks for measure, and brought him
back out to sleep under the sky. He almost wished he'd
stayed within, for the air stank worse than in the mine
itself, and he felt smothered.

The next day, his troops arrived. None of them liked
Blackbone Hill. He saw the looks sent his way, noticed
how they angled away from the line of march, as if they
didn't want to set foot on that dark stone. He hated it
himself, felt a subtle antagonism through his bootsoles.
What if he was wrong? What if the power of Blackbone
turned against them, preferred the lords? The gnomes
had said it would not, but they were, after all, rockfolk.
Their goals were not his goals.

Threesprings barton, kinbound to Blackbone, had sent
twenty-seven yeomen, the largest contingent. They were
all darkhaired, dour, barely glancing at Gird when he
spoke to their yeoman marshal. A third of them were
women, all as tall and thickset as the men. Longhill,
barely a day's march away, had sent fourteen: its best,
the yeoman marshal assured Gird. Deepmeadow,
Whiterock Ridge, Whiteoak, Hazelly, and Clearspring
had been on the march two days each. Some of them

had never been so far from home; they clutched their weapons and foodsacks as if they expected the rocks to sprout demons. Westhill, the most veteran of this lot, had marched four days across the rolling hills. Their sturdy cheerfulness heartened the novices more than Gird could; he did not explain that Westhill had no village to return to, for the lords had burnt and salted it over the winter.

Blackbone barton greeted these allies with restraint —or, as Gird saw it, with total lack of enthusiasm. A few words passed between the Threesprings yeoman marshal and a Blackbone man, a mutter of family news, as near as Gird could make out, but nothing more. Longhill clearly expected no better; the yeomen smirked and sat quietly without attempting conversation. The others, barring Westhill, clumped up nervously and stared roundeyed from the taciturn Blackbone yeomen to the higher slopes of Blackbone Hill. Gird made his way from one barton to another, doing his best to reassure and cheer them.

Blackbone barton itself actually broke the ice with a contribution to the evening meal. Short of supplies as it was—as any remote mining village without farmstead support would be—the village nonetheless made a very potent brew and had saved it, as their spokesman said "For the day." Now the chunky little jugs passed from hand to hand, raising spirits or at least numbing fears. Gird, mindful of watchful eyes, took but one pull at a jug before passing it on. The story of his drunken rage had traveled farther than he had; he knew he dared not risk another, and certainly not before a battle.

By dawn, he had them all in position. They looked fewer in morning light, when he knew an enemy was coming, and the land itself looked larger. Could they possibly hold the narrow throat, choke the lords' soldiers from the village?

Eight bartons. Near two cohorts, by his new reckoning, though he had none of his marshals along. And there, coming along the stone-paved trade road, were the mounted infantry, the archers he feared so much, the light cavalry, and—he squinted—and a small troop of the lords themselves, mounted. So—so the gnomes had been right. Whatever they got from the Blackbone mines was important enough to bring them out themselves. He could not read their devices, or recognize them by the colors they wore; the traders had told him all that, and Selamis had written it down, but Selamis was not here to remind him. Lords were lords, he thought to himself, and what difference did it make if he faced sier or duke or count—any and all would be glad of his blood, and he of theirs.

Because he was looking for it, he noticed that the lords' troops also disliked the touch of Blackbone Hill, and veered slightly until sharp commands brought them back. He told himself that the horsemen would have trouble on the slopes. Would horses, too, flinch from Blackbone? He hoped so; they were ruinously outnumbered otherwise. Perhaps he should have brought some of his regular troops—but there would have been no way to move that many that far without opposition, and he had had no time for additional battles. He looked over at Wila, who could see down into the cleft where his few archers waited, and held up his hands three times. Wila passed the signal on. If they could take the archers out, then his people could stand against a charge. Horsemen couldn't spread wide on that uneven slope. He hoped.

The clatter of hooves and boots rang loudly from the stones on either side of the track. Gird kept his head down, trusting his carefully placed archers to choose their targets wisely. He heard the twang of one bowstring, then another, then shouts from below. So it began, again, and he squeezed his own hands hard an instant, fighting down that last-moment fear that caught him every time. He stood, and waved his arm.

In that first scrambling rush downslope, Gird could see that his archers had done their work well; many of the lords' archers were down. Arrows flicked by, close overhead. A few of those below had found cover, and returned a ragged flight. Someone beside him staggered and went down, hands clutched to chest. Ahead of him, the front line of yeomen, with the best weapons, had engaged the mounted soldiers, unseating many of them and killing horses. The slope and surprise gave them advantage, and Gird's archers continued to pick their targets wisely.

"Get the lords!" he bellowed, reminding them.

But the attack lost momentum, foundered. No arrows found the lords on their tall horses; Gird could have sworn he saw arrows slide aside, as if refusing to menace the magelords. The lords themselves drew no weapon he could see—not then—but their soldiers regrouped with amazing speed. They paid no attention to the wounded and fallen among them, striding over the bodies as if they were merely more rocks. Gird had called for all his bartons to attack when he thought he saw the enemy crumbling, but now he had no unseen reserves, and the ground no longer favored him. Either his people were spread out along the road, outnumbered at each point, or he could call them to clump on the road itself, and try a frontal attack—exactly what he had not wanted to do with the weapons he had available.

Furious with himself, and with the gnomes who had advised his battle plan, Gird watched his ambush degenerate into a lengthy slaughter. Now that they were sure the rocky slopes held no more surprises, the lords and their soldiers pushed forward strongly on the road itself. Already they were beyond the range of Gird's archers, who would have to come out of cover to find targets. The yeoman marshals were looking over their shoulders now, expecting Gird to come up with something—some plan—and he could not think of anything. Could he hold them together? Would a rout be worse than this? Why had he ever thought the gnomes could design a battle plan for humans? He had to try something. He called them all in, trying to slow the enemy advance along the road. That might give someone a chance to escape.

It had been a mistake. It had been a disaster, and now the end would come. Gird held the retreat together, as foot by foot they were forced back through the village into the maw of the mine. He had been so sure that taking out their archers would be enough. It might have been, without the lords themselves there, with their wicked magicks. Their troops, who might have broken and fled—*would* have, Gird was sure—still moved forward, as if they had no thought at all, as if they could suffer no wound or fall to no death. Yet they fell, and died, and were trampled by their own. The faces he could see did not change expression even in death. Too far behind for any of Gird's weapons to reach, the lords sat veiled on their tall horses, watching, performing whatever magicks they could.

Here was still more evidence that some of the lords still had potent powers to call on. Rocks split, air hummed and thickened in his throat, unnatural light rippled over the battle, making it hard to see. And so he was going to die under a mountain of rock, because he had believed the wrong story. There wasn't any way out of this, but if he *did* live, he was going to have a few choice words for Arranha, if ever he caught up with him again.

He shifted to one side as the mine closed around them.

"Go on!" bawled the Blackbone yeoman marshal in his ear. "Let us take this."

"It was my bad idea." Gird smashed his club into a shoulder, and ducked aside from a pike. "I should be last—"

They fought side by side for a few moments, as the soldiers charged again. Then the momentum of that charge dissipated, and they could retreat further into the dark shaft without immediate risk. The soldiers were cursing the darkness, stumbling over loose rocks and the fallen.

"Hurry *up*," the yeoman marshal said. "Afore the lords get in, and make they magical lights—"

"But we should make a stand," Gird said. "I'll do it—a few others—"

"Never mind!" The yeoman marshal yanked Gird's arm hard. "Leave them to it; they'll find out—"

"What?" He couldn't see, in the dimness, anything but a flash of teeth.

"It's in the charm," said the man, almost gleefully. "Come with me." *What charm was that*, Gird wondered. It was that or be left in darkness, and Gird came. Dying inside a cursed mountain wasn't his idea of the way to die, but what choices did he have? None, like the rest of them. All around, in the darkness, he heard the rasp of feet on stone, the groans of the wounded, the heavy breathing. Deeper into the blackness, and deeper, twisting and turning through passages that were sometimes tight for a single man, and other times so wide that three or four abreast must reach out with hands to feel the walls. Gird clamped his fear within him, and tried to think, without success.

When the dim bluish light of a gnomish lamp blossomed nearby, he could not believe it. All around were faces equally surprised, mouths open. A firm, cool hand gripped Gird's, and he looked down to see the warmaster who had set this battle's plan.

"It is for you to command," the warmaster said. "No human noise!"

"Silence!" Gird bellowed, and no one spoke. He bent to the warmaster, full of his own questions and complaints, but the warmaster's expression stopped him.

"It is that they are within, the outland lords?"

"Yes."

"You marshal your humans, follow my orders."

"Yes." There was nothing more to say. Whatever the gnomes demanded, he would have to perform, both by his contract and by the logic of the situation.

"Then go. Follow that one—" the warmaster pointed. "Go far and swift."

"You don't need our help?"

The warmaster's face conveyed secret amusement. "Human help for rockwar? Go."

Gird waved, and the others formed up to follow him, as he followed his guide. It occurred to him, as they plunged once more into a narrow dark passage, that the gnomes might have planned all this just to lure a few lords underground—though he hated to think that.

All he could hear behind, though he strained his ears, was the noise of his own people shuffling along.

His guide carried a lantern, so he himself could see where to put his feet, but the others stumbled in darkness. At last, a dim shape of light ahead, that widened and brightened to daylight. He squinted against the light, and then, as he came out, stopped short. They faced a gloomy sunset, a few rays of somber light escaping beneath heavy clouds. And that meant—he shook his head, to clear it. They had walked *through* Blackbone Hill? He peered up and over his shoulder. There it was, that gaunt, misshapen spine arched slightly away from them.

Ahead the gnome set off downhill, in that measured but tireless tread, and Gird waved the foremost of his people on. He would stay to see the last of them out, and silence questions.

By dark they were far below the hill, coming into marshy ground. The blackwater bogs, Gird thought. The gnome stopped suddenly, and Gird nearly ran into him.

"Here is good water." The lantern light glittered from a pool that looked as black as the rock of the hill. But when Gird dipped a handful, it was clear, trembling in the light, and tasted sweet. Others knelt, dipped for themselves, and drank thirstily. He could hear the splashes, and the moans of the wounded behind him in the darkness. The gnome touched his arm to get his attention. "This is water that runs clean, and the bog clans know safe ways from here. Do you acknowledge debt?"

There was no alternative. "You have brought us from danger to safe water: I acknowledge owing."

"That is fair. This is the exchange: no humans to go beneath that hill. To gather the herbs of the field, to pasture flocks, it is permitted. It is not permitted to delve in the rock, or build aught of the loose rock of the surface. Granted?"

"Granted." Gird sighed, nonetheless, thinking how he would have to argue the miners into it. He wanted to ask why, but knew he would get no answer. And he was tired, desperately tired. He wanted to know how many they'd lost, and if the wounded would recover, and he wanted to fall in his tracks and sleep.

"What of the magelords?" he asked, determined to get something out of this exchange.

The gnome smiled. Gird remembered that smile from his months in their princedom. "It is not a place for humankind, within that hill. The magelords took what was not theirs; knowing, they took it. We return justice."

The ground heaved, thudding against Gird's feet, and a shout went up from his people. Trees groaned; their limbs thrashed briefly as if in a gust of wind. In the lantern light, the water in the pool rocked and splashed like water in a kicked bucket. Gird looked at the gnome, whose smile broadened.

"Justice," it said again. "No pursuit."

When dawn brightened behind Blackbone Hill, the marshy forest looked much less threatening. Delicate flowers brightened the hummocks of moss; butterflies flicked wings of brilliant yellows and oranges in and out of the sunbeams. They had halted beside an upwelling spring of clear water, that flowed into an amber stream between thick-trunked dark trees. A clearly-marked trail led away downstream from their campsite, and the gnome—who had stayed with them until daylight—said that it led safely to an old settlement of the bog folk, now abandoned, but on another safe trail to Longhill.

Gird counted up his survivors. Only five of Blackbone itself had survived. Their kin from Threesprings had lost but three, and still remained the largest barton. Longhill had lost seven of fourteen; Deepmeadow had lost eight of twelve. Whiterock Ridge had lost all its archers, but no one else, and Hazelly lost only one. Clearspring and Westhill had lost two each. But of those living, a quarter were wounded, unfit for work or fighting for many days.

And the survivors were anything but satisfied with the way the battle had gone.

"You didn't tell us they rockfolk'd be involved," said the yeoman marshal of Hazelly. For someone who had never fought at all before, he was surprisingly pert, Gird thought.

"Us wouldn't've let 'un fight in th'mine unless they'd been there," said one of the Blackbone survivors. "They told us away last winter they'd no more patience with the magelord's thievery." He peered at Gird through the morning mist. "But they didn't say what t'would cost *us*. They said you was the best leader—"

Before Gird could answer that, someone from Threesprings broke in. "Ah, them rockfolk! Suppose it was their plan, too, warn't it? And you their hired human warleader?"

"They didn't hire me," Gird began, wondering how he was going to settle this lot. They had good reason to grumble, but so did he; it was not his fault the gnomes had kept the main part of their plan from him. So had the Blackbone Hill folk, for the matter of that.

Westhill, more experienced in living in the country, had done most of the work to make the camp liveable. The others learned quickly, if unwillingly: the Westhill yeoman-marshal had a tongue sharpened on both sides. Gird began thinking what to do with this ill-assorted lot. Some of them, from the villages that no longer existed, could come directly into the main army. Others might go home for a time, though the areas of peace shrank day by day.

In a few days, the mood had settled; those who had been most badly wounded were either mending or dead, and everyone else had decided to stay with Gird or go home in a huff. There were only a few of the latter. The rest had begun to recast the tale as they would tell it to friends at home. Gird noticed that the lords' troop grew, and the lords' magicks became ever more spectacular, as they retold it to each other. The survivors from Blackbone Hill itself—including some who had hidden in the houses until the fight passed by, and then escaped around the hill—seemed glad to go to Threesprings, where they had kin.

Gird himself climbed back up the trail to take a last look at the west side of Blackbone Hill in broad daylight. It had not changed, that he could see, and he felt no desire to walk on it again.

He made his way back across country toward Brightwater, with the Westhill yeomen. On their way, they found ample evidence that the war was spreading. Twice they fought off attacks by mounted patrols; once they blundered into the path of a large infantry force, and got away only because they were fitter than their pursuers. Gird wondered where that force had been going; as far as he knew, he had no one active in that direction. They passed more than one burned-out village, inhabited by peasants who fled into the woods when they approached, and slunk out behind them to work the fields.

Gird led them in a careful circle around Grahlin; they were near Burry when they met someone recently from Brightwater, a yeoman Gird remembered only vaguely. His news was mixed. The king's army claimed to have killed Gird, between Gadilon's domain and the gnome lands to the south; it had then marched north, celebrating that victory by burning any village whose lord reported it as rebellious. For some reason, it had gone east, rather than returning in its tracks, and was now at the eastern border of Finaarenis, preparing to march home on the River Road.

"So," Gird said, putting a blunt finger on the map. "That group we saw was probably going to join the king's army. Well. When they get to Grahlin, the sier will have much to tell them, and we can expect them in Brightwater sometime after harvest, no doubt."

According to later reports, the king's army had met with scattered but brisk resistance on its march north; bartons Gird had never heard of had fought individual and combined engagements. In the meantime, Gird's main force had control of the valley in which Brightwater lay, from just south of the River Road all the way to the southern trade road. They had taken two lords' residences, although only servants were there: the lords were off with the king's army, and their families were safe (for the moment) in Finyatha.

Putting all this information together with Selamis and the senior marshals, Gird thought he still had numerical superiority, but most of his troops were ill-armed and had no defensive armor at all. They were short of supplies, in part because Gird did not want to squeeze the remaining farmers. Some smiths had come over to the rebels, it was true, but they had little metal for them to work.

As the summer waned, Gird remembered the gnomes' warning that he must win in one season, or find an ally with money or troops—or both. They had suggested one, which he had been reluctant to approach.

Chapter Twenty-seven

Not for the first time, Gird felt well out of his depth. These wooded hills had taller trees than any he'd known; following a gurgling creek between two of them, he felt he was sinking deeper and deeper into unknown lands. Far overhead, the leaves just changing turned honest sunlight to a flickering green, as unsteady as the water beside him. Most of the undergrowth still showed the heavy green of summer, but one climbing vine had gone scarlet, as if the tree itself were bleeding. Gird shivered when he saw that.

If he had not spent that winter with the gnomes, he would never have come here, so far east, to meet a lord reputedly not so bad as the rest. But if he had not gone to the gnomes, he would never have survived his second season of war. If they had been right about other things, perhaps they were right about the Marrakai.

"Ho!" Gird jumped as if struck, and then stood still, peering about him into the confusion of leaves. Then a man in green stepped out on the trail he'd been following. His guide? Or was it a trap? The man had a staff like his own, and a bow slung over his shoulder. "Are you from the Aldonfulk hall?" the man asked.

"Yes," said Gird. The man moved like someone well-fed and well-rested, full of confidence. The lord himself? Then he remembered what he was supposed to say. "Aldonfulk Lawmaster Karik ak Padig Sekert sends greetings to the lord duke Marrakai."

"Ah. And Kevre Mikel Dobrin Marrakai returns those greetings, through his kirgan."

Gird struggled his way through the names he had heard only in the gnomish accent, and the references, to remember that the kirgan meant heir of law and blood. He stared as the young man came forward. Black hair, green eyes as the lords had sometimes, a face young but already showing character. That sier in Grahlin would have been glad to have such a son. The young man smiled.

"And you must be Gird, the scourge of the west, that we have heard so much about. I'm Meshavre, called Mesha."

"But you're a—" He didn't want to say it, but the young man said it for him.

"A lord's son? The enemy? I hope not that, at least. Yes, Kirgan Marrakai, in formal usage, but this meeting you is hardly formal. Do not your people use one name only, at least in this war? Call me Mesha, then, and I will call you Gird."

He was used to command; his voice carried the certainty that Gird would do what he wanted because he asked it, and he (that voice conveyed) would ask nothing unreasonable. Gird could imagine him dealing with dogs and horses, with wounded men, with crying women, all of them calming under that voice and obeying it. Yet it was reasonable, what he said, and Gird could see no good reason to disobey, nothing that would not make him feel foolish.

"Well," he said, to gain time. "Mesha. Whatever you think of rebellious peasants, that's the first time I've called a nobleborn by a pet name in all my life." He met the young man's eyes squarely, to find surprised respect. Mesha nodded.

"My father was right, then, as were the kapristi. They said you were different, and told long tales of you; my father had heard some of those same tales from Finaarean lords."

"Who told them differently, I would guess," said Gird. He liked the young man; he couldn't help it. Was that the charming he'd been warned about? But the gnomes had said the Marrakai magic had gone long ago, that these lords were no longer magelords except by inheritance.

"I heard only one of them, from the sier whose life you saved. He was divided in his mind; if all the rebels were like you, he might be your ally. But come: let me bring you to a safe place to rest and eat. There's a forester's shelter, down this way." And without another word, Mesha turned and started down the trail. Gird followed, still half-afraid of a trap. But why then would the young lord meet him alone in the first place? Why not simply put an arrow through him from behind a tree?

The forester's shelter had three sides of stone, the front open to a firepit ringed with stones. Tethered beside it were two horses, a brown and a gray; a small fire crackled in the firepit, and something was cooking that sent a wave of hunger through Gird's belly.

Duke Marrakai was an older version of his son: heavy black hair and beard, green eyes, and a powerful body. Gird was aware that the two of them, father and son, could easily kill him if that was what they had in mind. But so far neither made a move against him. The duke was himself stirring a pot of some dark liquid, and Mesha moved quickly to unpack saddlebags: bread, cheese, onion, apples, slabs of meat. Gird unslung his own thin pack, and put his remaining loaf of bread with the other. Mesha looked startled, but his father nodded approval.

"We thank you, Gird, for sharing." His voice was deep, and Gird had no doubt its bellow would carry across a battle. "Mesha, show Gird the spring."

The spring came up beside a flat rock. Gird knelt and held his hand over it; the surface rippled a little with the flow. He muttered the greeting for its guardian spirit, and looked up to find the kirgan watching him curiously. "You don't speak to it?" he asked. Mesha shook his head. Gird looked back at the spring; surely it was glad to be recognized. He bent and scooped up a handful of icy, clean-tasting water. It made Gird's teeth ache. He filled his waterskin after Mesha drank.

"Do all your people talk to springs?" asked Mesha. Gird retied the thong that held the skin closed for travel.

"Whenever we take water from the earth, we thank the Lady, and the guardians. It's only courteous."

"Even from a well?"

"Of course." Gird looked at him. "If you give something to someone, don't you expect thanks? We cannot live without water, without the rain falling and the springs rising."

"Yes, but—is that why peasants—why your people— tie flowers and wool to the wellposts?"

"Yes, and if this were a spring on my land, I would bring gifts at Midwinter and Midsummer. Perhaps someone else does that here."

Mesha looked as if he would ask more, but didn't. Instead he waved at the clearing behind the shelter. "Over there, behind that cedar, is the jacks for this shelter. 'Tis far enough from the water, my father says." Gird had no need then, but wondered how long they thought he would stay.

They came back to find Duke Marrakai pouring the dark liquid into thick-walled mugs. "Do you have sib, in your country?" he asked Gird. Gird nodded. "Good. I like it with more tikaroot than most, though that makes it more bitter; this has honey in it."

It might be poison, but why? Gird took a mug and sipped cautiously. A strong flavor, thicker and darker than his people made it. After another sip or so, he decided he liked it well enough. The duke had his knife out, and cut the bread and cheese into slabs. Now it was Gird's turn to be surprised, for he held his hands over the food and used a form of blessing Gird had never heard: "Thank the Lady," had been enough for him.

Marrakai and his son took Gird's bread first, which forced him to share theirs. He wondered if they knew the significance of that among his people. Arranha had not, but these were supposed to be different. One bite stood for all; he might as well have cheese and apples. They ate in silence, as hungry men do; Gird, being hungriest, was most aware of his own eating. There was enough to fill his belly, and he took it. Mesha and his father ate slowly, so that they finished all together.

Then Duke Marrakai turned to Gird. "You are not oathbound to me, or to any with whom I share oaths: we are as strangers, among whom is no rank. Call me Kevre, if you will." Gird stared at him: a peasant call a great lord, a duke, by one name? He nodded, trying to cover his confusion. Marrakai went on. "We have shared food; among our people, that used to mean peace, and sometimes alliance. If it is not so among your people, I will not hold you to those obligations—but if you want first truce, and then perhaps alliance, let us speak of that."

Gird wondered if there had been ale in the sib; he could hardly believe what he was hearing. Alliance? With a duke of Tsaia? That the gnomes had had some reason for sending him here, he'd been sure, but this went beyond all hopes.

"Sir—Kevre—" That would take getting used to; the "sir" still came easily to him. "Among our people, shared food declares peace, at least for that meeting. And sometimes more—if something is being decided, then food shared means agreement." He did not mention obligation, intentionally: let the Marrakai duke show what he knew.

"Yet you were trailhungry when you came; it would be unfair of me to bind you by that—"

"Are you bound?" asked Gird boldly. Marrakai nodded. "I am. Both by custom and by my own honor. I knew what I did when I ate of your bread, and gave you mine; therefore am I bound. While you are here, in my domain, you are my guest; neither I nor mine will harm you, nor let harm come to you."

Gird nodded. "And I thought of what it meant, Kevre, when I put my food with yours, and when I saw you take it, leaving me only yours to eat. I said nothing and ate: that binds me, by the law the gnomes taught me, and by the custom of my people." He grinned at Marrakai. "Of honor I cannot speak, since I was taught that we peasants had none, but I can see right and do it."

"Which is honor enough for anyone," said Mesha quickly. His father gave him a sharp glance, but nodded.

"Mesha's right. So here we are, you my guest and I your host, both of us brought here by an interest in gnomish law. What law *have* the gnomes taught you? Is that your message?"

Gird tried to put his scattered thoughts in order. "Sir—Kevre—the gnomes taught me their law, and something of past times, and how the old customs of our people were like and unlike the High Lord's law."

Marrakai frowned. "Do they call Esea and the High Lord one thing and the same?"

"I'm—not sure. What they said was that the High Lord had been for the Aareans in the form of Esea. But they themselves consider the High Lord the source of justice. The judge."

"Yes. That I knew. The High Lord's Law, as they say. You know of the Rule of Aare?"

Gird nodded. "A priest of Esea taught me, but he was outcast, for claiming that the Rule of Aare meant differently than the king's law said."

"You met Arranha?" Marrakai shook his head. "Gird, I am well rebuked: I had not thought any peasant leader, no matter how worthy, would be familiar with Arranha's heresies *and* gnomish law. Are you sure you are not a scholar, rather than a fighter?"

Gird felt himself redden. "I did not choose fighting; I would farm if I could. But—"

"But you could not. My pardon, Gird; it is no time for jesting. But Arranha! I have not met him myself, although I have heard from his horrified colleagues all about his views. I think myself he's right. The oldest documents in my archives are from Old Aare, and from these it is clear that the interpretation of the Rule has changed, over the generations. I have tried to convince our king to return to the intent of the Rule."

"Would he?"

"Felis? No. None of them see it as I do, although some agree that great wrongs are being done in its name. Some would abandon the Rule entirely, seeing no hope of reform, and some are, unfortunately, profiting so well that they see no reason to change."

"Some like wrong itself," muttered Mesha. "The Verrakai—"

"I name no man's motives," said Marrakai firmly. "You know what I think, but that's not at issue here. There are bad men in any realm, and in every family."

"Not like that," said Mesha. Gird looked at him and wondered if he spoke as freely to his father in his own hall. "Taris is merely foolish."

"Judge all by the same rule," said Marrakai. "If you would name Verrakai wicked, for gambling with lives, then consider Taris's loss of those steadings—were there not men and women farming them, who came under another's power? How is that different? We have been fortunate to have so few, but we are not gods, to be perfect."

"You punished Taris; Duke Verrakai gave *his* son jewels when he—"

"Enough!" Gird noticed that Mesha was instantly silent, but clearly unconvinced. Marrakai turned to Gird. "My nephew, whose father was killed years ago, gambled away some of his father's lands—which to me is dishonor, for the care he owed those who lived there. Lands are not like ring or sword. As for the Verrakai— have you heard of them?"

Gird shook his head. "Only that Verrakai is one of the dukes of Tsaia, a great lord of the east."

"A great lord, if wealth counts for all. I would not speak of him, Gird, without need. Our families share no great love, and I cannot be fair."

Gird looked from one face to the other, and said nothing. After a moment, Marrakai sighed, and went on.

"That's beside our purpose. The kapristi may have told you that long ago my father's father's father resisted our king's attempt to invade their princedom across Marrakai lands. When they routed that invasion, and made a pact of peace with the Tsaian throne—as they did with the king of Finaarenis for the same reason—the kapristi noted our action on their behalf. They counted themselves in debt to Marrakai. My great-grandsire argued that what he had done was right—that he had laid upon them no debt—but they argued in return that by our law he had not been obligated, and so it went, until they agreed on a settlement. From that day on, we have dealt evenly with kapristi. As you know, they accept no gifts and give none, but with those they consider upright, they deal willingly and fairly."

"That is so," said Gird.

"Of course I knew of the unrest in Finaarenis; there is unrest in Tsaia, for the same reasons. And I had heard of you: after Norwalk Sheepfolds, everyone heard of you." Marrakai paused to drink more sib, and offered Gird another mugful. Gird took it, nodded, and Marrakai went on. "A peasant turned off his land turns outlaw: that's nothing new. That peasant joins a rebellious mob, burns hayricks, ambushes traders: that's nothing new. But a peasant training other peasants to march, to use their daily tools as weapons, to fight trained soldiers—not only training them so, but leading them: that was new. And not at all to most men's liking. Most lords, at least. And then you disappeared entirely, after saving Sier Segrahlin's life. Dead, most thought, or frightened into flight.

He had to ask, though he was sure he knew the answer, and the question itself could anger Marrakai. "Is it because you fear this for yourself? You would give me help, and for what—to let your domain abide?"

Marrakai was not angry, but his son was. He shook his head, at both Gird and his son. "What I fear is long war, with all the lands laid waste and no justice gained. They have not begun to fight back, Gird, not with the worst magic. You will see far worse than you've seen: poisoned wells, fields ruined for long years, unless you find someone with magic to restore them. You did not win quickly; they know, now what they face. Yet you must fight. I understand that—it had gone too far, and your lords have no intent to mend matters. Am I afraid? Of course. I have children too; I have lands I love, people that depend on me. Worse, I have an oath I swore to our king, when he took the crown. I cannot take my own soldiers into this, except to defend my own lands, without his permission, which he will not give."

"Why obey a wicked king?"

Marrakai sighed. "Felis is not wicked, merely weak. He has wicked advisors, some of them—if he had only had the sense to marry his rose, as he called her, instead of that sister of Verrakai's—but that's not wickedness. Gird, I pledged my loyalty to him, to the king of Tsaia both as king, and as the man Felis Hornath Mikel Dovre Mahieran Mahierai. If I go to war against his will, then I have broken my word, and if my word was ill-given, foolishly given, it is still binding on me. It would not be on everyone; some can free themselves with less trouble. I cannot. I cannot do it and be who and what I am, the self I respect. I have argued with him, pled with him, stormed at him, and finally left court—with his entire consent, because he was tired of hearing me. But that one thing I cannot do."

Gird felt the unshakeable substance of the man, as unyielding in his way as the gnomes. He had never found anyone to give such an oath to; the oaths he had had to give the steward he had never felt as binding. A peasant did what he must to survive; honor was something the lords sang of, in ballads.

"You disapprove?" asked Marrakai. Gird shrugged and shook his head.

"I have no right to approve or disapprove. It is right to keep a promise, that I'll agree, and if that is how you see your duty to your king, it may—must—be right for you."

"I wonder sometimes," said Marrakai. His lips quirked in a rueful smile. "What I propose to do is, in the eyes of many, just as bad as marching my own men out to face his. Fine wit, one of my tutors said, splits hairs, but split hairs make weak ropes to hang a life on." Gird said nothing; he could not follow that. Marrakai seemed to understand, for he shrugged in his turn. "Let me be clear, then: the gnomes sent word that you were the best of possible leaders to the revolt surely coming in Finaarenis. Last summer I thought you might come, and heard instead of your campaigns—"

"Not all of them mine," said Gird, rubbing his nose. "That fellow in the south—"

"I expected confusion of tales," Marrakai said. "But some were surely yours. The gnomes said you might—with the High Lord's judgment—win in one season, but they expected not. You would need gold for good weapons, they said, and possibly troops, and they were unwilling to provide either. They thought I might, for my own reasons." He looked at his son. "There is one of my reasons: Mesha will not succeed to my lands as long as Felis is king. He was too forthright at court, worse even than I am." A chuckle escaped him; Gird noticed that the young man's ears were bright red. Marrakai shook his head. "We are not good at hiding our opinions, we Marrakai; it has been so for generations. My grandfather said someone dropped yeast in the mix when the gods shaped the first of us; it bubbles out at inconvenient moments."

Gird looked from one to the other. He knew nothing of the lords' way of living, but he would expect no great tact from either of them. Curiosity pricked him. "What did you do?" he asked Mesha. The young man turned even more red than before, but his eyes twinkled. He started to answer, but his father waved him to silence.

"*What* does not matter, save that he spoke the truth as he saw it, and that was too stony a mouthful for the king's dignity to chew and swallow. I'll not have it a common jest, Mesha, I told you that: I'm proud of your honesty and courage, but it is wrong to make tavern gossip of your liege lord."

"He's not *my* liege lord," Mesha said, eyeing his father warily. "He will not take my oath—he said it—and thus—"

"I named you heir, and my oath binds you. Gods above, lad, this is no time for your antics! We are near enough the traitor's blade as it is." The younger man sat back, averting his face, and Marrakai turned to Gird. "I'm sorry, Gird: it is discourteous to withhold the tale, and yet I cannot let him tell it. Forgive me that discourtesy, if you will, and accept in its stead my support."

"Support?" Gird was still confused by the rapid exchange between father and son.

"Yes. You need weapons; I can supply some, and gold to buy others. You may need sanctuary; my woodlands are open to you, and my troops will not permit others to cross the boundary, if you should be pursued. If my peasants wish to organize—bartons, do you call them?—then I will make no objection. Your war will spread into Tsaia—it must, because our king is allied to yours—and you must win in both kingdoms if you are to win at all." He paused long enough that Gird wondered if he had finished speaking. "What I want is much like the gnomes asked of you: I want your assurance that you will do your best to organize a society *after* the war, in which order and law prevail—and that you do not urge your followers to massacres and destruction beyond the necessities of war."

"I'm doing that already," Gird said.

"So I had heard, but the stories were confused enough I was not sure which stories were of you, and which of your more fanciful selves. I can see for myself that you are not a man who hates easily, who would kill or rape for the pleasure of it; I know, from my own life, that war is a fire that cannot be caged in a hearth. This has already been bloody; it will be worse. I want to know I am supporting someone with a vision of peace beyond the war."

"Yes." Gird saw the futility of more words; how could he explain his vision? But his calm certainty seemed to convince Marrakai, who nodded shortly, and then stood.

"Gold I brought with me; you may take it as you go. Mesha will guide you to our borders, and introduce you to trusted men of my personal guard. Weapons—you will have to provide transport beyond my borders, but I can supply 250 pikes, whenever you can take them, and heads for the same number, if you have the poles."

Once again Gird found himself handling gold coins, this time in daylight, openly. Coins of both kingdoms were minted with the same values: Tsaian crowns were traded in Finaarenis often enough to cause no comment. He let his fingers rummage among them, enjoying the feel, and looked up to see a wary expression on Marrakai's face.

"They're so—heavy," Gird said. "And they feel—they feel so different against my skin. It's no wonder some men become misers, and want to touch gold all the time."

"Had you never felt gold before?" asked Mesha.

"Once. Someone tried to bribe me." Gird poured the coins from his hand back into the leather bag Marrakai had handed him.

"You cannot be bribed?" Mesha asked.

Gird met his eyes. "Between this gold and my heart is the memory of my daughter, raped and bleeding, her dead husband, my closest friend, struck down for nothing. I could be bribed, I daresay, but not with gold." The young man looked alarmed, but Marrakai smiled.

"I have trusted the right man, then. Fare well with that gold, and your memories."

Mesha, on the way to the Marrakai border, shared knowledge as precious as the gold he carried. "My father says I cannot tell you what I did to be banished from court and my inheritance, but he said nothing about what I *saw*." He explained the kinds of magicks the lords might use, and the tools needed for each, and the cost. He knew nonmagical counters for some of them, because the Marrakai, having lost their magicks early, had had to defend themselves from rival mages.

"It's said the best defense is a pure heart, but none of us has one pure enough, if we even knew what the gods meant by it. Men were not made perfect, I say, and come nearest perfection as fools when they deny their mistakes."

Gird nodded. "I've made plenty. It's a rare young man sees that, but you have a rare father."

"He's—different." Mesha walked on some strides before explaining that. "I knew that before I knew why; I could see it in the way others treated him. They're afraid of him, although they have greater powers."

"I hope for your peoples' sake that you are different the same way," said Gird.

Mesha looked at him, started to speak, and then, after several minutes of silence, tried again, his face turning red even as he spoke. "What is it like, being a peasant?" When Gird did not answer at once, he turned away, ears flaming, and hurried on. "The harpers sing of simple country joys, of the delights of the farm. My father's people seem happy enough, but they would not tell me, would they? I asked my father, and he said go and try it—but my tutor brought me back."

Gird thought at least part of Mesha's curiosity was genuine interest, something he had had no chance to pursue in a place he was so well known. He looked, to see the young man staring at the ground as he strode along.

"I liked farming," Gird said. "It's hard work, but I grew up with it; I was good at it. Have you ever milked a cow? Swung a scythe? No? Well, it came natural to me. Digging's no fun, but it has to be—plowing, planting, harvesting, all that's the good part. Seeing Alyanya's grace fill the baskets and barrels. Weather's weather, the same for all. What's bad comes from other men— from the lord taking more and more in field-fee every year, from death-fee and marriage-fee, from losing the right to gather herbs and firewood in the forest, all that. Having to take grain to *his* mill, instead of using our handmills, and having to buy ale from his brewery, instead of brewing our own. Going hungry, when there's no need but to pay the taxes, seeing our children thin and sick, while his plump younglings ride by on fat ponies, trampling our fields."

Gird looked over to see how Mesha was taking this; the young man's face was sober, neither angry nor disapproving.

"Never think the troubles of peasants are little ones, Mesha. Hunger gnaws at you; the hunger of your family, of your children, hurts worse than your own. To feel the winter wind strike through ragged clothes, to

SURRENDER NONE 437

have no fire in the house, and then the steward comes, smelling of meat and new-baked bread, to demand a special tax because the lord's courting a lady, or his lady has had a child, that's the bad part of it. Our lord, Kelaive, said peasants were lazy cowards: said it with his plump belly full of food we raised, with his well-fed soldiers around him, and we listened, shivering in a cold wind, or baked by summer sun. The steward said we should understand his greater problems. Greater than hunger? Greater than cold, than sickness, with healing herbs denied? Can there be worse than choosing which child shall have a crust of bread?" He could say no more; he felt the blood beating in his ears, the breath storming through his lungs.

"I'm sorry," Mesha said.

"It's all right," said Gird, blindly walking on.

"It is not, and it is not right that I did not know." Mesha sounded angry now, and not with Gird. "My father is a better man than that. I know it." But Gird heard the uncertainty in his voice.

"I hope so," he said, carefully making his voice light and easy. "As you will be."

"I would tell you of things my father has done, but I see now that it is not enough, not for me. I must *know* how our people live. He has asked me before to take over a village, but I wouldn't—"

Gird was surprised to find himself relaxed again. "You are young, Mesha. When I was young, I did not look for pain. I trained as a guard under that very steward—not looking, not seeing. My family—I thought they were fools, and I would show them all. After all, as a guard I ate their food, wore their clothes, brought money home—real coppers—to my father. And boasted of it. That's what hurt worst, later—that I had boasted, while my sisters and brothers went hungry and I was full."

"You—you do not hate me?" That was a boy's voice, a boy's naked desire to have an older man's respect.

"No. I do not hate you, or even—by this time— Kelaive. I hate what made Kelaive greedy and cruel, what made my father cringe before even his steward, what has kept you—who would, I daresay, be just and generous if you could—from knowing what you need to know." Gird smiled at the young man's worried face. "Be at peace, Mesha, while you can; long life brings enough battles to every man's door."

Once he crossed the border into Finaarenis, Gird began arranging transportation for the promised pikes. It would have been easier to sneak them across country before the summer's war erupted; the gnomes had advised him to go to Marrakai first. But he wasted little energy on regret. Before the leaves fell, all his pikes were over the border.

Chapter Twenty-eight

Meanwhile, his people told him, the war had hardly slowed for harvest. The king's army had split, one column going to Blackbone Hill, where they found only ruin. The other had started west along the River Road, but when it reached the lands controlled by Sier Segrahlin, the sier had refused the king's army passage. Rumor had it that the king and the sier would not mend their quarrel, whatever it had been, until an enemy army lay at the gates of Finyatha.

"We could arrange *that*," said Gird, laughing.

"Could you?" Arranha, to Gird's surprise, had come to Brightwater. He wore the same face Gird remembered, and seemed content to live with Gird's army and to endure the nervous glances of the other yeomen who distrusted anyone who had been a lord.

"We must someday," Gird said. "But having fought the sier, I would prefer not to do it again, if we can avoid it."

Arranha smiled at him. "You are acquiring prudence, then? I thought he might give you trouble. If his powers last, if he is not killed by a rock falling on his head, or lung-fever—"

"Can he be killed so? When my bowmen aimed at lords, the arrows flew astray."

"As I understand that form of magic—and it is not my own—one must know of the attack to defend against it, like a man holding up a shield over his head. If someone surprises him, he has only the strength of his bone."

Arranha had brought additional reminders and suggestions from the gnomes. "Not free gifts of information, you understand. I was told that they consider this to fall under the original contract; they're pleased with what you accomplished at Blackbone Hill."

Gird snorted. "They damn nearly got us killed at Blackbone Hill; they didn't tell me what they were doing, or that they'd been talking to the miners—"

Arranha laughed gently. "But you survived."

Another surprise of that homecoming was Selamis. After Gird had scolded him for not letting go his aristocratic background, he had seemed to fit in better. Once more, he was almost unnoticeable. Gird had begun to make use of his special knowledge, taking it for granted that Selamis would know which lord was related to whom, and what the news the traders brought meant. But until he left for Marrakai's domain, the other marshals had still been wary of Selamis. Several had come to him privately, and asked him not to make Selamis a marshal, or give him command. Gird had had no intention of doing that anyway. Now, however, they all seemed at ease with him. The marshals had discovered how handy it was to have someone able and willing to write and keep accounts—and someone whose face everyone knew, but who had no actual command. Selamis, Gird heard with some surprise, had stopped a street brawl—and he had patched up a quarrel between two of the newer marshals—and he had convinced the ranking merchants that the Brightwater yeoman-marshal was worth hearing.

"I thought you were crazy," Ivis said, on Gird's first night back. "A lord's son, troublemaker in his village—I know, you said he wasn't, but we had one in our village and you never did. Now—he's not that bad. You know what Cob's been calling him?"

Cob leaned over and punched Ivis. "Hush. Gird won't approve."

"What, then?"

"Luap," said Ivis, snorting with glee. "You know—the lords' own term for a bastard who can't inherit. Rank but no power. Cob's been calling him our luap."

Gird looked hard at Cob, who had the grace to blush. "It's not as bad as it sounds," he said defensively. "He's the one taught me the word, and made a joke about it. Spends all his time with us high-ranking folk, marshals and you, and has no command of his own. So I took it up, and he just grinned."

"Joke or not, I don't like it."

"Why not?" That came from the subject of discussion himself, who flung a leg over the bench, clapped Gird hard on the shoulder, and faced him squarely. "No one's ever liked the name my father gave me: you said yourself Selamis was a strange name. I am a luap: my father's bastard, and your trusted assistant in all but command. They'll tell you I've practiced, and learned fighting, but I'm still best at keeping accounts."

"Yes, but—" Gird shook his head, uneasy about something in the guileless, open face in front of him. If it didn't bother the man, it should. But this was one argument he lost; he found that many of the yeomen had fallen into the habit of speaking of "the luap" or "that marshal's luap." With Gird's return, and Selamis's return to Gird's side, it quickly became "Gird's luap." Gird still called him Selamis, though he sometimes slipped.

Later that fall, the lords changed their strategy. They had not been able to trap Gird's army all summer, and he had inflicted sharp losses on them. So they turned their attention ever more strongly to the land which supplied him with soldiers and supplies, forcing the evacuation of farming villages, burning them out if they resisted, stripping the countryside of resources. They had armed soldiers supervise the harvest, after which the fields were burnt; for hands of days the sky was streaked with smoke, and ash dusted travelers. Livestock they drove to the lords' fortified towns or dwellings, and any they could not confine under guard were slaughtered to feed the soldiers.

This work proceeded at different rates in various parts of the kingdom. Some lords were loathe to lose the produce of villages they had established, and counted instead on quartering more of their own soldiers among them. Some did not have the resources to reduce or move more than one or two villages that autumn. Those that survived could choose to try escape, or wait and hope that the coming spring would change things. But Gird found more and more refugees wandering, some seeking him and some looking for any safe place to spend the winter.

His own force controlled the valley lying south and east of Brightwater. This provided a large grain harvest—large, that is, until he measured it against his increasing needs. The town of Brightwater, all the little villages, his army—the grain would feed so many only if it were carefully managed, and by his own laws (he felt the teeth of a joke in this) he could not seize it. Some, of course, would not trust him, and yield it willingly. His own followers had sometimes less patience than he did; he found himself scolding his own as often as the others about the need for fairness, the evils inherent in bullying.

"It's not the same thing," Ivis argued, one dank late-autumn day, when a cold rain had blackened the falling leaves to a silent dark carpet. "If we're fair in distribution—in famine law—and all share equally, then it's not bullying. Bullying benefits the taker—"

"So it does—and so it does here." Gird blew his nose noisily on a bit of dirty fleece and rubbed it on his sleeve. His head was pounding, his ears felt full of water, and he was sure this was more than a fall chill. He could not feel this sick with a mere chill. "It benefits us—the takers—because then we have more to distribute fairly, and our own share—as well as others—is larger."

"But it benefits everyone."

"No. Not the ones who lose—who have larger shares now. Our way is right, Ivis, and better than theirs—I know that. But part of our way is how we do what we do, not just what we do."

"If we all starve it won't do them any good—"

"We aren't starving yet. Besides, while I won't bully

our people, I don't have anything against taking from our enemies."

"I thought you said we weren't ready to assault their fortified places."

"A grain caravan isn't fortified." Gird did not bother to explain, the way his throat was hurting, that he'd suggested to outlying bartons that they attack grain caravans. Some of them were successful—successful, too, at running off herds being moved from the deserted villages. More and more bartons began even bolder actions: ambushing any guard unit unwary enough to camp outside walls, or travel carelessly along the roads and trails. Clashes between small groups of rebels and small units of guards soon convinced the guards to move only in larger numbers.

Winter snows had always meant the end of military actions, but this winter brought no peace, only the slowing of movement. Gird, struggling to codify his laws with the help of Selamis and Arranha in Brightwater, sifted the reports from distant villages. Here a barton had ambushed a lord and two hands of guards, killing all of them and leaving that domain open; there two bartons had fought off a brigand attack, only to fall to the soldiers who came onto the scene when the battle was almost over. The merchants and craftsmen of Tarrho, a town about the size of Brightwater near the eastern border, had decided to overthrow their lord and declare their freedom—then the servants and laborers had rioted, overthrowing the merchants in their turn. Tarrho's small barton had tried to bring order, but had the trust of no faction; after bitter fighting that left many dead and the city without supplies of food, brigands rode in, looted everything, and set it afire. The king's messengers declared it was the fault of Gird and his rebels; the barton's survivors, who arrived in Brightwater before Midwinter, explained what had really happened.

"A good many of them brigand bands claims to be your yeoman, Gird," the yeoman-marshal said. "Nobody knows, for sure—I mean, if they aren't one of yours already, they don't. So they're afraid of your name, and the bartons."

"That's why we need to have our rules known," Gird said. "If they know we have rules, and what they are, and they see that we stick to them, then perhaps they'd trust us."

"Maybe." The yeoman-marshal did not look convinced. Gird peered at him.

"What do you think it would take?"

"Well—sir—I think they need something to see. We can say we have rules, but that's not enough, not for city folk used to looking up law in a book."

"Which is why I'm writing it down," said Gird, slapping the table and jostling Selamis's tools. He pointed at the younger man. "This is Selamis." He still would not say *my luap*. "He writes a better hand than I do, one anyone can read."

"That should help," the yeoman-marshal said, craning his head to see what was on the top sheet.

"It's very simple," Gird said. "I told him, we have to get it all into no more than four hands of rules—if people can count their fingers and toes, they'll be able to remember them."

And gradually, copy by copy, the first simple laws that later became the Code of Gird spread from barton to barton, even into the towns. Of necessity, these rules were suitable for a time of war; Gird could not possibly work out all the laws needed for trade and commerce in peacetime. But he was sure of his intent: cruelty was always wrong, and always harmed the community. Honesty and fair dealing were good, and helped it.

In the bitter cold and deep snows of winter, no army could march far. Stragglers came to Brightwater and the villages where Gird had some of his army encamped —starving, ragged, sometimes dying of cold even as they staggered to a fire. Gird himself traveled from one camp to another as best he could, trying to make sure that food and warmth were shared fairly among them. He knew, without needing the gnomes' advice, that he would have to win in this coming year—at least he would have to control most of the farmland, so that his people could grow food again. Otherwise his army would starve, and then the lords would win without a fight.

Food stores dropped lower and lower. His yeomen did not grumble much, seeing Gird's belt as tight as theirs. But the soft cries of hungry children pierced him as if they were all his own. He hardly saw Rahi or Pidi, these days; Giris had disappeared into the dust of war and he knew nothing of her. But the children in the camps were always with him, a reminder of what he was fighting for, and what would be lost if he failed.

It was in the first days of coming spring, uncertain weather that could bring thaw or hard freeze from day to day, that he took one of his cohorts out to seek food from one of the villages that had promised it the year before. They marched four days, south and east down the valley, across a ridge, and down another valley. Gird had sent a runner ahead. But instead of a yeoman marshal, or the barton, come to meet them, he found the entire village standing grim and unwelcoming in a snow-swept meadow nearby. They would not, they said, give anything—not one stone's weight of grain or handbasket of dried fruit. Begone, they said, before you bring the lords' wrath down on us. Gird nodded, and looked them up and down individually.

"What it comes down to, you don't trust me."

The cluster of ragged men and women said nothing. He hadn't expected them to admit it. No one met his eyes. Behind him, his cohort, even more ragged than the peasants from the village. He could hear their breathing, the rasp of pebbles under their feet when they shifted in place. He could feel, as if it were a hot iron, their rapt attention on the back of his neck. His own belly knotted with hunger; he knew theirs were empty too.

Gird tried again. "You agreed with us last year, you remember that?" He stared right at the headwoman, who stared at her feet. But she nodded, slowly. "Yes— you said you'd share your harvest with us, feed us, to help us win against the lords—"

"You didn't win." That voice was bitter, but low, from the back of the group. Gird could not tell which dark-wrapped head it had been, or whether man or woman.

"We haven't won *yet*," said Gird. "But we're a lot

closer—Lady's tears, did you think it would be all one battle? We told you—"

"'Twas a bad winter," said the headwoman, still avoiding his eye. "And them folokai got after flocks, near took the whole lamb crop."

"Tell 'em all, Mara," said the same bitter voice, louder this time.

"The lords come," the woman said. Now she looked up, and Gird could see a fresh scar across her face, the mark of a barbed lash that had almost taken her eye. "They said we had to have more than we could show. They said we'd been giving it to rebels, and they said they'd have no more of it. They took a child from every hearth—they come here, and where was you? Away, is all we know. No help. Help for help, that's what we say, and you've given no help."

"I'm sorry," said Gird. Now all the faces looked at him, all scarred one way or another, all bitter. All betrayed. He wanted to say *It's not my fault*, but knew that wouldn't help. They had protected many of the villages, in the past year: he thought of all those skirmishes and battles, the cost of it to his army. This year, given supplies enough, they'd control more territory, and fewer villages would suffer. But here they had not protected the people, and the people had changed their minds.

"They come oftener," the woman went on. "Check the fields, check the stores. Leave us bare enough for life, they do, and destroy the rest. Threaten the fields, if we give aught to rebels."

Could he promise they would not come again? Did he have the strength yet? Gird tried to think, but he wasn't sure. And a false promise would be worse than no promise. And if he told them how close he was to moving his lines on another league or so to the hills, would these betray him to their lords? Were they lost to him entirely?

"Gird?" That was Selamis, as usual. He had, no doubt, come up with some clever idea for saving the situation. Gird wished he could be properly grateful. He waved the man forward. Selamis muttered "The Marrakai gold?"

in his ear. Well, it was a clever idea. Probably not what the Marrakai agent had intended the gold to be used for, but it might work. Although—if they went buying food, to replace what he bought, their lords would surely notice *that*, too.

But he had to try. His mouth dried, thinking of all possible consequences. "We have a bit of gold we found—"

"Found!" That was not a promising tone. Someone spat juicily; it splatted on the rock a bare handspan from Gird's boots. "They told us you brigands'd have gold—and what they'd do if we come to market with it. You're no better than they are, that's a fact. Take our food for your army—they do the same. Both raids us, neither protects—not them from you, nor you from them, and there's not a hair of difference."

He could not, even hungry as he was, drive these folk farther. Like it or not, they were the reason for his fighting, and he could not harm them—yet. Could they use the gold at some market? One of them might pass for a trader, perhaps—someone robbed on the road? That was common enough. Would that pesky priest wreathe his magicks for them, make someone safe in the towns? He might, but he would want something for it, and Gird did not yet trust him.

"We're not the same, and I think you know it. But you've had more trouble than you could stand; I understand that. We won't take it by force, but you think of this—one child from each hearth *now*—do you think that will satisfy them? I lost more than that, before I broke free. You need not be as stupid as I was."

"You lost children?" Others shushed that voice, someone in a leather cloak, but Gird answered it, counting them on his fingers.

"My first two sons died of fever; the lord refused us herb-right in the wood. My wife lost two babes young, one from hunger and one from fever. My eldest daughter they raped; killed her husband. The babe died unborn. My youngest son they struck down; he lives. Another daughter they struck down, breaking her arm; I know not if she lives or dies. And my brother's children, that I'd taken in: two of them dead, by the lords' greed. And that's children. I lost friends, my parents, my brother. You ask yourselves: if they can take one child, will they stop there? Will all your submission, all your obedience, get you peace and enough food? Has it *ever* worked? You can sit here and let them take you one by one, or you can decide to fight back."

And he turned, glared at his own unhappy men, and marched them away. No one called him back, but he was not surprised to find three of the villagers following his cohort when they had gone some distance—and ready to join him.

Still, such incidents made him touchy. He was trying to stretch a small bowl of gruel one day, when two of his marshals reported that the villages to which they'd applied had refused to give or sell supplies, on the grounds that they'd been raided by brigands. His patience snapped.

"I am so *sick* of this!" It came out louder than he meant, and he'd meant it loud enough. Everyone fell silent, watching him, which only made him angrier. He lowered his voice to a growl, all too aware that his growl was audible farther than some men's shouts. "All this dickering, like a farmer trying to work down the price of a bull. All this haggling with thieves and bullies, craft guilds and village councils. Any idiot should be able to see what we're doing, and the worth of it. You'd think they *liked* being yoked and driven by the magelords, the way they kick and snap when we free them. The Lady of Peace herself would be driven to fury, the way they are. By the gods, we're trying to make them free, and make things fair, and they won't see it!"

"We might as well *be* brigands," said Herrak. It was not the first time he'd said something like that, and Gird disliked the whine in his voice. "The way they are, what difference does it make?"

"It makes a difference to *us*," said Gird. "There were brigands before; they never helped the farmers. If we're only robbers, all should be against us. What I can't see is why *they* don't see the difference."

"We need to win," said Selamis, smiling. He had the

honeysweet lilt to his voice that Gird hated; it worked on the crowds, most times, but it was not plainspeaking.

"What do you think, I should go to the brigands and recruit *them?*" He meant it as a jest, but the quality of the silence told him the others had thought of that before. Seriously. Selamis was paring his nails with a knife; he gave Gird that sideways look that Gird disliked.

"Some of them might be more like us than you think. Leaderless farmers thrown out of their villages—isn't that what you started with?"

Cob sat up straight and glared at Selamis. "We were not brigands. We may have been disorganized, lazy, filthy, and incompetent, but we were not brigands."

Selamis smiled at him. "That's what I meant. But your lord called you brigands, I'd wager." Cob was not mollified; he glowered at Selamis. But Ivis nodded.

"He did. And maybe—you were good with us, Gird, and if you found even another cohort by full spring—"

Gird mastered his anger with an effort. Late winter had always been the worst time for quarrels, even in the villages: empty bowls and enforced idleness made everyone irritable. "I suppose you have a particularly saintly brigand in mind for me to recruit?"

"I can't promise saintliness, but these last two villages both claim that the brigands near them muster a cohort or two. And there's a man who can guide you to their camp."

"I'll think about it." He would have thought about it between other things for a long time, but the next day a stranger came bearing an offer—written, Gird was surprised to see—from that very brigand captain. He had been a soldier, he said, and turned his coat when the war began. He had much to offer Gird, and would meet with him—in his camp. Gird talked to Arranha. The old priest shook his head and spread his hands.

"You put your life in the hands of Sier Segrahlin, Gird, and came out of that alive; if you want to chance this brigand I have no reason to think you'll do worse. Will you take a cohort of your own?"

"No. We don't have the food now to move them that far, and have them look like anything but starvelings.

That won't impress him or his men. I'll go alone, and wear my best boots."

"You might like to consider something." The big man's face was dark with more than weather; ancient dirt outlined every crease, and his heavy dark hair was greasy. But the dagger with which he was paring his filthy nails was spotless, its edge gleaming.

"I might," said Gird, accepting the dirty clay pot one of the other men offered without enthusiasm. Gods only knew what kind of brew would be in it. He sniffed as unobtrusively as possible. The big man's shrewd eyes missed nothing.

"If you want ale, we've got it. That's just water—spring water, from over there." His head jerked, and Gird's eyes followed, to a glisten of water among rank weeds across the clearing. Gird sipped, cautiously. It tasted like spring water, untainted by any herbs he knew.

"You're the peasant's new general, I hear," said the big man. He waved his hand, and a woman in a striped skirt, a pattern Gird had never seen, brought over a wooden tray. On it were a loaf and two wooden bowls half-full of stew. The stew had slopped onto the tray, making a gray puddle, but it smelled good. "Here," the man said, breaking the loaf and offering both chunks to Gird. Gird took the smaller; the man frowned, but passed him one of the bowls.

"I'm not a general," Gird said. He nibbled the bread: coarse and sour, but no worse than his own baking.

"General, captain, leader, whatever you want to call it. You're commanding them now—"

Gird nodded. No use hiding it, and by rumor this one would never tell the nobles.

"You need troops." The big man dipped his own chunk of bread in the stew, and stuffed his mouth full, then bit it off savagely. "I have troops."

Gird looked around at the men huddled at the cookfires, being served by the two women. "These?"

"Among others. More than you have, peasant general." The words were slurred with chewing.

"Then you want to join us?"

The man swallowed that mouthful, took another, and finished it before answering. "You need us. I think *you* want *us*."

Gird dipped his own bread into the stew and took a large bite. Better meat than he'd tasted since spring. "Good stew," he said. The man frowned at him, but said nothing. Gird looked past his shoulder at the others, and found eyes staring back at him that quickly looked away. He put his bowl down, and leaned forward, fists on knees.

"I need people who want to make a better land."

The man's eyes widened, and then he laughed, an explosive gust that sprayed spittle an armspan. "Better land! What kind of talk is that? Is that what you peasants think you're doing?"

"If it's not, we're nothing but outlaws."

"And you think that's so terrible? Simyits' fingers, Gird, we've been outlaws so long most of us don't know where we come from, and do we look so starveling to you?" The man pushed up his sleeve, and squeezed a meaty forearm. "See this? Show me the peasant with as much meat on his bones—not you, not anyone you know. Besides, you're all outlaws: the lords have a bounty on you, same as us."

Gird was aware of ears stretched long to hear their words. "We're outlaws because we had no choice. Because the magelords' law gave us no way to live within it. Given a fair chance, I don't know many as 'ud live outside the law. All I ever heard of outlaws, they was mostly men driven off their lands by some greedy lord."

The man hawked and spat, not too near Gird's feet. "Aye, it's unfairness drives most men to the woods. Some of us was stolen away young, or born to free fathers. But we're all free now, that's the thing. Free, and with no wish to put our necks under the yoke again."

"The magelords' yoke?"

"Any yoke." The man spat again, this time a hairsbreadth nearer. Gird thought it was deliberate. "See here, Gird, I'll be straight with you. We're free, and we want to stay free. You talk of a better land: just what do you mean? A better king? A better tax gatherer?"

Some of the others had come nearer. Gird had noticed before that they were well-fed; now he could see the glint of weapons in their hands. "No king," he said. "The mage-lords brought kings to our land; we had none before."

"Who told you that?" It was a long, lanky redhead well behind his leader.

"The gnomes," he answered. He would have gone on, but the collective intake of breath stopped him. "What's wrong?" he asked.

"You deal with *gnomes*?" The big man sounded both angry and afraid.

He was not sure how to answer. Would they understand that bargain he'd made, or would they fear gnomish incursions? "I learned of old times from the gnomes," he said finally. "And of law."

The big man's eyes slewed to left and right, meeting others and picking up control as visibly as a man picks up the reins of horses in harness. Gird felt a cold draft down his back. Something he'd said had changed their minds—and not for the better.

"I would not call it better for the rule of gnomes or gnomish men," said the leader.

"They seek no rule in human lands," said Gird. "They abide by their laws, which forbid that."

"But you learned law of them—and from them learned what you would do to make the land better?"

"It's obvious enough what would make it better. Honest dealing between one man and another, one craft and another. Fair judges. Taxes there must be, but fair, and no more than a man can pay and still live decently. From them I learned what is needed to make such things exist, what rules groups need."

The big man's teeth gleamed as he grinned. "Fair dealing, eh? And who's to say what's fair, with no king? The gnomes?"

Gird shook his head, pushing away his doubts. This was familiar ground, at least, and perhaps they would listen. "Not the gnomes; they have their law, for themselves. We need a law, a rule, for us—for all of us. We decide what's fair, all of us, in council—as our forefathers did, in the old days of steading and hearthing."

Talking fast, he explained more of the plan he and his friends had worked out. But he knew soon enough that they listened with only idle interest. When he finished, the leader was shaking his head.

"That's fine enough for farmers, and village bakers. Do you think the finesmiths will sit elbow-to-elbow with stinking tanners and pig farmers mired to the knees? And what about us? We have none of the crafts you mentioned. What do you think such as we will do, in your 'better land'? Do you really think I'll take up plowing and reaping, or Pirig will return to herding sheep?"

"Why not?" asked Gird, though he was sure he knew. "It's honest work, and without the magelords' inter-ference—"

"Because I'm not what you call an honest man," said the big man, leaning toward him. "You want honest, you go to the gnomes, and much good it will do us! Should I push a plow or swing a scythe, when my skill is with sword and handaxe? Will your better land have a place for soldiers?"

Gird raised his eyebrows. "Soldiers? Is that what you are?"

"Close enough. Strong men with weapons: call us brigands or soldiers, it matters not. Soldiers are but brigands in uniform."

Gird bit back the angry reply he wanted to give; this was no time to lose his temper, or his head might go with it. "Some are," he said in as mild a tone as he could manage. The other man sank back onto his rock. "But if life's to be better for all, *our* soldiers must be more."

"Your soldiers! Your half-starved peasants who know less about swordplay than the worst fighter in my band."

Gird smiled at him, with clear intent. "If your sword-play's so skilled, then why haven't you freed yourself of the militia's scourge, these past years?"

"It's not all swordplay!" yelled someone from the back of the crowd that had now gathered.

"Exactly," said Gird to that unseen voice. "Fighting a war's more than swordplay; my peasants may be clumsy with blades, but they know that much. You've tried your way, and it didn't work—now you want my help—"

"No!" The big man had jumped up; something had pricked him there, something Gird might use if he could figure out what it was. "I don't need anyone's help! We could sit here, fattening on the spoils of your war, *peasant*, preying on both sides. I offered *you* help, help you need: men and weapons. I don't need your pious words, your gnomish law."

"And what did you want, in exchange for your help?"

"Only what you give others who bring in troops for you: that you name me marshal—even high marshal—along with those others."

"I think not," said Gird, and bent down to pick up his bowl. As he'd expected, the big man came at him, seeing a clear target. As he'd planned, the bowl of cooling stew went into the big man's face, and he tucked and rolled away from the knife. His feet jammed into the big man's belly, and then he was up, balanced, fist cocked, as the big man choked and gasped on the ground. He kicked the man's knife away. The other men had started forward, but now ringed about him, uncertain.

"Soldiers must trust each other," said Gird loudly. "I must trust my marshals, and my marshals must trust the yeoman marshals, and those trust their yeomen—or nothing works in battle."

"I'll *kill* you," growled the man on the ground, between gasps.

"Get up and try," said Gird. Someone snickered, in the crowd, and he felt that others felt the same way. But the ring surrounded him; he could not have escaped if he'd tried. He didn't try, and they came no closer, more curious than angry.

The big man finally clambered up, his dirty face grim. "You—you should have killed me when you had the chance, fool!"

"It's not my way to knife a helpless man who is not my enemy."

"I am now," said the big man. He glared around the ring. "You—why didn't you hold him?"

"Why?" asked the same redhead who'd spoken before. "You started it. Take him yourself; he might hurt me." More chuckles, this time more open. The big man flushed.

"So I will, then, and you'll miss your fun after—I'll let Fargi take his skin. As for you, Gird, I hear they call you Strongarm, not rocktoe: if you have strength in that arm, use it."

"Aye," said other voices. "No more wrestlers' tricks: fight Arbol manlike, fist to fist."

Stupid, Gird thought, remembering the gnomes' acid commentary on human brawling. But stupid or not, his one chance of surviving this ill-chanced venture lay in the strength of his arms and the hardness of his fists. The big man crouched, then rushed him. Gird side-stepped, jabbed hard into the man's ribs, and took a glancing blow on his own. So that worked—if he ever saw the gnomish warmaster again, he'd have to tell him. *If you must use fists*, Ketak had said, *learn to use them well*. The big man was throwing a flurry of blows at him now, blows Gird took on his own arms, keeping them away from his face. His own punches were landing on shoulders, arms, and body; the other man was quick enough to protect his own face, ducking behind his fists like a river-crab behind its claws. He heard the other men mutter, call encouragement to their chief; he tried not to hear any of that.

Then the other man kicked out, catching Gird on the shin. He dropped his guard for a moment, and took a hard blow to the side of his head. For some reason, that made him laugh: the memory of his father once telling him he'd be safe in a brawl, having a head made of solid stone. He saw on the other man's face surprise and a touch of fear at his laugh—well, so he should be afraid. For all the big man's extra weight, he was no stronger, his shoulders not quite as broad—and *he* had eaten all his supper, and taken a kick to the belly.

Gird let himself grin. The man himself had chosen fists, when he might have skewered Gird with a sword— did he not realize he had chosen Gird's best weapon? The other man gave back, footlength by footlength, as Gird hammered him. He hardly felt the return blows; he had not had such a wholly justified excuse for pounding someone in a long time. In battle he had to be thinking of the whole, had to be looking ahead—in training he had to be watchful that he did not cripple one of his own. But now, here, he could let out all the frustration and rage of the past year, and whether he lived or died, he would have the satisfaction of pulping that arrogant face that thought itself too good to be a peasant.

Now the other man had given up attack, and was trying to defend himself from Gird's blows. Gird drove him back with two, three, four short jabs to the body, and then loosed his favorite swing, all his weight and shoulder behind it, to crack the other's jaw and drop him like a loose stone. The big man went down, twitched, and lay still. Gird flexed his hands, and sucked a cut. Nothing broken, though they'd be stiff in the morning. As his temper cooled, he could feel the lumps on his ribs that would be bruises, and the throbbing of his kicked shin.

The mutters around him now were awed. He looked deliberately from face to face, wondering if they'd attack him, knife him. He would not have a chance against so many. But although two knelt beside their leader, and someone brought a bucket of water, the ring widened, giving him space. He heard a complaint, quickly squelched, about a wager, and realized that some of them had gambled on the fight—he should have expected it, but he hadn't.

"Is that how you won your army, then?" asked one of the men. Gird shook his head.

"No. But I find it useful sometimes. My—Da used to say the only way to get an idea into some heads was to break them open and let the light in." Open laughter now, a little uneasy but genuine amusement. He felt slightly guilty for the lie, his father having been Alyanya's servant to the end, but his instinct said that letting these men know he'd ever been in the militia would be a mistake.

"An' now?"

Gird looked at the speaker, licked his knuckles again, and said, "Now what? He tried to take me, and I flattened him—that's between us. There's nothing between you and me unless you make it so—are you challenging?"

"Nay, not I. What I meant—d'you claim command of us?"

"He can't!" said someone behind him. Gird did not turn.

"No," he said slowly. "That's not what we fought about. You'll choose your own leader—for all I know, you'll choose him again."

"But about joining your army—"

Gird shrugged. "You heard what I said. I'm looking for men as want a better land later, and those that'll be honest yeomen now. Those that do can come with me; those that don't had better not. We may be skinny and hungry, but we do know how to deal with those as try to stick a knife in our back or steal from us." He nudged the fallen leader with his toe.

"We could kill you now," muttered one of the men just at the edge of his sight. Gird laughed, and saw the suprise on their faces.

"Killing's easy—you could kill me, and the magelords likely will. So then what? Killing me won't get you into my army. Make up your own minds; I'm going home." He turned, and stared hard at the men who had crowded close behind him. Like dogs, they wilted under a direct stare, and shuffled, making a gap for him to walk through. His back itched; it would take only a single thrown knife, a single sword-thrust. But he could not have fought his way out anyway. Behind him he heard a sudden argument, curses, and more blows ending in yelps. Someone else was taking over, he guessed, wondering if they'd come after him. He walked on, into the trees, not looking back. Looking back would do no good.

He had gone some distance when he heard running behind him on the trail. Gird slipped aside, crouching in the undergrowth to crawl back down parallel to the trail, and saw four men and the woman in the striped skirt jogging along. All were armed; the first watched the trail keenly, and stopped them about where Gird had left the trail.

"He can't be that far ahead of us," said one.

"Wait—I don't see—"

Gird stood up; they heard the rustling leaves and turned, clearly startled and alarmed.

"Why did you follow me?"

"We—I—wanted to join you," said the first man.

"I heard you let women join," said the woman.

Gird stepped out onto the trail, warily enough. "I do, if they're willing to take orders like anyone else. But we have rules you might not like."

"There's better than *him*," said the first man, jerking his chin in the direction of the brigands' camp. "I'd rather fight than steal."

Chapter Twenty-nine

Spring rains that year delayed everyone's movements. Gird drew and redrew his battle maps, revising his plans over and over again. His cohorts were most effective as he'd used them before, striking swiftly against small concentrations of the enemy, where they could outnumber them and control the surrounding country. But if the supply situation stayed as bad as it was, he could not do that another year; he would have to confront the lords' armies directly, win and control larger areas, to ensure the safety of food-producing lands and those who farmed them. Should he do that early, or late, after wearing down the lords' armies with raids? What would it cost him, in unsown grain, in next year's harvest?

In some areas, the lords were not allowing their peasants to plow and plant; in others, the farmers were guarded by soldiers. Gird shook his head at that. Why would they think he'd raid during planting time? His own forces protected an area in the Brightwater valley; over the winter he had urged all the farmers to form bartons and learn drill. Most of them had. Now his army protected them during planting, and he hoped they could protect themselves during the fighting season.

He began moving his army eastward, one cohort at a time, cloaked in the rains and leaving less trail than if he moved everyone at once. Ivis had found a good shelter two days' journey away, overhanging ledges that opened into a sonorous cavern. Gird himself went back and forth with the first two, then spent several days in Brightwater, settling accounts with Marrakai gold and hoping the town would be there when he got back. If he got back. Then he headed out with the last cohort, noticing that despite all his care, the tracks left by the others were as clear as any map ever drawn, one brown scrawl of mud after another across the new spring grass.

Roads, he thought to himself. *We'll need good roads, when it's over.* What they needed now was good luck, the gods' gift of miracles; remembering the other times he'd wanted miracles, and what he'd actually received, he was not willing to ask. He felt unusually grumpy; he had banged his knee hard on the doorpost going out of the barracks, and it still throbbed. The damp raw air seemed to bite into the bruise, rather than soothe it. He hawked and spat, catching an early fly; that cheered him.

By nightfall, he felt he'd been marching for half a year. His feet were damp and cold; he pulled off his worn boots and pushed his feet near the fire, rubbing them. A fine drizzle hissed in the flames; smoke crawled along the ground, making them all choke and cough. Gird thought longingly of the barracks in Brightwater—even that merchant's house, with the brazier in the center of the table, where several men could sit around it and talk. He would never think like a merchant, but he had gotten over some of his first astounded contempt. He told himself to be glad he had a good leather cloak; time was when the drips off the trees would have wet his bare head. But it didn't work. He was cold, stiff, damp, and without reason homesick for his own small cottage, with his own fire on the hearth, and his own family around him. He said nothing; the others were quiet as well, on such a dismal evening.

The next day's march brought them to the rock shelter and cavern, where most of his army was gathered. He plunged again into the familiar problems: how large to make the jacks, how many sacks of grain and dried fruit did they have and how long it would last, where the nearest sources of supply were. He was more than ready to pull off his boots and stretch out near one of the fires for a rest when Selamis insisted that he had to speak to Gird privately.

Gird followed his assistant deeper into the cave, annoyed once more at Selamis's fidgits. They didn't have time for such nonsense.

"Here." The younger man's voice, hardly above a whisper, halted him.

"I'm here," growled Gird, trying for patience. "What is it now?"

Instead of answer, soundless light answered him. Between Selamis's clutched fingers shone a rosy glow, steady as daylight. His eyes glittered in it, squinted almost shut. Gird, through his own shock, saw the taut lines of his face, the tears that trickled down those quivering cheeks. He looked down, terrified, at his own hands, but they were outlined only from without, by Selamis's light.

"What—" His voice broke, and he swallowed, tried again. "What *is* that—what did you find? Where?"

"In me." The man's hands spread a little; the light glowed steadily between them, sourceless, rose-gold: the light of spring evenings hazed with pollen, of autumn dawns among the turning leaves. Or of friendly firelight, welcoming. Gird shuddered, and fought back a rising terror.

"You're a—a *mage*?" And almost simultaneously, rage shook him. *You lied to me*, he thought. But Selamis's face showed more fear than even he felt, fear not of him, but of the light.

"I don't know." The man spread his hands farther apart, sighed, and the light vanished. Far back up the passage, Gird could hear Raheli arguing still about how many onions should go in tonight's kettle—so it was still the same world, the same time. "I told you," the voice went on in the darkness, "that I am a lord's bastard. But I didn't tell you—"

What this time, Gird wondered, remembering the many things his so-called luap had not told him until circumstances forced it. Would the man never find truth, and cease his lying?

"I was bred for magic." It came out in one gulping

rush. Gird said nothing, listened to Selamis's breathing as it slowed again. "They do that now—"

"I asked you about that," said Gird softly. It made sense, now. "Go on," he said, more gently than he might have a moment before.

"I—I had none they could find," his luap said. "That's why they sent me away—the real reason."

"You know," Gird began as delicately as his nature allowed, "if you'd just tell me the whole damn truth to start with, we wouldn't have these little problems."

"I know. But if you'd known—"

"*Damn* it, I'm not a monster!" His voice echoed off the walls, most monster-like, and then he had to laugh, muffling it as best he could. "Oh lad, lad, you are too old for these tricks. I can believe your heritage of blood, true enough, the way you never trust outright—"

"Trust is dangerous," muttered Selamis.

"And you trusted me with this." As always, the rage and mirth had passed quickly; he felt a pressure to reassure this frightened man, a certainty that he must be saved for them.

"It has to be the magic," Selamis said, his voice now steady but very soft. "But I don't know—"

"When?" asked Gird, rather than let him entangle himself in his uncertainties.

"Two days ago, when we came. Raheli asked me to come back here and see if anything threatened. I fell over a ledge, just beyond here, and suddenly felt I'd fallen a long way. It was dark—darker than this—utterly dark inside and out, despair and grief. What I fear in death, only worse."

Gird grunted. Darker than this end of the cave, after that uncanny light had left it, he could not imagine. Fear? They all feared, but Selamis was braver than he knew. He had a storyteller's gift of tongue, that was all, that let him talk himself frightened.

"Then I called on Esea," the luap went on. Darkness pressed on Gird's shoulders, so hard he nearly gasped. Esea! Was he so much a lord's son he still reached for their god in his trouble? "And the Lady—both of them. Light came to my mind—not as memory of light, but light itself, within." Gird felt the hairs prickling on his arms and neck as the luap talked. "Silver as starlight, cool. Then under the silver light flowers grew in a wreath, but colored as in sunlight, sweet-smelling: the midsummer's wreath, fresh-woven. But the light was silver yet." Gird's eyes filled with tears, and he felt them hot on his cheeks. Not magic, then, but the gods' gift? It had to be. "Then the light came, in my clenched hands, just as I showed you, and in the light I could see the symbols on the rock."

"The *what*?" Gird muted that roar even as it came out. Again the light bloomed in front of him, the same serene rosy glow, but this time the luap's face was calm.

"Come on. I'm supposed to show you. They said tell Gird."

"They?" He didn't expect an answer, and got none, following the luap over that ledge of rock to a bell-shaped chamber in the cave. In its center was a smooth polished floor, inlaid with brilliant patterns. Something glittered there, as if faceted, but the light was too dim to make it clear. Selamis stepped around it, and Gird followed, eyeing it doubtfully. Selamis stopped before a recess in one side of the chamber.

"There," he said.

The light in his hands brightened. Gird looked uncertainly at the wall, as the designs became slowly visible, then glowed of their own light.

"It's something about elves," Selamis said, when Gird said nothing. "And something about the rockfolk, and something about the gods—"

"And men," said Gird, tracing one line with a blunt thumb, for he did not put the pointing finger, the shame finger, on anything that might be sacred. Something rang in his head, a sound he later thought of as the ringing of a great bone bell, his skull rapped by the god's tongue—but at that moment he was conscious only of the pressure, the vibration shaking wit and body alike.

When it ended, he was flat on his belly on the cold stone, eyes pressed shut, and he heard Selamis's equally shaken breathing nearby. He opened his eyes deliberately, rubbed his palms on the stone, and then over his head.

"You might have told me you were the *king*'s bastard," he said, mildly enough he thought. Selamis had already come to a stiff crouch, the light still glowing between his hands.

"I should have." It was the first time he hadn't made an excuse. Whatever had happened had affected him, too. "I—I should have."

"You could be the heir. Bastardy's no bar, not with magic."

"I—don't have that much—"

"They should never have let you live." Gird heaved himself up, shook his head, and glanced cautiously at the graven designs. Now he could barely tell what they were, interlacing curves and patterns that meant more than any ordinary man could understand. Or should. He looked over at that mysterious pattern on the floor. "What's that?"

"I don't know."

"Huh. Bring your light, can you?" The light came, and Selamis with it, almost affronted to have Gird interested in something else. He could make nothing of it, even with more light and finally shrugged. "Well. Whatever that is, now we know what you are—do we?"

"King's bastard. Outcast. Light-maker." Selamis's voice was bitter.

"Do you want that throne, king's bastard?" The growl in Gird's voice made the chamber resonate. "Is that what it is, you'd like a peasant army to put you on your father's throne, let you rule instead?"

"*No!*" That howl, too, resonated, a reverberating shriek that seemed to pierce the stone itself. "No. I want—I just want—"

"Safety." Now it was contempt that shook the air.

"There is none." A mere whisper, but Gird heard it. He looked across the comfortable, cozy light into a face that had grown into its years. Almost.

"Right you are, lad. No safety, no certainty, and hell to pay if the others find out who you are. Is that what you see? Or do you also have the foreseeing magic?"

"Some, yes. Since the light came."

He would not ask. Pray to the gods for favor, yes,

and make the sacrifices his people had always made, but he would not ask the future. That was for the wild folk, the crazy horse-riders, and the cool arrogant lords who had no need to ask, because they knew.

"I will not be what he is," Selamis said. "I renounce my own name, and name myself luap—I swear I will not inherit that throne, that way, that habit of being—" It sounded like a vow to more than Gird, and Gird did not interrupt. "I am no true heir; I renounce it." But the light glowed on, even when he spread his hands wide.

Gird waited, then into the silence said, "Lad, you can no more renounce what the gods give—that magic— than I can the strength of my arm or the knowledge of drill that forced me into this in the first place. I've been that road; it turns back on you."

"I will not be the king!" shouted the luap, eyes wide.

"No. You will not be the king. But you cannot divide the king's blood from your blood, or the king's magic from your mind. You have only the choice of use, not the choice of substance."

"What can I do?"

Gird's belly rumbled, and he had a strong desire to hawk and spit. Clearly that would not do in this place; he didn't want to find out what would happen if he did. *Grow up*, he thought to himself, but to the luap said, "For one thing, you can guide us back out. I'm hungry." Then, at the indignant expression, he said "By the gods, you're half-peasant: use sense. You can be who you are, and do what is right. What's so hard about that?" Then he strode away, past the patterns on the floor that seemed to have tendrils reaching for his feet, and stumbled into the ledge. "*Damn* it," he roared. "Come on." His shin would hurt for days, he knew it, and there was too much to do and not enough time.

No one said anything when he came out of the shadows to the cookfire, the luap at his heels. The onions in the stew had everyone belching. *They can smell us in the king's hall, right across the land,* Gird thought, going out to the jacks, but he wasn't worried. He would have to think about the luap, but not now. Now he had to think about the army, and the king's army, and where would be best to meet them.

His one advantage was the willingness of the people to help him; he knew where the king's army moved, but the king's army must search for him. The king had left Finyatha again, and this time Segrahlin rode with him (so the word came), and every lord who could make magicks of any kind. And their well-fed soldiers, rank on rank of them, and their horsemen, who now had learned to armor the horses as well.

Thus he was in no mood to be cooperative when Selamis cornered him again the next night, and wondered, in too casual a tone, if Gird were going to name him a marshal in the coming campaign. Gird stared at him, momentarily speechless.

"I can't give you any command now," said Gird. "You can see that, I hope—"

Selamis glowered silently. When he was sulky, he *did* look almost aristocratic.

"And it's going to be damned hard to explain why I'm not. Blast you, you might have *thought*—"

"Would it have done any good to tell you sooner?" Gird did not like the self-righteous whine in that voice. Selamis had lied, and liars had no right to be self-righteous.

"Whether it would or not, you didn't. You didn't tell me, and didn't tell me, and if you hadn't had that—that experience—" He couldn't say it aloud, that Selamis had used magic, that he was a mage. It terrified him still, though he hoped he was concealing his reaction. The saying was that liars weren't much good at spotting others' lies. He hoped it was true.

"If I'd had no magic, it wouldn't have done any good to tell you."

"You think it's done *good*?"

"Well, I meant—if I didn't have magic, then my birth didn't matter—"

Gird rounded on him. "By the Lady's skirts, you're *still* thinking of the throne, aren't you? You still think your *blood* and your gods' cursed stinking *magic* give you some sort of right to power?"

"It wouldn't be the same—"

"You're right it wouldn't—because you're not getting within leagues of that throne, my lad. Forget that. You can make pretty lights, and your father is the Finaarenisian king. And that means *nothing*, not one damn thing, to me or any other peasant—"

"It means something to the nobles," said Selamis stubbornly. "You said that yourself. If they knew—"

"They'd slit your stupid throat. How can you be so *dense*? I've seen smarter stones, that had at least the sense to roll downhill. No. You're the king's bastard, and not alone in that, I'll wager. You've got a bit of magic, enough to scare girls with—"

Light blazed around them, and a cold fist seemed to squeeze Gird's heart in his chest.

"It scares *you*," said Selamis, furious, his handsome face distorted. "Quit pretending it doesn't. Admit it."

But there was rage and rage, and Gird's grew out of deeper roots than pique. He forced one breath after another out of stiff lips, and felt his heart settle once more into a steady rhythm. Without his thought, his powerful arm came up and smashed Selamis in the face. The light vanished, as Selamis measured his length on the ground.

"You stupid, stupid fool," said Gird, almost calmly. He squatted, made sure that Selamis was still breathing, then looked around. Could they be lucky enough that no one had seen the light Selamis made? No: there in the gathering dusk someone hurried toward them. Gird sighed, gustily. He ought to kill Selamis, quickly and painlessly, before he woke. He should have done it before, when he first realized the man had lied, and lied again. The fool had renounced his claim before the gods; that alone should have settled him. Now he, Gird, would have to explain everything, and it was the worst possible time to tell everyone that they had the king's bastard in their camp.

He was frowning over the supply rolls when he realized that Selamis was awake and staring at him. He glanced over and met a furious look.

"You hit me," said Selamis, in a hoarse whisper. His head probably hurt; the bruise on his face made it look lopsided.

"That I did. You showed me what you were."

"Why do you assume I'll be *bad*—?"

Gird put down the notched tally stick reporting the grain harvest in Plumhollow Barton and looked hard at Selamis until he wilted. "You know what you did: you lied, and lied, and lied again, and then lost your temper and used your magicks on me. Is that what any of us would want in a king, if we wanted a king at all? Should I believe that a crown will make you honest, teach you patience and mercy, give you wisdom? You seem to think you'll be a good king, better than your father. You might argue that it would be hard to be *worse*. But I'm not helping a liar, a lackwit, or a hotheaded fool onto a throne, where he can put his foot on my neck again. No."

Selamis's eyes closed, briefly, and the hand Gird could see stirred. Was he up to magicks again? But the eyes opened again, and the hand relaxed. "I'm sorry," he said. "I shouldn't have done that—"

"No more you should. Where'd you be if you'd killed me, eh?"

"I—I didn't think—"

"True enough. And does *not thinking* make a good king?"

"No." It sounded sulky, but then Selamis's face must have hurt a lot. A sigh, then, long and gusty. Gird didn't look up. "What are you going to do now?"

"I ask myself that," said Gird, picking up the single tally from the smithguild and running his thumbnail along the nicks. "I should have killed you, back when I first realized you were lying, and I definitely should have killed you last night. But I'll tell you what, lad, I'm a bad keeper of accounts, and you're good at it— and sometimes the best milker is the worst for kicking the pail."

"You'll let me live because I can read and cast accounts?"

"For now. But use those magicks just once more and you're dead."

"Did I hurt you?"

Gird's hand went to his chest before he thought; he glanced at Selamis and met his eyes. "Yes, and you might have killed anyone less stubborn. What did you think you were doing, eh?"

"I didn't really know—it just seemed as if I could press—"

"Don't. Don't even think about it. As soon hand a child of three Midwinters a pike to play with, and hope no crockery breaks."

"I'll be loyal," said Selamis, but it carried little conviction.

Gird put the tally down, and faced him squarely. "You will be loyal, lad, because I will break your neck myself if you're not. You have no more choices, no more room to maneuver. I've told the marshals what they must know; what you must know is that your life depends on my good word. And if they think you've charmed me, magicked my good word, they will kill you. And if you try charming one of them first, the same. If you find that too harsh, consider your father's way of dealing with traitors. We will kill you quickly as we may—but we will not let you loose again to misuse your talents."

Gird shifted east and south, taking two smaller holdings easily when the outnumbered garrisons fled, and winning another with a stiff fight: he needed the food enough to make the losses worthwhile. One of the fleeing lords had magic enough to poison the wells and blast a field to dry ash. Gird wondered if anything would ever grow in that gray grit. The others' fields might make a harvest, if nothing went wrong through the summer. The one that fought gave them, unwillingly, their first magelord prisoners.

The lord was dead; whether he had had magicks or not, he had fallen to pikes. His wife, several servant women, and the children—wholebred and bastard—had barricaded themselves into a wholly inadequate tower. Gird's yeomen battered the door down easily and dragged them out. Gird looked at the woman. But for her long robes, so unlike anything the peasant women wore, she looked like any other woman her age. She had borne children; she looked to be carrying another. The children were children: a stairstep gaggle, in all states from wild terror to infant placidity. The servant women were trying to gather them in their arms, soothe them.

Gird felt his head throbbing. He had never really thought about prisoners, and certainly not women and children. He had assumed that the lords would all be killed in battle, somehow, and he wouldn't have to worry about it. Now he did. The woman—the *lady*, he found himself thinking—looked as if she expected death. Or worse. The servants were unsure, glancing from the lady to his yeomen.

"She was about to stab the children," said one of the men holding her. Gird came closer. Brown hair, eyes with flecks of blue and green and gold. Her chin came up and she braced herself to face him.

"You didn't want to kill the children," said Gird.

"Better me than you," she said. Her voice was calm, almost toneless, the voice of someone who had given up.

"I'm not going to kill the children." What was he going to do with them? Where could he send them? But he was certainly not going to kill them; that was what lords did.

"What, then? Torture them for your amusement? I know what kind of games you peasants play." She had gone white, sure of what he would do; in the rage that followed, he almost did it, but one of the children broke loose from the servant women, and ran straight to him, pummeling his legs and screaming. Gird leaned over, wrapped the child in his arms and lifted him. Her? The mite had braids; did the lords braid boys' hair as well as girls'? The woman struggled frantically when Gird picked the child up, but quieted when she saw Gird hold the child carefully.

"Quiet, child," Gird said to the girl. He would assume it was a girl. She screamed all the harder, red-faced, tears bursting from under tight-shut lids. *"No!"* he yelled down at her. Silence followed; the child sniffed and opened her eyes. Remarkable eyes, blue flecked with gold, eyes he could drown in. He looked across at the lady. "You do not know the games peasants play, lady, if you think we torture children. It is the pain of our children that drove us to this war. Is this one yours?" White-lipped, she nodded. "A lovely child. I hope she has a long life." He set the child down and pushed her toward her mother. "Go, little one."

It was still no solution. He caught the sidelong looks, the low-voiced comments he was meant to overhear. As he toured the stronghold, learning more about fortifications than the gnomes had ever bothered to tell him, he wondered what he was going to do with them. The dungeon, when he found it, drove that thought out of his mind briefly, for there were the fates the lady had feared, knowing them too well. Gird swallowed nausea and rage, as his yeomen helped the pitiful prisoners up to daylight. He fingered the torturer's mask of red and black, wondering which of the dead men above had worn it. There on the wall was a larger version of the same mask, leather stretched over wood and painted in garish stripes. Beneath was a circle of chain, with barbs worked into the links. Behind him, his yeomen murmured, angry. Gird yanked the mask and circle off the wall, careful not to let the barbs prick his hands, and nodded to the other equipment.

"Take this all up and burn it. We'll leave nothing like this behind us." The words rang in his mind as he went back to his prisoners. *Nothing like this behind us* meant intent as well as material objects. He wanted to crush something, hurt someone, but that was what had started the whole mess.

The lady was crouched, with her children, in a corner of the outer wall, with a jeering crowd around her. They fell silent when they saw Gird, and he waved them away, but for a few guards.

"I think you know what I found below," said Gird. She would not meet his eyes, this time. She had known. Had she condoned, even encouraged? "I found the mask, the barbed chain—"

"I told him," she said, looking at her clenched hands. "I told him we were never meant to follow Liart. That our only hope was Esea's light, and if it failed, we should greet the long night peaceably. But he would not. He would not admit his powers failed, that his children might not have all he had been given. I told him nothing was forever, that men rose and fell like trees, like—like wheat, even, brief as that is. That we could not win safety this way."

Gird reached out and took her hands in his. "Look at me. Yes, like that. Did you, yourself, kill anyone? Did you send anyone to the torturers?"

Her head shook once, side to side; she said nothing, staring into his eyes with those multi-colored eyes of hers. Was she trying to charm him? Could she?

"Did you truly try to stop him, your husband?"

"Yes. But he would not listen."

Gird released her hands. "Well, then: you listen to me. If I find you've lied, that you helped with that filth, your life is forfeit. Otherwise, it depends on you. Will you redeem the evil your husband did?"

Her eyes widened; she had not expected that. "How could I do that?"

"Come with us, work to heal those who are hurt."

"I have not the healing gift—and besides, I am—" she gestured at her belly, just swelling her robes.

"Where do you think peasant women go, when they're thrown off their land and are pregnant? As for healing gift, if you can boil water and wash bandages, you will earn your keep—though I admit it's little enough, until this war's won."

"And I will be the slave of slaves, for your delight?"

His mouth soured. "No, lady, I would be delighted to have everyone safe at home, no one a slave to anyone."

"And if I don't agree?"

Gird shrugged, and stood up. "I suppose we can turn you out, chase you away from our camps, and let you find your own keep, if you can. Can you?"

"Not as I am," she said. "All right. I will take your offer." The unspoken *for now* seemed to hang in the air around them. Gird had the uneasy certainty that this would not be the last such problem, and he was not at all sure he had found the best solution.

The next day, he watched the lady—now garbed in the more practical peasant clothes—and her children set off with those of his wounded he was sending back to the rock shelter. He had had to argue harder than he liked with his own yeomen, to extract their promise to treat her fairly. The children they would have taken happily; he sensed that they wanted him to kill the lady, but feared to say it. Selamis—the *luap*, he reminded himself—had not offered his opinion, and Gird had not asked it. He had returned to being the efficient keeper of accounts and carrier of messages.

One of the new problems of this year, with the larger army was his inability to see what was going on across the field of battle. Now he knew exactly why the soldiers' officers rode horses: they were above much of the dust and all the bobbing heads and weapons. This count's stables had held many horses. Some of them were dead, but the others could be useful. He could barely remember how it had felt to ride that mule, back in his youth, but it would have to do.

The stables yielded five live, unhurt horses. Two were tall and leggy, one was a pony (*for the children?* Gird wondered) and the other two were nondescript animals of middle size. He was not even sure how to saddle and bridle them, but some of his ex-soldiers were, and quickly had all but the pony tacked up. These experienced riders mounted and tried the animals out. One of the tall ones began to fret and prance; it was lathered on the neck almost before it was ridden at all. The other tall horse seemed quieter, but on the second circuit of the courtyard went into a fit of bucking and dumped its rider in a corner. Gird knew he didn't want either of those. The other two horses were more obedient, but his experienced riders said neither was suitable for a novice. He could not afford a broken leg right now, Gird told himself, so he'd better keep using his legs for what they were meant for: walking. Maybe he could stand on a rock?

Two days later, as he was moving the army north again, he saw an old gray carthorse plodding through a narrow wood. One of the food scouts waved, hopefully. Meat? Gird waved back a negative. He really would like a horse; he had always wanted to ride a horse. Not someone's trained warhorse, but a plain old horse that would plod along, and let him learn without breaking his legs for him. He had no way to catch a horse, but he wasn't going to eat his desired ride, not yet. Besides, they still had meat from the horses back at the count's stronghold.

At the midday break, an old gray horse grazed only a few pike-lengths from them, ripping up the grass with delight. Was it the same horse? Gird could not tell. He could tell one cow from another across a field in the fog, but horses were horses to him, with color and size their only distinction. This one had the usual big dark eye, a pink-freckled nostril fluttering with each breath, burrs in the long hairs of its fetlocks—he realized that the horse had come a lot closer. He had to look up to see its back, its slightly swayed back. Ought to make it easy to stay on, he thought. The horse blew a long slobbery breath over his leg, mumbled the edge of his boot in its lips, and sighed.

He could probably grab its mane and hang on long enough for someone to get a belt or something around its neck. The horse's lips brushed his arm, gently as human fingers, and softer. Gird reached up to a tangle of yellow-gray mane that felt surprisingly silky. The horse yanked its head up, and Gird came to his feet. Everyone was watching him, silently. He looked at them, shrugged, and stroked the horse's neck. It stretched its head out, shook it sideways, and gave an elaborate yawn, showing a mouthful of heavy, slightly yellow teeth. Gird stroked its shoulder and barrel. He loved the feel of a healthy animal, and although this one had looked dirty from a distance, the coat felt sleek and clean under his hands. It must be someone's stray.

He found himself atop the horse bareback, holding the rope of an improvised halter, hardly aware of the sequence that put him there. The horse had sidled this way and backed that way until Gird had had to climb on a rock to keep stroking that sleek coat; he had wanted to keep stroking it. Then in some way the horse had indicated an itch, a flybite, on the opposite shoulder, and Gird had leaned across to scratch it, and there was a fly biting lower down, and he had leaned farther—and found himself lying belly-down across the horse's back. It had stood motionless until he made the obvious move of throwing a leg over.

It was much easier to see, from up here. He could see all the cohort beside him, and the ones ahead and behind. He could imagine how much easier this would make guiding a battle. But he had never imagined the effect of horseback riding on the unaccustomed rider. At first he was tense, then he relaxed and enjoyed it, and then—all too soon—his muscles and tendons began to complain. About midafternoon, he couldn't stand any more of it, and managed to slide off—which was harder than he'd supposed. His feet burned and tingled unpleasantly, until he walked the blood back out of them. The horse followed Gird as if he were tied, although Gird had forgotten to take hold of the rope.

He climbed on again the next morning. He was stiff in places he had never been stiff, but the horse had found another rock to stand beside. His legs loosened up quickly; he found the rocking motion pleasant. Something about the feel of the gray horse between his legs gave him confidence. He wondered if this was what the horse nomads felt, what made them raiders and not farmers. Of course, they rode real horses, war horses, and not gentle old carthorses. The back under him heaved a little, and Gird grabbed for mane. Surely the horse had not heard his thought, and taken insult! He tried to think of something complimentary, just in case, and was rewarded with a relaxed back and springy walk.

His original intent, in coming north again, was to intercept the king's western movement at a site where the ground gave him advantage. The king, however, had recognized that same situation, and put his army to a forced march to intercept Gird's. Unluckily for Gird, the runners who would have brought him this information were captured. If he had not chosen to ride, for the first time, out beyond his scouts, he would have led them into a trap. As it was, the gray horse stopped with a snort, planting its feet firmly in the road, and refused to budge. When Gird tried to swing off, it whirled, nearly unseating him, and then started smartly back down the trail at his first experience of a trot. He clung to the mane desperately, afraid to fall at that speed; when it slowed, where his forward scouts were, they had taken that return as an alarm.

"I don't know," Gird said, glad to slide down now that the horse was standing still. It looked past him back up the trail, and snorted. "It saw something it didn't like; animals can smell and hear better than we can."

His scouts slid forward, to reappear not long after with word of a large enemy force lying right across the route Gird had planned to take. Gird looked at his maps again. Any other route to the same ground would take them several more days, and the enemy might easily trace them and reposition themselves. Straight ahead he might get a slight advantage from a slope, but he'd have to engage in woods where the pikes were far less handy than swords. He frowned. Back down their trace a half-day or so was a passable field, a large natural meadow, backed by a steep forested ridge behind several lower hills. They had come the long way through it, to avoid the hills, but he could hide several cohorts back there.

It was the best he could do, and it would do only if the enemy decided to come after them; they could not sit for long without starving. He gave his orders, and then had someone give him a leg back up onto the horse. Old worn-out horse it might be, but it had saved him, and maybe the war. He stroked its neck, as he waited for the last cohort to reverse. Strange that an old carthorse should be so willing to carry an untrained rider, and so gently, but he would be foolish to question such good fortune. The horse heaved a huge sigh, and butted his foot with its soft nose. Gird scratched its withers, and his own head, contented for the moment.

His army reversed and marched back down its trace without attracting immediate mounted pursuit—the only kind Gird feared. They were on his new-chosen field a little after midday. It was not as good as he remembered: there were bramble patches near a small creek, and muddy areas under the fresh green grass. But such as it was, he had no choice. He moved his army back, under the edge of the trees, to encamp, sent his scouts well out, and set to work to improve the site as best he could. By nightfall, he had word that the enemy was coming, on more than one trail. The largest group followed his own trace, but another was moving in from the northeast, on one of the alternate trails. So, he thought. He had been right—no escape that way, even if he'd tried it.

Chapter Thirty

In the predawn stillness, he could hear a single bird calling from far away, high on the hill's slope. His army slept. As quietly as he could, Gird made his way past the banked firepits, past the line of sentries, to whom he nodded without speaking, and started up the hill. Here, beyond the camp, he walked through layers of fresh summer scents, the night smells of open country. A patch of pale tiroc flowers poured out heavy sweetness; in the hot daytime sun, they hardly had an odor. Down from the heights came a waft of cedar, a sharp bite of wild thyme. A goat had brushed against the bushes here; its sharp pungency banished the other smells for a moment, until he'd climbed past it.

Ahead, the hill was dark against the early dawn glow. Something rustled in the bushes, a frantic frightened scurry as some small animal fled. The bird called again, closer now. It was no bird he knew, with that exquisite rippling flow of music. Gird looked back. Light had seeped into the upper sky, and far to the west the land began to show its shape, the hilltops their color. He climbed on, very aware of the smells and sounds, the feel of the cool air on his bare arms, the texture of the leaves that brushed against him, the feel of the stone or soil beneath his feet.

He came to the hilltop sooner than he expected. Behind, below, the ragged and smelly army lay hidden in shadow. He heard a distant clatter of pots, and wondered what the cooks would find to put in them. More roots and herbs, no doubt, and they still had two sacks of meal. Not much for a whole army. But morning hunger had been part of his life from childhood; farmers were always out working at dawn. He had this brief, private moment before the day's cares.

Far over the rim of the world, the sun rose up, the light by which truth could be seen, as Esea's priest had named it. Against the low slanting light, Gird saw the myriad furred tufts of grass, rose-gold, forming a dancing curtain of rose, veiling the sun's impossible brilliance, transmuting it to grace and delicacy. He stood bemused, as he had once long ago on his farm, on that silver starlit evening. All was gold now, gold and rose together, shifting veils softening piercing brilliance; the scent of it rose up around him, a column of rose-gold incense. He had just time to think *This is a vision*, when the hill slipped out from under him and he hung suspended in gold and rose draperies. Now he looked west again, over the land new-lit by the sun, where soft gold light filled the valleys like wine, and a harder radiance chiseled the hilltops into clean, unblurred beauty. Despite the haze of gold, he could see far, to the distant mountains on the edge of Finaarenis. He had dreamed of them as cold, gray, uncaring crags, but now they stood serene and gracious, great castles awaiting their lords. He seemed to see within them, to the arched and echoing halls where the rockfolk harped and sang and crafted jewels and gold into treasures worthy of such castles. Now he looked north, across the light, to the great river and beyond, seeing at a glance all its laughing little tributaries, and the great loom of the moors and the broad steppes. There the horse nomads roamed, with bright embroidery on their boots, narrow streamers blowing from poles by their tents, herds of shining horses. Above them romped the Windsteed, flaunting a cloudy tail, and broad across the grassland the Mare of Plenty ranged on tireless hooves. Behind her, grass sprang tall and green, and her hoofprints filled with clear water.

He would have been frightened if it had been possible; he retained enough of his wit to know that. But it was not possible. He lay quiet in the gold and rosy veils, looking where he was bid, seeing the land as it was, as the gods saw it, as it could be: in the broad light of day, peaceful villages of farmers, orchards restored and fields once more fertile. Flocks of sheep on the hillsides, herds of cattle in river meadows. A market fair, in some town that might be built where a burnt village had been, with fair measures given, and fair weights enforced. Children splashing in a shallow ford, a woman riding a horse, a bright helm on her head, cottages with tight roofs and mended walls, rows of bright flowers. The vision pierced his heart, brought scalding tears to his eyes. This—he had almost forgotten —this was what he wanted, not an obedient army, helpful farmers, even victory in battle, but this peace, this plenty, this justice.

With the tears came his release from the dream. He felt himself falling, but slowly, like goosedown or a dandelion tuft; felt gentle arms around him; heard a murmuring voice he could not quite follow. Flower petals drummed feathersoft on his bare arms, against his face, drying his tears, and when he came to himself, he was standing in a drift as white as snow in the broad morning sun. He reached his arms into the cool petals, lifted them, buried his face in them. Alyanya's sign, it had to be—but beneath the fragrance was a faint bitter tang of cold wet earth in autumn. Promise and warning, then, and he but a peasant. Laughter rang about him, so joyous that he smiled before he realized the sound had been within him.

"Dammit!" he burst out, unthinking. "You won't ever make anything simple!"

And the voice that answered him then was cold, clean and precise as starlight.

—No. I did not make anything simple.—

Gird's knees gave way, and he fell into the flowers. *That* was not Alyanya, by any reckoning, and he could not pretend to himself not to know who it was. *Ask for a word from the gods*, he thought crazily, *and beware—*

But the knowledge he had asked for without really wanting it was pouring into his head, overfilling it as if someone stuffed a sack with wool.

Promise: it was possible to win that peace for his people.

Warning: it was not *his* peace.

His fault? he wondered.

No answer, only certainty. All the symbols the priest had taught him, all the gnomes had shared of their lore, flickered through his mind as quickly as the counters on a trader's account board, a rapid clicking that ended with the crashing finality of stone falling onto stone. As it was now, as reality lay, that peace was possible, but he was forfeit.

He had thought he did not care, until he knew it was certain. Now, in a silence he realized was more than normal, he lay face down in Alyanya's flowers and had leisure to consider if he meant in truth what he had said so often. I would give my life, he'd said. I will risk, he'd said. I could be killed as easy as you, he'd said to frightened yeomen.

But that had been *risk*; the spear might thrust in his gut, or not. The sword might slice another's neck. So far it always had been someone else, and he knew now he'd half-expected it always would be.

Now . . . *certainly* die? Never enjoy that peace? Never sit with his grandchildren around him, telling his tales of the old days?

He was suspended again, this time in the vast caverns of his own mind: cold, darkness, fear beneath him, and nothing at all above. If he fell *now* nothing would slow his fall; he would not land in Alyanya's flowers. His own mind—he knew it was that, and no gods' gift of vision—painted all too vividly a picture of the land after his fall. No peace, but the ravages of the magelords, the scavenging of brigands. More dead bodies bloated in the fields for crows to pick clean; babies and children and young and old: he saw all their faces. Innocent beasts, cows and horses and sheep, lame and wounded, wandering prey for folokai and wolves. And he saw his own death then, the death of an old man, bald and feeble, when he could no longer forage from his hideout in distant caves: he fell to folokai, and the crows followed.

Death either way, then. *It should be easy*, he told himself fiercely, *to buy that peace with an early death*. It was not easy. On his tongue he tasted the ale he would not drink, the roast he would not eat, and in his hands he felt the warm bodies of the children—o, most bitter!—he would never hold. *It is not easy!* he screamed silently into silence. His own mind replied tartly that nothing was easy, nor ever had been—and he opened his eyes and blinked against the snowy petals.

It was not easy, but he had done other things that were not easy. He had seen his mother die, and Mali that he loved, and his daughter near death at his feet. He had seen the best friend of his youth trampled under the lords' horses; he had seen wells poisoned and fields burnt barren. He took a deep breath, holding all these things in his mind, all the pain he could remember, all the love he'd had for family and beasts and trees and land—love that no one else ever knew, because he could not speak it. He tossed it high, with his hope for life. And felt it taken, a vast weight he had not known he carried.

The petals vanished, though he could feel their softness yet, and their perfume eased his breathing. He was all alone on the hilltop, though he heard someone crashing through the bushes on the upward trail.

"Gird! Marshal-general!" One of the newer yeomen, to whom that title came naturally. Gird took a breath, and hoped his face did not show all that had happened.

"What?" he called back, hearing in his voice a curious combination of irritation and joy.

"They're coming! They're already out of the wood!"

Gird swung to look north, and they certainly were. Horsemen first, the low sun winking on polished armor and bit chains, gleaming on the horses themselves, gilding the colors of banners and streamers and bright clothing. Some of those were surely magelords. Behind them, shadowy in the dust already beginning to rise at the edge of the wood, were the foot soldiers, rank after rank. His mouth dried. How many hundreds did they have? He had thought he had more—one thousand, two thousands, three—. The horsemen halted just far enough out on the meadow to let the infantry deploy behind them. Gird searched the wood on the far slope for the archers they would surely have sense enough to send out in a flanking movement. His own archers were supposed to be up on the end of the ridge, guarding against archers getting into his rear. He hoped they were alert. He had no fear of the horses or foot soldiers getting back there; the ridge behind him to the south was safe as a wall.

Below him, he heard his own army coming into order. He started down the hill, hoping the enemy had not spotted him atop the hill. He put his hand up to his hair, thankful that he hadn't put on his salvaged helmet yet.

At the foot of the hill, the gray carthorse stood as if it were waiting for him. Someone had found a saddle for it, and a bridle. Even so, the horse had positioned itself beside a rock. Gird climbed on, wondering even as he did why he found it so natural that the horse was making itself useful. Cob came running up with his helmet, and offered a sword. Gird shook his head. He hadn't learned to use a sword yet, and a battle was no time to try something new. The horse was new enough.

His cohorts had formed; he rode past them, checking with each marshal. The faces blurred in his eyes; his mouth found the right names by some instinct, but only Rahi's stood out distinctly. She gave him her broad smile, and the gray horse bobbed its head. Rahi's cohort laughed. He wanted to tell her, and no one else, what the god had told him, but he could not. That kind of knowledge had to be borne alone. He noticed, without really thinking about it, that over half of his yeomen had managed to find a blue shirt to wear; it was beginning to look like a uniform.

For a time it seemed that the enemy might simply stand on the far side of the field and stare at them, but after a time they moved forward. On the north, the broad-topped wooded ridge sloped directly into the meadow, but on the south, Gird's side, three distinct low hills lay between the sharp southern ridge and the more level grass, with the sluggish creek running east to west along it.

Gird had done what he could in the limited time he had to make this ground as favorable as possible. He had archers on the north face of all three hills, as well as the blunt end of the southern ridge. He had had pits dug, in the mucky ground near the creek, lightly covered with wattle and strewn with grass. This would, he hoped, make both cavalry and foot charges harder, and prevent easy flanking of his troop. His main force was arrayed before and between the two more eastern hills; the western hill seemed undefended, but in addition to archers had several natural hazards. Against the lords' reputed magicks, he had no defense but Arranha's comment that a mage could not counter what he did not expect. He hoped they would not expect the small, doomed, but very eager group that he had left well hidden on the south face of that north slope, directly in the enemy's rear, with orders to stay hidden until the lords were busy with their magic elsewhere.

Now the king's army moved; for the first time, Gird saw the royal standard that he had heard about, a great banner that barely moved in the morning breeze, then suddenly floated out, showing its device. Gird had been told it was a seadragon; by himself he would have thought it was a snake with a fish's tail. Each of the lords with the king had his own banner, his or her own colors repeated in the uniforms of the soldiers—and, if the gnomes were right, his or her own separate battle plan. That was supposed to be another advantage to his side. They looked pretty enough, like the models the gnomes had shown him: one hundred all in yellow and green, then two hundreds in blue and gold, then a block of orange, and a block of green and blue. Gird assumed that the lords were in the rear, those mounted figures in brilliant colors that seemed to glow with their own light. Even as he watched, he saw bright-striped tents go up, servants hanging on the lines. Smoke rose from cookfires newly lit. For some reason, that show of confidence infuriated Gird. *Win it before you celebrate it*, he told them silently.

The cavalry screen drew aside on either flank, and the foot soldiers advanced. Most of them still carried sword and shield; some units had pikes; a few had long spears. Gird frowned; those could cause him a lot of trouble. But watching them advance, he realized that they were not accustomed to that extra length. Evidently someone had decided to make a weapon that would outreach his pikes, but the men carrying them had not had enough drill. Behind the swordsmen and pikemen came the archers. Over the winter, Gird had tried many versions of a shield that would stop arrows but be light enough to carry, and easily dropped when both arms were needed for the pike. Nothing worked perfectly. His foremost cohorts had small wooden shields that might protect their faces from arrows near their utmost range, but most trusted to their stolen—no, salvaged—helmets and bits of body armor.

The first enemy flights of arrows went up; Gird's marshals shouted their warnings, and all but the stupidest looked down. The enemy made a rush forward, discovering a moment too late the pits Gird's army had dug. These were not deep enough or large enough to keep the enemy back, but they slowed the rush just as the archers, following it, came within range of Gird's archers.

More angry than hurt, the enemy foot soldiers floundered through the mud, hauled themselves out of the pits and flung themselves on at Gird's unmoving cohorts. The enemy lines were no longer lines, and behind them their own archers were falling to Gird's. They did not care; they looked, to Gird on his old gray horse, like any young men who have made fools of themselves in public. Their officers, bellowing at them from the rear, didn't seem to have much effect; a second and third line staggered into the pits, tried to jump across and failed, and fought their way out, to storm up the gentle slope toward Gird's cohorts.

The marshals watched Gird; he watched the straggling but furious advance. Those few seconds seemed to stretch endlessly, as if he had time to notice the expression on every face, whether the oncoming eyes were blue or grey or brown. Then the first ones reached the mark he had placed, and he dropped his hand, with the long blue streamer that served as their banner.

His cohorts moved. One step, two: cautious, controlled, their formations precise, he thought smugly, as any gnome's. Where the king's soldiers had expected last year's sharpened wood stakes, they met instead the steel pike heads that Marrakai gold had bought. The first died quickly, almost easily, a flick of the pike it seemed, from where Gird sat on the gray horse. He knew better, from having been there himself. Then the ragged lines caught up with each other, and the slaughter began.

Pikes outreach swords, but swordsmen and axemen can form a shield wall hard for pikes to breach, if all are brave. Whether it was courage, or the kind of magicks Gird had seen at work at Blackbone Hill, the soldiers of the king were brave. At first Gird's cohorts advanced, step by step, down that gentle slope, pushing the king's men back into the trampled mud and treacherous pits. Then the king's cavalry swept east, toward Gird's right flank, and back down the near side of the creek, avoiding the pits he'd dug at that end of the meadow.

This was not what he'd hoped they would do. He had hoped they'd be seduced by the apparent gap on his left flank, between that and the westmost hill. It should have looked like an easy way to get right round behind him. But apparently they'd been looking for something more quick than easy. And if he didn't do something—quickly—they'd be on attacking his flank with only the archers uphill to hinder them.

The gray horse seemed to understand this almost as quickly as Gird; he was picking his way neatly but rapidly across the gap between the center and the eastmost hill without jolting his rider at all. Gird looked around him. There—that cluster of bright colors up under the trees must be the lords and the king. So far they'd done nothing magical, but he had no doubt they would. And there, across the creek and coming his way, were the enemy cavalry.

Gird bellowed loud enough that the gray horse flattened his ears; the nearest cohort marshals turned, and caught his signal, then saw the rushing horses. He would have wheeled the gray horse around, but the gray horse leaped onward, straight at the oncoming cavalry. Gird hauled on the reins, to no avail.

"I know I said it would be nice to slow them down, but we can't—one horse—one rider—" Was this to be his destined death, charging uselessly an entire wing of cavalry? But they were almost on them; Gird shrugged, and swung the pole his blue banner was tied to.

Pole and rag took one horse in the face; Gird nearly lost the pole, and his seat, but managed to keep both, and duck a swipe from a curved blade. The gray horse swerved under him; he grabbed for mane and hung on. All around were horses, most of them swerving aside and one frankly running backwards before it slipped and fell, rolling on its rider.

Then they were in the clear, Gird with his banner and the gray horse with a disgustingly smug cock to its ears.

"I want to go back," Gird said between his teeth, as if the horse were a recalcitrant child. It shook its head, blew a long rattling snort, and picked up an easy lope back toward the battle. He saw a dozen or more horses down, some with arrows in them. He saw the back of the enemy cavalry, trying to charge again and again into two of his cohorts of pikes. The armor on the horses, heavy padded canvas, would have protected them from swordstrokes of other mounted fighters—not from pikemen on foot. Gird wondered if they realized that, or simply never thought of it. He felt the gray horse tense under him, and braced himself for whatever it might do.

What it did was outflank the enemy cavalry, working its way up and over the knee of the eastmost hill without putting a hoof wrong, and return Gird to his observation post on the central hill. From here he could see that that particular cavalry sortie would be thrown back without much danger. His own center was not advancing now, holding place to support the right flank under pressure, but that did not concern him. More worrying, some of that bright-clad group of nobles who had been back under the trees were moving forward. Several of them, clustered together, raised their arms.

He had not expected the well to spout water, the year before, and he did not expect the storm that gathered like a boil atop the ridge behind him, and spat lightning into the trees. Wind rushed irrationally *down* the slope, bringing fire and smoke with it. Shrill screams rose from both sides, louder from Gird's camp followers, who found themselves caught between a forest fire and a battle. Then the wind stilled, as suddenly as it had started, and Gird saw that the little group of mages had fallen to the ground. Behind him, the fires still burned, but less fiercely, and the new wind direction took the smoke and flame upslope, away from him.

His eyes still stung and watered; he could barely see across the meadow to the king's party. Had it been his hidden archers who killed those nobles, or someone else? The momentary lull caused by the onrushing fire had given way to renewed din of battle. His cohorts were inching forward again, by the half-step now, the wounded shifting back as they had practiced, the fallen trodden underfoot. He could do nothing about that, not yet.

The enemy spearmen had finally made it to the front of their lines; they proved as clumsy as Gird had hoped. Even so, they made rents in the cohort they faced, and it could not advance. For hours, it seemed almost for days, the two armies were knotted in battle. Their lines staggered back and forth, gaining and losing an armlength, a footpace. The noise was beyond anything Gird had imagined, so loud that individual screams and blows merged into a hideous roar.

He concentrated his attention on the details of it, sending his own voice above the rest when necessary. The enemy's reserve archers, mounted, tried a sweep past his left wing. This was the maneuver he'd been looking for: would they support it? At least half the remaining enemy cavalry, and—yes—behind the screen of battle, a cohort or two of infantry. They thought the west hill empty, available; Gird smiled to himself. He might be only a stupid peasant, but he had learned a few things. That trap would spring itself, but he had to set the main one now.

Once before, the arrival of his camp-followers bearing almost useless "weapons" had convinced an enemy that he had vast reserves. The lords had been telling themselves that the peasants were all rebels at heart; they had only to count to know how many peasants were on their own lands, and fear the worst. Gird had taken the chance that the king and his advisors would follow the trails they had followed through the ridges, trails where horses and pack animals could go, where armies could march without fighting their way through prickly undergrowth. Gird marched that way where he could, and he knew they had trailed him back to this meadow. So they would think that what they saw, and what might be behind the little hills, was the worst of what they faced. That was, in fact, the truth, but would they believe the truth when a pretense fit their deepest fears?

He rode the gray horse a little up the slope, above the dust of the battle, to where he had a clear view across the meadow to that forested ridge behind the king. The king would have scouts atop it, for a certainty —if his people had not found them yet. But that would do him no good. Gird waved the pole with its long blue streamer twice. An arrow whirred past his head as the horse neatly sidestepped. Evidently some archers had decided he was worth hitting—well, he'd told his own to take out archers first, and anyone on horseback next.

Shrill yips from the western hill told him that the first part of his plan was working. His archers were falling back, coming around the slope into the hollow between the two hills—not a deep hollow, but one with its own peculiarities. The enemy archers should be making for the hilltop; he thought the cavalry would swing around, trying to take him in the rear, and so came the signal he had been waiting for.

It was amazing how many pits five thousand yeomen could dig in less than a day. Gird thought they could have dug a trench all across the meadow, but trenches could be jumped, and pits cleverly placed where horses must go between rocks of a rockfall—pits just too wide to jump easily—are a most effective cavalry trap. Thanks to the land and the Lady, he thought piously, for that fortuitously placed rockfall between the hill and the ridge behind it, where many horsemen could get into trouble out of sight of the rest of their army. His archers, having slipped around the hill to the rockfall, were busy; the enemy archers above them, on the hilltop, found themselves unable to see what was going on. Those that tried to come down the south face of the hill to support the cavalry found the scour of the rockfall dangerous in more than one way. The others could—and did—let fly into the backs of the cohorts Gird had between the west and the central hill. He had anticipated this; those cohorts gave way, bending back around the hill; the archers found themselves having to shoot downhill into a confused mass of their own and Gird's troops.

One unwary captain in the king's forces saw that withdrawal as weakening, and urged his own cohorts on to flank those retreating. Gird smiled grimly. His left flank was now anchored by a wall of rock three men high—out of sight of that rash captain, up the little creek that looked so innocent. His troops stood on rock ledges, while their opponents were in the creek, or the mud on its other side. When they reached what they thought was his flank, they would find themselves standing on the far side of a pool of deep water, with no way out but the way they had come in. His archers would find them easy targets.

Meanwhile, the knot of bright-clad nobles across the field was moving again—perhaps it been only exhaustion that felled them. Gird squinted; he was sure he saw someone still on the ground. Out of the trees across from him came yet more cohorts of infantry, more squadrons of cavalry, and some—he squinted, shook his head, and looked again—some did not look human. Magicks, he told himself firmly. It's only magicks. Masks and costumes and fancy ways of frightening people into doing what you want. He wished he knew if the king's whole reserve was committed now.

Below him, the main forces contended as they had all morning, in a heaving, sweating, bloody, snarling mass. If it comes to plain fighting, he had told his marshals, if it comes to simple pounding each other, we win: we'll pound harder, and take more pounding. The king's army now outnumbered his in the center, but his center had not given back at all. They leaned into their pikes with every thrust, grunting with the effort.

Then the king's new reserves hit the back of his force, giving it that extra weight—man against man, those in front were forced forward by that pressure, onto the waiting pikes. They died, had to be shaken from the pikes, and others were already there, already being killed—and again, and again. Gird saw the shiver in his ranks, the realization that something new had entered. The marshals looked aside, trying to find Gird; he caught their eyes and waved with his free hand. Then he took the long pole and signalled his last reserve, across the meadow and up on the ridge behind the king's camp.

It seemed to take forever for that reserve to appear; he had told them to hide neither on the ridgetop nor near the bottom. In the meantime, his center sagged backward, and the enemy, heartened, drove forward with renewed energy. Gird had hardly time to see the first of his reserves clear the trees, yelling their heads off and sprinting downhill toward the enemy rear, before he was down in the thick of his own battle, supporting the center.

Fighting on horseback was completely different, he found. He had dropped the banner-pole, no longer needed—from here they would fight to the death, win or lose; he had no more decisions to make—and pulled his hauk from his belt. It was good for bashing heads, and bashing heads from above worked as well as when he was afoot. For one moment he thought of Amisi, and shoved the thought aside.

Later, when he heard it in songs, the battle of Greenfields (as the meadow became known) sounded much tidier than it had been in reality. The songs didn't mention the several times he was knocked off the horse, and remounted by some helpful soldier, or the blow to his knee that had him limping for a quarter year, or the near-rout when the enemy's last cohort of reserves turned out to be masked magelords with their power in hand. The songs certainly did not mention that long and miserable night after the battle, with the forest fire still burning its way south, or the cries of the wounded that never ceased. And somehow in the songs, that gray horse turned white. Gird was sure he had not aged that much in one day.

He remembered stumping through what had been the enemy's camp, swarming now with squads of his own yeomen gathering up supplies and weapons. The king's tent had gone up first, larger than many houses Gird had seen, with interior rooms walled in fluttering embroidered panels. He had had musicians with him (two had been killed, almost accidentally, when Gird's reserves tore through the camp; the others had been found crouched around their instruments), and a man who painted pictures on lengths of fabric. He had started a picture of the king, victorious, returning with Gird's head, but offered to change the faces for only ten gold pieces. Gird shook his head, and wondered what kind of king would take musicians and painters to battle.

The king was dead. He did not look much like Selamis, but fathers and sons did not have to look alike. He had been a tall man, dark haired as many magelords were, and in death his eyes had only the dull color of a fish found dead on the shore. Gird had found Sier Segrahlin's body, spiked with arrows from behind; he felt no guilt at that, but wished he could have talked to that brown man. They had almost understood each other, across a gulf no one else wanted to bridge. He still wondered, occasionally, if the sier had charmed him that night.

The songs listed the dead magelords, as if to remind the listener that these were all real. Gird did not even look at all of them; he had seen bodies enough. They had killed the wounded as quickly and painlessly as they could; they had killed all the magelords they captured; they dared not do less. At least there were no children with them.

He did not understand why he was still alive; his vision of the morning had been so clear, so certain. He felt curiously suspended, as he had after the Norwalk Sheepfolds, unable to rejoice in the same way as the others, though he felt a deep contentment. So many had died, and he had not, yet he had been sure he would—he had been almost *promised* he would. Nor had Rahi died, or Pidi; he found them both alive, marked but certainly not mortally wounded. But when he touched them he felt no more and no less than he felt for any of his yeomen: they were all his children, in some way he could not define.

He remembered coming back to his own encampment, holding the wounded and dying, speaking what comfort he could, until he fell asleep and woke to find that someone had covered him with a stolen piece of the king's tent. All that day and the next, as the crows and flies fought with them, he tried to bring order and restore health to that trampled and discolored ground. "Bury them all," he said, "Or burn them—even the magelords, yes: we had the gods' gift of victory, we owe them respect."

The songs began that first night, with the talk around the fires of those who could talk, and by the next night a few were trying to fit words to familiar tunes. The dead king's surviving musicians were glad to help. Gird was more than a little amused that the first version he heard of what became "Gird at Greenfields" was set to "The Thief's Lament"—the very song with which he had been taunted for cowardice.

PART IV

PART IV

Chapter Thirty-one

Greenfields broke the king's power, and gave Gird control of the main grain-growing regions of Finaarenis. But it was not the end of the war. Those lords who had not joined the king's army, for whatever reason, were now sure destruction loomed. Some walled themselves in Finyatha; others fled toward Tsaia. Heirs of lords killed at Greenfields squabbled over inheritances now in jeopardy; rich merchants, who assumed a peasant government would have no desire or need for fine goods, appealed to the remaining lords for help.

Gird knew all this, and much of it he had anticipated, but his first problem was securing the year's limited harvest. Where there were no lords, there might be brigands. He split his army into sections, put each under a high marshal, and sent them to settle the countryside. He himself rode for the north, crossing the Honnorgat for the first time in his life on the gray horse, which seemed less like a broken-down carthorse every day. He could stay on at a trot now, although he preferred the swinging canter. Most of his marshals had caught a horse and learned to stay on it, as well. It made supervising a march or a movement much easier, and messages could pass far more quickly. Feeding the beasts was another worry, but men could not eat grass, and horses could. In summer, at least, they could afford a few horses.

Rumors of the king's defeat spread even faster than Gird had expected. In the north, he and his column found mostly deserted, looted manor houses, and celebrating peasants. Few of his recruits had come from the north—in fact he had trouble understanding their speech—but they seemed genuinely pleased with his success. He wondered if the quickly-established bartons in each village would ever amount to anything, and prayed that war would not test them.

Finyatha offered a different problem. Largest and richest city of the north, the seat of the Finaarenisian kings, it hung just out of his reach like a tempting plum. Most of its people were common folk, as everywhere, but at the moment it swarmed with magelord refugees. He had no knowledge of siegecraft; common sense told him that assaulting those walls with pikemen would do no good—a much smaller force on the walls could defend it. He thought of trying to divert the river, but remembering Segrahlin's tricks with water decided that some mage inside could simply call water into any well he wanted. In the end, he left it alone, and like an overripe plum, it fell on its own. One party of magelords tried to escape along the River Road to Tsaia; most of those fell to raiding parties, Gird's or brigands. The rest were too weak to keep control of the city. When the disruption inside reached the gates, and the fighting erupted into the fields outside, Gird's column—which had been waiting at a distance—marched in with little difficulty, to the apparent delight of all.

The gray horse brought Gird into those stone streets as if carrying a king; cheers racketed off the walls, and the flowers of summer fell on his shoulders, Alyanya's blessing. Then the horse pranced into the courtyard before a towering stone structure that seemed to spring, like trees, from the roots of the world itself, and reach skyward with every stretched finger. Between its arches, great windows had stood; they were shattered now, glittering fragments crunched beneath the horse's hoofs. A few pieces still clung to their frames, reflecting brightness against the cool darkness inside. The horse knelt; Gird stepped off and looked around. It was a hot day, blue-skied, and the courtyard had blue shadows under every ledge of gray stone. The very air shimmered; he blinked. Was it the air, or his eyes?

Arranha stood on the steps, between splintered doors. Gird would have been surprised, but could not quite feel it. "This was Esea's High Hall," Arranha said, as if he were a guide. "It became something else, something worse, and Esea's blessing was withdrawn." He shook his head. "I warned them, but they thought they could extract more power by bringing darkness and light so close together."

Gird could not follow this, but he did follow Arranha into the partly ruined building. It soared overhead, high arches of stone, one after another rising from fluted pillars, making a space reminiscent of a great forest. At the far end, where a circular window had been, sunlight fired the lower arc to a silver crescent. Gird felt hairs rise on the back of his neck. He swallowed.

"You must see this," Arranha was saying, "because you must decide if the gods demand this building be torn down. I myself would hate to see that; it's the most beautiful in the north, to my eyes. But the people know what went on here; you must see for yourself."

What he had to see was evidence enough that the magelords had lost all sense of right and wrong. Arranha tried to explain what they thought they were doing; to Gird, who had never sailed a ship, did not know a lodestone from any cobble in the river, who did not *care* about the theory behind it, it was simply disgusting and grotesque. An excuse, as he saw it, for some to bully others, to excuse their own cruelty on religious grounds. Here were the same symbols he had found in that count's dungeon: the barbed chain, the masks with horns and spikes, painted to terrify, the instruments whose only purpose was pain. The place Arranha had led him to stank of old blood, death, and fear. He heard a nauseated gulp beside him, and turned to see Selamis at his side; he had followed Gird, as he often did, without speaking or asking permission.

"Don't make it worse," Gird said. "Go spew outside if you must. But this is your *real* inheritance from your father." The younger man made it to the outside before he threw up. When he came back—to Gird's surprise —he looked grim but in some way satisfied.

Gird came back out to find a crowd of those who had suffered under the old, and wanted his justice. His, he thought. The blue summer sky pressed down on him. Another than Alyanya had given him that victory; what did *he* want here? Justice, and all that came with it. The Hall?

The evil, he told them, is not in the stones, but in those who did wrong. Justice will rule here, the High Lord who judges all things rightly. He himself went to the crypt under Esea's altar and scrubbed it until it stank no more of all that had happened in it. He brought in the holy herbs for the dead, and lay them reverently on the floor. He came up to find the crowd still standing, and scolded them as if they had been his yeomen for years. Cleaning before building, he said, waving his arms at the shattered glass in the courtyard.

With Finyatha fallen, the other lords in Finaarenis fled to Tsaia, where the Tsaian king gathered an army to retake that land and save his own. Gird ignored that for the present. They had not time before winter to mount a campaign; the Marrakai told him all he needed to know of preparations. He himself was back in Brightwater before snow fell, with Selamis and Arranha, to plan for the coming year.

Despite the destruction of farming villages and fields, they had more food than the year before. The lords' granges had held a surprising amount; some had burned, but more had been saved. Many other goods were found in more abundance, though the distribution was not as even as Gird would have liked. But he did not interfere with anything but gross injustice. If these people were to help make their own fair laws, they would have to start by making some mistakes.

In spring, the fighting spread eastward into Tsaia. Gird had not realized how far the barton organizations spread—not only in Marrakai lands, but beyond. Barton after barton rose, combined with its neighbors, and elected a marshal: most were competent. The Tsaian royal army which had at first treated the very idea of a peasant army with contempt, even after the defeat in Finaarenis, fell back again and again. Gird did not want his Finaarenisian troops to invade Tsaia: they had fought

for their own freedom, in defense of their own homes
and families. That much he had felt confident that
Alyanya, Lady of Peace though she be, could understand and condone. Invading someone else's land, even
for the best reasons, did not seem the same.

But Ivis, his high marshal in the east, had no such
worries. Bartons were bartons; yeomen were yeomen;
in any fight between peasants and lords, he wanted to
be one of the leaders. Several cohorts volunteered to go
to Tsaia with him. Gird, working hard on the new
and—he hoped—simple legal system that would enable
men to live in peace and deal fairly with one another,
let him go with only a warning.

The legal code was, in fact, turning out to be much
harder than he had expected. If he made the laws
simple, they were so general that someone would claim
not to know how that general principle could be applied
in a particular instance. If he made the laws precisely
applicable to common situations, someone would come
up with an uncommon situation and claim to have found
no guiding general principle. Gird tried to ignore the
twinkle in Arranha's eyes, but finally admitted that he
had been as naive in law as in war.

"Not that you won't end up with better law than
we've had," said Selamis, quite seriously. "I think it's
coming quite well."

"Some of it," growled Gird. It had been so simple to
say that no one should beat up someone else, but now
he was faced with honest merchants who had pursued
thieves, and husbands convinced that they must beat
their wives. And how much beating was beating? If a
thief, once caught, kept fighting and had to be clouted
before he would come along to a magistrate, was that a
lawful or unlawful beating? Gird had insisted that the
right to beat, within marriage, was both limited and
equal for both sexes, but enforcement proved beyond
his means. He felt at times like the father of a roomful
of quarrelsome children, each of whom insisted that the
other one started it.

Mercantile law proved equally tricky. Gird himself
had gone around to three markets, taken a sample

weighing stone, and found that no two were the same. He had one of the Brightwater masons cut one that matched the middleweight stone, had several more made to balance it, and replaced all the Brightwater weightstones with the standard. As the mason turned out more standards, Gird sent them to nearby markets, and insisted on their use. Prices danced up and down with the new stones. Gird assumed they would settle to something equivalent to those before, but his mental analogy—a chip on a bucketful of water, after shaking—did not satisfy him.

At least this year most of the arable land was under cultivation, and his noncombatant camp followers had returned to their homes or settled in partially deserted villages nearer by. Some of the bartons had dispersed as well, those that had villages to return to. Food should not be a problem, if the war stayed in Tsaia.

As the war receded eastward, the land that had been Finaarenis settled back into farming and trade. Some lands were blighted, some wells ruined; peasants shrugged and moved on. Some fields grew rich green grass over bones the crows had picked; those they avoided for another year. Gird moved from Brightwater to Grahlin, amused now to see how small a town it really was, that had seemed a city to him. Esea's Hall there had been burned, by the local inhabitants; they showed him the charred foundations proudly. He moved on east, to camp near the Tsaian border for a time.

Tsaia fell, at last, with blue-shirted farmers calling themselves "Gird's Yeomen" holding the king captive in his own dungeon. By the time word came to Gird, the king had escaped—and been found dead, of a magelady's anger. The two messages came on the same day, in Ivis's difficult script. Gird had tried to insist that his marshals, at least, must learn to read and write, but some had struggled as hard as he himself. He looked up from puzzling his way through it, having read it aloud, to meet Selamis's steady gaze.

"So," he said. "You are the last surviving magelord of rank, if you look at it the way you once did."

Selamis shook his head. "No, you know I don't."

"You feel no slightest flicker of desire for that throne? They say it is lovely." The throne of Finaarenis had been hacked to bits before Gird saw it.

"None. That was not my throne anyway, even if they wanted a king."

Gird drew a long breath. "I suspect they do; there's a different feel over there. Marrakai said their king was foolish, not cruel, and Marrakai is anything but a fool. It's a land that might take lords, if they were not mages."

Selamis looked down, pensive. "And where is a land that will take mages, if they are neither lords nor evil?"

"You think of yourself? You are safe with me."

"I think of others like myself. I cannot be the only bastard with magic in his blood, that will someday bring him death at the hands of those for whom all magic is evil. Even some of the pure blood—that lady you sent away, and her children."

Gird cocked his head. "If I had magic in my hands—if I could bring light, as you and Arranha can, whenever I needed a light to find my way; if I could light a fire with it, and never be cold—I would find that tempting. I would want to use it, first for myself, and then for those I loved, and then—I don't know, friend luap, as you would be called—"

"I wish you would just call me Luap, as the others are doing now—"

"And forget who you are? I wish I could. But I see no way to use magic well, to have that much power others cannot share, with no force to bar misuse."

Selamis waved at the papers Gird had been working over, another revision of the first part of his Code. "Your law?"

"Law without force behind it is but courtesy: for love or greed, men do things they should not, and law must have a hard hand to knock those hot heads into sense. For ordinary men, the law can serve, but what force can bind a mage?"

Selamis laughed aloud. "You did it yourself, Gird—a good knock to the head, as you say, and there I lay."

Gird laughed too. "Yes, an untrained mage. By the

gods, d'you suppose if I'd felled that sier in the first place he would never have fought against us?" A ridiculous idea, but he was in the mood for it.

"Mages are children first, Gird—good parents can teach them law."

That sounded reasonable but he still had his doubts.

Then the Tsaian king's killer sought sanctuary in his camp. He wondered what she would say about his death. *Magedead*, the report had been, from someone who claimed to know what that meant. *A royal ring on his chest, and briars grown over him, in bloom even in this season.* The season was autumn. Late autumn.

"Bring her in, then," he said to Selamis-now-Luap.

"She's a mage," said Selamis. He meant more by that; Gird looked at him sharply.

"So?"

"She's one of them, but not one of them."

"One trying to do good, like the Marrakai?"

Luap looked away. "Not precisely. She had lived for years as a sheepherder."

"A *mageborn* lady?"

"So those who knew her say. In exile from the Tsaian court, for some wrangle there—"

"And she comes to us. Why? Did she say?"

"She says you must know how the king died, and hopes you will let her take service with us."

Gird stared at Luap. "Is she a fool, this magelady? Take service with *us*? Why not join Marrakai, if she's what you call a good mage?"

Luap shrugged. "I don't know. Will you see her?"

Gird shifted in his seat. "Oh, I'll see her."

She was tall, and even in armor conveyed a lithe lightness, a supple strength. It set Gird's teeth on edge. This one had never, he was sure, borne a child or suckled, had never so much as cared for a sister's child. Dark hair, braided snugly to fit beneath the helm she carried under her arm. Skin pale as ivory, flushed with rose at the cheeks, eyes used to command, bright and piercing. Before he could speak, she had spoken.

"The king is dead, and by my hand," she said. "If you

do not allow murderers in your army, you will not want me. Otherwise—"

Gird felt that his head was full of apricot syrup: sweet, cloying, thick. He dragged his thoughts through it, just able to think *So this is what that charming is about!* Whatever had happened to the magicks of the other magelords, this one had full measure and running over. He struggled with his tongue, which wanted to say "Yes, lady," and dug his fingernails into his palms. It helped a little.

"I wish you'd stop that," he said, somewhat surprised at the even tone in which it came out.

Her mouth opened, and her cheeks paled. "You—are not afraid."

Humor tickled the inside of his mind, thinning the rich syrup of her magicks. "No, but I am getting angry. I don't like tricks."

"It's not a trick," she said. The pressure of her sweetness increased; it was hard to breathe.

"Trick," insisted Gird, through the honeyed mist over his eyes. "Same as luring a fly to honey, and swatting it. You might try honesty."

All at once, the magicks were gone, his mind clear, and the woman's face had gone all white around the mouth. *That* had gone home hard, though most of the magelords didn't seem to regard honesty as much.

"I did," she said between clenched teeth. Without the magicks, her face was older, not unlovely, but no longer a vision of beauty and terror. The dark hair had silver threads in it; the face had fine lines, a touch of weather. "I tried honesty, back then, and that brought me exile. And when I tried again, my duty to the king—ah, you would never understand!" She turned away from him, a gesture Gird read as consciously dramatic.

"You killed him," Gird said, deliberately flat across that drama.

"I killed him." She faced him again, and now he saw tears glittering in her eyes. Did she really care, or was it all an act? Women he knew cried noisily, red-faced, shoulders heaving, not one silver tear after another sliding down ivory cheeks. "I trusted him; he was my liege. And then—"

He was tired of her dramatics, and wholly out of sympathy with her kind of beauty. "Spit it out, then, lass, or we'll be here all day—" It was the tone he used on his own folk, the young ones, the frightened ones. On her it acted like a hot needle: she jumped and glared at him.

"He sent me away because I would not give up my weaponcraft and magery to be his queen, or so he told me then. I loved him dearly, and thought he loved me; there was no Rule requiring me to give up the sword as queen. I thought it his whim, and tried to talk him out of it, but he would not. I went into exile heartsore, like any girl whose betrothed turns her away. When he was imprisoned I knew it; he called in the way of our folk, though he had no need to call *me*. I would have come. When I took him from the prison where *your* folk had him, when I'd fought our way past the walls to safety, he told me he'd sent me away because of foretelling. Because he'd been told he'd need me someday. So he set conditions he was sure I would not understand nor agree to, to force me to refuse him, and then to leave the court. I had been honest those years, true to him and his memory: he had lied to make use of me. No love, no children, no freedom for my own life—"

It was the sort of thing the women talked about, back home, stories and gossips about unfaithful lovers, men cheating women of a promised marriage, women's vengeance on them. The men, Gird had to admit, had their own gossip, muttered into their mugs of ale, or half-whispered from man to man during shearing time, with guffaws and backslappings. Still, it sounded just as petty from this magelady as from any village girl; he was surprised she hadn't come up with something better.

"And for that injury you killed him?"

"For that, and for the king he was not. By Esea's Light, he had enough of the old Seeing to know what went on. Marrakai would have helped him stop it if he'd wanted to, but he could not be bothered."

"And from that act of—honesty—" Gird let the word

trail out, and watched the blood flood her face. "You came here, and used your magicks on me. Why?"

"I thought you would not give me hearing, but kill me first. It was only to buy that much time—"

"And you found that time worth the cost?"

"It did you no harm," she said.

"You." Gird leveled both index fingers at her. "It cost *you*, mageborn lady. It cost you my trust."

"But—"

"NO!" He hammered the table with both fists. "No. You listen, mageborn, and then see if you want to dare our mercy. This you did, this use of magicks to charm me into listening, this is exactly what we despise. To keep yourself safe and put others in peril, to use weapons we cannot bear: this is unfair, unjust, and we will not let you do it."

"What do you know about justice?" she snapped.

"More than you. I would not use my strength against a child to take what was not mine—no, not if I hungered. I know what fair exchange is—"

"You've been talking to kapristi—"

"Aye, and listening, too. Weight for weight, work for work, honest labor for honest wages, no chalk in the flour and no water in the milk: that's fair exchange."

"And what did you exchange for this wisdom?" She was still scornful, ready to be very angry indeed.

"What they asked for it: when we gain the rule, to bind ourselves to respect their boundaries evermore. To allow gnomish merchants in our markets, at the same fair exchange humans use."

"*That* is all they asked?"

" 'Tis more than they got from you, all these years, so they said. They want a peaceful, ordered land nearby, one content with its borders; they want fair dealing." Someone came in then, an excuse to dismiss her. But he could not quite dismiss her from his mind. Her image clung there, disturbing. He wished she would leave; it was going to take all his influence to keep the others from attacking her. They might even think she had charmed him.

Several nights later he heard music from the far side

of camp. Strings, plucked by skillful hands, and sweet breathy notes of something not quite like a shepherd's reed pipe. A voice, singing. He stiffened. He knew that voice, knew that honeygold sweetness. *Damn the woman*, he thought. *Her with her arts, she'll get us all killed*.

He chose a roundabout way to her; he could not have said why. Perhaps the sentries would be less alert, listening to the singing? But no. They challenged him, every one, with a briskness he found irritating rather than reassuring.

She sat well back from the fire, cradling the round-bellied stringed instrument and listening to another woman play a wooden pipe three handspans long. Gird watched her from the shadows. That long bony face, the hollows of the eyes—she had grace, he had to admit. Her hands moved, her fingers began touching the strings again, bringing out mellow notes from her instrument. They wove around the pipe-player's melody and tangled Gird's attempt to follow either instrument alone. One of the men began to sing, a horse-nomad song. "Fleet foot the wind calls, run from the following storm—" The magelady joined in, again that golden tone he mistrusted. Her voice ran a little above the tune, patterning with it, but in no mode Gird knew. He scowled, ready to be angry. All at once her eyes met his. Her voice slipped, and found itself again.

No. He would not listen to her. He would not look at her. She was betrayal, treachery: she had killed her own king. Magelady, born to deceit and mastery. He was himself: peasant: Mali's husband. *Mali's dead*, whispered some dark corner of his mind. Raheli's father, then. Broad and blunt, and liking it that way—he would not let himself be seduced by mere grace and golden voice.

She was surpassing beautiful. He tried to think of her body as no more than the body of an animal, a sleek cow he had seen and coveted, a graceful horse. He focussed on her hands, now racing over the strings to finger some intricate descant to the piper. It was not the same song. For how many had he stood here, fascinated, watching her? Those long-fingered hands,

strong and supple, that long body. He met her eyes
again, dark eyes older than her years, full of sorrow.

She knew. She knew he watched, and how he watched.
Rage roiled up in him: she was charming him again,
even now. He glared at her; she looked back, sorrowful
and unafraid. Calm. *Kill me now*, her look said. *I did
not do this*. Yet, if it was not charm, why wasn't she
disgusted at his interest? A peasant, a coarse man old
enough to be her father—

Not so, came her voice in his mind. *You are not so
old, nor I so young*.

No disgust? *He* was disgusted, with himself. How
could he think of such a woman, as a woman, after
Mali's loyalty and Raheli's tragedy? What had he fought
for, if not to remove such women from power?

Time had passed, the fire only warm ashes under a
dark sky. The others had fallen asleep. Only she remained awake, watching him as he watched her. Magicks,
he thought disgustedly.

"Not so, lord marshal," she said. Aloud, in her own
voice, but quietly.

"Reading minds is magicks."

"That, yes. The other—if it be magic at all, it is older
far than mine."

"I—would like to hate you."

"With reason." She turned away, and folded around
the melon-bellied instrument a trimmed fleece. "But
you cannot, lord marshal, any more than I hate myself.
I did not come here to unsettle you."

"Wind unsettles water," he said, surprising himself.
Where had *that* come from?

She laughed softly; it had an edge to it. "Yes—wind.
But you are not water, lord marshal—Gird. You are
what you said—good peasant clay. Do you know what
the rockfolk say of clay?"

"No."

"Sertig squeezed clay to rock. And rock squeezed
makes diamond, fairest of jewels that gives light in
darkness."

He grunted, surprise and superstitious fear together.
He had consented to be rock; the other, half dreamed

of, still wholly terrified him. And diamonds were jewels, and jewels belonged to the wealthy, to such as this lady: he would not so belong. But his mouth opened, and he spoke again.

"I have dreamed of you." He had waked sweating and furious; he had not spoken to her since.

She looked away. "I thought you might. I'm sorry."

"You—you are like no one—"

"I am myself. Once—a name I will not use again. Now, what *he* called me, an autumn rose, a last scentless blossom doomed by frost—"

"You like that word. Doom."

"Gird, I know myself, and my future: it is the chanciest gift our people had, but in me it is, like the others, strong. I will have no children; my time is past." She met his eyes squarely. "And you, who have children—you think you could give me some?"

He felt suddenly hot. Now she was smiling, but it had no warmth in it.

"I know your dreams, Gird; your eyes speak of them. A magelady's body—a magelady unwed—what is she like? You see the foreign shape of my face, my hands, and you wonder about the rest." From musing, her voice roughened to anger. "Ah, Esea! You will believe it my magicks no matter what I do! And I have tried, if you had the wit to see it, to be invisible to you, to draw no eyes, least of all yours."

"It was your sorrow." That, too, came without his thought. Yet it was true. She had tried no charms on him or anyone, after that first meeting, but the stress of her sorrow drew eyes to her.

"Look, Gird: I will show you, and then if you are wise, if the gods are truly with you, you will know that in this I am honest."

He opened his mouth, but her gesture silenced him, for she had thrown off her cloak, and begun unlacing her shirt. If he said anything *now*, someone might wake, and the explanations would be, at best, difficult. Her fingers moved quickly, deftly, stripping off her clothes with no more apparent embarrassment than he would have had in his own cottage. It should have been too dark to see her, but she glowed slightly, a light he knew was magelight.

She had the body he had imagined. Long legs, long slender body untouched by childbearing; her hips were like a young girl's and her breasts—he ached to touch them. Even Mali as a girl had not had such breasts, the very shape of his desire. But through the beauty he had expected he perceived the barrenness she had claimed. Like some graceful carving of stone, set up in a lord's hall for amusement: he could engender nothing there. His hands opened, closed; instead of the imagined softness and warmth, there was hardness and cold.

She wrapped the cloak around herself again, dimming the glow until he could just make out her face. "You see?" A thread of sorrow darkened that golden voice. "It is not you, Gird; it is a choice I made, long years ago: obedience to my king. Service, not freedom. Death, not life."

"It's wrong."

Her brows rose. "You are my judge?"

"No, but—" There had to be a way to say it, that meant what he meant. "Serving things rightly, that can't be serving death. Loyalty's good, I'll agree there, but it's not all—what you're loyal *to* must be worthy."

"Wise clay, lord marshal." Her voice mocked him, but her face was uneasy. "Where did a peasant learn such wisdom?"

"It's only sense," Gird said stubbornly. "Peasant sense, maybe: we serve life in our work. Growing crops, tending beasts—that's serving life."

"I erred, as I've admitted. A mistake, believing the king was true, and worth my obedience. A mistake I remedied, you remember." Her voice had chilled again; he thought she did not truly believe it was a mistake.

"So you said." He was grumpy, annoyed with his body which had not admitted what his mind knew—no comfort there. A man his age, to be so put out—he was disgusted with himself, and with her for rousing that interest. On the way across camp, he stumbled into one thing after another, knowing perfectly well it was his own temper making his feet clumsy.

Arranha. The old priest was one of them; perhaps he could explain. Gird sought him out, not surprised to find that Arranha was awake, peaceably staring at the stars.

"And how is the lady?" asked Arranha. Gird felt himself swelling with rage, to be so easily read, and then it vanished in a wave of humor. He folded himself down gingerly, to sit beside the priest.

"She is herself," he said.

"Too much so," said Arranha. "A bud that never opened, eaten out within. She has the body of a girl, but no savor of womanhood."

Gird opened his mouth to let out surprise; his ears were burning. "She is lovely," he said, after a decent interval.

"Cold," insisted Arranha.

"Well—yes. And yes, I looked; she showed me—"

"She wants you?"

"No. I had never seen anyone like her—not to speak to—and I suppose—it was my own curiosity."

"Natural enough." Arranha shrugged that off, as he did other things Gird could not anticipate. "Which curiosity, I gather from your words, has now vanished. I would pity her, myself, were she not capable of better."

Gird chuckled. "I thought you said we all were capable of better."

"True. But great talents draw envy, even from tired old priests sitting up all night. Gird, she might have prevented much evil, had she listened to good counsel. It was not all heedlessness of love: she has the foreseeing mind. She chose not to listen; she chose in spite of her knowledge. She could not have saved the king, I daresay—from all I ever heard of him, as foolish a young man as ever sat on a throne. Not wicked, in any active sense, but silly and shallow. But she might have saved more than she did, and I can't forget that. Nor should you. If she ever quits making a singer's tale out of her lost love, she'd make you a fine marshal, but you'll have to change her course."

"I have enough to do, without teaching mageladies."

Arranha shrugged. "If a weapon falls into your hand,

you either learn to use it, or your enemy uses it against you."

Luap looked up as a strong, slender hand slapped down on the account rolls. He started to complain, but the look on the magelady's face stopped the words in his mouth. She was white around the lips—with fury, he was sure—and he half-recalled hearing Gird's bellow only a few minutes before.

"You!" she said, in a voice that had some of Gird's bellow in it, though not so loud.

"Me?" He could not help noticing the hilt of her sword, her fine and reputedly magical sword. The jewel set in the pommel glinted, as if with internal fires. And every bit of metal she wore glittered, bright even beneath the cloth that shaded him from midday sun. Her eyes, when he met them again, seemed to glitter as well, fire-bright and angry. What could he have done? She had always seemed remote, but calm, when speaking to him.

"You," she said, very quietly now, "you have mageblood."

Luap shrugged, and looked away. "Common enough, lady; if you look closely, there's bastards aplenty in this army."

Her hand flipped this half-truth away. "Bastards in plenty, yes, but those in whom the mageblood *stirs* and wakes are few enough."

He stared at her, shocked almost into careless speech. But he caught the unspoken question back, and tried to school his face. He could see by her expression that she wasn't fooled, or maybe she could see his thoughts. She nodded at him, mouth tight.

"Yes. I do know. You have the magic, the light, and you know it. You could be what I am, were you not obedient to that—that *churl* out there!" Her arm waved. Luap felt a bubble of laughter tickle his throat. "That churl" must be Gird, whatever he'd done this time to anger the lady.

"It may be so," he said, trying to keep even the least

of that laughter out of his voice. "There was a time I thought so, but truly, lady, I have no desire for it now."

She rested both fists on the little table and leaned close to him; he could smell her sweat, and the onion on her breath from dinner. It did nothing to diminish her beauty, or her power. "It has nothing to do with your desires, whatever your name really is. It is given to you, like the color of your eyes, the length of your arm: you cannot deny it." He said nothing, facing her with what calm he could muster. Her eyes looked away first, but she did not move. Then she straightened up, with a last bang of one fist that crumpled the supply roll. "No. You are more than just a bastard, and you must learn it."

Suddenly she was alight, blinding him at first, and then the heat came, scorching heat that blackened the edges of his scrolls. Without thought, he grabbed for power, and threw a shield before him, swept the scrolls to safety behind him.

"Stop that!" he said, furious and frightened at once. She laughed, a scornful laugh he remembered from his earliest childhood, the laugh of one whose power has never been overcome. Above his head, the fabric caught fire, the flames hardly visible against her brightness and the noonday sun.

"You have the power; you stop me!"

It was challenge, challenge he had never expected to face, that Gird would never have had him face. And he felt within a surge of that uncanny power, whose ways he had never learnt, never dared to explore. But as he had startled Gird, perhaps he could startle her, and so he let it out, in whatever form it might choose to come.

It came as a fiery globe, that raced at her; she slapped it away, first with a laugh and then, when it surged again against her hand, with a startled expression. She drew her sword, now glowing as brightly as she, and swiped at the globe. Luap would have been fascinated, if he had not also been involved. He could feel a vague connection between himself and the globe, as if he had a ball of pitch at the end of a long and supple reed.

With a final *pop* like a spark from sappy wood, her brilliance vanished. Luap blinked. Her shadow stood behind her, lean and black; the sun was overhead—he realized then that he was alight as she had been. She was staring at him, her first expression changing to respect, and then awe.

"You," she said, in a very different tone from her first approach.

"Yes?" Whatever was in his voice, it worked on her. Her mouth moved, but she said nothing. Finally she shook her head, and managed speech.

"Do you know *whose* bastard you are?" she asked. Luap kept his mouth shut tight; if *this* was where she was going, he was not going to help. But she nodded, slowly, as if this confirmed something she'd hardly dared imagine. "The king's," she said quietly. Calmly. "You have the royal magery; it could not be anyone else— and I think you knew, Luap. I think you chose your name of war precisely."

"And if I did?" he asked, relaxing slightly. The shadow behind her blurred, as if his light dimmed. He could not tell; his eyes still refused to answer all his questions.

"If you are the old king's son, born with his magery—"

"They said not," said Luap. "Like all bastards with no magic, I was fostered away—"

She laughed, this time ruefully. "Luap, they erred, as you must have known long since. You are his heir—in blood, and in magic—and the evidence is right here—in what just happened. Show this to any of the old blood, and you would inherit—"

"Inherit!" For an instant his old dream sprang up, bright as ever, but anger tore it away. "Inherit a kingdom torn by war? Inherit the fame my father had, that made men glad to see him dead? Inherit his ways?"

Her voice lowered, mellowed, soothed him as honey soothes a raw throat. "You have thought of it, Luap; you must have. He was a proud man, a foolish man . . . even, in some ways, a cruel man. He should have had more sense than to foster *you* away. None of our people have done all we should. But you—you know better. You could be—"

"I could be dead," said Luap. He wanted to hit her; he could feel her attempt to enchant him like a heavy weight of spring sunlight. It had been bad enough to go through this once. He shook his head at her. "If you had asked me two years ago, lady, I might have been foolish enough—I *would* have been foolish enough to agree. What my father did to me—the vengeance I wanted, the power I had always envied—yes. I would have. Even a year ago, maybe. But I've learned a bit, in this war. Even from you."

"*Even* from me? You mean, because of me, you would not—?"

"Not you alone. But, lady, I can see what Gird sees now; I can see the cost of your counsel, down to the last dead baby, the last poisoned well—"

"We are not *all* evil!"

"No. But—you tell me, lady, what it is that made you angry this time? What sent you here to work behind Gird's back?"

She whirled away from him; he let his own power flow out to her, and she turned back, unwilling, but obedient—recognizing even as she fought it the source of her compulsion. He released her, and she staggered. "He—he's an *idiot*! He knows no more of governing than any village bully!"

Luap chuckled. "He is an idiot, that I'll grant. But he's far more than a village bully, and if you can't see that, you're not seeing him yet for what he is."

"He lets those fools of merchants blather on, bickering about the market rules—"

"What should he do, crack their heads for them?" Luap could see she had thought of that, with relish. He shook his head at her. "Lady, Gird's as likely to lose his temper and bash heads as any man I've ever known. If he lets them bicker on, wasting time as you'd say, then he has his reasons."

"He claimed they would obey rules they made better than rules he gave—and yet he won't let them make the rules they *want* to make. Insists that they and the farmers must agree what is a ripe plum, nonsense like that."

"Nonsense like that matters, to those who grow the plums, or pay good coin for them."

"And that brings up coin. D'you know he's planning to call in and melt down all the old coinage? No more copper crabs and gold crowns, but stamped with wheat-ear and poppy. I tried to tell him what that would cost: the finesmiths don't work for nothing. He wouldn't listen. And he asks of me what he does not understand—"

"He wants you to give up your grievance, as he made me give up mine."

"Your heritage, he's made you give up."

"One and the same. My grievance: being born of royal blood, and thrown out to live in a peasant's world. Having the royal power, and being denied its use. The world, in short, not to my liking."

"It's more than that!"

"Not really." Luap grinned sideways at her. "Lady, I've known peasant lads enough, furious because their father favored another brother, because the steward was unfair, because the world was. Grumbling, sour, envious, resentful, quick to take offense and seek vengeance for every slight. So was I, though I hid it, thinking myself too good to admit such feelings, though they burned in my heart." He paused, to see how she would take this. She listened, though he suspected it was only because she knew he was a king's son. He took a deep breath, hoping no one would interrupt them, or come close enough to overhear what only Gird, so far, knew of his past.

"When I married, lady, I loved my wife as a prince might love a scullery-maid: just so much, for her beauty and her skill. Our children: I saw them in my mind, clothed in royal gowns, and hated the reality of their broad peasant faces, their rough hands. You are unwed: you cannot imagine what this means of love foregone, of wasted years, when I might have been rich in hearts-ease. Then as Gird's power grew, my master—who should, I knew, have been but a courtier at *my* court—commanded me to join the army, gain Gird's confidence, and betray him. I would have done so, for the reward he promised, but he did not trust. He took my wife, my children—killed my son, to make his point, and held them captive against my behavior. The wife I had never loved as I could have, the daughter I thought too plain: I saw in their eyes, as the soldiers took them away, a trust I had never earned. *Then* I began to love them, but it was too late." The old pain struck to his heart again, and tears blurred his vision. He blinked them away, and saw on the magelady's face a curious expression. He hoped it was not contempt: he could feel rage rising in him like a dangerous spring; contempt from her would set a fire under it. She said nothing.

"So I came to Gird, as one driven into rebellion by injustice, but I meant to betray him, only he was gentle, that night, with my injuries, and something—I could not do it. I told him, about my family, and he cried: great tears running down his face, his nose turned red—I could not believe it." He waited until she asked.

"And then?"

"And then they died, as my master had promised, and I could do nothing. In the market square at Darrow, before a frightened crowd—someone told me about it later, not knowing whose wife it had been. And I—I hated Gird, almost as much as my master, for having done nothing—though there was nothing he could have done. When I discovered my powers, I had thoughts of claiming my own place, somehow. Making things better, being the king that should have been, in a land where no one suffered. A boy's dream, after a beating. Crowns and palaces for all, meat and ale and honey on the loaf—"

"You could have—"

"I could *not*. Gird knocked me flat, when I tried my powers on him, and rightly so. I didn't see that at the time. But if you've wondered why I have no command, that's why. He could not trust me. The marshals still look at me sideways, but Gird knows I'm different now. So could you be, if you'd give up that old wound you cherish."

"I do not cherish it! The ruin of my life—!"

"Only if you choose so. Lady, listen to me. You have

lost something: who has not? It is what we make of what's left that counts. I lost my wife, my children, lost them even before they were taken, in the blindness of my pride in blood. I lost a crown, the way you see it. You stayed away from this war; you have not seen what I have seen, or learned the lessons it taught. My loss is as important as any other, and no more important than any other. King's son, bastard, widower, childless by war, a luap in every way: I have lost or renounced all command, being unfit for it."

"And this is what you and Gird want me to do?"

Luap stretched his arms high over his head, easing the knot in his back. By her tone, she was at least thinking about it, no longer quite so sure of herself. "Gird wants you to quit thinking you're a special case. I would have you consider the fruits of freedom: freedom from your past. What good is that old anger doing you now? What good is it doing any of us, when you would lure me into a conspiracy to undo what all these men and women have died to do? You, lady, best know whether you are as unfit for command as I was.

Her expression shifted, from half petulant to something approaching respect. "I—never doubted my ability to command, when it should be time. Not until now—"

"Yet you never took the field. And why come here, to your people's enemies? And why stay?"

"I'm not sure." She looked down, and away, and anywhere but his eyes. "I did not take the field . . . because the king did not call me, as he called other nobles. After I killed him, I thought . . . I knew that none of our people would accept me, the king's murderer. Why should they? I'd broken my oath to him, why not join his enemies? My own act placed me there, it seemed."

"And what did you think Gird would do, pat you on the head and tell you the king had treated you badly and deserved your vengeance?"

She flushed. "I didn't know. I don't suppose I was thinking clearly. As for why I stay . . . where would I go? Back to Tsaia to pick sides in that contention? Away

from here, where some peasant terrified of magery is
like to split my skull with an axe while I sleep?"

Now she met his eyes again, with an expression he
had never seen on her face, honest bewilderment and
the first glint of humor. "I set out to save the king, and
killed him; after that, what could I dare intend, that
would not go awry?"

Chapter Thirty-two

Gird had been right; Tsaia preferred lords to peasants, if peasants to mages. There the followers of cruel
gods had all been magelords, or their close kin. When
the bartons rose, some found their own lords with
them, against those they most hated and feared. Duke
Marrakai, though accused of treachery by Duke Verrakai,
proved his loyalty in most men's eyes by supporting a
Mahieran for the throne. The Rosemage, as Gird called
her, assured him that the candidate had no more magical ability than a river cobble. He was not sure he
believed her, but he did believe Arranha, who said the
same thing.

He was, as he had never expected to be, alive and a
hero. Everyone knew the big blocky man in blue (it
seemed simpler to keep wearing that color; when he
didn't, someone would give him a blue shirt "to remember by") on the stocky gray—almost white now—
horse. Children ran out to meet him on the way, calling
to him, running beside the horse. If his route was
known, there would be bits of blue tied to branches,
blue yarn braided into women's hair, blue flowers, in
season, thrown before him. If he surprised a village,
they would drop their tools and gather, beg for his
blessing, bring all their problems for him to solve.

He found that they wanted him—his physical touch, his presence, his listening ear—far more than they wanted his ideas. They had each their local heroes—someone who had fought with him at Grahlin or Greenfields, Blackbone Hill or Brightwater. Every little ambush, each battle, had its heroes, and they had all gone home, if they lived, to tell the tale their own way. Gird heard with some astonishment that he had thrown a horse and rider "so far the crash was not heard when they landed" in one battle, and someone who had lost a leg and survived (Gird remembered the man clinging to his hand, begging for death) came hopping up without it to hug Gird and pound his back and show off his children.

But when he tried to speak to them of the future, only a few paid heed. The others were busy with their work, with lives deferred. They had won, and life was good; they feared nothing but the lords' return, and needed nothing but Gird's friendship.

Some were interested in the legal reforms he instituted. Merchants, craftsmen, and even a few former farmers—but their interest in abstract justice and perfect fairness gave way to factional argument far more often than Gird had hoped. Eventually, after hours and days and even seasons of wrangling, one group would agree on a particular rule, only to have those who had not attended the original conference refuse to follow it. Then everyone appealed to Gird, and he found himself making the very judgments he had called on others to make.

Most folk understood the need to have some armed force for protection, both locally, against brigands, and regionally, in case of invasion. But fewer wanted to support the barton and grange organization Gird envisioned, with adequate, uniform training for yeomen, yeoman-marshals, marshals, with regular drill for all yeomen even in times of peace.

He was troubled, as well, by the feeling that he had had since surviving the battle at Greenfields. He had been told that he could not see the peace he would bring, and here it was, all around him. Either the gods

were wrong—and he could not believe that—or he had
misunderstood. He didn't believe that, either. Which
meant that the peace he saw was somehow not real.
Something was wrong with it, as something had been
wrong after Norwalk Sheepfolds. He had asked then if
it was his fault that he would not see true peace, and
had had no answer. He asked himself the same question now: was the wrong here his fault? Had he failed in
something he should have done, that would have brought
true and lasting peace—had he withheld something he
should have given?

His own memories reminded him of his mistakes; the
victories others boasted of in his name seemed to him
full of his miscalculations, deaths he'd caused by his
stupidity or carelessness. That one fit of drunkenness,
which left a legacy still; even now, even when everyone
called him Father Gird, someone would take the mug
from his hand with a kindly smile, when he'd had what
they thought was enough. He had done what he set out
to do—free the land of its bad rulers—but every time
his gray horse ticked a hoof on a skull, or he saw the
white end of a bone turned up as someone plowed a
field, he shuddered.

He traveled widely, urged on by that vague but
persistent uneasiness. Everywhere he went he seemed
to see prosperity returning, as farms returned to burnt-
over fields, as once-deserted villages hummed with life.
His people had more flesh on their bones; foreign traders complained of their scant profits, but kept returning. So did wealthy craftsmen who had thought a peasant
kingdom would have no need of their abilities. His new
coinage, which the magelady had so complained about,
circulated more freely than the old ever had. When
Luap first mentioned what he saw as the problem, the
continuing bitterness between former magelord land-
holders and tenants, Gird scoffed at him.

"They won't hurt children," he said. "The adults,
maybe, but—"

"I've talked with Autumn Rose." Luap said the name
without embarrassment; Gird still thought it was silly.
If she wanted to conceal her real name, she could have

taken any simple one. She had changed, over the years,
but she still had what he thought of as lordly arrogance.
He let himself remember the first time she had laughed
at herself, admitted that she could be as ridiculous as
anyone. Was it then that she began to change, to give
up her old grievance against the dead king. She had made,
as Arranha had predicted, a good marshal when she
finally quit dramatizing her lost love. He realized his
mind had wandered, as it did more often now, and
came back to find that Luap was watching him, pa-
tiently. Luap went on. "She thinks it will get worse.
There are too many of the halfbred children, and sometimes the power sleeps a generation or so, cropping out
unexpectedly. Besides, you said not all the adults were
guilty, that if they wanted to live under your laws they
would be safe."

"So I did, and so they are." He hated it when Luap
was patient with him, as if he were a doddering old man;
it made him grumpy.

Luap shook his head. "If they come so far as your
courts, they are. Many don't. There was a man killed in
the south, near Kelaive's old domain—" The regions
had not been renamed; Gird decided they needed to do
that next. The very name Kelaive wakened old angers.
"—a younger son, he could make light with his finger,
enough to light a candle. Stoned, Gird, and no one will
admit to having anything to do with it. You can lose
your temper and stab someone in a rage, or bash his
head with one rock, but stoning—that takes time, and
many people."

"What did they say he'd done?" He must have done
something, to arouse that kind of anger.

"They don't say, because no one admits to doing it.
Cob's your high marshal down there; you know he's
sensible." He had always liked Cob, whose blunt, matter-
of-fact approach to life had not changed through war or
peace. He still limped, from the foot broken outside
Grahlin, but never complained.

"What does Cob say?"

Luap pulled out the message and read it aloud. "Tell

Gird he must do something, perhaps send the mages away."

"Away *where*? Where would people trust me to send them? Those here don't want to live in Tsaia, won't go back to Aarenis—and they say there's nothing left in Old Aare. Besides, if I send them away, that kind of folk will worry that they're plotting together. I hear enough of that on the east side now, worrying that Tsaia will invade. It'll wear itself out, in time; what takes years to grow can't wither in a moment."

He went back to the maps, determined to eliminate Kelaive's name before the day was out. The old names, the folk names, belonged: Burry and Berryhedge (four families lived there now, in the ruins) and Three Springs. Get rid of the lords' newfangled names; he would agree that some of their family members were innocent, but no need to honor a bad name by putting it on a map. He was uneasily aware that some bartons had indulged in more looting and destruction than he would have approved if he'd been there, but he was sure—he hoped he was sure—that that had been a single overreaction to years of oppression.

Another year went by, and another. He put on weight; his old belt gave way one day in the middle of a court session, to everyone's delight. Someone ran to bring him a strip of blue leather; he insisted on paying for it (he was, after all, sitting as judge) and wore it thereafter. He still rode out from the city that had been Finyatha and was now Fin Panir, visiting villages and towns, following that old restlessness. He had to admit that Luap was right in one thing; it was taking much longer than he'd expected to reconcile the common folk to the continued presence of surviving magelords and their children. It would come, he was sure of it: at some point they would recognize what they lost in this continual picking at the past. Mali had told him that, all those long years ago, when he had held a grudge against Teris: all life soured if you held anger.

He was working by an open window one hot afternoon when he saw the furtive movement of those who know they're about to do wrong. One, then another, slipped past beneath him, heading around the corner toward whatever lured them on. He was not really curious; it was too hot, and his feet hurt even in slippers. Then he heard children's shrill voices, and someone yelled "I'll tell Gird!" in the very tone in which one wrongdoer informs on another. Sighing, he pushed himself away from his desk, put his feet into his largest pair of boots, and was downstairs when the threatened information arrived. "Something" was going on "down the market way" that he wouldn't like. The marshal, the barefoot child informed him "made no good of it." Then the child was gone, with a flick of a smile that could mean anything from "I started it" to "I know you'll fix it." Both could be true.

He followed the furtiveness he'd observed before, and saw more hurrying backs. Odd that someone's back could reveal intent, he thought. As much as a face, perhaps more. Then he saw a crowd, in the lower market, where the livestock pens were. At the moment, their backs had the look of guilty curiosity.

He felt the crowd's mood shift even before the growling mutter began. *Not again*, he thought. Couldn't the fools understand? Why did they start this nonsense again, now, when all was won, and only ruin could follow such anger?

Those at the back of the crowd moved instinctively away from his determined stride, even before they recognized him. Their voices followed, then raced ahead: "Gird—it's Gird—*he's* coming—" A lane opened for him, leading him toward the trouble.

There was Luap, as he had expected, and the Autumn Rose. She held the shoulders of a whip-thin, dark-haired lad whose face was a mass of bruises and scrapes, eyes barely visible in the mess. Blood dribbled from his broken nose and split lip. Gird could see the lad shaking, and no wonder. Across from them was a yeoman of the local grange, Parik, sucking raw knuckles. When he saw Gird, he glowered, no whit repentant.

Luap, uncharacteristically, said nothing. The Autumn Rose looked past Gird's ear, an insult he would have thought but for the warning that leapt into her eyes. So. He looked back at Parik, seeing in Parik's eyes the confidence that came from knowing he was not alone in this.

"Well?" Gird's voice cracked, as it had been doing since Midwinter Feast and that disastrous dance in the snow. He swallowed the lump and awaited an answer.

"That'n used magicks," said Parik, in a tone well-calculated to sting without justifying rebuke. He merely looked at the lad, and then gave a final lick to his own knuckles.

"You're accusing him of misusing magicks?" asked Gird mildly.

"Nah—they all seen it. He's a magelord's brat, should never have lived this long, and needs mannering, if he's to live any longer." Parik made a show of patting his tunic back into place.

"And you thought it your job—?"

"He put fire on me," said Parik, as if explaining something difficult to a dull child. "He put fire on me, so I put m'fist on him. Like you says, Gird, or *used* to say, simple means for simple minds." He laughed, a little too loudly, and Gird heard nervous sniggers elsewhere.

He closed his eyes, suddenly so tired he felt he must sink to the ground. He had told them, and told them, and explained, and argued, and shouted, and broken their stubborn heads from time to time, and even, when his breath ran out, spoken softly, and here they were, just as bad as ever. Just as bad as the magelords, barring they used fists instead of magic. *Gods—!* he thought, then stuffed the prayer back. Ask their help and get their interference, like as not. He opened his eyes to find everyone staring at him. Give them an answer, a judgment: he had to, and he could not.

"The Marshal?" he asked. His voice was unsteady; he could see their reaction to that, like a child's to a parent weeping.

"Don't need no Marshal to know right from wrong," said Parik, bolder now that Gird had not unleashed his usual bellow. "S'what you taught us, after all: don't need no priests, no crooked judges, no lords—and 'specially no magelords—"

Gird looked at Luap: Luap white-faced, gaze honed to a steel blade that sliced into Gird's mind. Luap, who had warned of this, whose warning he had ignored, thinking it special pleading. It was to Luap he spoke, in a conversational tone that confused the others.

"You were right, and I was wrong. Are you still of the same mind?"

Luap's face flooded with color: surprise. "I—yes, Gird."

"They are not *all* Parik." And that was special pleading, *his* special pleading. Luap nodded, taking it seriously. He had not hoped for so much compassion.

"Talk to *me*!" yelled Parik. Gird watched the Autumn Rose transfer her gaze to him, as deliberate as someone shifting a lance; Parik paled, but did not retreat. "Is that it, then? Are you hiding behind your pet magelords, using their power to charm us?"

"WHAT!" That time he had the old strength in it, and Parik backed up a step. Fury lifted Gird to his full height, pumped power into the fists clenched at his sides, as he stalked towards Parik, stiff-legged. "I never hide; I never did. There are no magelords, Parik, because *I* led you and the others to fight free of them. Mages, yes, and some mere children, like this lad here— but no magelords. No, Parik."

Parik backed up another step, blustering. "But—but that lady there—she looked at me—"

"I'm looking at you, Parik, and seeing a bully who'd be a lord as bad as ever we fought, had he the power."

"Me? But I just—"

"You just beat a lad half your size, for using magicks you said, but you brought no accusation to the Marshal—"

"Donag, he don't want to be bothered with little stuff like that—"

"Then Donag must not want to be Marshal; that's what Marshals do, is deal with 'little stuff like that' and keep big hulks like you from bruising their knuckles breaking lads' faces—"

Gird heard a growl from the crowd, concentrated over *there*—disapproval, backing for Parik. Maybe Donag as well? Could one of his Marshals be supporting this madness?

"He used *magicks!*" yelled Parik. "He put *fire* on me!"

"And what had you done, eh?" Gird glanced around at hostile faces, frightened faces, confused faces. "What started it all?"

"Parik's boy complained," said someone softly, just audible under the shifting crowd noise.

Gird swung toward that sound, and located a face that fit the voice. "Parik's boy?" he asked.

Silence fell, in the center. Parik scowled at the young woman who edged her way to the front. Neither beautiful nor ugly; a quiet face, clear-eyed and determined. She looked straight at Gird, as if afraid to look elsewhere—certainly not at Parik.

"It was Parik's boy, sir—Gird. He'n the others was playing, playing the stick game, y'know?"

He knew: a boy's gambling game, easily disguised as something else if disapproving adults came by.

"Julya—" began Parik angrily, but the girl went on, ignoring him.

"That lad, he has quick fingers—he's a tailor's apprentice now, and I've watched him with a needle—and he won twice running. Then Parik's boy said he was a cheat, and a magelord's bastard, and the lad said he was no bastard, and Parik's boy jumped him, and Parik grabbed him, held him for his boy to hit. That's when the lad made fire on his fingers, to make Parik let go—" Her voice trailed away.

"You—you just want to lie with a magelord's son, you Julya—" Parik's voice had a nasty whine to it. The girl reddened but stood her ground.

"I don't want to lie with you or any of *your* hard-handed sons, that's the truth. And I won't see you lying about what happened and not tell."

"Here now! What's going on here!" That interruption was Donag. Gird merely looked at him when Donag got to the center of the crowd, and Donag wilted. "I heard something—" he started to say.

"Awhile back, I heard something," said Gird. He

hardly knew what he was saying: a great space in his head rang off-key, like a cracked bell, and his vision was uncertain. "Awhile back I heard trouble—which you, Marshal Donag, should have heard. And then I heard that you did not care to hear such trouble. Or so Parik said."

In the quick glance that passed between Parik and Donag, Gird saw as much trouble as he feared. Anger gave him the energy he needed to round on them all, but before he had two words out, Donag interrupted.

"Gods blast it, we've tried for years! You keep telling us they weren't *all* bad. You keep telling us the children aren't their fathers. And yet we *still* have mages working their magicks on us and our children. Look at Tsaia—they have a king again, of the same mageborn line—"

"He has no magicks," said Gird heavily. "That was his great-uncle—"

"So he *says*," Donag growled. "So they all say. 'We have no magicks—we were born without—' And then some mageborn spawn of Liart burns an honest yeoman—"

"An honest yeoman who was doing coward's work, holding a lad for his lad to beat! And look at the damage: Parik has not even a blister, and just you look at the lad's face. By the wheatear and corn, Donag, if the lad had bitten Parik—as any lad would, to get away— you'd no doubt claim that was magicks."

"He could poison his bite," muttered someone.

"Donag, think! If the lad could charm someone, why didn't he charm Parik's boy—or Parik—into letting him alone?" Donag's face did not change; he was not thinking, or even listening. Nor were the others. Gird tried something new. "Suppose we exile them—send them all away. Will that satisfy you? Let the boy go, and any like him."

Parik and Donag both opened their mouths, looked at each other, and then Donag spoke. "If we let them go, they'll come back. Same as mice or rats or snakes— let 'em go, they'll breed and come back worse'n ever." Gird heard a murmur of agreement from the crowd. He wanted to tell them that what bred and multiplied here

was their own fear, but he knew it would do no good.
He struggled for words, and none came. He could feel
the mood deepening, one frightened and angry person
reinforcing another's fear and anger, as one bell vi-
brates when one near it is struck.

Black murder hung over the crowd, a veil of hatred
and fear. Some had wrapped themselves in it, as if it
were a literal cloak of supple velvet, welcoming the
darkness. Others stood hunched, frightened, unsure
which was worse, the growing darkness or the spear-
bright danger of the mageborn.

Luap gazed at him, calm, almost luminous. For the
second time, Gird felt that crevice open in his mind,
and Luap's voice flowing through, cool silver water
from a spring.

—We will not fight— he said. —We will not break
your peace—

My peace! Gird would have snorted if he could.
Some peace, with the city in wild turmoil; even Alyanya's
peace could not still this storm.

—*My peace*— echoed in his mind, in the great empty
cavern still clangorous with the crowd's noise. —*Do
you want my peace? Do you want justice?*— As once
before, he could not confuse that voice with any other.

Out of his emptiness, out of his pain, he cried—
silently, as the crowd listened in momentary silence—
for help. To the gods he had tried to serve, and feared,
and refused to ask before, he cried for help.

Again, as at Greenfields, he was snatched up from
ground, whirled in a storm of fire and flowers and wind
high above the city. But only for an instant. Then he
found himself standing where he had stood, but no
longer empty. Overflowing, rather, with utter certainty.
Full of light, of wisdom, of mellow peace thick as old
honey in the comb.

It was still hard. His head would burst, he was sure;
his mouth was too small for the breath he drew; he
could barely form the words that he must speak. They
had strange shapes, awkward in his mouth, as if thought
were sculpted into individual shapes not meant for human speech.

With the first words, the crowd stilled. He could not hear himself; he was balancing himself on those internal forces. Incredibly the thought sped by that this might be what women felt at birth—stretched beyond capacity, control relinquished to forces they could not name. Then he was drenched in a torrent of bright speech he must somehow say, its meaning racing past his mind faster than he could catch it. He felt the hair standing upright on his arms and legs, the prickle of awe becoming a wave of sheer terror and joy so mingled he could not tell one from the other. It was so *beautiful*—!

And as he spoke, and tried to hold himself upright, he saw the crowd change, as if someone had thrown clean water on a mudcaked paving. The hatred and fear lifted in irregular waves, leaving some faces free of that ugliness, others still stained but clearing.

After the first wrenching outwash of it, he was more aware of the crowd, of his own voice, of *what* he was saying. The words were strange to mouth and ear, but he *knew* what they meant, and so, somehow, did his hearers. Peace, joy, justice, love, each without loss of the others, engaged in some intricate and ceremonial dance. More and more the dark cloud lifted, as if his words were sunlight burning it away. Yet they were not *his* words, as he well knew. Out of his mouth, through his mind, had come Alyanya's peace, the High Lord's justice, Sertig's power of Making, and Adyan's naming: these powers loosed scoured the fear away.

That effect spread. Beyond the crowd gathered in the courtyard, beyond the city walls, across the countryside, the light ran clean as spring-water, lifting from fearful hearts their deepest fears, banishing hatred. Gird knew it happened, but dared not try to see, for the effort of speech took all his strength, even the strength he had been given. Sweat ran off his face, his arms, dripped down his ribs beneath his shirt, and still the great words came, and still he spoke them.

Now the darkness writhed, lifting free of his land, like morning fog lifting in sunlight. But it was not gone. He knew, without being told that when his words and the memory of them faded, it would settle again. And he could not stand here forever. Even as he thought this, the flood of power in his mind, faded, leaving him empty once more, but light, a rind dried by sunlight.

—It is not over— He had no doubt who *that* was. If he could have trembled, he would have. It had to be over: what else could he do? He could not live long as he was now. As he watched, seeing now with more than mortal eyes, the darkness contracted, flowed toward him. He closed his mind to it, as he had closed it to hatred so often before. It would not take *him*, even now, even weak as he was. But in his head the pressure grew again, forcing its way out, forcing an opening.

—Do not push that away: take it in. Take it *all* in, and transform it for them—

"I can't—" But he could, and he could do nothing else. With a despairing look at the crowd, at Luap, at the buildings that stood high around the market, even the top of the High Lord's Hall against the sky, he shrugged and relaxed his vigilance.

Now the great cloud of hatred and disgust pressed on him. He drew it in, doggedly, like a fisherman dragging a large net full of fish into a small, unsteady boat. It hurt. He had forgotten how painful it was to be that frightened, how hatred prickled the inside of the mind like a nestful of fiery ants, how disgust tensed every internal sinew. He had complained of his emptiness, to himself, but he had found those great clean rooms of his mind restful. There the spirit's wind had had space to blow; there he could go for quiet, for renewal. Now those spaces were filling, packed tighter and tighter, with stinking, slimy, oozing, crawling nastiness.

Envy, spite, malicious gossip like cockleburs, wads of gluttony like soft-bodied maggots, a sniggering delight in others' pain, thoughts and fears more misshapen, harder to hold, than the bright words he had found so painful. He felt himself grow heavier, as if he were filling with literal stones and muck, felt himself cramping into ever more painful positions as he tried to hold it all, and bring the rest of it in. Like a tidy housewife whose home is invaded by raucous vandals, he tried to protect some small favorite crannies of his mind, long-furnished with joyful memories—and failed. The stink and murk of it found every last crack, and filled them all. He felt himself creak, the foundations of his mind almost shattering from the weight. What would happen then?

He had it all. He dared not open his mouth, lest something vile leak out. The faces around him were stunned, horrified—he could not imagine what his face looked like, but it must be worth their horror. *Transform*, the gods had said. And just how? That ungainly, rebellious mass struggled to get out, and he *squeezed*. He did not feel the stones beneath his knees, then his hands—he felt only the terrible crushing weight of fear, the compression of hatred.

Through scalding tears Luap saw that homely, aging face transformed. *Like the High Lord's windows*, he thought. From outside, they looked dark—until at night a light woke them to brilliance. Now light illuminated Gird, almost too bright to watch, and from his mouth came rolling the words they all understood without quite hearing them. Beside him, the Autumn Rose murmured a counterpoint to Gird, her face radiant. Then she was silent. Luap felt his own heart lift, expand—and then his sight, as if Gird's speech awakened all his magegifts at once. He saw clinging darkness rolling away, lifting, knew in his bones precisely what Gird was doing, and what would come of it.

He could not bear it. It should not be Gird, who had earned a peaceful age, a time of rest. He should be the one. But when he opened his mouth, it was stopped, and the breath in it.

—You have other tasks—

He would have argued, but he had scarce breath to stay on his feet, and when he recovered, Gird was silent. Above them the cloud visible only to a few shifted, as if it were living spirit meditating attack. Gird was staring at it, mouth clamped shut just as so often before. Then—then his eyes widened, and his jaw dropped in almost comic surprise. Again Luap tried to move to his side, to help however he could. But again he could not move. Gird shrugged, then, and eyed the cloud doubtfully.

Even as he watched, Luap was thinking how he could record this in the archives. What would be believed, what would be too fantastic even for the superstitious, what would cause controversy, and what bring peace? He had no doubt that this was Gird's death. The man was too old, too battered by his life, to survive this.

—No one could— As he swayed under the pressure of that answer, he wondered if that was what Gird had heard.

And then the cloud settled on Gird, condensing, becoming, in the end, visible to everyone. That dark mass had no certain form, no definite edges. It weighed on him, pressed against him, until he sank first to one knee, and then the ground. They could not move to help, not until he lay flat, hands splayed on the stone, struggling to rise, to breathe—not until the darkness vanished, and Gird lay motionless.

Luap knew before he reached Gird's side that he was dead. His flesh was still warm, his broad blunt hands with their reddened, swollen knuckles still flexible, almost responsive, in Luap's. Luap blinked back his tears and looked at the crowd. Silent, awed, most of them had the blank and stupified look of someone waked from deep sleep. A few were already weeping.

But the air around them had the fresh, washed feel of a spring morning after rain. Inside, in the chambers of his heart where he had struggled to wall up ambition and envy, Luap knew that walls had fallen, and nothing was there but love.

The End

Epigraph

"Gradually it was disclosed to me that the line separating good and evil passes not through states, nor between classes, nor between political parties—but right through every human heart—and through all human hearts."

—Alexander Solzhenitsyn, *The Gulag Archipelago*

BUILDING A NEW FANTASY TRADITION

The Unlikely Ones by Mary Brown
Anne McCaffrey raved over *The Unlikely Ones*: "What a splendid, unusual and intriguing fantasy quest! You've got a winner here. . . ." Marion Zimmer Bradley called it "Really wonderful . . . I shall read and re-read this one." A traditional quest fantasy with quite an unconventional twist, we think you'll like it just as much as Anne McCaffrey and Marion Zimmer Bradley did.

Knight of Ghosts and Shadows
by Mercedes Lackey & Ellen Guon
Elves in L.A.? It would explain a lot, wouldn't it? In fact, half a millennium ago, when the elves were driven from Europe they came to—where else? —Southern California. Happy at first, they fell on hard times after one of their number tried to force the rest to be his vassals. Now it's up to one poor human to save them if he can. A knight in shining armor he's not, but he's one hell of a bard!

The Interior Life by Katherine Blake
Sue had three kids, one husband, a lovely home and a boring life. Sometimes, she just wanted to escape, to get out of her mundane world and *live* a little. So she did. And discovered that an active fantasy life can be a very dangerous thing—and very real. . . . Poul Anderson thought *The Interior Life* was "a breath of fresh air, bearing originality, exciting narrative, vividly realized characters—everything we have been waiting for for too long."

The Shadow Gate by Margaret Ball
The only good elf is a dead elf—or so the militant order of Durandine monks thought. And they planned on making sure that all the elves in their world (where an elvish Eleanor of Aquitaine ruled in Southern France) were very, very good. The elves of Three Realms have one last spell to bring help . . . and received it: in the form of the staff of the new Age Psychic Research Center of Austin, Texas. . . .

Hawk's Flight by Carol Chase
Taverik, a young merchant, just wanted to be left alone to make an honest living. Small chance of that though: after their caravan is ambushed Taverik discovers that his best friend Marko is the last living descendant of the ancient Vos dynasty. The man who murdered Marko's parents still wants to wipe the slate clean—with Marko's blood. They try running away, but Taverik and Marko realize that there is a fate worse than death . . . That sooner or later, you have to stand and fight.

A Bad Spell in Yurt by C. Dale Brittain
As a student in the wizards' college, young Daimbert had shown a distinct flair for getting himself in trouble. Now the newly appointed Royal Wizard to the backwater Kingdom of Yurt learns that his employer has been put under a fatal spell. Daimbert begins to realize that finding out who is responsible may require all the magic he'd never quite learned properly in the first place—with the kingdom's welfare and his life the price of failure. Good thing Daimbert knows how to improvise!

C.J. Cherryh's
The Sword of Knowledge

The Sword of Knowledge Cuts Two Ways ...

The Roman Empire. Imagine its fall. Now imagine that warring time with *cannon*—and a working system of magic. C.J. Cherryh did. In *The Sword of Knowledge*, we bring you The Fall, according to C.J. Cherryh.

A Dirge for Sabis, C.J. Cherryh & Leslie Fish
The Sabirn Empire is embattled by barbarian hordes. The key to their savior—forbidden knowledge. But will the Sabirn rulers countenance the development of these weapons, even to save themselves?
69824-9 * $3.95 ⸺⸺⸺

Wizard Spawn, C.J. Cherryh & Nancy Asire
Five centuries have passed and the Sabirn race lies supine beneath the boot of the Ancar. But rumors say that among the Sabirn are some who retain occult knowledge. The Ancar say this is justification for genocide. The Sabirn say genocide is justification for anything. . . .
69838-9 * $3.50 ⸺⸺⸺

Reap the Whirlwind, C.J. Cherryh & Mercedes Lackey
Another half milennium has passed, and new barbarians are on the rise to threaten the ruling tyrants. Once again, it will be a battle of barbarian vigor and The Sword of Knowledge!
69846-X * $3.95 ⸺⸺⸺

HOW TO IMPROVE SCIENCE FICTION

Want to improve SF? Want to make sure you always have a good selection of SF to choose from? Then do the thing that has made SF great from the very beginning—talk about SF. Communicate with those who make it happen. Tell your bookstore when you like a book. If you can't find something you want, let the manager know. But money speaks louder than mere words—so *order* the book from the bookstore, special. Tell your friends about good books. Encourage *them* to special order the good ones. A special order is worth a thousand words. If you can prove to your bookstore that there's a market for what you like, they'll probably start to cater to it. And that means better SF in your neighborhood.

Tell 'Em What You Want

We, the publishers, want to know what you want more of—and if you can't get it. But the people who order the books—they need to know first. So, before you buy a book directly from the publisher, talk to your bookstore; don't be shy. It doesn't matter if it's a chain bookstore or a specialty shop, or something in between—all businesses need to know what their customers like. Tell them: and the state of SF in your community is sure to improve.

And Get a Free Poster!

To encourage your feedback: A free poster to the first 100 readers who send us a list of their 5 best SF reads in the last year, and their 5 worst.

Write to: Baen Books, Dept. FP, P.O. Box 1403, Riverdale, NY 10471. And thanks!

Name:_____

Address:_____

Best Reads	Worst Reads
1)	1)
2)	2)
3)	3)
4)	4)
5)	5)